Arizona Rangers
BLAKE'S WAR
by William L. Casselman
"Book one of the Arizona Rangers series"

Arizona Rangers
BLAKE'S WAR

"Book one of the Arizona Ranger Series"

By William Casselman

©2017 By William Casselman

Edited by Susan Smith

Blake's War is a work of historical and Christian fiction. Names and characters are fictional, except for those names, being the author's friends and relatives, used in appreciation. Also, the names of famous historical characters and organizations, such as the Arizona Rangers of the late 1860s, American Indian tribes of the Old Southwest, and locations instrumental in the writing of this story, as well as historical moments; Mexican American War and American Civil War. But outside of these, any resemblance to actual persons, living or dead, or to actual events or locals is entirely coincidental.

Scripture usage for Blake's War comes from the Holy Bible National Publishing Company—Copyright 1943 and available only through Southeastern Distributors, Inc. of Charlotte, North Carolina. This personal Bible I have used belonged to a member of the Sander's Family for 70-years and now belongs to the author's family through his wife—Mona Sue (Sanders).

Published by:
Alaska Dreams Publishing
www.alaskadp.com

1ST Print Edition July 2017
ISBN numbers:
ISBN-13: 978-0-9903454-4-2
ISBN 10: 0-9903454-4-0

E-Book versions available. Please visit www.alaskadp.com for links.

Table of Contents

DEDICATION

As in my books, I first dedicate my story to my beautiful wife of nearly 35 years and my very large family of six plus children, 17 grandchildren so far and my first great-grandchild: 11-month old Solomon.

I also wish to dedicate this story to former Police Chief Alan Gray of Dillingham, Alaska. He saw who I was, a ten-year military veteran and Nam veteran, and still gave me my shot into civilian law enforcement as a member of the Dillingham Police Department in rural Alaska. They say in rural police departments that often whatever happened on your shift was all yours to handle, be it a traffic accident, disorderly conduct arrest or even a murder. The case was all yours to work, as we had no investigators, but we did have a lot of major felonies in this fishing community. I have always owed him for that chance and the vast experiences I gained there.

I would also like to list my oldest brother, Paul Ryan Holmes, who recently went to dance with my mom upon the marble floors of Heaven and a time to reconcile with our brother, Lawrence Joseph Coon.

Finally, I would dedicate this story to my father, Frank L. Casselman, who left us some time ago to have a word or two with the Almighty, concerning world affairs. My dad was a Korean War Veteran, and at 18 to 19 years of age, stationed in Japan with the U.S. Army, he was part of the first armor units to leave Japan and sail for South Korea when the bugle sounded as the North Koreans invaded. I owe my love for Arizona to him and my second mother—Bea, and my extended family. We spent a lot of time in the Arizona desert, among the ruins and learning the fantastic history of early Arizona. A beautiful land, where most of the men and women, of all races, were to hardy a group to have never said "I give up", as they faced the harsh elements to dig out a homestead and face their many enemies, or for the American Indians, an amazing people and some of the best fighting men in the world. It is my dear hope I show an honest interpretation of the Arizona Rangers and Apache Indians in this story.

AUTHOR'S NOTES

Blake's War begins in Arizona, but will quickly make trail for Texas and then into the Civil War, where JW and his gallant band will join with General Hood's Confederate Army of Texas. But during the Battles for Nashville, JW and his men are captured and land up in Elmira Union Army Prison Camp, New York for a spell, before returning to Southeast Arizona. This was more than a decade past the 1846 to 1848 Mexican American War, which had followed Texas gaining its independence from Mexico in 1836 and the famous Battle of the Alamo took place.

The Mexican-American War began on April 25, 1846, when a Mexican cavalry attacked a group of U.S. soldiers in the disputed zone under the command of General Zachary Taylor — killing a dozen U.S. troops. The Mexican Army then laid siege on an American fort along the Rio Grande. Taylor called in for reinforcements and with the help of superior rifles and artillery, they defeated the Mexicans at the Battles of Palo Alto and Resaca de la Palma. President Polk had his eyes on California, New Mexico — which took in Arizona at that time. He also wanted Oregon re-occupied by settlers. When Mexico rejected his offer of purchase, he instigated a fight by moving troops into the disputed zone between Rio Grande and Nueces River, which both countries had previously recognized as part of the Mexican State of Coahuila.

Following those two freshly won battles at Palo Alto and Resaca de la Palma, President Polk told the U.S. Congress that, "cup of forbearance has been exhausted, even before Mexico passed the boundary of the United States, invaded our territory, and shed American blood upon American soil." Two days later, Congress declared war.

At the time of war, only about 75,000 Mexican citizens lived north of the Rio Grande. Thus, the U.S. Forces led by Col. Stephen W. Kearny and Commodore Robert F. Stockton were able to conquer those lands with minimal resistance. Taylor likewise had little trouble advancing and capturing Monterrey in September. After suffering numerous defeats, Mexico called out for General Santa Anna, who was in exile in Cuba following the loss to Texas Independence. Santa Ana advised President Polk, if he was allowed return from Cuba, he would end the war on terms favorable to the United States. But Santa Ana double-crossed Polk and assumed control of the Mexican Army to lead it into battle once more. He would soon assume the Mexican presidency the following month.

In September, General Winfield Scott successfully laid siege to Mexico City and soon after, the Treaty of Guadalupe Hidalgo ended the

Mexican-American War. A new Mexican-American border was placed on the maps; establishing the Rio Grande as the official borderline between Mexico and America. Mexico also recognized the U.S. annexation of Texas, and agreed to sell the rest of its territory north of the Rio Grande for $15 million plus assumption of certain damage claims.

Now between the Mexican-American War and the later Civil War between the North and the South, Arizona was not known as a legal territory. Arizona was simply a westward part of New Mexico, which had also not reached statehood, but was loosely spoken of as a massive unforgiving desert region between Texas and California. Though New Mexico was primarily known for its Comanche Indian Tribes, the Arizona area was home to the Pueblo, Hopi, Navajo and numerous tribes of the Apache Indians. There were also the problems with Mexican bandits and a growing concern of White-Indian bandits known as Comancheros, who dabbled in slavery with the Mexican Bandits and the Apache.

Under protected by American forces, the citizens of Arizona became ripe pickings for the Indians and the bandits, burning new ranches and farmers from the east attempting to raise crops in the desert soil. People were either being murdered or taken off to be sold into slavery across the border. Some of the slaves went up into the tribal lands to a life of misery and eventually a hard death. These violent events continued taking place until the Provisional Government of Arizona, set up by the residents of Arizona, elected to provide a Ranger force similar to the famous Texas Rangers. This came about in 1860, when two fighting forces; one being called the Arizona Guard, stationed at Pinos Altos and the other, to be known as the Arizona Rangers and to be stationed in Mesilla. Their primary focus was to protect the citizens from Apache raiding parties.

With the outbreak of the Civil War in 1861, General Baylor's Confederate Army arrived in Arizona in 1862 and declared it confederate territory. Baylor became the Territorial Governor and formed Company A of the Arizona Rangers—first of three companies of the defending Arizona Rangers. A large group of Rangers did leave their post then to join up with Confederate General Hood, Commanding the Army of Texas. Men came from Arizona and New Mexico to join up with General Hood's command. Remaining Arizona Rangers went to Tucson to defend Western Arizona, but when the union troops belonging to the Army of California came through, the confederates were driven out of Arizona.

In 1862, backing a promise President Lincoln had made to America, Congress had finally passed the long-awaited Homestead Act. This new law provides all Americans the opportunity to become land owners of up to 160-acres of unclaimed public lands. The provision is that the homesteader must never have borne arms against the United States, must live on the property for five years and make improvements by building a 12-by-14-foot dwelling and growing crops. This was a dream come true for the country's immigrants from Europe. But sadly, there would be problems as the homesteaders were forced to deal with the approaching railroad, ranchers who didn't want to give up free grange on government property and those same Indians and Mexican bandits.

In 1863, the United States Congress officially organized the Territory of Arizona. The railroad would not run through Arizona until 1880, easing the remoteness of territory. With it came the town builders, school teachers, church pastors and merchants. Locations like Apache Junction and Globe began to grow and become good-sized communities, surrounded by ranches and even the farmer. In 1860 the consensus for Arizona's white population was 6,482. Now this didn't count Indians, Mexicans nor Blacks, or any other minority. But by 1870, Arizona had grown to 9,658, though they were still not counting minorities. During this ten-year period 870,000 head of cattle were raised on over 3,800 cattle ranches of all sizes.

A new reorganization of the Arizona Rangers would not occur again until 1882 and this was only because of Apache Indian raids led by the likes of Geronimo matched the violence of Cochise. In the early 1860's, Chief Cochise and his army of 200 war braves eluded the Army of the west for ten-years. Now Geronimo fought with less than 60 war braves and dwindled down to 30, eluded a post-civil war military force of over 2,000 and 7,000 Mexican soldiers on their side of the border. The Apache Nations were made up of the Chiricahua, Mescalero, Jicarilla, Lipan and Kiowa-Apache. The White Mountain Apache was related to the Apache of San Carlos, Payson and Camp Verde. The Apache is of Alaskan Athabascan decent, to be one group living aside the Navajo until the 1400's.

Gold was found in Sutter's Mill in 1848 and within ten-years 150,000 California Indians were annihilated. Between 1848-1900, bounty hunters were paid $25.00 an Indian scalp. Now, in 2015, this would be the equivalent of $2,500 and sex and age of the victim had no meaning. A lot of the victims were Mexicans because their hair color and texture matched, especially amongst the womenfolk.

In the 1860's the Apache population was estimated at 6,000 to 8,000 people, with the Western Arizona Apache believed to be 4,000 in number.

On February 4, 1861, Union Lt. Bascom lured and caught Chief Cochise with a lie and under a flag of truce. He falsely accused Cochise of kidnapping a rancher's son. But Cochise was not believed when he put up a defense and claimed his innocence. Cochise would soon escape, but his relatives were all hung by Lt. Bascom. Cochise retaliated by setting off a war responsible for the death of 425 people—killed by Apaches. The atrocities carried out by both sides were horrific. Even the famous Kit Carson, legendary friend to the Indian, carried out a "Scorched Earth" policy for the Army, destroying Indian homes and burning up acres of crops and peach orchards, which left 3,945 starving Navajo, who were forced to trek 300-miles from Fort Defiance to Fort Sumner, New Mexico. Many died along the way.

The Indian Wars lasted over a long period, but still the people continued to come and law enforcement grew to become Sheriff Departments and U.S. Federal Marshals. Additional U.S. Military forces came in to the territory and most of the Indians were confined to their federal reservations. Roads and highways were being built for the automobile that was replacing the horse and America was becoming a mighty country from coast to coast.

CHAPTER ONE

"Coffee's Burning, Got 'a be a Rattler in The Kitchen, Again."

Blake's Double "B" Ranch, Main Compound
Northwest of the Globe Settlement, Southeast Arizona
April 1862

With a late afternoon sun burning on the far hillsides to the west, a sign his long day of riding 400 head of cattle alone was done, a weary-eyed JW Blake casually rode into his front yard to tie up Knot Head. He couldn't help but pick up the vile stench of the burning coffee, when he tied up his 18-hand black stallion to the first rail closest to the porch and front door. He had to be wise with old Knot Head. The horse seemed to have his own set ways of doing things and dealing with his rider. Several times the horse had tried to throw JW, but the ranch's owner was an experienced rider. Still in all, JW liked the ornery bag of horse-flesh. He was fast and had already proved himself a dozen or so times when JW had engaged the local tribes.

John W. Blake, with the W standing for Washington, always kept Knot Head tied up for a spell before taking him over to the barn's water troth. He knew Knot Head needed to cool down before he sucked down a gallon or two of lukewarm water and got his self all swelled up.

But right now, the unsaddling would have to wait a moment, the stench was foul and that meant his lovely wife was probably on the other side of the room from some rattle snake and she's too far from her rifle. *Course, she's used a chair a few times. Don't know how those snakes keep gettin' in. Ah keep checkin' but can't find no holes I haven't shored up. Must be knockin' at the door and just walking right in. Surprise is the best weapon an' those rattles are plumb smart.*

Knot Head tried to rear back, but the tied down reins stopped him. But his attitude was sure making John wonder. He knew Knot Head didn't act like that around rattlers, he normally just stomped them. Almost as an afterthought, John pulled his Navy Colt Revolver, checked his loads, and walked towards the front door, but very quietly, he backed off. He feared there may be a couple of Indian bucks in there and his Sherry Ann might be holding them off with her Springfield. He knew those Indians had to be insane, if that's who it might be, to get between a she-bear and her cubs.

He looked through a window corner—one of two windows he had ordered from Kansas City last year, before the trouble began. All he could see was his ten-year old son, Steven. His eight-year old daughter, Jessie, was out of view, along with Sherry Ann.

John didn't like mysteries. His son was not much help, as his eyes were glued on something to the right of the front door. This left him with two options: leaping through the front door, possibly getting someone shot or going around to the back door and coming in through there. He decided on the latter.

JW—as he was often called by his friends--was a good-sized man, stood six-foot-four, broad shoulders, not much noticeable fat. At 34-years old, his eyes were clear, steely bluish colored, his jaw was square with a two-week's beard growth, and his hands were large and calloused. He wore handmade grips on his weapons to fit them. His dark brown hair—gray strands filtering through—hung to his broad muscular shoulders; a trait he sincerely hoped his daughter would not inherit. Usually, he had a calm temperament; but he was known as one to finish his fights quickly. He was a good man with rifle, revolver or knife, but he was also known for his intellect. It was his brain and care for his soldiers that got him noticed during the Mexican-American War. His Company of cavalry lost both their officers. JW was promoted from sergeant to Captain on the battlefield by the Commanding General. He was Captain Blake, which was a title that stuck with him until he was officially made Captain of the Arizona Rangers.

Between working his 650 acres of ranchland, he cleared the land without much help, building his ranch house, barn and bunk house for his future cowhands. This plus his Ranger duties meant he didn't have a lot of family time.

Now, they seemed to be in danger, once again. He quickly walked around the house, stooped down at the back door, slipping off his sweaty, dusty leather boots. Once off his feet, he glanced at his mildly deformed boots, realizing he needed a new pair. Then, shaking his head to clear his thoughts of stupid things, he stepped on the back porch; which was only half the size of the front porch. He cleared the land for a good 25 yards in a half-circle area so the Apache would not have anything close by to hide behind.

At the top of the left-hand corner of the door was an eight-inch long piece of old rope, which went through a hole and down to the inside locking bar. At night, they slipped it off the bar so no one could sneak in while everyone was asleep, but right now it was coming in real handy.

Blake quietly pulled the bar up, inches at a time until he knew it was clear. Then he gently pulled on the door. Once it was open wide enough for him to sneak in, he cautiously snuck into the back bedroom. Well practiced, he glanced down at his revolver and very carefully cocked it, but as to not make any sound. He was now ready.

JW looked down at his bed, the one he shared with Sherry Ann and then looked back to the short narrow hallway. The bed was made tightly, just like Sherry Ann liked it, so just maybe she hadn't been raped. White Men like their privacy, usually, but Indians could care less.

JW's family remained in absolute silence. This bothered him, but he was ready to deal with any problem.

He held his revolver, well-balanced in his right hand. His Bowie knife is partially pulled from its leather sheath on his belt should he need to throw it. He was one of the best with a knife in the territory—taught by a gray-haired Mexican mountain fighter. He now stepped into the room. With revolver at his waist, ready to gun down any danger to his family, he hesitated. What he saw was a confusing sight—a nearly naked white boy, maybe 14 to 16 years old, covered over in blood, holding a hunting knife for his defense. He appeared a whole lot more frightened than his Sherry Ann.

She sensed his movement, but kept her eyes on the boy, "Don't shoot him, JW...He's a frightened little button and I'm tryin' to talk that knife out of his hand. He's terrified an' yuh just made it worse. Now holster that dog killer so I can continue makin' friends with 'im. Whatever he saw has left him a fearing the human race."

"I only shot that one dog and it was rabid," JW said in a low voice and then he added, "You was real glad I shot it back then."

In a calm voice, she replied, "Yes, JW, when that happened I was grateful, but you done killed a whole lot of men since then." Sherry Ann shooed him away with a wave of her left hand and then sent her kids outside to give their dad a hand.

"Okay, young man, it's just you and me, so let's talk. You hungry, I made some great biscuits and I got's me a jar of cactus jelly."

He decided to leave when he noticed the small Colt.38 Revolver in his wife's waistband. She was a fine shot and a strong enough woman that if there was trouble, she'd be like any other she-bear and would've shot big holes in this strange boy. But now the kids were with their father and she could try a few different things to help this kid open-up. Sherry Ann already suspected he was from one of the smaller wagon trains that had gone by, heading west for the gold and silver fields, or the rich California soil to grow their giant fruit orchards.

JW looked down at his son, "Unsaddle ol' Knot Head and walk him over to the water. He's calmed down some by now."

"Dad, were you gonna shoot that boy?"

11

"Naw, I didn't know who it was in there with your mom. But if he'd had a gun and moved the wrong way, I'd probably of grazed him for safety-sake," JW said.

Eight-year old Jessie sauntered up with an armful of fresh hay for Knot Head. She asked, "Dad, what's the matter with that boy?"

"Honey, I'm thinkin' that boy saw something pretty awful and your mom's tryin' ta get it out so we'd know how to help him and who ta get for 'im. But sometimes, it takes a while."

But right then a burst of loud wailing came from the house. JW knew his wife had broken through to that boy's inner being. He still didn't know what to call it, but people from all over South East Arizona and farther, came to her for help. Sherry Ann had this bizarre gifting with the critters; it was almost like she could talk to them. For some she was a healer for the mind and the physical needs, and others saw her as someone gifted in helping the powerless with their inner demons. Early on, she'd been called a witch, but no one used that word in JW's presence. Although he couldn't understand it, JW watched many times when she lay her hands on people, praying. The air would become hot, much hotter than this desert produced and with those prayers, healing would happen. He did know his wife was never paid for her services. At times, she thought JW's head was made of granite as she repeatedly tried to explain God's gifts — how it would be wrong to ask or receive payment for doing the Lord's Will.

"But the Parson gets paid, he takes his share of the offering plate to live off of an' you make sure at a minimum our ten percent is in there every Sunday, plus whatever else we can add. What's the difference?" This was a question he tended to bring up once a year. Her reply was nearly always the same, "Our ten percent — our tithe — allows him time to serve the church community and still eat, but you provide for everything we eat and the Good Lord provides us with healthy cattle, good crops and safety when you're on the ranger trail."

But he knew his wife of some 12-years was right, as a ranger he had been forced to kill or wound 19 men, while performing his duties — thirteen lay six feet under, two were hung, the remaining four thugs and killers were spending out their lives in Yuma Penitentiary, a federal prison rumored to be "Hell on Earth".

JW had 22 rangers under him, or with him, who rode the desert for pennies a day. Their only food being what they could shoot. Their water supply often a stream on the other side of an Apache war party. Each man is down to a few bullets in his rifle. Still, they were rangers. Doing the impossible was expected of them. In carrying out the law, they left their graves scattered about the Southeast corner of Arizona. Here were growing ranches and a few farms willing to take on the rough sandy soil of the desert floor. The various Apache tribes wanted the White Man out and Mexican bandits would lay siege upon their growing towns.

Rangers were needed everywhere, but Arizona couldn't afford another company to handle the border area with Mexico or a company to be up north to work with the wagon trains heading to Oregon, Nevada and Utah.

Most of the time, JW was sending out teams of three rangers to handle bandits and a team of ten to handle a recent Apache raid. But the Apache would be long gone, the bodies of families mutilated and the homes ransacked or burned to the ground. Horses would be taken, mules would be eaten on the trail and children kept to be eventually sold as slaves through the Comancheros. If womenfolk were pretty, it could become a curse, their life would go to the highest bidder.

A good raid for the Apache War Party often involved three or four small ranches or farms. Success depended on how many warriors were lost. The rangers always carried shovels. After a raid, they would bury 20 people or more. This was especially hard work when dealing with bodies treated by the Apaches' gruesome ways and spending two or more days under the hot desert sun. Such duties were never forgotten. Some rangers carried a few of those horrid scenes to their own grave.

JW was treating Knot Head to a good rubdown with a curry comb and a soft piece of deer hide in their small gray plank barn—big enough for three horse stalls and a Blacksmith's workshop—when Sherry Ann walked in. He could tell she was tired by the wearisome look to her eyes. This was happening more and more after she performed healings for God. He wasn't much of a believer, but he tried for her sake. He kept feeling his duties. What he did on his job was always keeping him from tasting the real thing. Trouble is, each time he came upon a massacre, he'd view the bloody scene and ask himself, *"How could a loving God, a deity she loved so much, allow such things to occur on his watch.*

"How'd it go?" he asked.

She had walked up, with two partially full coffee cups in her hands; one for him and one for her, with cow's milk. The kids were out taking care of their chores.

"He's asleep...finally." She took a long warm gulp, then she answered. "He was easier to break than most, but I suspect it's because it all just happened." They both took another sip.

"They had a party of eight wagons break-off from a much larger train. His family wanted Southern California and the wagon train was headed for North of San Francisco…Napa Valley. So, they agreed on a split.

"Oh, he's 16 years old and his name is Liam McFaul. It was his dad, mom and two sisters, who were killed, plus a lot of other relatives. He was serving as an out-rider…south side I believe. They ran with six out-riders and a scout, who had been to Southern California twice before. It was right after breakfast two days ago that he took a position, when something hit him in the head. By the looks of his wound he was headshot, but his thick skull saved his live."

"Did he happen to see what kind of Indian, what tribe…maybe it was bandits or the Comancheros decided to attack this small chain on their own."

"Nope, when he came to, the sun was going down. Before him lay the most gruesome scene of blood, torn and ripped flesh. He estimated seven-children were gone. All the bodies were scalped, lying face down. Some appeared tortured in heinous ways he refused to describe to me 'cause I's a woman. My Bible talks of such things. All the blood came from the young bodies he tried burying and those of his family. They took his youngest sister and killed the other two."

"We need to find the scene. It will help us to know what tribe these Indians are from or if we are dealing with Mexican bandits operating out of their normal range or possibly Comancheros. Looks like I need to send out a Rangers Needed Call." JW looked at his wife. She knew from his eyes what he was going to ask.

"I think he can ride tomorrow, but be gentle with him. He's a city boy from the northeast, who can ride a gentle horse and maybe shoot a shotgun. But he's never had a Navy Colt tied down to his right leg or faced an enraged Apache. So, promise me, you'll be really careful with him."

He held her in his arms, giving her one of those: *Hey it's me, Honey* looks. She grinned in response.

She pulled back, slapping his left shoulder, "You'se better gets a move on if you'se want your rangers here by tomorrow, and don't you forget—no drinks in town. You come home smellin' of liquor and you might as well make your bed in the barn. An' I hope you get your fool head shot off…jus' a little bit." She held up her right hand with her index finger and thumb far enough apart to see the clearance.

JW shook his head in response, for he was used to her threats made in jest. She knew when the job was at hand, he kept his mind on prepping for the trip. Then he headed out leading his company. But besides the danger, JW was having to deal with low morale. The government had cut their pay to $22 a month, while most ranch cowboys were making a starting wage of $30 a month, plus room and board. The rangers were down to just the one company for the entire state, outside of Tucson. The government made sure Arizona's largest city had its own ranger company to handle their outlying areas. The lieutenant commanding the Tucson Company was still under JW's overall command.

JW wasn't sure how many men would show up. He knew that many of his disillusioned fighters were going off to fight in the Civil War under the great General Hood of Texas. Men from Arizona and New Mexico and a few California confederates, headed east, hoping to fight under the Texas southern flag to kill Yankees.

For the moment, the Union troops — a point element for the soon to arrive California Union Army sent into his area — was barely more than a platoon of cavalry and a platoon of infantry, along with two field pieces of artillery. They rarely left the populated areas of Southern-Central Arizona. They would make a run as far east as Fort Bowie, on the wagon trail going east for New Mexico, bypassing the trail to Sonora, Mexico, near Texas Canyon vicinity. The Union Cavalry traveled north with wagons, their infantry protecting the new growing settlement of Globe. After a couple days of drinking in the café/bar, they'd wander back to Phoenix — population over 2,000 — stay a couple nights, then march down south to Tucson. The hard ride or even a walk between Phoenix and Tucson was believed to be approximately 170 to 180 miles and could prove dangerous for the Army. But South-East Arizona's desert offered little protection to people with a couple wagons or a section of a wagon train numbering eight wagons, to be out in the open. The main wagon trail road was nothing more than wide dried out dirt ruts in the summer and deeper mud ruts in the winter. In both cases, it was a dangerous travel for both small and large trains, but the smaller trains were of course hit more often because of fewer guns to protect themselves with.

SETTLEMENT OF GLOBE, ARIZONA

JW expected to be going out on burial detail. He made sure everyone brought a shovel, carried in the ranger's wagon. Food, extra ammo, blankets, extra water and chow for the horses would all be carried in the ranger's tarp-covered 18-foot long wagon. They seized it for the state after finding it abandoned after a Ute Indian attack. The rangers dug 19 graves that day, three of them being for babies, that were gently placed in empty flour sacks. JW made sure the ranger wagon had an ample supply of flour sacks for such a duty and other grizzly tasks as well. When they found a decapitated body, the head was usually found within a couple hundred yards. JW had seen Comanche, Ute and Apache playing a strange game with mounted Indians using their spears to knock the head or heads about. He knew the French had once played it as their mounted Lancers used Indian heads.

JW wasn't all that sure which civilization started all the barbaric acts. He tended to believe claims that White Man brought the act of scalping to the American Indian. From what his wife and their Parson had told him, barbarism began a very long time ago and mankind continued to bring it forward with every century.

Rangers over all tried not hating the Indians. It became hard. They knew Whites were doing much the same thing to Indian villages, including the U.S. Cavalry. JW saw this was not a time to be proud of the human race.

Stomping his feet on the wooden plank porch, JW entered the town's combined bar and café, which was open to a trading post and attached gun shop, and capable of being transformed on Sundays into the New Globe Christian Church. JW flung back the sides of his knee-length rough-cut brown dyed cow hide coat to shake the dust off. This noisy action allowed everyone to see JW had come packing all his weapons of war. On a ten-year old wide leather waist belt hung his highly decorative beaded holster, tied to his right leg by a leather string with two three-inch wolves' fangs. He carried his Navy .44 Colt, loaded with five rounds. Like most men who spent a lot of time on their horses, he kept the hammer of his revolver sitting on top of an empty chamber so if he fell, he wouldn't blow his leg off. His ornate Mexican belt with several engravings burned into it, including a longhorn steer, a buffalo and grizzly, held and extra 20-rounds of 44 caliber ammo. On the opposite side of his waist, he wore that large Bowie knife in a leather sheath of buffalo hide, with the outline of a buffalo head branded on the sheath's outside front.

Tonight, he wore a bandolier for his new rifle — a model that was held back from normal sales because of the war. The Henry Company refrained from selling this highly efficient rifle to either side. However, they gave a few newer experimental rifles to a few special people. This 44-70 golden brass, high-gloss wood rifle was sheer beauty to behold. It could be loaded with 15 rounds down a tube, running below the barrel, along with one round in the chamber. It used lever action, which was extremely fast. A competent shooter could down 16 opponents before reloading. If he had extra ammo tubes ready to go, a battle against a single-shot enemy army could be over in short time.

JW, previously a Law Enforcement Officer following the Mexican-American War in Nashville, Tennessee, saved the life of a man who was about to be knifed for the wad of money he waved about to impress a few ladies. The man tried thanking JW with a large cash payment, but JW already left with two prisoners. News of the Arizona Rangers being formed with Captain JW Blake taking command of one of the three companies, reached the man, who was Executive Vice President for the Henry Company. He used Pinkerton Investigators to verify JW was the man he owed his life to. Knowing a ranger would not take a cash payment or a high-paying company job, he sent one of these new rifles, along with 100 boxes of the special 44. caliber ammo, ten-loading tubes and loading instructions, with a well-trusted company security official to locate JW. Even by special carrier it took nearly three-weeks to locate JW, who was stunned to find the rifle and ammo inside the wooden crate addressed to him. While he recalled the incident mentioned in the attached letter, he just shrugged his large shoulders, grinning at the new rifle in his hands. He grasped the rifle in his left hand. It wasn't even being sold in the stores, yet. To him, the rifle was worth its weight in gold, maybe it a bit more. He knew someday his son would inherit it and then his grandson.

Tonight, was the third time he brought out the rifle. He did it mostly to show this little chore the rangers were needed for was important and they were headed for Indian Territory.

"Rangers, we got us a small wagon train, filled with ignorant easterners and some foreigners who apparently got tangled up with our Apaches. That means we got a lot of graves to dig and hopefully we can find the trail those Injuns used to find the children they stole. We is meetin' at my place at dawn, bring your own shovels." JW looked about the room and spotted five of his men, who all nodded at him. JW tipped his hat with his right hand, leaving the joint. He had a couple more stops, one a bit less savory than the bar.

He always wondered how the people could hold church in such a place. The town's elderly preacher would flash him a big grin and answer, "We go where the heathens are, for who better to hear the Lord's Words. You should come by sometime, JW. The experience may startle the town and I believe yourself."

"Sherry Ann is lookin' forward to the church gettin' finished so she can bring the kids in, Parson."

"With all the financial help we receive by such families as yours, we should be putting the roof on in a few months. Bless your ride tomorrow, Sir."

With his Henry Rifle still grasped in his left hand, the butt plate leaning on his left hip, JW moved a heavy woven blanket aside, stepping into his second location. His preacher friend referred to it as Satan's hellish home for Sinners. Several times the parson was seen standing outside this place during daylight hours, a raised Bible in hand, praying up a storm. JW could never understand what good that did, as all the ladies of the night were snoring away and the men were back home with their wives.

But he respected the Parson and everyone knew the Man of God was under ranger's protection.

JW was going to need his town's other Man of God for the long wagon trip out to say some words over a lot of people who were not going to be making it West. Preacher Joe never gave his age, but JW suspected he was between 70 and 100 years old. He was a medium-sized man of thin build. His hair was short and all white, kept well-trimmed. No one in town could remember the man without his well-groomed white beard. But what marked Preacher Joe were his scars; the backs of both hands were covered over in burned scar tissue. So was half of the right-side of his face, along with most of his forehead. Those that knew compared it to oil fires they had seen in the past, but with such severe burns the victims had rarely survived.

Over the years JW and Preacher Joe came to know each other pretty well. They become good friends. JW thought about asking him about the scars, but held off. He liked the old man and didn't want to offend him by delving in to his private affairs. Besides, he was the only man in the area who could play a decent game of chess. Their current win-loss ratio was breaking even-Steven and that made for a great challenge on the occasional quiet nights when the wife and kids were visiting elsewhere on church business.

Preacher Joe always wore the robe of a Spanish Catholic Priest and had a long silver chain draped around his neck that dropped below his chest holding a very large silver Mexican Crucifix attached to it. Yet Preacher Joe was not a Catholic. When he asked Preacher Joe about that, the old white-haired man told JW, "When I came here…from far-far away, the town's priest was dying. He was very old. He spent much of his time with the Apache. The silver Crucifix was a gift to him on his 65th birthday from the Apache and Mexicans in this area…he called it his Parrish. He wanted me to have it to help his people. After the old Priest passed on, I felt by wearing his crucifix it immediately became a symbol of my office the locals could recognize and accept me as one who was accepted by their old Priest…and it worked."

"What about visiting Catholics?" JW had asked.

"Those that stop by feel I am a priest. I see no difference as we both believe in Christ. Yes, I will listen to their confessions to help them. God already knows, it's only the true forgiveness we desire that accounts for our hearts to be closer to our Lord. I've studied up on their various practices. I see no difference in why we take communion. The Word of God is still the Word of God. I will let the Good Lord judge me when my time comes. I have been used to make a lot people contact with services, marriages and bringing non-believers to the Lord."

"But, were you a Man of God before you came here?" JW Asked.

"John, between us two I will answer that truthfully, for God already knows what it is true. I was in South America, a little country on no one's map, where, to protect a friend, I was forced to kill a federal officer...a corrupt one who demanded money. I was sentenced to be killed, except for some strange move, I was sent to the darkest of prisons to serve a life sentence.

"At the time, I would've preferred quick death, but my Lord had a plan for me. A couple months after arriving there, I met an older Pastor during our single meal time. If we wanted more food, we needed to bribe the guards. This Man of God saw something in me, something I'd never admitted to. It was a love for God. My folks raised me on the Word of God...right up until French Officers destroyed our Christian Mission in Southern Mexico. I was quite young, but we had come from St. Louis, Missouri to set up a school-mission for the Mexicans and Apache Indians who learned to live together. From memory, he taught me the Word of God that I no longer remembered, helping me to forgive the Lord for what had happened to my folks.

"It took nearly 30-years, however he advised me I had the education and spiritual knowledge to walk this earth as a Christian Pastor. We prayed together that night and he anointed me. By this time, we were sharing a cell. The only cost for this privilege was praying every night for a number of guards who respected the two of us. The next day, when I awakened, I found him lying there with a soft smile on his face and no beat of his heart. A week later, I was released, provided with escort to an American Navy Ship, that transported me to Galveston, Texas.

"It took me a month and a half of travel, but I made it to the big Christian Mission School that had sent my friend and his parents out. I told several people my story. They long wondered what happened to that mission school and the family they sent down there. Because of my story and my knowledge of the Word of God, I was promptly enrolled in Seminary, which was to last four-years. I finished in less than three years, after which I was formally anointed a Christian Pastor for the Lutherans. I remembered my friend telling me how he had problems with some Lutheran doctrines; however, their ministry field among the lost and schools for Mexicans and Indians, encouraged fair treaties among all races; as long as, a single faith in the Lord reigned above all. So, during seminary I kept my mouth shut.

"When I graduated, I imagined my dear friend being up on that stage as I accepted my diploma. I was the oldest student they had ever graduated. When asked where I wanted to go, I told them I would leave it to God, but now I would go out among the Indians. They brought me here. Now you know."

JW recalled that conversation as he stared down the long straw covered wooden plank hallway that separated five rooms. Off to JW's right side was a sort of waiting room. Here sat four semi-intoxicated men; two White and two Mexican. Thankfully, JW didn't see a ranger in the bunch, though he wasn't ignorant enough to think he was going to leave here 100 percent happy. So, he stepped into the hallways, yelling, "Rangers, I don't want to know who you are, so do not answer me back, but we got us a job. Be at my place, ready to go at dawn and bring your own shovel. We will be out for five…maybe six days. Good night, gentlemen!"

He began to hear someone reply with a goodnight through the thin wooden doors, when a second man yelled, "Shut-up!" This caused all the ladies inside the narrow rooms to burst out laughing. But the voices sailed through the building and JW now knew who he had in here. It wasn't too bad. These two rangers were his youngest sprouts; two unmarried friends with older brothers in the outfit. He hoped these boys didn't catch anything from their nighttime encounters with these Dark Ladies, as they were often referred to as.

It always made JW chuckle to see his wife talking with one of these dark ladies in a store, never realizing how that woman spent her nights. He never told her, not that it would've mattered, as Sherry-Ann saw the best in everyone and enjoyed spreading local gossip as long it wasn't harmful to anyone, and listening to new stuff made her happy. JW used these ladies for Intelligence gathering, because these ladies knew just about anything there was to know about the different menfolk in town. He bagged two wanted Mexican Bandits, turning them over to Mexican Police at the border, which enhanced their relationship. A few months later, the Mexican Police brought over a semi-conscious American outlaw who was wanted in Texas for murder. This continued until the Civil War broke out and Mexico began having its own problems with the French and Spanish.

Fortunately, Globe was a young settlement and small enough not to have a town council, a mayor or even a "Women for a Better City, Stop Drinking Now!" group. The Globe Bar and whatever other function it formed worked as the courthouse, when needed and even the Town Bank. There were always half-a-dozen or more men lounging about until closing time, so JW knew it would take a real fool to attempt robbing the Town Bank, which was actually only a steel box wrapped in pad-locked chains, held behind the bar. Within seconds they would be looking down the barrel of many firearms, possibly dead. The banker came in from Phoenix with two body guards once a week to secure the transactions. He hoped the new Globe bank would be built soon, so he could get clear of his father-in-law, who was head-teller, loan officer and owner of the bar.

Most monetary valuables coming in were either silver or gold nuggets or dust, and some green backs the settlement's business owners needed to pay workers or trade for valuable minerals and gems. In-store credit was offered and most prospectors took the offered in-store trade-off, where half of what they brought in would be stored away to assist others with loans. They were referred to as banking investors and their funds were paid back to them with three percent interest after a minimum of six-months and five percent after one-year. Most miners had no understanding of interest bearing loans or investments. They saw this as a precaution against a mine running dry or the great mother lode that continued eluding them. These miner's stakes involved a large amount of money; however, locals could put any amount of funds in a saving account with a promised 1.3 percent interest rate every six-months. Such things as savings accounts with interest rates are new to many people in Arizona Territory. The ranchers and farmers adding their funds already brought prosperity to Central Arizona, which could easily pay the cost for a six-foot tall, built-in wall, steel and cast iron bank; with combination lock from Wells Fargo.

JW's last stop was the new livery stable, which served a dozen purposes besides storing horses. The extra-large corrals held cattle, sheep and goats, wagons and provided hay piles for men to bed down on. Women slept in wagons. A night guard on duty kept the women safe. Of course, once or twice, the men needed protection after a local gal got fired up on homebrew.

Calling for the owner, JW found the filthy hunkered over and shirtless owner working his manure pile, which he mixed in boneless table leavings from the café to make up the decent fertilizer he used for a two-acre vegetable plot. He learned all about making this *compost* from three Chinese families who passed through with a train of 48-wagons. He sold veggies to the café, locals, and wagon trains passing on their way south for the entry into Southern California or north across Nevada and into Northern California.

"Look, I need the ranger's wagon ready to go within a couple hours. Preacher Joe will pick-it up. Load it with oats for 12 horses, four water barrels strapped, two on each side, plus two horses pulling the wagon." JW asked for the big black draft horses again. They worked pretty well last time they were out for over a week. "We'll need to rent a couple extra saddles, too, some extra horse blankets and if you've got some extra shotguns, I'd liken to borrow three or four of them for a week, plus powder and shot."

"Not a problem, JW. I'll toss in a whole tin of buckshot and one of black powder. Bring it back if you don't need it." Mr. Johnson of Tucson had come to the Globe settlement to leave behind a dead wife and four dead children — victims of a Bandit raid back in 1851. He had too many memories around his old place, which is what he told Preacher Joe and later to JW. He had used his grief to build the livery stable one section at a time. The big corrals were put up last year and five months ago he signed a contract to work with the stage coach line; which stopped to change horses and grab a bite in the café for passengers. Johnson appreciated the business. There were a couple times the stage came in days late, drug in by ranger escort. The coach and horses escaped from the Apache; but the coaches had dozens of arrows and bullet holes in them. Sadly, everyone aboard was dead. They couldn't find anyone. The usual Apache practice was setting fire to the coach, which added to the mystery of the missing passengers. Searches were made, but none found. According-to the stage-line, five people, plus driver and a young man riding shotgun had been aboard. All seven were lost; a brief note in Arizona history.

Passengers going both directions are warned about the stage being unpopular with the Indians. From Globe, they headed south for Phoenix, then into California through a crossing near a horse trough called Blyth. More than one stagecoach hit the outer walls of many a town, with a band of Apache's or Utes on their heels, screaming and yelling their threats. The back of the stage resembled a porcupine with arrows sticking out of it. The shotgun rider, if still aboard was either wounded or dead. Many times, the stagecoach driver and the man riding shotgun both were killed. Some unidentified brave cowboy exited the coach to assume the duties. More often, he had to ride one of the stage horses as the reins were dragging the ground. He used his shotgun to keep the Indians from the horses, or killing him.

If the Indians managed to stop the stagecoach and everyone was dead or seriously wounded, they would look for their personally marked arrows, returning them back to their quiver. Damaged ones would be salvaged for what could still be used, such as the arrow shaft, feathers or the arrowhead.

JW was back on the town's main street, a hard-packed and wind swept section of dirt between two short lengths of hard plank wooden walkway. During heavy rains, this roadway became four to six-inch deep mud, perilous for buggies and small wagons. Womenfolk were picked up by men, often or not strangers, and carried across the road to keep them from slogging through the thick mud. This was one of the very few times a stranger got away with handling a local woman. He is usually thanked for it. Being a gentleman, he seldom mentioned the act, again.

The wind picked up since he left the livery stable. JW pulled his flat brimmed leather work hat down, securing its leather string below his chin to keep it from blowing off. The hat had a hammered silver band he'd bought in Tucson, after selling off 58 fattened head of cattle for 62 cents a pound. He needed horses to build his heard. He used the cattle money to buy 14 horses. Not the best to breed with, but they would do for this area of the territory. Good stock was still hard to find in Arizona. The Indians seemed to hold sole ownership on the wild mustang market.

While fighting in Mexico, JW learned about the Appaloosa horse with its beautiful colors, tied in with amazing strength. He personally found they could go all day and night, and be ready for a fight in the morning. He bought and rode one through the end of the Mexican-American Campaign. He made it known through the right circles that he wanted to buy 15 to 20 Appaloosa prime mares and four Appaloosa stallions for his ranch. He and his future rangers later came across a band of Mexican banditos, who possessed unmarked Mexican Gold bricks. Since they defeated the Mexicans, they chose to keep the gold, dividing it amongst themselves; which allowed most of them the beginning of their ranching and farming business ventures.

In truth, they talked among themselves about turning the captured gold over to the territorial government or even the federal government, but each ranger had a different sad story to tell concerning corruption they witnessed by such so-called appointed officials. They knew Federal Marshals were hired thugs, who stole property and money from the people of Arizona. They were the strong arm behind both the territorial and federal governments. A vote was taken. It was unanimous—withhold the gold and use it to begin their farms and ranches. Several men who served in the Union Army and fought in the Mexican Campaign, still had over a year's worth of wages due them. They considered the gold an overpayment of sorts.

Two months later Captain Blake took possession of a fine herd of prime Appaloosa mares from a group of Hispanic gentlemen at a price JW could handle. Each horse was in great shape to breed with his males. The delivery made one very energetic stallion he had purchased from the Navajo, extremely happy.

The wind had a foul odor to it. This troubled JW, causing him to wonder if it was the smell of death coming from the big war to the east, or some of the butchered dogs the local group of part Mexican and part Apache were hanging south of town for tomorrow's feast. JW didn't mind the taste of dog. As long as it was hung right and seasoned over a low fire. He couldn't understand why Eastern Americans had problems with eating dogs. He read about how all over the Orient the people ate dogs and it was also consumed in different parts of Europe. Hearing his men complain about beans on ride, JW often thought Americans were a bit prudish when it came to fashions, customs and especially their food. While he studied European History, he marveled at the citizens of Britain and Europe and their disdain to bathing, or of how they built their massive castles to be so airy, as to freeze all winter, due to poor heating plans. History showed most great civilizations absurdly foul when it concerned their plumbing needs and how open sewers ran down the center of London and Paris streets. "And they referred to American Indians as 'heathens' and 'savages'."

He found Preacher Joe inside his grayish weathered cedar wood plank house, sitting beside an oil lamp, blocking the flame from the wind, reading from his dog-eared Bible with yellowing pages. His was a leather bound Holy Bible, containing both Old Testament and New Testament. JW thought the leather hide may be from a giant elk he heard about and the sewing must have been done by someone who really knew their business. He briefed Preacher Joe on what he requested for the wagon; just to make sure he double-checked Mr. Johnson's loading work. There were times Old Man Johnson used the old memory-loss excuse; not that he wasn't old enough. Or, he used how he had suffered greatly and this caused his memory problem. But in truth, he was too much of a skinflint to hire someone to do muscle work. JW caught him rolling equipment into a barn's tack room that was supposed to go on the trailer. One time, the water barrels were only filled halfway. So, JW checked everything before leaving. To keep things cordial, he advised Mr. Johnson he's required to verify all the equipment and goods going into the field, to ensure every single item is accounted for.

An hour later, JW headed home. Preacher Joe was heading to bed for a few hours of shut-eye. He informed JW he had several armfuls of white crosses already made, after the last massacre. He wanted to be prepared. It was hard to find decent wood to make a cross out of in the desert. "I also have 'Stars of David' for any Jews found in a massacre site."

JW warned his old friend he'd most likely have a young passenger with him. He didn't go any further into details. As he approached his ranch, he picked up the sounds of his wife singing one of her child's songs. She hadn't done this for some time. Then he heard the echoing sound of a desert hawk off to the north — one of the prairie's predators. It sounded close. All JW's critters were too large for a hawk to carry off. He figured the bird must've spotted a jackrabbit and was circling overhead. Its eerie cries could freeze a small animal in its place and the hawk would buzz right down and scoop it up.

He took Knot Head into the barn, unsaddled her and did a quick rubdown with a handful of straw, followed by his curry comb. He pulled out the other half of an apple he bought in town and held it over the horse's eyes. Fresh fruit wasn't cheap, but a good horse often saved a man's life.

JW gave her the first half back in town. He now rewarded her with the second half. "I know, I'm a sure spoilin' you, just don't you tell Sherry Ann, or you'll be on salt rations for a week." Sherry Ann had been on him about buying too many expensive food items in town. Bags of sugar, salt, pepper and anything else had to be hauled in. The customer always was the one who paid extra for it.

"You want those apples and pears, you buy the seeds and grow the trees," She growled at him after paying the monthly bill at the store and seeing what he spent their ranch money on.

JW walked across the yard after locking the barn for the night. He gave the area a once over before walking up the front steps and opening the door. The wind died down between the settlement and his ranch, but it was still a might chilly with a cloudless sky from horizon to horizon.

Inside he found his wife sitting on the floor, singing to Liam McFaul, who was now asleep, lying prone on the floor; covered by two light-weight wool blankets she crafted.

"All okay?" JW asked in a whisper.

They walked into the kitchen area of the house to finish their conversation about the boy. "He was havin' a bad nightmare and woke up screaming. He said he saw people being scalped, but he doesn't recall seeing the real thing, since he was knocked cold."

"Mind can play a lot of games, with only a fraction based on reality. He may think this is what happened and now his mind is fillin' in his lapses. But I need him ready at dawn. We might not be able to find the site without him, based only on directions from a sprout with no roots in this whole area. One stream will look like another, same with the hills and that earlier wind most-likely filled in his tracks. I am hoping I can follow his trail, but he will be needed to identify who for the reports and for the names on the crosses."

"I'll get him up for you and get you both loaded down with hot coffee, bacon and biscuits. I've already got fresh bread in the oven, so you'll have plenty of food for both of you."

"Oh, I'm takin' along Preacher Joe, would you…"

"Sure, anyone else you want me feedin'?" She asked, with a sigh and her arms spread out and hands facing upward.

"Well, I thought about taking along some of those dark ladies to entertain the troops…" He stopped when a loaf of rising unbaked bread smacked him in the face. He had taken his coat off, leaned his rifle against the wall, before locking the front door and turned just in time to catch the bread ring true between his nose and chin.

With a playful wife pounding his back, JW lifted her up and tossing her gently over his left shoulder, he carried her into their bedroom and dropped her not so gently onto their newly acquired feather bed. A fellow rancher had three of them shipped in with bedding. JW made it four upon hearing about it. This was a rare surprise anniversary gift. Sherry Ann completely flipped over the exquisite comfort and the bedding was really beautiful. The top comforter was dyed in a strange softened blue color, which made both JW and Sherry Ann think it resembled the overhead sky on a clear spring day.

Then he remembered this Liam McFaul character out in his living room. He walked back out there in his skivvies to grab all his weapons. He bolted the bedroom door behind him. He was sure to awaken if this Liam woke up and began tramping about, but he did not want to take any chances.

DAWN AT THE DOUBLE B RANCH

It wasn't the kid who woke JW up. The sound of a dozen or more horses standing outside in his yard woke him. His rangers were on time.

Sliding on a pair of dark brown canvas pants, over his flannel one-piece skivvies; which concealed his outcropping of brown and gray chest hairs; he walked to the front door; and unlocked it. He looked down at Liam, noticing the boy was glaring up at him from the kitchen table. "Good to see you're awake. Now get yourself ready because you are about to be raided by 12 or more Arizona Rangers and they're liable to be hungry for breakfast and coffee. Now I told you to go finish dressing, you got a long ride to make." When Liam just sat at the table staring back at JW, the man of the house raised his voice and said, "Get movin'!"

JW turned away, walking out to the wooden porch; just as Sherry Ann belted on her night coat, walking out of the bedroom to see what was happening. Big yawns escaped from her as she listened to JW speak to his early arriving troops. She then looked down at Liam, a frown formed on her face. "My husband said get dressed. Now you might remember he is the Captain of these here rangers and they love him. If they find you're not listening to him and obeyin', they might just take the matter into their own hands and paddle your backside. You're too old for that. Time for you to be a man, now. You've seen how unforgiving the land can be. It's only the strong and good people who make a difference. Now, you have to decide if you got what it takes."

Liam stared at her for a moment. He'd never been talked to as an adult before. But he now sensed what was expected of him. He went off to get dressed. Sherry Ann had cut down and sewed up some of JW's older clothes for the boy after she burned all of Liam's bloodied garments outside with the help of a pouring of coal oil. As she watched him head into her boy's room, she grinned, walking into the kitchen. She had a lot of coffee to make and that meant sending Liam off to the well for a couple more gallons of water and another armload of firewood for the stove. Two of the milk cows would have to be hit right off to provide for breakfast needs.

With a big ceramic bowl JW bought for her in New Mexico several years back, and a hand carved wooden spoon from a mesquite log, she commenced making a mess of flapjacks for her rangers. She always kept a five-pound barrel of corn flour inside her kitchen and a 45-pounder in the barn; all sealed up to keep the bugs out. Corn flower was a few cents cheaper a pound right now than wheat flower. But she knew the prices both went up and down to fight for customers. Next month she might be using wheat flour, which JW preferred, but the man would eat anything and everything she prepared for him.

Once a month, JW would haul the nearly empty big barrel into Globe to be refilled. Sherry Ann liked to keep the five-pounder in the kitchen in the event the Apache lay siege and they couldn't leave the ranch house, while standing off the raiding Indians. However, she had long figured out those Apache had a deep respect for her husband and used such attacks on their place as a passing of manhood for the new braves. After two or three days, they'd vanish with the coming of a new dawn. A couple times they left half-of-a buffalo; meat and buffalo robe included in respect for JW and his wife. Out of some unspoken agreement, they had never attacked when JW was not home. That was not to say they would not kidnap her and the children, but it would not be a murder raid. JW had lived with several of the Apache Tribes and new most of their laws, customs and traditions. Kidnapping of his family was another way to bring him out to test their individual warriors, but the kidnapping raid had never come because JW and his rangers had provided meat and water to many of the small Apache Tribes that were not on the warpath. However, they were starving or thirsty because too many White Men had forced them from their lands because some ignorant White Men identified these people as part of the Renegades.

The Rangers from Texas, New Mexico and into Arizona, had long known the difference between the People and the Renegades. They did what they could for those trying to obey White Man's laws.

Sherry Ann knew they'd use up her supply of chicken eggs this morning, but it wouldn't take her laying hens long to refill her egg bin again. The hens that quit laying, out of age or contrariness, found an invitation into the frying pan or her stewpot.

When she watched Liam pass through the kitchen, wearing her husband's clothes and his knife sheath shoved down into his pants, held in place with a rope belt, she was now realizing she had probably just gained a new son. Liam had shared with her earlier as to how he had no other family, but those who got themselves slaughtered. She had mentioned it late last night, when JW came home from town and his only reply was, "We'll see."

Most of the men had arrived and they had prepared their own coffee over an open fire pit, out in front of the front porch. But they all would admit, their coffee never tasted as good as Sherry Ann's brew and she would never share her secrets with anyone. Not even JW.

Liam McFaul was introduced to the rangers and with several of the men offering him a nod or a handshake, one or two back slaps, but not one of them offered him up an ounce of pity. They had learned the hard ways of the west, and pity, well that only went to kids who had lost their family, or parents who lost a son or daughter. But Liam, he wasn't kid age any-more and needed toughening up real fast to survive out here in hard-times. If JW gave the say-so, they'd help in his training and make him a ranger, but only if he had what it took to be one. Right now, he was coming along only in hopes he could locate the remains of his wagon train.

As called for, every man brought a shovel, but not knowing how long they'd be gone the ranger also brought with them two of the prospector-style one-gallon canteens or Indian-style water bladders. Those water bladders had been the stomachs of long-horn steers or the larger woodland buffalo. Once boiled a few times they performed their duty for holding water pretty well. The ranger's wagon carried an extra 55-gallon wooden barrel of water for the men, giving them two water barrels on each side. Two were for men and two for the horses. The men knew how to stretch their drinking water thinly, but not too thinly for their mounts. A dead horse could leave them a-foot and this could very well turn into a death sentence for a man under a hot desert sun with the nearest creek being more than 30-miles away. Often not knowing which direction the creek or water hole lie or if it ended up dry, poisoned or drinkable?

Most every man had their own hand drawn maps of the region from all the trips they had made, but JW knew it would make no sense to Liam.

He had to follow his own trail, what he recalled going from hill-top to dried creek bed. The Ranger's had two great trackers, but only an Apache could follow someone over the old lava fields and rocky embankments. Liam mentioned having taken several falls, which his bloodied knees, elbows and jaw being ample evidence of that. So, for now JW would let Liam lead for the first couple days. JW also knew the approximate location where the wagon train trail is and possibly the spot where eight-wagons may have departed the big train. This at least gave him some northern reference point. That along with Liam's account of how they headed southeast, hoping to eventually locate the Santa Fe to Tucson Trail. Once on the trail they planned to head for Los Angeles.

Unfortunately, being just a sprout himself, Liam wasn't in on any of the grown-up chats and didn't know of how far east their train planned to cut southeast of the Grand Canyon—possibly with a stop-over in Phoenix and then Tucson—before that last big desert crossing to a mule-stop watering hole he heard of called Blyth. After that it was supposed to be 12 to 15 days to the outer walls of Los Angeles and the bigger cattle ranches. His family and that of his uncles were fishermen. Liam told Sherry Ann how they planned to build two-fishing boats south of Los Angeles and fish the Pacific Ocean. "They hoped to sell their catches to the various stores and restaurants in this Los Angeles. They fished the Atlantic Ocean, but there were too many fishermen, too many boats of all sizes and the catches were getting smaller."

After breakfast was over, Liam helped Steven, JW's ten-year old son he was sharing a room with, gather up the trash, plates and cups. JW came over, touching Liam's right shoulder, "Come along, Lad." He led Liam into the barn. While outside, the rangers finished preparing their mounts for the long ride into the desert. For those who hadn't already done so, they were slapping on their riding leathers and killing weapons. Steven had watched this before, many times. He knew these men were preparing for war. His dad explained it to him that as much as the preparing was a physical effort, it was also a mental thing.

"Rangers need to put themselves into a right frame of mind for what lay ahead…not only for the shooting, but for all the burying of the mutated bodies—men, woman and children—they'll need to do."

When JW led Liam inside the barn, the young man was surprised to find a mounted Appaloosa, with full water bladders and a shotgun tied barrel down to the saddle. "Sherry Ann wanted you to use her second mount. It's a mare, about 16 hands named Sandy. She'll run all day, but you best be nice to her or I'll have you walkin' or riding the wagon with Preacher Joe. Until I know what you're made of, you'll ride with us during the day or out on track with point. If on point, and an attack comes, you are to run as fast as Sandy will take you back to make a report. Do not stand to make a fight of it…Indians liable to haul you both off and I'll never know what happened to you. Other tracker will do the same if you are jumped. But you'se only got to worry 'bout that when you on point and we're having trouble finding your tracks and you need to look for something might be familiar."

JW pointed to the water sacks, "Treat that like life's blood. Sips at a time and if I think you're sippin' too much I'll give one warning and then you lose them. I'll give you a drink when I take one and I been known to go all day without a sip, can't even pee for darn near 24-hours."

He turned away so Liam couldn't see the smile on his face. "Now you said you had some experience with a shotgun. But all I got is this 12-guage double-barrel. It's filled with buckshot…each round with nearly 20 pellets and each pellet could kill you. You fire both barrels at once and it'll break you in half. So, it's one barrel at a time. Now tell me the truth, is that the kind of shotgun you carried before?"

"No, sir…mine was loaded with varmint loads. But I shot my dad's and his was very much like this. But only one barrel at a time, like you advised me."

"Liam, now that you're calmed down, I noticed you've been to school. What were your parents…farmers or ranchers, maybe educated people?"

"Sir, my mother home schooled us and I was taught to read from the Holy Bible when I was five years old. She was once a school teacher, but left that job when she married my father. He was a fisherman, but he had gone through all the grades and had obtained his high school diploma. He hoped to go for a Medical Degree from a well-known Medical College on the East Coast, a religious one, but the family business needed him. All I can remember is how we were brought up on the Word of God, how to patch nets and clean the decks of the family boat.

"My little sister fell quite ill and she seemed to be improving as we came west. I heard a word…consumption, but couldn't find a meaning for it and I never asked, as I did not want Mom and Dad knowing I was listening to their late at night conversations."

"Well, as long as you're with my family, you'd just better not listen to any of mine and Sherry Ann's later night conversations…either."

"No, Sir," Liam said, as he slowly stroked Sandy's neck.

"There's a bag tied to the back of your saddle, got some apples in it. Now it ain't for you, it's for Sandy. But don't serve them whole. Make them last longer by giving them to her in halves or quarters. But cut the seeds out. Now I don't believe with my dear wife, but she's taken it on that if Sandy or any other horse eats fruit seeds the trees are going to grow inside her. Plain foolishness. But by cutting the seeds out, you won't be lying to her."

"No, Sir…I mean, yes, Sir."

"Well, like I said, you and I will do some shooting practice along the way to get you used to that shotgun. I've also brought along a six-gun and holster rig to see if you can hit anything without blowing your leg off, but that's for later."

Liam spotted a tied off canvas bag, near Sandy's front legs. "What's that?"

"It's my old riding leathers from when I was about your age. I grew so fast I didn't spend much time in them, but I held on to them. Steven's two to three years away from being big enough for 'em and the wife thought you might need 'em. Wearin' what you got on now, two to three days of hard ridin' and you done worn a hole right through you'se backside. So, you wear those and here's a hat." JW went over to a wooden post and pulled off an ancient, flat brimmed leather hat. This one's seen several hundred thousand miles of desert travel, thunderstorms and a few dozen Indian battles.

"This'll keep the sun off your face. Now bring Sandy out and get lined up with the others out front." JW started to leave, but then turned to face Liam. "One more thing, try not to embarrass me by falling off your horse…okay?"

"Yes, Sir," Liam said, but JW had already opened the barn door and was headed for the porch.

"Did he like the gifts?" Sherry Ann asked. She stood on the porch with their two kids.

"Like a six-year old on Christmas mornin', Sugar."

"Always the same, you call me that southern Sugar name when you get ready to leave on the warpath again." She locked her hands around the back of his neck and stood on her tip toes. "You had better come back to me, Ranger and bring that sprout with you. I'm a thinkin' the Good Lord has plans for him."

"I just hope he can ride and we can teach him to shoot." JW gave her a deep kiss and then picked up each of his kids for a big hug. Steven complained about the hug, saying he was now too big for his father's hug and a handshake would be more appropriate.

"Son, you just don't get too big for those words 'fore I gets back an' we'll have us a talk about it. I've just learned young Liam is a learned young man and maybe he can help with the home schoolin'."

"So, you'se already a thinkin' he can stay with us?" Steven asked.

"We'll talk about it, some. Got' ta go now." JW gave her one final kiss, a wink and headed over to his mount Knot Head. He noticed Preacher Joe was still up on the wagon, reading from his Bible and blessing the Blake Ranch. JW knew Preacher Joe had a black powder and ball, 1853 Enfield Musket by his knee, a wood axe on the floor of the seat and a ten-inch blade hunting knife strapped to his right side. Primarily, Preacher Joe would be watching over the campsite, doing the cooking and Liam would be his assistant when not being used for tracking.

ROLL-CALL

Sitting atop his mount, he glanced at the line of mounted men to make sure they were all sober. He followed up with a quick visual check of their riding clothes, hats and the weapons they carried. Oh, he knew each man had at least one hidden revolver, possibly a broken-down musket behind their saddle and two or three extra knives. He knew one man carried a meat cleaver, in the event they took down a desert dear or were forced to eat one of their horses, and they all carried ultra-sharp skinning knives with blades no longer than two-inches. His own skinning knife had a two-inch blade and doubled as a surgical knife, with sharpness took him a lot of hours of hard laboring work to obtain. JW hoped one day to claim one of those Indian lava stone knives that could make his blade dull as a shale slab by comparison.

JW also looked at their boots, knowing some of his men could ill-afford a new pair of leather boots. He had already done a spot check on several of the horse's horseshoes. Extra horse shoes and farrier tools were aboard the wagon, because the lava beds were known to present a serious problem on past rides. It struck JW funny how he had ridden most of the Arizona flatland and had come across miles and miles of ancient lava beds in various locations, but rarely did he see a dormant or extinct volcano anywhere in the area. He figured based on where possible volcanoes could have existed inside such range like the Superstition Mountains, these lava flows traveled hundreds of miles. He learned of such old Indian tales of flaming stones flying out of flaming mountains and flying over the horizon, which might explain these lava beds. However, it was all stories. Yet, in his time in Arizona and dealing with the Apache, Navajo, Hopi and others, he learned not to laugh at their ancient tales and legends.

Each rider in front of him was pretty much a volunteer, their ammo was paid for and the cost of a new horse if theirs was lost, stolen or killed during the line of duty. Those who survive a whole month might see that $22 fee now due them. But the pay had little to do with why a ranger hit the trail. He rode to protect his territory and his country. He wanted the land safe for everyone, especially the families coming west to settle. Some did it for the action, while others did it for the camaraderie between rangers.

Liam looked at these men on horseback and saw that same hardness. They also carried iron jaws and cold eyes that could look-into the heart of a storm and tear its guts out with a strong right hand. So similar to the sailing men of the sea, fishermen who had spent years watching fellow sea warriors go to their boats to face weeks at sea, battling the storms with 30 to 40 foot waves to make a catch. Iron-willed men who held fast upon their decks, with a fist raised against a mighty icy tempest, the man knowing the heart of the storm was out to drown him and the rest of his crew, for simply daring to sail into these blackened waters.

No, Liam saw a great resemblance between his family and these new friends he was guiding out to where the massacre had occurred. He believed his father would be proud to be buried by such warriors as these.

JW had to leave two rangers in Globe to handle any problems that might come up. Soon, Globe would be big enough to have an election, become a township and hire themselves their own Sheriff, who could possibly get himself a few Sheriff Deputies if the town council allowed him to.

Globe's rapid growth sort of worried JW, for his property now had new neighbors on the road. With every new trip to town he saw more immigrants with various languages, different style clothes, a dozen new dreams. He had no idea what they were saying as he returned their waves. In the last six months, farms had popped up with German, Swiss, Quaker, Mormon, Dutch and a family from Scotland. At his last count, at least ten new farms and ranches had been built within the settlement area. JW couldn't see anyone to the east of him, but property to his south was being bought up. He would have liked to have bought the land up, but all his financial strings were stretched to the limit now. He only hoped for good neighbors. Three years earlier he had hung a close-by neighbor's adult son for horse and cattle stealing, killing one of JW's ranch hands in the process. Ranger's caught him raising a ruckus down in Tucson, after he sold the animals across the Mexican Border.

"Seems he rose too much of a ruckus down there, so the French kicked him north," the arresting ranger told JW. The trial lasted three-days. He was hung on Saturday morning in Tucson. JW was present, along with the parents of the boy.

JW had left his second in Command—Ranger Sergeant, James Arthur Lee Dreeke—to select the two men who would stay in town. When Sgt. Dreeke arrived at the Blake Ranch he briefed JW on how he had selected the oldest and youngest Ranger to stay in town and both grumbled. He also sent the message JW had written to Tucson, via Phoenix stagecoach. The new telegraph wire for Arizona was still months away from being constructed and the Pony Express route didn't consider Arizona part of its route yet, due to the low population; in 1860, the census had shown only 6,482 White Americans.

James Dreeke — known to JW as Jamey — was 32-years old and a third-generation German-American. He stood five-foot, nine-inches in his rumpled-up socks, carrying 162lbs of leanness. But though a small man, JW knew Jamey to be a bobcat in any given situation. A scraper from head to toe, he wore his shiny black hair to his shoulders and was known to be a great scout and tracker. His wife named Becca, with flowing red hair and a home full of God fearing song, they raised two daughters — Ava, all of six-years old and Clair, a rambunctious three-year old in the joys of knowing the Lord. After a prior home burned down, with help from over 20-Mexican bandits, who made off with 34 horses and a young cattle herd of 146 cows and steers, they were now living in town in a rented log home. James was working with his younger brother, attempting to raise money to build up their stock and rebuild their ranch on the same foundation.

Ranger Joshua Troy Dreeke was 30-years old, five-foot, ten-inches and 220 pounds, barrel chested like his old man, kept longish strands of reddish-brown hair like their mother. Joshua seemed to look a bit more Irish in appearance than German. His face carried a stern look, which ended in a pointed chin. His cheeks always seemed in need of shaving and his eyes, carried an almost impish look to them, as if he always knew a secret no one else knew, or he was about to pull one of his witty pranks on you. But when out on a ranger venture, he grew a beard that was a sight to behold and when he returned, many of the children in town thought he resembled a pirate. Joshua had large feet and hands, passed down from his mom's side which gave him a problem finding boots and riding gloves. His newest set of both had been handmade for him during one of his pilgrimages across the border to pick-up a saddle he had ordered for his golden palomino — Star Fire.

However, not supporting a family and being a pretty good gambler, he did quite well at the table in the bar in Globe's Trading Post. He never show-boated it. Once he won a few hands, he'd lose a couple small ones on purpose and then call it a night. Becca Dreeke was holding all the funds for the Dreeke future, but Joshua was happy to have his store-bought 52-cards for a few games by firelight. All losses to be paid back upon returning to Globe and an IOU could be held for up to 30-days. These are the rules the rangers played by and no firearms at a game, plus no booze on the job.

Both Dreeke brothers were anxious to get going. The day was moving along at a rapid pace. Joshua's mount was beginning to bite at a no-name brown mare ridden by Ranger Lawrence Joseph Coon; was also known as Indian Joe because he was half-White and half-Navajo. At 25 years-old, Coon was six-foot tall, which was large for a Navajo. He weighed 158 pounds, wore long black hair to his waist, which he kept in a thick single braid. From his White side, he gained unusually large ears, which got him into many fights brought about through teasing from White students in school. His broad shoulders and dark looks attracted the womenfolk, even the married ones. But Lawrence walked his own road and in time he gained a reputation of being a fair hand with working cattle, could ride any horse, wild or tempered, and from Mexico he had learned to be a competent knife fighter with the Spanish nine-inch blade killing weapon he carried on his left hip in an ornate cowhide sheath. Many a woman had lost their hearts to his cold black eyes and in some cases this had led to duels with Coon having the right to choose the weapon. Knives were always his choice and almost always a bit of a nick was enough for his opponent to withdraw his challenge. Still, once a man tried to cheat with a hidden firearm and he died for his mistake. After that, Lawrence Coon worked hard to avoid engaged and married women. JW had laid the law down on him. "Ranger or criminal, you can't be both."

Jim Williams was another knife fighter and there were many a night the two of the men would entertain the rangers, with a practice of their skills by the light of a campfire and a clash of blades. Sometimes it would end in a cut here or there, but if it was getting too serious JW would have them stop. William was raised by the Apache, stolen from a burning wagon when he was less than two-years old and brought home to an Indian woman who had lost her son a few days before to a strange illness. The Indian camp was raided when he was 12 years old, just when he was now beginning — with the other braves — their first years to become warriors. His mother had died when he was seven-years old during a Mexican Bandit attack, however the young warrior braves chased them off. He also lost his sister of six summer seasons, who was carried off by the retreating bandits. At five-foot, seven-inches, 171 pounds, Williams was now 26 years old, could speak American, Apache and some Mexican. He was an expert with any weapon put into his hands and during his time with the rangers he had been wounded seven times. He was formally engaged to a beautiful 23-year old Navajo lady, who taught school at the nearby tribal lands. Her White name was Vicki, but her Indian name was Singing Star.

One of the men who always preferred to ride scout, considering it his lucky spot, John A. Holloway, a White Russian of 44 years old, owned a 100-acre farm within spitting distance of JW's property line. A deep crevice separated their two properties and no fence was needed because the cattle gave the cut in the ground a wide berth on both sides. Holloway, who had Tartar blood deep on one side of his family line and relatives who rode in the ceremonial guard for Moscow's royalty, wanted something different. He docked in Texas as a 28-year old and based on his former military experience, he was soon made a Deputy U.S Marshal. Eventually though, he grew weary of Texas and the law's desire to hang people a bit too fast, especially the immigrants, so he resigned and headed west. He bought a 140-acre farm that came with 102 head of cattle and nine horses. This included a log home, a good-sized barn, three corrals, and four additional out buildings. He never found out why the seller had such a low price on it, but Holloway later heard the seller's wife was Chinese and the farm was worked mostly by Chinese laborers. Then it all suddenly stopped and everyone disappeared and the legal owner was in a real hurry to leave the area.

Holloway carried a sawed-off double-barrel 12-guage shotgun and a Russian .44 caliber revolver in a left sided shoulder holster. But on his waist, he carried two matching knives, which were almost swords because the blades were over 16-inches long and had golden colored sword-like pommels. He had once told JW the swords had come down through the family through multiple generations and now he used them against the Apache. He rides a black mare of 18-hands in height, with a white star and four white socks on its feet. He had named the horse Comet and had raised it from its youth. Holloway had joined the Rangers for neighborly involvement and to learn more about his enemy — the Apache.

Feeding his horse, Little Texas, from his dusty Stetson, Globe store owner and part-time Ranger, Chad Leaders glanced about the group. At 34-years old, Leaders was all-of five-foot, five-inches, 160 pounds, had medium length blondish hair that was balding and radiant blue eyes. He enjoyed being a Ranger, but his wife insisted he put half of his time in at the store, or he might face family problems.

Leaders moved into Globe with the first hardware store in three wagons. He would put in the first man's shopping emporium north of Phoenix. Whatever he didn't have, he could order and he carried half-a-dozen catalogues. But the store's argument always started when the subject of barbed wire popped up in a conversation between farmer and rancher. That's when Leaders would pull out his Navy Colt and slam it down on his wooden counter just hard enough to get everyone's attention. Store owner Leaders had now just become Ranger Leaders and everyone quieted down right smartly.

Leaders and Brady Williams glanced at each other and both smiled. They both enjoyed a good desert ride. Although his last name was Williams, Brady was no relation to Jim Williams. He was still adjusting his saddle for the long ride ahead and waving his hand at JW. "I'm about ready, Captain. She done and drank too much water this morning…was 'bout ta pop." Brady was half white and half Dakota Sioux from the northern plains country. He had spent several years with his mother's people in a Christian Indian school. But when his mom died from a Crow Indian arrow, he went to live with his White father in Tucson. The man was a traveling fur and hide trader, who because of injuries in the field had to take root and he no longer had room for a grown-up boy. But he did right by him and got the older youth a job working for Ranger John Holloway. In time, he joined the Rangers and proved himself on his first venture by saving two Ranger's lives, when they were ambushed by a small Apache raiding party. Brady killed two Indians and wounded one more, securing for himself full right to be considered an Arizona Ranger.

His Half-Sioux blood line provided Brady with shiny black hair worn long in two braids tied off by leather strings. He stood a hair over five-foot, nine-inches, weighed all of 156 pounds and was now engaged to a local mule skinner's daughter in Globe. Her name was Sue. She had a real nice reputation as a good Christian. She was still looking over five younger siblings. Her mom died when she was kicked by one of their mules, leaving her dad no choice but to take the mule out and shoot it right between the eyes. The carcass was left for the wolves and coyotes. Brady was an expert with the fighting knife and trader tomahawk, but he would never practice with the other rangers — except for throwing skills at playing cards for coin. He also often carried a Sioux tomahawk with three eagle feathers tied to it and carried no pistol. But he did carry a double-barrel shotgun loaded down with nails on his saddle. He found a load of nails a good killing machine for more than one target.

Then there was John L. Gibson, who was the oldest in another part of a brother team. He and his younger brother Michael Henry Gibson had come to California on boat from Mississippi when they were young. The call of the Pacific Ocean brought their parents west to settle in the Great Los Angeles area. But this had not worked out for the family and they lost their homestead in a land swindle. The family split up, with John going with his father and Michael staying with his mother. But, when their mother fell sick and died, their father was killed a month later in a shooting. This brought the boys back together and they joined up in Arizona, first to Tucson, then up to the new township of Phoenix. Along the way, they met JW Blake, who told them about the Globe area and building of the Arizona Rangers. Well the two of them had learned very little about side-arms, but their grandfather had taught them all there was to know about rifles and both boys could knock down a desert hawk flying overhead by better than 100 feet on the wing. The side arm issue came later and within the year they had become rangers.

Now 28 years old, John Gibson was a tall one, standing six-foot, five-inches, he had to duck his head for nearly every doorway in Globe or in every ranch or farm in the territory. He preferred a Spencer Carbine, but sure had his eyes on JW's Henry Rifle. Every ranger did. John also carried the Navy Colt revolver, which fit with his long lanky legs. With dark blondish hair worn longish and under a flop of a flat-brimmed leather hat, he kept an eagle's feather coming out of a blue-ribbon trim. With eyes, bluish in color and his beard, that never seemed to quite reach adulthood—sort of scrawny-like in nature with a hair here and there—looked younger than he was. John rode a male gelding of 18-hands, bought from a Mississippi man who honestly complained that horse was still filled with too much piss and vinegar. John was warned several times after the transaction was made, "Don't you ever turn your back on that Devil. He'll kill you'se for damn sure." John named the horse—General Lee, after a famous Union Officer who turned Confederate fire breather.

But the giant in the family was six-foot, eight-inch Michael Henry Gibson. At 26 years-old, he was the gentler of the two young men. He enjoyed a good clean shave once a day, even a dry shave and took to his family's religious ways of carrying a Book of Mormon with him. At 273 pounds, Michael was a giant that many a man feared. When walking the street with his brother even the horsemen gave them ample room. Matching in description with his brother, but a smite broader at the shoulders, Michael had taken a liking to carrying two Navy Colts, plus a good size hunting knife he wore inside his left boot. After his first engagements with the Apache, he had switched rifles and now carried the 1855 Model U.S. Springfield Rifled Musket.

When not carrying out their Ranger duties, the two brothers hired out as horse breakers, wolf hunters and riding as shotgun guards for the stagecoach lines. Anything to keep them fed between JW's call-outs. Nothing they liked better than a long ride with their comrades and the aspect of an engagement with the Apache. Michael rode the largest horse he could find in Arizona, which was half Appaloosa and half dinosaur. It breathed fire from its massive snout. This was not a handsome horse, but it was bigger than most wagon pullers and could still build up a head of steam to get him out of a close call. Before he found the horse at a Quaker farm south of Tucson, Michael was stuck driving the ranger wagon. Now he was mounted. He named his shy pony after the new Commander of the Army of Texas; General Hood.

Next man in line was one of the older men; Troy C. Crutchfield, current owner of Crutchfield Merchandise and a fur buyer for Central

Arizona. A former Missouri Deputy Marshal for the area of Sedalia, he began his law enforcement career as a jail guard in a Mississippi prison and worked his way around the state. True, he was born a southern boy, but now he felt a bit too old and frizzled to run off to sound of the bugle to defend his former home. No, he had come to Arizona nine-years ago, building his first small store in Tucson, only to see it burn to the ground during an Apache raid. He took his wife and kids north to Globe, where it was reported to have the protection of the U.S. Army. But the Confederacy took over Arizona in 1861, only to lose it to the northern forces with their arrival in 1862.

At 49 years-old, Troy stood a mite bent over at five-foot, eight-inches and didn't know his weight. But he took a lot of ribbing, because he rode with a soft blue pillow under his hind-end to cushion his long days in the saddle. His riding leathers had long fringe on them — circa time of the older plainsmen. He also wore knee high moccasins, very ornate and topped in beaver fur, made of bear hide and hand sewn together with porcupine quills. Troy liked to carry both long knife and tomahawk when going after Indians and sported a .54 caliber Sharps Buffalo Rifle to do his killing. His saddle was also equipped with two holsters to the right and left by his knees and in these he carried Navy Colts of .44 calibers. He believed in being ready for anything. He slept under three Indian blankets. During winter months, he brought along his buffalo robe to keep his old bones warm. JW liked having him along, as there was little about the Apache and this country this man didn't know. He wasn't quick enough to ride scout anymore, not that Troy cared. He liked to be close to where the hot coffee would be ready.

With his mother a Spanish lady of stature and his father an Irish boat owner and skipper, Patrick O'Miller grew up as a child of education and wealth. He knew of homes in Spain and Mexico, but also in Ireland and on some island in the Caribbean he had seen only once. But a terrific storm off the west coast of Mexico ended all that. His father's ship was sunk, killing all his family, but himself, who was saved by a second mate. The man and the boy made it to shore and then after a lengthy rest, they stumbled their way north until they reached a small town. Here, the mate abandoned the boy to an abusive blacksmith, who beat and tortured the lad for seven years, until the townspeople had enough of the foul man and killed him late one night. At 13 years-old, the boy was given a dozen pesos, a bag of food and a skin bladder of water, and was pointed north. Having him in town reminded them of their murderous act and they wished to forget it. The traveling Priest would not be by for several months to take the boy with him. Still, one kind local man gave him a ride in his wagon for the first ten miles, but then he had to turn around. His last words of advice, "Go to the Americans, they will help you."

Fourteen years later, Patrick was approaching his 28th birthday and standing by a smart buggy driven by his wife, Canaan, and sitting beside her was their 11-month old child, Solomon. Patrick had JW's permission to say a final goodbye and ensure Canaan had everything she needed. Sherry Ann had offered to let her stay, but they had a growing café business waiting back in Globe and she needed to be back by dinner time. As owner, she was still the head cook, night clean-up and money changer. Down at her feet was a new style Colt revolver, which she kept inside a black cloth bag. Behind the seat was a loaded Spencer Carbine. She also carried extra ammo in the cloth bag. Though there had been no report of Indians seen anywhere near the road to Globe, she didn't take any chances. She had two good horses fastened to her buggy instead of one for a fast dash into Globe. Nearer to town she would fire off three rounds. The townspeople would know there was trouble and a dozen men on horseback would be on the way to help her.

Patrick had come to Arizona aboard a gold train. He was one of the young guards, along with Union troops. They spent a week in Phoenix and Patrick stayed. He liked the people, the city and the climate. He could speak both languages and got along fairly well. Within a week, he found employment in the sheriff's office as a jail guard; a year later as a deputy. Law enforcement jobs hopped around, but he decided he wanted to own a business, one that would serve both Spanish-Mexican and Whites. He soon learned that to buy or build a business, he needed to move outside the established business areas and on good advice from friends he eventually moved to Globe with his savings. There he later met Canaan, who had dreams of her own and tremendous cooking and business skills. The Irish Café became a big hit because it offered more than stew and customers were being served fresh eggs for once. Still, Patrick liked to keep his hand in police work and once he proved himself to JW, was soon accepted as a Ranger. The only condition being the wife had to cook for the annual Ranger cook-out on the Fourth of July.

JW sold Patrick one of his prized Appaloosa stallions, standing 18-hands, with a longish mane and black tail that came within a couple inches of the ground. With a darkening gray front and white back, black spots all around, the horse loved to run as if chasing the wind. The horse had also come to love his owner and friend, who would spoil it with desert fruit and a lick of sugar. Now for call-outs, which began terrifying his wife, Patrick rode with two Navy Colts, a favorite firearm of the Rangers, in his recently purchased Mexican made two holster belt rig with fancy leather imprints burned into place. The back of his belt displayed a sailing ship of the type he believed his father once owned, plus a sea anchor. Then in front was an engraving of a deputy's badge and beside it a horse's head of what he thought his Storm looked like. Hooked inside his saddle rig was a .30 caliber Sharps black-powder rifle and on the other side, a sawed-off single barrel 12-guage shotgun for close range action.

"Move out...Scouts stay within a half-mile of us. I'm concerned they may have left an ambush, knowing we might be coming. "JW yelled and then he addressed Preacher Joe, "You keep that wagon in the middle of us. You get slogged down, you whistle out and four or five of us will get our ropes tied on to you an' help pull you out." Preacher Joe waved casually in response.

JW found Liam's trail and followed it back a good five to six miles, so he knew it would be an hour before they hit new ground and from what Liam described, they were headed into the northeast and up near the shared land of Apache and Navajo. These two tribes were sworn enemies, but both had no love for the White Man. JW knew from his few chats with both tribes what they thought of the wagon trains and their reply, though in different dialects came down to meaning the same thing, "Invaders. Takers of land they do not own, or been traded for. Thieves!"

Whenever he went toward the Northeast, possibly entering the New Mexico Territory, JW was also concerned of running into a wayward band of Comanche. They would occasionally come west to make war with the Apache and Navajo, as well as the white settlers. The growing war to the east was drawing the soldiers to the east and the Indian tribes knew that only the ranger companies were standing in the Indian's way from slaughtering these Invaders.

CHAPTER TWO

"You sure this easterner brat knows where he's going, JW?"

THIRD DAY INTO THE JOUNEY TO FIND THE WAGONS, AN ESTIMATED 23-MILES NORTHEAST OF THE BLAKE RANCH

JW, standing beside Knot Head, shared a handful of water with him from his nearly empty water bladder, and followed-up by wiping his own forehead down with his moist hand. "Look, Brady, give the kid a little break...all right You can see as well as I can, we're still followin' the boy's tracks. Sure, we done lost 'em for a bit through the rocks, but he remembered those and showed us right where he entered them. So...what's got a burr under you?" JW glared at Ranger Brady Williams, who knelt-down to inspect the boy's track.

Brady ran a dry tongue across parched lips. He was one of those who timed his sips of water and midday would be his next drink. But he needed to give his mount a small portion of hot water from his hat. So, before answering JW, he filled a single knuckles depth of water into his hat; holding it up to his horse's snout. It was far from cool, but it was wet. Still, he withheld his response to JW. He knew the Captain could see what he was doing. Brady let the mount finish and then put the damp hat atop his head and for a brief-moment, it cooled his burning head.

"Sorry, Cap, I guess knowing what we got waitin' for us at this first juncture makes me head hurt. Too hot, I guess. Oh, I don't mind diggin' the graves, I just hate puttin' all those kids and ladies into them. Thinkin 'bout all their dreams shattered in just an hour or less of sheer terror. Makes me wonder why do we live in this land, Cap?"

"I want you in the wagon for a while and under the tarp. I'm bettin' you're runnin' a fever and your head's burning up...and that's an order, Ranger."

"Yeah, sure...I'll admit I ain't feelin' all that good...but those tracks have me confused, Cap."

"Why, they look like a set of a young man's tracks...they..." JW glared at Brady and then at the tracks. They were too perfect, as if made only a few hours ago, instead of four to five days ago. "I was so eager to get out there, I nearly blew it. Thanks, Brady, but you still get time in the wagon. You're all flushed with fever now and we'll probably have to spend tonight burnin' it out of you. That means wagon time again tomorrow ta get your strength back up, but you'll have three to four shotguns keeping you company if they hit us tomorrow."

"Why not wait until we reach the massacre site?" Brady asked. "They can ambush us right from the burned-out wagons or those tarantula-holes they dig. They cover themselves over with a piece of tarp and then some sand to make them look like part of the landscape."

"You're right, we'll be weary, and our timing and edge will be off because we think it's only dead people here and we know, the Apache are really superstitious about their dead. But this is our dead, they'll have had removed all of theirs, which we would of expected. No, they're leading us, keeping an eye on us and making sure we can't miss Liam's print by cleaning them out. But the wind blew last night and there's no sand in these prints." JW glanced around the desert, but he saw nothing. He did know the ranger patrol was coming up behind them and the Apaches know the ranger's strength.

Right after he mounted Knot Head, he gave the desert another looksee and sidled up beside Brady, "I can't see anyone, but I believe we got Apache eyes on us. Probably only a scout, who'll run ahead of us and at dawn he's checkin' ta make all the prints easy to see. This bunch must have no respect for our tracking skills, or at least yours today. But I'm a thinkin' we're either evenly matched in numbers or we got us a couple more than they do and they need this sort of surprise move to catch us off-guard."

"My thoughts, too, Cap…They might have even trailed the boy to make sure he arrived alive to bring us back. You think 'bout it, with all that blood on him as you described, I'm surprised a wolf or a band of coyotes didn't take him down." Brady was beginning to feel a mite dizzy. "We'd better get movin', Cap, or you'll be babysittin' me until the wagon catches up."

"Rap your reins around the pummel of your saddle. Then hold on. If you fall off, you'll never live it down. Okay?"

"A man of all kindness, Cap…remind me when you get an arrow in one of those indescribable locations and need help pulling it out." Brady began to circle a top his mount and quickly made a fast two-handed grab for his saddle-horn. "I'm seein' two of things now, Cap…if we run into the Indians point at the real one for me.

BACK AT THE ENCAMPMENT SITE

Preacher Joe gave Brady a pretty good going over to make sure he had not been bitten by a flea, stung by a scorpion or bit by a young rattler. Not finding any evidence of this he could only blame it on the sun for now, as his limited supply of medical books were all back at Globe. A lot of the peaceful Indians and Mexicans around the town could ill-afford seeing the weekly doctor who visited from Phoenix, so Preacher Joe did what he could and had become quite comfortable in making medicines and pulling teeth. He had even pulled teeth from a fair share of cattle, horses and sheep, and helped one desert tortoise get his head unstuck from a length of rolled barbed wire waiting to be loaded on to a wagon in Globe.

"I've got Brady bathed down in water and stripped of his heavy clothing. The wagon's tarp will provide some shade, but the ride will be rough. If I could I'd knock him out or get him drunk to handle the dizziness. But we don't have anything. How close is the nearest stream or river?"

JW shook his head at Preacher Joe, "Not until we reach where I believe the massacre site might be or at least three-more days. But the Stumpers' place is not too far away and they always have booze. They make their own. Not that it won't kill him, either. But does he really need it?" JW asked.

"We can stay here for three days, leave him here with myself or we take the responsibility for inflicting him with some of the most severe headaches that could have him down for weeks. Being drunk, he won't feel a thing and he should make a fully recovery in…probably three days and by then we should be at the site."

"That's another thing, Joe…seems like we have an Apache ambush waiting for us. They're guiding us and I'm betting right now they have their coyote-eyes on us. "JW called out to the rangers, "Everyone, move in closer. I want you to hear me real good." *But not our spy somewhere out there watching us.*

JW waited a moment and then addressed the problem of the suspected trap at the site and his suspicion of an Apache following to ensure we don't lose the trail. "These Indians probably realize we're rangers and are hopin' on it. They know by now our numbers are low, but we've got plenty of horses and a lot of guns and ammo they can surely use. I'm bettin' the people in those eight wagons put up a good fight and this killing raid's numbers have been reduced some, otherwise they'd have taken us on earlier. Now they're usin' the wagon site for their ambush. But we'll keep our eyes open for everything an' anythin' that might hide an Apache. Tomorrow, I want two two-man flankers out on both sides…good 500-yards out. Signal out with a single rifle shot if you come across any tracks of a party of Apache headed back towards Globe. They might choose this time to get around us and hit some of our own ranches. I also want two riders 500-yards behind on tail, to keep those Indians from sneaking up our rear. I'm thinkin' one of you better ride in your saddle facing backwards ta keep from being rode up on."

44

JW glanced over at Ranger Sergeant James Dreeke, "You pick out the riders, while the rest will ride front and rear of the wagon. I'll be scouting with the kid."

"Ah'll get it done, Captain," Sgt. Dreeke replied.

A moment later, Sgt. Dreeke walked up to Liam and none to gently, grabbed him by his left shoulder and whipped him around so the boy was facing him. Holding him by his leather shirt, he said in a low, but threatening voice, "You watch the Captain's backside, boy. If you come back without him, you'd better have at least three bloody wounds in yuh, and one had better be in the front...or don't come back at all." James Dreeke dropped his hand and walked away from the startled youth.

JW had seen the exchange, but decided not to say anything to either the boy or his sergeant. He knew James was only being overly protective of his Captain and friend, but he was often like that. As for Liam, he elected to see if the boy would come running to him to complain. But Liam didn't. He adjusted his leathers, glanced about to see who might have noticed the exchange and then went about his business. That left JW nodding his head with approval, *Maybe, this kid's got more backbone than we thought...It did take a lot for him to hike that desert alone, all bloody and no water or food. He just might be Ranger material, when this rescue is all said an' done...an' he grows a few years.*

Within the hour, JW had briefed Sgt. Dreeke and Preacher Joe of his intention to make a fast ride over to the Stumper's place. He'd take Rangers Crutchfield and Jim Williams with him for this trip, and hoped to make it there before sunset. This left Sgt. James Dreeke in command and once chow was served Sgt. Dreeke knew guards would need posting in four-hour shifts. All the men knew that falling asleep could easily lead to never waking up and his hair dangling from an Apache scalp pole. This inspired the men to stay awake and alert.

Liam McFaul wanted to ride with JW and the two other rangers, but JW shook his head, "Better to have you here if we don't make it back. And if we don't, you follow Sgt. Dreeke's orders until he releases you, then hightail it back to my ranch to defend my family. Nine rangers ain't goin' to be enough to take on a raiding party in the open desert. All the men will be going back to take care of their own, cause these Apache ain't done yet."

Now Stumper's place was neither a ranch nor a farm, but more of a small fort planted in the Arizona desert 40-miles northwest of the Globe settlement and 28-miles east of the Pueblo ruins of Montezuma's Castle. Some believed the ancient ruins at Stumper's place had originally formed the outer walls made from when the first Spanish forces came into this land long ago. Over time, weather and the Stumpers needing building materials, the old adobe walls were destroyed. To build the fortress,

Stumper Family members replaced crumbling adobe with wood planking shipped over from Phoenix to Globe. It was then taken the rest of the way via armed convoy by family and various outlaws, who used the security of the fort to keep them safe from Federal Law; as well as, Apache and Ute Indians. New adobe was also added to the fort and the Stumpers soon had five outbuildings built inside the walls and three large corrals outside, and one inside. A massive two-sided wooden gate 15-foot, tall was rebuilt three times since the Stumpers owned the place. Apache set fire to the gate, and burned it down to ashes, but still couldn't break through the hail of bullets coming from the out buildings.

One of the businesses the Stumpers were known for was making a rare form of cactus whiskey, able to drive a man blind if he didn't stop after a jug in one setting. Of course, few people could stay awake and sober after that first jug. There were rumors that rattle snake venom was part of the concoction, but that was never proven to be true. Still, it was hard to find a live rattlesnake within a square mile of the fort, or see a jack rabbit leaping about.

One of the outbuildings served as a bar. The only law enforcement officers allowed on the premises were Rangers. They had given their honor bound pledges to never come raiding Stumpers, without at least 12-hours forewarning. Since the U.S. Army never came near the joint, only the occasional U.S. Deputy Marshal would wander by. He was only allowed in, without weapons, which were handed to one of the three or four gate guards, to water and feed his horse and himself. But most avoided the location completely, not wanting to risk their lives against 20 to 30 armed outlaws and scoundrels, or be out there on the desert when the Apache are on the prod. However, the Stumpers enforced very few laws inside the fort, but one of them was no knifing or shooting inside the fort. A "Violators Will Be Hung" sign was hung on the gate, inside the bar and the small supply store. "No Violation of Women Folk", and "No Stealing from Other Guests", were also grounds for being hung. Bare knuckle brawls and one on one fighting was allowed; however, all damage had to be paid for before those involved could leave the fort and arrangements were made for reimbursement. Cussing and bad mouthing the cook was okay, card playing was allowable with table-stakes being the rule and anyone caught cheating would be tossed outside, without horse, water or weapons.

The sun was tipping the horizon to the west, when the three rangers were allowed through the gates and sociable greetings made. While the rangers stayed with their horses; walking them about before watering them down in the open warm water troth, they shared a chat with several of the fort's occupants. Most of them had heard about the massacre of the eight families, but no one had gone out, knowing the Apache would have taken everything they wanted and left the rest to the desert predators. Life in the desert was hard and old timers and Indians alike never faulted a coyote, the desert vulture or the snake for finishing off human remains.

JW walked inside the bar and looked about the darkened room, where halfway closed shutters produced a strange array of shadows against the side and back walls. He spotted four men in the corner playing cards, but he knew one was an older Stumper boy who was on good terms with the ranger. They both exchanged an easy nod, while the boy clutched his hand with both hands. JW counted another seven men at the bar; six 100-gallon weathered whiskey barrels holding a bar top of four-planks wide and 12-feet in length. Many a cowboy and outlaw had carved their initials and foul sayings into these planks.

Most of these desert cowboys were not serious bad guys and would never draw on a known ranger like Captain JW Blake. There were also two women, both working the bar and the older one waved at JW, "You want ta drink, big fella, and lay claim to some outside information or buy you some jugs for the boys?" Old Mother Stumper smiled with her near toothless grin. She was gray haired, plump as two fully ripe pumpkins and barely cleared the top lip of the bar by mere inches.

"Already heard where you're goin'. Thought you might need some jugs for afterward. Bad mess...I hate Indians!"

"Naw, only needin' one jug this trip and I already know what I got's waitin' us up ahead. Can smell the Indians; expect them to hit us at the massacre site." One thing JW knew and trusted about the Stumpers, was their sheer hatred for the Apache and any man who would trade with them. This is one of the reasons why the Stumpers always welcomed the rangers, not only did the rangers fight the Indians, but they caught and killed the raiding band of Apache braves who had caught one of the Stumper boys and his family coming home from Globe. Rangers had rescued this old woman's grandson, but everyone else was dead. She looked upon them as her knights in shining armor. More than once the family had kicked people outside the fortress in the middle of the night for defaming the ranger name. And never once had the rangers violated their so-called treaty with the Stumpers by arresting any of their family or close friends for out of state or federal warrants. Rangers would leave that to the federal officers and U.S. Army. Only once did a Stumper family member cause a problem, by shooting an unarmed man down in a bar and then making a run for the Stumper Fort.

By himself, JW rode out to the Stumper Place, was let in and he stated his reason for being there. Old man Stumper, who was no longer alive now, brought his 20-year old nephew up before the family in the bar and gave the boy a chance to explain himself. He accused the man of being a foreigner — a Swiss Jeweler stopping in Globe and on his way into Phoenix to start his business up. An argument ensued over the Stumper boy not being able to understand the man's accent, so he shot him. He didn't know he had killed him.

"But you thought you'd better ride back here so we could protect you, am I right?" Pa Stumper asked.

"Sure, we's family!" The Boy replied and put a big smile on his face.

Pa shook his head, reached under the bar, removing a French black powder pistol. Before the boy could react, he was thrown backwards with a massive hole in his mid-section. Black smoke filled the room, as Pa dropped the pistol on the bar top and spoke to JW, "Will you let us bury him with his father?"

"Sure, Pa...case is closed. Sorry it had to come to this."

"He put man size pants on this morning and saddled himself with that piece of iron. Now he knows the responsibility that comes with it, wherever he is. Thanks, JW." Pa knew the ranger captain long enough not to ask him to stay for a drink and he watched him leave the bar. Pa looked to the others, their eyes showing how stunned they were. "I only wished one of you all could've turned out like JW, but his breed comes from a thin line of gentlemen and most of you started with the likes of me."

When JW had his jug inside a potato sack for the ride back, he came outside to mount up. He knew his mount was watered, but he handed Knot Head a chunk of dried apple for the ride back to camp. They'd be taking the return trip slower, following the stars and a rising piece of moon splinter to see by. The camp would have a campfire going, probably being the only light in the whole valley floor and JW figured it should not be too hard to find as long as they read the night's sky right. He only hoped they wouldn't stumble upon a couple of Apache braves out and about, or a wayward bear. Now and then a grizzly got sighted, but for JW, it had been a few years, since he had to tangle with one.

About 4 a.m., the three weary rangers rode into camp and unsaddled their tired mounts. JW took the jug over to Preacher Joe, who commenced giving it to his patient in small doses. Within two hours, the man was totally unconscious and wouldn't be likely to feel some of the deeper three-foot deep holes in the trail, but he sure carried a stench of Stumper Home Brew. Preacher Joe thought this stuff was potent enough to make a grown man sob and help a woman to forget all the pains of child birth. But JW had tasted better coal oils and matched its odor to elixir known as Old Rocky Mountain panther piss — *good for what ail yuh.*

It was past noon hour, when lead scout, Ranger Coon, reined up as his eyes looked on a perspective ambush site cutting across the boy's trail.

Young Liam had stumbled across a dried-out streambed, between sandy bluffs and some hard-packed sandstone, among dried brush. Ranger Coon knew that once the wagon was crossing the dried-up stream, the Apache could hit them hard and fast from those firing pits they like to dig, from the two opposite bluffs, but also from the streambed itself on each side of the path Liam had dragged himself through. He waved his rifle to Ranger Chad Leaders, who was a good 50-yards to the east, but not as far up the trail. Ranger Leaders spotted Coon and understood his signal to ride back a-ways and then join-together on the foot trail.

"Good ambush site...I don't like it," Ranger Coon said. Both had stepped down to give their mounts a hatful of water. It was hot out here on man and beast, but the horses came first. "I say we ride back and see what the Boss wants to do."

"Sounds okay, but let's take it at a careful mosey, Coon...This loose sand is rough on the horses. Wish that boy could've found some hard pack to find his way to the Cap's Ranch."

"You want ta stay here, Mr. Leaders and wait on us. Probably only 20-Apache over that away. They don't mind boiling away in this hot sun. There all just a hopin' to get ranger's scalp to show off to their squaw. But if I don't find you, I'll make sure to take two of 'em down in your name and let your wife know how gallantly you fought and died."

"Move off, I'm right behind yuh...better, yet I'll lead. One of them Apache might see you and think you're a one of them and might holler out before they shoot." Ranger Leaders took the lead position as the road single file. They made less of a target that way.

"I've tried to teach you, Apache don't yell out...nope, they just suddenly appear and you is dead."

"But you're half-Navajo, right?" Leaders asked in a non-chelate way, as horse and rider swatted flies in the heat.

"Sure, but Navajo don't holler out either, White boy. Only Indian who hollers out is Sioux and you know why?"

"Nope, ah sure don't. So, why is the Sioux different?" Leaders swatted at a fly on his temple and nearly knocked his hat off his head, which got a laugh out of Coon.

Sioux is a plains' Indian, lots and lots of open plains and nowhere to hide. So, they cut loose with these god-awful screams to scare the hell out of the White Man and he just falls over dead from a heart attack. Works every-time from what I'm told."

"Okay. So, I've heard about some scuffle between the Sioux and the Apache, but how'd the Navajo fare off? Leaders wasn't used to talking so much, so he took a sip from his canteen, which he had refilled this morning from the wagon.

"Oh, Navajo never fought the Sioux," Coon replied.

"Why not?"

"See, the Navajo's a hard of hearing, those poor Sioux had just hollered and whooped themselves up until they'd grown so weary they were falling off their horses. More than half of them had to walk home and wouldn't you know it, the Navajo didn't even know'd they was there."

"You know, Coon, you got to have guts to go around tellin' tall tales like that. Must be why you'se a ranger."

"You bet, they'd string me up for sure if I wasn't." Coon sighted the bunch and picked up the pace. A moment later, Coon was sharing with JW and the rest what he had spotted. They were all dismounted, sharing a dry lunch of dried out, nearly tasteless jerky. But the meat protein would keep them going. Many of the men preferred buffalo or elk jerky when they could get it and then deer. But beef was better than no jerky at all. A cook fire could soften the jerky up and provide a lick of taste from the fire that was used to cook it with. But unless there was no other choice, none of the rangers liked to cook their jerky or other meats over cow or buffalo chips. It left them with an unsettled feeling and made their guts rumble.

After some talking it over with Sgt. Dreeke, JW finally brought them together to explain how they'd make the dried stream crossing. Preacher Joe stayed with his patient, Brady Williams, who now appeared more intoxicated than in great pain.

"Ranger Coon spotted a good ambush site for the Apache to surprise us at. After giving me the layout, I tend to agree with him. So, what we're going to do is send two flanking groups out east and west; three-men to each. You will ride over a hundred yards from the entry to the site and hold there until the wagon begins approaching. Both groups will separate from the wagon when I give the signal, when Coon makes sure I see the target site. The wagon won't enter; we can't afford to lose any horses or Preacher Joe, plus Ranger Brady Williams. The wagon will hold back with Liam and Ranger Mike Gibson..."

"What, I'm being left behind with some brat kid!" Mike Gibson complained.

"I have to leave one ranger behind and I want it to be you. Or you can head back to town right now and I'll cut you from the rolls unless you can follow orders."

"Aw, Cap...I'll get it done."

"I know, that's why I'm placing Preacher Joe, Brady Williams and the Brat in your custody. I know you can get them back if everything goes south."

"Thanks, Cap," Ranger Gibson replied. His feelings were no longer feeling hurt.

"All right, unless anyone else wants to comment on his assignment, I want Ranger's O'Miller, Crutchfield and John Gibson to the east. From the west, Ranger's Leaders, Holloway and Jim Williams. You'll start closing in as you see us leave the wagon. Now Sgt. Dreeke, Ranger Coon and myself, will approach from the trail, our young Mr. Liam McFaul was fortunate enough to leave behind. Once I either figure we're close enough or I smell Apaches, I'll signal with a wave of my rifle...No, better yet, I'll have Coon signal with his. My Henry sparkles like gold with a shimmer of sunlight and it may give us away. When you see the rifle waving, dismount and head in on foot. One of you to the north of the streambed, one in the dried stream and one south of the streambed, as your positions move in. If shooting starts, you pour it on and make sure you all watch for those firing holes of theirs. They call them tarantula holes for a reason, because they come springing out just like those horrid spiders and that's what they are. Those Apache can spend all day in one of those and pop up ta make their kill. Often or not, when they first come up, they're disoriented just a bit for a split second from the heat to aim for horsemen and wagons, so you hit the ground and look for targets. But remember, we have more ammo in the trailer. Do not hold your shots, you can waste a few rounds to you keep them ducking."

"Liam, how far do you think we have to go still to reach your wagons?" Sgt. Dreeke asked.

Liam looked first at JW and then back at Sgt. Dreeke, "If we stop for tonight...I mean if there is no fight here...I think tomorrow by noon day."

"Good, but can you recall any other stream beds or other obstacles?" Sgt. Dreeke asked. He was only asking the questions because he noticed the boy was in pretty fair shape for having just left the brutal massacre of his family and so many others.

"I cannot say for sure and I'd rather not speculate, I was not in very good shape. My mind was unsettled and I may have wandered about for a time before I was able to continue on."

"JW, you is sure right, he does talk like he's got a lot of school-learnin'," Ranger Jim Williams said in his southern twang. Most of his friends knew he liked to stretch it some, having lived in eastern Arizona a whole lot longer than he ever did the South. But to get Sgt. Dreeke and Jim

Williams going in a lively conversation, a northerner might only catch a word here and there.

"Okay, we move out in a bit, make sure all weapons are loaded, you have extra ammo on hand and hand weapons sharp, plus give your horses another slurp of water and a handful of oats. This could be a long afternoon or a short stop in the dry trail for safety sake."

JW walked over to Knot Head and saw to his own horse, while Liam made sure his new ride was well-taken care off. Liam enjoyed admiring the collection of horse flesh the rangers rode, including the two giants pulling the ranger wagon. He had seen similar horses back east and owned by dozens of the wagon owners for the long trail westward. On the train there was a double wagon, held end-to-end by long thick rails and hooked together by chains to allow for turns and curves in the road. It was the only double-wagon he'd ever seen, which was being pulled by six of these mighty steeds and he never did find out what was in the wagons that required such strength. He heard it joked it was full of Gold, but Liam doubted it because he never saw extra guards on it at night. But for some people, it was gold. For these men and women in their group were all hoping to find a new future in the New West. They'd come from Italy, bringing with them seasoned ancient wine presses, molds for news one, bottling designs and wine recipes brought down from one generation to the next and saplings of 18-champion vintages for the New Napa Valley outside San Francisco.

For the non-wine lover, the horses were worth more than the contents of the wagons. But at least these wagons had stayed with the main train and the wine presses would eventually make it. Very few people in the main train would ever hear of the massacre of the right wagons and the foolish people who chose to breakaway in Indian country and head for Los Angeles. They were warned to wait for two-weeks, when they would reach a U.S. Cavalry fort and hopefully pick-up an army escort to Phoenix. But they couldn't wait, they were in a hurry and it had cost all but one, their lives.

"Saddle up," JW ordered. "No shooting unless an emergency gives cause for it. No sense lettin' the Apache know where we're at, if they're not here."

But within the hour, they knew the Apache had chosen not to use this crossing for an ambush. Not a shot was fired and the Rangers were now en- route to their evening camping site. The closer they got, the more careful JW became. Guards rotated three hours on and six hours off, making sure to have three-men — fully alert for three hours all night long. The rangers were used to losing sleep on the trail and have even gone three days without it, while being pursued by White Mountain Apache for three days and nights. Two rangers and seven Apache were killed in that pursuit, but the rangers finally reached a Confederate Army Fort. But that was before the U.S. Army of California marched into Arizona and chased the rebel forces into New Mexico and eventually Texas.

JW took first shift and Sgt. Dreeke took last shift. Ranger Brady Williams was showing signs of improvement and was even able to finish off two biscuits, with a cup of hot coffee. JW was hoping to see him in a saddle before they engaged the Apache if possible. But if not, he could shoot from the wagon. Both Preacher Joe and Liam would be in the wagon, with Williams' horse and Liam's mount in tow. An extra rope was used to secure the two horses to the wagon — a move to make it tougher on an Apache horse thief.

Preacher Joe's pale skin was tough as dried out rawhide, covered over in brown age spots, with more appearing every year or so he complained. His aged hands were curled in sheepskin gloves to protect him from two sets of leather reins, while Preacher Joe sat on the hard-wooden bench seat, tossing a grin toward Liam, saying a kind word, "Don't you worry none, lad. The Good Lord has his warriors with us, this day."

There was no smile on Liam's face, he only shook his head and glared down at the shotgun barrels in his hands. Sure, he had been a believer, up until the massacre. His folks raised him on the Word of God, but now he was having trouble believing in a God who could allow such barbaric bloodshed.

Liam held the double-barrel 12-gauge handy for Preacher Joe, in the event some Apache sprang up out of one of those spider holes Captain Blake talked about. Then Liam would take up the rifle beside his right leg, knocking against the seat of the wagon bench, as Preacher Joe began shouting at the horses to lead out. He whipped the reins against their backsides and they knew it was time to step out. The wagon had a whip, but so far Liam hadn't seen Preacher Joe use it. Later, he would learn the whip was kept handy to dislodge Indians during an attack. The Apache would often use a move to get a warrior onto a wagon horses' backside to override the reins and divert it away from the rangers, then kill the driver in the process and getaway with what goods it carried and the horses, too. Most often the heavier draft horses were used to feed the tribe, because they were too slow to hunt with or use as a war horse.

Liam didn't have any time for Preacher Joe's Bible lessons, not after losing his family and all those others to the Apache only days before. *Where was this God of his then, or these warriors he's speaking about? If there were any of those holy angels flying about during that massacre, they must've been on the Apache's side an' not ours! Nope, now I just hope I can get my kill to avenge my folks and this old geezer lays off on the Bible thumping, he sounds like Pastor Bittney on the train. All holy this and that...I think I'd rather walk, because this seat feels like when Mom walloped my rump for stealing cookies. By the time, we reach the massacre site, I'm going to be all black and blue from hip to hip.*

Ranger Brady Williams was sobering up now from the evils of that homemade concoction, but his head felt like he'd been struck with a crossbar. Still, he had his hands grasped tightly around his rifle and felt a brief wave of security when he realized he was lying between extra rifles, some shotguns and plenty of ammo. Preacher Joe had brought him up to date, while he forced a large gulp of water down him. "Ah got to dilute your blood, Brady...have-to drive Stumper's poison out of you. It done did its job, now it's time for you to do yours. Your fever's almost gone and now we need that shooting eye of yours."

JW led out, then stopped, nearly 20-feet out in front of everyone else. He stuck his right arm straight up, glanced around, making sure everyone got his attention. This was his signal for everyone to stop and be quiet. JW wanted to listen. He needed to take in the sounds of the desert, to see if he could detect anything that didn't belong. He knew he rarely could hear an Apache, for they owned the desert and could move across it mounted on their ponies or on foot and only make the sounds of a breeze if they wished to. Or they could come on with the very sounds of hellish creatures of a man's worst nightmare to drive terror into the hearts of their human prey.

A trio of desert birds, brown in color, the size of a sparrow, were off in the distance to the north, nervously fluttering through the sage brush as they nipped at dried bark and small bugs. But then he noticed it, his time in the desert and knowing his enemy paid off, he saw how the birds were avoiding a particular-patch of desert floor and sage. Here, he knew, his enemy had dug in. But how many of them were there?

Once more he stuck his hand up straight, but this time it held his revolver. This was the signal that they were to assume there was enemy ahead. Making sure everyone saw him, he waved his weapon hand in the circle, the signal to hit fast, when the order to move in was given, and then he pointed down. The Rangers were being warned to watch for tarantula holes up ahead.

He wrapped his reins around the pummel of his saddle, taking a brief swipe of his forehead with the back of his free hand to clean some sweat away, then signaled Preacher Joe to hold his position with the flat of his same hand off to his side. Hand signals were often used in desert fighting, since too many Indians had learned to understand the "American" language. With the War of 1812 still so recent in the past, most westerners refused to use the word English, but replaced it with American and some of these rangers had grandfathers who had fought and fallen in that war. Sgt. Dreeke even lost a grandfather on his pop's side who had been killed in the Battle for New Orleans. Yet there were a few rangers who suspected Preacher Joe had been a drummer boy for General Andrew Jackson at that battle, which he never admitted to or denied. He only grinned, whenever it came up again with a new ranger recruit.

Preacher Joe grabbed his shotgun, climbing into the wagon, dragging Liam with them behind the wagon seat. Preacher Joe and Ranger Brady William knew if this was an ambush they could expect an attack from the rear by Apache on foot. They'd be coming from nearby crevices, tarantula holes or behind rocks, but they would suddenly appear to seize the wagon, the horses and everything it held. They knew without water the rangers would die, even if they survived the ambush. But the Apache also needed what the wagon carried; food, water, ammo and guns.

JW slowly moved ahead, the one thing he didn't know was when the Apache would spring the ambush. A seasoned desert fighter would wait until the rangers, were in the middle of this dried streambed and on the way up the other side of the shallow embankment. But a young Indian might begin shooting right away, giving up the element of surprise too early. Yet, JW knew whoever was leading this killing raid was experienced enough to let Liam go, so he could bring back others with horses and guns, and hopefully rangers. There were a lot of Apache who wanted revenge killings for their brothers and fathers killed by rangers, or taken into to be imprisoned in White Man's prisons. Far too often this meant a slow death for the Indian, even when the jail sentence was only ten to 15 years. Yuma Prison and its guards were tough, especially on the Apache. A lot of the guards and prisoners had family tortured and killed by the Apache and White Man's respect for White Women meant nothing to the Indian, just as it meant nothing to the barbaric White Man who tortured, raped and murdered the Indian Women.

At a slow walk a vigilant JW slowly rode Knot Head down the sandy embankment. He knew this streambed may not have seen water for a hundred years, or maybe a storm's flashflood had sent a five-foot wave down through here only a few months earlier. It didn't take long for the burning sun to dry up a stream or riverbed. He had even seen small lakes turn into mud flats, and then cracked earth in a single summer. This made finding watering holes an interesting proposition, especially for the inexperienced and their bones now littered the desert floor. Not just man, but animals, too. Well-known watering holes could be dried up one summer and have water in them for the next three torrid summers.

But a nervous or over excited Apache was the wrong one to put so close to the trail left by the young-man escaping the massacre scene and JW picked up the movement of a sage bush that covered a prone Apache. He wasn't even in a hole, simply covered in loose sand and buried under a pile of sage brush. But his odor for what it was, possibly last night's dinner, made the birds nervous enough to avoid his covering. It would be a costly mistake, one he was taught never to make and he had apparently not listened well.

The Apache Indian died with the first two shots fired in the exchange, as JW took aim to where he glimpsed an elbow. Then other Apaches sprang up, but the rangers were already coming in from the east and west, dismounting quickly and dropping to one knee as they used their rifles to claim targets here and there. JW was on one knee and then lying prone, but he heard a warning shout and turned over to see an Apache brave running at him with a broken lance, the point intended for JW's back. His last rifle round entered the Indian's chest and the brave fell, the broken blade of an old bowie knife strapped to the end of a lance, with the point grazing JW's left shoulder. Blood was drawn and it burned, but he still had a battle to fight and he was right out in front of it all. Without time to reload his rifle, he switched to his revolver and went to hunting.

For a brief-moment it was utter calamity, with the 16 Apaches giving a good account for themselves as the battle entered hand-to-hand combat. When it seemed-like the Apaches didn't have enough rifle ammo to compete against the rangers, arrows began to fly and a ranger horse, "General Hood", went down with a shaft sticking out of its left rear flank. Preacher Joe cut the shaft off, packed the wound and tied the horse to the wagon. Michael Gibson would be riding on the wagon seat, while Liam rode *Sandy*. Gibson was much too heavy for Sherry Ann's horse, though JW had to listen to Gibson's complaints for a bit. A well-made stone knife opened a nasty hip wound on Ranger Troy Dreeke, but with some stitching he'd heal up fine and he shot the Indian at close range. But when the Indian was buried, Troy Dreeke insisted on the man having his own grave with rocks on to protect it from the critters.

"That Indian fought hard an' nearly kilt me...I respect his tenacity and hope whatever heaven there is for Indians he finds a happy place." Michael had thought to keep the knife that stuck him, but he asked Chad Leaders to put it in the man's hands, along with his other weapons, before he was buried.

JW was impressed with Michael Gibson's inner growth and nodded his head at the funeral for the Apache, a practice JW insisted upon.

When it was all said, and done, there were seven dead Apache being buried and the rest now running north across the desert, for where their horses were being held by the youngest brave on his first raid.

The battle for the wagon renewed as five Apache braves sprang out from behind a rocky embankment. On foot, they charged the wagon from the east. They had 30-yards or less of open desert sand to cover. As far as they could tell, the wagon appeared empty. Approximately five-yards away, Preacher Joe rose up, letting go with first one barrel and then the second barrel of his 12-guage shotgun. He killed two Indians in mid-stride and wounded a third in the shoulder and hip. Before Liam could rise up, Ranger Brady William fired off his first round, from his lever-action rifle, then reloaded his next round, fired, and killed the fifth Indian with a chest shot only a foot before he would have reached the nearest water barrel.

When he returned to the wagon to check on everyone and have Preacher Joe bandage up his shoulder wound — a minor wound that bled a lot, ruining a perfectly good shirt — JW looked over the scene, wondering why the Apache didn't just pepper the water barrels with rifle shots to have them leak all over the desert floor. Liam came up with one of the Apache rifles, "They had no ammo, Captain. Every rifle in this group is empty. I believe their whole plan was to untie the barrels or drag them off and leave us without water. Possibly get away with the wagons or hopefully some ammo we might have had in the wagon."

"Don't you'se folks an' those people in those other seven wagons carry rifles and bullets?" Ranger Brady William asked.

Liam glanced about, growing agitated by the looks he was receiving from the rangers. He knew they all judged his family to be a stupid, ignorant group of immigrants, but they were his family and friends. So, he turned and walked away.

A moment later, JW came to stand beside him, "Liam, all of us at one time or another was a kid, and sometimes we tend to forget it, or how at 15 or 16 years old we were not responsible for our parents and other adult's actions or decisions. But, as a Ranger Commander, I do need to know…How were your people armed? The why to it is because those Apache survivors will not be going home until they obtain enough arms and ammo to defend their tribes from other tribes and feed their families. The Indians we just faced were poorly armed and I'm thankful, as we only ended up with a couple knife wounds and a wounded mount. With better arms, it could've been much worse."

"Captain Blake, I only saw half-a-dozen older rifles and a few shotguns…There were only a couple handguns carried by the leaders of the group. However, I did hear the men talking of how low the ammo was. The only round I had was the one in my shotgun and I see now I and the other flankers were more of a sacrifice to possibly save the main body. Ironic in how I was the one to survive. Preacher Joe says my experience was one of the *God's Mysterious Ways* the Word of God speaks about."

JW didn't want to get into a discussion about the Bible right now, he had a job to do and his Christian beliefs were mostly minimal at this point. He left the bible teaching to his wife, Sherry Ann.

So, this isn't over. Appears these raiders plan to strike and terrorize, burn and kill, until they've satisfied their urges and are ready to return to their villages victorious. "With these raiders being from the Chiricahua Tribe, we're up against some of the most ruthless killers we've ever come across in this territory. So, we need to bandage our wounds, get a good meal in us, water our mounts, finish burying the dead and pursue the hostiles." JW took another swipe across his sweaty forehead with his left hand and followed it up with a well-soiled faded dark blue handkerchief he had pulled from his left rear pants pocket. "I got ta remember ta carry extra handkerchiefs with me out on the trail…two ta three just don't do the job."

"So, Liam, how far do you think, now?" JW asked.

Liam felt like falling-down on his knees and was about to, when he un-buckled his cartridge belt and found a place to sit down. His horse was okay. Sandy was his main responsibility, side-by-side with his new weapons, loaned to him by the rangers. During the attack, he didn't even get a shot off. He watched Brady work that lever-action. He never saw anyone move that quickly and sight in a new target.

"I was out of my head through this part, so, I believe we're within three to four miles of the wagons," Liam answered.

"Then we should begin seeing the undertakers in another mile or two," JW said and then explained his remark, when he saw the look of confusion on Liam's face. "I'm talking about desert vultures, Boy. We'll be seeing dozens of them circling overhead, waiting to take their turn or ta fight for an opening at an exposed body. We often call them undertakers because the clean up the remains, leaving only the bones for us to bury and hopefully some sort of identification to tell us who had been killed so we can notify the next of kin."

"What happens after we bury the dead…my family and friends?" Liam asked, but his face was looking down at the ground as he asked the question.

"First off, we can expect our next ambush. There were more pony and horse tracks at the last ambush to have been made by the ones left to hit us. The next force will be a superior number. If we survive and some of the Apache escape, we'll go in pursuit," JW said in a low voice. His weariness was showing, but this was no time for a nap.

"I expect we'll stay out until our supplies tell us it's time to call it quits. But we will first fight some more Indians and bury your family. Liam, always be ready…between here and those wagons, those Apache can still jump us and probably will at the massacre site. I'm still somewhat surprised they hit us here. This might have been a maneuver to throw us off, give us a case of overconfidence, where a greenhorn ranger might ride right into the site not expecting any trouble. I'd wager $10, the sub-chief running this raid is a new boy out to prove himself and his guiding elders are not saying anything. They're along only to see how he handles the situations and report on the raid to the tribal senior council.

"But, between you and I…I'm suspecting this new sub-chief has made his second mistake. Oh, the massacre of the eight-wagons wasn't a mistake as we see it, but warriors want weapons and young slaves to sell. Your horses were almost all wagon pullers, which were sent back to the villages to barbecue, but, and excuse my cold way of talking, you had few slave age young girls, few weapons and little ammo. They stole some bright colored cloth, cooking pots and pans, and some kitchen knives…plus all the leather they saw. Reins work really well on making moccasins and great for trading with other tribes."

Liam stood there glaring at JW, fighting hard against the nightmarish scenes of finding his murdered family and friends, of the young man he had become close to. The two boys had made a lot of plans for when they reached California. No, he refused to put that murderous scene back into his mind. He only knew he wanted revenge and studying those earlier dead Apache, he wondered how they could've ever gained such a fearsome reputation.

Dark skinned, longish black hair, small in stature and very thin, the Apache were fast and capable of surviving on the open desert, where western men believed no human could possibly live. He was rated by his enemy to be the finest guerilla fighter in the known world, the finest cavalry soldier. In Liam's one brief glance of the last Apache alive out of the five who attacked the wagon, running toward the water barrel, the Indian gave off the illusion of a towering grizzly about to make a kill. Liam continued recalling the viciousness in the man's eyes, how his nostrils flared and muscles were so taut, nothing would stop him but death.

AT THE MASSACRE SITE, ONE DAY LATER, MID-AFTERNOON

They approached the site extremely cautiously. Rangers Jim Williams and John Holloway tracked the Apache party of 23 mounted horses, north across the desert from the last ambush site, for three hours before returning to this site. Part of the mounted Apaches was the half-dozen or more who escaped the last site, but the rest were members of the raid the sub-chief would use for this secondary ambush. He was pretty angry when he learned he had failed to destroy the rangers in his first ambush. All he received from the two tribal elders was a blank look. Of those who escaped, they reported losing most of the Apache force and only wounding two of the rangers. One of the sub-chief's scouts soon reported the wounded Captain was back on his horse. The other wounded man was still riding in their single wagon.

When the rangers were in view of all the settler's wagons, no one was surprised to see how each of the wagons was burned to mere black and gray ashes, leaving only the metal axels and wagon strappings. Over two dozen desert undertakers had to deal with a pack of scruffy coyotes for rights of ownership of the decaying bodies. They were chased off with several shots fired into the air. Between the desert's hot sun, dozens of birds and that pack of coyotes, there was little left beyond bones and clothes for the rangers to bury.

It was decided to place them in a mass grave, because the danger of attack could come at any moment. The individual crosses previously constructed by Preacher Joe would now bear their names. Most of them could be identified by papers on them, the family wagon they were in-- identified by Liam — or flesh left on their face for Liam to make an identification. Their names were burned into the wood.

Preacher Joe held a solemn ceremony. What valuables that could be found, along with proper identification, and where it could be mailed, were wrapped in bundles and placed in the ranger wagon. JW and Sgt. Dreeke would write out the Death Notifications once they were back at Globe. Remaining unidentified valuables, such as watches, jewelry not found by the Apache or coin and cash, was given to Liam as sole survivor. Liam wrapped up his family's articles, which included a framed family photograph of his family before they left Independence, Missouri. This photo was left abandoned in one of the four trunks tossed out of their wagon. A family Bible belonging to Liam's folks was found under a false bottom in a small trunk, which had held his mother's wedding dress, but it was apparent the material of the wedding dress went back to the village to delight a young Indian maiden. Below the Bible was found a packet of cash, amounting to $1,000. This was his folk's seed money, to get them started in California. Now it belonged to Liam and he wasn't sure what or how he would spend or save it.

The rangers claimed extra shovels, pick axes, lanterns, some unbroken dishes and miscellaneous items that the value of mailing them back to family members exceeded the worth of the article. Another bonfire was set and the rest of the articles were tossed into it. JW had hoped to find at least one usable wagon or several wagons they could've salvaged to construct one working one. For they had found the dried food stuffs the Apache had no knowledge of and the rangers hated to leave them, but they could not overburden their own wagon with dried food, canned goods and cause an extra strain to those four horses.

So, they decided to bury the goods. Preacher Joe estimated the dried goods to be at least 1,000 pounds of food stuffs from the eight-wagons the Apache had left in ashes. As to why they tossed them out of the wagons, Preacher Joe could only figure they were concerned all the canned goods would keep the flames from catching. They also discovered dozens of cans being carried several yards off into the desert, giving the impression the Indians had tried to open them with their hands and knives and in their frustration had simply tossed them off into the sand. The water was also a big loss as the water barrels were poured out, broken up and tossed into the fires.

With four rangers on guard, the other rangers talked among themselves, as they imagined how angry the Apache might have become when they found little honor in slaughtering defenseless trespassers. There was little or no fight, as far as the rangers could find. Ranger Coon, using his Navajo tracking ability found exactly where Liam had been taken down. He located the very rock the Apache brave had taken him from and then found the foot prints of at least four braves who stood around Liam's unconscious body as they made their plan. Ranger Coon even followed the brave's path for a distance to see how well he remained parallel with Liam. Later, as he reported this to JW, Coon said, "I bet I could follow that Apache brave's trail, or another one's trail right up to your back door. I tell yuh, Cap, we're messin' with a smarter Apache. Someone's teaching these braves, someone who knows somethin' about western-style of fightin'."

"Get yourself fed, take care of your mount and grab some sleep," JW said casually. "We move out in the morning, heading north. But keep your guns handy. The back of my neck is itching somethin' bad, so I'm thinkin' we got us a war party around us and they're waiting for somethin'."

"Cap, I don't know why we should head back after this. The only thing up north of us is the Navajo, a few towns that even thu ghosts had left an' those three or four large cattle ranches. We also got the Apache Fortress, with more than a couple thousand warriors. You've been there and know it ain't a nice place for us White Men.

"What do you expect to find out in the open desert, Cap? We turn east we've got New Mexico and those dang Comanche and there's not enough of us for that…and west, we've got more Indians. Plus, there's Mexican bandits and those Comancheros, and an American Civil War ta think 'bout."

"Are you wantin' a promotion, Coon?" JW asked with a straight face. "Maybe you can run this outfit."

"No, Siree...I got one side of half Navajo and that frightens those people down in Tucson to have a half-Indian non-com or officer runnin' the rangers. Can you see their faces? Me comin' in with my scalp pole filled with Apache and Mexican scalps? They'd fire me first and then hang me, without even a trial."

"Go take care of your horse, I'll tell you all what I have planned tonight after chow."

"Thanks, Cap," Coon tossed him a casual salute and led his horse away.

JW shook his head. He couldn't think of a better group of fighting men to be with—facing Indians or bandits. They were the most curious, least courteous, foulest smelling, worst tempered group of galoots he'd ever been around, including his time on cattle drives.

Avoiding the wagons, partially because some of the men were superstitious, even though all the bodies were buried, the ranger encampment was placed south of the site. JW still suspected the Apache were in place around the burned wagons or possibly placed inside the blackened ruins, waiting for a signal of some kind to spring up and begin killing rangers.

But for the moment, dinner was frying pan biscuits, hot jerky beef roasted on sticks and boiling hot coffee. Tonight, it was Ranger Leader's turn to cook, with Liam helping-out with the cook fire and other duties as needed. Afterward, JW and Ranger Troy Dreeke had their wound bandages changed, and General Hood, Michael Gibson's mount, was looked after. They had gotten the arrowhead out, but it would be another couple-weeks before the horse would be able to carry a man's weight. In the meantime, Ranger Michael Gibson continued riding in the wagon with Preacher Joe. Ranger Brady Williams was nursing a headache, but said he would rather ride in a saddle than on that hard bench seat of the wagon. Michael tried to talk Liam out of his horse, again, but the young man wouldn't go for it. He knew Gibson was much too heavy for Sandy and he still wanted to be by himself, riding a few yards off from the others. Liam continued-on with his grieving process and was sure wearisome of Preacher Joe's sermons on how the Lord moves in Mysterious Ways business. All Liam knew was how his family lay dead back there, he was alive and they were still in pursuit of the Apache who had done it. When that was said and done he planned to return home, this west was no place for him.

With the stars shinning overhead and a moon just breaching the mountain peaks to the east, the men sat around a small fire. They all sat back from the flames, so it wouldn't cause problems with their night vision in the event of an attack. But three men—Sgt. James Dreeke, Ranger Crutchfield and Preacher Joe—were on guard duty for the first shift and the rest of the shifts had been assigned for the night before Sgt. Dreeke went on duty.

A hot cup of coffee in his tin cup, blackened up the side from years of usage, JW took a sip, glancing about the circle. He wasn't sure if he could see each man or smell them by their individual stenches, but everyone carried a particular-stench. No bathing, burying the dead, smoking a pipe or enjoying a chew of tobacco, tooth decay and sweat, and wearing old or new leather trail clothes. It all added up to make a certain odor for a man, even himself.

"I sure do hope we find us a river before we get home, or the settlement of Globe won't let us enter the new walls with the way we stink." Jim Williams said. His rifle was loaded and lying across his lap, plus his revolver had its sixth round shoved into its chamber.

JW glanced at Williams, worried the man was reading his mind. He then heard a light noise behind him, thinking it sounded like a slight scratching and he wondered if it was a man moving the camouflaged roof off his tarantula hole. He reached down, pulled out his revolver and took to loading a sixth round. Every one noticed this and for those who had not done this action, they copied him, but very quietly.

"Don't need to smell good to fight good," Ranger Michael Gibson said. He'd been unusually quiet on his side of the fire and it was unlike him. JW noticed that both brothers were acting mighty peculiar since leaving his ranch. They did their job, but these two were often or not the group clowns to break-up the tension, when things were running badly.

"Besides, Cap, those new people in Globe…they don't cotton too much to us southern rangers, not like the old folks do. With more and more Union Troops comin' in from California, things are getting' sort of tight feelin'."

"All right, I was going to let this hang for later, but what's ever eating you two has got to wait." JW pointed to one side of the fire and said, "You four move to our wagon and protect our goods."

JW pointed to the other side of the fire, "We will stay low and advance from the west. Remember not to shoot toward the wagon and keep one eye behind you. Those people could wait and pop up right behind you. Have your knife ready and once your rifle is empty, switch to your revolver. Be prepared for a knuckle draggin' brawl and here the loser is dead.

Liam hadn't been at the fire when JW heard the noises. He was at the wagon filling water buckets to water the horses tied to the horse line. This would be their last watering for the night and one of Liam's duties. He didn't want to make a lot of noise so he hung the bucket off the wooden water faucet. The warrior was only armed with knife and a tomahawk. He threw the tomahawk. Liam knocked it aside with the barrels of the shotgun. Liam then bent his knees, bracing himself, firing off the other barrel of the 12-guage. These pellets struck the Apache from less than three-feet and the carnage to the man's face and shoulders removed all tissue and went to the bone. This caused Liam to drop to the ground and vomit.

Once these two shotgun blasts were fired off, the ambush was ignited. Apache warriors who had been in hiding for hours were now springing or crawling out of their camouflaged holes and ditches. Some held one, while others held two or three warriors. If the warriors were not armed with rifles or pistols, even bows and arrows, they attacked with knives and tomahawks. Eight Apaches attacked on horseback, led by the sub-chief, only to have the rangers kill or seriously wound six of the mounted warriors and the sub-chief was dragged out of the fight by the orders of one of the elders to save his life.

It was the ranger's superior firepower that again won out and Liam's advanced warning had saved the wagon and possibly five ranger's lives that would end up needing the medical supplies Preacher Joe carried with him. Holloway had taken a six-inch spear slash above his left hip; Jim Williams rolled over the fire, while fighting a large brave. His back was burned. Brady Williams was shot with another arrow. This one, hitting the lower left leg, went all the way through. Which meant one side had to be cut off in order-to pull it out. John Gibson took a knife to his left shoulder, which was not his shooting side. Both Liam and Chad Leaders took extensive bruising and abrasions to their bodies from physical fights with the braves. Leaders had the tip of his left ear bitten off. For a time, Liam could not see from his right eye, because an Apache shoved his thumb into it. They would both require nearly 100-stitches over their faces and upper bodies from their brawls with the Apaches. It became a case of knives, lance ends and broken arrows, boot heels, elbows and fists, in an attempt-to survive.

When it was over, JW counted seven dead Apache from the spot in the sand Leaders and Liam had commenced taking on the Apache Nation. He also noticed there were other blood trails leaving the area, which included from his two rangers.

For nine-hours the attack raged, with one piece of the desert erupting in yells and blood curdling screams, followed by several rifle or pistol shots. Ranger names would be called out, but each unit knew to stay in its place until morning to make sure they were not shot by a fellow ranger. There would be long quiet spells and JW hoped it was over, only to hear the war erupt once again from another side of the fight. But with the rising sun, the surviving Apache once again fled north; with JW hoping they would be on their way to the northern fortress, which lay up in the Painted Desert.

With the battle lasting so long and the action covered by nightfall, a lot of the Apache dead were carried off. This prevented JW of knowing exactly how many of the enemy was killed or wounded. This also meant the rangers had no prisoners, but on a positive note, young Liam had proved himself to be a fighter. Though still only a kid, JW would recommend him as a recruit for becoming a ranger. A recruit was given various duties, but was always with a senior ranger for a period of 12-months. Based on senior's reports the recruit was either denied entry or sworn in as a new Arizona Ranger.

The wounded rangers needed at least one more night staying off their horses. The more serious cases would be loaded into the wagon. Their horses were tied to the wagon in tandem for the trip home. Liam continued carrying out his duties of helping Preacher Joe, whoever the cook was and his chore of caring for the horses.

But it was late that night, after chow and before bedding down, JW was hit with another blow of bad news.

"Captain, mah brother an' ah...well, me...we's wasn't goin' ta say anythin' until we gots home, but this is our last ride with thu Rangers...at least until we can convince dem damn Yankees to leave our Southern States alone." Ranger John Gibson said in that terse Mississippi accent of his. He may have left the South when he was young, but the voice still stuck. "Me and mah little brother, we's joinin' up with General Hood's Army of Texas. He's taken in riders from New Mexico, Arizona an' ah hear'd some of dose California cowboys."

"I'm not surprised, but how those southern ladies are ever goin' to find enough confederate gray to put you two into uniform...you might break the Confederacy war budget," JW said in jest.

"Why don't yuh come along, Jim," Michael asked of Ranger Jim Williams.

"Mike, I'll worry about that fight when we done fightin' this one. Now, Cap, you got orders for us?"

"We were supposed to ride north for three days. But we don't have enough supplies to handle that. You men know this is a murder raid and those Apache ain't done yet. No, they're gonna make us think they is done and went back to their villages, until next time. But I don't think so. I'm thinkin' those braves, is as I suspect bein' led by a young chief's son who's out to prove his oats. If he returns now, he'll be laughed at by the older warriors behind his back. No, I'm thinking he plans to cut back and hit the settlements north of Globe or some new settlement somewhere near Phoenix. The Township of Phoenix has grown too big for his remaining warriors, so he'll hit a lot of ranches out…take them by surprise. Half-a-dozen cowboys minding a herd would never have a chance and this can provide this young leader with horses, slaves, guns and ammo. Enough to make him big medicine and we'll have to deal with him later."

"What if he hasn't changed their trail after three days?" Ranger Brady Williams asked.

"I gave that some thought and decided to go with a hunch, we'll cut west and head south for two days and set ourselves up north of the settlements. We'll be thin, two man posts, but soon as we see a ranch or farm on fire, we run for the others until we get a sizeable fighting force to take on the Apache. We can live with the ranchers, do a little work for 'em, as long-as we are able to ride an' watch the desert country. What do you think?" He looked to the Gibson's, "Can you hold on for a week or so, this war in the east sure won't be over that quick?"

John glanced at Michael, who nodded his okay. "You got us, but what about all that food stuffs we buried back at the…wagons?" John nodded toward Liam, apologizing for bringing a sore subject up. But in the darkness, he doubted the boy could see his face. With the possibility of Apache still in the area, they kept away from the torch light set around the camp's perimeter and sat back away from the fire. They also relied on their horse's reactions to the smell of the Apache to alert them, but one of these days Preacher Joe was determined to raise a couple large hounds that'd starting baying as soon as they picked up the odor of Indian. The only problem lay as he saw it, was how to teach them to know the difference between friendly Indians and renegades.

"We'll leave it there for now. Pretty-soon the Southern troops will be here again and they can send troops out to pick it all up after we give them the directions," JW said.

"Hey Liam, is you a northerner or is you a southerner in this man's war?" Michael Gibson asked. Though he spoke in a low voice, Michael's question came from deep down in his chest and blew across the distance between the two men like a mini-sandstorm.

Liam thought about his reply for a brief-moment and then answered, "I'm 16 years old, Ranger Gibson and last I heard California was neutral in this Civil War."

JW shook his head, for he expected a different answer and said to Liam, "I'm afraid before this is over there's going to be a lot of 16-year old boys on both sides fighting in this war. One side believes it involves the enslavement of his fellow man, while the other side replies it's about state's rights to govern themselves. But I know there's a lot of patriots from the north signing up simply to prevent the states from dividing, knowing both sides would soon become targets. This war and a lot of American youth your age are going to turn our countryside red with their blood and dampen many a mother's cheeks with her grieving tears."

They rode for three days, following the Apache trail as it headed toward Hopi and Navajo Territory. Some of the wounded were now on horseback again. The order of the day was to take down any meat seen running about. JW knew this route was not the most intelligent move for such a small Apache war party to be making. By now JW was convinced the Apache was trying to pull them away from the settlements of Globe and new Phoenix.

The trip back home was uneventful. They needed to move cautiously, following the Apache as they worked their way back to the settlement of Globe. Thankfully, they found themselves a river and got themselves cleaned up, horses to match, before returning to their various ranches, farms, businesses, or that bar stool with their name on it. Preacher Joe returned the wagon and with Liam's help, carried all the personal bundles belonging to the dead over to the store post office to prepare for shipment to their next of kin. Preacher Joe agreed to write the letters, which would accompany each package.

Liam returned to JW's ranch, where he and JW proceeded to do a good week's worth of chores in two days before saddling up and heading northeast of Globe with two pack horses lashed down with food, ammo, extra rifles and plenty of water. JW always wanted to keep his ranch and his family behind him, with him between the Indians and his lovely Sherry Ann. Liam understood and never had to ask any questions about which directions they were headed as most of the time he was completely lost anyway. They selected four different observation points in the rugged ridgelines, leading off to the Superstitious Mountains; a holy land of sorts of majestic desert peaks for the various desert tribes, now believed to be haunted and cursed. The mountains were known to house several high-grade gold deposits, but it seemed none of the gold prospectors ever came out, which added more weight to the hauntings and curses.

JW wasn't in search of Gold and he was still quite a-ways from the actual mountains. Still, the ridgelines provided them with a maximum view of a hundred miles of desert flatland to the north, in which JW could see half-a-dozen large ranches, some farms, a growing religious commune who disliked strangers and the back-road routes into Globe.

Off to his left by ten miles, was where he had positioned the Gibson brothers. They were staying in a ranch's line shack. Next were placed Rangers Coon and Jim Williams, who took up ownership of an abandoned homestead. The owners couldn't make a go of it and returned to the East Coast. This post was followed a few miles further up by Rangers Holloway and Leaders, whose wife was becoming extremely upset with her husband. She let the whole settlement of Globe know of her anger by openly accusing Ranger Leaders of going off to play ranger and not running his business enterprise as he should. She was now threatening to sell the store cheap and take a stage for California. But Leader's would have to be the one to sign the deed over and he wasn't about to, he happened to like it here.

Rangers Jim Williams and Coon, who didn't always get along that well, were monitoring the desert from a trapper's hillside homestead. This belonged to an old hunting partner of Ranger Williams, who Coon thought resembled more bear than a man, but was married to a very large Russian wife he bought by mail. They had taken up residence outside old Hopi ruins built a century before and later abandoned. Ranger Coon spent most of his time on horseback, he thought the ruins were haunted and felt real uneasy being around the loving couple. Daily they consumed their own homemade intoxicant; a dark liquidly substance, with a stench to bring tears to Coon's eyes, and he noticed how they also used it to cure his many varmint pelts.

Now Coon could tell Williams just loved the guy by the way they swapped old hunting stories, held spitting contests and kicked rattlesnakes around. When they began throwing tomahawks around the shack at each other, Coon moved outside. Then the Missus talked about doing a mail order bride set-up for her sister, like her husband had done for her, bringing her over for her husband's good friend. After that He was spending more time on horseback and smelling fresh air again.

"I tell you, Coon, lookin' at old Jack, I'm not sure how we ever survived our youth. You think all those Russian women that big?"

"Ah never plan on going to Russia to find out. Their kind of whiskey is downright deadly. I think I saw one of his dead varmints stand right back up and waddle out of that house."

"Ah wouldn't of doubt it, no siree."

The farthest west post was the ancient ruins of a Spanish Fort. No one knew what had happened to the gallant Soldiers of Spain or what tribe had participated in their sad demise, but the ruins lay there still, made of log and adobe, and here set Rangers Brady Williams and Joshua Dreeke.

Sgt. Dreeke was assigned as rover, checking each post to ensure they had what they needed and had not run off to play war for the South or gone off to Mexico for a week of frolic. Not that they all didn't need a time of frolicking in Old Mexico. But the men had proved faithful to the promise they made to JW. Not so much as to Arizona or the Rangers, but to their Captain. They would hold these posts for seven-days, watching over the desert to search out the Apache and catch them before they could strike. JW knew they would lose a farm or a homestead, because it was the killing fires the Apaches so loved that would bring the Rangers in on them. But if they had not come after seven-days, he knew the men had decisions to make and money to earn. As of today, the Rangers held their posts for the five long days, doing nothing but watching. This gave a lot of time for a man to think about future-plans. For Ranger Williams, this meant avoiding his friend's overbearing wife and nuptial plans for her sister and him.

Seventeen-miles north of Ranger's Holloway and Leader's position, 63 Apache Braves were moving south. With pillage from the massacre well appreciated in the form of horsemeat, material goods and many strange shaped pots and pans, and wanting to help his son was well accepted. Additional braves volunteered to go with him south. This included the 23 survivors, who were the first to join up. Their reason was vengeance. Yet, for the journey guns and ammo was still a major obstacle. They rode south, armed mainly with bow and arrow, lances and scalping knives. Though known for fierceness, the Chiricahua was only one of several Apache tribes. They most often fought in small numbers. In the past, only under great chiefs were all the Apache brought together, but this was not to be one of those times.

The young sub-chief, desiring to impress his father and his warrior clan, was planning-out the battles. Though he carried out the killing of eight wagons of intruders into Chiricahua Apache lands, he lost several valuable warriors to a second poorly planned ambush. So, he knew this next raid must be for something very valuable; in order-to make him appear great in his father's eyes and those of a young maiden he wished to wed. He had the necessary bride price, but the father desired more in a son-in-law than three-horses, some Spanish blankets and an older rifle, black powder and shot he had taken off a grizzled old Hispanic gentleman during a raid on a homestead several months ago.

He led his greatest party of 62-warriors south toward several of the White Man's ranches. He wanted to kill them all, burn down their homes, their dwellings, steal their cattle to feed his tribe. He would kidnap their small children and the women who could be sold as slaves to the Mexicans, and be long remembered for a great murder raid upon the Arizonians who had come to settle upon his people's lands.

Once again, beside him rode two of his father's senior warriors, men who have fought in dozens of battles and several wars against the White Man, Mexican and French trappers, now even the American soldiers of both gray and blue colors. For the young sub-chief saw patrols of both armies of this American Civil War cross upon his people's lands and today he hoped to come upon one such patrol and steal their weapons. Still, his main goal, his heart's desire, was to add the Ranger Captain's scalp to his scalp pole, for this man had killed his brother in the last ambush and he now sought revenge.

CAPTAIN JAMIE HEMPSTEAD, C COMPANY COMMANDER ASSIGNED TO GENERAL HOOD'S ARMY OF TEXAS, MORNING OF THE SIXTH DAY

C Company had broken camp early, before the sun had even shown itself from the east, but its illumination was already now chasing the darkness across the sky. Captain Hempstead of San Antonio and his 22 riders had taken a southern route to enter Nevada and waylay a few of the silver wagons being sent out of Carson City en route to the west with the vast riches they carried under military escort of a dozen U.S. soldiers. Once the wagons had traveled some 50 miles they were to join up with wagon trains traveling to Portland, Oregon or San Francisco, California. Both destinations would provide transport aboard U.S. Navy ships for passage to Washington D.C. The bean counters at the nation's capital believed an ocean voyage was safer than risking attack by Indians and Southern troops.

Southern spies were already in Carson City though and had sent word back to the South concerning how much silver was being carried in these transport wagons and the best locations in those 50-miles to attack the small escort. C Company was tasked with the chore of securing that silver and once they had attacked three separate wagons, to then return to the South with their treasure, which would be used to purchase weapons and needed equipment from foreign allies.

A young man of 24, Captain Hempstead had inherited his ranch when his grandfather had passed on. His father was killed by bandits before young Hempstead was even born and Grandpa had become his Old Man. He was considered tall for that day and age, hitting six-foot, two-inches, with muscular arms, and broad chest from working ten to 12-hour work days. He sat a horse well, having been riding since he was four years old. He wore his hair longish, and maintained a short beard and moustache, and his eyes were clear with a radiating blue, and a break in the middle of his left eyebrow was a wide scar caused by a rock throwing incident from when he was seven-years old.

Many ladies in San Antonio had targeted him for marriage, but he was set on one woman only. She was a daughter of the man who sold him horses every summer. She was half-Spanish and half-white, had long black hair that hung to her hips, deep brown eyes and took no guff off anyone. They were married when she turned 18 years old and he was 22, which the affair was one of the biggest hoorahs in the area in sometime. Hempstead's new father-in-law even staged a rodeo to round out the reception.

With time being short before the next wagon was due to leave Carson City, Captain Hempstead drove his Company from early morning to the twilight at the end of the day. It was weary men who dragged themselves to small newly made Indian-style fires and often or not most of the soldiers fell asleep before they finished off the semi-warm rations piled upon dented tin plates laying on their dusty laps. Their horses remained quiet; having carried their man for over 25-miles across a boiling empty desert. They took their last drink of water from their soldier's sweaty hat and a handful of dry oats, before the scratchy saddle was removed and mare or gelding could stretch their sore backs some. Sleep came hard for a cavalry horse out in the field, for every sound would jar them awake and they'd let go with the whinny. A good horse was almost as good as a trained guard dog for detecting movement outside of a campsite.

Staff Sergeant. Samuel C. Butrick, three large stripes and a rocker on his arm of his filthy and soiled gray uniform, had assigned the three men for the first two hours of guard duty. There would be two men on the campsite, posted on opposite sides and one man watching the horses, which were hobbled and tied securely to a rope line, which was ground-secured between two large rocks. Captain Hempstead decided two hours of guard duty would be about as much as these men could handle from all the long riding they'd been doing. Unfortunately, for Sgt. Butrick he'd be losing a lot of sleep as he made sure the posts were relieved and no one was falling asleep on guard duty.

Captain Hempstead hadn't even known Sergeant Butrick before this assignment. The man had been dragged out of his own unit due to his western experience with the Indians of New Mexico and Arizona. A former Scout and hunter, he had been in 17 confrontations with Comanche, Ute and Apache, and survived them all with only two arrow wounds and a knife wound to the shoulder. Sam still carried the knife on his belt that had belonged to the Indian he had scuffled with.

Sam knew the desert and he knew the best route to South Nevada. Still, the old geezer was now a hair over 60 years and long hours in the saddle were getting to his backside and pain cost him his alertness. He would often ride ahead, play scout, ensure the trail up ahead was clear of Indian sign or possible trail for a US Cavalry Troop. Recently he simply pointed out the direction across the flat desert the Captain would lead his men, then walk a spell to relieve the fiery pain to his spine.

As he traveled across all this emptiness, suffering under the burning sun, Captain Hempstead missed San Antonio and the cattle ranch he had left behind to ride behind General Hood and his Army of Texas. He had never owned any slaves and almost his entire ranch was manned by paid Texans and the rest a few Mexicans who lived on the ranch with their families. Captain Hempstead went to war because like so many others he felt the Federal Government should keep its nose out of their state affairs. He couldn't stay home. Not while so many of his friends and relatives joined up under General Hood. But his young wife didn't understand and the icy disposition she held for over a week did not make it any easier. Only the night before he left did she melt to grant him a memorable send-off. Afterward, she wept off and on for the next two-days. The older senior hands knew how to keep the ranch going and all big decisions she would make. She had not told him she was in the early stages of her first pregnancy, for she refused to use that to pull him home and then later he would resent her and the child. Still, she thought he looked so handsome in his new gray officer's uniform, when he mounted his black stallion, saluted her and road off to join Hood's Confederacy.

But before a saddle-sore Captain Hempstead and his valiant C Company riders ever reached northern Arizona, they had fallen victim to a well-laid Apache ambush. Sixty-three Apache Indians, laying, sitting or standing behind rocky fortifications along the walls of a narrow canyon, well-concealed, their mounts hidden a mile away, held by their two youngest braves, opened fire on C Company. The soldiers had no chance of escaping. With the Southerners trapped in the center of the canyon, the Apache closed-up both ends, continued firing both arrows and their few single-shot rifles until not a single Confederate soldier remained a threat. With only two Apache wounded in the ambush, this was considered a major success and the young chief received approving looks from the older one, who had ridden along with him.

An Apache Scout saw C Company from a great distance, knowing they followed one of the old wagon train routes, used before the White Man's war between the Mexicans to the far south. The Apache had not seen anyone use this route in some time, mainly because it was open to Apache and Ute attacks in this area and Comanche attack to the east. The scout brought back this news, surprising the young chief. He recalled when he was half his current age how he rode through a narrow canyon still north of the soldiers and sensing uneasiness. Even then he knew this was a perfect ambush site and he planned to use it against the White Man.

For the last 100-years or possibly longer, the Apache and Comanche had an unwritten agreement not to enter each other's hunting grounds. This provided the Comanche with New Mexico and a good part of Texas, while the Apache held Arizona, South-East California desert regions and Northern Mexico. Sharing these lands were the Ute tribes who had no such agreement with either tribe. They too were warriors. Ute fight in small groups, almost never ride horses; however, can run across the desert floor for miles without stopping. In many ways, Utes can be compared with the African Zulu, except in size, as Utes are small people. They are deadly and extremely fond of torturing their enemy for lengthy periods of time. When working in small parties; they move silently, falling upon Indian, White Man or Mexican, if   their numbers are right. Other Indians in the area— the Pueblo and Navajo--are looked upon as being non-warrior societies. Yet, both tribes proved themselves to be warrior-breeds, when the need arose over past centuries.

This ambush was carried out by the Apache and the warriors were letting out their victory yells, as they moved among the dead, dying and wounded too secure treasures—scalps, weapons, ammo, clothing, jewelry, blankets and horses. They killed the dying and wounded, except the old sergeant. When they came to Sam, a warrior spotted an Apache holy medallion worn on a necklace, a special token given to a person for saving an Apache warrior's life. The older ones saw this and ordered that Sam be moved outside the killing field, left in the shade with ample water, some food and his horse tied up nearby. His weapons were also left with him, including the Apache knife he had won in battle.

A favor was returned for a favor as they saw it. Ironically, Sam was unconscious during the whole ordeal. He'd taken an arrow to the upper left chest, which was removed and his wound bandaged somewhat. So, when Sam awoke, feeling the sharp pain of the wound and a badly folded bandage over his chest, he was startled at first and then surprised to find he was still alive, but seemingly well cared for by the Apache. His canteen was full, some desert food the Apache consume was wrapped in a cured piece of antelope hide and his horse stood secured by his rope to a large rock nearby. Only then did he notice the Apache medallion was missing. He realized it was meant for a one-time affair and kept him alive when he saw the rest of his troop were all dead.

73

He couldn't help but cringe when he saw the scalped mostly naked bodies of the troopers nearby and seeing his young captain with three broken off arrows in his chest. This told him the Apache had shot him full of the deadly things, but were unable to remove them from his chest, so, broke them off to save the feathers. At least he knew the young man was assuredly now dead. It was the Indian way to abuse their enemy's bodies, but he had seen a lot of White Men and Mexicans do far worse to Indian bodies. He noticed even the men's boots were taken. They left the rest for desert predators to consume. The old man knew within a week, only stripped bones would remain for those who followed. This pass would be forever rumored as haunted by the 21 somebodies who died here in some unnamed battle.

Sam had to get his mind off the dead and figure out what he was going to do. He sure didn't want to spend the night beside his dead and mutilated friends. The intense summer heat and movement of the sun, removing the shade, already started producing a vile stench. He counted over a dozen vultures flying overhead, and. Sam knew they'd be attacking the bodies soon. He wanted to be on his way when that began. He expected coyotes and possibly wolves to pick-up the foul scent also.

The ride to Carson City was too far, especially in his condition. He felt he might be able to reach Globe — If he could stay in the saddle. He needed to get moving right away, before he used his water up. He needed to share it with Ol' Jelly Bottom, his mare these last seven years. Sam hoped if he passed out, his horse would find the way. They had been over these trails a couple times in the past, when he scouted for the Union boys and the occasional immigrant party headed to California. Every time he crossed this inferno desert with an immigrant train, scouting for 12 to 20 wagons of foreigners, he met up with the Apache. But he had to admit, those foreigners knew how to fight. He never lost a whole train. They did leave a parcel of crosses behind to mark graves. He'd never been hit in this pass, which provided a short-cut to Carson City. *Except now and it cost me mah company. Must've been my age, getting' too old ta see the Indian signs an' they all died 'cause ah failed dem.*

Feeling lower than a lizard, Sam pulled himself to his feet, cringing and grinding his teeth to stifle off the cry the pain brought on from straining the muscles of his wound site. He had started bleeding again. He had no choice. He was thankful they left him with his service rifle, a single shot Enfield Musket. He used this as a crutch, but made sure to keep the barrel end out of the sand. Even as he fought with the intense pain, he wanted to keep his rifle loaded in the event an Apache brave came back for another trophy. He never saw any sign of them. It took him three attempts to get mounted. He upchucked, when in the saddle. Sam cussed out Jelly Bottom for glaring at him and letting out a whinny, as she shook her head.

"Yeah, I know, I stink...whole place stinks, but some brave men died here today and you're not going to badmouth a one of them. Now get me headin' south or I'll toss your oat ration into the wind." Only then did Sam check his sidearm; relieved to find it loaded with five chambers full. He turned, tried straightening up some, presenting his best salute to the men of C Company and their young commander, Captain Hempstead. Sam hoped he survived long enough to go by the Hempstead Ranch to tell the story to the widow. "Of course, I'll liven it up some, tell how he killed his fair share of Apache, while trying to save a couple of his men before being killed. "Sad, the Captain being shot and killed right off. Maybe he could've got some of the men out the south-end before they closed it off, but those Apache, they've learned to go for the officers. Young Hempstead was probably dead before he hit the ground, at least I hope so." Sam said to his mare, as he rearranged his bandage. Being a desert scout, he was used to talking to his horse and Jelly Bottom often nodded her head as if she understood his talks and ranting's. They were still conversing when Sam rode out of the canyon, leaving C Company behind to man their new posting forevermore.

The Apache diverted from their path to fight C Company, but once more headed south. The two wounded warriors, along with the young ones, who guarded the mounts, were taking C Company's horses back to the tribe. They would share the story of the attack on the soldiers, and show the treasures they returned with. The warrior's families of those on the killer raid would receive first pick. Half the mounts would feed the hungry tribe. In the eyes of the senior chief, he was proud of his son. He knew in a couple years he would be ready to take over as one of the senior leaders of this tribe.

Several of the rifles were brought back, were superior to the ones they traded for last year with the Mexicans from the South. The rest of the weapons remained with the raiding party, to replace the bow and arrow. Twenty-two warriors now carried handguns. They had no expertise using them. In celebration, they shot all five rounds off. They soon learned they were not quite sure how to reload them. Men attempted shoving rifle rounds into pistols, to no avail. Two braves saw firearms used and conducted classes on reloading them. As far as accuracy, the whole raiding party had drawn up short. They all liked carrying the new trophy, but the old ones feared that unless their enemy stood right in front of their warriors, they would miss their target and that was if they remembered how to use the firearm in the heat of battle. There were a few warriors who refused to give up their bow and arrows. Some who were deadly accurate.

With the loss of four braves, and the men he sent back with the horses, the young chief now led a raiding force of 55 warriors, which was still an amazing number for a killer raid. Most raids numbered less than 25 warriors and often less than 15. They learned to watch their targets, study habits of White Man or Mexicans of ranches and farms and hit fast. Once they completed a few days of successful pillage and plunder forays, they headed home to escape rangers or possibly, Union Cavalry. If they could defeat them, the young chief felt the desert was open for them to strike the White Man living around the new settlement of Globe. Maybe even attack this Globe itself, if its defenses looked weak enough.

CHAPTER THREE

"Get's much hotter, let's stop for chow. I can fry mine on a rock."

CAPTAIN BLAKE'S RANGERS, HEADING NORTH, SEVENTH DAY ON THE TRAIL

With neck scarf damp from perspiration and backside sending painful signals to his brain, Captain JW Blake called a halt, ordering the men to walk their horses. Sgt. James Dreeke walked up beside Blake, sensing his captain needed to talk. As usual, he was right.

"This is the seventh day and you know I promised the men we'd pull back and head for home if we found no sign of the Apache…But I still got that itch. You got any ideas, Jamey?"

"Captain, ah think dese fellas would follow you on ta thu surface of dat blazin' sun up dere, if'in it had a point. But by all appearances, dose Apache has done headed for home an' dis bunch of ours is much too small ta follow dem into deir mountains. We'd need a thousand men for dat an' all we's got is us. You'se also known as a man of your word an' dey're countin' on dat. Besides, by thu way you'se ridin', it's getting' tougher for you ever'a day ta stay mounted, JW…ah, Captain, Sir."

Blake grinned at his faithful sergeant, "You're right, we'll head back in the morning and make an early camp tonight. Should be a watering hole coming up in a mile or two and we can rest up there."

"Sounds a good to me, ah'll pass thu word along. It'll make thu men all feel better, maybe even gets a little poker goin' tonight."

"Sergeant, you just make sure those guards are posted. This is still the Apache's stomping grounds and my wife might behave a might unpleasantly with you if I lose my gorgeous hair."

Sergeant James Arthur Dreeke chuckled and said, "She mite at dat, Sir." He then pulled on his reins and turned to pass along the line to give them the news. On the morning of Day eight, they would head home, taking the direct route to Globe from the northeast. It would involve rough travel, over low rocky hills and a few lava beds, JW hoped to bypass if they could.

JW soon found out Preacher Joe was extremely relieved to be turning back. His lower backside was under attack from the aged bench seat's wooden splinters and several blisters from handling that wagon for the last seven-days. He used two folded Army blankets to cushion the ride and was still wincing with nearly every bump, and the old cuss was much too ornery to let out even a whimper. Each night he built a small private fire, treating his own wounds, refusing to let any of these rangers from coming anywhere near his bottom with one of their Bowie knives. Young Liam offered to help, but when he made the first attempt to cut a splinter out, his hands were shaking so bad Preacher Joe removed the knife out of self-preservation. "I thank you, Liam, but you're not ready for something so-sensitive as my butt. Why don't you jus' grab up the axe an' locate us some firewood."

On this seventh night, Preacher Joe wore bandages on both rear butt cheeks. He planned soothing his wounded flesh with hot water, boiled in the late night hours by Liam to help the old man.

Liam never asked, but was always curious why the old Preacher had not begun right off riding on a thick layer of cushion. What he was using wasn't much more than a horse blanket and Liam knew those side rails the old man's hips slammed into at every sudden jerk or bump were plumb full of splinters. But he didn't say anything. He didn't want to sound like an upstart around an older gentleman he was beginning to like. By now, the two were friends and Liam would do anything he could to make the old Preacher more comfortable. But cutting the splinters out with a small knife became an obstacle he couldn't overcome and was thankful when Preacher Joe relieved him of the duty.

The Watering hole wasn't much more than a mud hole, but after an hour's worth of work by two teams of men with tools, the water spring bubbled up with filthy dark creamy colored liquid; which was boiled in the soup pot from the wagon. The filth was spooned away from the top with a large hand-carved wooden spoon. Once it cooled down some, they refilled three buckets; starting the process all over again. By late nightfall, all their canteens were full, horses somewhat content and their two water barrels were half-full; which was enough to get them back to the last river they crossed, four days back.

Guards were posted and the men's spirits were up, heading for home always had that effect on the rangers. Horses were tied off on a ground line from the wagon to a good-sized boulder and the mounts also individually hobbled by their owners to ensure they were not an easy target for an Apache horse stealer. JW knew of one Apache horse thief he had never been able to catch and he knew this man had gotten away with over 200 horses across Arizona and New Mexico. He often wondered if the man was still alive, or if he had finally retired to instruct other young ones in his trade. He hoped the old Indian was now chasing horses in the sky, for the man was a real slick operator and rarely needed to kill during his thefts. He had even gone so far as to steal a Union Officer's horse out of

Fort Bowie in Eastern Arizona. With the officer being a major, all the night guards received 30-days extra duty.

For the first night since leaving his ranch, JW slept the whole night through and he felt pretty good upon opening his eyes with the break of dawn. This was part of a ranchers and a farmer's life, one did not waste daylight hours by staying in bed. He was in the process of rolling up his blankets when he heard a loud commotion over at the watering hole, dropped his blankets, grabbed up his rifle and dashed over to the puddle in the sand. There he found a man curled up in fetal position, with a horse blanket over most of him and his horse standing by nearby, untied and not hobbled. He also saw how the man was unconscious, not just asleep, otherwise all the noise would've awakened him. He held an empty revolver in his hand and was wearing a Confederate sergeant's uniform, with a sun-bleached *Reb* cavalry hat resting over his face.

First thing JW did was to carefully un-cock the firearm's hammer and gently remove it from the man's hand. Only after he had done so did he pull the man's hat off his face, "Sam!?" JW said with surprise. "What the…" He didn't go any further, now seeing the blood soiled bandage and shirt Sam had on. "Get Preacher Joe up here, we have a wounded man, here."

It was Brady Williams who hustled back to wake up the Preacher and once told why he was non-too gently awakened, Preacher Joe grabbed up his doctoring bag and came hustling over at the best pace he could handle, considering his own shape.

"It's Sam Butrick, used ta scout for thu rangers 'fore he went off ta join thu Confederacy. He's been shot up pretty bad…chest wound an' appears he's a ridden quite a way's." Sergeant Dreeke muttered, "I is not all ta'gether sure how he dun wandered in ta our camp wit 'out bein' a heard by our guards. But it sure do makes you wonder, don't it, Cap?"

"I'll talk with you about that later, Sergeant. Right now, I need to know what Sam is doing out here and where's his troops?" JW glared up at his troops, especially those knowing they had pulled the last guard duty before dawn. Someone had been dozing and they were all lucky it was a Confederate soldier and not a bunch of Apache warriors, or Union troops. Tonight, those same men would be pulling double duty to remind them of their mishap and Jamey will be conducting more inspections of his guard. A loss of sleep was always a good punishment and JW pitied the ranger Jamey caught sleeping tonight.

"He's coming around, JW," Preacher Joe said.

"Sam, it's John W Blake, can you hear me?"

"I'm a bit tired, JW I isn't dead. Not yet anyway. Sure am hungry, though."

"Hold off on all the talking, for now and we'll get you fed," JW ordered. He then looked back up at Jamey, "I need him carried over to the fire so I can get this wound sewn up before he loses anymore blood. Send a couple men over for the wagon tailgate and bring it over here to load this man on it. I want him to stay level. He cannot afford to have any more of his insides be torn up by being carried roughly."

JW gestured at Coon and Holloway to do what he ordered. Thinking he was helping, Liam began tossing some extra chunks of wood on the fire in the event Preacher Joe needed them to operate with, but Sgt. Sam Butrick yelled, "Keep that fire down, boy...You got a large band of Apache around here...and they..." Sam fell unconscious again. Preacher Joe checked him and announced he was only unconscious and not dead.

Having worked with Sam on numerous occasions, JW knew the man was an experienced Indian fighter. So, he ordered four men to saddle, with rifle and canteen, to the four points of the compass to surround the camp. "You remain 50 yards out, keep mounted and keep riding slowly in a circle. No fixed positions and do not gang up on one another. If you see any dust, a sparkle of light or hear anything that shouldn't be there, you pull in and report, but only the one who saw or heard it. The rest of you, start building up barricades, dig some rifle pits in a tight enough circle we can defend with our mounts in the middle. Leave the wagon horses harnessed up, but keep them hobbled for now. We can cut the lines if we're in a rush. We'll move Sam into the wagon once Preacher Joe finishes up his operatin'."

"JW, Sam's awake again...needs to talk, but he's bleeding again so make it quick."

"Okay, Preacher." JW knelt beside Sam and gently rested his hand on Sam's left knee. "Tell me what you have, Sam."

"Thought I was dreamin' when I heard your voice, kid. It's been a long time since we rode the desert together. But you've got to get out of here. Is this a ranger outfit?"

"Sure is, I'm commanding the ranger now, not much of a kid anymore, Sam. So, who got you, last thing I heard you were back east fighting in the big war under General Hood's Army of Texas."

"I was, but they yanked me from my unit and assigned me to this young captain and a mounted company being sent west to borrow some silver from the union silver mines in Nevada. We were supposed to hit three loads and then take our load back to Richmond. There was 23 of us, including the Captain. Now, except for me, their bones are drying out in a narrow canyon up northwest of here. They wiped us out…Except for me."

"How many, Sam?"

"I was riding up front with my Captain, a nice young man from San Antonio, but we went down fast. It's only an estimate but it would have to be more than 50 braves, JW. It's a war party, not just a killing raid or a bunch of horse stealers. I'd used this trail a lot, but a man gets old and he loses something. I never saw it coming and they had warriors on both sides, plus closing-up the front and back ends to prevent us from escaping. When I first woke up, it wasn't a pretty sight and you understand what I mean." Sam was talking in a low whisper to preserve strength.

"But Sam, how did you survive?" JW asked.

"You recall that medallion I wore with the pretty blue stone. How I told you an Indian gave it to me for saving his life…I guess they honor their promises. I woke up with my wound bandaged, my weapons still beside me, along with a full canteen and some food, plus my horse Ol' Jelly Bottom tied up nearby. But the medallion…It was gone. They had paid me back."

"That's enough palavering," Preacher Joe said. "JW is liable to finish what the Apache began with all his questions."

"Sure…but Sam, do you know where they might be headed?"

"I was a headed for Globe and they were still in front of me, so I cut off heading east. I…I…I couldn't warn Globe, but maybe…Maybe some of the ranches east of Globe."

"Globe!" JW exclaimed. He then gestured for the men to gently place Sam on the wagon gate and with others helping, to carry him over to the fire. They then left him in Preacher Joe's care, while they listened in as JW talked with some of his seasoned Indian fighters and Sgt. Dreeke. They had some fast decisions to make. "Stop on the barricades, but keep the riders out there for now or do we make a run for Globe and risk running into the war party?"

First they had to wait for Preacher Joe to finish his operating on Sam and get him settled for a rough ride, using most everyone's sleeping blankets. JW then summoned Jim Williams over to where he had his saddle braced against a ledge of dried clay. Sgt. Dreeke stood nearby to listen in and add anything if he was asked.

"Take a seat, Jim or stand if you're more comfortable, but you're liable to be riding real soon in any event." JW pulled out his Bowie and began sharpening it from an aged sharpening stone that had belonged to his grandfather, who had also owned the knife. JW often liked to have things in his hands when talking with men. Somehow the palavering went easier.

"Jim, you've already probably heard, we've got a good-sized war party headed south for Globe. Sam is an experienced man and he estimated over 50. But their Confederate Company of 23 was wiped out, leaving only Sam alive, but wounded severely. The Apache owed him a death honor, so they allowed him to live, but it's a one-time thing and he's used it up. So, Jim we believe they're headed for Globe to make a major score on scalps, cattle, horses and weapons. They know there aren't any Union troops there and they've just killed off the one bunch of Confederate soldiers. With a party this big I doubt they're all that fearful of us rangers. You understand all this so far?"

"Sure thing, Captain. You want me to ride."

"Not just ride, Jim, but to ride like the devil. You'll take your horse and Sam's, towing his on a lead. You'll carry three canteens, two of them on Sam's mount. He calls his mare Ol' Jelly Bottom. They've been together for at least seven years I know of. But when your mount wearies, you switch and let yours one free, but you can't stop for anything. You were raised by the Apache. You know your stars so I know you won't get lost in the dark. You're to head Southwest at the gallop and use the Devil's Frying Pan to gain on the Apache. You'll be edging the sides. I do not expect you to cross the center of it and stay clear of those Apache. You must get a warning to Globe that the Apache are coming in force. You also have-to stop by at the ranches and farms north of Globe and warn them. You'll have enough time to stop for water and a bite in the saddle, but it's up to the farmers and ranchers to heed the warning or die on their property.

"You're going to be our version of a Paul Revere, Jim and once you hit Globe and give the warning. You move on to the farms and ranches east of Globe and advise them to either move for Globe if they can make it within two hours or head for my ranch. You're to advise all the rangers not in the settlement to head for my ranch. It's the best spot to make a stand if one is needed. You tell our wives were coming fast, but we'll be coming up behind the Indians to hit them by surprise from the rear. Between all of us, we might be able to finish this tribe's killing days off."

"You got all that, Jim?" Sgt. Dreeke asked.

"Sure enough, I got book learnin' now."

"That's right I forgot, so why don't you find a pencil and some paper and take a brief-moment to get some one line messages written down to the men's wives. I know that will mean a lot, especially later-on." JW said and Jim understood what the later-on part meant. Some of the rangers might not survive this last shootout with the Apache, as the warrior tried to escape and flee north.

Within half-an-hour, Jim hit the trail and was taking the prayers of all the men. He had a good 60 miles or more to travel in less than 48-hours of hard riding. This was going to be one of those times the hard training of the Apache, who held him prisoner for several years of his youth, would be needed. Whatever pain he might feel, he would have to shoot it to the back of his mind. He carried no bedroll, only one saddle for the horse he rode, no rifle and only a handgun with six rounds of ammo. The final round was for himself, for he refused to be taken prisoner by the Apache. But he also carried a small sheath knife, for he learned how important a knife was in desert survival. Jelly Bottom wore an Indian fashioned rope saddle, to which he secured the two extra canteens. He kept an extra shirt for wiping down the white frothy sweat buildup from his mounts' chest, neck and out of their eyes.

Before nightfall, he would stop, take a drink for him and both horses, wipe them down and feed them a handful of oats he carried in a green canvas bag hanging from his saddle. He watched as the sun passed down beyond the western horizon; a strange quiet twilight arrived. It was time he took a study of the stars to give him his route for the night. He first looked for the North Star to keep it always over his left shoulder. He could not ride as fast now, not wanting to break a horse's leg in a small rocky crevice or in a varmint hole. He was also concerned with rattle snakes, which were out searching for their nightly meal. They might strike at the horse as he rode by and he would soon lose one of his mounts to the snake's venom. Jim also learned how the darkness played tricks on a weary man. He heard numerous stories of ghosts who wandered the deserts searching out travelers, hoping they might once more return to the real world by taking the body of a dying human. Indians had hundreds of such stories, along with the Mexicans and it was often the White Man who spread them to frighten the tenderfoots coming to the new land.

Jim had been told dozens of such tales by Comanche and Apache elders and their medicine man, because his time of testing was at hand; when he would wander the desert alone, to survive, to prove he was worthy of being called a warrior. Jim, taken originally by the Comanche, was sold to Mexicans as a slave when he was nothing more than a toddler. But the Mexican bandits grew weary of dragging such a young sprout. When they came to a trading meet with the Apache, they let Jim go cheap. Years later, Jim was rescued. He was forced to learn the ways of the whites. This was not an easy time for anyone involved in the process. He was more Apache than white at the beginning and White Man was considered the devil.

Jim often thought back on those times, of how he had bitten, clawed and kicked many of his teachers. If he had gotten his hands on a sharp object, he would have done even worse harm. But he wasn't the first, or the last white teen to be rescued. They all know time was required. Time, a lot of understanding, plus a good amount of love. But a stern right hand was also required when Jim got too wild and he needed his rear end spanked for improper behavior. It was then that JW stepped in and they took the boy home, filled him up with good beef. JW taught him manners, giving him his name. Now he rode as a Ranger. Still, Jim had never forgotten his time with the Apache. He remained fluent in several of the desert Indian dialects. This skill was often needed and even encouraged by JW and Jamey.

His horses rested, Jim remounted Comanche, his own gray Appaloosa gelding, with black mane and tail. He grabbed up the lead for Jelly Bottom and proceeded south. He knew the Apache would not ride at night and this would give him his edge on catching up with them and hopefully bypassing them in 30 hours — Hopefully. But his time in giving warnings to the people of Globe was extremely short. Jim knew his mount would ride until it dropped dead, but he wasn't so sure about Sam's horse. He had met Sam a couple times before, when he came by JW's place. Jim was working as a hand then, with kitchen privileges. He still had his own room built up on the back porch. Now Jim lived at the Ranger's Compound in Globe, stretching his arms out to be a man. He still considered JW and Sherry Ann his Uncle and Aunt. Though he had no memory of his parents, he just never took to calling them Mom and Dad. They both understood and never brought it up.

Looking off at the night sky, glancing around for campfires to avoid, Jim decided he'd ride Comanche for another couple of hours, at least to the next mountain outcropping he could make out in the distance and then switch mounts. He named his horse Comanche because he admired a large Appaloosa ridden by a Comanche chieftain that stuck in his memory. He couldn't recall what the Indian looked like or if he had been the Indian who killed his family, but that horse was spectacular.

Later, when he was riding Jelly Bottom, he was greatly surprised by the horse's energy and its desert knowledge. He quickly came to respect the mount's skills in avoiding holes, sand slides and even a rattler or two. "Sam must've taught you good, missy, you sure know the desert."

Before the morning sun breached the horizon, Jim came upon a burned-up miner's shack, still smoldering from last afternoon's attack. He couldn't tell right then where the man and woman's bodies were, but he promised to come back soon and give them a proper burial. However, his first task was to help the living. The horses shied away from the stench.

The two bodies were left inside the shack to burn with their collection of belongs. He spotted half-a-dozen rattlers that came for the heat, so he moved on. As he rode away, he wondered how many other small places he would find. Almost a mile later, he located a freshly dug Apache grave. While on the trail they often tried to hide their warrior's graves, but Jim was a scout and he had followed the tracks right to it. "So, the miner or his wife killed one of them…that's one."

Time was coming up for Jim to finish sweeping around the next bluff and find before him the Devil's frying pan. It had many names, nothing ever official, but by midday during the boiling season the temperature out there could reach better than 140 degrees. Many a tenderfoot wagon train had attempted to cross the center of the pan during the wrong season and their trains would be found in the winter or fall, with everyone dead and all the horses baked to a tanned leather-like tightness. As in other parts of the desert, the pan had more than its share of crosses marking the graves of stupid people who never listened to an old timer's advice of staying clear of the pan.

Jim wasn't about to make any attempt at crossing it, but he could ride the outside fringe and keep his mounts wetted down with those two canteens. When he got around, he'd be dry, but it was only a few miles to the next water hole and if that one was dry he could make the next one within a couple hours. He knew he couldn't count on any of the settlers, because that would put him directly behind the Apache and he needed to get in front of them. Once he got watered up, he'd return to the pan and keep heading south. This would put him in front of the Apache soon enough. If the Apache made additional stops to burn out settlers he had a good chance on making it to the Globe settlement and preparing them for a real Indian war.

Finding their tracks, he realized the Apache war party numbered at least 60 warriors. This was indeed a major raid. While he was with them he had never seen such a sizeable force to go out on a kill raid. Only when the Apache went against another Indian tribe had he seen these numbers. When they returned home, nearly a third of them were gone. He often wondered if it had been a victory or had the two tribes separated and fallen back after losing so many warriors. He did recall there was no celebration that night and many of the wives were screaming out their grief throughout the darkening hours. Half-a-dozen of the wives had even taken their own lives, but these were the ones without children.

When Jim was asked to compare Indian life to White Man's world by his friend at the local drinking hole in Globe. His usual response was, "Apache make life simpler."

JW'S RIDE SOUTH IN PURSUIT OF THE APACHE, THE NINTH DAY

Though the Rangers were tired, having ridden all night and now into the day, there was an anxiousness amongst them. They knew a lot of their family members and friends were in Globe and the surrounding ranches and farms just to the north, who would be hit first if Ranger Jim couldn't get through in time to rouse up a fighting force. But they also knew he was the right man for the job and fought hard to keep their minds on their own task at hand. JW was pushing hard and in this country, where Indians could spring up on a party at any moment, in any arroyo or come across any flat shooting and yelling like banshees, one had to have eyes in the back of his head.

Preacher Joe, drove the wagon horses hard. Sam lay in the back, fighting to keep from being beat to snot by the rough travel. Liam did what he could to help, while keeping a shotgun within grasping range. They were followed by two rangers, holding to a lope, while Preacher raced ahead. JW ordered the two rangers to stay back with the wagon, in the event some Indians might be about and tried to get behind the wagon. Four horses and whatever the wagon carried would be a nice prize. But when the men and mounts with JW needed water, they'd pull-up and wait for the wagon to catch up and bring the water barrels to refill the canteens and give the horses a drink. Liam would water the wagon horses, too. This gave Preacher Joe time to check on Sam's wound and re-bandage him if needed.

"Captain, we can't keep a goin' at dis pace," Sgt. Dreeke advised JW. He was concerned after checking the condition of the men and horses. Most were covered in white froth.

JW considered it for a moment, then replied, "Another hour and we should hit Dutchman's Gulch. There's usually a mountain stream running through there and hopefully enough water to refill the water barrels. We'll break there until sunset, cook up a meal Indian-style and give everyone a nice rest. Then we ride until we make-contact with the Apache and hopefully they're retreating from the newly formed Globe Militia."

"Globe Militia?" Sgt. Dreeke said with some hesitation. As far as he knew, no such force existed. "Sounds good, Captain," Sgt. Dreeke agreed. "A'll sure get thu word out...Sir," Sgt. Dreeke replied. He then led his mount to be toweled off and wet down with a damp rag, not bothering to say how often he found Dutchman's Gulch dried up and dead animal carcasses lying about from those critters that could not go any further and gave up.

Rangers knew the Southwest Indian would go so far without water and then slice their horse's throats to drink their blood for their own survival. Oddly enough, few White Men would do this. They would shoot the dying horse and then walk off to die in the desert, sometimes within a mile of a watering hole. This was one of those things that confused the Indian, the attachment a White Man would form for his horse, while the Indian saw it as a piece of equipment-like a good knife or fine hand-carved bow.

JW wiped down his Appaloosa, gave it a drink from his hat, which cooled his hat. He then walked over to check on Sam. "How's he doing, Preacher?"

"Either a lot of prayer, JW or they just built them tougher back there in the day. But it appears he'll live to fight again."

"Sure ah will. Now if yuh give me my horse, ah'll get out of this rockin' chair. It's got me where ah'm not sure which way I'm goin'."

"Not yet, Soldier Boy," Preacher Joe said. "You still got some healing to do. You get on some horse and you'll probably start bleeding again and ruin all my needle work. You might bleed out before you get back to me. That would be bad for my medical record havin' you die after I done operated on you."

"JW, you ain't goin' ta listen ta him are yuh?" Sam pleaded.

JW grinned and then replied, "In medical matters and Godly items, I surely will. Now hold on, we got us another couple hours-of tough ridin' to do before we take a longer break." JW then shot a glance at Liam, "You doin' okay, boy?"

"Sure, Captain, but I'm hopin' for a chance to use this here scatter gun on some more of those Indians who killed my family."

"You will, Liam...but remember, revenge can become a bittersweet pill to take." JW then mounted and rode to the front of the group. "Mount up and let's ride. Those that can't keep up, stay back with the wagon. We'll break in a couple hours at Dutchman's Gulch. If there's no water there, we ride for another hour to Apache Springs. I've never seen it dry...but sometimes down to a trickle. Now let's hit it!" JW turned and led his rangers southwest.

DUTCHMAN'S GULCH

There was water here, but barely enough to fill one water barrel to quench the thirst of the horses and half the ranger's canteens. This meant the men were now sharing until they reached the next watering hole. JW hoped Apache Springs would be running tomorrow morning. But this evening his rangers, plus Sam, Preacher Joe and Liam, were taking a well-needed rest. JW hoped to lead out at the midnight hour, reach Apache Springs within a couple hours to refill canteens and water barrels and then make a long fast and tiring ride for the flats north of Globe. Several of the farms and ranches were located on this massive stretch of flat desert land and from the hill top to the north, he'd be able to see any structures on fire or a large party of Indians fleeing to the north. Or so he had hoped.

JW fought the Apache for years and believed them to be the best guerilla fighters in the world; as well as, some of the greatest warrior horsemen. He'd seen warriors holding on to the belly of the horse, the Indian's head only a foot from the ground, firing off an arrow at their enemy; or holding on to the horse's neck, using it for cover; standing upright on his mount's shoulders, while throwing a six-foot long spear at a soldier, killing him. JW saw them bounce all over a horse, showing off their skill, while entertaining a prospective wife; or stand on its bareback at full-speed without holding onto anything. There were a few times when he watched from a hill top observation post, the Apache skillfully and tactfully attack their target. But when they returned home from a kill raid or horse stealing raid, they would stupidly use the very same route from which they came. This is what JW was counting on. He hoped this large party of Indians, escaping from the Globe force, would flee north along this same trail. His Rangers would be ready for them in an ambush site.

Ranger Coon, who was half Navajo, searched out a rattle snake nest just inside the entrance to the Old Dutchman's abandoned mine. This mine was worked in the early 1800's. When it played out, the party of Dutchman prepared to leave, but were slaughtered by a party of Ute. Another group of homesteaders passed through en route to California, stumbling upon the 14 skeletons, leftovers after the desert predators were finished. A small diary was found and one of the homesteaders could read the lingo. They buried the remains, put up crosses and a sign reading "Dutchman's Gulch". Fear of Indians kept them from staying around long enough to look for the mine, but Coon had no trouble in finding it. He returned to the temporary encampment with eight dead snake carcasses.

"My folks said this would taste like chicken, but it don't...at least not my mom's fried chicken. Tastes good, but has its own distinct flavor." Liam said.

Coon gave the boy a hard look, "What's this word 'distinct' mean?"

JW didn't want any problems this evening and Liam's education could cause some difficulties between the troops. They might look at him as a know-it-all and begin to dislike him. He replied before Liam could, mostly because Liam was finishing off a very hot piece of rattlesnake. "'Distinct' is simply another word to mean or say one-of-a-kind, like its own flavor that doesn't compare to any other critter."

"Oh, I could'a told you that. Never did understand people saying it taste like chicken. It sure don't look like no chicken and in my book, it taste a shy bit better than fried chicken. But you got' a remember to take those poison sacks out before you cook it up. I've seen some idiots get mighty sick when they don't. Even heard of a few who done dropped dead."

"Mr. Coon, how'd you know where to find so many rattlesnakes," Liam asked. There were enough snakes cooking over the low fire, built Apache style so there was little smoke to give their position away to the Indians, to feed all the rangers.

"I've come here, knew of the old mine. Used to be silver, but all gone a long time ago and now area haunted by the Dutchman's Party. Rattlesnakes like shade of the mine during heat. This is why you be careful when climbing rocks, snakes like to be in shade," Coon said. He then added, "At night they seek you out to stay warm beside you. If you wake up, see snakes, don't move. They go soon to find shady spot. I once wake up with three rattlesnakes around me, they leave me for shade."

Liam nodded his head and with his eyes big in awe, he said, "Thank you, I'll remember that." He reached over and pulled another piece of snake off a grill. They had searched for and found thin and narrow sheets of rusted metal that once burned, had blackened nicely and worked well as a grill.

Thirst quenched and now fed, the men took turns getting some well needed sleep. Even Sam was out of the trailer and walking around with a lengthy chunk of wood from the old mine. But Preacher Joe would still not release him to ride his mount. "I'm saving you for when the rangers run into the Apache. They'll need your guns then, but not now. So, walk around, stretch your muscles and go over to the fire and eat some cooked snake or we've still got some hard-tack rations down you."

"You all bedside manner ain't thu best, Preacher...Ah can't wait ta hear one of yuh all's sermons on oh hellfire an' damnation." Sam turned around and very slowly walked over toward the fire.

All the mounts were cleaned and wetted down, plus given several drinks. Now most of them stood there with their eyes closed, but ears flapping about toward any sound being made. These horses may be weary, but they were still alert for danger and though they made great guard dogs, their whinnies and snorts were not as loud as a guard dog's growl and bark.

Captain JW Blake dug into his saddle bags until he found a small wooden box. It was covered in brown leather and bore his name on it. A few years ago, it was given to him from the people of Tucson, when he had left there as a Deputy U.S. Marshal for the Arizona Territory to become a cattle rancher and farmer, both. Inside the box was a beautiful gold plated Swiss pocket watch. The inside cover was engraved with a simple,

"Thanks, JW". He always remembered to wind it up before leaving on a journey so he could keep track of the time, but he almost never wore it for fear he might damage it or lose it. This was the first pocket watch he had ever seen, much less owned and was speechless the evening it was awarded to him at his surprise Going-Away Dinner.

His inner-clock told him he was approaching midnight and a look at the watch told him the time was indeed 11:33 p.m. The hands of the watch were black and delicate, on a light tan backing with a small inner gauge, telling if it's a.m. or p.m. The outside case was slick, with only the company's name in Switzerland, but the front outside case displayed a raised five-point law enforcement badge, with "Deputy U.S. Marshall" written in a narrow banner across the upper part of the badge. JW thought the gift was glorious and one day he would pass it on to one of his children that pursued a law enforcement career.

JW began waking the troops and had Liam, who was already awake, start putting the fire out with shovelfuls of dirt. Preacher Joe was already awake, making sure Sam was comfortable. Preacher had his own watch, but it was one of those tin-plated jobs made in Boston. Weapons and sacks of extra rations were returned to the wagon. They were placed outside to give room for Preacher and Sam to sleep comfortably. Liam took only a catnap underneath the wooden heap among the ration bags. Most the men were hoping they would come across a wayward unbranded steer, some wild pigs, or a few desert antelopes. The antelopes didn't come very big so the Rangers would need to harvest a small herd to feed this bunch, especially with the young Dreeke brother with him. He was rumored to be able to down three of the desert antelopes in a single sitting, but only after they were skinned, beheaded and disemboweled. His brother complained he was a shy picky about his meats.

With the pocket watch back in the left saddle bag, JW estimated it was approximately 12:15 when they left Dutchman's Gulch at a gallop, heading south for Globe.

It was daylight on the horizon when Jim Williams bypassed the Apache. He was mounted on Jelly Bottom. They had had their last drink at lower Tonto Basin. His horse needed a break, but Jim was greatly surprised by how strong this old horse was at the gallop, with the occasional bump up to faster lope speeds across outlying areas of the flats. It was while coming down from a small hill top he saw several structures afire in the distance. Jim estimated the burning buildings to be two to three miles off. He could even make out mounted men riding about the fiery ruins. If he was right this was the *Salflour* farm — some 4,000 acres of farmland, with a family of man, wife, four daughters and three sons. There were also five or six farmhands. But against 60 Indians, they had little chance. As much as he felt he should ride down there, he had his orders to follow. *Globe had to be notified, to save the largest number of people.*

Jim sighted a riverbed running south, now mostly dry, that would allow him to bypass the Salflour Farm, and the Apache. He would be in front of them for the first time, making all speed for the next farm or ranch.

JW COMES UPON THE SMOLDERING SALFLOUR FARM HOUSES

It was around seven hours later when the Rangers smelled the smoldering ambers of the farm structures. When they reached the scene, they found every building, right down to the outhouses, reduced to blackened ambers. JW believed the Apache had struck this place right at dawn. Half of the farmhands were killed in their beds, with their throats slit, while one half-dressed farmhand was killed with a knife out in the outhouse. Two died in the stable with arrows in their chests. JW suspected they were out doing the milking of two cows for breakfast. But by all appearances this had been a quiet attack and few shots were fired. Still, of course, all the scalps had been taken before the raiding party moved toward the main house. One of the little Salflour girls could not be found and the men suspected she'd been kidnapped.

It took them an extra hour, but the rangers could not leave the dead and mutilated children, or their parents found burned in the ruble. No one tried to figure out how they were killed, except it was brutal. Individual graves were dug, while Liam and Preacher Joe worked on building crosses from unburned lumber. The Apache left the animals behind. JW believed they figured on claiming them after their attack on Globe. He suspected the leader did not want to reduce his numbers by sending a couple riders back to their homeland with the horses and cattle.

Ranger Chad Leaders came up to JW, "Mr. Salflour and his hands carried those new Colt Rifles. He ordered them from New York and supposedly they're not even on the market yet. But he had some connections, I guess. These things shoot five to six shots before reloading, an' now the Apache have at least seven of them or maybe more."

"Great!" JW shook his head in disgust. "Let's get this family buried and hit the trail. Another twenty miles and we can set up our ambush."

"Yes, Sir." Leaders replied, as he moved off to find his shovel.

PAUL REVERE RIDES AGAIN—EARLY EVENING OF THE ELEVENTH DAY

Once more back on his beautiful Appaloosa—leading Sam's Jelly Bottom on a long rope—Ranger Jim Williams rode into the northern outskirts of the settlement of Globe. He led four wagons from families he startled, having given them ten-minutes to get loaded. Sixty Indians were not too far behind. "Everyone is needed at Globe to form a Militia ta fight the Apache. Rangers are comin' up from behind for a surprise to keep them from retreatin'. Now hurry up or you'll be left behind to battle it out with the Apache all by yourself."

At one ranch, Mr. Isaac Cootzer, a German immigrant and his family of six, plus seven hands opted to fight it out from their farm house. Jim Williams could only shake his head and move along, but the others came into town. As JW moved closer, he came across the smoldering rubble of the Cootzer farm house. Rangers were convinced flaming arrows were used to set the ranch afire. Only three dead Apache were found and once again all the animals were left. Old Man Cootzer was dragged from his house and impaled to the side of a barn wall with Indian spears. Then the barn was set afire. This was a hard way for a man to die and at some point, his scalp was taken before the fire reached him.

While the Cootzer family was hastily buried in one mass grave, due to the need to move forward and set up the ambush site, JW and Ranger Holloway scouted the country ahead. They found the trail and Holloway estimated the party was still in the high 50's. They further found additional discarded bows and arrows, evidence the Apache were switching over to rifles and pistols they stole from the farms and ranches they raided. This brought a breath of relief for JW. He explained his sneer to Holloway, "These Apache are dead shots with a bow and arrow, but taking on a rifle without days of practice, their accuracy and even usage of the weapon will be on our side. The warriors who stole the modern rifles earlier won't even know how they work…I don't, but I can read instructions and they don't know how to read English, much less French or German. I bought one of my shotguns and everything came in German, a couple years later it came in German and English.

"No, this is in our favor. I'd rather face them with these new rifles than their bow and arrows any day."

CHAPTER FOUR

"That's a whole lot of angry Apache Comin' at us, I sure hope you're right about this."

Five shots from a Navy Colt Revolver were fired off into the sky, as Ranger Williams galloped into the main center of the settlement, with the wagons sliding side to side to as the driver pushed the horses to speeds they rarely traveled before. Dust plumes and grime from the dirt roadways rose up in clouds and quickly invaded some of the stores, where their doors were still standing open. One owner of dress shop raced around her cutting counter to get the door closed before her store filled with road brown colored dust.

Ranch and farm hands escorting families and female house workers let loose with a couple shots themselves to get the settlement awakened from its late afternoon siesta.

Ranger Williams reined in his horse and let go of the lead for Ol' Jelly Bottom, before standing up in his stirrups, calling upon his remaining energy reserves to finish his task, he shouted, "Apache are coming. Fifty to 60 Indians in a war party. This is a killing raid. They've already burned some of your northern neighbors out and killed the families. You know me, I'm Ranger Williams and Captain Blake is out tailing the Apache now. He plans to set up an ambush to the north, for when the Apache retreat from hitting here. So set up barricades in the streets to keep them out of Globe. Put all the horses away, protect women and children and grab your guns. I think the Apache will be here soon, unless it gets dark. Then we can expect them to come in early morning." He looked over the people, who seemed stupefied and unmoving. Jim fired a couple rounds at the feet of two civic leaders he knew about. Now they were awake.

"Can you take over, now? I've still got work to do." Jim asked the two men, who came out of the drinking and gambling establishment with a light reddish glow to their cheeks.

"Sixty Apache...They're hitting Globe very soon or early morning. Yeah, we've got it...Go finish your job and thanks, Jim," Mayor Peterson said. He turned to everyone standing in the street, sitting in wagons and yelled, "All women and children go to the church, bring any personal firearms with you, extra ammo and bring food and water for the night. Oh, make sure you have blankets and I want you there in one hour or you'll be locked out."

He glanced up and down the street, pointed at Mrs. Waterson, who was out in the middle of the road. "Mrs. Waterson, I'm putting you in charge. In one hour I want the church doors closed with armed women at the windows." He then addressed the crowd, "I want all men from 12 years old to 70 back here in 30 minutes loaded for bear. Ammo, knives or whatever you call a weapon and every rifle you have in your house, except the one your wife may need. Now move!"

Ranger Jim slumped forward over his saddle, knowing the biggest part of his task was accomplished. He may have just saved the majority of the Globe population. He dismounted and walked his two horses to the troth in front of the town stable to let both mounts get a good drink. After a timely refill, he pulled them back. He still had some riding to do before dark.

Jim was headed for JW's ranch. Along the way he would stop, warning every home he came upon. Ranchers were to bring what they could to JW's place, making their stand there in the event the Apache headed east in their escape.

THE DOUBLE B RANCH

Sherry Ann Blake just gotten Steven and Jessie to bed, when she heard the wild commotion coming up the road to the ranch house. She grabbed her 12-gauge shotgun off the wall, made sure both barrels were loaded and swung open the front door, half expecting a gypsy troop to be out front. Instead she found her neighbors, also armed to the teeth and Ranger Jim Williams standing to the side of the open door with his hands up in surrender.

"Where's JW?" That was her first and major question.

Jim grinned to relieve her, "Last time I saw him he was somewhat weary, but fine. He sent me here, after I alerted Globe…Can I put my hands down now and will you lower that shotgun?"

Sherry Ann gave the shotgun a serious glance and apologized, "Sorry Jim. I forgot it was even in my hands. Now give me the quick story and why are all these people in my yard?"

Jim began the telling of events, while Sherry Ann listened, along with a dozen or so others, who gathered about to hear all the details. "…so, that's why I'm here. We need to set this place up as a fort to repel the Apache. From what I have seen so far, the Apache number 50 to 60 warriors and they now have a good supply of rifles and pistols they've removed from the people they have killed. But, I'm hoping and I imagine so is the Captain, that they'll have trouble using them. However, they're using fire to destroy the structures, so boarding up in the houses may be a bad choice."

"Jim, what do you suggest?" A ranger's older boy asked.

"Well, Zack, when I lived with the Navajo, I saw them sometimes use ditches to fire from. Ten to 14-foot long ditches or trenches, and we dig them about four to five feet deep, sometimes deeper. We have the men in there and haul all the women to the upper woods in our wagons, which will keep the nearby horses away from the Apache. Let's put three ditches on each side of the road in a staggered line and 100-yards from the structures. When the Apache charge forward, we pop up and shoot. Makes us a harder target to hit and flaming arrows won't have much effect on our dirt holes, or setting fire to the farm."

There was silence and then a voice popped off, "I like it, let's go dig. Where's all the shovels?"

"I'll show you," Steven Blake said from inside. He was up and dressed, which surprised his mother. She then looked inside and found her daughter, Jessie, the eight-year old, in the kitchen putting food together for the trip to the woods. She felt very proud at the-moment.

"Friends, we may have little time or possibly all night. My hands will help with our personal livestock, but you should quickly move the wagons up into the woods and get them concealed from view." She glanced at her son, "Older boys should be armed to protect the women and children, wagons and horses you've brought with you. All the men need to stay here to set up a defense along the trail as Ranger Williams suggested to surprise the Apache if they come this way. Our husbands are counting on us to carry out this chore, so let us get this done."

Everyone began hustling at once; running into one another until they got the wagons turned around and led out of the yard for the journey up the road to the upper hills and deep into the wooded areas. This was one of the few areas in the whole desert that provided a couple acres of cedar trees and a small lake, and where JW kept his cattle fenced in. Once the wagons were concealed and the women and children constructed an overnight camp, with no fires. The older boys, between ten and 15-years of age, began guard duty under a farm hand's leadership. None of them ever faced an Apache before. Most were really excited with anticipation.

AMBUSH

JW rode ahead of the detachment, distancing them by over a mile. He had his rifle out in the event he was jumped by an Indian left behind to keep this site secure. Apparently the Apache leader felt it was more important to keep his number high for the raiding party and the arroyo was found empty of Indians. A good sized stream was running north to south down through the center of the arroyo, where the bottom, if the arroyo was empty, was nearly 15 feet below the level desert ground on both sides. Entry into the arroyo from either side was sandy with a gradual grade, making it very safe for the horseman or even a wagon. The streambed, when full, ran 20 to 25 feet wide, but was usually only inches deep, except for flash floods brought on by heavy rains. The only danger-point at this crossing came in the towering rock formations on the sides of the north entrance; which looked right down onto anyone coming across the arroyo. Troops or Indians caught in the streambed would be shooting almost straight up, while shooters on the ground could block their escape to the north from behind large outcroppings of boulders on each side of the arroyo.

JW hoped to put his two best riflemen up on the top the eastern rock tower. Two more riflemen would close up the escape from behind the boulders. The earlier camouflaged wagon, would be shoved across the escape route to slow Apache from risking a charge across the arroyo. In the meantime, JW and the rest of the rangers would cross the arroyo farther north and come down to get behind the Apache as they began crossing. His plan was catching any remaining Apache in the Arroyo and finishing the raiding party off from all sides.

Sam, Liam and Preacher Joe, armed with 12-gauge shotguns were to be hidden behind a sand hill just 30 or so feet to the west of the wagon. It was their task to protect the wagon and to keep any Apache from coming from the south, that crossed the arroyo, from getting behind the blocking force and killing the rangers. They used sand covered blankets to camouflage themselves; another trick the rangers learned from the Apache. Rangers Brady and Coon held the rock tower; while Holloway and Leaders stood behind the rock and boulder formations. This left Sgt. Dreeke and Ranger Troy ready to cross and climb the second tower. The two towers would have the company's best long distance shooters. This left JW with the Gibson Brothers and Patrick, to cross the arroyo during the night and conceal themselves. They were to hit the Apache in the arroyo from a long pile of stone boulders located on the wagon side of the arroyo.

Sam wasn't happy to be sweltering while lying under a sand covered blanket. He was sweating and his wound had discovered a new level of discomfort of itching. Not only all this; but, he grew weary of listening to Preacher Joe lying in the burning sand, praying every moment or quoting scripture from memory. No, he'd rather face the Apache in open warfare. But JW was off playing Davy Crockett and the ranger sergeant was scaling a rock formation in the dark. "Nope, I'm wrong, ah'd rather face a Union cavalry platoon on some Field of Honor, then fight another filthy Apache." Sam whispered to himself. "These Indians probably gave me some disease, an infection of some kind and that's why I'm still sick."

Sam never heard the rustling and it was a sign his Indian fighting skills needed some work, but he suddenly felt a very sharp blade at his throat and a whispering voice at his left ear, "JW told me all about this great Indian fighter, but if you get Preacher Joe killed because of your talking, I'll drive this knife right through your heart...now shut up!" The blade disappeared and he again heard a very slight rustling as Liam slid into his spot and pulled the sheet back over him.

I had no idea...Sam shut up.

SETTLEMENT OF GLOBE, 5:40 A.M.

Every roadway leading into Globe was barricaded. With the arrival of darkness, the men had presumed they had all night to work. Guards were placed on the outskirts in mounted parties of ten riders. If one shot was fired, the town's fire department alarm bell would be rung to let everyone know the attack was on. A double charge of dynamite was placed under the church's pulpit, with a self-explosive detonation charger. Five different women were assigned the task in the event the Apache began breaking down the re-enforced outside doors. The church had twice been used as a fort to fight off both Apache and Ute, which caused the decorative window shutters to be heavy with rifle ports, able to be secured inside by double bracing. The doors were reinforced by two, six-inch by two-inch, 12-foot long lengths of pine.

Water barrels were filled and placed up and down the streets for putting out fires on roofs from expected fire arrows. Medical stations were set up; however, Preacher Joe was the only citizen close to being an actual medical doctor. Still, many women handled neighbors' childbirth or bandaged a damaged husband from being thrown from a bronc or coming home from the losing end of a Saturday Night free-for-all.

Main Street barricades were manned with 20 men or older boys, while smaller barricades on side streets had from five to 12 older boys and men behind them. Barricades were constructed from gambling tables, dinette sets, traveling trunks and lumber, wagon wheels, chairs and couches, plus anything else that could stop an arrow, spear or possibly rifle, or revolver rounds.

Windows and doorways opening into the desert had to be barricaded, too. Beds, dressers and dining room tables were braced against doorways, as well as the few windows there were open to the desert. But most were covered with wooden shudders; which were nailed closed;

except windows being used as shooting ports for selected marksmen. All the doors opened inward, which prevented Apache from easily opening them. The wooden braces were nailed across them, too. By the time the town was turned into a fort, the hardware store was nearly out of nails and spikes. And, the carpenter shop was out of finished and raw siding, used for the wood bracing all around. In some locations, whole logs — piled up for the lumber mill and carpenter's shop — were hauled about and used to brace between wagons to stop charging mounted Apache. Fire pits and shallow trenches were quickly dug at various points. These would be lit, using coal oil and some of that new ground oil shipped in from Texas, for quick accelerants. This would attempt stopping the initial charges on each end of town and enable shooters to lower the number of Apache warriors right off; possibly getting the Apache leader to retreat.

Thirty-militia riders — all volunteers — had mounts saddled inside nearby building, to give chase when the Apache run off. Hopefully running right smack into Captain Blake's ambush. Then they would have the Apache in a squeeze play, if enough of the militia riders survived the Battle for Globe.

Two older men — with long white beards and pony-tails, attired in old deerskins — were both fighting Indians since the War of 1812, had their 50-Caliber Sharps Rifles with them and plenty of ammo. They were leaning side-by-side in the Church steeple to defend women-folk and children. With the Sharps, they could hit a target and kill it assuredly at 950-yards, but neither man could see clearly a hair over 100-feet. They could drop any Apache making a move on the church and might just take a chance on any mounted men out in the desert screaming up a war cry that sounds more like some coyote gone bonkers from getting its tail caught in a cook's biscuit fire. Those old timers had commented to anyone who would listen on how they had heard a raiding Indian hit the high notes no human should be able to reach. They were heartedly annoyed to have missed the Alamo. They had been up in the Dakota Country dealing with the Sioux and Cheyenne over a herd of buffalo. As to their stories and yarns, there wasn't a bar or drinking hole in the Arizona Territory that had not given witness to their acts of bravery against every known Indian Tribe in America, with exception of the Alaskan Natives. They'd been thinking about heading up that way soon enough.

Minus the rangers, all women-folks and children, Mayor Peterson did a rough count of the citizens and estimated he had 140 to150 men and older boys, defending Globe. He hadn't realized how much the town grew since the last election when 94 people voted, 73 of them put him into office. "So, with women-folk, Globe might have 280 to 300 or more people. We're nearly becoming a town." He spoke to no one in particular, but there were those who followed him around, listening in. Mayor Peterson turned to a downcast man who wore brown broadcloth over a soiled pair of blue-canvas overalls.

"Michael, where is your gun...a rifle or something?"

Michael brought his hands up, looked at both, and then replied in a low voice, "Don't own none, Mr. Mayor."

"What do you do, except follow me around?" Mayer Peterson knew Michael had been around him for a couple years, but he couldn't recall why.

"I clean your office...I'm you're 'go do this', guy, Mr. Mayor...also...I'm your first cousin on your dad's side. I'm a Peterson, too."

"I forgot, Michael...so, can you shoot?" Mayor Peterson was having trouble believing he had forgotten his own first cousin, or that he'd been using him as his runner. He figured it must have been the stress of the impending Apache attack.

"Yes, Sir...I can knock off a rattler at 50-yards with a 30-caliber Sharps."

"Okay, run to my office and you'll find one 30-cal Sharps with a full powder horn and ammo, an Enfield Musket, which I prefer, and a brace of two Navy Colt Revolvers, with gun power and ball. You'll carry one and I'll take the other. Can you remember that?"

"Yes, Sir," Michael replied. He nodded his head several times and took off running.

He looked at the others around him, there were about three hangers-on. He said, "I got so excited in all this I forgot to arm myself. I do so hope you men are carrying at least a pistol, for I see no rifles in your hands." With that the threesome was off to find their own firearms. Peterson said to himself, "I must find out who these men are and why they hang around me. Are they my cousins, too?" With that, he continued walking down Main Street to observe the newly installed fortifications.

AMBUSH SITE TO THE NORTH

In the same way, Mayor Peterson inspected the town's defenses, Captain Blake used his binoculars to observe his rangers and where they were positioned. In his gut, JW believed the Apache would retreat when they had lost half or more of their force, attacking Globe. That meant they had to lose over 30 warriors and that would be a tough chore for the defenders of Globe to take on. Then that would mean approximately 30 Apache warriors would return this way, where he'd spring this trap. Or they might head eastward, possibly swinging by the Double B Ranch. Here, a smaller defensive force would wait; amongst them would be his family. For JW the next 24 hours would be the longest day in his life.

JW talked with Preacher Joe, Rangers Holloway, Brady Williams and Coon, all of which were half-Indian, raised in this desert region. He needed local intelligence into what they each felt the chances were for the Apache breaking-off from the attack, head eastward toward the Double B. They all knew he worried about the fighting force that should be ready at JW's place and the possibility they could face as many as 30 Apache warriors. But, it was agreed, if The Apache headed that way and a rider was sent to notify them, there was no way for the Rangers to dash across the desert and be in time to reinforce Ranger Williams and the Double B Ranch group. The Rangers only chance was, upon notification, to shoot across the desert heading northeast for the Keams Canyon area to attempt getting in front of them.

Watering holes would be a problem and so would the Navajo, the further north they went. While the Navajo preferred fighting in large groups against the Apache, taking on this small group of White Men would prove a good testing of manhood for their young men.

ATTACK!

With only a glimmer of daylight barely touching the eastern horizon, a 30-calber gunshot sang out from a mounted guard, north of Globe. He missed his target in the semi-darkness, yet only a second passed before an arrow flew-through the air impaling him in the back, splitting his ribs and killing him instantly. The kill-shot drove him off his horse. He did his job though and did it well. He went unseen in the darkness to the west, until he sighted a crawling Apache, who attempted making a silent advance on the township. With him, he brought ten other warriors. It was their task to tear down a smaller barricade, allowing an Apache band to ride through the center of town, providing chaos and fear among the White people. But now, shooters from the walls were firing all around their position, forcing Apache to withdraw to join the other waiting Apache.

Men had to be ordered to cease fire. They shot at early morning shadows, going through their ammo too quickly. Mayor Peterson, mounted on a 15-hand brown mare with a white face, named Judy, rode up and down Main Street, shouting orders, waving his Navy Colt through the air. Behind him, on foot, Cousin Michael Peterson tried keeping up; running, carrying the Mayor's two rifles, powder and shot, plus a canteen. Somewhere along the line Michael Peterson picked up a brass U.S. Naval sword that banged against his leg. It made him feel like a proper soldier.

The Apache attempted charging through the northwest end of Main Street; but fires were set when the first band of Apache's were sighted. A couple Indian fighters hadn't ever seen such a site — over a dozen mounted Apaches, waving rifles or bows, screaming battle calls as on they came. When they hit the fire trenches, the flames were five to six feet high and the horses wanted nothing to do with these orange and yellow flames of death. Apache were thrown from their horses, as their mounts made sudden stops and warriors landed in the flames or flew over them. Mercifully, the White Men shot the screaming Indians, ending their suffering or stopping the noise. Three Apache jumped over the flames, clearing the barricades, only to face four times their number. Enraged, they lifted their hand weapons and attacked. For them, the battle ended in a matter of face. They dropped before a wall of lead balls knocking them to the ground. Even their mounts were shot in the excitement.

Along the north side of the town, Apache on foot moved up in a flanking position to take the town under fire by bow and arrow, and rifle. Thirty Apache were devoted to this, while the young chief sent the remainder of his band around the southeast end of the city and on foot up the south side to find a point of weakness. The young sub-chief was surprised to find the city, this township of Globe, transformed into such a fortification. He realized he had been foolish to come this far to hit such a large group of White Men. At this point, he also knew he needed to withdraw before he lost too many more warriors, or the Old Ones and his Chief would never allow for him to lead a single warrior out on another raid. He then sent three of his best remaining runners out to voice his decision to withdraw. They were to move back to the black ridge and then decide their next course of travel. They were told to pull-back with all wounded, all mounts and weapons.

The warriors on the south side of the town, met a heavy hail of fire from selected shooters manning positions in various buildings. One determined warrior — though wounded twice — broke through shudders, forcing himself over a wooden headboard he splintered apart with a Trader's steel hatchet and entered battle with a Swiss assistant storekeeper. The fighters tore up the main room — neither one giving ground — both fighting for possession of the Indian's hatchet. The warrior's two bullet wounds — one to his left upper leg and the other his right side just below his chest — took his strength away. He dropped to one knee, the Swiss store keeper towering over him. Still all four hands were locked together on the weapon's handle. The Swiss was about to rip the hatchet away and kick the Apache in the gut to end it. He knew the man was in bad shape and saw no reason to kill him. He thought in a flash, the possibility of getting the man healed and used for trading for White captives. But right then, as

Indian and Swiss went eye to eye, a look of admiration of the strength of one's enemy shared. Swiss saw a look of great pain and horror come over the warrior's face and then saw the tip of a sword's brass blade come out of the man's chest. Michael Peterson, a look of triumph on his face, stood there with the sword in his right hand, driving it in the man's back.

"No-o-o-o…" the Swiss storekeeper bellowed as the hatchet fell into his hand.

The Apache fell to his side and Michael had to fight to get his sword yanked out of the body. He couldn't understand when the store keeper shoved the hatchet into his chest and said, "You made the kill, you keep it. Tell everyone how you destroyed a wounded man from behind. But if I ever hear a different story come out of your mouth, I'll make you eat that hatchet."

When Mayor Peterson eventually heard the story about his 1st cousin, he found him another job in Tucson, getting him out of Globe on the next stagecoach. Sadly, that stagecoach never made it to Tucson, it was ambushed by Banditos and only the driver's body was found. Five Passengers and a shotgun rider were missing and it became another mystery of the Arizona desert.

THE APACHE

When the Apache parties withdrew to the Black Ridge, which was about half-a-mile north of Globe's northern outskirts. A count of the warriors revealed that 17 were unaccounted for and four wounded were carried back. Of the four wounded, three did not appear they would make the ride back to Chiricahua Apache Territory. As sub-chief and leader of this raid, he ordered the three wounded to be made comfortable; left with knives, water and food. The remaining wounded warrior was helped to ride his mount by two other braves.

He lost 20 of his warriors, leaving him with an effective force of 32-Apache braves to make the long journey home. A small fire was built, where he and his older one could take measure of today's failure and plan their retreat. It upset the two elders to learn a fellow elder — one who chose to lead the fighting force from the south of the town — failed to return. This warrior entered in hand to hand combat with the Swiss store keeper. Tonight, once the decisions were made the two men would mourn for their dear friend.

Sub-Chief needed their say on whether he should take his band eastward and strike at the ranches along the way for additional cattle to help the tribe survive winter, more horses and always their drive to kill Americans and obtain better weapons. Or, should he head directly back with their one wounded man, picking up some of the horses and cattle strays he knew they left at the farms and ranches they had already hit?

For most of the evening they talked about this, unknowing that they had a small party of observers on an upper ridgeline. These three men were from Globe, scouting for the new 22-militia riders, who were now camped out southwest of the Apache. The Militia and the Apache were separated by a 300-foot ridge, a deep arroyo and some foreboding chunks of massive granite. Four militia riders were wounded in the Globe attack and one man, who worked in the newspaper office, was killed. For the first time, he would now have his name in print, but under the obituaries. In the first paper to be printed after the attack, which didn't get printed for six days because of printer damage, the obituary column would carry 38 people and this number only concerned the town, not all the ranches and farms to the north. Until the Apache cleared out, no one knew about the number of deaths to the north, as JW and Sgt. Dreeke kept record of everything they found. It would shock a lot of townspeople.

Taking the advice of the elders, the young sub-chief chose to head straight back the way they had come. They hoped to gather up to 200 head of cattle for the tribe and 50 horses that they left. They also left other prizes they could collect to make the women-folk happy.

Word spread that they would leave at first light, with three scouts in front, two in the rear and single flankers east and west along the ridges. One of the three forward scouts rode ahead — up to four or five miles — searching for danger from other tribes, nature's hazards and white men soldiers. Many older Apache remember a story or two of a band of braves riding up an arroyo when the sky was clear, only to be met by a towering wave from a flash flood. The Apache was taught from a young age to respect the desert and know its many dangers.

Once the observers saw them moving north, they sent one rider the long way around to the south — to locate the Globe Militia and advise them. The Apache were moving toward Captain Blake's ambush site. The Globe Militia was expected to make a stand once the ambush was sprung.

All day they rode across the desert, heading north. The Apache Raiders went through burned out farmlands, rounding up milk cows, beef cattle, and a single burro at the first place; and tripled their number of animals at the second place. A string of large wagon horses stood in the field of one blackened set of ruins. None of the Indians remembered seeing the ten-massive draft horses earlier.

They drove a herd, numbering well into 150 to 200 head, mixed with horses, some sheep and a few goats. They had trouble getting the herd to keep up. One Indian had picked up a goat and laid it across his horse, a prize for his daughter. Once completed, several more were picked up just to keep from losing them. One brave became upset with the critter's noises and sliced its throat before tossing it to the ground. He received a look of disapproval from the brave who had picked up the first one. Soon after, some lambs and goats were tied to the backs of milk cows. Larger sheep could keep up. They tried using the horses, but quickly realized these horses were still wild and liable to kick their heads in for trying to put smaller creatures across their backs with ropes. The Sub-Chief hoped to trade horses to Navajo and Hopi, allowing them to break the wild ones. But the giants, he would present those to his Father. He wondered if these mighty beasts could be trained and used to fight the desert cave bears--the grizzly. He wondered if he could tie knife blades to the sides of their massive hooves, to fight the grizzly's claws.

They stopped for the night, three miles south of the ambush site. JW had a man watching the three fires and the Militia watched from the South. During the day, the Militia moved around to join the trail, staying approximately five miles south of the Apache. When they heard the first gunshots, they would move north at the gallop, joining the charge once within site of the battle. The Globe Militia had one bugler—a boy of 19. Hiram was in his first year of trumpet lessons. He spent several hours a week working out the "Charge" call, much to his parent's test of nerves. But for a Jewish youth, it made him popular among the Militia members and other townspeople. Before long, no one made any Jewish jokes in Globe. If they did, they quickly learned why it was unacceptable. A single warning was offered, after that it was "hit the road, Jack".

When JW received word on the Apache's location, he sent Sgt. Dreeke on a dark journey into the night to gather any possible intelligence. "Look, I know it's a long shot, but we've got to know if there are any Apache coming down from the north to meet up with this group. We can't be caught in our own squeeze play. Just ride north for two hours, give a good looksee for any fires and then ride back to be here before dawn. Okay?"

"Sounds easy enough," James said. "You want me ta fire off a couple warning shots when I return?"

"I sure hope there's a smile on your face, Sergeant. But, no, I would rather not alert our enemy with those pearly whites of yours. Wouldn't want those Apache slipping out in the middle of the night because the moonlight bounced off all that ivory. No warning shots unless you are in trouble and the best I can do is send you one ranger…or Liam. Now good luck."

"See you in the morning, Captain." With that he was gone and using only three minutes to throw a blanket on and saddle his horses, he was on the trail north.

Now Sgt. Dreeke knew there were a lot of reasons why the Apache did not like fighting at night and true, part of it had to do with their superstitions, tales concerning ghosts and ancient hauntings. But there were many other dangers out in the desert night; most of them due to lack of vision, caused by the wall of darkness that dropped upon the land. Between hungry wolves, scavenging coyotes and nearly silent rattle snakes out there until you're upon them, the desert night was a perfect hunting ground for the 800-pound desert grizzly and some of those bears could come even bigger. For the first 50 or so yards they could even run a horse down, but then the grizzly tired out. Banditos also worked their trade at night, knowing the Apache would be camped, leaving them to rob and kill the innocent traveler. Lately there was word of a new sort of evil running the border, from Texas through to western Arizona and it was called, "The Comancheros", a group of Apache working together with Mexican and White banditos. These men raided and killed large ranches, took on small wagon trains and seized the womenfolk to use as slaves and future wives for the men. Their encampments were below the border and the Mexican Federal Police weren't powerful enough in this region to take them on. They issued warnings, then shied away from these Comancheros.

JW didn't really think another Apache force would be coming from the north-country, but he had to prevent being entrapped. He learned a lot while fighting the Spanish and French during the last war. Sgt. Dreeke knew all this too. He still rode slowly under the stars. He had too much respect for the Apache. His 30-caliber single shot rifle lay across his saddle, with the cocking hammer within an inch or two of his right hand. His five-shot Navy Colt was snug in its cowhide holster. It wasn't tied down. If he needed; he wanted it fast. On his other hip, he wore his Bowie Knife, and a Trader's Tomahawk with a formed metal head. One side was blunt like a hammer, the other side, a sharpened tomahawk blade three inches long. He kept one of those in his rolled-up blanket, in the event he was looking forward to some rough and tumble work. Riding out by himself, he might need every weapon he could carry, including his pearly-white teeth.

SUN-UP AND ALL "HECK" BROKE LOOSE

JW had the men up an hour before sun-up. He never figured out how he knew, but he seemed to just know when the sun was about an hour from breaking the horizon. Some rangers wished he hadn't learned that skill, because an extra hour of sleep could help on a day when they expected to battle the Apache. Thirty-minutes after using his right or left boot to awaken the foul-mouthed bunch, they knew there would be no morning chow. JW was always concerned civilization's strong odors of cooking coffee, roasting hard tack and baking oats or biscuits, would quickly reach the Apache. No smoking or chaw this morning either--only until the attack was in process. Then the chaw came out.

JW had rock climbers on their way earlier, then ordered Preacher Joe, Liam and Sam into the trailer. Followed by the others taking their positions to await JW's first shot.

DOUBLE B RANCH—SAME MORNING

Jim Williams was up early — about the same time the rangers were moving about with JW. He wasn't surprised to find Sherry Ann at the stove getting her biggest coffee pot out and a going on her kitchen's wood stove. She was expecting to coffee down and feed breakfast to 16 men and nine-women, and 23 kids of all ages. Two older women were also up, setting up Sherry Ann's cooking bowls for several extra-large orders of flap-jacks.

"Here's your coffee, Jim," Sherry Ann said. "Now can you send a couple of the boys out to gather me some eggs for the flap-jacks?"

"Sure, but you'd better give me a broom. I start getting them up this early they might come up swinging. I'll use the broom to hold them down with."

"It's over there in the corner, but you shouldn't have any problem. These boys are rancher and farmer kids. Getting up with the sun isn't new and having all you men here is real exciting for them."

"I'm just glad we got word the Apache are heading north. Our party here is too small to take on a group of revenge seeking blood crazed Injuns." Jim said. Then he remembered JW. "Oh, I'm sorry, Sherry Ann, but JW and his Rangers will take care of what's left. They've got the militia coming to back them up. If you want I can take half the men with me and leave the other eight men to defend the Double B. It would take me a couple days, but I'll probably be able to meet up with them."

"No," Sherry Ann said. "This is your posting and JW would scream to high-heaven, turn red-faced and blusterous, shouting out his orders to fire you four-times on the spot and threaten to throw you in the hoosegow for disobeying his orders. Then the next day he'd hire you back and thank you for hustling so fast to insure I and the kids were okay and then thinking about him and the rangers being up against superior numbers. You know, that's how he is."

"Sure do," Jim said. "That's why I like working for the man. I'd follow him right into the flames of Hell, as-long-as he had a plan to get right out again."

APACHE ENCAMPMENT

For most of the warrior clan they found it nearly impossible to sleep, having lost so many brothers in the strike at Globe. They asked one another repeatedly how the White Man's town had heard of their coming. They had killed everyone as they moved south, so no one could've ran or rode ahead giving advanced warning, yet that is what happened. There was only a little food and water, which they shared with their horses. Still, several mounts were worn-out, suffering from minor leg fractures and could not go on. Five Apache horses that helped the warriors escape the disaster at Globe, were put down. Their throats were cut and they bled-out. The choicer cuts of horse meat were taken, wrapped up in horse blankets from the dead mounts, and tied to other live horses. The sub-chief then selected five warriors to ride double with horseless Apache. This gave them some meat to consume last night and early this morning.

There was still hope that once they gathered the cattle, cows and other animals running loose to the north — from ranches and farms they had previously attacked — the horseless Warriors would claim new mounts and they would have plenty of meat for the ride back home. Even though their Murder Raid to Globe met with disaster, they still returned with a treasure trove of animals, weapons and needed articles for the tribe. At least the sub-Chief hoped the senior tribal council would see that and gives him other chances to make war on the Whites.

They broke camp with very little talk among them. The morning air was warm. The wind came from the west, soothing the skin, but causing the morning dew to drip away. For the Apache, returning from days of warfare, the desert's morning enchantment was all but lost to them. Being Apache, they continued watching in all directions for any sign of danger, knowing that until they returned to their mountain fortress they risked being attacked from all directions.

The Elder was surprised the people of Globe had not sent a force after them, if only to check on the homes they burned and looted. But there was no sign. Still, he was suspicious, as the desert felt strange to him. During this night's rest, he mentioned it with the young man he was observing. A Holy Man prophesied how this young man would become a well-known chief and fight many battles against the White Man. This is how he rose quickly through the ranks. But he was also brave and intelligent, and showed a care for the women and children of the tribe. No, the Elder found no error in his attack on Globe. Somehow the town was warned and this would be a question that would haunt him until his death — which came all too soon in this life. So, he was never able to express his opinion to the Tribal Seniors, which would have helped the sub-chief as his raid was carefully examined from start to finish.

THE ARROYO

Rangers were now all in position, every single one of them silent, as they watched the Apache warriors move into the Arroyo, moving toward the ancient crossing. But this time, the large towering rocks and surrounding ridgelines of stone boulders were occupied by rangers. The sandy embankment across the watery arroyo became a killing ground, where JW's Rangers were poised to attack. Liam, Sam and Preacher Joe gently cocked the hammers on their double-barreled shotguns. Extra rifles, powder and ammo were set beside them, for quick grabbing, after the order was given.

In a low whisper, Liam kept saying to himself over and over, "No one shoots until JW fires."

As if by providence, Sgt. Dreeke rode up at that time, dismounted, sliding up beside JW. He tied his mount to the wagon, hidden behind the large rock, where three other rangers waited with extremely itchy fingers.

JW waited. He knew how hard it was for the rangers, but he wanted the Apache close. He preferred quick kills instead of wounds, because a wounded Apache was as bad as a she-bear who just lost her cubs. He spent long hours training these men on how to make kill shots and this is what he expected, now. He glanced to his right, saw Preacher Joe praying with his double-barrel shotgun in hand. He was to hold off firing, protecting the others, while they reloaded. Killing any Apache who charged the sandy hillside, hoping to climb the tower and kill the rangers—close-up to show valor to his friends. Usually they died for this when dealing with the rangers or military.

JW laid there, recalling a poem or story from the Revolution, something about holding fire until you see the whites of their eyes. But then he remembered, and spoke out loud, "Apache's eyes aren't really white..." He aimed at the nearest mounted figure, fired, striking him in the chest, driving him backwards off his horse. He rolled several times before resting in an awkward position that clearly said this Apache was dead.

This started the rest of the Rangers opening fire in mass, with rifles blasting at startled Apache warriors. It was nearly 20 seconds before the Indians returned fire; which was inaccurate, missing every ranger's emplacement by two to three feet. Once they cut loose with their first volley, the Apache were off their horses. By then, the 32 surviving Apache numbered 25. Two of the Apache warriors were wounded, attempting to drag themselves out of range and further into the arroyo. This was one of the Elders. A 30-caliber bullet knocked him off his horse, striking him low in the left shoulder. His collar bone, broken, he suspected his upper ribs on the left side were damaged because breathing was difficult. He still had his rifle, took the time to load it—a Sharps 50 Caliber Buffalo Rifle he won long ago against a group of White Men. They were traders, leaving the Apache Camp as friends. Three years later they were killed by the Comanche in Texas.

A fierce fire fight continued between rangers and Apache. The rocks were a strong defense. Not one ranger was wounded or killed, yet. However, the Apache were using only the ridge walls of the arroyo. The Sub-Chief considered charging after the next ranger volley, but his warriors told him he must survive to fulfill prophecy. They were willing to stand their ground so he could make a run for to the west. After an exchange of heated words, he agreed to abandon them, for that's how he saw it. He would take two volunteers with him. They would leave when the remaining 16 Apache charged on foot. They were too easy a target on horseback.

Seconds before the Apaches were to rise-up and the Sub-Chief was to flee westward, the Apache Elder decided to return to his fellow warriors. He began using his heavy rifle to boost himself up. As he did, he felt the painful strike of a rifle barrel hitting his broken shoulder, driving him to the ground. He turned looking up, seeing a rifle aimed between his eyes. This was the last thing he saw as Mayor Peterson pulled the trigger of his rifle, waving on the Globe Militia, who approached the Apache from the immediate south on foot.

JW spotted the Militia, smiled and loudly ordered, "Aim Low, the Globe Militia is here and they're right on the other side of the Apache. Now let's finish this off!"

Preacher Joe rose-up on one knee and shot one barrel-load of shot, then the second load, before dropping down to reload. Liam fired four times, thinking he may have hit an Indian, but wasn't sure. He was reloading, again.

The Apache were caught in a crossfire. With all the good people these Apache killed on this murder raid, no one wanted them to surrender. Yet it wasn't even a fight or an event to be considered a battle. The Apache were being smacked down from both sides and one Warrior was shot in the chest and the back before he finally dropped down to die.

It was during this time the three riders crawled on their stomachs up the arroyo to where the frightened horses gathered. They quickly mounted three of the warrior's horses, with the Sub-Chief locating his own mount. He made a mad dash to the west. They ran up the arroyo, then climbed through the rocks to avoid being hit in the back. They hoped the rising sun in the East would help their escape. When they cleared the arroyo, entering the thick bushes, the boarder of a wide stream—one Apache was dead and another badly wounded. The wounded warrior remained on his horse, staying with his leader, as they changed directions, heading north.

"You'se want me a goin' af'ta dose two, Captain?" Sgt. Dreeke asked JW. The field of valor was now silent, the guns were quiet and the bodies littered the sands of the arroyo. Three Militia men went over, gathering the Indian mounts.

JW looked about, waved, providing a friendly smile to Mayor Peterson. "No, let them go home to tell their stories about what happened down here. Maybe we will get fewer attacks in the future. Only two of them survived. Two out of…some 60 warriors. But we were lucky here, today. They could've bypassed us or gone further east…Well, this one is over. Check on the men, Sergeant and give me a report."

"Yes, Captain." Sgt. Dreeke was off. He looked over the field of blood. It didn't surprise him any, seeing the Militia guys going through the Indians, collecting trophies. Some even scalped them, upsetting Dreeke's stomach, while others simply removed weapons, bead work and misc. items. Sgt. Dreeke wasn't a trophy taker. He had certain Indian items presented to him over the years. Still, he knew better than challenging another desert fighter over what he considered proper, unless it involved taking women or children. He would not stand for that.

The whole Arizona Ranger Unit heard about the slavery issue down in the far south. However, not a one agreed with it. There were those who left Arizona to fight with the Union Army. But JW and Sgt. Dreeke—both prior Union veterans—were not happy with the current Union policies regarding the Federal Government telling the state government what to do and how to do it in their own neighborhoods, cities, counties and states. It reminded a lot of people about why Americans went to War against the British in 1776. Some rangers from Arizona, New Mexico and Texas had joined the Army of Texas under General Hood. But JW and Sgt. Dreeke once worn the Union uniform and swore allegiance to the Stars and Stripes. Both had seen America and knew the South would not win in the long run. They knew the South did not have the manufacturing capability of the North, or the numbers of troops.

GOING HOME

The ride back to Globe was a long one. They still had to be careful. Other Apache tribes roamed the area, as well as the neighboring tribes. It was decided the Militia would ride with the rangers, as a larger force would most likely be avoided. They would have Indians watching them, but no attacks. Another agreement was made. They ride from 7 a.m. until 7 p.m., with a luncheon break and rest breaks as called for by the two leaders—JW and Mayor Peterson. JW had no problem with this as he was already pretty worn out and didn't want to show up at home looking like death worn-over.

At the pace they moved, to save their horses, the ride to Globe took three days and two nights on the trail. They entered town just after dark. However, within moments a 100 people knew the Militia and rangers had returned, and they had destroyed the Apache. JW was watering his horse at the stable troth, along with Dreeke, when a rush of thankful people suddenly appeared from all directions, clapping hands and slapping them on the back. He was kissed on the cheek half-a-dozen times by town women and one bar girl, who also gave him a wink and a nod. But he was gratefully saved when he heard the loud voice of Jim Williams shouting out for him.

"Captain Blake! Captain Blake! Are you anywhere in all this mess?" Jim yelled and gently nudged his horse into the mob. The street display of affection was for every one of the rangers and Militia volunteers. Mayor Peterson was really soaking it up. He tried reaching a nearby porch so he could step-up and deliver a different rousing speech.

"Hey, Jim, I'm down here…What's going on?" JW said in a loud voice. He continued gently dividing the crowd, towing his horse behind him. Sgt. Dreeke was right behind him, enjoying every bit of this celebration. He'd never been kissed so many times and he hadn't even shaved or washed up.

"I'm glad to see you two survived and all the rest. You can tell me all about it later. Sherry Ann sent me in here on the double and said if you're not shot, stabbed or horse kicked, you'd better get home before she come in here and causes you an embarrassing scene for all to see."

"Yup, that sounds like Sherry Ann. So, I'd better ride for home." JW turned to Dreeke, "Can you handle all this, Sergeant?"

"Ah can't believe you'se still is here a talkin' ta me. You'se better get gone 'fore she do some Lady Godiva act ta get you back home."

JW thought about it for a second, "Nope, not right for the kids. I'm going." With that JW speedily galloped toward home.

About that time, the Mayor found his perch and began singing a song of the Militia's courage against the fearsome Apache. He mentioned the Rangers here and there, which told Sgt. Dreeke it was time to stable his horse and head for the café for a good meal, followed by a few hours in the bar. When he and Jim Williams opened the doors to the Globe Café, he found most of the Rangers and some of the Militia Volunteers chowing down. The proprietor met them, walked them to a table near the rest and surprised them by saying, "Tonight, your dinner is free. My way of saying thank you." His strong German accent made each word stand out strong.

"Well, thanks…then I'll let you decide what I'm going to eat."
Dreeke said in German, which made the man smile and then Jim William
said in English, "Whatever he said."

Sgt. Dreeke was at the bar enjoying his second beer, a pretty, black-
haired, Polish barmaid on his arm, when the telegraph runner showed up
at his side. "This just came in, from the Territorial Government. I thought I
could give it you, instead of riding out to the Blake Ranch."

"Good thinking, I don't want my Captain disturbed tonight. I'll take
this out to him tomorrow afternoon." Sgt. Dreeke replied.

"It's your message now, you can deliver it when you want. But I
have to verify soon that I provided it to you."

"Not a problem. I simply want my Captain to have some family
time before the government sends us back out chasing bad guys or
Indians, again." Sgt. Dreeke said. He then stepped away from the bar and
his Polish lady friend and walked over to the wall to read the message.

"Captain John W Blake and Sgt. James A.L. Dreeke are to report to
territorial official as soon as this message is delivered. Consider this a
priority, come by stagecoach and bill to territory authorities in Tucson. Do
not delay."

Sgt. Dreeke did not like the way this sounded and it failed to say
who to report to in our prestigious government body. But he still wasn't
going to bother JW until after 4 p.m. Besides, he knew the next stage
wasn't due for two days and it was scheduled for 1 p.m. He put the
message in his pocket, returning to his Polish beauty, whose English skills
were seriously lacking, not that it mattered one bit. She was over six-foot
tall, with blue-eyes, long black hair, and very long legs covered in black
silk stockings. He planned to have a nice evening, but he couldn't recall
where Poland was.

IN THE CHIRICAHUA APACHE FORTRESS

By the time the weary, but uninjured Sub-Chief and his dying
warrior friend entered their fortress, the two men rode double. The
wounded man was tied to the Sub-Chief. Several warriors came forward,
gently removing the man from the horse, carrying him to the Medicine
Man's tent. There was little they could do for this man. He died during the
night. His family was very thankful that his Sub-Chief brought him home.
He nodded his thanks. However, his mind was on the upcoming Council
Meeting, where he would appear before the Senior Council Members.
There was a new member on the council. He became a great chief, well
respected by his tribe. His name was "Cochise". The Sub-Chief only talked
with him a few times. He feared what he had lost over what he had gained

in the Murder Raid. He believed he might lose his standing — returned to the warriors, showing his prophecy as misguided.

The meeting continued into the early morning hours. He was questioned, over-and-over again as to how the town learned of the coming attack. Each time, he had no answer. He didn't blame it on any other Apache. It was this that won Cochise's favor.

When the Sub-Chief left the council meeting, he was not proud. He had lost over 60 warriors. Much grieving must be done before he could lead another attack. But he would make the people of Arizona pay for what they did to his people. He would accomplish what was needed to insure his prophecy played out and every white man in Arizona would shake at the mention of his name. For his name was "Geronimo".

CHAPTER FIVE

"The Gray's a bit tight in the shoulders, but I love these swords!"

ARIZONA TERRITORIAL STAGECOACH, FORTY-SIX-MILES NORTH OF TUCSON, "IT'S A HOLD-UP"

For Albert and Stephen Boyd, recently of Bethlehem, Northern Idaho, a nearly abandoned mining town of 68 people, today would be a very bad day to venture into the criminal enterprise of stage robbery — especially a stagecoach carrying two Arizona Rangers. Captain JW Blake and Sgt. Dreeke — heading south to report to territorial authorities and as seasoned Indian fighters — expected the possibility of Indian attack or Banditos between Globe and Tucson. They were well armed, carrying rifles and revolves, knives and tomahawks, which alarmed one of the passengers — a well-dressed woman traveling west from Vermont to California, her fiancé as her escort. The young man was armed with a small revolver hidden inside his traveling coat. Both rangers wore their work clothes, leaving their Sunday go to meeting attire rolled up in bags stored in the back of the stagecoach. They'd change before going over to the Territorial Offices. It would be three days before the next stage traveled north for Globe. They both knew the food and lodging was decent enough in Tucson.

The Boyd Brothers — Albert, 26 and Stephen, 22 — were bungling criminals. They failed in nearly every caper they attempted; including a brief stint of going straight, mining for Gold up in Northern Idaho. Upon arriving in Bethlehem, the town had nearly 5,000 people, with nine bars on the main — but "nameless" drag — teaming with shady ladies, poker tables and armed guards to protect the gold being handed in for chips. Multi-colored chips bought booze, a higher value colored chip bought a brief time with a dark lady of the night and colored chips of all colors were available to gamble with. There was a store, where gold was weighed and goods were purchased. Within six-months, the river beside the town played out. People started leaving. The first to go were the bar owners. With them went the ladies and gamblers. Next went the stores, followed by lines of miners in wagons, dragging carts, riding horseback and hiking out to find the next "Bonanza".

Out of their short stay of panning gold from "Three Rivers Crossing" — actually, one river with two streams running into it — one of the first miners arriving was born at a place called Three Rivers in California. He named the place, passing a bottle of booze around to seal

114

the deal. The Boyd Brothers made less than $83.00 from all their hard work, using every dime to live on along with the occasional bottle to keep their spirits up.

Originally from Ohio, the brothers had no love for President Lincoln and didn't hanker joining the Ohio Militia. They left the state to avoid the war, trying a stint as cattle rustlers, but lost their small herd of 19-steers to a group of Sioux Indians. They held up a Utah farmer, and his family fled with three chickens, a bag of apples and a $1.70 in cash and coin. Albert wanted to take the farmer's 16-year old daughter. Stephen talked him out of it. He reminded him these people were those Mormons he'd heard about and they'd get up an army to give chase, but not for three chickens, some apples and so little in cash and coin. In fact, the brothers were invited to stay for a meal and lodging after committing the robbery. As they moved along, they were able-to avoid the Indians, except for a pair of them here and there; which, they shot and killed out of revenge for losing their herd of cattle. It didn't matter that these Indians were of a different tribe. An Indian was just an Indian to them. They should be killed. The held up a stagecoach station, but all they discovered was a week's worth of food supplies, a nice Bowie knife with a grizzly bear hide sheath and a necklace of grizzly claws around the neck of the dead stage handler. The second man survived, because he took the stage to the next town for supplies. He planned riding back with eight freshly shoed horses from the blacksmith.

Now the brothers were hungry, and broke. This oncoming stage was the perfect answer. All they had to do was to take out the guy riding shotgun. They planned robbing every one — taking all their valuables, killing them, and then searching the cargo for any rewards their cases offered. The Brothers hoped the attack would be blamed on the Apache. They'd have to scalp the passengers; which was something neither man had done before. They didn't look forward to the activity.

Luckily, they saw the dust of the stagecoach coming south from nearly five-miles away. Once they topped a pile of large rocks beside the trail, they watched the rig itself to see how well the driver handled his team across the sandy desert surface. The man easily held the shotgun in his hands, ready in the event some Apache sprung out of a tarantula hole they'd become famous for. He carried eight extra rounds of 12-gauge load, sitting in a small wooden box beside his right leg for an easy grab.

Sgt. Dreeke tried getting a conversation going with the nice couple from Vermont, but they made it clear they weren't interested in conversing with some Desert scum.

Captain JW Blake couldn't care less. He wanted to catch some more sleep. He felt uppity people like this didn't belong in Arizona. He was glad to hear they were on their way to California. He couldn't understand why parents would allow such a young lady to be traveling with her fiancé--not her husband. From what he read about customs in Vermont, propriety was strong in their culture. This arrangement these two had seemed to violate this propriety. It wasn't any of his business. However, he felt sorry for his Sgt. Dreeke, who always enjoyed conversation with pretty girls—especially ones who didn't know him.

At that moment, a single rifle shot rang out from a short distance. The two Rangers had their Navy Colt Revolvers out and ready. JW watched as the man riding shotgun fell from his seat, onto the desert floor. The stage kept going. A second rifle shot was heard. The lead horse pulling the stage fell hard and slid, dragged for over 14 feet, until all the horses stopped. The horse behind the lead dropped also, tripping over the leader, breaking both front legs. The Stage wouldn't go anywhere for the moment. The driver stood up, his hands up. He watched two men—without masks—boldly walk to the driver's side of the stage. Albert yelled, "Throw down the box…or the bank bag, whatever you got."

The driver knew he would die—the robbers took no pains to disguise themselves—nodded his head. He would comply. Reaching down, he grabbed a second eight-gauge shotgun. He knew it was loaded, because he loaded it himself with rounds he filled himself. He knew what an eight-gauge blast would do to a man. His mind raced. Who would he shoot? They were both in the same proximity, but too far apart to get both. He glanced to the left. The Brothers both had their rifles up to their shoulders—the lethal ends pointed right at him. He only had seconds before he would die; however, he would die anyway. He'd rather go out this way, than as a helpless victim.

He took a deep breath, quickly standing up, his left hand holding a bank bag from Globe. His other hand held the trigger guard of the shotgun, which was now behind his leg. He hoped they'd be excited, seeing the bank bag. They were. It provided the second or two he needed to jerk up his double-barrel eight-gauge shotgun with 18-inch barrels and fire off the first barrel at the nearest robber.

Albert watched in horror as the blast nearly tore his younger brother in half, being only ten to 14 feet away from the shooter. Stephen's rifle flew out of his hands. He was launched into the air, thrown backwards a good 12 feet, rolling backwards another six to seven feet before coming to stop—a pile of blood and mangled body parts. One arm was missing from the right shoulder, as was most of his entire right side down to his pelvis. Ribs were open to the air. Several were broken or missing. Pellets mangled his face. No identification would be possible. This amount of harm to the human body shocked the driver who previously only shot targets with the heavy shotgun.

With a loud scream, Albert turned away from what was left of his brother. He pointed his rifle at the driver, who didn't even lift his shotgun to make the second shot. Before he could pull the trigger, avenging his younger brother's death, the blast of a black powder Navy Colt is heard. The bullet carries through the air, striking dead center over Albert's heart. He dropped his rifle — a round going off — before being driven backwards several feet, falling on his back, clutching his chest with bloody hands. Within seconds, he is dead. Thus, ends the murderous actions of the Boyd Brothers — wanted in four states for Robbery, Theft, Cattle and Horse Rustling, and Causing Great Harm to Womenfolk. A Reward of $10,000 was offered, except to non-police officers, rangers or military. This meant JW wouldn't be seeing any part of that reward money.

A frightening scream came from the other side of the stagecoach. Both Dreeke and JW responded, hustling over to find the fancy dressed gentleman on the ground, a bullet hole in his face, a small five-shot revolver lying inches from his right hand. The woman, attired in her Sunday best — or so Sgt. Dreeke thought — stood two feet from his head. A look of horror on her face, she held a pale light green handkerchief to her mouth. She whimpered and shook.

JW knelt checking the gentleman. JW knew he was dead by the placement of the wound. The Bullet entered his face at the upper right side of the nose, traveling through his brain, leaving an even larger hole in the back of his head. The spot in the sand was growing from the blood coming from the back of his head.

"Ma'am, I am sorry, but your man here is dead. He must have been hit with that stray bullet the other robber fired off when he fell. But again, I am very sorry. My Sergeant here will help me bury the four dead men and we will mark them well in the event you wish to come back and relocate his body to another location. I'll even provide you with a map which should enable you to find his body."

She couldn't speak. She watched the two men in western ware walk away to check on the driver. Her whole trip — her reason for her leaving Vermont and going to California — was now in dire jeopardy. She felt so totally lost. She glanced about the desert, knelt-down to retrieve the man's five-shot revolver. Though she never shot one before, she knew the basic principle of point and shoot at the enemy. However, she didn't know who the enemy was. For the last five weeks, the enemy was this dreadful, disgusting Californian, who came to Vermont to purchase her contract of money owed to a criminal enterprise. Monthly payments were slow and her new bosses paid off the debt completely.

She took out a large loan to save the family's farm. The banks wouldn't help her and she was led to another source. Now, she owed a

Tong crime lord—an elderly Chinese Black Dragon of the Tong in China Town of San Francisco, California. She would be a very special gift. She was checked by several older Vermont women, during a startling surprise inspection of her womanhood. She was found to still be a virgin. At 23-years old, this made her a highly-rated gift to bless the Black Dragon. She would bring great favor upon the Tong family who presented this gift. She wouldn't be touched sexually by the man responsible for her travel—a White private investigator, who's office was just a few blocks outside China Town. He was known to assist the Tong numerous times in the past, in cases where the Chinese were not welcome among the Whites.

JW and James Dreeke helped the shell-shocked driver down from the driver's seat. Unable to speak, he allowed JW to remove the shotgun from his hands. JW removed the second loaded shell to ensure no one else was shot by accident. James carried a canteen over to the driver. He got several sips into the driver's mouth and down his throat. The driver mumbled about how the men were shot to ribbons and how he had never seen such carnage before.

James and JW had seen a lot of the same kind of damage during the Mexican-American War—from cannon blasts and other large bore weapons used against infantry and cavalry. They had also seen worse damage in wars against the Apache and Ute tribes—who could be barbaric in torturous ways, leading up to death, even scalping their enemies while still alive.

A large grave was dug behind the rocks, west of the trail. All four bodies were placed inside with clothes from the private detective's suit-bags were used to cover the face and upper shoulders of each man. JW said a few words over the dead, holding the two killers separate from the other two. He and James began filling in the grave. The driver was much better, and made a large cross to mark the grave—a single cross. Once the dirt and sand work was done, the driver worked on his surviving horses, cutting the reins away until he had four-horses pulling the stagecoach into Tucson. JW and James were busy carrying rocks from the same formations that hid the Boyd Brothers. They used them to cover the grave protecting the grave from desert predators. Once satisfied, they walked to the stage, checking on the lady.

The lady, startled by JW's sudden appearance at the stage door, pulled the pistol she had recently acquired, pointing it at his face. Her hand shook. She had failed to cock the hammer back, which saved JW because she pulled the trigger several times.

"Lady, give me that!" JW yanked the revolver none-too-gently, from her right hand. He tossed it to James, "You deal with her. She tried to blow my head off and I'm none too friendly with people who try that." JW turned his back on the girl and walked over to where the driver was working with the shorter team. Six horses had been used. They were down to four. They located the Boyd Brother's mounts. However, the mounts could only be tied to the stagecoach to run in behind the stage. They would be sold by the Stage Company to regain some of the money from losing the two horses. They couldn't use them to pull the stage as they had not been broken and trained to pull as a team, nor were they strong enough for such a duty. The Brother's weapons would be auctioned off and monies made would go to the stage line.

When JW walked up the driver turned to him, "I wanted to thank you for saving my life. I'm not sure what happened to me…but, thanks."

"Sgt. Dreeke and I saw a lot of the same reactions during the last war…Mexican-American War. But, you're welcome. Still, for your personal use, you might want to get a 12-guage shotgun and leave that eight-gauge at home. I'm surprised it didn't blow you right off the stage."

The driver nodded, a smile on his face, "I agree. But I wanted to talk with you and your partner about something else. We need to lighten the stage…as much as possible. Losing two horses will make it tough on some of the hills we have-to climb and go back down some steep slopes into that new town they're building in the flatlands. I've heard it called Phoenix and its already got close to 2,000 people…Whites, Mex, Navajo and some of those runaway slaves from the south." He stopped with a set of leather reins in his gloved hands and spit some tobacco juice onto the desert floor. "Heck, people around here still can't decide which way the want to go. I've seen the confederate flag flying over Tucson and sometimes the Union flag, plus both sides patrolling the roadways and deep into the desert." He looked at JW with a half grin on his dirty and bearded face. "I'd been stopped and mah money box took by both sides, but I suspect those troops kept the gold and coin for themselves."

"If yuh was carryin' Ranger pay, there was little enough to buy a troop a single round at the bar. We gone as much as seven-months without pay and my boys get a might surely. No girls, no booze an' no poker. Got so bad they was playing stud poker with IOU's." JW then went to work helping the driver get the leather reins pulled away from beneath the dead horses and cut off. The heavy leather reins were then pulled to the side of the road and buried in a shallow grave. The next stagecoach heading south from Globe would locate and transport it back to Tucson in the coach's boot. Nothing was wasted in the desert country. Good strong leather reins, lashings and bridles were expensive. The driver finished by stacking a pile of rocks on top, making it easier to find. The driver's main concern was weight—removing every pound possible was the next chore.

James made sure the outlaw's horses had a good drink from inside his hat, pulling the scarf from around his neck. He knew this would be the last trip for this long silky blue scarf with gold five point stars embroidered on it — a one-time gift from a lady — had quite a stench about it from his sweat and his own horse's drinks and rub-downs from several months' wear. Worse, he couldn't recall the lady's name who bought it for him during one of his visits to Tucson. Thinking about her, taking a sip of water from his canteen, he finally focused on her face, "Pretty lady, but kind of old for workin' a bar…must've been one of my talkin' nights and I balled on her shoulder."

"What did yuh say?" JW asked from on top of the stage. JW was removing the baggage belonging to the lady's escort along with baggage belonging to the shotgun-man. There was a saddle tied down, belonging to the man riding for the stage. JW thought it was worth more than one of the Mexican saddles on one of the outlaw's horse. He switched them out. Meanwhile, James searched the fancy dandy's two suitcases for any valuables that could be turned over to the lady.

"Hey, JW, lookee here," James said in a raised voice to get his friend's attention and was flapping around a leather folder in one hand along with an elegant written piece of paper in the other. "This dude was a Private Investigator out of San Francisco. Certified by the State and he's got travel documents for he and this Miss…Miss Dearmond…Ruby Dearmond. There's also over a thousand dollars here in cash and several letters of credit if needed."

"Well, just give it all to the lady. The outlaws are dead and her part of this doesn't concern the Arizona Rangers," JW replied.

"What about the weapons, Cap? There's two other revolvers in here, plus ammo and cleanin' kits."

"Same thing…no, find the lightest case or bag we've got and put everything in there. Then we can give it all to her once we reach Tucson."

"You got it, Cap," James replied.

Once all chores were complete, the valuables were buried together with the stagecoach property, leaving it all look like graves. The driver started the horses moving south. One of Ruby's trunks — a beast of a thing — was hidden behind the rocks, covered in heavy brush. It took both JW and James to carry it. JW couldn't understand how one woman would need so many dresses, shoes and feathery hats. It was James whose mind was busy on why this woman was under armed escort of a state certified Private Investigator into California. There was something in this business that was making the hair on his arm stand straight up. That usually meant danger ahead.

Ruby spent most of her time sitting in the coach, in a quandary over what she should do. *Should I keep heading west for San Francisco? I could stay in Los Angeles...take a boat somewhere. I still have the Tong's money and their Letters of Credit...I might be able to use them for boat fare and save my money. I could even travel to Europe. But will the Tongs come after me? I have heard of how deadly they are and they'll never accept betrayal. Maybe I can send the money back and then they'll leave me be. But all I know is farm work...milk cows. And I've seen no churches out here...not one. Oh Lord, what will you have me do?"* Tears were running down her cheeks by now. She tried hiding them when James climbed into the stage, taking a seat on the hard, semi-stuffed wooden bench, across from her.

"I'm right sorry you had to witness all this, Miss Dearmond. Our stagecoach robberies are on the decline, since the Rangers formed up. Used to be one in every ten stages got held up on the run between Globe and Tucson, or comin' back north. Rangers caught a mess of the outlaws or we left 'em buried out beside the road."

She straightened herself up, blew her nose, clearing her voice from a squeaky note to a tone of gentleness. "From what you say then, you and the man up with the driver are both Rangers. Is that so?"

James grinned and took his soiled flat-brimmed hat off as he introduced himself, "Yes, Miss Dearmond, Captain JW Blake is up on top. He's probably the best Indian fighter in the State of Arizona. And I am Sergeant James Arthur Lee Dreeke of the Arizona Rangers. Sorry, if-in we seemed a might late in catchin' the stagecoach, as I know they done held it for us, but we'd been off fightin' a sizeable bunch of Apache...men needed some down time and that goes for Cap an' me, too."

Ruby liked the smile on James' face and the tone of his voice. She knew he was southern born and wondered why he wasn't wearing the Confederate gray right now. So, being a deliberate girl, she asked him. "I figure you to be a man of the south, Mr. Dreeke...which I think is of German ancestry, I am naturally curious why you're not fighting for the South right now instead of Arizona."

James glared at her for a moment. Had she been a man and a stranger as she was now, he might have punched him for just asking such a personal question. But she was a woman, a breed he knew to be nosy and quite an attractive woman at that. "Miss Dearmond, I'll answer your question, but on one condition...you have dinner with me in Tucson...and it's your treat."

"My treat, why I never..." Ruby began to get upset, but he cut her off.

"If you want the answer, that's my offer…and besides, I put the $2,000 or more that your friend had in your bag. But your guns and knives you'll get back when we all reach Tucson. So, what will it be?"

"I'll have a condition also, Mr. Dreeke, that when we reach Tucson you'll help me sell those weapons and any other valuables. I want to send that money back to his office in San Francisco. As to the $2,000…that's my money." She glared at him and waited.

"Reason I mentioned you buy dinner is 'cause we ain't been paid for almost two-months. We pass IOUs in Globe, but they won't accept them down here…even from our boys stationed here."

She had a look of disbelief on her face as she slowly nodded her head. She had recalled reading a story about the Boston Police not being paid and how they had gone on strike. Trouble began right away and the pay checks showed up on the second day of the strike. But these men down here knew that they were the only defense between the Whiteman and Hispanic against Apache Indians. She wasn't aware of the other tribes in Arizona, or how many bandits were running their operations all over Southern Arizona. Cattle rustling became a major operation. With border so close, it was easy work to gather up 500 head of steers and run them across the border before daybreak.

She presented a sweet smile, dropped her large blue-green eyes briefly, then looked warmly intro James' face, "So, I'm waiting for my answer now, Sir."

James laughed briefly, looked over at his hat, then lay his eyes on the nice-looking woman sitting opposite him. The Stagecoach was going through a dusty stretch of roadway. Dust blew into the passenger compartment. "Miss Dearborn, before I respond, I really must ask yuh ta change seats with me, before yuh become buried in this dust."

"Then you'll be the one all covered. No, I believe we know each other well enough to sit on a stage seat together. So, you jus' sit there an' I'll move to your left. I do not wish to interfere with your firearm hand in the event you need to pull it out to save us once again." She pulled up the fluffy sides of her dress, moving to the opposite bench in quick order.

James looked out the stage window, watching the thick dust and sand blow by, behaving totally blind to Ruby's transfer. Except she was only inches away from his left arm and leg. For the first few seconds he stuttered, but was then able to get control of himself. "Miss Ruby, I do apologize for my behavior. My only reasoning I…I may offer in mah defense is how I am not ever in the presence of a lady of your quality. As a Ranger, I live on mah horse. Ah sleep with the wolf and coyote, and ah hunt down bad guys who come into our state or cause a problem right here. Ah'm jus' not sure how to behave 'round you." James had not mentioned one of the papers inside the leather folder, a medical report of some kind that showed Ruby was in perfect condition, no diseases and confirmed to be a virgin. This paper had the signatures of four people and two of them identified themselves as medical personnel.

"James, you have saved my life and treated me as a lady. But I am only a lady from Vermont. My family owned a large farm, where we had 378 milks cows and 1,000 acres of land granted to us from my great-grandfather's service in the Revolution." She was about to tell him more, but stopped herself and only added, "Now you owe me an answer Dear, Sir and I await you."

"It was during the Mexican-American War…Ah had come from thu south to fight for dis country an' wore the Union Blue colors. JW was mah captain then an' I worked myself up to being his lieutenant. We were cavalry and during those long hot days and nights we lost some good horses from underneath us. A lot of our fellow troops fell before thu Mexican cannons or dose sword-like bayonets, an' we done made good friends who still to this day wear thu Union Blue. But ah think thu major reason…You can only give your oath and allegiance to one country, one flag and ours was thu north. Now we's both sided with the south, but this Arizona of ours done needs us more." He leaned back against the bench seat, drained of energy and ready right then to climb into a hotel bed for a couple of days' worth of sleep.

"James, would you like to sleep now, you may have the use of my leg to lay your head upon, or we may continue to talk to help the time pass by," Ruby said.

With a shy grin, James again looked in her eyes and replied, "Ah believe, Miss Ruby, the things ah might utter in mah sleep may hurt your ears, and have an effect-on our new friendship."

"That is so very sweet of you, James Dreeke. You remind me some of my younger brother. Ross was such a dear lad, but in such a hurry to be a soldier. He joined up, but my parents had to sign for him since he was only 16 years old. So eager…he fell in the first battle of Bull Run. Some say he stood his ground and tried to give the men time to escape…Dad was so proud. I was sick."

"Ah'm so very sorry for yuh loss, Miss Ruby."

"Thank, you…but I must acknowledge both sides have suffered terrible losses in this senseless war." She took her hankie out from inside her sleeve to wipe her lips. This desert trip was drying her skin and chapping her lips, making her wonder how any White woman could ever live out here in Arizona.

"You believe it 'senseless'?" James asked. He knew he had several cousins fighting with General Hood in the Army of Texas, and now he wanted to know why this lady felt this way.

"Why, yes...I do," she replied. "One country, who had gained its freedom by defeating an English tyrant and now separated over issues that should have been worked out in the Halls of Congress. Not on the battlefields of the east and possibly into the west. Far too many men, and women and children will die before this war is over. In the meantime, who will do the farming, raising the cattle and making enough money to buy food and clothing for the families left back home while their husbands, fathers and brothers are off playing at war?"

"Though ah'm a sittin' this one out, ah'm a sure this is no game. This be some serious business."

"I do apologize if I made you believe my remarks meant I thought this war was in any way a game, however I still stand by my statement of saying it is a senseless war." Ruby adjusted her dress, which was now transforming into a dusty grayish color from all the sand and grime coming through the stage window. There were leather sun blinders on one side, but on the opposite side they had been removed and not replaced. Had James pulled the working side down, the blowing sand would not have blown through, but piled up inside the coach and made it worse for both. It was better to let the desert dust blow straight through. However, they used a whole canteen in a very short time. James knew it was much worse for JW and the driver. Before they were out of this sand storm, Ruby would have allowed him to cut material off her soiled dress, which was ruined beyond what any washing could've have done for it.

Ruby held up her left hand, sideways against her face, to keep grit from blowing into her mouth as she spoke. This was the first time James noticed two rings on her left hand; a red ruby ring where a wedding ring would normally be and a smaller red ruby ring on her pinky-finger. He didn't wonder what they were worth, but simply admired their beauty. *Ah'm a bettin' her father gifted her that big ruby, her namesake ring an' a former beau spent three months pay to buy her the other ring...Ah do believe it's real.*

"I have talked with numerous people...most of them of my age, but some of them much older concerning the issue of slavery. It was their opinion and I share it, that this issue could've been settled by the South given the time to do so. Instead a decision was forced upon them. Have you ever owned slaves, Sir?"

"Ruby, down in this here country, possibly California too, yuh mus' never ask that there question. Its best ta leave your loyalties...um, locked up in your heart. Unless, you is with your fellow sympathizers. A wrong word cun get yuh kilt."

She was startled, but then asked James the same question again and this time he replied, "No, ma'am. In thu South we was one of the poor families, but ah had a lot of darkie friends, we done a lots of fishin' together on the river so our families could eat. But most of 'em got sold off. Ah never did cotton to dis slave thing. But later, ah had ta agree with the South, even though ah was here in Arizona by then and fighten' thu Mex, no federal government politician has a right to tell an elected statesman what to do concerning our issues. If it be a fed issue, we need to listen an' act upon it, but be it a state issue, than thu fed's need ta butt out."

"Do you think that's why so many states annexed themselves...because the federal government was attempting to govern the states of non-federal issues?" She had to stop to spit out a wet spittle of sand from her mouth and then she sneezed. In very lady-like fashion she used her handkerchief to wipe her lips and then her nose. Afterword, she threw the hankie out the window, which surprised James. But she then promptly open her bag and withdrew another light blue handkerchief, with tiny blue birds in flight embroiled on the four corners. Once again, she had two handkerchiefs to deal with the ongoing storm.

"No one, not even a state, likes bein' told how ta do things, Miss Ruby. Only the rich or well-ta do own slaves an' dat's 'bout one in fifty in thu South...maybe worse," He wetted down his scarf to wipe his face and then slid to the window, to yell up at JW, "Ya doin' okay up there? Anyone need a break?" He waited for a moment. Not getting any answer, he climbed halfway outside the coach and grabbed ahold of the JW's left arm to get his attention. Suddenly, James was looking up at the lethal end of JW's Navy Colt Revolver. James didn't move, a tight two-handed grip on the coach's window edge, but he did pop a wide grin for his Captain. The pulled revolver was an automatic response, but upon seeing James, he shook his head side to side, holstering his revolver. "WHAT!" JW yelled in hopes of being heard over the storm.

"Do yuh want ta change places, take a break and have a talk with Miss Ruby?" James had to let go of the window edge to use the sleeve of his rawhide duster to clean his face. The wind from the storm combined with the speed of the stagecoach was a bitter ride.

"Nope! We should be pullin' into the next station stop in a few hours." JW hollered. He used his left hand to gesture James back into the coach.

"Mr. Dreeke, my first thought was that I must have been boring you, but now I realize you were willing to share the torture of this sand storm with your Captain and I find that a gallant gesture."

"Ah sure wouldn't call it no gallant gesture, ma'am, but thu Cap an' ah've been through a whole lot over thu last 20 odd years. If 'in ah don't bring 'im home in one piece, his Sherry Ann is done liable to blow mah head off. That's his wife an' she done kilt her own share of Apache at d'eir ranch…thu Double B."

"With all this Indian fighting going on, how does anyone have time to be a cattle rancher or a farmer", Ruby said.

"Ma'am, unless you want ta resemble a dried up peach when we reach Tucson, ah think you'd best get you face covered. Driver may decide to hold over at the station if-in this wind don't back off."

"You tied all my garments up above and my handkerchiefs are not of a length to cover my face. What would you suggest?" Ruby glanced about the coach, looking for something that might work.

"Well, ah don't mean to be improper, but in all your shifting around ah notice you is wearin' at least one silk slip. If ah may be so bold, ah length of your silk would make a swell head scarf to protect your whole face an' still enable you the ability to speak."

Ruby was speechless for a moment, but her eyes glared coldly at Sgt. Dreeke, until she realized his suggestion was one for her safety and not for his delight. His eyes softened and she pulled the side of her puffy dress over to the front of her and exposed her top slip, which was indeed genuine silk. It had been paid for by the man left buried back the trail, to enclose the Black Dragon's gift in fine trappings. "Please, Sir, cut enough for both you an' I. No sense in us both being blinded by this blowing sand."

James' eyes went wide, hearing the offer and then he pulled his Bowie knife from its sheath and very carefully began working on the silk. Being such a delicate and fine silk, which Ruby knew had cost the gentleman a surprising amount of cash, adding in the other dresses, and waist coats, extra dresses, a traveling full-length coat which was left in her trunk and three of those frilly feather hats. James was astonished in how hard it was to cut the silk with his Bowie. He had just put a very fine touch on the ten-inch blade, which would sail through leather as if it was butter. But this silk kept sliding off and this slowed him down.

Ruby giggled upon seeing his troubles and reached into her traveling bag to come out with a small pair of sewing scissors. She took over the cutting. He was the one with his mouth open, seeing how easy that little pair of scissors could cut faster and finer than his Bowie.

With his help, Ruby removed her hat, allowing him to cover her head and face with this silk head scarf. Her vision was only slightly impaired. However, she no longer received mouthfuls of desert sand in her mouth. She helped him secure his head scarf, though he kept blubbering his concerns about being seen by his Rangers. The fine silk head scarves were secured around their necks by a separate ribbon of silk, making James feel real odd. He knew if JW or anyone else caught him wearing something so feminine he'd be forced to leave the state out of embarrassment. However, for the moment, it was working.

They rode in silence for a moment. Then she asked, "I recall I had asked you a question concerning how people could have time working their homestead and dealing with the Apaches."

James nodded his head, remembering the earlier question. "Yup, it's not easy. But d'ese Injuns have d'eir seasons. During thu winter they hole-up in d'eir encampments an' rarely come down unless d'ey is a starvin' an' durin' thu summer, you keep watch for 'em. Rangers keep a movin' aroun' to catch-'em."

"But how many Ranger does the State of Arizona have?" Ruby asked. She had heard the Indians could put thousands on the war path and she was worried for her new friend.

"We's got about 30 aroun' Globe…if everyone shows up, an' d'eres 12 Rangers in Tucson."

Ruby's face showed her alarm; even through, the silk head scarf, "You've only got 42 Rangers in the state?"

"Well, we'se got us ah couple militias…one in Globe with possible 30-40 men, an' 'nother one in Tucson…couple hundred men."

"Possible 280 men to handle all the Indians in the State of Arizona. Is that right?"

"When you say it like that but all our Indians, well d'ey jus' don't get along. Mostly dose Injuns will kill each other before makin' ah war on us."

Before she could reply, both she and James heard JW's voice shout down into the coach, "Station ahead…everything looks okay."

James quickly removed his silk head scarf, but she kept hers on. She wouldn't remove it until she was inside the adobe and wood constructed station. Each window was covered by heavy wooden shutters, as well as the door—for Indian fighting. There was also a dried-out wood rail corral that held several loose horses and a six-horse team waiting for the stage. JW was hoping for chow and a drink of whatever the house bar had, but that wasn't what they found. Sitting at a table was a family of five— parents, an older boy and two younger girls—whose covered wagon had broken a wheel nine-miles short of the station. There were three station workers, one of them doubled as a cook. But there was no bar or any liquor on the premises. Turned out the Station Master was Mormon.

Chow was a tin plate of hot beans and some sort of mystery meat, which James advised Ruby not to ask about. From the taste, he was pretty sure it was coyote with a handful of snake tossed in. But overall, the taste was not too bad. The drink was grimy water.

Outside horse troths were all covered over. The younger station worker stepped outside to water the horses using a two-gallon bucket. He finished by giving water to the outlaw's horses, who were looking a bit rough from the trip south through the growing storm.

The man with the family negotiated terms with the coach driver to ride back to Tucson to purchase a new wooden wagon wheel. The two men from the station offered to help him boost his wagon up to change wheels. They had the station's extra horses to get back and forth on.

James looked at the father of the family, wondering how he expected to get the family back up this way. Mostly the stagecoach hi-tailing it up north for Globe, traveled east and then turned north in a wide loop. Rarely did the stage head directly back north, unless it was under special orders; which meant this family would have some expensive stage fare to pay for a family of five.

For the ride from the station south to Tucson, James would ride the best of the two outlaw's horses. The coach's cab could only carry six-people. Concerned she may not see James ever again, Ruby asked James and JW to sit with her during meal time. Both were happy to join her. She confided with them—between bites and then after putting her fork down and sliding her tin plate away—how she managed traveling on this stage with them.

"Miss Ruby, I see no reason why you must continue on. These Tongs—as you call them—have no idea what you look like. You've said there's been no photos. This man's death will not reach them because it will not be reported. I have no name, do I James?" JW asked his sergeant.

"No, Sir…skipped mah mind completely…must be mah age."

"That is very nice of you, but do you have any idea what I should do now. I cannot go back to the farm as I will endanger my family. They must consider me lost in the orient."

Both JW and James remained silent for a brief-moment, but then James popped up, "Seems to me dat $2,000 is your money…for puttin' you an' your family through all dis. So, come back ta Globe…invest in a business and become involved in thu community. Dese Tongs don't have your name an' ah doubt dese Chinese can handle our homegrown Apache, so dey won't come across thu state lookin' for yuh for $2,000."

"Sure, you can stay out on the Double B, help out an' learn something about cattle ranching, while you look-into a business venture." JW put his right hand out and after a brief-moment, she shook it.

"Now you cun spend some of dat money buyin' yuh some cattle ranch clothes."

They waited for two hours hoping the sand storm would let up and ended up spending the night sleeping in the station with the menfolk trading off on guard duty. Another Apache tribe was active in stealing horses and killing the lone miner or hunter.

The station's telegraph line — wired in place only eight months earlier — was disabled eight-days ago. Indians were the suspects. JW promised the stationmaster a visual check of the telegraph lines to see if he could find the break and turn in the location to the Telegraph people. The Indians knew how important these lines were to the White man. They knocked them down as often as they encountered them.

They left the station on a beautiful morning — the desert put on quite a show, displaying all its beauty. Not a cloud in the sky, the temperature still cool, not an Indian or smoke signal in sight.

By early evening they were riding into the outskirts of North Tucson. James changed horses once. The other mount developed a case of wobbly knees. For a moment, he thought about shooting him. Instead, he tossed the saddle on the top of the stage and let him loose. All the way into town, the horse stayed with the coach. James put him into the corral with the outlaw mount he rode in on.

Once they had said their so longs to the grateful driver — they'd see him again soon enough — they said a quick goodbye to the family. They escorted Ruby to the nicest hotel in all of Tucson. They knew she could afford a nice couple of nights. Reservations were already made for her and her now deceased traveling partner. JW explained what happened in the robbery attempt. The hotel clerk knew JW as the Ranger Captain. He rendered immediate sympathy on Ruby and promptly ordered her one of their famous, "inside the room" hot bath rooms. A young boy grabbed her suitcase and soft bag and carried it to her room on the fourth floor. The trunk would soon follow, once it was dug up at the robbery site. The bath tub would be wheeled into her room within the hour, immediately followed by a moving train of young men with hot water from the kitchen.

"Now do not worry about those other items. As we promised we will get those sold either tonight or tomorrow, and bring the funds straight to you."

"Thank you, Officers. Besides saving my life, you have proved to be perfect gentleman." She then shook hands with both men, keeping it very professional in front of the hotel clerk.

BAD NEWS COMES HARD- LIKE A BELLY WALLOP ON A RUG OF SPIKES

Sgt. James Dreeke, dressed in a clean light blue Ranger shirt with three large faded white chevrons of a sergeant sewn to each arm and the sleeves rolled up just over the elbow. His blue denim pants still showed wear from the trip south, as he sat beside his captain in a stuffy, will-lit room. Before them was a taller slender old geezer, with white hair and a long white beard. He sat behind a large oak desk—nearly eight-feet long— which was cluttered with piles of papers, numerous folders and other clutter. This made no sense to James. Captain JW Blake was utterly speechless. The tall, older gentleman, had just informed them of how their whole outfit was being fired from territorial employment.

"You're tellin' the Cap an' Ah we've been thrown out with the bath water…Why, we're only a year old." James said in a raised voice—he elevated it a bit more, so the men outside could hear his objections. "Do you gots any idea jus' how many Injun fights we'd been in? How many Utes and Apache we done killed. How many Banditos we'd killed or arrested? Why, we done jus' saved the Town of Globe and kilt over 60 Apache. Don't that mean nothin'?"

"Yes, Sgt. Dreeke…It means you have earned your monthly pay of $38.42 and have gained the thanks of the people of this territory. But you have-to understand, the territorial government can no longer afford the Rangers. The war back east is taxing all the states and now the territories. But, we've had no taxes and there is no money. We just can't afford to pay for many of our public safety needs. We have written to the Nation's Capital and have asked for additional Union Troops to be sent here to help with the Indian problem, to protect the Capital, the stagecoach route to Phoenix and Globe and the road continuing into California and up north into Nevada. These routes are needed to enable the Territory of Arizona to grow and eventually become a state."

"Which side…Union or Confederate?" JW asked. "Earlier on we represented the South, now Tucson displays the Union flag. Is it a matter of moneys or the one with an army here?"

"Captain, you're a smart man. You'd know it concerned both." White hair replied.

"But what about the cattlemen and farmers to the east and southeast…Who's going to protect them from the marauding Apache and

Utes?" JW asked. James simply kept nodding his head, letting his boss ask the questions. But down deep he didn't think it was going to do any good.

"Captain Blake, farming in southeast Arizona is a useless endeavor. There is simply not enough water for a farmer to grow anything but cactus and scrub bushes. But cattle move around from waterhole to waterhole and a smart cattleman can make a profit, and with taxes coming we here at the new territorial capitol, yes, official now, we really hope they do well. Tax rates have not been set, as-of-yet. As to public safety, Towns will elect Sheriffs and counties will have Marshals appointed by the Territorial Committee for Law Enforcement. It was they who decided the Rangers could be released. We've also been advised we can expect U.S. Marshalls to be making their appearance very soon and in larger numbers to handle our criminal element." He rifled through his papers and came up with an envelope. "Inside you'll find you and your men's paychecks for all monies owed. Please have them sign the line beside their name before you give them their check. You can cash the checks at any bank in the territory. But please, mail the completed form back to me. I do try to keep the territory records together."

"What about our horses, officially some of them belong to the Territorial Government? There is also other equipment items…and scalps."

"Scalps!" White Hair nearly shrieked. "I certainly do not need any scalps, thank you. I imagine you should bury those. As to the rest of the equipment and the horses, I have no invoices on same and I'd rather not spend my time with it. I then make a gift of them to whoever." He looked about the room and then with elbows on his desk, stuck out his head and said in a low voice, "Gentlemen, I am a Texican and I lost my old brother at the Alamo. I know I sound like a stuffed-shirt, but I've been informed they expect my conduct to be that of an English Gentleman. I've met one English Gentleman, he had come west to escape the monarchy…king and queen. He had seen the questioned look on the sergeant's face when he said monarchy…and was now about to be hung for horse stealing. Otherwise a decent chap. I had gone to see him because we were about to do a church play and I was playing the role of an English butler. A single conversation with him had helped me a great detail. Trouble is, I have a very hard time dropping the whole English bit. Hench, I got this job some time ago when no one else would hire me because I was 68 years old. But a man still has to eat."

"How old were you when you came to Arizona?" JW asked.

White Hair thought about his answer for a moment, looked around the room again and then said, "I was 56-years old and had spent, 20-years as a public-school teacher and then a live-in private tutor for well-to-do cattle barons of Texas. But at 56, I followed my last student, who was

Second-in-Charge of a new cattle ranch to be set up on Southeast Arizona...the Broken Arrow. Bad omen for Apache Lands. Only five of us survived that last attack on our new ranch and I ended up here. My pupil went back home with some families who gave up on their journey to California. I've done lawyer work, some accounting and private tutoring, then I was approached about being the...Assistant General Office Manager for the Territorial Government."

"Impressive, Sir...so, who wanted to give us the cut, or can you tell us?" JW asked.

White Hair sat back in his chair and shuffled his paper again, while he thought about an answer. Both ex-Rangers sat quietly, as they waited, but James was getting a mite thirsty.

Then with a sincere look in his eyes, White Hair looked from JW to James and back to JW before he replied. "You may not appreciate my answer, but it is the only way I can reply and keep my oath I made in being hired to this job. As I've said, I am from Texas and have all respect for the Texas Rangers. A majority have left that service to ride with the Army of Texas, under General Hood. I have also gained total respect for the Arizona Rangers in reading your reports and seeing what you have done to save this wild territory with so few numbers to serve. But, as you know the first flag to wave over Tucson was the Confederate Flag and personally, it was my flag because Texas had sided with the South. People...some people saw the Rangers siding with those Southern boys and going out of their way to help them out, even if that meant ignoring the complaints of the local citizens. So, now that the Union flag waves over Tucson, the locals have complained about keeping the Rangers here. Now I do not agree with this and some of the men on the council agreed with me, also. But we were not in the majority, so the Rangers have died and the economy is being blamed as the culprit."

"Thank you, Sir...I appreciate your honesty and your holding to your oath by not identifying those who had voted against us. We may have had to pay a visit to them at some point. But we will now move along so you can return to all those documents on your desk." JW grinned and he added, "I have heard how much paperwork a government can generate and now I see an example." JW stood up, which was followed by a disgruntled former Sgt. Dreeke.

"Oh, before you leave, the Territorial Council wanted to offer you both Territorial Marshal jobs. JW, if I may, would be able to remain near his ranchland. Sergeant, you'd probably be able to name the area you wanted, since you'd be the second Territorial Marshal chosen. So, what do you think, I do need to have your answers before you leave town."

"Sir, you have been a fine gentleman during this whole time and I do not wish to tarnish this exchange in any way, but you can tell this council they can take their marshal's star and put it where the sun don't shine no more, no more."

"Me, too," James said.

"It brings me pleasure you have replied so and I cannot wait until the next meeting so I can present your reply. After reviewing your records, I did not feel you would accept mere bread offering from their plate of poisoned lamb. For it is them who have stabbed you in the back and I can see a lot of people who will suffer once the Apache learn the Rangers no longer ride."

Both men shook White Hair's strong right hand, a grin was shared, then they left his office to find a bar. By now, James' thirst had grown to a mighty test of his spirit. He was holding off under great temptation not being drunk before Miss Ruby, but his insides were all dried up from all the sand they'd eaten and plain water would not do.

Three beers later in a darkened booth of the Silver Spur Saloon, both men considered moving on to something hard to toast the end of the Rangers. Still, James held to his resolve and told his former Captain about his new-found love in this Miss Ruby and needing to stay reasonably sober for a later dinner with her. But JW was also invited.

"Jamey, I've know you since you were old enough to climb aboard a horse, shoot your first gun and fall in love with your first gal. Now if I remember, this would make the eighth gal you sworn your undying love to and guess what, old buddy, you're now unemployed. Hard to impress a gal when you've lost your job."

James finished off his third beer, which was now warm and had the nauseating taste of sweat built up on a two-day old sock. "Dis is really lousy beer, JW."

"Took you three beers to notice that...I was bettin' on five the way you gulped down the first two." JW had taken a sip of his first beer and poured the rest down through a break in the floor boards. For the cost of each beer, he wondered how this place was still in business. Had it been in Globe, the townspeople wouldn't have stood for it and burned the place to the ground.

"It's dat lady...Miss Ruby...ah jus' don't know what ta do. Ah gots no job, no ranch and nutin' ta do. You wanna hire me?"

"You'll see your Miss Ruby in a couple hours and that means getting yourself cleaned up, well, best you can. We'll decide about our future when we get home and have all our Rangers together. But tonight, it's just you an' Miss Ruby. Okay?"

James looked lost and he glanced about the room. JW fallowed his looks to see if trouble had arrived in the bar, but then James said, "Ah forgot...Ah forgot, JW. Ah gots ta get dose guns sold ta give her some money. We gots ta go."

"Slow down partner, I thought we were doing that tomorrow. What's the hurry?"

James looked at JW, worry radiating off his face. "She's scared...She's dun scared of everythin'. An' ah done promised her, might hurt her feelings if' in ah break mah promise. Will yuh come wit' me?"

JW studied the worrisome look in his friends glistening eyes, taking in some illumination from the nearby overhead oil lamp. It was a look a younger brother would give his big brother, when asking for help in a girl problem. JW wanted to smile, possibly chuckle, but he fought both off as they would cause hurt to his good friend.

"All right, Jamey, let's go grab the hardware and see what kind of cash we can raise for your Miss Ruby. You just remember, she's got a check for $2,000 and the bank here in town can cash it. But that's her business and not ours. Let's take care of your promised task, then you can have your evening with her and we can leave tomorrow."

"How we getting' back, it's a week 'fore 'nother stage heads north for Globe on thu short route. Long route means we'd stop at every minin' town, reservation office an' goat farm along thu way. Take us nine-days to get back ta Globe that way and we is beat to a pulp."

JW shook his head, "Nope, I cashed my Ranger check and bought us two nags for the ride back. We can sell them in Globe ta got my money back, if yuh want."

The two of them left the bar, but not before voicing their discontent for the lousy beer. Seeing how well armed the two men were and knowing the larger one was a Ranger Captain, the owner just nodded his head in agreement and watched them leave. Yet, he had to agree with them. His last batch of beer came out with such a stench he suspected one of his workers had slipped and fallen in the tank. But a search revealed nothing, so he had to blame it on the ingredients and come to find his latest cactus skin was all dried up before being shredded and fouled the batch. He normally used fresh cactus shreds. But he wasn't going to toss this mess. No, he served it anyway. Oddly enough, he found most of his patrons didn't notice a difference. A few of his favorites sung his praise for serving the new batch.

When James left the bar, walking out onto the wooden porch, the fresh air nearly toppled him. "How long were we in dat dive?"

"Long enough to give us this stench. We need baths, but first your promise."

They went back to their room, which was clean, but not nearly as nice as Ruby's suite. Two bedrooms separated by a large shared room, with three couches, two over-stuffed chairs and a beautiful full-sized Grand Piano, and a small open kitchen, only large enough to prepare platters for small parties brought up from the restaurant kitchens below. The kitchen area also had a wine storage cabinet and spaces for metal platters, utensils, plates and cups. Crystal ware was brought up from the big kitchen. But Miss Ruby had no plans to hold any parties to celebrate her escape from the Tongs, but following five-years of piano lessons, she could not resist playing the Grand Piano. The sounds coming out of her room caused many of the hotel guests to stop and listen. This was how the two former Rangers found over twenty people outside Miss Ruby's door, listening to the beautiful music being played inside. Most of these people had never heard such music before as she went from Bach to Mozart, adding in Beethoven and several other great composers.

No one left as-long-as the music came through the door and seemed to transport the listeners into a different world, if only briefly. But then she stopped, her fingers were sore, as well as her arms. She had not played in some time. She was startled by the wave of applause coming from the front door, it continued to go on until she opened the door. The applause lessoned until one man looked inside and confirmed no one was at the piano, it was she who had blessed them so. Once again, the applause came and now the people were all looking right at her.

JW stepped forward and in a low voice, said, "I recommend you take a bow, let us inside and then politely close the door or you might not ever get rid of this crowd."

"Oh, yes…thank you." She gave them room to enter and provided them with a formal show-woman's stage bow and then with an appreciative smile she slowly closed her door to a continued applause. Once the door was closed, the applause died away and she held her left hand to her upper chest, a fresh pink handkerchief clutched in her hand and a look of relief on her face. But there was still a twinkle to her eyes, for it had been quite a while since she ran her fingers across such fine ivory keys. It made her wonder why the Tongs were treating a White slave so well, when they could've tossed her into a pig pen, while they waited for the next stagecoach west.

"Your piano playing was like nothing I've ever heard before…Almost a sense of magic to it. I could feel the flying carpet taking me off to a foreign land. It was beautiful," JW said. He now stood beside the Grand Piano, having never been so close to such a music piece before.

He had seen pianos in bars and down in the stage pits, but nothing as so fine as this piece. He figured he could shave off the glassy reflection the angled top provided.

James, he was standing between JW and Miss Ruby, and he was speechless. The music she had played had moved her up into the angelic category and now he didn't know if he could talk to her ever again. His hat was off and he was fidgeting with it between both his hands, waiting for JW to saying something else, so they could finish the matter and get back on the trail home.

"Gentlemen, I really wasn't sure what time you would show up, but would you allow me to order us up some dinner. I understand the restaurant here is the best in Arizona and we could be served within the hour. I also wanted to discuss some business with you, if I may, but only after we finish dinner. My Pa told me that one should never do business while eating a good meal, as a poor business proposal could sour one's stomach and ruin a perfectly good meal."

"Miss Ruby, that'll be fine," JW said and then he shot James a raised eyebrow look that said, *What am I supposed to say? I can't be rude to the lady, not after playing so pretty and offering me dinner from downstairs.*

James shot him back a sneer, which disappeared when Miss Ruby asked him a question. He was glad she didn't see his expression, he knew such facial expressions made him look older and slightly plague-ridden.

"So, how well did you do with the weapons and belt ware, James? Oh, and please be seated, we have so many places here to choose from.

As they took a seat on a soft brown couch with Spanish designs on it, they watched as she walked over to the kitchenette area and pulled on a cord. "This, as it was explained to me, reaches the kitchen below and rings a small bell to notify the cooks what room is desiring to have their meals served in. A young man will be here in a few moments with menus and he will take our orders. Later, he will return with our meals on a wheeled cart. I have seen such things, but this is the first time I am the one being treated in such high-tone fashion. My dear father would probably be dragging me out of this hotel by my ear, suspecting the worst. That I had gone off and married some rich dude with a good yarn…and probably three other wives spread across the nation."

JW figured the boy must have run up the stairs because he was at the door before they could even get into the gun venture. The menu had a French side and an English side, but JW couldn't recall that many Frenchmen coming into Arizona right now. But their language sure looked really fancy on the page.

James also admired the fancy French writing and he was being polite by waiting for Miss Ruby to make her order, but his stomach was growling something bad and that 24-ounce steak cooked with apples and onions was causing him to salivate a bit. Finally, Miss Ruby ordered the barbecued chicken, a side a baked shrimp from the Gulf of Mexico and these new style of French fried potatoes. The young man recommended it, and the new gourmet dipping sauce down from Chicago that was called "Ketchup".

Giving into past rank, James waved his hand in a gesture and adding a bowed head, JW smiled in return and then made his order of the 24-ounce steak, with onions and apples, a side of those shrimp and a helping of those French Fries. He'd never heard of them, but he was willing to try it. He also ordered a plate of fried catfish, with sliced lemons. Then it was James' turn and all he did was order the very same thing JW ordered. Plus, he ordered two pitchers of ice water and two loaves of fresh bread with an extra helping of butter."

The young man looked at the two men, shaking his head from side to side, "You cowboys can sure put away a lot of food. But I guess you don't get a lot of it out on the trail."

"Oh, no, sir..." Miss Ruby said, "This is Captain Blake and Sgt. Dreeke of the Arizona Rangers. They stopped a stagecoach robbery and saved my life on our way here. Before that they had put down an Apache raid and killed over 60 Indians. They are not mere cowboys." Right then the boy's eyes grew twice in size and the hero worshipping began.

"Wow! Wait, till I let the other guys know, how I served you both dinner. They won't believe me." He was out the door before asking if they wanted to order their dessert now or later.

"Miss Ruby I'd appreciate if you wouldn't tell anyone else about our activities. But you should know that later this afternoon, we found out why they needed to see us here...It was to let us know the Rangers were being fired. The Territorial Government feels they can do without us. Now I have to go back and inform my men...my friends, I'm giving them their last pay checks."

"Now look what you done, JW...You done an' went an' soured mah tummy, just like she warned. Mah mind is on the men back home...What dey gonna do?"

"Jamey, I can kick you in your stomach, but when that steak roles in, you'll be perked up and ready ta go," JW said. "Now let's cover the guns, so we can put that behind us."

James pulled out his long cowhide wallet from his right back pocket. He had to adjust his holster and belt some, to pull the wallet clear. This was when Miss Ruby made the suggestion, "You Gentlemen may take your weapons off and set them aside. It will make you more comfortable for dinner."

Both men agreed and they stood up to remove their well-used belts, which held their clean and oiled Navy Colts and pouches for ammo and powder. They thought about putting them on the nearby couch, but realized their weapons would spoil the fine upholstery. They lowered them to the floor instead, with the belts wrapped around the full holsters. Once that was done, they then took their seats and James opened his wallet to withdraw the funds they had collected from selling all the firearms and leather gear, along with other expensive items found in the Private Investigator's bags. Once they had heard Miss Ruby's story and seeing no reason to doubt her, especially when her fact coincided with the papers in the dude's belongings, they left it to her to decide if any money would be sent back to San Francisco. But upon dwelling on it some, they realized that would only alert where Miss Ruby was last known to be and a new investigator would've been sent out.

"Here's $341.80 from everything sold. It was $20 more, but it cost us that much to keep your name and the investigator's presence out of the stage hold-up and both the town's reporter and a drunkard of a newspaper editor each wanted $10. It was easier paying them than bending a barrel over their heads." JW said, while James counted off the money into Miss Ruby's right hand.

"Do you think they'll keep this promise, you did say the editor was a drunkard?" Ruby eyes showed the fear she felt concerning being discovered by the Tong warriors or another gang hired by the Tongs. Since learning of her new business loan owners, she had done what reading she could find concerning Chinese gangs and she was scared. This is one of the reasons she had not tried running away once she was outside the state or trying to secure help from anyone on the stagecoach since leaving home. These Tong Warriors were modern day assassins and seldom had they tasted defeat.

I brought a couple of friends along with us and they'll keep an eye on the paper. If they tried changing the story or printing a follow-up, they have our permission to hog tie both-of-them and drag them over a patch of cactus...several times." JW said.

"He done made his point, Miss Ruby," James added.

She used a handkerchief to hide her grin, then offered each man $25 for their fulfilling their promise, but neither of them would accept it. "Now, you still got's dat map of where ta find dat trunk if in you please some day? You could give a stage coach driver $20 to bring it here." James asked, as he helped Miss Ruby sit back down into her chair, while JW poured each of them a tall crystal glass of red wine.

"Now this is what I wished to talk over with you, Gentlemen," Ruby said, as she accepted the wine and then waited for both men to be reseated.

"I've decided not to go on into California. I feel it might be too easy for the Tongs to locate me and possibly kill me as an example to other slaves thinking of running. Or they'll murder me for the death of their Private Investigator. A lot of money was paid out for my travel and to safeguard me until I arrived in San Francisco untouched."

"What you're saying is true, Miss Ruby an' staying here isn't much better...Nor is returning home. Where you'll endanger your family. Thinking about it, maybe it might be better to have the stagecoach story say both the Private Investigator, listed him by full name and where he is from, and the unidentified woman, only your description, shot and killed in the outlaw chase. That reporter was hungry to write him up a real excitin' yarn. What do you think?"

"I think that's what should be done, my White Knights in Armor. For I have decided to...well, to ask you to use what funds I have-to purchase me a wagon and four horses, plus the food, water and gear I'll...we'll need for the trip back to Globe. I plan to find a job there...teaching school, piano lessons...even singing lessons. I can cook, I've worked on a farm all my life an' I can even open up a dress shop for the ladies. My mom and her three sisters taught me a lot about sewing. I'll also need a good rifle...a .30 caliber if you will. I used to go deer hunting with my brothers and it was I who usually brought home the first kill."

Both men, a bit astonished by what they had just heard, especially looking at Miss Ruby in this fine city dress and this this hotel suite that was costing $35.00 a night, didn't know what to say. But finally it was James who broke the silence, "Den ah 'magine yuh cun handle ah wagun string of four hosses, then?"

JW still had a blank expression on his face, but his mind was racing with the idea of bringing this special lady back to the Township of Globe. He knew that within a week the menfolk would be fighting over her in the bars and fighting gun duels out on the streets, simply to take her out to dinner. He also knew right at the top of the pile of suitors would be his former Sergeant. Yet, for her sake, it was the smartest thing to do. Besides he had other plans for Former Ranger Sergeant James Dreeke.

For the next few minutes they conversed about her needs for the trip and how it would be James to be with her the next day to buy a wagon, horses, equipment and food, while JW made another visit on the newspaper staff and buying a Sharp's .30 caliber Rifle in used, but fine condition. JW had to swallow some pride, but apologized to the newspaper editor for his previous threat and again pay both men $10. But he reminded them of how the Tucson Star was brought up to Globe on the stagecoach and if he didn't like the story he'd be back down here to fulfill his cactus drag promise.

They spent one more night in Tucson, giving the three of them time to give the 14-foot long wagon with a curved canvas topping a thorough going over. The wagon was outfitted with four 40-gallon barrels of water and feed for six-horses. Miss Ruby bought two trunks worth of material bolts for the making of dresses, shirts and pants, vests, skirts and blouses. She even bought leather tanning kits, one of the latest things for making fine leather wallets, vests, belts and dinner jackets. She bought an armload of music books; from beginners to the Great Composers of Europe. Her wagon was a treasure trove and there was enough inside there to start-up a fine dress shop and music store. She spent $235 ordering a small straight back piano out of New York and it was expected to arrive in Globe in nine-weeks.

"If in yuh don't min' me uh askin' yuh, 'bout how much yuh got's left of dat $2,000?" James asked Miss Ruby, as they wrestled that last trunk into the wagon.

"James, I don't mind you asking me anything…We've been through too much together in such a short time. I already feel a kinship to you and JW." She smiled and added, "I like calling him JW…Has a real western feel to it. But back to the money, we're down to $685 and I am going to need most of that to get a new building built in Globe, plus a small house attached to it. If business is slow I can do odd-jobs around the town. But I'll sell the wagon and horses, then buy a riding horse for myself to get around on. I guess I'll just have to wait and see what's available."

"Ah've gots ah great mount for yuh back home an' it's all yours…for-r-r free…ah birthday gif'."

"It's not my birthday, James and won't be for some time."

"Well, Miss Ruby, den ah gots it covered when it is, ain't ah?" James said with a big smile on his face.

"Yes, you sure do. Thank you, James."

"Yuh know, yuh can calls me Jamey, too. Only JW an' his family can, but ah'll let yuh, too."

She reached forward, grabbed him in her arms and kissed him on the cheek. "Thank you, Jamey, that makes me feel pretty special. Now we'd better finish up, so we can leave here early in the morning."

James was rubbing the cheek where he'd been kissed. Oh, he'd been kissed on the lips, but a kiss on the cheek by Miss Ruby made him forget all those earlier kisses and for a moment there, he felt he was walking on a cloud.

That night it was decided by a flip of the golden eagle $20 piece that James would start off driving the wagon for the first section of roadway. Miss Ruby sat on a soft pillow beside James. On steep hill climbs she'd be out on foot, using a fine hemp whip to induce the horses to work a bit harder. JW used a rope lasso looped around the front lashing for the horses and his saddle to assist in pulling the wagon. The wagon was loaded heavy, however they made it over the first range and up into the higher desert. They took a long break, eating their lunch. Miss Ruby did the cooking, while James watered and fed the horses. JW rode a widening loop around the encampment to ensure they weren't surprised by any Indians or Bandits. He didn't find any and returned just in time for a tin plate of fine food.

"Miss Ruby, if we ever served food like this on a cattle drive, we'd never get the men to leave camp. This is great," JW said.

James was unable to add anything because his mouth was full of an east coast version of chili—hot and sassy.

The trip went fast. They made it to Globe without incident in four-days and three nights. Preacher Joe was on hand to welcome them. When he heard the bad news, he asked, "When's the meeting and where? I'll get the word out fast an' you know it."

"Tomorrow night, my ranch an' I cook us up a last barbecue," JW said. He went to the stable, exchanging his mount for his beautiful Appaloosa. "Water the brown up, feed her and give her a good rest. I'll decide what to do with her in a couple days. Just add it all to my end of the month bill. Okay?"

"You know it always is."

JW grinned, tossed his friend a friendly salute to the brim of his hat, mounted his old buddy. Less than an hour later, he was riding up to his ranch. He stopped at the cattle gate to ring the large brass bill announcing his arrival. Even guests were advised to ring the bell or they might be met by a couple rounds shot just above their heads.

JW's family came out on the porch. Seeing it was the Family Patriarch, they began waving and shouting out their greeting, "Dad! Daddy, you're home! Darling!" He rode up quickly, making sure he closed the gate first, spun out of his saddle and ran to meet his family. He'd only been gone a week, but it felt like so much longer and he kissed each member. Then when he got to Sherry Ann, he lifted her off her feet and spun her around in the air, followed by planting a big kiss on her lips.

They never minded expressing love in front of their children, at least to a certain degree.

JW then stopped, held her in his arms and looked deeply into her beautiful eyes. It was then she could tell there was a problem, a hurt he was carrying deep, but he couldn't say anything in front of the kids.

It was right then that JW heard a thumping noise coming from the door leading into the barn. He pushed Sherry Ann behind him and went for his Navy Colt revolver. It was then — weapon clearing the holster — JW realized he was looking into eyes-of-terror. Liam stood there with a pitchfork in his hands. He had just knocked the forks against the barn door to clear the forks. He knew he was looking at sudden death. His mind was mostly blank. Then everything began clearing as JW holstered his revolver. He stepped forward, reaching with his empty hand to shake Liam's. His expression cried out — *Will you forgive me, Boy — I'm jumpy and I forgot you were here. I am very sorry.*

Liam dropped the pitchfork. With some hesitation, he lifted his right hand up to shake hands with his boss and the man who had avenged his family's massacre. "You done an' made me wet myself, Captain Blake. Now I got ta go change my pants."

"Had a bad trip going south, Liam. Stage robbery…had to kill two outlaws, but not before they killed two people. I need a good bath now and some time with the family. But I need you to make some visits for me. I'll write you down a list, but all the Rangers will meet here tomorrow night and well have a barbecue. You and I, will spend the morning getting the beef ready to feed 70 to 80 people. Tell them they can bring their families, and any side dishes are always welcome. Now can you do that?"

"Sure, Boss. Just make out the list and I get a going," Liam replied.

Sherry Ann knew what her man needed and she took her man in to the kitchen and fed him a plate of leftovers from dinner and then shoed all the kids to bed. She knew Liam was already off on his task and that left them with the barn alone.

"Now you follow me, Captain…Time for you an' me to have some time alone. And you won't need that." She unbuckled his wide-leather gun-belt, while he continued chowing down on a piece of pan-fried chicken. She hung it on its assigned hook, dragging him outside and across the yard, over to the barn. Once she tossed him down onto the loose hay, she closed the wide, heavy doors, taking matters into hand. It would be early morning before she unlocked the barn from the inside, wandered over to the kitchen to make her man some early morning coffee. Instead of a smile on her face from a pleasurable night, tears cascaded down her cheeks.

142

CHAPTER SIX

"You're an' Office and a Gentleman, now, so act like one...before I slice off those big ears of yours an' fry them in Buffalo Fat."

For over four hours, JW and Liam worked feverishly, slowly spinning a side of beef over a spruce wood fire, adding branch from other trees to soak the meat with various scents. Sherry Ann made over a gallon of her special barbecue sauce, with some of the ingredients taught to her by the Rangers who previously lived with the Indians. By the time the meat was considered roasted, JW was using his smaller knife to cut away chunks for him and Liam. "Needs a bit more spinning, sauce needs to blacken a bit more." JW said, and then he went back to spinning the spit. When they loaded it on to the spit, JW estimated the side of beef's weight at 260 pounds. The roasting reduced it to under 200 pounds. A lot of the fat dripped off.

It was approaching dinner time. Most of the Rangers arrived, either with a girlfriend, a wife and kids, or alone with big appetites. Boards were used as temporary tables, supported by hay bales. They held hard boiled eggs, veggies of all kinds from whatever was growing, platters of corn on the stalk, pies and cakes, plus various breads. There were soft drinks bought in town. The bottles had to be returned for the nickel deposit on each one. There was hot and cold coffee, some tea and milk for the kids. Someone brought a two-gallon cask of beer, but it was moved off the table for later.

Now it was time to haul the meat in and remove the spit. JW had the honors of doing the cutting. He wanted Liam to share in the honors. By the time they were both done, they had some mighty big steaks and over an inch of meat on the side's ribs. JW was forced to use a wood saw to get the ribs off, not wanting to make a show of it with a wood axe. It was the ribs the Rangers went for first. The ladies shared the steaks with their families. There wasn't a single complaint about the taste. Most of the ladies tried talking Sherry Ann out of her recipe for the barbecue sauce, but she wouldn't give.

The dinner finished up with desserts, resulting in a pie throwing fight between Brady Williams and Joshua Troy Dreeke (James' little brother). A friendly debate about the South and its ability to win this current war — Brady saying the North had too much of everything to lose. This caused young Dreeke to pick up a dried apple pie and nail Brady right in the nose. Once he licked off the tasty filling and cleared his eyes,

Brady quickly scooped up a potato pie and smashed it into Young Dreeke's mouth, neck and down his chest.

That began the war, with Rangers taking sides, women and kids fleeing the scene. They knew there would be no gunplay. These men were like brothers. But for the moment, it was pies, bread, cookies and brownie bombs zeroing in on their opponents. Then it came, someone from one of the sides threw a fist and now the war had elevated into a down and dirty tumble.

Luckily JW, James and Liam, also Preacher Joe, stayed clear of the fight. But, JW could tell James wanted to get into the melee. As his guest, he brought Miss Ruby to the Barbecue. She stood over to the side with Sherry Ann. Ruby noticed Sherry Ann was in possession of a dangerous looking 48-inch double-barrel 12-gauge shotgun.

"You think they've gone long enough, Ruby?" Sherry Ann asked. After only a couple of hours they had taken to each other and were discussing new dresses for her and her daughter.

"If they keep this up someone is liable to get hurt and they still have the meeting to discuss, so I believe it's time to end it, Sherry Ann."

Sherry smiled and hefted the shotgun with the weapon pointed to the heavens. She pulled the inner trigger, grimacing as she absorbed the recoil of the blast. However, the loud blast got everyone's attention. The first thing they all thought of was how they were all unarmed. Their weapons were back in the wagons, on their horses and carriages. Then they saw who fired the shotgun and knew their fight was over. Time to clean up their mess, forgive each other and prepare for the Captain's talkin' to.

It was then that Preacher Joe came out of the house with a large plate of food in his hands. He said loudly a prayer of forgiveness, shook his head and went back inside to eat with the kids. This caused both Sherry Ann and Ruby to look at each other. They broke out into laughter, which became famous. Before long everyone was laughing or chuckling.

JW told them to leave the food on the ground. He'd just run his hogs over the area. He did ask for the bales and boards be carried into the barn, set up as stadium seating for the 30 or more Rangers. He advised the ladies that only the Rangers could come into the meeting right now, which seemed to perturb the women-folk

.

THE MEETING

JW did not look forward to this meeting. He remembered how bad he felt when he received the news. Once the doors closed, he looked over his men. He let out a deep sigh. He was losing these men, his friends who accepted him as their leader and together fought over 100 engagements against the Indians and Bandits. Now he must tell them it is all over.

"Good news first, I've got your pay checks right here and they're up to date…a sizeable amount of cash for some of you…Now…Sgt. Dreeke and I took the Stagecoach south to Tucson. There was a hold-up and four-people died and we killed two outlaws. Thankfully, we were on scene to save the life of Miss Ruby, who is standing over by my beautiful wife. Rather than continuing-on, she has decided to become part of Globe."

JW pulled a dark blue handkerchief out of his back pocket and wiped his face. "Now as to the pay checks, as I said we will handle it right after this meeting. But now the bad news. Upon our arrival, I learned…the Arizona Rangers have been terminated due to budget cuts. Now there's more to it than that, as some of the Union big wigs in Tucson feel we have a certain leaning toward the south and might become spies against the Union Troops when they soon arrive. When I reminded them of how the cattle ranches and some of the farmers to the Southeast will no longer have any protection if we're fired, it did not seem to bother them.

"They expect the Union boys to patrol all the roads, escort the stagecoaches and even pay visits to the Apache and Ute home grounds to ensure they're staying there."

"Cap, you've got a cattle ranch and even a farm going, but most of us only have the Rangers and part-time work on these ranches and farms. Without the Rangers, I'll have to head out…I'm just not sure what I'll do," Lawrence Coon said.

"Okay, I've given you the bad news. The Territory is going to start taxing everyone and just about everything. So, I may lose all my cattle and every other critter on my land. Then they'll go for my land. All because I have Southern sympathies. Now if the South does win I can probably start all over on my own land. This all means I am going to break my oath to the Union and volunteer for the Confederacy. I am leaving tomorrow for Texas, to join General Hood's Army of Texas. Anyone who wishes to ride along with me needs to be here with the breakin' of daylight. For those of you who may or cannot ride along, you will always be my friend and I salute you. I further salute the men who have ridden with us and have fallen as Arizona Rangers."

All the men rose-up and saluted the dead, and the memory of the Arizona Rangers. Then one by one they left the barn to collect their families and depart JW's ranch. Tonight is a night of decision making and it would involve their wives and a good amount of tears.

DAYLIGHT

For over an hour and both unable to sleep, they were in the barn giving the Appaloosa a thorough rub-down, a good drink and just enough food to burn in her engine, but not enough to have her break down with a stomach ache. Sherry Ann trimmed her mane and tail and surprised her with half an apple, but she removed all the seeds first. He finally placed a clean horse blanket on her, followed by the old saddle, with a few new additions. The front of the black saddle fancied up with tooled leather, now carried two extra black holsters, one on each side of horse's neck. This provided easy access for JW to pull either one of the Navy Colts the holsters carried. Then right behind his left leg was a sheath for his sword; a golden pommel to it now and a slightly curved blade nearly two-feet long. He spent two hours over the grind stone sharpening the blade. And behind his right leg a similar sheath held his personal hand axe he made for him several years ago. The one thing he could say from all the engagements he had been involved in, he had learned from the Apache how there were times when one would have no firearms and you'd be facing more than three of the enemy.

JW saw one Apache defend himself against five soldiers, each armed only with bayonet tip rifles, and no ammo. He was too far away to help, seeing the fight through binoculars. In a matter of minutes, the Apache brave wounded two men and was able to escape. JW had seen many of the trade tomahawks, which were far better in one on one battles than a soldier's bayonet. But he added several other features, including an all metal handle, slightly larger blades. Instead of a hammer on one side and blade on the other, JW had gone with a double blade. By now several of the Rangers were armed in a similar way, if they could afford it.

Sherry Ann finished by putting a bag of cookies into his left side saddle bag. It was her last offering of love before he rode off. There was a large soft roll tied down to the saddle, right over the saddle bags. This included his blankets, two extra shirts, one extra pair of pants, more shot, ball and powder wrapped up, plus four apples for his mount.

The two doors were pushed open, exposing the inside of the barn to increased daylight, and as their vision cleared, both JW and Sherry Ann were amazed by the number of riders he had in his yard. Some of them he didn't know.

James walked over, leading his Appaloosa by the reins, "Dere's eleven of us an' a Mr. Lloyd Grimes, a former Ranger, who'd like ta come 'long. Boy's say he's got some good history an' resigned ta be a town marshal."

"Dese 13 riders are Rangers from Tucson...Dey rode north to catch up wit' yuh, once dey got fired. Dere boss is a Lt. Bret Sampson, says he knows yuh."

"That make us 26...a sizable cavalry unit for General Hood, nearly a platoon of cavalry. "I'll go have a chat with this Sampson, but let those boys know you're my acting sergeant and have everyone come together for one of my trail chats. They can chow on some jerky if they have some, but water their horses, we still got some riding to do."

Once he had gotten closer to this Sampson fella, he did remember him and the games of poker the two of them had played while guarding over a gang of owl-hoots on the Arizona and Mexican Border. They were supposed to turn them over to the Mexican authorities and be rid of them. They were bandits, who had come across the border to steel cattle. But on the Mexican side they had killed three Border policemen. It was half an hour later when, on the other side of the river, the outlaws were executed by firing squad. All said-and-done—In only thirty minutes or so. JW shook his head and rode back his way, while Sampson left in another direction. This was the first time they had seen each other since then, though Lt. Sampson knew much of Captain Blake's record. "My grandfather recommended I head north to find you right away. He expected you to join the Confederacy and we might be better off with a larger force. We're also expecting more volunteers along the way, most of them with previous law enforcement experience."

"Would your grandfather happen to be a rather tall, white-haired, gentlemen?" JW asked.

"Why, yes...he is. He also said with your experience, you should be the leader and how I would gain much by watching you."

"Your men all agree with what we're planning on doing? Going to Texas to join up with General Hood?" JW asked.

"Yes, Sir...I'm always honest with my Rangers...former Rangers, or I don't say anything to them. But I did lose my sergeant, who elected to stay behind to become the new Tucson Deputy City Marshal. He's got a family, with seven kids and a sickly wife. No one could fault him for staying behind. Still, all together I lost nine Rangers for various reasons and brought 12 riders with me...all good men. Plus, a good scout who knows New Mexico and Texas Territories."

"Well, let's bring 'em all together for a chat an' then we can move out," JW said as an order. To which, Sampson replied with a, "Yes, Sir."

A rope line was laid across the desert sand, tied between three large rocks and a heavy shrub. The horse's reins were then tied off to the line. Several of the horses were even hobbled, to ensure they didn't try to run off and this was evidence of a new mount. However, an experienced Ranger knew to be left on foot in the desert because of a skittish mount could mean his death; thus he took a lot of precautions. Some even ran a rope from a stirrup, which he held in his hand, during the upcoming meeting. Most of the Tucson Rangers had never seen the Captain before, but they had all heard stories of his adventures up north against the Apache, Ute and Bandits. While the Tucson Rangers were expected to stay close to the territorial capital and nearby ranches or farms, it was the northern Rangers who made war on the renegades and got them back on their lands, and stopped the killing and horse stealing raids. Some of the Tucson boys really envied their northern brothers, but transfers were rarely approved. Mainly because the Southern Rangers had grown up mostly fighting border bandits, some stagecoach robbers and heist men of the banks and mines. They knew almost nothing of fighting Indians, unless they were over 40 years old and that was considered too old to be pulling field work.

"Gentlemen, for those of you who do not know me, I am John W. Blake. You may call me JW, unless we become a part of the confederacy and I dearly hope you will address me as General JW." His own men started laughing, which got the new additions joining in.

"Now I've been made aware; you all know where you're going. But to reiterate, this unit of former Arizona Rangers, the finest fighting force in Arizona and possibly all the Southwest, is headed to San Antonio to join forces with General Hood's Army of Texas. Now is there anyone here who objects to this? If so, they may depart now without any hard feelings." JW remained silent for a moment. When no one in the large circle of sitting and standing men moved, he continued.

"It is my idea to run this unit of ours as a Ranger Company. I will be the Company Commander and this has been okayed by Lt. Sampson, who'll become my second in Command and B unit leader for his Tucson Rangers. A small unit will be led by Sgt. Dreeke, who served as a Union Lieutenant in the U.S. and Mexican War. He served with great distinction and saved my life, his commander, a couple of times and was wounded in the process. Listen to him, he speaks from experience in fighting in more than 100 engagements with Mexicans and Indians, plus the occasional husband he wasn't made aware of earlier." Again, another round of laughter and several of James's friends slapped him on the back in jest.

"We are privileged to have three gifted scouts with us. Two of them, Scouts Holloway and Jim Williams can take us through the Apache and Comanche territory and I am told Scout Salcedo also knows this same area, plus Texas. So, we should be well covered. I want the three of them working together from the start, this way they'll get to know each other's signals and signs before we hit Comanche territory." He looked to his two men and released them with a wave and Lt. Sampson followed up with a wave to Salcedo.

"You three meet back with us after sundown," JW ordered.

"Now I plan to run this company as if we were still a Ranger Company. You'll accept the orders of the ranks above you at all-times. If you feel you are being taken advantage of, you may contact me through Sgt. Dreeke and then Lt. Sampson. Even if it is their order you are objecting to, they will not refuse your right to see me, but you'd better be sure you have a valid reason. Rarely have I been brought such a complaint, but there have been a corporal or two whose new promotion got the better of him and this was straightened out. Also, if at any time, you wish to ride on to join the confederacy on your own, you may, but you'll never ride with this unit ever again once we join with General Hood. I do not work with quitters."

Sgt. Dreeke handed JW a canteen, which he accepted gratefully and after a sip he returned to his talk. "We will ride Ranger style, two ranks, as it makes our unit look larger and may keep the Apache or Comanche from attacking us. Personally, I'd rather get to San Antonio with all of us, as I hope to remain together as a cavalry company and not mixed up among other groups in need of reserve riders."

JW then gestured to Liam to come stand beside him. "As you can see, this young man is a wee bit young to be a ranger. Will, you'd be right. He is like an adopted son to my wife and I, but more importantly he is this company's runner and should be considered as the young man delivering my orders and returning with your responses. He has no rank, but do not let his youth lessen your opinion of him. Within the last month, he has displayed great valor in three engagements against the Apache. He has taken vengeance upon the very Indians who had massacred his small wagon train. He was involved in the attack where we ambushed 60 Apache and killed two Apache I know of, one in hand-to-hand combat with a knife. So, I wouldn't get him angry."

Sgt. Dreeke pounded Liam on the left shoulder, nearly driving him to the ground and shoved him into the waiting arms of Cpl. Leaders. The Globe Rangers treated their mascot like a conquering hero.

Strangely, Liam could recall nothing of the ambush, as it was all a blur. But he knew he was fortunate to be alive and he really enjoyed the acclaim he was receiving from his buddies.

"Now, we will ride hard from daybreak to sundown, for we have a very long distance to travel. I hope to stop the stages we encounter to see if they carry any newspapers. I know we'll all be interested on how the war is faring. But we need to be clear of Arizona and stay to the south while going through New Mexico to avoid any union troops. Although we are not in uniform, or flying a confederate flag, if we fire upon the union troops and any one of us were captured, they would definitely shoot us as a spies. So, we will avoid them at all costs until we have given our oaths of allegiance, received our uniforms and gone to war."

"Cap," PFC Coon said in a raised voice to get JW's attention. Once he was acknowledged with a simple hand gesture of JW's right hand, PFC Coon asked, "What about food…Are we foraging…What are our limits for this journey?"

"There will be times for foraging, but only from farms or ranches that can afford to feed us, and our mounts. We're not out here to make war on the civilians we are supposed to be fighting this war for. There should be plenty of rivers for water, we may even stop to fish and slaughter a heifer from a larger herd. But we will find someone to ask first. Now if it ends up being a Yankee herd being brought up from Mexico, then we might just be California volunteers heading east to sign-up for the Union Cavalry. That means you southern boys keep your mouths shut." More laughter.

"That's it for now. We are going to see a lot of action and I'd estimated only a half of us will be coming home when this is all over. I'll give you another few minutes to think about it, then we ride east. Anyone wants to back out, you have my wishes for a safe ride back to your home. Arizona still needs brave men to defend our homes from the Apache."

ONCE MORE BACK ON THE TRAIL

Speed was kept to slow gate; a step above a walk and less than a gallop to save the mount's strength and still cover ground. JW was in the lead, with Liam at his side, his horse two-hands shorter than JW's Appaloosa. Behind them rode Sgt. Dreeke and two ranks of A Platoon. Then approximately 20-feet back rode Lt. Sampson, followed by two ranks of B Platoon. Two men rode nearly a half mile back as rear guard, with loaded Sharp .30 caliber Rifles standing up at the ready in the event of attack. Their task was to notify the main body of danger coming up from behind. All they had to do was pull-back on the rifle's hammer and pull the trigger. But an arrow in the heart or throat often made that impossible, and that is why there was two of them, in hopes one could get a warning shot off.

The rear guard was replaced every hour to ensure they stayed alert and both platoons pulled the duty. Actually Brady Williams, liked rear guard duty, because all the horses up front stirred up the sand and dust caused him to sneeze a lot.

When they pulled out, both platoons were at full strength. No one had returned to Tucson or Globe, though JW didn't think any of his Globe Rangers would pull out once they committed. He did wonder how many fights rang out across the desert last night. With Sherry Ann, she simply cried. She knew he had to go, but she was so frightened he wouldn't come back. But she did argue about Liam, saying he was too young. He won out in simply reminding her the boy was not theirs and would follow them one night all alone. "He'd probably get drafted into the Confederate Infantry, end up cannon fodder. At least this way I can protect him." Again, more tears.

When James told Miss Ruby about it outside her wagon, now parked in the ranch yard belonging to JW and Sherry Ann, she hugged him in a tight embrace. Then taking his cowboy flat brimmed leather hat off with her right hand, she followed the embrace up with an actual lengthy kiss of his chapped lips. Now, astonished beyond his dreams, the older man, whose eyes are now bugged out, watched as she gently pulled away. Without saying a word, she briefly held his rugged face between her small hands, smiled at him, nodded and then pulled away.

Then, without him being able to say a word, he watched as she climbed up the attached ladder into the back of her wagon, glanced once more at him and then went inside. The tarp was pulled closed and he could hear her weeping inside for him and this was a first, he had never been so touched. A woman, a lady was weeping for him and he didn't know how to respond. His instinct said, *back away, let her cry* and that is what he did.

So he walked over to the porch, set down and watched the stars. He was still sitting there in that chair when the first Ranger arrived and he walked over to stand by the yard's coral. Just him and Holloway, discussing the long ride ahead. Every once-in-a-while, he looked over his shoulder at the large wagon, but it was all quiet now.

NEW MEXICO TERRITORY

Leaving Arizona went off without a hitch. However, in New Mexico, they nearly ran into a Comanche hunting party. The scouts didn't take time to count them, but estimated their numbers at over 100 Indians. They were after buffalo. Scout Salcedo knew of this area, which was used often by the Comanche for Rites of Passage for their younger Indians into Manhood. Salcedo had been nearly trapped in the valley during one such event, but had learned of an old trail behind a low mountain range to the south. With Salcedo's guidance, the Rangers were able-to escape an encounter with the Comanche and three days later they entered Texas.

151

It was after their fourth night inside Texas, while stopping for the night, the three scouts came in with a Confederate patrol of cavalry. JW, who was kneeling by the fire, stood up. He saw the gray uniforms. They were led by a very young lieutenant. JW made a quick count and saw there were ten confederate soldiers.

"Sir, your scouts have informed me you're all former Arizona Rangers, seeking out the Army of Texas. Well, Sir, you have found the Army of Texas, at least a small part of it. Allow me to introduce myself. I am Second Lieutenant Pinwell, of Mobile, Alabama. This is my scout patrol, Sir and we all are assigned to scout and detect Union activity west of San Antonio. Can you all inform me of any such activity you may have passed through?" He spoke with a definite down south accent, but with a strong sense of education to his words.

"Lt. Pinwell, may I speak with you, alone?" JW asked. When the young officer complied, JW was prepared to rip him apart for violating so many protocols when meeting unknown parties during a time of war.

"Lieutenant, you are extremely lucky to have come across me and not some union patrol in civilian clothes. If that was the case, your whole patrol would be dead or at least held prisoner. Not only that, you advised me what Army you are assigned to, being the Army of Texas and approximately where I could find San Antonio. You also provided me with your General orders.

"In some instances, you could be shot for providing too much information to the enemy had I been a Union patrol or simply Union sympathizers. Do you understand what I am saying here, Lieutenant?"

The expression on the young lieutenant's face told it all, he was truly expecting to be shot at any moment and couldn't reply.

"It's all right, Lieutenant. I and my men have not enlisted in the Confederate Army, yet. We are truly former Arizona Rangers on our way to join up with the Army of Texas and we will all forget the events of this night. Now I would appreciate one or more of your men provide escort into San Antonio for us to accomplish our task. Would this be all right, Lieutenant?"

"Umm, yes, Sir...I'll take care of this myself. I believe I owe this to you and my sergeant can take over the squad."

"How long have you been an officer, Lt. Pinwell?" JW asked. He admired the man's uniform, surprised by how clean it was.

"Sir, I received my Second Lieutenant's Commission only last month. I finished college last year, but I avoided going into the military service until I had no choice. My father said it would be a grand adventure and he would no longer supplement me. It became the military or having-to work, so here I am. But I find myself a terrible officer, the men dislike me so and I am such a terrible rider. How is it for you, Sir…as a Ranger?"

"Slightly different, Lad. But no time for that now." JW gave his troops a once over and then asked Pinwell, "Any Comanche between here and San Antonio?"

"Only a few horse-stealing parties but they'll avoid a unit this size. We'll have to make a wide loop to the south to avoid a Comanche graveyard, it's very old, but still holy ground. They keep guards on this one and if someone steps on the land that shouldn't be there, the word goes out and within a night, you've got an angry war party at your camp, an' they come with scalp knives all shined up. No, our problem will be Union patrols. They've become a major pest here in Texas."

"Then let's get some sleep. I'll post four guards, changing them every three hours so they'll stay alert and we're up at daybreak for a quick cattleman's breakfast. Scouts out first, rear guard on hold and we leave shortly after the scouts. Sound good to you, Lieutenant?"

"Yes, Sir…with my men that will make us nearly a full company strength. Only those Yankee boys will mess with us, but the scouts should pick them up first." JW said. He walked over to his sleeping place, which had been set up by Liam. Saddle for a pillow, his thick roll laid out for a nice mattress and all his weapons handy in the event the camp was attacked. His horse blanket was shaken free and then laid back down on the horse's backside to help with the morning dew. Liam placed his roll to the right side of JW and Sgt. Dreeke slept on the opposite side.

Dinner was trail rations; jerky and hard tack. But when roasted on a stick the bacon jerky wasn't too bad. Hard tack, well, there wasn't a lot one could do to make hard tack palatable, but it did fill the stomach to some degree.

JW was up, just as the first graying of a new day sun began to appear in the East. Sgt. James Dreeke was next, followed by his younger brother. A fire was started and two five-gallon blue metal coffee pots— hanging from a camper's spit frame and showing the blackened burns of heavy usage—began boiling with this morning's hot coffee.

Breakfast done, horses fed, watered and saddled, the troop led off with 2Lt. Pinwell and his ten-men in the lead. Quite often, Pinwell fell back to chat with JW. Pinwell knew every moment with this old Ranger was a valuable lesson he'd never learn in a book or from the mouth of a professor. No, Pinwell sure wished the professors who taught military history, strategy and leadership were veterans, men who had gone off to see the elephant and experienced the bloodshed of war. Second Lieutenant

Pinwell still hadn't experienced such an event. However, he kept his Navy Colt and sword ready for when his time came.

SAN ANTONIO

The ride took over a month. They made it without losing a single man or horse. Yet, arriving at the outskirts of the biggest city most of these men had ever seen; they wondered if they won the war with Mexico. There were hundreds, if not thousands of Hispanics in the streets, pulling carts and driving wagons. The single-story adobe led into two and three story adobe buildings, some of them quite old. Multi-colored blankets hung from window openings. There was also a maze of balconies, with ribbons of gold, red and blue, yellow and orange flying freely in the breeze with one end tied to the building's roofs and upper porches.

As they began riding deeper into the town, the crowds became thicker and the streets narrower, smells changed from a pleasant to a pungent order. For here is where animals were slaughtered to feed locals and Confederate soldiers. Goats were halved and hung, pigs, sheep, beef and hundreds of chickens and ducks. Never had JW seen such a supply of butchered meat. The bugs, the flies, were terrible.

Scarves covered their faces. The flies attacked their eyes. The horses began going wild. Several of the Arizona riders had to dismount their horses to cover their mounts eyes, leading them on foot until they reached a wide river. They crossed on one of three heavily built wooden bridges, protected by a squad of Confederate soldiers, who recognizing Lt. Pinwell, allowed the whole unit to pass through without challenge. JW thought this to be another security violation, but said nothing.

On the other side of the blue-green river, where the Texicans lived as White men and only a few invited Hispanics, the Confederate Army of Texas, commanded by General Hood, made its temporary home. The Rangers couldn't help but notice all the gray uniforms everywhere, for Hood commanded thousands of men and was preparing for a new offensive against the North.

Lt. Pinwell stopped inside a large pavilion, dismounted and walked back to JW. "Would you and your Lt. Sampson be pleased to join me and we will report into the Officer of the Day?"

"This sure is an interesting town, I've never seen so many people all gathered together in one place. Where do all the troops live and stables for the horses?" JW asked as he dismounted and handed his reins over to Liam. The young boy was from the east, so he had seen a few big cities but the smell of the meat processing area was something he wouldn't soon forget.

"You all want me ta come in," James asked.

"No, you stay with the men. We've just passed a row of bars and right now I don't need a bunch of drunk enlistees spending the next ten days in jail for tearing up some Texas bar. All right?"

"Yes, Sir," James replied.

JW, Sampson and Pinwell walked through the front door of Headquarters, Army of Texas, with full intention of simply seeing the Officer of the Day, which is normally a Confederate major. However, with JW bringing to the Army of Texas such a large mounted unit of experienced riders, the well-known Arizona Rangers with combat experience in fighting the Apache and border Bandits, JW and Lt. Sampson were soon standing in front of General Hood himself.

By the time their short meeting was over, speeded up due to an attack up north upon General Hood's most northern perimeter guard, the men of Arizona were sworn into the Confederate Army by General Hood Himself and assigned the prescribed ranks as assigned by their Company Commander: Captain JW Blake, 2Lt. James Dreeke as A Platoon Leader and 1Lt. Bret Sampson as Second Platoon Leader. As the Rangers were unfamiliar with the east, a Colonel from Operational Command, assigned two ancient sergeants to the company to be the platoon Sergeant Majors. MSgt. Gary Wells would be assigned to First Platoon, while MSgt. Wallace Michaels would be assigned to Second Platoon. "You'll have your senior NCOs by morning, they'll be coming right off the battlefield," the Colonel said.

"Thank you, Sir," Captain JW Blake said. He then walked over to Strategic Placement and Plans to get the location for where his command would be bivouacked and who his regimental commander might be and where he could be found. Along with where he could find uniforms and weapons for his troops.

Once he had the information, he walked outside with Sampson at his side. He found a large gathering of men standing around, where he saw Liam still mounted. He hustled over to see what kind of problem his young hot shot had gotten into. When he arrived he found Liam still holding onto his horse's reins, attempting to keep a uniformed officer from mounting JW's horse.

JW burst through the last line of onlookers and noticed his men were keeping a company sized group of soldiers from rushing in to grab the horse for their officer. JW shook his head, stepped in and quickly took the reins from Liam's grasp, noticing the boy's hand was bleeding. He turned to face the officer, "Where I am from, Sir, attempting to steal a man's horse is a hanging offense."

"This is splendid horse flesh and I decided I desired it. So, now hand your horse over and we will forget about this matter, or do you wish to anger me and risk a firing squad?"

JW grew angry and in a raised voice he said, "Major, you're an officer and a gentleman, now act like it...before I slice those big ears of yours off and fry them in buffalo fat."

"What...What did you jus' say to me!?"

"Major, you throw your rank around like a Roman Caesar and you might do to remember as to what happened with them. Now my men and I have come from Arizona to fight for the Confederacy and we were just sworn in by General Hood himself. So, Sir, I request you drop this matter, because in the west we do not cotton to being threatened with a firing squad. Nope, I've killed too many Apache and Ute to just stand in front of a wall and let you drill me in the chest. So, I guess I'd have to do it the honorable way, Arizona style, I'll simply call you out and see how brave you are for a good old fashion gun fight. And, Major, this youngster here just saved your life, for this situation would've resulted in one of two ways. Had your men stolen my horse, my men would've killed every one of them with pistols and Bowie knives...and that means you too. Now had you been able-to get on my horse's back, I would've had no work to do, because he's killed every man who has tried except for me because I trained him Indian style. So, you might say thank you to this lad."

The look in the major's eyes was one of sheer hate, but the rising applause JW was receiving was even coming from some of the major's own men. They knew they would pay for it, but they respected valor and even tipped their hats to the boy.

Once the major was gone, marching his troop out, JW couldn't help but wonder how many of his men had whip marks on their backs. He had a feeling this was not the last time he'd be dealing with this arrogant jerk.

"All right, follow me and let's get our mounts down to our assigned stables. I am betting they'll need a good cleaning, so no griping. Once they're settled down we will claim our tents and set them up. With all the horse stealing around here I do not want to be too far from our horses and that'll mean nightly guards. A lot of us are riding Appaloosas and some other expensive costly stock. If a major tries stealing one, you can bet we got horse thieves in all the ranks."

Later that evening, after the eight-man tents were up and the cots finally figured out and set up, most all of them were ready for chow and a good night's sleep. When they made it to chow, most of the food was gone. The tin platters of beans, some pieces of bacon and cups of coffee were all that remained. Still, it was better then what they had on the trail.

Back around the main fire, JW told his troops the order of command. He doubted anyone was taking any notes, "We are F Company, which is the smallest of the six companies in Fifth Regiment, inside a six regiment Division. We are then inside Second Division inside a four Division Cavalry Force in the Army of Texas. Mounted soldiers account for 8,640 troops. The Army of Texas also has Artillery Units and Infantry, giving the Army of Texas roughly 24,000 troops in all."

"Wow!" A man in the back said and several agreed with him.

"Right, I agree with you and the Army of Texas is only one part of the Confederacy. This war is being fought with hundreds of thousands, if not millions of soldiers. Ours is just one small part of the larger scheme and this time, it's not against the Apache or Utes. We will be battling cavalry troops equally armed and going up against artillery. I've also been told we will be fighting against Blacks, who have been freed up north and they're fighting for this freedom. Do not misjudge them because they come from a foreign land and once were slaves. You might need to remember we came from foreign lands, some became slaves and we too fought for our freedom. So, be strong, be wary and never take anyone for granted. Always look for traps. Don't get sucked into a situation you cannot get out of. Alright, that's enough for tonight. Get some sleep. Tomorrow we will start training."

Another thing they had to do that night was get their uniforms prepared for duty. PFC troops wore one stripe on each sleeve, while the corporal wore two white chevrons. Basic sergeant wore three stripes and the count of chevrons went up based on how high their sergeant rank was. For Lt. Dreeke, this was the first time he had worn a lieutenant's bar since the earlier war. However, back then, he was in a Union blue tunic with a silver bar on his collar.

Scouts were allowed-to remain in civilian ware, but they risked being shot as spies if caught. So, Scout's Salcedo, Holloway and Jim Williams got their uniforms spruced up with the red scout tag sewn to the upper left shoulder — no rank shown. But the uniform kept them from being picked up as a spy.

Cavalrymen were issued swords, worn on the opposite side of their sidearm. The rifles they carried were the Spencer Carbine, a single-shot short barreled weapon. It was a hard weapon to reload on the run. Most cavalry troops used the rifle for the first long shot, then switched to their revolver for the charge, followed up by the sword for close-up fighting. This meant today JW needed his troops working on the sword dummies on the practice field. He knew his Globe Rangers would also be carrying their tomahawks, which meant the rest of them would want the blacksmiths making up a batch before his unit became operational.

For four hours in the morning and four hours in the afternoon, F Company worked hard to be ready for war. Even General Hood came out once to watch them work over the dummies with those tomahawks and swords. If he had time he would've ordered more of those weapons for the rest of his cavalry, but he now knew why the Rangers were able-to keep the Apache and Comanche at bay throughout the Southwest. These men of the Texas, New Mexico and Arizona Rangers were fearless and he was blessed to have them on his side.

ORDERS ARRIVE—F COMPANY IS OPERATIONAL

Their two weeks of training over, F Company is ordered up to join their regiment to the north for an upcoming engagement against the Yankees. It is now October 3, 1863.

BACK HOME IN ARIZONA

Mail has been slow and very few letters reached the families of the Rangers, or going the other ways to the ex-Rangers. The Army of California arrived in Arizona pushing out the remaining confederates and their sympathizers. A new pro-Union government is in place, curfews are in order and new federal taxes are installed. As taxes rise beyond what people can afford to pay, their properties are seized and the time of the carpet bagger begins as profiteering becomes a sudden reality. Two-bit lawyers working for major law firms and well-to-do families arrive in Arizona to buy up seized land at rock-bottom prices, including cattle herds. Arizona banks go bankrupt trying to help bail out old and trusty friends, and Union troops are protecting slippery lawyers as they throw whole families off land they have owned for decades. Some Hispanic lands showed histories going back several hundred years, but none of that matters now. Even though the land was granted to the family after the earlier war for services the family had provided in helping with that war. It didn't matter, as some of the land even dated earlier, belonging to Hispanic gentlemen falling inside Indian Missions in-order-to protect the White man. Now it was all gone, because of inflated tax and someone up in New York or Chicago who paid the tax bill so they could own the land, the cattle or even the water rights. This was a sad time for Arizona and it was only worsening.

THE ATTACK

Artillery cannons from across the field announced the Union Army's advance across the grassy plain of West Virginia — one of the few cleared spots amongst the forests of green. "This is not a good spot for mounted troops to engage the enemy." MSgt. Gary Wells said to Lt. Dreeke.

"Yuh gots mah vote," James replied. By now he and Gary had become good friends. Both served in the US-Mexican War as Second Lieutenants, each former enlisted men, who now, babysit young Captains. James followed JW into the Rangers. Gary entered the Holy Roller business becoming a horse-riding pastor. When this war broke out, Gary built his first church outside a small town. He could not desert his southern boys. He followed them into the Confederacy. Based on his education, past rank and former experiences, he was offered a First lieutenant's commission. He declined it, accepting his current rank. Every Wednesday evening and Sunday morning, MSgt. Gary Wells—sometimes called Pastor Wells, when not on the battlefield—conducted prayer services and Bible teaching. He was ready for counseling and helping with letter writing. Hearing about this man, even JW attended the services to listen to the man's preaching; which eventually brought the whole company together for Sunday morning services.

"He had his own church back in South Texas…liked to consider himself what he called a non-denominational pastor, or so I am told," MSgt. Michaels had told Lt. Sampson and Lt. Reeves. "He told me once he didn't want to be confined to one church's doctrines...some which he felt might conflict with God's Law. I never understood that, but he is a travelin' man."

Companies E and F were sent to a southeast position, which amounted to 85 cavalry troops. More than half of this number were from E Company, which was commanded by Major Bannon of Austin, Texas. Most of his troops had come from the Texas capital. The Bannon ranch was well known, carrying the Sleeping B brand on more than 50,000 head of cattle and nearly an equal number of horses. As far as size went, the Bannon Ranch currently spanned 125,000 acres. If Bannon's marriage to Kathleen Turner—oldest daughter to retired Colonel Isaac Turner and former State Senator of four terms—their combined ranch would be nearly double in size. Colonel Turner had no sons, so his Will had his ranch going to Kathleen, upon her marriage or her 25th birthday. Until then, ranch affairs would be managed by the local bank. As-of-yet, the good colonel was still alive making everyone's life a miserable state of affairs—especially Kathleen's.

Major Bannon was the ranking officer. He had no love for Arizona cowboys, so he assigned F Company to hold the open area between E Company and D Company. Normally, the situation would've been just the opposite. Major Bannon wanted his command to be closer to the tree line if artillery bombardment became too intense, so his troopers could withdraw into the thick grove of trees.

Captain Blake didn't complain, though he fully understood a frightened man when he saw one. So far, he was not overly impressed by the majors in the Army of Texas. Rather than object, he complied, stationing his men in two ranks. He rode slowly back and forth in front of his company. In a raised voice, he reminded them, "Relax some, but remain mounted and in your lines. Listen up for your orders and all Glory to the South...Let us show them Yankees what some Arizona Rangers can do against their artillery. Remember, its rifle...then revolvers, then swords and tomahawks. If you cannot hold both, I recommend the tomahawk for the sheer shock value it causes. It's our intention to get those soldiers running, to abandon their field pieces and provide our army with new artillery. Kill if you must, but prisoners are important for what they may know and using them to trade for our own."

Before JW could ask for questions, the first trumpet blow sounded off, followed by several others echoing the warning blow. The next tune would be for the attack and then, with rifle raised over his head, JW would lead his two ranks of F Company out into the battlefield, and within range of the Union five-pounders.

According-to intelligence reports, the Union Artillery consisted of 45-guns, each with a four-man crew. They were supported by several squads of infantry, and a dozen in all snipers. Two hundred-yards behind the artillery, wagons filled with gun powder and the heavy five-pound balls followed. Supplies were carried to the guns by assigned infantry men. Three first aid wagons were available to deal with any wounded. There were 45-carts and horses used to pull each of the artillery pieces.

Unlike the Union side, where only a small force on foot supported their guns, General Hood assigned an entire infantry regiment follow-up behind the cavalry. Hood knew how important this clearing meant. He wished to position an airship here for observation — one of the few balloons the South had in their possession; a gift from the French.

This was considered a strategic target. He also needed those 45 pieces of artillery, along with all the ammo and powder the wagons carried. He needed a strong, rapid hit to secure those guns and wagons, but there was only enough room in the clearing for the Fifth Regiment to be used. He further felt secure in the knowledge the Arizona boys were in on this attack.

The awaited sound of the second trumpet carries across the field. Each Company Commander raises his rifle, issuing the order, "Move out." For the first 100-yards, they moved at slow gait, gradually speeding up as their commander pumps his arm holding the rifle up. The first artillery-round is fired; followed almost immediately by 44 other cannons. Five-pound balls burst over the surface; shrapnel springing out in 360-degree radius. Other balls hit the ground, bouncing, knocking horse and rider to the ground.

"Charge!" JW Ordered. If he wasn't heard, the men assuredly saw him dashing toward the guns, his rifle now lowered to the level of the butt of his revolver. "Come On, Rangers!" He yelled as his second order. With so much noise out there, he wasn't sure if anyone could hear him.

One cannon ball struck the grassy dirt only a few feet from him. It was a bouncer. He turned, watching it mow down two horses and their riders. He didn't have time to consider who it might've been that went down.

F Company was within rifle range. He raised his rifle up over his head, giving the signal to his troops. He brought it down, sighted in on a soldier carrying a five-pound ball to the cannon right in front of JW. Having shot a lot of Apache from horseback, JW was not surprised when he saw the Union troop drop to his knees, a .30 caliber ball in his chest. The five-pound ball rolled out of his hand and he fell on his face. A second Yankee looked down at the fallen soldier. He then looked up at the Rebels coming right at them. They shouted and screamed their rebel yells. He dropped his cannon plunger and ran.

Captain JW simply let go of his rifle, drawing his Colt Navy Revolver. It had five-shots loaded. He cocked it with a hammer pull to move the first ball into play. He shot the third man at the gun. That was enough to send the fourth man running back towards the wagons. He left his rifle beside his artillery piece stacked up in the grass as required per regulation. Not having anything to fight with, he kept running away from the battlefield. He was one of the first troops to begin a massive retreat.

Revolver holstered, tomahawk and sword in hand, JW used his knees to direct his beautiful Appaloosa. He charged in amongst the Union artillery crew. Some of the Union boys couldn't reach their rifles before the cavalry was in their midst. At two points in the battle, horse riders were destroyed, nearly disintegrating, as they rode right up in front of the cannon, just as the weapon was ignited. The cavalry troops rode past artillery pieces as the troops charged to secure the wagons, carts and horses tied up in the distance that were used for work detail.

Brief battles were fought here and there, but once the Fifth Regiment broke through the line, breaking the spirit of the Union soldiers. Over a hundred escaped on foot into the woods behind the wagons; however, 189 prisoners were captured in this battle. Commander's Call reported the Fifth Regiment secured 41 of the 45 artillery-pieces — four were destroyed. All but two of the wagons were secured, along with all carts. Most of the mounts were recovered, however it appeared some escapees rode away. They recovered all three hospital wagons, capturing one doctor, two aides, and three nurses. They were busy assisting both Union and Confederate wounded. They set up a field hospital in the middle of the clearing.

On the negative side, the Fifth Regiment lost 34 troopers and sustained 87 wounded. Fifty-nine horses were killed in battle and another 68 had to be destroyed. A massive gravesite was dug for the cavalry mounts, while individual grave sites were dug for troopers and the infantrymen.

"You will return to your commands and take stock of what you have lost. Send your runners to my Command Center with your replacement needs, for troopers and mounts. I expect you to work with supply for your equipment needs.

Regimental Commander then called in Major Bannon into his tent and had heated words with him regarding his taking it upon himself for altering the alignment of the regiment, on the battlefield. The Commander was loud enough for half of the encampment to overhear him and he came out of the tent with a dark shade of red to his cheeks. He found JW and in front of his troops, Major Bannon apologized for violating orders and placing his command in jeopardy. He then left to rejoin his command. Before morning his officers would find that he had deserted his command and fled Texas. He was never heard from again, but one story was told of how he was shot over a bad poker deal in New Orleans after the Civil War ended.

When Captain JW Blake left Commander's Call and returned to his Company, he met with his two officers and asked for the names of the men they had lost in this attack. First Lieutenant Bret Sampson, being the ranking officer, replied first. "Sir, it is my sad business to report we lost three brave men and their mounts: PFC Dan Richards…an Arizona Ranger for two years, PFC Rudy Halverson…a Ranger for five years, and PFC Jimmy Carswell…a Ranger for five years and former Union Sergeant. PFC's Klein, Ringer, Becks, and Chris Wakefield are marked as being wound. We should have all four of them back within the week, but two of them will need new mounts."

"You fared better than I expected, Lieutenant. I am glad to see you survived our first engagement. Riding against those guns reminded me too much of the Mexican War. Now how about you, Lt. Dreeke?"

James couldn't speak at first, he had been with each-and-every one of these men through thick and thin. They had fought through the icy cold nights of a desert winter and hiked for miles in search of water during the scorching summer days, only to be ambushed by Apache warriors. Yet they had survived.

"Sir, ah need not tell yuh how long dese four troopers we los' have a ridden wit' us as Rangers, an' dis is no negative reflection on thu Rangers from Tucson. For dey have proven demselves to be Rangers an' ah was proud ta know each an' every one of dem. But for thu Captain and ah, as it is wit' yuh an' your men, we have a ridden far an' wide wit' dese gentlemen. Today, we said goodbye ta Corporal Gibson...big guy, who was said ta have taken a cannon ball in thu chest ta knock him off his mount. PFC Miller, who could ride further than any man ah knew wit'out water, an' had dis mystery 'bout him in thu way he talked ta horses. We also los' PFC Lloyd Grimes, who had jus' returned ta thu Rangers from ah job as ah Deputy Marshal. Ah guess he miss't thu long rides." James then hesitated.

"Who else did we lose, Jamey?"

"Sir, we lost...Ah buried Sgt. Joshua Dreeke...Mah baby brudder. He was kilt once we had made thu breakthrough an was ridin' for thu wagons. He took two mini-balls ta thu chest...Ah believe he was dead 'fore he done hit thu ground, or at least ah hope."

JW looked down at his scuffed-up riding boots, unable to think up what he should say. He could feel his eyes were welling up and reached up to wipe the tears away. That gesture was better than anything JW could have said and in response, James replied a whisper of, "Thank yuh, Sir."

JW look over at Lt. Sampson and said in gentle tone, "You know our runner, Liam. When I first met young Joshua Dreeke, he was even younger. We'd come home from the Mexican War, Jamey and I. Most of our original unit had been wiped out, seems we're always being volunteered for behind the lines stuff and this old man spent most of his time protecting my life. Then we became Rangers and he did the same thing. When little Joshua was old enough and we couldn't talk him out of it, he joined the unit and big brother made it rough. But the kid had killed his fiftieth Renegade Indian by the end of his first year."

"We all hated the gun runners, bandits coming across the border to steal cattle and those new Comancheros who were White men who rode with the Apache, but Joshua, he had this strange sixth sense in finding them." JW was quiet for a moment and then he said, "We will all miss him."

"My condolences, James." Lt. Sampson said.

"Thank you, Bret." James said slowly, losing most of his accent.

"What about wounded?" JW asked.

James shook his head in wonder, "Except for you and I, our bunch all came home with some piece of lead in them. But none too seriously. Everyone should be horse ready by the end of the week, but don't plan on any square dances and we'll need eight…maybe nine mounts. Five had to be destroyed, including my beautiful babe. I gave yours and Liam's a good going over, but nothing serious. Oh, Liam has some scrapes, a few cuts and a gash here and there, but he is sure proud of them. He now had real war wounds to talk about when we get back to Arizona."

THE ENCAMPMENT

That same night, the regiment of cavalry filled the clearing, with the five-pound artillery pieces formed in a massive circle and now pointed outward. Horses were staked out inside the circle, tied off to ground lines between field guns, with all the hospital wagons positioned with canopy tents for the wounded to protect them from the night's sprinkling and morning dew. The dead were all covered so the scent of decay was not present as-of-yet. Meanwhile, a Company of Infantry was given the task of performing guard duty in four-hour stints; then replaced by another unit.

With the news sent, General Hood decided to let the Fifth Regiment and the assigned Infantry remain on scene for five-days to recoup and receive replacements. All JW had to be concerned about was his mournful Lt. Dreeke and what kind of replacements they would receive.

He shared a log with MSgt. Gary Wells, in front of a low evening fire as the moon first made its appearance. "I've never lost so many men in one scrape before. Four very good friends…all dead and this was our first fight against the Yankees. Maybe I was wrong to bring them here, having them follow me."

"Captain, from what I've seen of your Rangers, they would've followed you to the surface of the sun. Now try to think about what would've happened to them had they stayed home? Most of them would assuredly be dead now for defending their homes and their families against this rash of northern carpet baggers. I understand they call them that because their bags are made from old carpet material.

"Now it's not the Union soldiers fault, they're as poor as we all are and living on $7 a month. Maybe we cannot even blame Lincoln, but he's the one who's signed these tax bills in being…granting seizure laws the rich and their lawyers can use to move in and buy up the U.S. southlands. Here, you're thinking about Arizona, but wait and see what happens if the South loses this war. Those rich bottom dwellers will be down there buying up whole plantations for penny an acre and they'll get the land because the property owners are broke. In so many cases, big plantations were owned by men who became Confederate Colonels and Generals and they used all their money to raise up their regiments and divisions."

"What about this slavery issue, will the North be able to help on these southern slaves?" JW asked. He had pondered this question often, but had never actually brought it up to anyone.

"I've been told by my Northern Christian brothers of how Lincoln had never planned to free the slaves right off, for fear the Black men and women would find themselves out of work and the White people fearful to hire them. Soon, they would then cause problems simply because they were going hungry and needed housing. Then came a time when Lincoln was told the Army needed additional troops and granting freedom could spur the northern Blacks into enlisting into the Army. Which is exactly what happened. But there are also Blacks loyal to the south, who have enlisted to form up Black regiments. Now I don't know if the Blacks will be used to make war on one another, guard supply trains or guard prisons. But things are happening."

"I still have my family back home outside of Globe, Arizona…I haven't had a letter from them since I left. I know mail is slow, but I had no idea it was this slow. As far as I know, they could've been kicked off my land by these carpetbaggers, killed by the Apache or kidnapped by the Banditos. The list is long and worrisome." JW picked up his now empty camp coffee cup, which came with an array of dents and burned-black marks, and asked Corporal Brady Williams for a refill of the boiling hot, but savory brew. Thanks to taking the Union wagons, the Fifth Regiment had scored on a good supply West Virginia Hams and some decent smelling coffee grounds. There were enough ten-pounder bags of coffee to go around so each company obtained three-bags. Spits were built for the hams to be reheated, though they had already been well-smoked.

The wagons also held an ample supply of feed for the horses, even based on the amount ridden off by frightened deserters and those killed. So, JW's Appaloosa was eating well tonight, much better than he ate back home on the trail.

There were mostly Globe Rangers sitting around the fire tonight with the Captain, the Tucson boys knew both fires had their own wakes going on for the men they had lost. But it was Lt. Dreeke, who suffered the loss of a younger brother that made the first move. He came over to JW, stood over him and patted him on the left shoulder, "C'mon, JW, we're one big family now. You know Joshua would've wanted it this way."

As James walked over to join in with the Tucson wake, JW and the rest of the men followed. Once there, MSgt. Gary Wells told a Bible story, of Jonathan and His Armor Barer. By the time he was finished all the men were thinking of today's attack and how they had done it together, just as Jonathan and his Armor Barer had. Gary then jumped into leading the song, "We're Tenting Tonight," which almost immediately had everyone singing in low reverent voices. After tonight, it was F Company and no longer the Globe and Tucson Rangers.

CHAPTER SEVEN

"Captain, you don't think those dumb Yankees are smart enough to pull no weasel in the Henhouse trick on us, do yuh?"

ENTERING TENNESSEE, ARMY OF TEXAS—UNDER GENERAL HOOD, NUMBERED TWENTY-FOUR THOUSAND CONFEDERATE TROOPS

Rain had fallen for the last week or so. The ground was mushy, with the hooves of the horses sinking in a good two to three-inches. There was a good possibility of sliding along for up to a foot until a tree stopped you. On such a surface, no one was about to make a "charge" through these Tennessee forests that one never saw an end too. The trees went up one valley and down another, and where a desert horse could break its leg or worse. They'd been warned there were Indians in this area of woods, but the Scouts had not found any evidence of them, except for the occasional arrow shot into the tree as warning to leave the area.

Since that first attack against the artillery position, the Fifth Regiment had engaged the Union boys in 19 total engagements, most of them quite costly. But they were the winners—If anyone could say such a thing was victory—of the first eight engagements, but then things began changing.

The soldier's uniforms began rotting. There was no sign of replacement uniforms or gear coming from supply. So the dead were stripped of their uniforms and service equipment, especially their boots. Food was also on short supply. The men foraged from wherever they could. Even the officers turned aside so as to not identify the culprits if harm was done to a farm owner or his workers. Worse yet, some officers became involved, leading in the looting and destroying small Southern towns. When commanders learned of it, the renegade troops were sought out for court-martial. Those involved were punished severely. For the officers, this severe punishment meant death by hanging for dishonoring the officer corps of the Confederate Army. But worse was yet to come. The South lost at Gettysburg, with the destruction of three whole Confederate Corps; which broke the back of the South.

Still, battles raged on. The North now had the advantage with fresh supplies and new replacements coming in from Ohio, Iowa, Oklahoma and the north east coastal regions. The Northern sea blockades kept French and British supplies from getting in and Southern cotton from getting out. Great sea battles were fought on the entrance of the Mississippi, in the Gulf of Mexico off of Louisiana and around the tip of Florida to Virginia. This was the time of metal war-boats and ships made of hard oak, referred to as "Ironsides". The North had the advantage in numbers and the manufacturing capabilities.

During one battle, Captain JW Blake lost his beloved mount, shot by a sniper hiding in a tree. On foot, JW led his men on, swinging of both his scratched and nicked up sword, and his blackened tomahawk, now drenched in blood from a duel with a Union Colonel. The man sought to run his saber through JW's chest, but it quickly became apparent he had no experience in close combat. JW, now on the ground beside his dying horse, deflected the sword easily with his own sword and swung around with a death blow from his tomahawk to the startled Union officer. He was dead before he fell off his horse to roll across the grassy ground.

The field was filled with the dead and dying that day, but there were many acts of valor by gallant troopers on both sides. JW respected a Union Private who was wounded on his shoulder and leg and still attempted protecting three wounded comrades. For this bravery, JW ordered his troops to bypass the four wounded men; allowing Union aid workers to reach these men. JW, backed by Lt. Dreeke, whose left arm was wounded by a sword cut, approached the wounded Union soldier and JW knelt beside him. He first removed his weapons; then offered him a drink of water from his own canteen. This surprised the soldier, but he accepted it. "You are a courageous young man, Sir. Had you lived in Arizona, where I am from, I would've been proud to have had you in my Rangers."

"Rangers?" The man whispered in reply.

"Yes, Arizona Rangers. We dealt with the Apache, Ute and border bandits. So, get healed up and after this war is over, you come visit us." JW placed his right hand on the youth's chest, said a brief prayer and then stood up to return to the war. His strange act of kindness did not escape notice; because this fallen troop did not escape a Union sniper's vision. He lowered his rifle, released a sigh and found a different target. A fellow Christian, he wouldn't kill any man who could be praying over his enemy, today.

By the time the Confederacy retreated, Fifth Regiment lost over a-third of its 360 troopers. A-Platoon had not lost a man, though every single man came away with a wound or wounds. Only Corp. Leaders, Scout Jim Williams, Corp. Gibson, Runner Liam and MSgt. Wells, along with Lt. James Dreeke were still riding their personal mounts.

Over half of the horses they rode into the battle were dead. Several troopers were caught-up with rider-less mounts. If time allowed, they transferred their equipment over. Or they quickly fled from the advancing Union infantry and their barrages of .54 caliber mini-balls. The Rebel infantry in the rear provided a protective barricade for the riders to fall back to and the Union boys were ordered not to advance any further before sunset.

However, B Platoon took a licking. They lost MSgt. Wallace Michaels, who was believed to be seriously wounded and a Prisoner of War, along with PFC Sigmund Udo, whose mount was shot from under him. He was bayoneted to the upper thigh by a frightened 15-year old kid from Iowa. PFC Andy Salcedo was hit over the back of the head with the stock of a Union rifle by another young troop who had forgotten how to reload his rifle. Salcedo was seen being dragged off toward the rear. JW suspected the Union Commanders wanted prisoners for the same reason the Southern Generals wanted them — Information in the ranks concerning morale, welfare and is the South ready to surrender. But the Southern Boys had a big surprise for their interrogators; they turned out to be a most stubborn lot and there was a lot of fight still in them.

PFC's Zack Ringer, William Klein, Sam Donaldson and Jerry Beck were all killed in action, and the act witnessed by at least one other trooper. Corporal's Leo D. Wakefield and his brothers, Chris Wakefield and Dan Wakefield all received nasty wounds requiring multiple stitches or field surgery. Chris was on his third wound and a surgeon wanted to remove his left arm, but his brothers threatened to kill the doctor if he tried it and Captain JW Blake supported them. But he lost most of the use of his left hand due to nerve damage, though he could still hold a horse's reins if wrapped around the hand. Lt. Bret Sampson received several minor wounds and a near-death miss with a mini-ball that slid across the side of his skull and right above his left ear.

Captain JW Blake's F Company was now down to 14-troopers and before their next action they needed time to heal. But on their second day off the battlefield, they pulled back to the Divisional Encampment in the Southwest tip of Tennessee, Captain Blake was summoned to Corps Command. This was where he met with General Hood, Commander of the Army of Texas.

The meeting was brief and it was over a table top sized map of the State of Tennessee. It was here JW learned F Company no longer existed. He was now assigned to Hood's headquarters as a Scout Platoon. He was to receive four new men and two Indians who knew Tennessee, and Hood wanted to know where Grant had his main force situated. Hood planned on attacking Nashville, but not knowing where Grant's cavalry troops were, would make planning his attack difficult. General Lee had his primary generals situated further east, but Hood would be involved in a three Division attack to secure the city and waterways. It would be a major morale booster for the men of the confederacy. He was ordered to move out in four-days, for Hood knew the condition of his troopers and added, "You'll leave behind any man who is unable to make the ride, Captain and knowing how you and your Rangers worked in Indian Territory, I know you can move very quietly to be avoided. Am I understood?"

"Yes, General." JW said and then he left the Headquarters Tent, walked outside to examine the busy encampment and walked over to his horse, which was being held by Runner Liam. Rather than mount, he accepted the reins of the 16-hand golden mare with one white sock, and began walking across the field. He was looking for the Enlistment Tent. When he located it, he noticed there didn't seem to be much interest or desire in the Tennessee boys for signing up in this here war. At least for the South that is. He tied his mount to a provided wooden horse rail and told Liam to do the same.

Less than an hour later, riding into their encampment area, Runner Liam was riding tall. He was a brand new Private in the Army of the Confederacy and earning $4.65 a month. If he survived and did well enough to be recommended by his commander for promotion, he could be promoted to Private First Class. Of course, he still looked as if he was 12-years old, but now he was in a cavalry uniform with full weapons. JW didn't want to spoil the moment by telling Liam of how the uniform and equipment was all second-hand and was taken off the dead. He already had a good mount and had sustained two wounds in combat. But now, if JW wanted to, he could file reports on his acts of gallantry. "The kid is like some weird magnet, Jamey…he's always feeling a coming battle long before I can hear a sound."

James, who was sitting beside him outside JW's tent, said, "Maybe you're tryin' ta say he's ah Prophet an' knows what is 'bout ta happen. Good t'ing den ta keep him up dere in front of us."

"We've got three more days to heal up and get these new mounts trained up. You and MSgt. Wells work on our rations and supplies. Our guides should be here tomorrow, but I'm a wondering what sort of Indians we get that live in this area. Sure beautiful land for trapping and raising a family. I don't imagine there partial to seeing two armies fight all over the land and scaring the game away. I ain't seen a deer or a bear since we arrived here."

Before James could respond, Scout Jim Williams, with his left arm in a sling and slightly limping from a bad spell, was leading two attractive looking Indians across the large Divisional Encampment and up to where the new Scout Detachment was calling home. Behind them came Scout Holloway, some ten-yards behind. He carried the Indians' rifles, which were decorated with turkey and eagle feathers. They were escorted by a party of ten Confederate soldiers, young troops who had never seen wild

Indians before. Each Indian wore face paint of a brownish and green color, and they wore their black hair in long braided ponytails. They wore no shirts, but carried powder and shot pouches across their shoulders. Leather pants with fringe covered their legs and a fancy braided piece of material dropped from the top of their pants to cover the manhood area. On their right side, they wore metal knives traded for from a fur buying trading post, and a trader's metal tomahawk hung from their left hip. Their moccasins were colorful with great works of beads worn calf-high, with a leather tie strap to hold them in place. JW believed the leather was mostly, if not all, deer. Yet, he was later surprised Elk was a major supplier of the Choctaw's leather, backed up by deer and the occasional black bear. JW suspected and learned the thicker soles of the moccasins were buffalo hide or bear hide, as it appeared to be tougher than Elk. The Choctaw, though they occasionally used horses were mostly foot warriors who used horses to haul their meat and furs.

JW and James stood to their feet, "Do you speak American?"

The taller of the two spoke and his words amazed the crowd of men, "Yes, we speak your language. We are the two guides you were told to expect."

"You are welcome in my camp and I am happy you speak our language so well. Please, you must understand my lack of knowledge, for I am from the Arizona Territory and the Indians we know of are the Apache, the Ute and Navajo, and some other peaceful tribes. But I have never come across an Indian such as you. Please tell me what tribe you are and why do you...your tribe wish to help the Confederacy?" JW reached out with his hands and without an argument, he took possession of one of the rifles the Indians were carrying and he was at a loss for words. He could see his reflection in the heavy brass work of the incredible Henry repeater.

JW continued to speak as he examined the Henry, "My name is Captain John Blake and I'll be leading this scout unit ahead of General Hood's Command. What is your names?"

"In the missionary school, I was given the name Peter, but when I returned to my people I was given a warrior's name that in English means Black-Eagle." He then looked to his companion, gestured with his right hand and said, "His name is Man-Who-Runs, but his English is not too good for he only spent two years in the missionary school. His father died and he had to return home to take care of his family." He glanced at Private Liam and saw a young man equal in age to Man-Who-Runs and it saddened him.

"We have heard of these great nations and of this Arizona you have come from. We come mostly from Oklahoma, but before this we had covered many of your states. We are the Choctaws and in my grandfather's youth it was said we numbered in the hundreds of thousands. Our cousins were the Comanche of Texas, but war came between us and now both our tribes dwindle in size." He looked over the rifle in JW hands. "I was educated in Christian Missionary School from the age of five years until I was 16 years. I am what you would call a General in my tribe, but the Choctaw are no longer at war. Our numbers are too few to fight. We have farms and ranches in Oklahoma and Southern troops have come to offer us peace if we help your side. But the Northern side, all they promise us is federal reservations to live upon because they are afraid of us. We mean no harm, our time to fight has come and gone. We had fought the Mexican and drove them south long before I was born. Now we use our weapons to hunt the animals to feed our tribe. Much as it will be for the Apache and Comanche. Even the great Sioux will find their days drawing fewer and fewer, and they still number in the thousands...but they stay to the north."

"This rifle, it's amazing...I've never seen anything like it before...The workmanship is superior to anything I have ever seen...But I have read of one like this rifle coming to the West. How'd you get it and tell me about its firing." JW asked, as he ran his hands up and down the side of the Henry Rifle. He then noticed how easily he left his fingerprints and hand prints all over the brass work. So, he pulled his rifle cloth he kept in his rifle pouch and began cleaning all the brass work before he handed the rifle back.

"This does not belong to me...I am...testing this in the field...I was told to say. This is one of many prototypes...a word I do not understand, but was said to use when asked, being used for several months to see if the rifle can handle the...rigors of the field. This word 'rigors' also another strange word for me, though I like how it sounds. It can carry 15 bullets in the long casing below the barrel, but bullets that come also in brass cases. You no use black power, nor a ramming rod. Plus, one ready to fire and this lever action reloads each bullet one at a time and the shot shell is...ejected is the word, out the top." He then added, "You can reload these 16 bullets faster than it would take you to reload three black powder."

"This would turn a regiment of infantry into a whole Division...but how long before a thousand of these rifles will be made?" He returned the cleaned off rifle to the Choctaw warrior and added, "You speak our language better than some of my own men do. Your missionary teachers taught you very well."

"They were a fine couple, but school is still there with new younger couple. Old Couple have gone on to be with God and receive their great reward for such work as they did."

"I am impressed, Black Eagle. How many Christians among your tribe?" JW asked.

"More than half of my tribe is Christian, but the Choctaw have many small tribal groups and the Christian missionaries have walked among them as friends. No harm will ever come to a Christian Holy Man in the Choctaw land...at least by a Choctaw. But now we have Blue and Gray soldiers on our hunting grounds which covers much of Tennessee. But with the coming of your civilization, we studied much on this...and this war, our hunting grounds have been lost to use. Now we are Oklahoma and here we will stay. They talk of building a Indian College in Oklahoma, so we become educated in White man's way, to learn and progress to walk among you as equals...someday."

"I fear that day will not be soon, my friend, but I do wish it will come while you still live so you would see our promises fulfilled, our treaties among friends upheld. I value the Indian courage, your valor and refusal to give up. But it is the savagery I fear, that which was taught to you by bad White men and those people from Europe who came first. I have had to fight the Apache, the Ute and even the Navajo, but in most of those battles I respected my opponent. Can you understand that, Black-Eagle?"

Black-Eagle studied JW for a moment and looked deeply into his weary eyes. He then replied, "I see what is in your heart and now know you to be a true man. I and Man-Who-Runs will work with you and show you Tennessee."

"Thank you, Black-Eagle and you also, Man-Who-Runs." JW said and then reached out with his right hand to grasp the right inner arm of each Scout, Indian fashion. He then introduced them to Lt. Sampson, Lt. Dreeke and MSgt. Wells. Over the next week, Black-Eagle and Gary Wells would become good friends, sharing in their common belief of the Lord Jesus Christ and reading of the Bible together. Other members of the platoon would also join and along the way PFC Coon prayed the sinner's prayer and was welcomed into the Army of God. It amazed everyone to have a Choctaw Indian praying over the man and from memory saying the Lord's Prayer.

Later that evening the four scouts sent over by General Hood made their appearance and reported to Captain Blake's campfire. "Sir, I'm Corporal Eric Stonewall of Nashville, Tennessee, this is PFC Zachary Jackson...yes, he's a distant cousin to the former President, and I thought I'd tell you before he started bragging about it." Stonewall spoke with a Tennessee-twang to his voice and JW liked the way it sounded.

"Here's PFC Leonard Sanders and his cousin, James Sanders of Missouri. Both from the Ozark Mountains, but they both know Tennessee pretty darn well. And, Captain, I'll tell you right now, these two boys are mighty embarrassed 'bout half their family goin' to fight as Yankees. So, I wanted ta get it all out in the open. We've been a scoutin' for the General for the last six-months."

"I am pleased to meet you men and thankful you arrived a couple days before we were due to depart. I'd like you to draw me up some maps of the 60 or so miles in front of us and the best routes to take to keep an eye on those Yankees. Our job is to ensure the General is not surprised. I'd also like to of any Southern troops out in front of belonging to another corps." JW then introduced the four scouts to the unit's command staff. When he began to introduce the two Choctaw, he realized the six Scouts all knew each other by the arms grasps and shoulder slaps.

"I see you all know each other." JW said.

"Oh, yes, Sir," Corporal Stonewall replied. We've done scouted together for the last couple of months. Good men to be out in the wilderness with and they've taught us a lot about being as quiet as a mouse when you got Yankee riding over the top of you. And I've tried to talk that rifle away from Black-Eagle the whole time. I've offered him money, trade of horses and even tried to get him into playing cards, but he don't gamble. First Christian Indian I ever knowed. But he's also the best shot I ever seen…takin' down our dinner or nailin' a Yankee scout at 500-yards."

"Yes, I look forward to the day we're all issued those rifles, it will forever change the West," JW said.

Stonewall was about to say something, when MSgt. Gary Wells offered him a boiling hot cup of coffee. Steam was still coming from the top of the cup when Stonewall took his first sip. He whispered, "Ahhh…man's coffee. Burn the lips, char the teeth an' make the tummy forget its problems."

MSgt. Gary Wells spoke up, "I was talking with a headquarters Sgt. Major and he'd heard the Winchester Manufacturing Company was supposed to be coming out with a new lever action rifle to rival the Henry and cost less. Won't have all that fancy brass work."

"But I like that fancy brass," Lt. James Dreeke said.

"All right, all of you hold it down. Wars always bring out new killing equipment. It's how those big companies make their money for their stockholders. But we'll never be able to afford one on military pay or Ranger pay. Even $30 a month cowhand's pay won't be enough for a $300 or more rifle. Those first Henry's like the one Black-Eagle is testing for the Henry Company will be costing $500 or more and then there's the ammo. For the first year or so the ammunition for these lever-action rifles will be considered rare and you'll have to order it from a big city and get it out here by stage and that when this war ends."

"Not to forget which side wins and what kind of rules the victor lays down," Lt. Sampson said.

"Right, if in thu Northern boys win, we may not be able ta own no rifles…maybe no shotguns for fear we kick somethin' up 'gain. We'd have ta get Black-Eagle teach us how ta make bows an' arrows for huntin'."

JW was shaking his head and then held up his hands to get everyone attention, "Let's bring it back to the now, Gentlemen." When they all quieted down and fresh coffee was handed out to all, except Man-Who-Runs, who disliked the burning hot coffee and could never understand how the White man enjoyed this stuff. Even Black-Eagle seemed to enjoy it, but he had been exposed to it by being invited into the Missionary homes numerous times during his last year at the school. He was being prepared to take the Word of God back into his tribe. On those nights, he was taught on what was expected of a missionary. He often wondered what the old missionaries would have thought about the American Civil War. He had come to respect and like many of these men who fought for the Confederacy and wondered of the men wearing the blue tunics. He knew it was the politicians back east that desired to put them on reservations, where they would be clothed and fed by the American Government, but it would forever change the Choctaw People. He had heard of what the American politicians wanted for all the Indian people from the East Coast to the West Coast and it saddened him greatly. There were times he wished the great tribes could put aside their old feuds, their dislikes and quarrels to fight as one tribe. If this was possible, they might possibly be able to earn the right to one corner of the US of A. But the great chiefs would not hear of this and the inner squabbling amongst the tribes continued. This alone allowed the settlers to spread further into Indian Territory, along with Army forts and roads and soon the towns. Such thoughts caused Black-Eagle to suffer depression and he always wondered why his God would do this to His Indian people. But his questions remained unanswered. Still, Black Eagle did not lose his faith.

Before JW continued-on, he had MSgt. Gary Wells gather up Scouts Holloway and Jim Williams and escort them over to the fire. Here they were introduced to the two Choctaw and the four other Rebel Scouts.

Scout Holloway had already met and was impressed by the Choctaw and knew this Black-Eagle to be a mighty Warrior in the Choctaw Nation by the amount of beadwork he carried and the Eagle feathers on his weapons. He was also impressed by how well Black-Eagle spoke English and knew this displayed the man's intelligence. Both Scouts knew they'd enjoy working with the new Indians of the Choctaw and were happy the Arizona Rangers had never gone to war with this tribe.

Now JW continued-on, "This is my order for tomorrow. I want Man-Who-Runs and one of our new Scouts…your choice Corporal Stonewall, to leave at day break and proceed westward. I need a route large enough for the Army of Texas, with wagons and artillery to travel by. You will also take my two Scouts, Holloway and Jim Williams, so they can learn this area. They're both good men in the woods and one can be used as a runner to bring me information or in event you have need of anything." JW stood up and tossed his half-empty coffee cup down on to the rocks surrounding the fire pit and it bounced into the flames. James retrieved it with a long stick and set it on the ground to cool down.

"Remember, we can cut down trees if need be, but it slows us down. Rivers can be crossed, but lakes will really slow us down if large rafts must be made for wagons and mounts. This means we'll have to go around. But we are headed east, not north where the Yankees probably have five to six Army Corps up there on rest and leave. They probably have swimming parties going on in the rivers and lakes Tennessee is famous for. You just remember we are scouting for nearly 20,000 soldiers and all the equipment General Hood can bring into the field. Think about that as you make our trail."

JW looked to Black-Eagle and said in an officer to underling voice, "You can follow his signs…right!?"

Black-Eagle did not like the tone of voice he was being addressed in, but he recognized the weariness his new friend was in by the worrisome look in his heavily bloodshot eyes. "I can follow Man-Who-Runs."

"Good," JW replied. He then nodded his head to Black-Eagle and moved his eyes to Corporal Stonewall, "You four leave at daybreak and travel for three days. You will then leave Scout Holloway to wait for us, while you three go ahead for three more days and will then leave Scout Jim Williams to wait for us. Ride for three more days and then you two will stop and wait for us to catch up. Then all four of you can be resupplied, rest for a day and provide intelligence on the pathway you have made. We will then send you out the same way the following morning for nine-days, with one man being dropped off the same way each, three days. Stonewall, will designate the man to lead the detail.

"If you run into Yankees, you are ordered not to fire on them unless your life is at stake. Hide and then get away so your report can get back. Your Intelligence is worth far more than you killing some poor Union boys. Is this understood?"

Each of the four understood and replied with a "Yes, Sir." To ensure Man-Who-Runs did, Black-Eagle repeated the orders in Choctaw.

"Now you four get your gear together and then get some rest. MSgt. Wells will send you off in the morning and good luck. I expect to see all four of you in nine-days." JW tossed them a casual salute to release them and knelt-down to find his coffee cup, as he was thirsty now. His mouth always dried up when he sent men out on a dangerous mission. His first such mission ended with the Ranger being caught by the Ute. He was found buried up to his chin, both his ears chopped off and ants feeding off-of him. He still wasn't dead, but he died shortly after they removed him to find that he'd been severely tortured. They soon realized the pressure of the sand against the body was prolonging his death and once the pressure was gone, his many broken bones caused his body to collapse and finally die. It never ceased to amaze JW the degree and type of torture the Apache and Ute used on their enemies. This death had caused JW to have nightmares for some time, but he continued to do his job.

"MSgt. Wells, I want you updating me every day on the condition of our troops and our mounts. I want to know who is truly ready for the long ride...We will depart at daybreak on Friday morning." JW then gestured to James, "Lieutenant, I want you to check on our men's equipment, weapons and uniform condition. Now I know it's doubtful you can get anything from Supply, but if need be check the morgue. I'm really tired of our boys looking like beggar trash in some Yankee big city. They need boots and for that you'll have to hit the morgue...Take what men you need and write down the other men's sizes."

A sip of the boiling coffee caught him off guard, he wasn't prepared to pucker-up his lips and he let out a, "Damn!" And he almost dropped his cup.

"As for me, I plan on taking Black-Eagle over to Headquarters tonight and using their maps for our new friend to show me what kind of territory we're looking at. I'll draw us up some smaller maps and have them available for the Scouts in the morning and I can give the General some idea of the basic route we're going to be covering. Supposedly the General has some spies out ahead, which means no shooting of civilians as they might be our spies. These people know if they are caught they'll be hung or shot as spies...It's one of the roughest duties in this war. That and those poor balloon fliers, they're just big targets up there for Yankee artillery and sharpshooters." He was sipping from his canteen, letting the cool water help with the burns brought on by the coffee.

"That's the end of this meeting. Everyone get some sleep, guards posted. Dismissed." JW issued his orders, said his goodnights and then led

Black-Eagle over to Headquarters to look over the larger maps to rough out a route the scouts were to check out.

ADD-ON

Moving the Army of Texas was not any easy thing, but since the war began in 1861, the Confederacy had spread itself thick and thin along the battles they shared with the North. As of late, the South had run out of replacements. More and more cavalry troops were pulling infantry duty because there were no more horses. Artillery pieces were being left along the roadside because they had fired off their last supply of cannon shot or used up their last wagon of gun powder. In some battles, Confederate soldiers were attacking with bayonets and swords, even broken rifles used as clubs, because the ammo supplies were no longer coming through. Soon enough, the men would be throwing rocks, but the Confederate spirit would not be broken—He continued fighting on. Barefoot, pants torn to ribbons up to the knees, shirts sleeveless, these men still charged against lines filled with new replacements, armed with new unfired rifles and tipped by unused bayonets. The banshee-like yells were known to send a Yankee line in retreat and for the night, those Rebels would have Yankee rations to fill their empty stomachs and fresh coffee to warm their freezing bones.

The battles through Missouri, Virginia, West Virginia and Tennessee was rough on the Army of Texas. These men could handle the August and September heat of an Arizona, New Mexico or Texas desert, but the constant downpour of cold rain, ice and slush, and the occasional snow crippled these desert warriors. Men were dropping like flies to fierce colds, flus and bouts of pneumonia and all too many died. Even digging the graves proved difficult, for the mud filled in nearly as fast as the diggers could shovel the mud out. And the graves had to be dug deep, because earlier on the flood caused some of the bodies to resurface, sending many young troops fleeing through the woods.

Cooks had to use their imagination to keep their units going and any varmint that could be caught or shot, even found drowned, was skinned and thrown into the stew pot. Tree bark was used for seasoning many a time and few people complained. All too soon, a mule or a horse had to be slaughtered to keep the men's strength up. During the Battle of the Wilderness, as many men died from the elements, sickness and starvations, as battle. This was also a bad mark on the time of the battle field surgeon, who through neglect or simple overwork, opted to remove arms and legs in an extreme number. This in turn led to a growing trend of suicides of the men who felt they could not go on without their missing limbs, especially for those men who lost both legs. This occurred in both armies during the four-year war and the word "Doctor" became a hated term among the troops, where men would often hide their comrade and treat him themselves. Sometimes Christian families would assist and were known to take in wounded troops from either side or a time or two have patients from both sides sharing space in their barn, while a local, who knew something about mending cows and horses, would do his best to save the soldiers. During this time, there was a state of peace announced for these homes and it seemed to be respected. When the patient was up and limping, he'd make his way back to his unit, but not before thanking the family who took him in and saying a goodbye to the soldier or two who he had a shared horse stall with for two weeks.

BATTLE OF NASHVILLE

For 15-days and into the last evening the Scouts rode hard, without making any contact with the Union boys. JW knew he had a whole Army Corps up ahead of him and three more directly to his north. But his orders were to reach the low mountainsides southwest of the City of Nashville. The horses were plain worn to a frazil, just like the troopers. Yet, he wasn't surprised to see how well his two Choctaw were taking it. For them, this was simply another hunting party. He learned over the nights he shared a fire with Black-Eagle, of how Tennessee was their provider of elk, deer, bear and buffalo. But with the spreading out of the White man, the Buffalo moved on and only rarely did they find a small herd. As a youth, Black-Eagle could still recall seeing the great herds of thousands of the great bushy headed beasts. He had killed his first buffalo two-days back from where they now camped. There was no fire now, for there was far too many Union patrols out and about these hills. To fight one would bring in a major force and they would never escape to warn the General.

JW finally got to see one of the big Tennessee Elks Black-Eagle spoke of. It was wandering in a heard of about 25 and the largest and most majestic beasts he'd ever seen. They were bigger than anything he'd ever seen before. "That rack shoots off its head for nearly five-feet…It must weigh over a-1,000 pounds. He's surely as big as one of those Alaskan moose I heard of," JW said to no one in particular. "This war ever ends, I'm a comin' back here to do some hunting. I could make a full-years' worth of clothes off his hide and feed the Rangers for a month."

"You think we'll be Rangers again, Captain?" Corporal Dan Wakefield asked.

"Arizona will need us, Dan. As-long-as they have bandits, cattle rustlers and warring Indians, the Rangers will ride."

On the 15th day, the Scouts were together, except for Black-Eagle and Man-Who-Runs. They knew where they were and had received permission from JW to forge ahead on foot to get a good idea and how far the city was. Slipping in and out of the trees was a lot safer then riding, but they wouldn't be back until nightfall.

Though he knew how good his two Choctaw were in the woods, having witnessed their expertise for the last 15-days, JW was relieved when they walked into the camp. They had even caught the sentry off-guard, but the Indian's sneer and shake of their heads was enough of a scolding for the man. He had never heard a thing until the two Indians were walking by him.

"Three hours by foot to Union lines, but they have many patrols out on foot and on horseback. City is all lit up, like a big party was going on. Every street has lights on it, all houses have lights. I never understand how you White people waste your candles and oil lamps. Makes me think you are all afraid of the dark," Black-Eagle said. He stood by JW's side with his left elbow rested on the barrel end of his Henry Rifle. JW had also given him a semi-new Navy Colt, with powder and ball, plus a loading and cleaning kit, after letting JW and his officers shoot a load of 16 cartridges through the Henry Rifle. Each man felt their shooting score had improved with the new rifle and JW had to agree.

"How many troops do you estimate are in the town, Black-Eagle…How many Cavalry?" Lt. Sampson asked.

Both Indians accepted a cup of hot coffee, but Man-Who-Runs kept blowing on his before he took his first drink. He began acquiring a taste for coffee since joining the unit. It helped when food supplies were running low and you mixed it with jerky. One of the Rangers suspected the cooks were making the jerky out of desert buzzard now, he recalled the taste.

"I counted horses until I became bored. So, I say there is nearly 2,000 Cavalry in Nashville; maybe more — not less. The city is ringed in Artillery and those strange guns you call mortars. Those are a very odd looking cannon, but the balls very large. I could see those used for forts, or maybe ships, but to shoot at men and horses…very odd."

"What about other men, did you count them?" MSgt. Wells asked, as he poured coffee into Lt. Dreeke's cup.

"No, too many to try. But if I was to give you an estimate — I watched for some time, with Man-Who-Runs agreeing with me — I'd saying easily close to 30,000 and more to the northwest. We made our way up that way to give a looksee and the hillsides are covered with campfires, enough to rival the stars on a moonless night."

"Well, that verifies the report of at least two and maybe three more Army Corps in the Nashville area. It looks like the Army of Texas is riding into a trap. Ol' General Grant wants to hammer a nail into the heart of the

Army of Texas. Once he takes control of this part of the country, his three corps can sweep down south and from the west, deliver a killing stroke to the south. "JW looked around his men and senior officers. "Anyone disagree with my summation?"

"Sir, what's this summation thing?" PFC Scout Leonard Sanders asked.

Corporal Stonewall, slapped him over the head with his filthy and torn-up Confederate cavalry hat. "Never you mind, Boy. Ah'll do your thinkin' for yuh."

"Thank you, Corporal…but, Leonard, a summation is…well, an idea or plan I laid out in brief details. Did you agree with what I said?"

"Why, sure, Sir. Ah sure do."

"Thanks, Leonard." JW then glanced around his dwindling unit and for a brief-moment he wondered how many men he would have left when this was over and if he himself would survive? *I got no time for this.*

"My plan for the moment is to leave you all here, but ready for action. Dug in, but ready for a quick escape after your first brush with the Yankees. Withdraw and keep withdrawing until you see my smiling face. I'm taking Black-Eagle and Man-Who-Runs back to see the General, so they can brief him. You know how long this will take." JW looked to Lt. Sampson and said, "This is now your command, if you feel you need to withdraw at any point, any time, you decide. There is no sense throwing these men's lives away to take on several hundred Yankees. You know as well as I do, once the Union boys know were here, they'll throw everything at you and that includes bringing troops down from the north to cut you off. They won't know if you're a scout element or a point troop, until they take you prisoner and get a good look at you. Thankfully, you are all in uniform…mostly, even if you do look like dockyard thugs. Too bad we don't have a barber in the unit or a decent razor among us. But hold your heads high and we'll be back in a couple of weeks with whatever supplies we can carry. Good luck and God bless, gentlemen."

Once the horses were made ready and goodbyes were all made, JW and the two Choctaw rode west at a quickened pace. Black-Eagle rode up front to show the way and he appeared able to see in the dark from the way he missed all the trees. JW rode in the middle and Man-Who-Runs brought up the rear. He would stop now and then to listen for sounds of anyone following and then catch-up. It was decided to ride for 16-hours and sleep for eight, trading off on guard duty. No fires, so it was cold jerky and troopers hard tack, which the Indians didn't seem to mind. As for JW, he felt like his molars were going to break in-half and he really missed his hot coffee. But he also knew how far the scent of coffee could travel through the woods, plus the smell of burning-embers and how easy it was to see a cloud of smoke in a clear sky. If they hit any rain, then they'd risk the fire, but not until then.

All three knew there was a possibility the Union cavalry could have their own scouts out and if they ran into them their only chance was to flee and hope their pathway would get them away.

JW knew the Army of Texas was moving along the path, but at only one-third the speed. Most of the time it involved waiting for the caravan of wagons and artillery catching-up. General Hood did not want much of a break in the line as the army moved along. He estimated finding Nashville in under 24-days and would attack as soon as possible to prevent the city from being alerted. But that didn't happen.

It took nine-days for JW and his two Choctaw to reach the forward scouts for the Army of Texas and they were brought right to the General, where their report was made. The news shocked General Hood and all he could do was shake his head as he stood up with a lighted cigar between his clinched teeth and then pounded his traveling desk with his right fist. He then looked to Captain Blake and in an unusual act, he whispered, "General Lee has given me my orders, Captain. Nashville must be taken or the South will lose Tennessee and possibly the war. I have no other choice and I know this will mean thousands of brave men will soon die. I am sure you understand this, knowing you have had to accept and give such orders in your wars against the Apache."

"Yes, Sir. What is your orders?" JW asked.

"Return to your men and keep an eye on the city. If they begin to show sign they're stirring up to prepare for our attack, send me your Choctaws. They would be the best in getting the news back to me. Will you return to your Command, Captain?"

"Sir, I obey my orders," JW replied abruptly. He felt as if his loyalty and bravery was suddenly in question.

"Sir, I do apologize, I meant no such wish to make you feel uncomfortable. I know from your previous record as a Ranger Captain and as a Scout Company Commander of your great acts of bravery...Please excuse a weary old man who has grown tired of asking so many men to die." He offered his hand and JW shook it, then smiled.

"I am on my way, General and will send my two Choctaw, who are the most amazing Indians I have had the good fortune to ride with, back to you as soon as there is any sign of battle preparation. Good fortune to you, General."

"Good luck, Captain and may the Lord bless your travels, where ever they will lead you." General Hood then arm grasped both Choctaw and then returned to his desk, to review the latest dispatches coming in from his units.

JW quickly dug up some extra chow and coffee beans; extra powder and ball for their weapons, and feed for their horses. Thanks to their Choctaw, they were almost always camped near to water and their current site had a fresh stream within 50-yards and a cool pool for the horses.

James told Gary Wells that had this been the Rangers, they'd be sharing a two-inch wide mountain stream coming down between two rocks and the water was probably hotter than their boiling coffee. "We'd hav' ta kilt 50 Apache jus' ta get ah drink, an' 'nother 50 ta wader our horses."

Wells looked over at Pvt. Liam, "Does he always lie like this?"

"No, Sergeant...sometimes he lie even better." Liam replied and then he took off running to escape Lt. Dreeke's temper.

"Boy nev'a did hav' no re'pect for adults." James said, but then broke out laughing. "But, I tellin' yuh, Good Lord, nev'a did put much water in Arizona. Mus'ta saved it all for dis Tennessee."

"Oh, I guess Texas an' Arizona about thu same. 'Cept we gots Comanche an' you gots Apache. Too bad we didn't have those Choctaw, I like those two fellas we got workin' with us. Good men to be beside in a scrape." MSgt. Gary Wells said.

"Yuh got that right," Corporal Stonewall added in. He was sharing in a cup of plain water with the command staff, what was left of it.

Lt. Sampson then came to sit down and accepted a cool tin cup of spring water. "Thanks, Sergeant. Now is everyone dug in? Guards out and relief appointed?"

"Yes, Sir," Lt. Dreeke replied. But then he took in a big gulp of water and gestured for Wells to take over.

"Sir, good trenches dug in in the event we get charged day or night, two men to a trench. Guards are out and relief assigned. Lt. Dreeke and I will switch off on making sure the relief gets posted. Horses down at the pool, tied down to submerged line and cobbled in the event we get rushed and they try to scare our horses off. They'll be surprised. I've also got Holloway and Brady Williams about 50-yards out front, listening in for any advance. They'll let out with a rebel yell if those Yankees come a visiting."

"Sir, ah'll dat done," Lt. Dreeke said.

"Sounds good, men...Now what's our food and ammo shape?"

Both Gary and James looked at Pvt. Liam, that task had been designated to him and hoped he had remembered getting both chores done.

"Sir," Pvt. Liam said without hesitation. "Our ammo shape has not changed since the Captain left, due to us not being engaged with the enemy or going on any hunting trips for fear of alerting the enemy to our whereabouts. Each man still has his personal load for both rifle and pistol, along with his sword and tomahawk. Both of which have been sharpened into fine blades due to boredom on the men's part. As to food, this is a different matter altogether. Most of them are out of their provided rations and are now chewing on evergreen bark soaked in hot water or cold. Onion bulbs or other vegies pointed out earlier by Man-Who-Runs are being consumed as they can be found. Personally, I am concerned the men may be interested in one of the sickly horses and you may consider cutting its throat and harvesting the beast. That is my report, Sir."

"Liam, I am extremely surprised of how you remain a private. Such an articulate report bears witness to your intelligence and keen witness to survival in the wildness. I strongly believe you should at least be promoted to the rank of PFC, once this little skirmish is behind us. Thank you." Lt. Sampson then looked to both James and Gary, but also Stonewall. "Do you men agree with our young soldier's view on harvesting the sick horse for our consumption?"

"Lieutenant," Gary said first, "I do not believe the horse is so much sickly as just plain old and worn out. This being the case, I do not feel the horse would cause any of us ill-health, but we should avoid consuming any of the blood and stay with solid meat pieces. But, we still cannot build a fire unless the rains hit us and someone will have to use a knife or tomahawk to put the animal down. Should be done quickly as this animal has done much to serve the south."

"I'll put it down, I've done it many times in survival situations and the animal will not suffer more than a mere second, and it's quiet. Who is the rider?" Stonewall asked.

"Horse, it belongs ta Corporal Leaders, but he unda'stands dis. He been ah Ranger for 'long time." James nodded his head and left to go have a word with him.

Gary gestured to Pvt. Liam, "Get two men to started building a horse size trench. We'll do everything there and when we're done we bury our friend with honors so the Yankees don't find the grave. Now go get 'em." He ordered and Liam was off at the run.

It was over an hour before the meat was being served raw, but the men didn't care. They were hungry enough to eat their own stomachs at this point. Liam was amazed by the way Corporal Leader's mount was put down so silent and so fast. Ropes were tied around his legs, with front legs tied together and both rear legs tied up, which forced him down onto his side into the large trench, which was about four feet deep. One man held the horse's snout, petting his forehead and snout, while he wrapped a set of reins around the snout to keep him from trying to bite anyone. Stonewall sat down on the horse's neck. The horse tried to buck, but was unable to and this was when Stonewall pulled a long knife from inside his right boot. Liam learned later it was known as an Arkansas Toothpick. He placed it inside the horses left ear, the closest one to Stonewall and he then used the base of his revolver like a blacksmith's hammer and used one blow to drive the knife through the horse's head. Death came instantly and a lot of the men had never seen anything like it. They've had to shoot horses that still took breath for another few seconds, but this was merciful, when death was a necessity. Stonewall then pulled his knife out, climbed off and wandered over to be by himself. He knew it needed to be done, but he had a real fondness for horses and he didn't want anyone else trying to do it and end up being cruel to the animal.

Once the meat was removed, the animal was buried and a cross was whittled into the tree right close by. No one would see it unless they were right in front of it and they had the horse deep enough to keep the predators from finding it. Large rocks were placed over the body before the dirt was filled in, which would keep the wolves from being able to get to him.

"Pvt. Liam, you and Corporal Leaders will have-to double up now, since you're the lightest of our men. Okay?" Lt. Sampson asked in the way of giving him and order.

"I understand, Sir."

"Thanks, Liam…thanks." Corporal Leaders said. He had ridden his "Smokey Boy" for 12-years. He just couldn't believe the old horse of his had given up the ghost on this last scout. But he went out as a Ranger, probably saving the lives of his fellow rangers. Had they gotten back to the Army of Texas, he wouldn't have gone out again and he might've died among strangers. This way was fast and all his fellow Rangers would never forget him.

By the time JW and his two Choctaw were back with their scouts, the men were again hungry and this time they were chewing on their leather gloves and looking for another sick animal. But there wasn't one and no one wanted to volunteer their own horse. But they didn't have to. JW had carried rations and had Liam hand it out, while Lt. Sampson briefed his commander on the events that transpired while he was gone and lack of movement by the Union troops.

"If they have anything planned, we're sure missing it. During the day life goes on as usual and at night the same fires burn. Even to the north, not a sign of movement and this worries me. The army is sitting still too long, makes me feel a trap is being set somewhere and for someone," Lt. Sampson said, between bites of some hard bread and meat rolled together.

"General said we could move-up some if we felt it was safe, and a little north. I'd like to see if they're really troops up there to the north? Maybe they've only got a couple hundred men up there lighting fires and cutting wood to feed them...make us believe a couple Army Corps are there and really their Army is coming down behind us.

"Captain, you don't think those dumb Yankees are smart enough ta pull no weasel in the henhouse trick on us, do yuh?" Corporal Stonewall asked.

"Gentlemen, Yankees do have brains and they have pulled their share of wild tricks in this war. Burning fires on a hillside to make the Army of Texas think they have two whole Divisions camped out there for nearly a month actually shames me. I should've known better by now, we all should've. Can you even imagine General Grant, who I have heard is as great a strategist as our beloved General Lee, keeping two whole Corps out of the war; even if it was to protect the City of Nashville. This can only mean he knows General Hood is advancing with his whole Army of Texas and he has made steps to position his troops behind the General to smash him when he attacks Nashville." JW went silent for a moment and held his right hand up to ask everyone to remain quiet as he thought things over.

"Alright, this is what we have to do to prove whether we're right or not about the Union boys. I will take...Lt. Dreeke, Pvt. Liam, MSgt. Wells, Corporal Leaders, Corporal Brady Williams, Scout Holloway, Scout Jim Williams and Black-Eagle with me and move in on the City of Nashville. Once I can show the Union is preparing for an offensive from the West, we will fall back to this position. No retract that, Pvt. Liam I want you to stay here and watch the camp and make sure no wanderers steal our horses."

"But Captain..." Liam began to interrupt, but JW silenced him with a hard stare.

"This will leave you, Lt. Sampson, to move north with Man Who Runs to guide you, plus Corporals Gibson, Wakefield brothers and Stonewall. You'll also have Jackson, and the Sanders cousins. You are to move on foot north to verify if the whole army is up there, or only a couple hundred men who are watching a thousand fires to trick us and it's a mighty good trick, too. Then once you've got it confirmed either way, you make it back here to meet up with us."

JW looked around the troops and made a decision, "I am giving you a direct order, Gentlemen. I do not expect you to fight off a regiment of Union troops. General Hood will have gotten this information somehow. If it looks bad, I am ordering you to surrender. For when this war is over, we will be going home to Arizona and our territory will be in dire need of its Rangers. You need to live for our Arizona, so no heroics at the last minute and that's an order. Am I understood?"

Some of the men didn't like it, but they all nodded or whispered their acceptance. Pvt. Liam had serious trouble with it because the Captain was leaving him behind to take care of the horses.

The soldiers under Lt. Sampson prepared to go and took a moment to say so long to their buddies. Then everyone stopped as MSgt. Wells said a prayer over the unit and blessed them along their way. Both JW and Sampson shook hands, "I expect to see you in four to five days. I'll send a couple men, with Black-Eagle on ahead with whatever we find and wait here for you to join up. So good luck, Bret."

"Good luck to you too, Sir. If we get back first, I'll do the same. I'll send Man-Who-Runs on ahead with two of our men, and then wait. If you're not back in a week, maybe I'll just set a big fire to burn Nashville to the ground."

"Can't do that, Bret...we got Southerners living in there, too." JW then waved as Bret walked on down the trail they made over the last week. Bret hoped it would be smooth sailing for the next day or so, as they stayed in the gullies. After that, it was going to be Indian style as they moved up the hillsides to see who was sitting around all those campfires.

JW walked over to Pvt. Liam, who was sitting on a rotted log. He was using his knife to whittle on a piece of scrap wood. "Listen, Liam...I know you resent me right now, but I can handle that. But you need to know why I did this, so open-up your ears and listen or I'll stand you at attention. If that doesn't work, I'll throw you over my knee and paddle you all red and blue like the kid you're behaving like right now. I've been so proud of you this whole venture...until now. You are behaving like the kid I worried about you becoming. Now what's it going to be?"

Liam thought about for a brief second, chewed on his inside upper cheeks, then dropped his eyes and jumped to his feet to assume the position of attention. "My apologies, Captain."

"Now that's much better," JW said. He set down on the chuck of rotting wood and told Liam to relax. "Listen, kid. I left you here because I want you to survive this war. It's nearing an end and our beloved South will be the loser. Arizona, even the United States, is going to need strong young men like you to rebuild this nation and Arizona. Being dead will not do anything for either of us. If I fail to survive, I'll need you to help Sherry Ann to keep the Ranch going. Hopefully they'll be new Rangers and you'll be one of the leaders. It's simply a waist to have you killed in the last days of this horrific war. Hundreds of thousands of people have died, and there will still be problems. Arizona will be filled with new immigrants; Blacks newly freed coming from the South and they'll need protection from the Wild Indians, but not only them and the bandits, but those hateful White, who'll not want them settling in Arizona. We, as Rangers, will need to protect them because they will have the same rights granted them by our Bill of Rights. A whole new world, young one. This is why I needed you to stay here. And the same order applies to you. A group of Yankees show up, surrender your arms. You won't be in prison camp very long, probably less than a year before total surrender."

"Why'd we lose, Captain?"

"We lost our allies; French and British. Sea blockades kept our cotton from getting out to pay for goods, which meant no weapons, food supplies and other war equipment being brought in. The Union had better manufacturing and so many more people. We ran out of replacements, out of horseflesh. No shoes, so our men became ill. Too many of the wrong people were granted commissions, simply because they knew someone and knew nothing of how to lead a unit. Far too many decisions needed to be made and no one who was willing to make them. But the Union had their own troubles and these will be brought out in the years to come. Newspapers who once praised great victories and the leaders who directed the armies, will now be investigating these same people for misuse of funds, fraud and many misdeeds. Though the war will be over, a very hard time is coming for our country's economy. I will be happy to return to Arizona and chase bandits, deal with Apache and wait for the day I can afford one of those fine Henry Rifles."

"Sir, we're ready to go," James said to his friend. He then walked up and shook hands with Liam. "I recommend you build a wood platform up in the trees and sleep up there. Walk the horses in small groups and don't shoot anyone unless you have, too. Make sure an Indian isn't one of ours and do not sleep with your trigger in your hand. You wake up all-of-a-sudden, you might shoot and then everyone will know you're in the area."

Soon, the patrol had vanished over the far hillside and Liam knew he was all alone, a fact he never enjoyed.

CHAPTER EIGHT

"So, this is what a train ride in a cattle car feels like…ain't no wonder why the cattle hate it so."

Lt. Sampson and his patrol traveled on foot, very quietly, crossing several creeks and one shallow river, drawing ever closer to the Union ranks. They spotted several patrols and took to the trees to avoid being seen. The men were hungry, now down to dried jerky meat they had stored in their belt pouches. The salty meat, roasted until the meat was nearly brick hard and capable of breaking teeth if a soldier didn't suck on it long enough, using his mouth juices to soften it up. Those who tried biting off a chunk often loosened their front teeth, so the smart ones cut off a chuck with the sharp blade of the knife and then sucked on it for an hour or two. In most cases the savory juices roasted deep into the meat would then be released into the troops' taste buds. A single piece of jerky, be it beef, turkey or pork, could last for more than a couple of hours. Yet some of the men couldn't wait, they were too hungry and angered their jaws by forcing the meat into swallow-able chunks and forced it down. Only to regret it later, when Mother Nature took action.

Hard-tack was all gone and no one dared fire a shot to bring down a varmint to eat raw. But then came the last late afternoon, when they drew close enough to see the wood being brought in by the wagon-loads from beyond the northern hills. Men from the wagons, three to four to a load, would drop off several large armloads at each fire pit and there were no other troops around. The patrol was up in the trees again and they had a good 50 to 70 yards of distance to see.

Lt. Sampson counted 12-wood wagons and approximately 40 to 48 men on the nearby detail. Once the wood was dropped off the wagon would move along until the wood was all dropped off. Then the wagon would depart back over the nearest hill-top, leaving the Union boys to set the fires. Lt. Sampson had no trouble imagining how this same detail was happening all along the whole hillside area and it would probably require a single regiment of infantry to handle the duty. This meant nearly 100,000 Yankees were available to catch General Hood and the other Rebel Corps by surprise, unless they got word of this.

Lt. Sampson looked down at Man Who Runs, "You understand what is going on here? Can you get message to General Hood that this is all a fake?"

"I know…I go now?" Man-Who-Runs asked.

189

"You go now as fast as you can, but I'll send Leonard Sanders an hour behind you. We will then all follow an hour after that. Hopefully, one of us will make it through." Sampson reached down and shook hands with Man Who Runs. "Leave as soon as you consider it dark enough."

"Okay," Man Who Runs replied. He then began inching himself down the tree as quietly as possible.

WITH CAPTAIN BLAKE

Blake's patrol, with Black-Eagle leading them, had followed a stream bed, which lay at the bottom of a deep gully. During the days, they dug shallow holes for them to lay in, covering themselves with their camp blankets, which in turn were buried under sand and dirt from the gully walls to camouflage them. While most of the men would sleep, at least two remained awake to watch for Union patrols. Once, they had taken haven in the tree tops to escape a Yankee horse patrol that far outnumbered Blake's unit at better than five to one.

It took Blake and his men five-days to reach the outskirts of Nashville and with the moon waning, the weary soldiers were now low crawling their way toward a large warehouse. Sampson thought it strange there had not been any roving horse patrol surrounding the city, or guards on the warehouse, but he wanted to know if the building housed Union supplies or was it sitting empty. If it was empty and a couple more, it could mean the Union was out in the field and on the move. Plus, the artillery pieces they had passed by were abandoned. Once entry was made, and the emptiness confirmed, Blake decided he still wanted one more warehouse to make sure. They entered without incident, finding the floors vacant.

"That's it then, the Union boys are out there in mass, waiting to jump down on our General Hood with both feet and a barrel of rocks to boot." Blake grasped Black-Eagle by the shoulder and turned him around to face him. "Now it's your time, my new friend and you've got to fly like your namesake." Blake said. "You leave now an' when you reach Liam, you tell him what you saw. If Scout Jim Williams doesn't arrive at our camp to claim his horse within four-hours after you leave on your horse, Liam is to follow your trail. It will mean Williams was captured. But he is your back-up in the event something happens to you. We will slowly make our way back to avoid capture. God Bless, my brother."

Black-Eagle grasped his arm and replied, "Blessing be upon you, my brother. We will see each other, again."

Rather than leave the building through the same back door they had come through, Black-Eagle quietly snuck out through a front open cargo loading dock and made his way past several other buildings by crawling through the dock shadows. It disheartened him to see more than ten-platoons of Union Infantry proceeding toward the building he had left. He then caught eye of a large Company sized unit of cavalry and knew he would not have to be concerned with Scout Jim Williams coming later. He would brief Liam and then the boy could try to keep up with him as they tried to head-off General Hood.

WITH LT. SAMPSON'S PATROL

It was nearing midnight, according-to Lt. Sampson's Southern-Pacific golden watch he held in his hand as he fought to see off the glare of the fires behind them. It was difficult. The watch with the attached gold chain had been a retirement gift to his uncle, who had served 27-years with the railroad. He had no family and in his Last Will And Testament had left the watch and chain, along with a brace of dueling pistols made in England, to his favorite relative — Bret Sampson. There had also been a Sharps .50 caliber buffalo rifle, that Sampson still carried, but the brace of ornate dueling pistols stayed back home in a Tucson bank for safe keeping. Sampson hoped to some day pass it along to his own sons. The pistols were used three times, to prove his Uncle had won all three duels. The victor always walked away with the weapons used in the duel, be it sword or pistol. Bret had seen one duel fought with Indian tomahawks and another with short spears, both of which had been extremely bloody and all four men had died of their wounds.

He decided it was time to head back for a rendezvous with Captain Blake and the horses. Bret also hoped Man-Who-Runs would get through to Liam and then on to General Hood's Headquarters.

Bret waited until the campfires were quiet and then began moving his small squad south. But during their second day of travel, the patrol stumbled right into a well-placed ambush. A full-company of Yankee-infantry was in position, after two Union scouts had seen the Confederates moving in the early evening. The Union Captain's orders were to capture the Rebels alive for questioning over what they had seen and what unit they were assigned to.

During a rough climb, while they made their way down through a dark ravine, the Union boys swept in, at better than four to one odds to catch Lt. Sampson's squad without a shot being fired. Now disarmed, Lt. Sampson and his men were tied up, and escorted to Union Regimental Headquarters for the unit handling the hillside charade. There they were interrogated for hours, only to learn nothing from the stubborn Rebels. Finally, a Union Lt. Colonel ordered the Rebel Lieutenant and his men on to the Nashville prisoner's holding camp for eventual travel north to one of several Union Prison Camps.

ALONG WITH CAPTAIN BLAKE

"Listen up, you Gray Backs, this is Major Corrick of the United States Army and you are now surrounded by two full companies of Union soldiers. I am giving you exactly 60-seconds...one minutes from right now, to surrender and come out of that building with your hands up high and all weapons of any type or kind left inside that building. You now have exactly 50-seconds and counting." Major Corrick waited for a few seconds and then added, "When my men attack the building it will be with the orders to shoot to kill, there will be no prisoners. You now have 30-seconds."

Captain Blake looked to his men and shook his head, he had already warned them what he would do against impossible odds. He was not going to have them killed for simply the honor of the South, not when the State of Arizona still needed them. He dropped his rifle and began to unbuckle his belt.

"This is Captain JW Blake of the Confederate States of America and I am surrendering my squad. We are disarming ourselves and will be on our way out." MSgt. Gary Wells didn't feel like surrendering to no Union major, but Lt. Dreeke explained it better to him by laying a right hook on his jaw and laying him out. "Ah'll hav' ta pay for dat one lat'r, but he'll know it was bes' t'ing ta do. He jus' onery."

Both Dreeke and Brady Williams lugged him outside to be searched by the Yankees, along with the rest of the men. A squad of Union boys went inside to gather up the weapons. It was a sad thing to watch, for the men knew it would be the last time they would ever see those weapons, spoils of war for the victors. Captain Blake looked over at Major Corrick, saluted, and asked, "Do you have any boys, Major?"

"Why, yes, I do, Captain. I have three sons, all safely back in Pittsburg with their mother. Why do you ask?"

"The men you have captured tonight will probably see the rest of the war in some prison camp. We're members of the Arizona Rangers, and those tomahawks we carried have seen 100 engagements against the Apache, Ute and Navajo. I'd be proud if you would take my tomahawk and Bowie knife and carry them on to your sons. I have my own son and daughter, and right now, along with my wife, are defending my ranch against the Indians and bandits of Arizona. There is a lot of blood stain on them from some very courageous Indians and I would appreciate their courage being remembered."

192

"Captain, I am touched and I'll take possession of both knife and tomahawk. I wish I could do something for you in trade, but you are the prisoner. Maybe someday I'll see you again once this dreadful war is over. I am glad you surrendered, I wouldn't have wanted to carry the slaughter of such brave men on my conscience. But now you must be taken to headquarters for questioning, for which I can already see is a waste of time. Not with men such as you and those with you. Prison camp will be terrible, but it will eventually end. Remember that, if not for any other reason than seeing that family of yours again. Goodbye, Captain Blake." Major Corrick saluted his opponent, which surprised his Union troops.

Captain Blake came to attention and presented his best parade ground salute for a fine gentleman. He had finally met a major he liked and it just happened to be a Union officer.

"Who hit me!?" MSgt. Wells asked in a growl, as he came to and no longer needed help as the squad began following their Captain and the Union escort.

"Big Union Sergeant, Gary...blind-sided yuh," Corporal Brady Williams said. He then grinned at Lt. Dreeke, who nodded his approval.

As with Lt. Sampson, Captain Blake's interrogation and that of his men proved fruitless. Six-hours later, the somewhat battered troopers and their two officers were taken by wagon to the cattle yards in Nashville. Here, by climbing over one fence and under another, Captain Blake's squad and Lt. Sampson's squad joined up with over 500 other Confederate prisoners taken in the area South of Nashville. This was prior to General Hood's attack on the City of Nashville.

For two days, the men went through long lines and were served a plate of oatmeal mush, a chunk of dried bread and a tin cup of water. The food and water had to be consumed in the area and then the tin plate and cup were tossed back into large wooden bins for later washing. If the plate and cup was not returned, the prisoner was taken off to the side for searching. If the metal dishware was found on him, he was given kitchen details to work with the Blacks, hired by the Union Army or enlisted into the military service. If the dishware was not found, he was taken and placed into a deep hole, without food or water and used as a military latrine for the Union boys. He would remain there until he told the sergeant where the plate and cup was. Either of which could be turned into a weapon to assault a guard and generate a prison break.

This was not the last of the inhuman treatment the prisoners would endure by either side, because the men forced to work as prison guards did not relish in the duty and blamed the prisoners for the reason they were forced to be pulling the duty. In Northern prisons, racist Whites were ordered to work alongside Union Black companies, which in turn were almost always hated by Southern troops. But there were times the racial barrier was abridged by Christianity or the rare Jewish soldier. The Jews fought their own share of racism, since the time of the Crusades.

Though the Jews were blamed for the crucifixion of Jesus Christ, the Catholic Church seldom remembered Christ was of the Jewish faith when he was killed.

TIME TO LOAD THE TRAIN CARS

When they finally had close to a thousand prisoners, Grant sent word down it was time to send a prisoner train up to New York. This load was going to the infamous El Mira Union Prison Camp, which may have been one small step above the Confederate's Andersonville Prison Camp for Union prisoners. Between the two of them they could be blamed for over 30,000 prisoner deaths, and much more. Prisoners died of malnutrition, infections and disease, beatings by guards and murders by fellow prisoners who fought over any slight, or over any crumb of food.

At El Mira, outside New York City, the prison camp filled with a lake of sewage that spread pestilence, mites and lice lived in the mud to spread from soldier to soldier. The food being served was often rotten as some high-ranking officer stole the funds being allotted to feed the prisoners and made lower bargain food deals that could barely keep the Southerners alive. The winter snow, ice and severe cold was killing off these Southern troops who had never lived in such frigid temperatures before and the blankets paid to be delivered to them, never arrived as the money was looted by either politician and senior officer, or both working together. In some cases, a crate, of blankets made it to the prison, only to be sold off to the guards to keep themselves or their families warm. Winters in New York were tough on the Ohio, and Iowa regiments and even troops from Pennsylvania.

To stay warm, the troops used body warmth and the blankets they brought with them, now in most cases torn to shreds and often used for bandages. In El Mira, Confederate troops were dying at better than 1,000 a month.

The prisoners at Nashville had been held in the cattle pens adjacent the railroad tracks. Here the great herds from the west would be loaded and shipped north for slaughter, to enable the great steak houses in Boston and New York City to serve up their famous mouthwatering 16-ounce and 24-ounce steaks. But until they arrived in the cities, they were kept on the hoof for easy handling. Same with the prisoners, they went from the massive cattle pens into 40-foot long railroad cattle cars. No benches, no bunks, simple open cars with a thin layer of hay on the floor and armed Union guards walking the roof of each car. There were also five railroad passenger cars, placed among the cattle cars, which carried Armed Union Troops, to keep the prisoners in line at any food and water stops. The Confederates were released — one car at a time — to prevent a riot from developing into a mass escape attempt. This way it was four Yankees to every Rebel.

Not knowing it, the prisoners on this long four-day ride, were receiving the last of their decent chow. Had they known what to expect at El Mira, they would've attempted an escape, no matter what the odds.

"So, this is what a train ride feels like…Ain't no wonder why cattle hate it, so," Corporal Brad Williams said. The train car they were forced into, with barely enough room to sit down in, was rattling side to side.

"You ain't been on no cattle train before?" Corporal Leo D Wakefield asked of him.

"Nope. Loaded my share 'for I joined the Rangers, but nev'a rode wit' 'em."

"Me an' my brothers, we done ride wit' 'em, good way to a city or two. Got sick first couple of times, felt like I was out at sea in a storm…or so I was told. But Ah've been caught out on a lake when a wind caugh' me an' nearly tipped mah boat over. Then I gets used to it. But Pa took us ta Arizona and soon, we start riding for thu Rangers."

"What state was you from," Brady asked of Leo D.

"We had a farm in middle of Missouri, but even as the Rangers broke up, my brothers and I couldn't side with them Yankees. It was dem Feds who took our Farm…done wouldn't extend our loan. Sold it to some city slickers out of Kansas City, but we burned the house and barn down 'for we left. Pa built them, he said he wasn't goin' ta leave dem behind."

"Your Pa still alive?" Brady asked.

"He was when we left, but we nev'a see no letter since joinin' up. But we pray he is well an' the ranch is okay. Our brand is a Broken W with an arrow runnin' down the middle. If you ever see a steer with it that was one of ours."

"No one in our Globe outfit got any mail. Ah don't think we'll get any in the prison camp. Jus' hav' ta wait till the war ends and we get back home. I sure do miss Arizona…Ah could stand for some of dat good ol' desert heat right now."

"Now you're talkin'," PFC Coon added in. Except for Pvt. Liam, PFC Coon was the low-ranking man on the totem pole and this usually meant he and Liam had most of the "go for" and "do-this and do-that" chores when arriving at their destination.

195

The majority slept between food breaks, but once a big city was hit the troops lined the sides of the cattle cars to see the sights. Being cattle cars there was large spaces between side boards to allow fresh air in to clean out the stench the cattle produced. But for the men, these same spaces between side-boards of three to five inches, allowed the icy air to blast in. With the speed of the train and outside temperatures dropping down to below zero the closer their destination grew near, the wind produced temperatures in the minus 20's. Soon, only when the train was stopped did the men leave their huddles to examine the city lights, but only for a short moment. Huddles usually numbered ten to 15 men and each car held four good sized huddles. People in the center would have their time at warmth and then they would rotate to the outer circle and slowly work their way back in by ten-minute rotations. If anyone refused to leave the inner spot, they would be jerked out of the huddle to be on his own. When they reached their final stop, Captain JW Blake's cattle car saw six-men freeze to death, curled up against the side walls of the train car.

Blake was the ranking man in the car, but not the train. There was a major, two – Lt. Colonels and a full colonel on the train. The Colonel was offered a chance to ride with the senior Union officers, but the Confederate Colonel refused, deciding to stay with his men. In doing so he had earned a lot of respect from men who had never actually seen him before and they kept him in the inner circle since hitting the severe cold.

Many of the Union officers spoke out against this movement of Southerners north to New York in the wintertime. They compared it to moving the New York Divisions to fight in Arizona in the hottest part of summer. But no one listened to them and the Union troops were not about to give up their one blanket they were using to stay warm. Still, a young Confederate Pastor, a Major Dave Johnson, went back to the first cattle car and enquired through the boards of who was sick. When he was told it was a Corporal from Alabama, the Pastor shoved his wool blanket through the boards. "Have him use this and I hope it helps. Tell him I will be lifting him up in prayer this day. I, too, am on my way to this prison camp, but not only for the Union Army. I will also be available to you Confederate, as my first oath was to God."

Before the train reached El Mira, that same blanket comforted seven-dying men, who each said they could feel a strange warmth emanating from it. At the camp, it came in with a prisoner so it was allowed to be kept and it continued to provide a ministry to the dying soldiers.

A LOST SOUL

Pvt. Liam had set his horses free, except the one he was riding. The mounts remained in the same wooded area. When he rode off, the horses moved to the west, remaining close to him. He no longer had time to mess with them. Nor could he fire off a shot to scare them into a wild break.

He saw which way Black-Eagle, and then Man-Who-Runs, had charged off, mounted upon their horses. This was the direction he was to follow. Unfortunately, he was a tad too late. The two Choctaw escaped an ambush; but Pvt. Liam made a tight turn over a bush-lined ridge and swung down into a shallow gully. He was covering ground at a gallop; which provided no time to react as he stumbled right into the back of the Yankee ambush. Seven Union troopers hid in the shallow gully. When they heard the horse galloping toward them, they turned to see a gray-back mounted upon his horse charging right down on top of them. Only the fact that they had been ordered to take prisoners saved Liam's life. So rather than have a bayonet to his stomach or several mini-balls blasted into his chest, he was jerked, rather roughly, from his mount and thrown to the ground.

Pvt. Liam shook his head to clear his vision, only to find several Union rifles pointed at his head. Right then, a Union Sergeant walked up, yanking Liam off the ground to stand in front of him. Liam was quickly disarmed of his tomahawk, Bowie and Navy Colt. "Ain't you too young to be out here playing soldier, sonny?" The Sergeant asked. "That's a lot of weapons for a boy to be carryin' around."

Liam glanced at the man's arms, counting the chevrons. He knew the man was a MSgt. "Sergeant, my name is Private Liam…Blake. I am a Runner an' Scout with the Army of Texas, under General Hood. Before that, I was with the Arizona Rangers…as a mascot."

"Well, at least I got some honesty in all that. So, you're real active duty now?"

"Yes, Sergeant and I've already killed my first Apaches to avenge my parents. Arizona Rangers carry tomahawks and we are proud when we have bloodied them. So, now I am your prisoner."

"Afraid so kid, but I'll keep your tomahawk for you. Look me up some day. I have my own blacksmith shop in Sedalia, Missouri. I'll hold it for you, okay?"

"Thank you, Sergeant that is very kind of you."

The sergeant glanced about, after taking the tomahawk off a Corporal and telling him to divide up the rest of the booty. He pulled Liam over to the wagon he'd be hauled away in. Fortunately, it was empty for the moment. "Listen here, Liam…you've got an education…I can hear in your voice. I can tell your own unit likes you, and this is why you've been made active. In my army, you might be old enough for a drummer boy, but not carrying a rifle. Anyhow, it's too late now. But the place you're goin' is a hell hole and getting' there…travel alone can kill. You are going to New York, place I think is El Mira and everything I've heard is how bad it is." He looked around again and then asked. "You got any Union money…cash or coin? And no, I'm not going to rob you."

"No, Sergeant…I have not seen any U.S. Dollars since joining up. When the Rangers paid us it was with Confederate money an' I left mine with…well, she's sort of like my adopted mother and my commander's wife. They found me after the Indian massacre, took care of me…raised me up."

"My own little brother and his new wife were in a wagon train heading for California, but a Comanche attack took them both…so, we have a bit in common." He pulled out $5 in $1 bills. "Here, this is all I can afford right now. Hide it. Put it down in your crotch. Soldiers hate to search there. You'll need it, but be wise. You can buy some food, blankets and medicine if you have the money."

"Now my name is Master Sergeant Douglas Packa. Remember that and you come see me when this is over an' I'll have this waiting for you. Man needs a weapon he's already bloodied. Especially if you're heading back to Arizona."

"Oh, we will be…how many of us have survived?"

Packa reached over the wall of the wagon, coming back with a pouch of beef jerky. "This is pretty good stuff. Hide it where you can, but remember you will be searched for weapons before being put inside the prison. You'll need that meat. Between here and the cattle pens, eat as much as you can out of the pouch. I'll make sure the guard won't bother you. There's also a canteen. Except for what's hidden on you, you cannot take anything with you. But, kid, don't try to escape. These guards are under orders to shoot to kill any escaping prisoners."

"Why are you doin' this, Sergeant?" Liam asked. He stuffed the dollar bills in his front crotch area and began sliding strips of beef jerky down the back of his pants into his inner buttocks region. "I doubt I'll be sharing this with anyone."

Packa grinned. "You look a lot like my kid brother, maybe that's why. Now get into the wagon and chow down while you can. It's going to be awhile before you eat so well again."

"Thank you, MSgt. Packa…Stay safe."

MSgt. Packa nodded his head and then ordered two young guards into the wagon. He knew before long the three of them would be talking about their homes and experiences. He knew this was one of the problems about this Civil War: Americans were fighting Americans and no one was going to come out a true victor. He wasn't much of a philosopher-type.

Though he knew buildings could be rebuilt, the time it would take for healing amongst the two sides would take decades, if not centuries. A lot of his customers were from Southern States. He wondered if they would ever return to use his services. Although they were small to medium sized farms, they worked them with families. He did not know one who had the money to buy a slave or even wanted to. They wanted the Federal Government to butt out of state business and excessive taxes needed to stop. As result, even if the state didn't fall to the South, whole communities may have or a select group of farms.

Overnight, Liam was the lone prisoner. He was transported into Nashville. Once given a nightly tour of the big city he could smell what was coming next. Cattle yards. He soon shook hands with the two guards and the wagon driver. He was then hastily escorted to a full cattle pen. He was roughly patted down for weapons, told to remove his boots, which were quickly searched. Having no weapon. He was shoved bodily into a crowded yard that had the vile stench of cattle feces. There was ample evidence to prove their temporary jail was once used to house cattle and at one time, a pig or two.

Had Liam known he was only two cattle pens down from Captain JW Blake he would have found a way to join up with his superior and comrades. But it wasn't until the third day at El Mira that he learned of their existence and that was by ending up sharing the same "latrine hole" with Corporal Leaders. They were both pulling their pants up, with two other men between them, when Leaders glanced over and saw the young Liam.

"Liam! That is you, right?" Leaders said in an excited voice.

"Corporal...howdy! Nice place to meet old friends." He tightened the rope on his pants, tied it off and came over to give Leaders a brotherly embrace.

Leaders wasn't used to such affection, but he knew Liam was a young-one and being separated, even a short time must have been rough on him. He pushed Liam back, but held on to him. "You look good, Liam...No wounds or anything?"

"Nope, I ran right into a bunch of them. They had orders to catch us Rebels alive. But I met up with a swell Union sergeant. He fed me, gave me extra jerky I can share with the unit...If you don't mind where I had to hide it. Plus, he gave $5 in Union pay. Said I reminded him of his younger brother who was massacred by Comanche on the way to California. I thought he was goin' ta ask me about Black-Eagle an' Man-Who-Runs, but he never did. Said if I had been in the Union ranks they would've made me a drummer's boy. Other nice thing he did was ta keep my tomahawk. Told me he's a black smith in Sedalia and once the war ends to come by and pick it up on my way home."

"Now that is a decent Yankee, but let's go find the unit. Captain Blake's been worried about you."

"All this time I was worried about you fellows."

CAPTAIN BLAKE'S RANGERS

Frostbite was already a serious problem and for the men who had no boots or any form of shoes, some sort of footwear had to be produced to keep them from freezing their feet. First degree frostbite was not that abnormal for the men of the desert. Occasionally, the temperatures dropped low enough for prolonged exposure to bring about a case of first degree frostbite to those points on the body not covered. Usually this was seen on the ears, nose, hands and feet. In the high desert mountains, second degree frostbite could strike. This caused blistering to the skin and was extremely dangerous. In both cases, heat must be restored to the body, even if that should mean a sharing of body heat with another person and gentle bandaging of clothes dipped in hot water over the exposed parts. But only in the icy and snow areas of the high mountains does the possibility of third degree frostbite enter in, where the body part is exposed to frozen ground, ice crystals or snow for a prolong time. This can cause severe skin damage and loss of entire limbs or death to the victim. The skin goes through the first two stages and if nothing is done the skin will begin to turn black and eventually swell.

The ice on top of the septic marsh was now causing men with uncovered feet to freeze until they blackened with third degree frostbite. If they make it to the prison doctor in time and he is willing to operate, he will remove whatever limb or limbs that froze. Without medications, the prisoner would often die of infection.

Soldiers made a dangerous game of sliding across the ice, knowing that a fall might cause them to break an arm or a leg, but the depression brought on by the imprisonment here at El Mira brought such steps forward as a way of playing with suicide. Men gave up, attacking guards; not to escape the prison, but to escape the trap their mind was now in, where the suffering was far too great for them to handle anymore.

JW Blake wondered if El Mira Prison Camp would ever be remembered. The treatment of fellow Americans, of fellow humans, went far below the acceptable treatment of animals. Men were dying all over the camp and more than half of those who were sent to the hospital never came back.

He traded a silver piece—a Mexican peso he had brought back from the war and carried, sewn into his shirt, since then—for a tin cup. He hoped to eventually present the coin to his son, for him to carry and deliver to his son. JW wondered how many generations that coin might be carried, but now it was gone. He needed to trade it for a dented up tin coffee cup. This allowed them the capability of carrying a hot cup of chicory coffee to a sick man. Several men carried the chicory in uncomfortable placements, tossed into cattle cars during stops and shoved into their hands while they lined up for food. The hardest part was bandage material, but it was some of the Union Yankees who funneled bandaging material to them. These ended up being Christian soldiers who now saw brothers in need and not opponents. JW couldn't believe some of the events that transpired on the train cars. Guards on the roofs looked the other way during water stops for the engine in towns, where people ran up to shove food, old shoes and boots, coats and sweaters, and even blankets. These were not Rebel sympathizers, but members of the different Christian faiths. They knew these men were headed to El Mira or other northern prisons, but El Mira was already legendary as a death hole, or Hell Hole.

But it was true, JW Blake found El Mira to be exactly what it was rumored to be. "This must be Hell," JW said to Lt. Dreeke.

Once every three days, the officers of El Mira held a General Officer's Call before a two-star Confederate General. At last count, there were 139 officers present. During the last meeting, the officers were advised of the Confederate attack on the City of Nashville and its failure. Most of the Army of Texas was routed by a vastly superior force, which caused General Hood to finally withdraw. There had been some initial talk from a captain who'd been captured of how General Hood was considering resigning his command to General Lee.

This really shook JW up and his head was down as he returned to his campsite inside their designated area. He was surprised to hear a celebration of sorts was in process and lifted his eyes to see Liam looking right back at him. Liam then ran to him, but rather than embrace the man he saw as he adopted father, he came to stop, braced himself and raised his right hand in a parade ground salute. "Sir, Pvt. Liam…Blake, returning to duty and reporting in, Sir."

JW smiled as he returned the salute and braced the boy's shoulders between his two hands, "You have no idea how happy I am to see you…alive and well. Now what is this Liam Blake stuff?"

"Captain, my family was massacred and so was my name. When captured, I gave your last name…so Sherry Ann might get notice of it and know I am still alive. I lost her horse though and for that I am sorry. But if it is all right with you, I would like to keep using your name as mine. I claim no rights with it, only for others to know I have a family alive in Arizona."

"Liam, you have made me proud so many times, I'd be honored to call you family. But I have an oldest son, so if anyone asks, you are my adopted young brother. Is that okay with you?"

Liam was speechless, all he could do was embrace his captain, which got a soft applause from the Arizona Rangers.

Later that night as the Rangers sat around the fire pit, burning scrounged up wood tossed into the yard from old rail cars being torn apart. Liam noticed that several of the men had picked up a cough, which had JW concerned. He had already told his men about what had happened at the Officer's Call and how it was feared the Army of Texas had been decimated by Grant's troops. "The General also issued an order, we are to escape in any way possible. To return to our old units and once more fight for the south." He waited as this information spread through the unit. He knew the Sanders Cousins were not going anywhere. Their cough had spread into full blown pneumonia and JW didn't know how many days these Missouri Ozark boys had left.

"Now for some good news, with the General's permission I had word put out for all Rangers, from Texas to Arizona, to join up with us. We Rangers will work together on putting an escape plan together and try to get out as many Rangers as possible. Any objections?"

"What about traitors…spies, anyone who will sell us for a decent meal or a warm night's sleep?" MSgt. Gary Wells asked.

"That has me concerned, I won't lie to you. This place has put us through an inhuman strain and can break a good man. I think every man who wants to join must be supported by two others. I don't know what else we can do. But the best thing for us, we're putting Rangers together.

When it was all said and done, Captain JW Blake now had a Brigade Command of two full-sized Companies; 122 Rangers from Texas, New Mexico, Arizona and half a dozen from the expired California Rangers. Blake would lead. He had seven lieutenants of second and first ranks. Experience was not a problem with 17 sergeants able to hold the ranks together.

First Lt. Jack Borders of the Texas Rangers would command A Company; while MSgt. Sam Watkins of New Mexico Rangers, would be his First Sergeant. First Lt. Bret Sampson of Arizona Rangers would command B Company, with MSgt. Gary Wells as his First Sergeant. Rather than non-commissioned officers, squad leaders would be first and second lieutenants, supported by seasoned NCOs. Three squads of 19 each per company, with back-up officers ready to take command in the event of losses. Second Lt. Dreeke was assigned to Captain Blake and Pvt. Liam Blake was assigned the Brigade Runner. Each company was also to assign a runner.

All of this information and who was assigned per squad was presented to NCOs and officers at the Ranger's for Commander's Call. Squad leaders were designated to contact the men assigned to them to make it official. "Now this is a toughie, Gentlemen. When the time to escape does come and I expect it soon, we will not be able to take the sick ones with us. This will be an all or nothing attempt and as much as I hate to say this, we cannot have the injured or unhealthy ones slowing us down. Also, if a man is wounded before we're able to locate our horses, those wounded will have to be left in the hands of…I pray the chivalrous and honorable Union soldiers." Blake looked about and then added, "I am awaiting further orders so for now take care of each other, and this is the most import thing…survival."

A TUNNEL FOUND

For two days, Scouts Holloway and Jim Williams had been conducting a search of the walls surrounding El Mira Prison Camp. Often or not the guards ordered them away, but during one foray they found the entry of an ancient tunnel, covered in dirt over logs. It was the shape of the entry that caught Holloway's attention, as he had seen such an opening to underground root cellars among the Navajo people.

Holloway grabbed William by the elbow to pull him back and he carefully gestured to the dirt covered door. "Could be nothing but storage from the old days, before the war, or it's an old tunnel used by prisoners when this camp was first used. The location is good, the guards will have a hard time seeing us and we can use the shadows to make our way. Only problem I see is moving from this spot we're standing. I'll start stargazing and if I can get the guard to look up to see what I am looking at. You can hustle over there. But I'll stay here."

"What do you want me to do when I get there?" Williams asked.

"You could stargaze with the guard and me…or you can open the door and see what's inside. If it's a tunnel, we'll come back tomorrow night prepared to check it out from that side. Now you ready?"

"Yeah, show that Yankee where Jupiter is and wish us luck." Jim Williams waited until the guard was curious enough to look to the sky and see what had Holloway's attention. Then he quietly ran.

Jim had to leap over an ice-covered obstacle, that was now unknown to him but he thought it might've been a wheelbarrow now buried. He made it to the wall and quickly found the dirt covered door. It surprised him to find the wood door was made-of thin tubes tightly woven together and initially covered in a woven carpet material. He had heard of these tubes and remembered they were called "bamboo". He wondered how a plant that normally grew far into the deep-south could be up here in New York. But that question was for later. The door was five foot in length by three-foot width and extremely light to move as he slowly opened it. He suspected that was why the dirt was put on it; to camouflage the door and weigh it down. Yet, he wondered why no ice or snow covered this door, while the hillside around it was still covered in the wintry effects.

Once it was open wide enough for him to slide through, he entered the hole and saw — pitch black darkness. He reached out and could tell this was a tunnel or cave for there was a-distance-of-some-sorts, but without light, he risked too much to venture further. Thankfully, when he turned around he could see a dim light coming from the surrounding seal of the door. The lights of the encampment provided his exit. Now he simply had to work his way out without being spotted and then crawl over into the shadows to wait for the guards to be on the far side of their coverage, so he could silently dash back to the Ranger camp to deliver his report. "But what did I find?" He asked himself in a whisper.

The next night there was Captain JW Blake, Liam for his small size and ability to squeeze into narrow spaces, Jim Williams and Holloway. There was also MSgt. Gary Wells and five good-sized Texas Rangers of B Company, in the event some force might be needed.

With so many people, it took them nearly ten-minutes to get everyone through the bamboo doorway. They had candles, bought for $1 a piece on the trade market in the camp and three torches. Rangers combined their cash to reveal a bank of $63 and 45 cents American money and $230.00 in Confederate dollars that no one was taking now.

The area ahead of them was now well lit and everyone could see it was a tunnel of some size. They also felt waves of warmth and this troubled all of them. From the smell, Holloway mentioned he had smelled the same thing in thermal tubes that crossed underground from volcano to volcano. But no one had ever heard of a volcano in New York.

"These tubes here must run for hundreds of miles, but I think this gas we're now smelling will probably disable us with ten-miles. We need to find a departure point, where the other prisoners got out." JW Blake said. He had been inside such tubes in South Arizona and in Mexico and knew they could kill silently.

"Captain, we cannot tell time, they've stripped us of everything but our minds, So, I recommend we take turns counting to sixty at an even speed, out loud and then someone else take over. Liam, you count-off on your fingers when we reach ten. Then we'll turn around and make a speedy return," Jim Williams said.

"Okay, with me, who's going to start?" Liam asked.

"I will," Jim replied and he began. "One…two…three…four…five". They continued moving forward as he counted off the numbers.

By the time Liam counted-off eight minutes, one of the bigger men brought along as an enforcer, began to feel feint and he plopped down. "You all go ahead, ah'll wait here."

But right then, Holloway yelled out, "I found it, come on ahead for some fresh air." The opening had been camouflaged and Holloway might not have found it. He tripped over a rock and fell against the door. His weight dislodged the door and he fell out into a grassy plateau. Without knowing it they had been traveling upward and now looked down upon the prison camp. From where they stood, JW Blake could see the deep blue green water of the Atlantic Ocean and one of the first Union warships he had ever seen. Even at this extreme distance, he knew that the Union having such powerful creations, the South was undone. He didn't say anything to the others.

The plateau was covered in deep snow. There were homes below where they could steal warm clothes and food. They would not harm civilians. JW Blake remembered reading how the New York militia had refused to join in Lincolns War, causing an American president to send American warships in New York harbor to fire upon the City of New York. Only then did the New York Militia join the attack on the South.

When Captain Blake and the others returned to their camp they found another surprise waiting for them. MSgt. Michael Wallace, PFC Andy Salcedo and PFC Sigmund Udo had finally arrived at El Mira Death Camp. They transferred through four other Prison Camps before being dropped off here. All three still had their limbs, no disease or coughs, both eyes and ears and no frostbite showing. Captain Blake took them aside and explained what was about to happen and after the surprise wore off they were ready to join in. MSgt. Wallace was assigned B Company, Third Assistant Squad Leader behind Second Lieutenant Joe Masters. PFC Salcedo and PFC Udo had been assigned to B Company, Second Squad, under First Lieutenant Bart Masters, who was seconded by his younger brother Second Lieutenant Bret Hansen. They even had a younger brother; Sgt. Bo Hansen, assigned to A Company's second squad.

Captain JW Blake had soon learned the Texas Rangers had a lot of brothers and cousins in the Rangers. The Adams Brothers numbered four, plus that had three cousins who were brothers. He also had the three Nestle Brothers and two New Mexico Rangers who used fake names, calling themselves—Corporal Lad Zinc and Oldster Copper. But he didn't have time to get into this and the New Mexico acting commander said Zinc and Copper were excellent Rangers.

Three days later, the General gave the Rangers the okay to make their escape. A disturbance would be initiated at 11:45 in the area used primarily by the Rebel artillery men, who spent their time arguing about distances and the right loads, and what it would take to blow this wall apart. They were also working on an escape, but the Ranger were first in line.

"Once you hear the shouting and threats from the guards, it's your time to move. We will do the best we can for those you must leave behind. You must get out of those clothes and travel in small groups...Good luck and God Bless your journey south." The General offered Blake his hand, which Blake shook and he then popped a salute, which the General returned.

"I wish you were going with us, General," Blake said.

"In some ways, I also do, but my new command is here now and keep as many of these men alive as possible is what I must do. Still, a large escape may have the American congress looking into the shape their prisons are in. I also know the sad shape our Andersonville is in and it is a black eye to our beautiful south. Now get going, Captain. You do not have that much time."

"Yes, sir and I've ordered my men not to kill or wound any civilians during our trip south. I pray we can all keep that promise."

"I do to, Blake, otherwise you will be looked upon as thieves and murderers, not escaping soldiers."

JW left the ratty headquarters tent, where cold icy air blew through the holes and evening snow would often burry the General's fire. JW prayed this good man would survive the surrender of the South and be able-to return to his home in Louisiana.

When he made it back to his camp, JW realized he had lost feeling to his left foot. The lack of feeling spread up over his ankle, but not to his calf. He could still walk on it, in fact he hadn't realized it was frozen solid until he had accidently thumped his foot into a small ice spike sticking up and felt absolutely nothing. Now he was frightened. Unless he was able-to thaw out his foot, which was going to be sincerely painful, third degree frostbite would begin and the only answer was to cut his foot off. He briefly wondered if he should stay back with the other wounded, but he wanted to see his family to ensure they were safe from the Apache and whatever the federal people were doing to take his property. No, he would go on, but he would seek shelter in one of the homes below to bring his leg back to the living and send the others on. Liam would stay with him and that is all he would need.

The prisoners were sectioned off in their squads. Goodbyes were shared with those being left behind. It was tough for everyone. Then came the first shout, followed by hundreds of yells and shots fired up into the air. Men were yelling out their protests against bad food, poor conditions and prisoners freezing to death. It was time to move. JW Blake new they only had moments.

They went out with A Company following Scout Holloway, who went back and forth, but not before cleaning his lungs out on the plateau or he risked passing out in the thermal tube. Torches were now lit in place, marking the length of the tube and the soldiers were advised to move fast to get the whole Ranger command through the tube before the disturbance ended and the guards in this area returned.

A Company was through and was now moving southwest down the plateau toward the city to find clothes from wherever possible, remembering the order not to steal, rob or kill; which would put them all before a hangman's rope and no longer looked upon as Rebels trying to escape and rejoin their outfits. This was sort of expected of them by the rules of war.

Now B Company was in the tube and a volunteer recovered the opening and camouflaged the door once more. But now the southerners knew where the escape tunnel was, found by some prisoner who knew something about volcanic thermal tubes. The Rangers would forever owe their escape to the scientific fellow.

WHEN MORNING CAME

With the first break of sunlight, the Union guards new something was wrong. Numerous prisoners were suddenly missing. All the guards were accounted for, and none of the gates were damaged. Within moments, the main alarms sounded all over the valley. The wind-up alarm up high on the El-Mira Town water-tower was being turned by a barely awake volunteer fireman and as people looked up to him he shouted down, "Prison break! Over 100 prisoners vanish without a trace. Union troops ordered in!"

By now, most of A Company was already riding a cargo train heading due south for Nashville, loaded down with supplies for the Union troops. The men fought a strong desire to blow the train up, but they would keep their promises to Captain Blake. Such an explosion would destroy the tracks and impede food supplies going back and forth between towns and cities. He asked the troops to wait until they could rejoin

Southern forces and then they were released from their promise and Ranger's pride kept those promises held fast. But the Texas, New Mexico and California Rangers would never return to their units. In two days, the North and South received news of General Lee's surrender of the South to General Grant at Appomattox. A strange bittersweet victory for the North and a sad and painful loss for the South. Now it was time to rebuild America, but the rebuilding would come slowly.

Captain JW Blake and his Arizona Rangers, who refused to abandon him, rested inside an abandoned mansion. From what they could determine, the home once belonged to a large family with extensive interests in the Georgia cotton industry. From the broken windows, fire damage and foul words painted outside the homes, the family was convinced to abandon this beautiful home to flee for their lives to the south; which left the men a choice of nine bedrooms, plus a beautiful master bedroom decorated to look like a sea captain's cabin. There was a Teak king size bed with four huge carved beams shooting up to the ceiling, handsome artwork from all over the world and fireplaces in every single room. The men wondered if they used the fireplaces, would the thugs might return. After some searching, they discovered the owner's hidden arsenal—a walk-in armory—with four walls of various types and sizes of rifles and drawers with handguns. There were also standing cabinets in a second room, where ammunition was stored.

"It appears the man took what he could, but left so much more. I also came upon a drawer filled with gold coin. Must've been his saving account and he was worried about the weight." Lt. Bret Sampson said to JW. At the time, JW was in the living room, soaking his frozen foot in tepid water. He soaked it every other hour for 30-minutes and still, only now was he beginning to feel anything at all.

"It will take time and we have time. At Hell's Hole, we have now stumbled upon Heaven to restore ourselves. When we are in readiness, we will return to the subject of war," Lt. Sampson said, as he carefully poured some hot water into his foot bath.

But it was right then, in the late afternoon, the main town area of El Mira erupted into song, dancing in the street and great revelry. A whole city-wide celebration. Captain JW Blake needed to know in the event they needed to quickly move along. Possibly the other Rangers had been caught and they were being brought back. If so, they would need to rescue them before they were tossed back into that frozen marsh. "Liam, you sound the most northern and still look too young to fight. Go out the back…leave the pistol," He saw the bulge of the pistol butt sticking out from under his pants belt. They all took advantage of the male clothes left behind, by either servants or the owner himself.

"Sneak on out of here and then act carefree, like a visiting relative. Anyone asks, you have an uncle who works at the prison...you must remember a guard's name?"

"Sure I do, a whole lot of them and the whips they used on me."

"Old news, son. Now go find out and get back here." JW glanced at a couple others. "You go into the kitchen pantry and throw whatever you can into strong canvas carry bags. Not just beans either. Grab some of the hash, the stew...don't forget all that fruit. Rest of you get yourself armed up. Rifle and set of revolvers for each of you. I saw he's got a rack of those new Winchesters, so make sure you each got enough ammo for them for some time, plus power and ball for the revolvers. There's a Henry in there and that is mine. I'll pick up my own ammo...And, I haven't seen any hunting knives, so we'll have to make our own or buy them."

JW gave the house a good hard look. I don't like the idea of thievery and breaking my own promise, but this man made all his money off Southern backs. He never fought for the South and from what I have seen I doubt he took very good care of his slaves and his type owned a lot of them to pick his cotton. But I may be jumping to conclusions. So, we will not take all his weapons, all his food nor all his gold. Each of you will take ten-to-20 gold pieces. That's $200 each and more than you will probably ever see again riding as a Ranger. But I feel you earned what we found here from that Northern Hell Hole. Too many of our comrades and our friends died there because the Union didn't bother to take care of us. I am told our Andersonville was of the same level, but I pray it wasn't. So, this is all we take...agreed?"

They all agreed and by the time JW had counted out the gold pieces for Liam and selected a nearly new Winchester lever action 30-30 for him, Liam had come back to the mansion right through the front door.

"Hey, Kid...what are you doing? You want people to know we're here?" Jim Williams asked.

Liam looked at all of them, his face a pasty white in color and then his eyes locked on JW, who asked him, "What is it, Liam...did they catch the other Rangers?"

"No, Sir...far as I know they are on their way south...But Captain, General Lee has surrendered the South. General Grant took his surrender at a place called Appomattox. The Civil War is over."

CHAPTER NINE

"Sure dun feel a lot's longer ridin' home, dan ridin' off ta way. My durn bunns hurt!"

RIDING THROUGH UPPER MISSOURI ON THEIR WAY BACK TO TUCSON, ARIZONA AND THEN UP TO GLOBE

It had taken the men all night and into the next day to realize their war was lost, but then they realized there was nothing to stop them now from going home. But they needed horses or at least a couple wagons. Instead, Captain JW Blake decided they would take a train into Pennsylvania, for he had heard a man could purchase good horse flesh there.

He brought his Ranger Command back together and announced, "Things have changed for us and the owner of this manor. As I understand war and what occurs afterward, this man will be forced to pay an amazing amount in tax money. This means all that gold coin will be divided up between a Yankee court judge, some to a Yankee politician and a small percentage probably sent on to the Nation's capital for road improvement and rebuilding of federal buildings. So, we just might as well keep all that money to keep it out of the hands of those thieving Yankees. Along the way, we can hand it out to deserving people in bad ways. What do you think about that?"

Everyone of course agreed and the extra weapons, shot and powder was loaded into one of the three wagons left behind. There were no horses, so Holloway, Brady Williams and Corporal Gibson went into town and found their way to the stables of a well-known horse peddler, who had kept his best horses hid from both armies in a hidden valley. Once their gold was displayed, they were taken by coach out to the location, where the Rangers purchased 12 heavy well-matched half-ton Percheron draft horses that quickly satisfied all three men. Total cost was $820.00 for the horses and all the leather work they would need for the wagons. Everyone knew the horses were worth far much more, but no one else had money to throw around so close to the war's ending and the stable owner was happy with the deal. He could finally put some decent clothes on his kids and purchase a couple flatbed wagons of feed bales for his other animals. A year from now he would laugh at the offer he'd taken, or maybe he would've cried.

With weapons, ammo and powder, clothing, blankets and a ton of canned food, the plunderers of the cotton tycoon headed southwest. What they never learned was how the greedy cotton tycoon, who had owned over 200 slaves, while en-route to England, ran right smack into a major storm and his ship was lost at sea. There were some survivors, but sadly his entire family had gone down to a watery grave. No one ever knew about the lost gold coins, or any of the items stolen from the home. But the U.S. Government did seize all his property for taxes owed, which included 2,650 acres in Georgia, his mansion and 60 acres in El Mira and a small island off the West Coast of California known as the Isle of Catalina.

JW had declined to purchase any mount for himself and encouraged the others to wait until they reached the famous horse farms in Pennsylvania. "For once we have the gold to buy the finest horseflesh in the world and I for one, am going to wait. I know the travel by wagon will be rough, but we should be there in three to four days, maybe less. One of the first things we need to do when we hit a big city is buy us some maps. I'd hate to miss Arizona and fall off into the Gulf of Mexico." That got him a laugh. They all knew they would hit the Texas panhandle first and from there, finding Arizona would be easy enough. The real problem would be avoiding renegades and Indians, especially the Comanche and later, the Apache. But at least they would be well armed this time and JW figured his Band of Brothers could stand-off a killing raid of 50 to 60 warriors with their lever action repeaters. They were also hauling 500-rounds per rifle.

At the first horse farm, some of the men had bought some handsome mounts, but JW was holding out and so was Liam. He also wanted to bring home the perfect mare to replace the one he lost belonging to Sherry Ann.

At the third horse farm, JW was astonished at the herds and the breeds he saw running free between the white painted fences. He saw Golden Palominos with their long golden manes upon bronzed bodies; many of the beautiful Appaloosas in all different dappling's and shades. Great black stallions and beautiful brown mares with white stars on their foreheads and from one to four white socks above the hooves. There was one small herd of pure white horses running free through the trees, gracefully staying apart by several feet in protecting the younger colts, while following a towering giant of a white stallion. JW had found his horse, only to find out the owner of the farm would not sell the stallion because of its age and how it was now used for breeding. JW couldn't believe it, but this stallion of 20-hands, was 15 years old and not been ridden for the last two-years.

"This was my wife's last horse, sir. She died when news came both our sons had died nearby at Gettysburg. Later, I and some of my friends rode over to hear the President speak. It was an eerie feeling, sort of. That speech was like no other I have ever heard or seen in print...kind of like right up there with the U.S. Constitution...but maybe my son's dying there made it more personal."

"I would think so, Sir...I am fortunate my son was much too young to serve," JW said.

"Well, I mentioned it felt eerie-like because there were still so many bodies lying about from both the Union and the Confederate sides. So, many died in those three days, it must've taken them nearly a month to get everyone underground. Before then, I had felt strongly against my one son running of to fight for the South, but on that battlefield, I saw blue and gray soldiers embracing each other, knowing they were dying and it weren't no life or death struggle. It was a hug, a wanting to hold some one for those last breaths on this earth. I kept thinking about family who found family out there in the hellish field of men stacked upon each other. It made me think of my sons and I asked myself, 'Did they locate each other in those last moments?' I sure hope so. But now is the time for our country to heal, to lay aside these last four years and help each one rebuild."

JW was weary of telling lies to people about him and his group as they made their way south and he was ready to test this man's convictions. "Sir, you are a gentleman, who has made for yourself a fine business here, but you have not asked me of what side my friends and I had served with...so, I will tell you. I am Captain JW Blake, former Arizona Ranger and these are my men. We are returning home. But, during the war our Rangers were dismantled and we went to ride with General Hood of the Army of Texas. For eight months we were held as prisoners at the El Mira Prison of War Camp in New York. As I've been told it is comparable to the South's Andersonville Prison Camp. Both being Hell Holes of Humanity, where prisoners died of neglect, starvation and greed of the camp supervisors. This was done by both sides, not one and someday, I pray those responsible for so many deaths will be held to account. Now, do you wish to continue our deal or have us leave your property? I will truly understand if you would rather have us leave."

The man cocked his head to one side and gave JW a hard glare, but then it softened and he spoke, "I say what I think and what I say I follow through with." He offered his hand to JW and the two men shook hands. "Now let me show you one of this stallion's better squirts. I think you'll like him. He's 19-hands, near 500-pounds of ornery cursedness. He can run faster than his Dad and for longer because of his mother's breed...she's a beautiful black and gray Appaloosa. So, if you're returning to Arizona, he's the one for you. But he's got to accept you, otherwise you'll never get on his back."

"Sir, you've issued me a challenge ah can't refuse," JW said. "Is it okay to let my men wander about some, I'd like my men to have two mounts each before we leave this fine state of yours,

"Did you ever reach our state in any of your forays, Captain Blake? I ask because I do not recall reading anything about the Army of Texas making it this high up."

"We scouted for the General, he liked using Arizona, New Mexico and Texas Rangers for scouts, but Virginia and Tennessee was as far as we got. I'm right happy to have missed Gettysburg, but that was mostly an infantry engagement. I have heard it was not one of General Lee's best decision to hold there for three days and continue attacking the Union lines. The Union held the high ground, with artillery and sadly, the killing field was so large and open. Far too many gallant young men on both sides perished during that battle. But I will have you know, I have had the grand experience to meet some fine and courageous Union Officers during this war. Some I believe if the situation was different I'd be able to call them friends. I would further go on to say I would be saddened to hear they had died before the final bugle was blown in this hostility."

The elderly man who owned the farm shook his head, "Your men must love you, Captain and I trust your Indians and bandits despise your directness. Now let's go look at your horse."

That night the men of Arizona stayed in the bunk house with the workers, but they received orders there would be no fighting with the ex-Yankee workers. There was also no drinking of beer or other alcoholic beverages allowed, at risk of job termination. So, the evening dinner, which was pretty good, was very subdued, until a couple guitars came out and some harmonicas. A commonality between enlisted men's songs began to ring out and carry over the ranch yard.

In the old man's dining room, JW, Sampson and Dreeke were invited to have a semi-formal dinner with the old man and his foreman. The home was good-sized, with a dining room table capable of sitting 30-people and a living room able to play host to some 50-people. There were three indoor outhouses, a kitchen that could handle five cooks and seven-bedrooms on the lower lever and two-bedrooms on the upper level— which included a massive master bedroom.

JW learned how the house began as an early patriot's log cabin back in 1765 and the family had grown and built around it. One of the signers of the Declaration of Independence was the first family member, who had built the cabin and later fought the British. The story as told to JW was how the man had lost his life to Shoshone Indians during a hunting trip before the U.S. Constitution was ratified in 1786. But it was in the early

1800's the family had gotten into horse breeding. General Grant was riding one of the farm's horses, which impressed the three guests.

The meal of beef steak had also impressed the guests, but none of the men could finish their hunks of charred beef. Their stomach had not healed yet from the starvation diet of El Mira. Even the cans of stew at the rich man's manor were taken in slowly, but hunks of rich beef could cause their systems some real difficulty and the farm owner understood, when JW explained the difficulty.

"I apologize, Gentlemen…I had not thought about your previous…difficulty. I had simply wanted to provide a good meal to prove I am truly happy this exhausting war is really over and wish you well."

"Sir, you have done that by providing us with such fine horses. We will be the envy of all Arizona and we are all thankful." Lt. Sampson said.

For James Dreeke, he had pushed the steak aside and was shoving a forkful of apple pie into his mouth. He decided to let those two do all the talking, knowing they would be back on rations soon enough. But he did appreciate the two mounts he found today, they were like twin goddesses. Two buckskin mares with black manes and long tails. He had always wanted a light brown buckskin and these two were both 18-hand mares and only five years of age.

By daybreak the ranch-hands were up, having had their breakfast and were now busy at work. First off, the chore was to feed and water the ranch horses and clean the stalls. For the Rangers, gold coins were flipped to see who would drive the wagons for the first stretch. The driver's mounts would be tied off to the wagon's gate. The rest of the men would pull their extra mount behind them and this involved a little bit of training. Some of these horses were not used to being ridden with another horse in tow. So, the first stretch on the road was an example of loud voices and in Liam's case, being tossed off his saddle to the hard ground. His towed horse had simply dug its hind hooves in and braked. Pulling Liam backwards and rolling him over his new horse's left hip.

The horses being towed by wagon often object, too. This was a whole new experience for them. But for JW, his new horse pranced along as if he was king of the roadway. There were a few times when he objected to a direction of travel JW wished to take and in that case, JW simply removed his long dark blue scarf from his neck and wrapped it around the horse's head, blinding the horse. The frightened horse would dance around, trying to dislodge the scarf and JW, but when that failed he would cease his actions. A moment would pass and JW would remove the scarf and provide a slice of dried apple to the horse. Over a short time, they had no further problem. JW had learned this teaching aid from the Yaqui Indians, who would also use rivers to ride wild horses into and keep them tied from both banks. In this way, they would learn to trust the man on their back or risk drowning and the tight ropes prevented the horse from escaping.

When there was only one or two people a small corral, just a bit larger than the horse, could be built in a five-foot deep pool off the river. The horse was dragged by a rope into the corral and tied-off to the front logs. Now depending on Indian or White man who would be riding it, the man would first get the horse used to having a saddle blanket placed on it, followed by the saddle. Then when the rider was ready, with extra padding tied about his legs for when he'd be slammed against the corral logs, he would mount the horse. The ride could be short or long depending on the spirit of the horse, but some smart horses had been known to behave broken in the corral and then go crazy with the rider on him or her outside the corral. Men have been drowned and horses hurt beyond usage, forcing them to be killed. But odds were this was the safest way to break a wild horse.

The blacksmith at the horse farm had over a dozen ornate saddles with silver rings and gaucho shells, plus strips of shiny silver and highly polished buttons running the side of the saddles. Stirrups were covered in the fine silver and all this made the saddles weigh nearly twice as heavy as before. Every one of the Rangers was impressed with his work and all the ornate saddles were purchased, along with his fine leather ones for the second mount. Bridles and reins were thrown in for free, along with new shoeing for all the horses. This would allow the men to be able to leave by noon.

A local leather smith heard by word-of-mouth of the horse buyers with gold to spend and he came over with a wagon of cartridge belts, leather vests, flat brimmed western hats dyed in various colors, rifle slings for the saddles, knife sheaths, plus a selection of Bowie knives and other miscellaneous items. Every man bought a rifle sheath for their new Winchester and JW's Henry. He also had the Leather Smith sew two nice looking holsters to the front of his working saddle and then walked over to the equipment wagon and retrieved two Navy Colts with ten-inch barrels. They slid perfectly right into the holsters and JW handed the Leather Smith a gold $20 gold piece, stamped with the U.S. Mint on one side.

"It's been a long time since I've seen one of these…my wife's going to just flip."

"Then here, give her a second one a let me have one of those Bowie knives with a sheath," JW replied.

"But, Sir…with a sheath the knife is only $8."

"You got kids?"

"Why, yes...I do, sir."

"Spend the change on them. The war was rough on all of us, especially the young ones." JW turned and walked away to allow the man some pride. He knew that such a man had probably begun to weep and he did not need anyone seeing it.

It was closer to 2 p.m. before the Rangers left in a small convoy. The ranch owner had directed JW toward a large town where he should be able to find maps for sale and a place where the Rangers could lay their hands on some decent boots, gloves and wind breakers for the long ride south.

That first night they camped under the stars, but off the road. Still, they could hear a lot of troops headed north as veterans returned home. Men with no money for trains were walking all the way back to Iowa and Ohio farmlands. It made JW think about all the Southern troops hiking back to Southern California, Arizona, New Mexico and Texas. He couldn't help but wonder how many of these foot soldiers would make it and did they still have their rifles when the mustered out. He had heard the Southern troops were either allowed to keep a bayonet or a sword, but no firearms. The Federal Government was fearful of Southerners joining up together to become gangs and attack settlers heading west.

But now with President Lincoln dead, assassinated in Ford's Theater by the actor John Wilks Booth, fear spread through the south in what was to become of the Black worker who was now free. So, some of the wagon trains were made up of Black families trying to find a future out West in California or Oregon. But the trail was a tough one and dishonest men posing as legitimate western scouts robbed these people and then abandoned them in the middle of East Texas, with no town or any civilization around as the scandalous thieves rode off with the wagon train's cash box.

ON THEIR WAY

Map in hand, new boots on their feet, several pairs of gloves and jackets, along with insulated long riding coats for those cold Arizona mornings, plus each wagon now covered. Everyone better armed than they had ever been, having traded in their long-barreled Navy Colts for either the newly issued Colt .44s or Colt .45s, with six-inch barrels. New holsters were required but that wasn't a problem as-long-as you had money. When questioned by the law, their story was of taking a major sized herd to Nashville and being paid off there. As for not serving in the war, their excuse was Nevada wanted them to stay on as cowboys to deliver the herds through Indian Territory. So far, the story held and now the war was long over.

Each wagon carried three barrels of water, which gave them five barrels for the horses and four barrels for the men. One wagon carried the extra weapons and half of the ammo, plus half of the shiny saddles. Wagon #3 carried half of the ammo, plus the other half of the shiny holster, extra gear and night sleeping roles. James Dreeke and Gary Wells worked hard to divvy up the load evenly. They were not too worried about the horses, knowing these beasts could tear down the pillars of Rome, but they were antsy about the wagons themselves. Weapons and ammo, plus water were a heavy load, along with the remaining gold.

With pushing themselves by riding a half-hour after daybreak, giving everyone enough time for a quick bite and a hot cup of coffee, horses watered and fed, the men and animals would ride until the sun was about ready to drop behind the horizon. This gave them just enough time to get a fire built, a camp set up and chores completed. Lunch break was when JW's new silver and gold pocket watch said it was 12 p.m. and lasted for 45-minutes. Horses were rested, fed and watered by the owners, who then fed themselves and took all of 15-minutes to ease their backsides from the morning ride. Now it was time to switch wagon drivers and Liam was not looking forward to his stint on the hard seat. He had ridden up behind Chris Wakefield and watched as the big guy was shaken up and down, then crossways, as the wagon covered the ground. Liam wondered if it might be a softer ride if he climbed on the back of the front draft horse and led the wagon that way, but he rode up beside those massive horses and didn't like the looks in their eyes. "You got some evil ways in you, horse...so I'll keep my whip handy if you decide ta act up." Liam rode on ahead to ride beside JW.

By nightfall they sighted the Great Mississippi River. They were now on the western side, using a series of bridges to work their way over. A check of the Missouri map showed they were only 60-some miles away from this town of Sedalia. "Do you think he's had time to muster out and get back home, JW?" Liam asked. He was referring to Sgt. Packa, who had disarmed him, kept his tomahawk and given him U.S. $5 and some beef jerky. He was living in Sedalia as a blacksmith and would return the tomahawk to Liam when he came for it.

"Do you think he expects the $5 back?" Liam asked James Dreeke, who was riding on the other side of Liam.

"Ah would imagine so and yuh cun afford it now, my youn' sir." James replied.

"Oh, that's right...I forgot."

They made camp that night off the shores of a stream. Dinner was red bean hash, with canned peaches and hot coffee. Mosquitoes were bad and it was bothering the horses, also. It got so bad the men finally gave up, broke camp and headed toward Sedalia at 4 a.m. So, rather than take a second night in the woods to reach the town, they pulled into the main street a few minutes after 7 p.m. Their appearance got the immediate attention of the town constables; seeing how well armed they were and a group of 16 men, plus three wagons and extra horses.

Knowing of the need to be direct with the law, JW dismounted and walked right up to the ranking constable and offered his right hand, which was obviously his shooting hand and introduced himself. "Officer, the name is JW Blake, late Captain of the Arizona Rangers and recent cattle boss for a herd my men and I delivered to Nashville, Tennessee. We're on our way back home, but needed to stop by here in your beautiful town to see a blacksmith by the name of Packa. Now with it being so late, I was hoping you could point me toward a campground where my men and I, plus all-of our horses could rest for the night. Tomorrow, we'll look up Mr. Packa, visit with him for a moment or so and then we will depart your fair township. We still have a long way to go to reach our homes in Arizona and have a lot of Apache and Ute to deal with once we reach our homes."

Tongue-tied briefly, Constable Martin, who wore the double stripes of a corporal on one arm, nodded his head. "Yes, sir…I've heard of the Arizona Rangers and your fights with the Apache…a fearsome bunch. I can see why you're so well armed. You even carry the new Colts, but were stuck in the dark ages with ball shot and black powder."

"Would you like to see my revolver, Constable Martin?" JW read his sewn-on name tag, that was no longer bouncing about from nerves.

"May I?"

"I'll have to unload it…my personal policy of never handing a man a loaded firearm and this is a Colt 44, which also fits my rifle."

"Yes, sir, I understand that." Martin waited for JW to remove the firearm, open the cylinder and unload five rounds. Though it fired six-rounds, he never kept a round under the hammer, when traveling.

"Why, it's heavier than I thought," Martin said. He turned and stretched his arm out to point the weapon at a blank wall. "You must cock the hammer each time before you fire it, correct?"

"Yes, but they will soon come out with a newer model where you will not have to cock the hammer, but I am not sure which of these will be considered safer to carry."

"If you do not mind me asking, what do you carry for a rifle?" Martin asked as he glanced over at JW's most beautiful horse and saw two Colt .44's, attached to his saddle.

"I'll be glad to chat with you, Constable, but my troops are weary from days of riding. Could you show us to a camp and recommend us a fine eatery?"

"Of course, I do apologize. You've brought some excitement into a dreary shift of duty. I spend most of my time helping young people reclaim their cats from trees, hauling drunks off to jail and standing around to show the city taxes are being well spent. Please follow me to the train yard, which I believe is the best place for you to stay tonight. If you need more than one night, I am sure we can find a more suitable place. Now as to a fine restaurant, I would suggest Mrs. Audrey Bascoms' Fine foods. They'll be serving dinner until 10 p.m. and have a wonderful steak and catfish dish."

The men built their cook fire and the two fires they slept around. Coins were tossed for guard duty, but they were assured they would make it into the restaurant before dinner was over. The men were also warned, "One beer only, we need to be on our best behavior here. No shenanigans."

By fate or miracle, Liam was sitting down beside JW, napkin draped around his throat and a corn of cob between his fingers, when he spotted Mr. Packa come walking in with a woman Liam presumed to be his wife and two small kids—a boy, and a girl. Liam put the corn down quickly enough and tore the napkin free, before he looked to JW and said, "Sir, that's him…right there. That's Sgt….Mr. Packa."

"Mr. Packa!" Liam shouted and waved from across the room and then he scampered over.

Mrs. Packa looked alarmed, seeing that the boy had come from so many rough looking men. But Mr. Packa, he wore a blank expression on his face and then his expression changed when he suddenly recognized the youth. "Liam, is that you!?"

"Yes, Sir…I came here to see you, just like I promised I would." Liam stopped suddenly, shot a questioned look at Mr. Packa and asked, "Do you still have it, Mr. Packa?"

"Oh, yes, Liam I have it on display in my Smithy and it's all yours." He reached up and gave Liam a powerful handshake, which then turned into an embrace. "I was always afraid you wouldn't have survived El Mira or one of those other terrible prison camps."

"Please, Sir…there are some people I'd like you and your family to meet. Could you join us for dinner…it's all on me, Mr. Packa for the service you have done me. These are most of the Arizona Rangers I ride with against the Apache and though we look a bit weary, unshaven and rumpled, they are the greatest men in the world to ride the territory with."

"Sounds good, Liam, but no more of this Mr. Packa. My name is Doug and you have earned the right to be considered an adult. So, let me bring my family over…I'll be right back." Doug went back to where his wife and kids still stood and told her about what was happening, she was somewhat in a mild case of shock now and kept glancing over at Liam. She had heard the story before, but had thought Liam was much older. Yet now she could see why her husband had taken such care over him, he had really resembled Doug's younger brother.

Another table was added, introductions made all around and Doug received great thanks from all the Rangers for having taken good care of Liam. As it was, Liam's tomahawk would be the only one to have survived the Civil War. It was after dinner when JW, Liam and Doug, plus his young son, walked over to the smithy to fetch the tomahawk. It was found on a piece of flat-wood mounted on an upper beam. On the flat-wood was a shiny bronze plaque two inches high and four inches long, with the name "Liam's" imprinted on it. Four hooks held it into place and Doug had no problem pulling it down to present it back to Liam.

"Carry it with honor, Liam for if not as a Ranger then as a man." Doug said.

"Doug, I'm not sure what to say. You were right though about El Mira, I never experienced such evil as I did there. But it just wasn't the north, we heard how our Andersonville was equally a hellish spot. So many prisoners died in both of these places. We will never forget and I hope no one ever does. But now I have something for you and I believe it should be held for your son and daughter." Liam reached into his pocket and pulled out his coin purse. From it he pulled out ten $20 gold pieces and handed them to Doug.

"No, we did not rob a bank, nor did we hold up a stage. There is no one looking for us or this money. You might say it was owed to us and a lot of other people we're trying to help on our journey south. When I saw that tomahawk set-up there, with my name on it, I knew you had fulfilled your promise…even if I never showed up or arrived on my 90th birthday. You had kept your word. I have seen so few honest men in my life. Captain Blake here is one of them and I am proud to serve with him and live with his family. It was also because of him I was able-to avenge my family who were massacred by the Apache. Now I know another man who means what he says and does what he means to do. Please accept this money, use it as you may need, but I hope it may help in sending your kids to school." He reached forward and closed the hand that held the gold coins. Doug had never seen such money at one time and this paid to him by a youngster for keeping his word.

"Did you ever tell your friends where you hid some of that jerky?" Doug asked.

"Nope."

"Where did you hide that jerky?" JW asked.

"Ask me again when you're 90 years old and on your deathbed...then I'll tell you, but only if we're alone."

That next morning after breakfast at Mrs. Bascoms' Restaurant, Constable Martin and the Packa family saw 16-men and their three wagons off. Mrs. Packa was amazed with the beauty of the horses the men were riding or having pulled behind their wagons. Doug had decided to wait for a bit before showing the gold coins to his wife, knowing she'd be wanting to take the stage to St. Louis to Kansas City to buy do-dads for the home and clothes for the kids. But he had his own plans, he had the idea of sending his son off to U.S. Military Academy in ten years and that meant a lot of schooling now and extra tutoring to cut the muster. He suspected the USA couldn't stay out of war for too long and already he had been reading about the problems in South America. He also knew lieutenants on up to colonels sure lived better than sergeants and corporals. And the blacksmith business was sure slowing down since the war ended, but he would not touch one of those coins unless it came down to his kid's health. So much for that new 90-lb vice he'd been thinking about all day.

From Sedalia, they rode down through South Missouri, through the beautiful and rugged Ozarks. The men remembered the Sanders Cousins and tried to find a relative or two, but no one admitted to it. JW figured their group probably resembled some sort of federal tax collectors, who wanted to arrest the Sanders. So, they left the Ozarks, but not before spending the day in one of the big lakes Leonard Sanders always bragged about.

Two days later they were in Northeast Texas and the desert felt like home. Some of the Rangers kept looking about for an Indian they could hug, but the vanishing Americans seemed to have really disappeared.

They hooked on to a wagon train trail to head west and spotted a small Union cavalry troop. JW was taking his turn on the front wagon, his whole backside radiating with pain, when he took a breather and reined his black beauties in as the troop approached. "Everyone play it nice and cool, we're all one family now.

The ten-man patrol was being led by a young lieutenant and a middle-aged sergeant. The rest of the men were mixed ages, but all of them seemed to be having problems with the heat.

"I am Lt. Gray, out of Austin and this is Sgt. Grimes, we are out here in search of a lost wagon train. Report says there are 22-wagons, some handcarts, who were victims of fraud and theft. Have you seen any wagons at all since you entered Texas, gentlemen?"

"No, sir. I am JW Blake, late of the Arizona State Rangers. These were all my men, except for this young man who was much too young back then. The territory dismantled us in 1862, so we went north to Nevada to run cattle. We recently took our own herd of 5,000 head back to Nashville and took in a big payday. Now we're on our way back to Arizona, hoping to reclaim our Ranger jobs. But you strike my curiosity, how or what did these thieves do to commit fraud against this train?"

"I'll make a deal with you, Sir. I'll tell you all the information I have if you would share some water with my men. Our canteens are empty and our mounts have gone too long without water, also."

"Sir, you need not make a deal with me. Out here in the desert, we share alike or someone dies and I will never let a horse go thirsty. We have plenty of water to fill your canteens and give the horses their fill."

"Sir, this is a generosity I find unusual, especially out here in the desert." He ordered his sergeant to have the men dismount and fill their canteens and take one drink only. Then give their horses a drink from their canteens into their hats until their canteens are empty. Then with this gentlemen's permission, they may refill their canteens and then return to their mounts, but stand by their horses."

JW could see the Lieutenant's thirst was and led him over to the barrel on the front of the wagon he was driving. We are bringing a lot of horses back with us so we have five barrels for them and four barrels for us, but they've just been refilled."

"Refilled?" Lt. Gray asked. "Is there water near here?"

"If you were to follow this trail for five-miles back…approximately, you'll see where my tracks came in from the North. Go over the ridge line and you'll see some rocky hills. If you go to the far left of that rocky ridge, you'll come across a good-sized pool of water that is fed by the rocks and then the mountains above. We left a good-sized supply of water when we left and at least you'll know for future times where a watering hole is. A Texas Ranger told me about it some time ago."

"Well, thank you, that's very nice of you. I have heard the Rangers are a decent sort, who must do a hard job with few numbers. Why didn't you join in the last…war?"

"Some of my men bend to the south, while some would go with the north and it was decided we just didn't want to be shooting against each other. I once wore the Union jacket of a captain in the war against Mexico, so we all decided to go north to North to Nevada and play cowboy. We took several herds across and in those last miles we were protected by

General Grant's troops because word was General Hood was preparing to attack Nashville. But this last herd was all ours, bought along the way from bankrupt ranches we had learned about along the last couple runs. Oh, we had to bring 1,000-head of steers that belonged to our old boss, so we have-to take some of these fine horses, home to him to set up a breeding farm. Now what about this fraud business, I'm always interested in crime stories."

"Yes, well three or four scouts hired on with this train...going to Southern California or was it Oregon, not that it matters. They paid these scouts good money and somewhere along the line, they apparently abandoned the train." He glanced about and added, "Somewhere around here I guess.

"One of the scouts got himself really drunk in Austin and through a slurred voice spoke of how they tricked all these people and robbed them blind. He was arrested and the next day confessed to everything. One of his accomplices was rounded up and after several hours with a muscular bruiser of a deputy, he confessed in how they had hired on with full intent of ripping off these people. They knew all the people's money was in one wagon and during an evening dance, they knocked out the guard and rode off."

"When did the Army get called in on it?" JW asked.

Lt. Gray shook his head. "I am ashamed to say things greatly slowed down when it was learned the entire wagon train was Black families heading west to seek their fortune. But a lot of pressure came down from Washington when the wagon train failed to report in at its Austin contact, nor its New Mexico contact point. This was when the U.S. Army was called in...Seventeen-days after the wagon train was abandoned in the desert."

"Well, which way are you going, Lieutenant?" JW asked the young man, who was pouring tepid water into his canteen.

"Hey, Jamey, ride up ahead that way," JW point the direction the Lieutenant and his men had ridden along, "and tell how long ago the last wagon train was. Take Holloway with you."

"Yuh got it, Cap!"

While the two men were gone, Lt. Gray asked, "What sort of horse is this? I must say it is the most beautiful piece of horseflesh I have ever seen."

"It's a special order from my boss in Nevada, big silver mine owner who got himself into cattle and now horses. But this one can't be bred, it's solely for his personal usage. Sort of a half-cast, but ungelded to keep its sport up. One half is from those famous all white German jumpers...I never can recall the name and the other half is Arabian Appaloosa. He's 19 hands and nearly 1,000 pounds of pure evil. I had to spend most of a month breaking him and thankfully the Apache ways actually work. But right now I am the only one who can ride him, he's nearly killed three others who have tried."

"Nearly every horse you have is a show horse, you must tell me where you bought them."

"Well, if you ever get assigned near Pennsylvania, there are three horse farms who have the finest quality. I've promised not to give names out, but all three are in the same valley and same town. That should be a big help. Thankfully, they knew we were coming. We also had to wait for the ordered leather work to be finished and then the weapons. Those miners, they have too much money. Except for what you see on me and my work horse, also the same for all my men, every-single-thing belongs to the miners."

JW pulled out a can of peaches, opened it and asked Lt. Gray and Sgt. Rimes to split it. Both were very appreciative. Their rations were down to dried out hard "teeth busting" jerky. Then JW presented them with two tin spoons and their smiles were near childish.

"Break out some peaches, one can to two men." JW ordered and Liam was busy getting the order carried out.

James and Holloway returned quickly with favorable news, "Lieutenant, had you made uh right turn ta follow thu trail 'stead of comin' ta us, you'd been right on top deir trail. Looks like a wagon train come through over two-weeks ago, possible three...maybe" Holloway said.

"Is that an Arizona accent, Sir?" Lt. Gray asked.

"Nu, Sir...It's Americun," Holloway replied.

Lt. Gray grinned, "Yes, I must agree with you, Sir. That's pure American."

"Lieutenant that is how a country grows. Another is finding that train and getting them moving in the right direction. Without a scout, they could end up in Mexico."

"Mr. Blake, I have word of a sizeable force of Comanche in the area and they may have already slaughtered these people...but I am asking if you might ride along with us until we find that train. Your extra weapons will be a big help if we encounter the hostiles."

"Lieutenant, we're going in the same direction, but have your men take it easy on the water. It's at least two days to the next watering hole and that one may be dry as a bone." JW replied. He then looked at Liam, "I know it's not your turn, but I want you up on this wagon seat following this troop. I'll be riding with the Union Lieutenant." JW rode over to where James and Bret Sampson stood, along with MSgt. Wells and MSgt. Michaels.

"Listen up, we will for a time, be riding with the Union Troops who hope to find a lost wagon train of 22 covered wagons, plus foot carts. They've been missing for 17-days and for an added touch, this is an all-Black wagon train heading for Southern California or Oregon. They hired scouts who abandoned them, but not before stealing all their money. Now I do not know what kind of weapons they have, but I have just learned there's reportedly a bunch of Comanche out here and this wagon train might be looked upon as smooth pickings."

JW let out a deep sigh, "This ride home has sure been an interesting journey…Now I got you escorting Union troops." He then gestured to his men to move them into two ranks. "Until I give you different orders, you are now in the Union Cavalry and will ride like one. You will take Lt. Gray's orders, unless I tell you otherwise. But if an attack is brought against the Comanche, only one boss is needed and this is his command and I want the Comanche scouts to thinks this is one good sized unit and they might just leave us alone. Before you mount, load up with extra rifle and pistol ammo, you may need it."

JW Blake then waved to Lt. Gray, "Sir, would you come over here, please and bring Sgt. Rimes with you."

He met them at the back of the wagon he'd been driving, "Sir, together we are 26-mounted men, but a Comanche Dog Soldier force can be one of the fiercest mounted cavalry units ever witnessed. If they have 30-soldiers, we will not survive. If they have 60 dog soldiers they could give Austin a good run. You may recall their famous 1,000 Comanche raid that destroyed most of Texas and drove all the way to the coast. They are hard to kill and never stop killing them. Never think you've stopped them by wounding them, because they will stand back up and drive a knife through your heart. This is a vicious tribe and even the Apache and Comanche respect each other."

"All right, but that's not much of a pep-talk coach."

"I've told you this to explain why I am loaning you these weapons, but it is only a loan. The miner in Nevada already owns them, but I cannot afford them to fall into the Comanche's hands." JW open the lids off two boxes. "These are the new Winchester 30-30 lever-action repeater rifles. They carry six-rounds including one loaded. I'll teach your men how to use them right here and now, but I want your word I will get them back…agreed."

"You have my word," Lt. Gray said.

"Right, you've got my word," Sgt. Rimes said. He was mesmerized by simply looking at the rifles.

"These will be eventually issued to you, but the army moves slow. Probably be another ten-years, be my guess."

Jamey, get our men over here to start basic instruction. Shoot against that hillside over there. If a Comanche scout is watching us, his jaw's about to drop."

It only took them ten-minutes to get all the rifles handed out, along with a basic load of ammo. Their own carbines were placed in the wagon for safe keeping. JW didn't want to think about what he might be forced to do if the Union boys went back on their word once they got to the Wagon Train and found everyone healthy.

Each Union soldier fired the basic field load through their Winchesters and JW could tell by their expressions they had fallen in love with their rifles.

"Lt. Gray, I am putting my men under your command. I will ride as Second-in-Command. But my people will follow your orders unless I believe you are doing something really stupid. I will first point it out to you and if you do not agree, you may carry-on with your ten-men. Still, each of our soldiers with these new rifles is worth four to five troops and the Dog Soldiers will be using older muskets or a few carbines they have stolen or traded for."

"You mean with 26 soldiers, armed with these lever action rifles are equal to…130 troops! With your men's experience in Indian fighting, we just might be able to stand-off a full-fledged Comanche Dog Soldier attack," Lt. Gray said.

"Are you frightened anymore, Lieutenant?" JW asked.

"Yup, but more hopeful…thanks."

"Good, stay frightened. But keep it under control. Nothing wrong with being scared, as-long-as you can control it. My men and I have been in over 100 engagements against the Indians and I've always been scared. I use it to keep me alert and prevent me from making stupid mistakes. Oh, I've been shot with both bullet and arrow, felt the killing edge of a knife across my back and have enough scars to send little kids running for momma. But I am also proud of each-and-every one of them because they were earned in battle. You'll do just fine, just remember your training and I'll be around to help you out."

"Time to go?" Lt. Gray asked.

"It's your command, Lieutenant…boots and saddles, time."

"Sgt. Rimes get them all on their horses in into two ranks with wagons in the middle."

"Yes, Sir," Sgt. Rimes replied. He glanced over at JW, grinned and touched the brim of his hat in a snap salute. "Everyone…mount up, two ranks with wagons in the middle. Volunteers to the rear, troopers to the front. Stretch it out some, so we look a bigger than we are and sound-off if you see anything and I mean anything."

Sgt. Rimes then fell in behind the Lieutenant's horse, leaving his space for JW to ride in. Liam was bringing up the first wagon, he had his Colt revolver on his right hip, his new ten-inch blade Bowie on his left hip and right behind it was his old Tomahawk. He glanced over his left shoulder to see Chad Leaders riding right behind him.

"You know what, Chad?" Liam asked.

"Naw, what, bucko?"

"Sure feels a lot longer riding home; than riding off ta war…my darn buns hurt!" Liam complaint.

"Not so loud in the ranks," Sgt. Rimes ordered.

"Sorry, Sarge," Liam hollered back, which got Rimes to shake his head.

Twenty-minutes later they were past the point where the troop had turned off to check-out the Rangers. Now they were following the wagon train trail, used for many years but the last wagon train had left behind the most recent horse and oxen dropping that allowed the scouts to date the passage.

"Lieutenant, might I recommend you send out my two scouts Holloway and Jim Williams. You have to use his first name as I've got two Williams and they're not related. I'd also recommend you send two of your men to follow behind us to keep an eye on our tail and give us warning if the Comanche rush us from behind. Have your men hold their rifles at the ready, but no finger on the trigger. That way an overexcited soldier doesn't shoot one of us in the back and he can hopefully shoot a round off before an arrow ends his life."

"Did you get all that, Sgt. Rimes?"

"I did, Lieutenant."

"Get it done."

"Yes, Sir." Rimes rode out of the line and addressed the first two men in ranks. They soon fell out of line and followed the Sergeant back to where he reached Scouts Holloway and Jim Williams. "Lt. Gray and…your Boss, have ordered Scouts out and I suspect you two know what that means."

"Oh, yes, my good Sergeant. We're on our way," Scout Williams replied.

"Sgt. Rimes, are you stationing these good men to the far rear as a tail for us?" PFC and Scout Andy Salcedo enquired.

"For a Mexican, you don't have much of an accent."

"You shame me, Sergeant. For I am not a Mexican. I am an Aztec warrior and proud of it. We are a super race of old world Indians, unfortunately mostly wiped out by the Spanish. But I was educated in Missionary Schools and now have a high school diploma. Currently though, I am an Arizona Ranger, for which I scout for."

"You can sure rattle on, but what did you want, Ranger?" Rimes asked.

"That I be able-to fall back with these gentlemen and show them how the Comanche work, set up their traps and fight. This might help them survive their upcoming encounter."

"Sure, get out of here and take them back as far as you usually do."

"Usually we fall back 200-yards or so. One keeps watch on this 180 degrees and the other watches that 180 degrees. We'll stop and walk our horses at times so we don't close up the distance...Those wagons will slow the front element down some."

"Aztec huh?" Sgt. Rimes asked.

"Yes, Sergeant, I was told it was rumored I was the grandson of a King, but the Spanish ruined everything. I hate the Spanish an am likely to kill one on sight. Aztec ways of death are very painful."

Sgt. Rimes shook his head and rode back to report to the Lieutenant. While behind him, Scout Salcedo was using hand gestures to move the men back to the correct position to assume their duties.

Once they were moving forward, he studied the one shorter and heavier soldier for a brief-moment with a hard glance, "Are you Spanish...maybe from Madrid?"

"Uh...no! I'm half Filipino...my mother sailed to California from Village of Luzon and met my father."

"Was he Spanish?" Salcedo pulled out his Bowie knife and began running it by his thumb to check its sharpness.

"No, he's white...now knock it off with this Spanish kick I take enough heartache for being from the Philippines."

"Why, it's jus' another place...like Canada or France."

"Don't ask me, but people don't like half-breeds."

"You tell-um ta come see me. I don't like people who think like that...Unless it's against thu Spanish."

When Sgt. Rimes reached the Lieutenant, he briefed him on the assignment and how Salcedo had volunteered to go with the two men to show them the ropes. But JW shot him a hard look and said, you sent Salcedo with them...alone. Didn't he tell you he was an Aztec?"

"Well, yes, Sir...he did."

"Well, you'd better get him replaced before nightfall. I won't be responsible for your men out there after dark. This is all on your head, Lieutenant."

"Why, Mr. Blake...what's wrong with Aztec?" Rimes asked, his voice now jittery.

"They carry a curse and it comes upon them at night. I have to keep him tied up between the hours of darkness, and it's especially bad when the moon is shining brightly."

"But, Sir, what does happen to him?"

"Rimes, the Aztec people died off because of the curse..." JW was interrupted.

"Salcedo said the Spanish wiped them out, wasn't that true?" Rimes asked, he was now shaking slightly.

"They used that as an excuse between then to hide the curse, but Rimes, during the hours of darkness, the Aztec become monstrous, nearly unstoppable without a Golden cross blessed by the Bishop in Holy Water brought from Rome. During this time...They become...cannibals!"

"You mean they ate their whole civilization up...but Salcedo is still alive." Rimes wasn't sure who or what to believe.

Right at that moment, Salcedo was very carefully, Indian style, sneaking up behind Sgt. Rimes.

"Yes, but there had to be someone left for the cities were massive and some fled to the north. We rescued Salcedo from the Comanche and he told us about his curse and begged us to tie him up and we have watched the transformation. Monstrous...monstrous."

Right then Salcedo snuck-up and rose-up beside Rimes and he was perched on his saddle. Salcedo grabbed him from the left leg and pulled him off the horse, growling during the time. Men pulled their guns, but JW Blake ordered them to not fire, laughing as he did. He looked over at Lt. Gray, smiling, "This is a prank we pull on new Rangers who have come out to fight the Comanche or Apache the first time."

Salcedo had Rimes all bounded up, using only his arms and legs, and he held his new Bowie knife only inches from his neck.

"Okay, let him up, Salcedo, you proven once again how the great Aztec Warrior can still sneak in and catch the unaware." While Salcedo unwound himself, making sure the good sergeant wasn't going to shoot at him or even swing a good right hook, while JW continued talking.

"This is conducted whenever a new Ranger is brought into the field. Sometimes to frighten him, to show him the chip on his shoulder better vanish or his comrades may not help him in the real thing, but mostly to show him how real it is. You have just seen how an Indian, be it Comanche Dog Soldier or an Apache Warrior, possibly a Ute, sacrifices himself to kill the enemy of his people. You have seen an example of how sneaky they can be. They can spend all day sitting underground in a spider hole; also, called a tarantula hole, and covered over by a dirt camouflaged piece of material. Suddenly they will spring up while your unit is right in the middle of them. Watch the ground around you, watch for air holes and movement. These people are fantastic at making traps, they are fine shots, but this desert is their home. They can go without water for three days and still fight. They will ride a horse until it dies on its feet and when it drops the Indian will eat it if he has time or slice its throat to drink its blood to handle his thirst."

"His horse?" A young private asked.

"Youngster, we make friends with our horses. For the Indian horses are simply meat on the hoof. They are looked upon by the old timers as the best cavalry that has ever rode and I'd have to agree. I've seen them shoot arrows from under their bellies, from under their necks. They use the horse as some would use a shield. Simply put there are few things an Indian cannot do with his horse except plow a field. No warrior will ever be a farmer…Not unless they break the back of the Indian nations and I do not believe I'll see that in my lifetime. Still, maybe the day will come we can make peace with them, if Washington can actually keep its promise and uphold its treaties."

"Sergeant, are you okay? Any ill feelings?" The Lieutenant asked. JW glanced back over the wagons to see his men had remembered their job well, to stay in their places and observe the desert hillsides in the event the Comanche rushed. They all knew what Salcedo was doing. He had worked for Tucson, but JW brought him up to Globe when he was needed. In another six-months he would've used him on Liam, but now it wasn't needed.

"No, I'm not above learning things and if this is how the Indians fought I am glad to learn it this way. But what's with the Aztec stuff?"

"Salcedo was born to a family that worked for a Missionary Family in Tucson. His father was Spanish and White, and his mother an Apache. Both parents were killed by avenging angels, a group of sanctimonious racists who tried to clear Tucson out of minorities, which included anyone from Indian, Mexican, half-breeds, even Jewish and Blacks. Basically, they wanted a white Utopia. It never happened and the avenging angels were driven out into the desert to vanish. Salcedo was only two years old, so he was at first hidden by the church family and then raised by them for 16-more years. He knows the entire story, and has spent time with his mother's family to learn the Apache ways. But, he has learned the Missionary ways and cannot grasp the Apache religion, but still his family accepts him as-long-as he keeps his word to never tell of the Apache hideout locations and I have never put the pressure upon him to tell me. He has great integrity.

"But he is still bothered, even though he is a Ranger, for being an Indian. So, over time we came up with the Aztec legend to have fun with trouble makers and, also new troops to teach them. When things were quiet, I was even allowed to visit with the Apache headship, which was a great honor for me and we talked of future time. They have learned I am a man of honor and my word is sound. None of my Indian prisoners will be abused and I am willing to make deals with the Apache for prisoner exchanges. As to being Aztec, I've never met one in my life and wouldn't know them from a Florida Seminole I once saw long ago in a special conference. Now you talk decorative, those Seminoles are truly colorful, but I was told the jungle they fight in; their colors are natural camouflage. They are also some of the cruelest warriors, enjoying throwing live prisoners in deep crocodile pits to watch the critters feed."

Lt. Gray looked to his troops, "I hope you have learned something, men. Never stop being alert, or in this country you will die. Let's ride!" He ordered and then rode out with JW at his side.

"That was one of the more serious object lessons I've ever seen taught, but it was needed. I know it rattled me. Thank you, Mr. Blake."

"Don't stare or react, but glance at the crest of the ridgeline to your right. We have picked up our first shadow. I'll fall back and advise your men not to react, mine already know this. But at least it finally happened, which tells me the wagon train people are still alive or they wouldn't bother with us."

"Do we have a fight up ahead then?" Lt. Gray asked in a low voice.

"Yup, but not too soon. When we have a whole ridgeline of Comanche is when it's time to worry." JW drifted back and spoke with each set of two men, as Sgt. Rimes moved up into his old spot, to be briefed by the lieutenant.

When he got back to Liam, JW tied his horse off and climbed up into the hard wagon seat. "You've got everything ready?"

"Rifle's loaded, extra ammo in my chest sling, plus extra ammo for my revolver in my cartridge belt rings. Plus, I have more ammo ready in my small pack, ready for a quick grab if I have to jump under the wagons."

"Sounds good, boy. But one of your jobs is to protect these black beasts. I want then back on the ranch pulling hay wagons for all of us. We'd never be able to afford these monsters. So, once the attacks comes, you take the rope below you and the horses off so they cannot move an inch. I'll tell the other guys to do the same. I'd rather have them all dead out here than hauling supplies for these Comanche. Now keep your cool and that's an order."

"You've got it, Big Brother."

That made JW laugh and then he remounted to ride over to the next wagon. When he got back to be with Lt. Gray, a second Comanche had appeared but he was on the opposite ridge and this one was a good 200-yards farther away.

"Salcedo, bring the rear guard up 150-yards. I don't want them being a free turkey dinner for those Comanche ghosts."

"On my way, Captain."

Now the Lieutenant was worried about making camp for the night, knowing the Indians were out and about. He began to think he preferred it when he didn't know. But he was sure glad he had JW Blake and these extra 15 seasoned veterans with him. Still, he wondered if there would be enough of them to save the wagon train.

CHAPTER TEN:

"Hey Juke, that white boy drivin' dat wagon better stop soon, or those big black horses of his comin' like thu demons of hell, gonna run right smack into us."

Wagons were set into a wide triangle, with saddles stacked with anything else they could use from the wagons to provide protection for the soldiers and Rangers behind them. Percherons were all tied up on lines and their massive shadows dancing off the wagon tarps, as the flames from the large fire rages. The remaining horses were also tied up inside the enclosure, but they were also hobbled so they wouldn't break away off the lines if the Apache attacked. But the Rangers kept their primary horse tied up close, right beside their point of defense and for the night they would be on a 50 percent watch. Every other man would take the first six-hours and then the next man would relieve him so the first weary-eyed man could go grab 40-winks. But if the Apache attacked, no one would sleep.

The fire was fed with dried brush, small trees, and pieces of wood they could safely remove from the wagons. A three-legged fire-spit hung over it with a five-gallon coffee pot the Army had hung on a supply mule. At least this way the men all had steaming hot coffee all through the night, but no sugar to add to it.

Lt. Gray and JW conducted an inspection of the defenses and except for wishing they had another 100 men, they seemed satisfied. Before nightfall settled over the valley, a third and then a fourth Comanche had appeared, but each one staying out of rifle distance and keeping the same pace as the troops until the Union patrol stopped to make camp.

Canned food was running low, now that the Rangers were sharing it with the Union boys. Lt. Gray was hoping to replace it when they reached their new posting west of Austin. But JW advised the lieutenant he and his men would be continuing-on once they locate the wagon train. "We'll continue following the trail west, Lieutenant and make our run through North New Mexico to avoid the Comanche and Ute in the southern area."

"I'd sure like to purchase those rifles off-of you, JW," Lt. Gray said with a hopeful smile on his face.

"I'll tell you what, Lieutenant, let's see how we fend with our current problem. Otherwise, your Company Commander might be the one having to deal with those Winchesters."

"Yes, Sir...But do you think we might be attacked tonight?"

"Knowing the Comanche, they'll send a couple dog soldiers in to check our defenses…Try to steal our horses our even dry them off. So, we'd better be ready. But I don't expect a full-fledged attack, yet."

"We have enough cleared space between the wagons and the bush lines," Lt. Gray said in a hopeful voice.

"They'll wait until the moon goes down, Lieutenant," MSgt. Wells said.

"Right, that's when we'll go to 100 percent watch. The men will lose some sleep tonight, but my Rangers know all about that," JW then gestured to Lt. Dreeke, for him to tell second shift to catch some winks while they can. James replied with a snap salute and walked off to spread the news.

Before the men went to sleep they checked the loads in their revolvers and followed this up with an inspection of their rifles. They had already picked up extra ammo and topped off their canteens. Horses were all fed and watered for the night and most of them were asleep. Union horses had not been in the field long enough to picked up the sixth-sense of an enemy in the area or the smell of an Indian. Nor have the new Ranger mounts, but after five or six attacks they will know and could smell the individual odors of an Apache, Ute or Comanche from half-a-mile away. They would begin to act as if a bee was buzzing around their ears or a horsefly was attacking their rear hips, and the horse was giving a dance.

JW told Lt. Gray and Sgt. Rimes of how he had once owned a four-year old mare that was trained to hate Indians by a peaceful Navajo Brave. He would dress up as a Comanche then as an Apache, to abuse the horse while breaking it. "Well, that horse was broken to a saddle and bridle in three-days, but she was violent whenever an Indian of Comanche or Apache tribal affiliation came near and the horse tried to attack, because one night out in the field, a young Apache brave snuck into our camp to prove his manhood by stealing a horse. My mare pinned him to the ground and stomped him to death before we could stop her."

"But how…What did that Navajo do to make himself different from other Indians," Sgt. Rimes asked.

"Seems he would cover himself with the various peppers and flowers the individual tribes ate and would then beat the horse regularly in breaking it, so it put the pain and smell together. I had always thought they consumed the same desert plants, but it appears there are some differences."

"So many things they fail to teach us at the Academy…Maybe you should come back and teach for a year or two. It would be of a great benefit to the troops who have to fight the Indians in this vast desert."

"Lieutenant, I once thought about that…But, I am heading to Globe, Arizona, to see if my family can still remember me. Then I need to rebuild my Ranch, pay my taxes and in all hopes, rebuild the Arizona Rangers to combat the Indians and Bandits."

Lt. Gray nodded at him, smiled, which was lit up by the flames and said, "I do wish you hope, Sir and I pray we all arrive at our destinations without further injuries."

"Amen," added MSgt. Gary Wells.

A glance at his pocket watch illuminated by the dancing flames of the fire showed the time to be 4:10 a.m., and the three-quarter sized moon was heading for the horizon. JW put his watch away and woke-up Lt. Gray. "It's time…100 percent watch…Everyone up."

Lt. Gray, his inside eyelids having the texture of sandpaper and his eyeball dry, sure hoped the coffee was hot and plentiful. But first he woke up Sgt. Rimes, who in turn made his way slowly around one side of the wagons, while MSgt. Gary Wells took the other side. MSgt. Michaels was handling the big fire duties, with one of the Union lads.

As they were awakened, the men were not handed their rifles until their eyes came into focus and they remembered where they were. They were then advised to move in silence, so the Comanche, if they were close to the perimeter, wouldn't know where the men were if the opted to pepper the camp with arrows.

But by 7 a.m. and daybreak, things had remained all quiet—no attack had come. So, breakfast rations were served, with a cup of coffee per man and a piece of hard-like steel beef jerky given to each man to hold them over to noon meal. They would cut a piece off, put in their mouths and suck on it, until the meat texture would soften. By then the flavor was all gone and the bite was swallowed.

By 8 a.m. the caravan heading west had now acquired a fifth Comanche; two on the north and three on the south.

No one had said anything about the scouts not having shown up, but JW was used to his scouts staying out overnight. Their return trail may have been blocked off, a horse could've broken a leg and they're waiting for the force to catch up with them, or both men were tied, stretched out over a burning mound and long dead. But Holloway and Jim Williams were two of his best scouts and he wasn't going to give up on them. Nor was he opting to send out another scout.

"Lieutenant, I recommend you pull-up your read guard to twenty yards and keep Scout Salcedo with them for a three-man unit. That way the Comanche can't sweep in and get between us as we shoot those river beds up ahead."

"I agree," Lt. Gray said and then he ordered Sgt. Rimes to deliver the order. But before he left, JW stopped him and said, "Ride slow, Sergeant...We don't want to those Indian's thinking they rattled us at all."

"I understand, Sir." Sgt. Rimes casually turned his horse and rode to the back at a slow cantor.

"Mr. Blake, do you think we'll pick up additional babysitters?" Lt. Gray asked.

"Indians are hard to figure, Lieutenant. Just when you think you've got them nailed down, they'll pull a switcheroo on you. They have their own rules, code of conduct and the Comanche Dog Soldiers are sticklers for enforcing that code. But it's not something we'll ever understand.

"Now in some Indian tribes I can be invited in for a conference and if I come in unarmed as their rules call for, I will be untouched. For a brave to harm me while I am under that covering is death to that brave, for I've brought shame to the whole village. Now after I leave that village, I have until the following morning to get away, because then the Dog Soldiers may be coming after me, for my covering of protection has passed. But in other tribes, my protection ends when I leave their village and I'd better be riding fast. In those cases, I usually leave my weapons concealed in a tree, behind a rock or something."

"Then why do you go to the conferences?" Lt. Gray asked.

"Same reason you rode up on me...I was a total stranger and outnumbered you. But you had a job to do. I hope to keep the peace and some of my conferences have worked out, others have only shown to then that I am not afraid and that my word was good. I'm sure you've been told, the Indians have no word for 'lie', but we seem to be teaching it to them with all the treaties we have broken."

"You're a mighty imposing man, JW."

"Lieutenant, I've been gone for a while and there's no telling what the Apache have been pulling in Arizona. Maybe some of the older Comanche remember me and while trading with the Apache, they'll let them know I coming' back and bringing my Rangers. That might unsettle them. The Texas Rangers will be back out here in no time and I hope the Army gets along with them. True, a lot of them rode with General Hood, but their allegiance is to Texas. They know the Comanche better than anyone...Be smart and use them."

"Thank you, Sir...I will."

They then rode in silence for some time, for the sun's rays were growing hotter with every half-hour. When the noon-hour came the men were ordered to stay in line, but to dismount and rest their horses in place and share their canteens with them. The Sgt. Rimes spread the word, "We will be moving off soon, but be prepared for the order to pick up speed. We'll be hittin' it hard and fast for a while until we get to the river up ahead. If you fall back, you're on your own."

When Sgt. Gray reached Liam, he gave him a separate order, "Mr. Blake wants you to bring him up his White stallion and you to be on your best mount. You'll drag your number two mount behind you, now get it done and mosey…I said mosey up there to your boss."

"Yes, Sergeant."

"Be safe, Sprout, that man thinks the world of you."

"I think the world of him, too."

Once all the horses were fed, watered and the men had taken a good drink themselves, JW knew all the troops were making a last-minute check of their weapons. JW let out a Rebel whistle to move the men ahead as a gradual rate of speed. Over the last few days the Union troops had learned the different whistles and soon, they'd be hearing what a Rebel yell sounded like, at least those who had never faced a Confederate cavalry charge.

The sand was only an inch or two deep and they could still see dried feces dropped from the last wagon train's horses and oxen. But along the way they also began to see the settler's signs of defeat; people from the wagons were throwing personal items out of their loads to reduce weight for their beasts. Dishes, suitcases filled with clothes, piles of valuable books and even a handmade rocking chair littered the trail. A Union troop stopped long enough to toss the chair into the back of one of JW's wagon and one of the Rangers picked up a pile of strapped together medical books. "If nothing else, they'll make good fire," Dan Wakefield said. But his brothers new better. Dad had always shown an interest in the medical field and had dreams of some day of going to medical school to become a doctor.

The farther along the troops followed the trail the more they found, but not just from only this last train but earlier trains too. But earlier trunks were ransacked and JW said to Lt. Gray, "Comanche most likely, they went through them and took what they wanted for their womenfolk. They'll also decorate their horses up with the colorful materials, tying them on to their manes and tails, wrapping around their necks and even use some of it for their head bans and sewing it along the borders of their vests. Now they have no value of our books, still they're fond of our photos and will hang them in their lodges. I've seen photos of someone old grandma hanging, right beside some Italian couple's wedding photo, knowing all three people might've been killed by the old Chief I was visiting to exchange prisoners with. They also like our mirrors, once they learned the things weren't going to rob their souls."

"You make them sound like such an innocent people, JW," Lt. Gray said as they rode along and observed the miscellaneous articles in the sand.

Had they the room, JW would have picked up one or two of those hand-built wooden trunks with the fine carved inlay. "No, Lieutenant, not innocent by any means, just…just like a tourist, visiting Boston or New York City for the first time. Able to defend themselves if challenged, but marveled at all the new and colorful treasures." JW pulled out his ten-inch blade Bowie, "Comanche, Apache or the Ute and a dozen other tribes in this here country, will cut your heart out, boil it and it eat in a ceremony. They'll also scalp you, but I've heard this was a skill taught to them by the early White man. I don't know, long before my time. Yet, I have learned they have a respect for an enemy who shows great courage and honor. Some White men have been allowed to move on, while others were accepted into their tribes. I know of one Union soldier who became a sub-chief in the Apache nation."

"What!?"

"I met him at a prisoner exchange, where he acted as their interpreter. I found him to be a man of integrity and he didn't like the way the Indians were being treated. He married a Chief's daughter, took on the tests of Apache manhood and now has two sons I know about. To the Apache, he is one of them. But his goal is to bring peace between both nations. Thankfully, I've never had to fight him, it's rumored he was quite the strategist as a Union Officer. Academy graduate, too."

"What was his rank when he left the service?"

JW grinned, for he'd been asked that every time he'd told this story. "Lieutenant, the man was a one-star general, from his home state of Maryland."

"Wow…I hope to meet him someday…in a peaceful situation."

JW was about to say something, when he spotted two horse-mounted figures on the wagon-trail up-ahead coming their way. Lt. Gray lifted his hand up and brought their party to a halt.

"Looks like Holloway and Jim Williams," JW said. Both men had their rifles out of their slings, grasped in their right hands and resting on their leg. But they were not moving too fast.

JW looked to the north and south ridges and spotted four more Indians, two on each ridge joining up with the five Comanche the patrol already had. This meant the north ridge had four Comanche and the south ridge showed five mounted Indians.

"That's nine Indians. Do you think they'll attack at sundown to run-off our horses?" Lt. Gray asked.

"Possibly, but we'll be ready, but let's see what our scouts have for us," JW said. The two of them remained silent then, as they watched the scout come forward and gave the Comanche a hard look over. Lt. Gray kept looking for a hundred more Comanche to come up on the ridge line at any moment, or even a hundred from both sides. He had to admit to himself he was nervous, if not frightened. But he noticed JW was like a rock and his nervousness subsided some to have a man of such experience right beside him.

"Sorree we couldn't get back las' night, Cap, jus' too many Indians between us an' it would'a been a runnin' fight all thu way. So, we camped in thu rocks an' these fine Winchesters kept 'em back. Must'a kilt 'bout fifty ta sixty of dem," Jim Williams said. Whenever he grew over- excited, Jim's southern drawl became more apparent and hard to understand.

"Cap', I believe we might've wounded an' kilt ten ta thirteen Comanche, but den dey backed off an' dis mornin' dey stayed out of rifle range. Our single-shots was good for 500 to 700 yards, maybe up to 900-yards with a deadeye, but dese here Winchesters drop their rounds at 200 yards an' the Comanche know that." Holloway held up his Winchester in front of him to make a point."

"Dis rifle is thu next best Indian killer, but we still need a long rifle for dose kill shots," Holloway said.

"Any sign of the wagon train, men?" JW asked.

"Sure thing, Cap, dey all formed up in a defensive circle down at the river…dis side. Trouble is, dere's 200…maybe 300 Comanche between us an' thu wagon train." Jim Williams added.

"Are they all on the road, or up on the hills?" JW asked.

"Spread about," Holloway replied. He also expected JW next question and said, "River is running too fast to build barges and come down the river and join up with them. We'd lose have the force."

"You've been with me too long," JW said to Holloway. "Then it sounds like a straight shot in." JW turned and gestured for James Dreeke to join him and both he and Gary Wells rode up.

"Our wagon train is up ahead with the raging river behind them. But there's also 200 to 300 Comanche in the way. I figure the Indians haven't attacked because they're afraid all the shooting will scare us off and the chiefs want our horses and especially these repeating rifles. So, they'll take us both at once." JW looked at the Indians up on the hills, and then continued.

"We're are going to turn all three wagons into war machines. I want six men, plus a driver for each wagon. The driver will begin on the driver seat, but once you hear my rebel yell, you'll haul the reins into the back and from there you will drive that wagon. The six riflemen will use the wall boards to protect them and cut the tarp away to give you clearance to shoot. One of the two men in the back will also have to watch the back gate to keep you from having a Comanche come jumping in on top of you.

"Next, I want your horses tied to the back of the wagon by rope, do not rely on your reins. The Comanche will try to cut them free, but the rope will slow them down for a shooter to handle them. The shooter wagons will be a surprise against the Indians, the sheer amount of firepower coming from these three wagons may be enough to run the Comanche off. Officers and senior NCO will have a quick briefing in five minutes. Troops to get their horses watered and fed, then divide the revolver and rifle ammo up between the wagons. Move it!"

COMMANDERS CALL

As the men were busily moving the ammo about in a work detail under the command of Corporal John Gibson, Lt. Gray, Lt. Dreeke, Lt. Sampson, met with MSgt. Gary Wells, MSgt. Wallace Michaels and Sgt. Rimes all met with JW Blake, Temporary Commander of this detail as elected by the above officers and non-commissioned officers.

"We do not have a lot of time by my estimation. I suspect the Comanche War Chief will figure we are nearly close enough to attack us with a small force and attack the wagon train with his main force. Now I have no idea how well armed the occupants of the train are, but I see it doubtful they'll be carrying these Winchesters. But if we can get these Winchesters to them, that's ten more riflemen who are equal to sixty. Comanche.

"So, my plan is to charge our three wagons into the wagon train and hopefully someone there is smart enough to open up a door to let us in. Otherwise we might end up killing four of our magnificent draft horses and injuring seven of our men.

"Now Liam will drive the front wagon, following me on my white stallion. Lt. Gray and Lt. Dreeke will ride behind me and shoot any Indian who tries to jump on one of our black devils and try to steer it away. My job will be to keep the trail clear of any Comanche.

"First wagon will hold Union troops. Sharp, Hills, Duster and St. Paul, Brady Williams and Salcedo will also be aboard. Ranger Liam has the reins. Get your horses all tied up and make sure the black devils of the next wagon will not run them over.

"Second wagon will hold Union troops...O'Brian, Ridgeway, Bitters and Homer. Rangers Holloway and Salcedo assigned to that wagon. MSgt. Michaels has the reins.

"Third wagon will hold MSgt. Gary Wells at the reins, Leo D Wakefield and his brothers Dan and Chris Wakefield, Chad Leaders, Lawrence Coon and John Gibson. Following the wagons to keep the Comanche off the horses being dragged along on the ropes, plus the draft horses on the second and third wagons, were Lt. Gray, Lt. Sampson and Sgt. Rimes. Both John Gibson and Lawrence Coon, known for their shooting skill, were also advised to man the back gate of the third wagon to monitor the three mounted men to keep them out of trouble, whenever possible. Is there any questions?"

"Sir, we've been told this is an all-Black wagon train, do you have any idea as to whether they'll welcome us or feel were part of the Indian attack. White men, like the Chicanos we've heard about?"

"No idea, Sgt. Rimes. But we will find out real soon." JW looked to his senior command and asked, "Gary, will you offer up a prayer?"

MSgt. Gary Wells nodded his head and stood up. He'd been sitting on the top of a discarded wooden, tin and fabric trunk. "Thank you, Captain. Yes, I have a prayer..."

HERE WE COME!

First thing to do was use their old black power single shot 50 and 54-caliber rifles to kill those nine Comanche look outs. One was missed, but JW went out after him and chased him over three hills before he was now close enough to shoot him down with his Henry. He then saw that the 50-caliber mini-ball had shaved the back hip of the Indian pony and that's why the animal was traveling so slowly. JW then returned and issued the order for the patrol to head out. They all knew their speed would be picking up as soon as JW spotted any Indians on the trail.

There was 22 – 14-foot long covered wagons set-up in a long rectangle, with its backside row at least two-feet from the fast-moving river's bank. A wagon was pushed into the two openings at each end to keep the Indians from breaking through. This left ten end-to-end wagons on the train's front side to block any charge attempts by the Comanche Dog Soldiers. All the women and the children. Plus a handful of men and older boys were available to watch the riverside, in the event some of the Comanche tried to swim along the river bank to attack from the rear. They had tried that the first night to steal some forces, but the attack had failed. Two Black men and five Comanche died in that attack.

An old white haired Black man, his face covered in wrinkles, who had been a slave since he was six-years old when his tribe was defeated by another larger tribe and he was sold off to White men on the coast. He had never seen such a large ship before and didn't think his parents would survive the trip to the far-off continent. As it was, more than a third of the slaves had died the rough handling on board and were thrown overseas. He also heard his mother's screams on several nights as crewmen came to unbuckle her chains and take her to the crewmen's quarters. His father tried to fight, but he was beaten severely.

Once they reached shore, they were split up into groups and he never saw his father again. But he stayed with his mom for years to come as they were sold to a large cotton farm in eastern Louisiana. Juke, the name given to him by the plantation foreman, stayed with that same farm for 82-years, which made him now 88-years old. His first wife had died after 40-years of marriage and now he was married to 76-year old Sarah. Both were favored to the land owner and upon being given his freedom, Juke was given three bags of gold, with the explanation, "Juke, my father always appreciated your honesty and insight in doing the best for your people, even building the school and housing for families. After he died, you became my teacher and your son, he was my best friend and the racial barrier meant little to the two of us. If not for this war, in another decade maybe the south would've done away with the whole slavery issue. Being said, I will always miss Johnathan and our times together. I am so sorry, he had to go fight and lose his life."

"Thank you, Mr. Wilkerson that thought means a lot to me."

"Yes, our two families have lost so much since you joined our plantation. But now you have your freedom, but as we have talked, this will not be a safe place for the free Blacks to remain. Whites will rise-up in resentment and I've already heard of mass hangings by White so-called authorities. They call them nightriders, who burn crosses on the properties now owned by Blacks. For a Black to show any slight to a White woman, even by accident, they can be gunned down in the street and no one is going to do anything. It will be another six-months or better before the Union troops get down these ways to support the laws and a lot of the Union boys will not be Black lovers.

"So, to honor our long friendship, my father, who saw this coming and I've added to it, had set this aside for you to purchase a wagon train to take our Blacks westward to the State of California. There you may get a clean start, buy some property I know about and I've read where California now has minorities of Blacks, Chinese and Japanese, civilized American Indians and Hispanics. So, please accept this as here gold as a token of our love." Mr. Wilkerson patted a very heavy set of saddlebags on the hand-carved tabletop. "Don't open them now. Have a meeting with your seniors and talk over what I've said. There's over $100,000 in there. I've already set for one of your grandsons to come carry it. You'll need it to buy wagons, horses, supplies, hires some scouts and purchase some weapons."

"But, Sir, you'll need to pay the Yankees all the taxes they want."

"I'll be paying their illicit taxes for the next 50-years. But I'd rather you have this and it was my father's wishes for me to honor. Once you're all gone, I plan on leaving for New Orleans with the family to catch a ship for England. We still have our old cotton farmers over there and plan to look-into the coffee business and importing silks from China. Who knows, we may end up living in China."

"Thank you, Sir. I do not know what else I can say for such a gift. You have presented us with a new life."

"Juke, maybe in a very small way it will pay for all those slaves who died on this land for the last 200-years."

"Sir, you and your father will never face judgment for that crime," Juke said. Then Grandson William showed up, bowed before Mr. Wilkerson out of respect and not obedience. "William, be so kind as to take these saddlebags over to your grandfather's house. Do not open them, but they are very heavy."

With a hoist to his shoulder, William released a blow of air and agreed with the heavy load observation. Mr. Wilkerson then stood up and waited for Juke to stand to his feet before offering his hand. "Juke, when you've decided, I'll have my foreman and hired hands accompany your men to New Orleans to purchase all the wagons, supplies, horses and weapons you will need. But I want to express my thanks in making my farm the most plentiful Cotton Farm in this state."

"The cotton return was a clear demonstration on the respect my people had for your family."

"It's too bad the other farmers couldn't have learned this. Thrown away the whips, selling families apart and misuse of Black women. Allowing the White and Black pastors to conduct Christian services on the farms helped, but fear was the problem, fear all around. Whites fearing the Blacks and Blacks fearing the Whites. And it's taken this bloody Civil War to teach us a lesson."

Now Juke, with a .50 caliber Sharps buffalo rifle in his hands, stood beside the gate of a monstrous wagon facing the Indians and for the first time seeing all the dust clouding up on the wagon trail. But the Comanche wasn't shooting at the wagon train, they were having a hullabaloo with whoever was charging their way. Juke kept listening for a bugler, hoping it was U.S. Cavalry, but not hearing one he began to suspect an Indian trick.

"Everyone get ready to fire. This may be a trick. But no one fires until I do. I don't want to shoot any help if this is who it is."

When JW and his people cut loose with their 30-30s and the single Henry .44 rifle, they caught the Comanche completely by surprise. The extent of their fire power also had the Wagon Train people thinking a whole regiment was bursting through. Then Juke gave the order, "Hit the Indians on the hillsides, and avoid hittin' the trail. We got help comin'!"

Wagons were barrowing through as fast as those black demons could run. Liam was having to stand up behind the seat to maintain control, but JW rode right behind him to keep the Comanche off the Percherons. He's already shot six Indians off the back of the giant horses and taken one arrow to his upper right arm. But to ensure he wouldn't fall off his mount he had used thin braided rope to tie himself to his saddle. Both Lt. Gray and Lt. Dreeke had accomplished the same thing, knowing they would be riding right into the thick of the Comanche.

Two of Liam's lead Percherons had arrows sticking out of their rear hips, but it didn't seem to slow them down. The riflemen in each wagon was doing a superb job at wounding and killing the Comanche, until some of the Indians were riding away from those terrible weapons.

Now they were within easy sight of the wagon train and 100 men and women were using their single shot rifles and black powder Navy Colts to hurt the Indians. As of now, the Indians had focused their attention on the Rangers and Union troops, but now new orders given had the Indians rushing the Wagon train. Before long the people of the train were locked in bitter hand-to-hand combat beside and behind wagons. Women with boiling hot water were throwing kettles full of it on Indian faces, while nasty meat cleavers were used against Dog Soldiers trying to kill their menfolk. Store bought hunting knife against trader knives and tomahawk, decorated Indian spears versus oxen harness and bench seat 2x4s. Even burning fire wood was smashing into the sides of Comanche heads, or the heavy barrels of an empty Sharps rifle smashed into the skull of an Indian strangling a Black wagon driver. It was a major melee as JW's forces drew near.

"Hey Juke, that White boy drivin' dat front wagon better stop soon, or those big black horses of his, comin' like the demons of Hell, gonna run right smack into us!" Bobby, a nearly six-foot, seven-inch Black former picker shouted from ten feet away. He had a Comanche under each arm and was busy knocking their heads together.

"Move my wagon...Hurry, move my wagon out of the way to let all those boys through," Juke ordered, and 12 men grabbed the wagon from the inward-side, front and back and began moving the heavy beast backwards. Two other men, who had just finished off the two Indians they were fighting, began steering the wagon to the left to clear the wagon behind it. Four minutes later, the third wagon and the last rider was through and they were closing off the hole. By now what was left of the 26-man command was returning fire at an alarming rate, shocking the Black men standing about them, while JW began handing new Winchesters out one-handed and having a Ranger offering a quick demonstration how they shoot. Liam was handing out ammo and he and MSgt. Gary Wells was helping them load the rifles.

But by the time the other new shooters were back on the wall of wagons, the Comanche had backed off to the hillsides over 1,000 yards away to check on their injuries. This gave the Wagon Train and their rescuers time to check on their own wounded and dead.

Liam had taken a bullet crease over his right shoulder, but he was more worried about his two wounded Percherons. The arrows had to be dug out, but the horses were tough and they would live. Of the prized 32 mounts from the horse farms, 11 were either killed or captured. JW's second mount was gone, but his white stallion had escaped harm. But for the men, they did not fare so well. Of the ten Union Troops, Lt. Gray was wounded twice, but would survive. Sgt. Rimes was killed. Troopers Hills, Duster, Bitters, Ridgeway were dead. Troopers Sharp, Homer, O'Brian and St. Paul were all wounded to some degree, but all could ride within a few days. They had been moved to an aide station set up in the center of the Wagon Train yard. Of the Rangers, Dan Wakefield had died, while leaping out of his wagon to ensure the third wagon made it through. He took a spear to the chest and was killed instantly. Rangers Salcedo, Jim Williams, Leaders, Chris Wakefield and Lawrence Coon were all wounded and now being treated by the grateful women of the train.

For some of the southern troops, they had never had seen so many Black womenfolk all around them, but they were never slave owners or ever considered racists. Most of those who were conscious were really appreciating the great treatment.

JW set still briefly while an old medicine woman treated his wound, he thought was a bullet grazing, but then passed out when she removed the arrow head. He came to an hour or so later, but the Comanche were still in the hills.

Lt. Reeves gave JW a full account on the patrol's status. He was then introduced to the Wagon Leader with the name of Juke. The old man was somewhat surprised when JW offered to shake his hand, but with his uninjured arm. "You've set up a fine defense here, Juke. One would've thought you have served in the Army."

I was told stories of how my tribe's warriors used to fight opposing tribes. One of the most feared tribe and the largest was the Zulu. They were great strategists and even defeated the British Army."

"Your English, I do not even detect a southern drawl. I'm surprised."

I was taken as a slave to a Louisiana cotton farm at the age of six-years old. My mother and I…My father was sold to another location and I never saw him again. But my owner's father was near death and his son and grandson were Christians. Very kind men who never used a whip on a slave, or molested a female slave. We had Christian church services, missionary schools and most of our teachers came over from London area. I, myself, finished high school and earned a degree in accounting. So, I ran my owner's books. But he was much more of a friend. I was brought up with his son and then saw him leave, when he was forced into the Southern Army. He never came home and I will never forget our friendship."

"If you do not mind my asking, was it him who set you up with your Wagon Train?" JW asked.

"Their whole family has put money aside for us because they knew this day was coming and they fear for our lives once we were granted our freedom. They felt in California we would be safe. California is filled with various minorities and there is a future there for the American Black man."

"I sincerely hope so, Sir. But it may take time and the acts of bravery of such people as yourselves. Crossing this desert is not an easy thing and crossing the Plains trails you deal with the Pawnee, Crow and Sioux. And, there is also racism up there. But why didn't you book passage around on boats?"

"Several reasons, Sir, one being we might not have enough money left to set up homes, plow the lands and have supplies…Much less buy the properties. There is also the boats. A lot of my people are not nearly as old as I and their slaver's trip was not all that long ago. A lot of our women were abused by the sailors and this memory could cause problems. We, as the seniors, felt it best and this is what was recommended by our previous owners. We would have to leave from Texas and Louisiana ports and 130-Blacks with money for shipping may become prey to the criminal element."

"Yes, you have thought this out well." JW said, as another older woman in gray hair brought him his hot cup of coffee.

"Mr. Blake, this is my wife, Sarah," Juke said.

"I just wanted to add my thanks, as I am sure Juke has. But he's probably forgotten to tell you why, he is getting old."

"Hush, You, old woman and please do not embarrass me." Juke face broke out into a grin, but then it turned to one of solace. "We reached here with 22 wagons, Sir...Holding more than 140 families from the Wilkerson Plantation. We were 155 older boys of 16 and above and 128 womenfolk. But at last count we are down to 102 womenfolk and 94 menfolk and older boys. We have wounded numbering in the thirties and we've lost a third of our cattle, 12 of our 40 oxen and eleven of our horses from the fighting inside of here, just as you arrived. But without your arrival I fear we all would've been killed, or some of the women and children carried off as slaves."

"Yes, Sir. Those of you they do not keep for themselves, would be sold to the banditos for work in Mexico. But your skin color would be a novelty for the Comanche and they might keep more of you. I'd recommend you tell the married men and women, it is better to die than be captured by the Comanche or the Apache, which you will find further west. Western women often carry a pistol to shoot themselves to avoid being captured by the Indians and it is far worse than I believe the sailors might have caused on any slave ship. For when the Indian is done with...Its worse, believe me. Even a man does not want to be captured by an Indian and he will turn a pistol or rifle on himself, saving that last round for himself. Yet, the Indians consider suicide cowardly and they will do savage things to the body so it will not go to Heaven, or if it does all will know this person was a coward."

"You know a lot about the Indians, Sir," said Zeke, another senior, whose gray hair was extremely thin on the sides and he had no hair on top. His beard was full and curly, mixed of white and silver and he looked to be nearly as aged as Juke.

"Gentlemen, this is my co-leader Zeke and the man behind him is his son, Sam. This other young man is my grandson, Bobby. We pretty much make up the Wagon Train Council, with Bobby representing the young people."

That's a good idea, the youth need representation. Now as to Zeke's questions, yes, I've lived with Apache and Comanche, also the Navajo, but during the peaceful times. I've fought them as a soldier and then as an Arizona Ranger Commander. So yes, I've seen all sides of the desert Indian and no, I still don't understand them. They have their own codes of honor and integrity, but as you might have heard, their language has no word for 'lie'. But stealing horses doesn't mean the same thing to them as it does to us. To them it can be considered an act of bravery and a foolish act on the ones who left their horses unattended."

"Why are they hittin' our train, Sir?" Zeke asked. "We've done nothing to offend them."

"You're wrong, Zeke and you may call me JW…please. But you failed to send a representative to them to ask for permission to pass through their lines. Quite often they will respect the white flag and then a time of trading would follow for granting you their okay. Now they do not own the land, no Indian owns the land they occupy because they feel only their creator can own the land. But this is their land to hunt and occupy. They would've probably accepted some token gifts, that's if your representative had been allowed to return. But better to sacrifice one man than several."

"What else did we do wrong, JW?" Bobby asked.

"For you younglings I prefer Mr. Blake, it is simply the way I grew up. A sign of respect for a person's years on this earth…But as to your question, you showed a great weakness for leaving behind so much of your belongings. Most of which was gone through by the Comanche and what they wanted carried away. The Indians never leave anything behind that is visible. They'll bury it in a pit and mark it so they can reclaim it later.

"They had never seen so many of your race together, or for some they had never seen a Black person at all and this frightened them. Their medicine man may have told them you all must be killed to take away this fear. And believe me, the Comanche hate to be afraid of anything.

"They also wonder what else your wagons might have in them and for this alone, the war chief may be willing to throw away fifty of his dog soldiers…or even more."

"So, JW, what do you suggest?" Juke asked.

"I'm willing to try a meeting with the Comanche war chief, right out in front of here and on the trail. But I'll need two of you to go with me, to show you're not afraid either. No weapons other than what I bring to trade, but you can carry a knife. We will post a white flag and I speak Comanche well enough and may even know the war chief. If he honors the meeting he will approach on foot with his two senior men, also unarmed. More than three men come, we hightail it back inside the train for it's a trick."

"What will we take out to trade with and what are we trading for? Juke asked.

"First, we're trading for passage through his hunting grounds, which end inside the New Mexico Territory. They take in a lot of land, especially when one is hunting buffalo because the herds move with the seasons. Now as to what we're trading with, I suggest half-a-dozen cast-iron posts and frying pans of various sizes…Make that about 18 altogether to keep the wives of the sub-chiefs happy. I'll donate three of our large Bowie knives with sheaths and two of our Winchesters with 100 rounds each. They'll shoot-up that much before they even attack their next wagon train, but it will take down plenty of buffalo."

"What are we asking for right off, JW?" Zeke asked. His facial expression, especially with all the wrinkles, showed how curious he was over the whole thing.

"We need to stay here for another four days for our people to rest up. Then we'll travel south along the river to where the bigger trees grow. We're going to need rafts to get these wagons across and the river's too wide for a rope tow. This means 25 good sized rafts to float further down river to a suitable river bank to land at. Going to be a rough haul on your horses, but if need be our Percherons can help bring your wagons up and over the embankments. Then we forge our own trail until we can locate the old trail. I just can't figure out what they used before, or if these waters are at flood stage from the mountains rains high up above and someone had a large raft and rope tow service running until the waters rose-up, and washed away the business. Indians might've got him, too. I've still got to find out what set these Comanche off, but I'm figurin' it probably had somethin' to do with our Civil War."

"When do you want to do this," Juke asked. He was standing uneasy, knowing he was going to be one of those men out there to parley with JW and those Indians.

"You dig up those pots and pans, maybe some nice jewelry the womenfolk will part with…the gaudier the better…while I go get the weapons and advise my men what I'm doing. Lt. Gray and Lt. Sampson will assume joint command of our people if anything happens to me. Both men carry a lot of experience, but the best Indian fighter is Lt. Dreeke." JW turned to face young Bobby and asked, "Can you find me a white bed sheet and tie off one end to tall pole? Not sure what you can use, but find something. I'll have you carry it out to hold the flag, but you'll be standing way behind us. Things go wrong, you're not to come to our rescue, just drop the flag and get behind a wagon. Okay?"

"I'll nail two two-inch by four-inch pieces of railings together. We carry extra to reinforce damaged wagons."

"Sounds good, Bobby, now get it done," JW ordered and Bobby was off at the run.

JW stood up from the box he ended up sitting upon and suddenly hurt all over. He felt as if everything was sprung in the wrong direction and now wished he hadn't sat still for very long. It wasn't only the arrowhead they cut out, no, he'd had too many of those removed and knife or tomahawk wound stitched up, but he suddenly realized it was his age. His years were catching up with him and this last run for the wagons had been stressful, and maybe too stressful. Yet, his heart felt fine, it just seemed to be everything else crying out in pain. But he didn't have time for this now, he needed to look strong before the Comanche War Chief or this whole thing could be worthless.

JW knew from experience that he and the two others would be under the sights of mixture of a dozen rifles and bows and arrows. Personally, he preferred being shot with the arrows, for the times he was shot with mini-balls the doctors thought he would die and had spent weeks in the hospitals. With the arrows, he was usually up and out of the aide stations within a few days at most. He had kept every arrow head they had cut out of his body, including the one they took out today. But he had no time to lay down and recuperate. Plus, he couldn't look sick.

He went to the rifle's wagon and secured two Winchesters. Then he looked to MSgt. Gary Wells, who had just come back from the first aide area. "I told you to get these rifles handed out to the men in the train…All of them, until they were all issued and all the ammo."

"Sorry, Captain, I was over praying with the dyin'."

"Ain't no time for that, now. Master Sergeant. For now, we take care of the Living. Then as time allows you can help with the dyin'. You understand me?"

"Yes, Sir, I do. Though I may not always agree with you, I'll obey your orders."

JW grabbed a canteen off the water barrel and poured water all over his face and washed down his arms and hands. "Listen, Gary…I'm tryin' to set-up a parley with the Comanche. I'm gonna have all the women and children back at the aide station. I want you and Liam, stationed there, along with Coon and Holloway, and two of Juke's men, both armed with Winchesters. If the Parley fails and they break through, make sure none of the wound, or the women and children are still alive. You understand what I am asking of you, and I also want you to handle Liam for me. Can you do that?"

Gary Wells stood in thought as JW wiped off his arms and went to obtain the two Winchesters and 100 30-30 caliber rounds for each rifle. Gary Wells Then came to attention, popped a formal salute and stated, "Your orders will be obeyed, Captain."

"It's been a privilege, Master Sergeant. I still hope to swear you in as a new Ranger, once we get past this small obstacle." He returned the hand salute and patted Gary Wells on both shoulders.

"Captain, if this is a small obstacle, I cannot say I am looking forward to one of your large obstacles in Arizona."

JW glanced about and finally spotted Liam working with his Percherons. He had unhooked them from the wagons and one team at a time, had removed their rigging and tied them by leather reins to a rope line he had running between two wagon's wheels that were set up on the river side of the wagon train. He knew being tied off separately, there was less chance of the big draft horses from becoming frightened with all the shooting and screaming, and running wild over people inside the wagon defensive perimeter. Twelve of these massive beasts could do a lot of harm, forcing the troops to shoot the horses down. But now, that hopefully wouldn't happen. He had them tied off and hobbled. Only thing else he could do was tie their tails together, but he thought that to be foolish and he'd probably end up being kicked in the head.

"Liam...Liam, come over here!" JW ordered.

Hearing his name called out in that familiar loud roar, he looked to see where his Commander might be and spotted him over by their wagons. He waved once and then hustled over to find JW examining two Winchesters. MSgt. Gary Wells was also pulling the rifles out and stacking them to lean against the tailgate of their wagon.

"Sir, Pvt. Blake reporting as ordered," Liam said. He stood at attention, with a Winchester at the side of his right leg. Liam had not learned the rifle salute movement as JW had not bothered to teach him.

"I am assigning you to MSgt. Gary Wells. You are to stay at his side until I release you from this order. Do you understand?"

"Yes, Captain...What are we doing?"

Gary replied, "I'll brief you on that myself. Right now you will carry 200 rounds of ammo out to where our Commander so designates and then you will report right back to me. Understand?"

"Yes, Master Sergeant."

"I need a whitish blanket also to sit upon, I'll go check with Juke. You two wait here."

Meanwhile, up on the hills the Comanche reviewed their prior attack and wondered who these new White people were and why they had come to help these Black people. Three Horses, War Chief for this war party had been told by his medicine man that White people hated the Black people, yet now he sees the opposite. There were also the new rifles the Union soldiers carried, along with those civilians. One such rifle was brought to him, but he could not get the rifle to fire and it would not take his black power nor his mini-balls. The weapon had belonged to Sgt. Rimes and was empty when he was killed and thrown from his saddle. A

Comanche Dog Soldier had secured his weapons and brought them to the Indian War Chief, but not knowing how the lever action rifle worked he had damaged the rifle by pouring black powder down the barrel and into the loading slip. He had even tried to insert one of the 30-30 cartridges into the loading slot, but he did it backwards and when it didn't slide in and used the hilt of his knife and tried hammering it in. Had he known how close he had come to death at that moment he would have offered great praise to his gods for saving him. However, the Colt .44 was much easier to use and he was extremely happy with this gift from his warrior, who had grown in stature in the war chief's eyes.

Then news came to him, a late parley was being requested within an hour before sundown. A Whiteman's white flag was being waved and there were three people sitting on a white blanket and there appeared to be gifts.

Three Horses then knew a White man had come who knew how the Comanche did things. But first before going to the parley with his two sub-chiefs, he checked to see how his wounded were doing. The medicine man was busy for there were over 60 men wounded and most of them after the new rifles showed up. As to the dead, he knew they were on their way to the spirit world and would no longer care for who won or lost this single battle.

JW set in front, with Juke and Zeke sitting cross-legged right behind him. In front of them were 19 cast iron frying pans and stew pots of various sizes. There was even one of three gallon size and it was the largest pot JW had ever seen. Then there were three brand-new Bowie knives with the ten-inch blades, but the big trade gift was two brand-new Winchester 30-30 caliber Rifles. Only when he unpacked them did JW realize these rifles carried serial numbers with only three digits, which made him wonder how many digits these serials numbers will grow in a hundred years.

Bobby held the 15-foot tall flag pole made of two eight-foot long 2"x4's. One foot of the top board was used to nail it to the bottom rail. Attached to it was a full-size white bed sheet, loaned by one of the families right off their bed. Bobby hadn't realized it and so, he hadn't told the family that if peace was accepted, the white flag would have to be waving over the train as it traveled and in the camp. In this way, any splinter Comanche hunting party would know they had obtained Three Horse's permission. He would put his mark in the center of the flag to be seen by all.

"Bobby, you remember to step back to the wagons before the Indians get here, but keep that flag up so it can be seen. If peace is agreed upon, the war chief will have the flag brought forth so he can put his mark

on the flag for all his Indians to know we have his permission. All right?"
JW asked.

"I'm ready to move, Captain...Your three Indians are on the move."
Bobby said.

"Is it only three?" JW asked.

"Only three," Bobby said. As he was standing, he could see a lot
better than the three men sitting on the ground.

"Step back to the wagons and have the men lower their rifles. I don't
want to have a single rifle pointed at these Indians. They're our guests and
we must treat them as such. Remember, the White man has broken every
treaty made with the Indian. Maybe having a wagon train of Blacks will
have a different effect."

It took the three Indians nearly 15 minutes to ride down from the
hills and rein up their mounts a short distance from the parley blanket. All
three dismounted and JW could see they were all about his age, but the
one who was clearly in authority seemed to be. *I know him...at a prisoner
exchange with border bandits.*

(Speaking Comanche) "Three-Horses, many moons have passed
since last time you and I talked as friends. I do hope your sons are strong
and have killed many buffalo," JW said to the front Indian and offered an
arm grasp to show his friendship was still there.

Three-Horses stood less than two-feet away from him and with a
hard look on his face he examined him from head to toe. His eyes then
softened and he returned the arm grasp of friendship.

"Had I known you were with this wagon train we would have talk
first to find out where these people are going? You understand why we
fight for our land? Even now the buffalo herds grow smaller, antelope and
deer moving away because of your war. And Yes, I do remember the time
we had together and how your Indian name is, 'Man-Who-Follows'. Do
you still follow the bad man?"

"We fought in the Whiteman's war, now it is over and we return
home. I will follow the bad ones again and they will be of any color."

"I also now remember how you step in and give us extra money to
trade for two women taken by bandits. One was pregnant and she make
me a grandfather. My sons all make me proud, but only two of them still
alive. One died in buffalo hunt and one was killed by Apache scum."

"Will you now join us and sit at the parley. It has been a long time
for me, so I hope I have done it well."

JW then turned to face the Parley rug and walked on the right side
of Three-Horses. When they reached the white sheet, Bobby made sure

everyone received the order to lower all weapons. The Indians were to be treated as guests and the whole train was at risk if someone shot at one of the three Indians. The White flag was now being held in place by one of Bobby's friends, another giant of a young man who looked as if he could grab a steer by it horns and launch it over his shoulder for a ten-yard toss.

When he looked over the wagon train, MSgt. Gary Wells knew by all the muscle on display, they'd have no problem cutting trees down and making rafts. But that was for later, the Comanche was still the problem.

With all three Indians sitting down, they gave Juke and Zeke a good once over. For Sub-Chief Sun that Sets, these were the first Black men he had ever seen. Three-Horses had seen Black people before at prisoner exchanges, but not men and for Sub-Chief Walks-Tall, this was only the second time. Walks-Tall had attacked a small wagon train with his war party several years earlier and a Black man died trying to protect an old couple from harm. For his bravery, the war party had left him alone, but the older couple, though dead, were treated as cowards. They had no weapons. Walks-Tall wondered why such a small train would risk danger by crossing this part of Texas? But the Comanche had unknowingly done the Union a favor by knocking off a Confederate spy force, which was on their way to Northern Nevada to pose as a Missionary School. Another such school in its early growth was attacked and burned to the ground by the Apache in Northern Arizona, this was after the Arizona Ranger had been dismantled and Union patrols were nowhere near the area.

For over an hour the six men talked with JW doing all the interpreting. There were several times of laughter and other times of agreement. Finally, Three-Horses asked for JW to show him how the Winchester was loaded, while his sub-chiefs watched. "Can you call to your men and tell them all is okay, while I show you how to shoot this rifle?"

Three-Horses said something to Walks-Tall, who walked fast over to his horse, where he mounted and rode back about 50 yards. He then waved both hands and shouted several words out in Comanche, which JW understood.

JW looked to his two men and said, our test firing will not cause a war. Would one of you ensure the same here?"

Juke turned to face the train and bellowed, "We're going to test fire a couple Winchesters, so keep your hands off your rifles. Everything is looking fine so far."

"John Gibson, bring me your Winchester and claim another one or grab one of our shotguns. I've got to give your rifle away."

"Okay, Boss, but I sure hate to see it go," Gibson replied. He then came forward with the rifle out in front of him in a presentation-like appearance. He then handed it to JW and returned to the wagon train.

"(In Comanche) Chief Three-Horses, friend of long ago, I am escorting this train through Comanche and Apache lands. They are on their way to California and will not stop for hunting parties, but may hunt one or two buffalo as hunger comes. I had not planned to escort them, but their scouts were thieves and stole their money and left them in the desert alone. They would be lost and the Union cavalry commander is now dead. These things happen because…they do. Had they known how to parley, you may have let them pass and no battle would've been fought. But I know, some battle is good for young warriors to learn, to carry wounds of battle and take first blood. But now I ask your permission to pass through your land, to travel south to a place to cut trees and build big rafts to take us across your land's mighty river. In return we give to your womenfolk these pots and frying pans that will not break. I give you these Bowie knives that are brand new and best of all I present you with three of these magic Winchester rifles. Here, now I show you how they work." JW made sure his rifle was empty and knelt-down next to a 30-30 caliber wooden box of ammo and pulled off the top and then pulled back the piece of tin that covered the cartridges.

"These are 30-30 caliber cartridges and there are 100 cartridges in each box." JW handed a rifle to Sub-Chief Walks-Tall and Sub-Chief Sun-that-Sets. He then addressed Walks-Tall, who now carried the full rifle from John Gibson. "Your rifle is full but we must empty it. So, keep your hands off the trigger and grasp only the lever." He then inserted the single round from the box into the side loader, with Chief Three-Horses watching him. He demonstrated the unloading of his rounds—unloaded six.

"Remember it carries one in the chamber and five down in the loader. Do not try to over-load it. It a six-round rifle and then you reload.

"Now the rifle is loaded and watch how I fire. You should fire slowly at first or it can throw your aim off." JW aimed at a bush some 100 yards away from him and began to fire-eject, fire-eject…, "Now load your rifles, but always remember they are ready to shoot, so do not aim them at anyone for you can risk an accidental shooting."

Once the three Indians had their rifles loaded they brought their Winchesters to their right shoulders and began shooting, but the last three rounds were done in a faster maneuver, as JW expected. They then quickly reloaded and fired again, decimating the poor bush.

Then Three-Horses stopped them and examined the weapons closely, "Is this what the Union Army will have-to fight the Comanche with?"

"Not yet, these were a special gift to me and my men. But the U.S. Army, especially the cavalry will all carry such a weapon."

"Have your White flag brought to me and I will give you my mark. But a war party will follow, if these people stop to settle, to make farms, our treaty is no more. This is only for travel. You will have five moons to leave Comanche lands. But I fear your people in Ute and Apache lands."

The White flag was brought up and Three-Horses used charcoal from a camp fire to draw his name into the middle of it. Where once it was simply white and blank, now rode the large diagram of three white stallions.

"One last thing, Man-Who-Follows, my Granddaughter insists you come for visit tonight. My men will come get you in one hour."

"Umm...sure, yes and thank you." JW looked at the two older men and smiled. "Indians can be a very hospitable people, especially if they've just brought in a buffalo. If I know my Comanche, I won't be able to eat for a week."

Meal time was not Buffalo; however, it was great helpings of antelope, deer and lots of various desert birds. The dinner drink was mostly water, but afterward it turned to an alcoholic-type beverage made from various desert vegetables and JW could not afford to get drunk. He was the only White Man in a camp of about 1,000 Comanche. But he was being treated as a visiting royal ambassador. Knowing the language helped a lot and shortly into the meal he was introduced to Three-Horses' granddaughter...The one he had helped buy back from the bandits. But back then he didn't even notice her, he only wanted to gain a friendship with the Comanche. At the time, Sub-Chief Three-Horses was one of many, but JW sensed this Indian was going to be on the rise. Now there was only one chief higher than him and that man was in his 80's.

Now, the Granddaughter was extremely noticeable, in fact JW thought she was extremely beautiful. She was dressed in a white leader form fitting dress, covered in light blue pieces of turquoise and a long necklace of silver chain. On her feet were white leather calf-high moccasins and both dress and boots were adorned in magnificent multi-colored bead work. Her long black hair went to her hips and her deep brown eyes and full lips only enhanced her beauty. And to add to her attire, she also wore a wide metal headband made of shimmering silver, with stones of gold and turquoise. JW was utterly speechless when she came forward to stand by her grandfather's shoulder, who set on the floor at the head of his grouping. But then she surprised everyone when she sat down between Three-Horses and Man-Who-Follows.

JW wasn't sure what to say, other than, "You honor me above all honors."

"My husband is dead, a strange sickness we do not even whisper of or know, but my son lives and he is strong. But if not for you, I may have died for I promised myself I would rather die than return with those men. So, I and my children owe you a debt, as my Grandfather does. Maybe, this is why you are here, this night. Many men and boys wish to marry me, possibly for me or maybe to become a sub-chief to my Grandfather. But I am happy alone. Are you married, Man-Who-Walks?"

"With such beauty around me it is hard to speak, but yes, I am married and her name is Sherry Ann. I have two children. Steven was ten-years old and Jessie my little girl was eight-years old when I left for the war. Though I've had no mail since we left and wonder how things are on my farm."

"I had hoped you to be single or a widower. But it is wrong to wish such a thing, knowing what I gone through and the pain I suffered so. I do hope you find that all is right with your farm and your family well. But if you ever come back this way and wish to see me, I give you this...As a way...to find me. If all is forever well, you may sell it to reclaim the money you paid out to save me and know I will forever thank you." She took her headband off and presented it to him, which caused Three-Horses to look upon Man-Who-Follows with a strangeness in his eyes.

Four Comanche escorted Man-Who-Follows back to the wagon train, where he thanked them and they in turn wished him well, having seen the friendship shared between Three-Horses with this White man, who knew their language so well. JW then saw how the white flag had been mounted to the right side of Liam's wagon, which would now lead the wagon train. The second Ranger wagon would be in the middle of the train, right after the eleventh California bound covered wagon and the last Ranger wagon would pull tail-end. Union troops and Rangers, mostly all bandaged up from their wounds with the help of that Black medicine woman, were separated between the three wagons. Their horses running loose were now running with all the extra mounts brought along by the Black families. Before they headed off down river, the trailing herd was numbered at 84 horses and there were six-outriders keeping them together.

The riverside was mostly flat land, with heavy brush, large rocks and the occasional soaked up log washed ashore. Holloway reminded JW of the forest ahead. "A lot of big trees. Take some time to bring down, but we'll build the rafts we need and take 'em down river to the next beach. Way this river is raging we might find a decent shoreline to beach our rafts, but that means a lot of raft making. Have you checked these people for saws and axes?"

"Not yet. I'll talk to Juke or Zeke about it," Holloway said.

"Let's get these wagons moving before noon and maybe we can get within sight of those big trees." JW said, then walked off looking for Liam.

Sure enough they had two-man saw tied up underneath the wagons and single bladed and double bladed axes in every wagon. All of them brand new, without even an ounce of sweat on them. But that would change very soon.

They stopped a half-hour before sundown and there was no sight of the trees, but Holloway and Jim Williams returned to report they could see the big trees to the south and estimated their distance at 20 miles. They had also spotted 30 to 40 Comanche, but when they displayed a large white banner with Three-Horses' diagram on it, the Comanche rode off.

The trip was rough going and had to stop along the way to replace half-a-dozen broken wheels, so they didn't hit the trees until the next day in the afternoon. They took their wagons into the trees and set up a perimeter defense, using the river as their backside. A double corral was built, allowing a space for the guards to walk between the two corals and there was plenty of water to keep the horses happy. Once the encampment was set up, dinner was made and guard duty was assigned. Two hunting parties were assigned to leave in the morning in groups of ten-men each, with two draft horses from the wagon train assigned to haul the meat back. It was taking a lot of food to feed this group. Older boys were already trying their skill at fishing and big boys were around to jump in and pull the foolish ones out. By 10 a.m., the first of the river trout was caught and from then on fish became a main staple until the rafts were all across.

The rafts were to be 18 feet long and some 12 feet wide. Horses swam pretty well, so they would be herded across. Half the herd before, and half the herd at the end. JW knew they would most likely need the big black Percherons to tow and hold the rafts to the opposite shore. Holloway and Jim William would swim their primary mounts across and then scout the other side in hopes of locating another wagon train trail. They wanted to head west, but if the only trail led south into the bigger population centers, they wagon train occupants were willing to do what was necessary to survive.

Locating the big evergreens was not hard and by dinner time that had dropped more than half of the needed logs. Then the draft horses and Black Percherons were used to bring the logs over to where the raft would be built.

A pit over two feet deep, 16 feet wide and 20 feet long was dug out of the ground, leaving a dam of dirt nearly two feet wide between the river and the pit. Then men and horse laid branchless logs no more than two feet wide across the pit. This was then followed by men, with horses helping them, lay one log at a time lengthwise with the end of the log facing the river. Then a second log was run up beside it and the two of them roped together. This continued until the whole raft was all roped together. Once completed, four massive spikes were driven into the ground and with the usage of pulleys and the Black Percherons, the first wagon was pulled backwards up onto the raft and then secured with wooden braces and spikes, also additional rope pieces.

Before the first wagon went across, half the herd was launched into the river and they ended spread over a quarter-mile of riverbank. Logs had to be floated across, which was no easy feat and they lost three of them in the attempt. They also lost a rider, but he showed up after a mile swim down the river. His horse had come back with an empty saddle, but all ended well. Men on the rafts had the ropes to throw, but if they missed they then had to jump into the water and pull the rope to shore.

Before long they were slowly taking a hold of the rafts and 20 horses were pulling them up river, against the current until they could be locked into placed for unloading.

All together it had taken them a week to make the transfer and even Three-Horses and a party of 100 warriors had appeared in peace to simply watch the operation. Three-Horses was really impressed with the whole river crossing and he wondered of Man-Who-Follows could build them a bridge along these waters. (Speaking Comanche), "I would like to take my hunting parties across river to go after the buffalo that stay on that side. Meat and robes too heavy to bring back across on horses and we lose both many times when we have tried."

"Three-Horses, I do not have the knowledge to build a bridge, but I have the words to speak to say the Great Comanche seek such a bridge and may trade for such a thing to be built. Would you be willing ride the peace trail if bridge over the river is built for your Tribe?"

"I would have to seek council, but before you leave my hunting grounds you will have my words to give the people who make such things."

"I wish it be so. Once I have a good answer I will provide it to the Indian Department now in our Nation's Capital. If small party of US Army comes out with White flag, you must be ready to receive them in peace…at least for the time you parley."

"One day you who saved my Granddaughter will become my brother and you will always be welcome in the Lands of the Comanche."

"I will look forward to that day coming as it will honor me...How is your Granddaughter?"

"She has been sad since you left, but she will be happy to see you asked about her. It is too bad you are married, but again this shows you are honest man. A worse man would lie to her, maybe marry her to have only a couple nights with her. Many White men would die for such wrong doing to one of my family. But you a good man. I hope you find all well when you reach home, but I have word for you within the week."

Jim Williams and Holloway rode hard for eight days and then they stumbled upon a wagon train trail headed west. There was also recent dropping from oxen, horses, and steer. When they got back to the wagon train that was already proceeding south along the river, but on the opposite side and JW had received his positive reply from the Comanche Nation, he had sent Scout Salcedo with official mail to Austin. Salcedo also carried two saddle bags of personal mail, but no more and a three-foot wide white banner with Three Horses diagram reprinted on it for free passage through Northern Texas. Now his only concern was of the Ute and Apache. But he made it to Austin and presented the official mail which included the Comanche bridge idea in trade for peace and it was formally turned over to Indian Department of Affairs, which was a two-man office in Austin. The request was then sent by stagecoach to Washington D.C. for the big thinkers to look at the idea.

JW didn't know about it for several years, but after months of foolish debate, the bridge idea was voted down for fear the Comanche might use the other side of the river to conduct raids deeper on into Texas. But evidence was shown the Comanche didn't need the bridge for their war parties, only their hunting parties. Still, it was not passed and White and Black men continued to die in Mid-North Texas and even parts of South Texas. The 1,000-Comanche raid that hit Austin had rattled the local politicians and their fears were felt in the Nation's Capital.

When Scout Andy Salcedo made it back to the wagon train they were entering the New Mexico Territory. Now they needed to be watchful for Comanche, Ute and the beginnings of the Apache Nation. For the wagon train going to California, they still had nearly 1,000 hard desert miles yet to go.

CHAPTER ELEVEN

"Do you think old man Abraham would have a heart attack if'in ah asked his granddaughter fer a dance?"

NEW MEXICO TERRITORY, BIG DANCE, WITH FIDDLES PLAYING AND GUITARS

Through New Mexico, with the exception of a few Indians seen at a distance, they had no problems with any of the Indians tribes. Then two-days from the Eastern Arizona Territorial border, the wagon train was met with a Union patrol of cavalry out of the recently built Fort Defiance. According to the Patrol Commander, Captain Sedwick Jones, who had been at Fort Defiance for only three months and this was his first long range patrol for the fort was positioned approximately 240 miles northwest of Globe.

"Headquarters in Tucson wanted a fort in position to separate the Navajo and Hopi from the various Apache tribes to the south and southwest. But as of yet we have not seen any Indians at all."

A large meal was provided for the 32-man patrol by the members of the wagon train and the Southern Blacks were surprised to find seven Blacks among the Western cavalry.

"Captain, how long have you served in the desert?" Lt. Sampson asked. Though he no longer wore his gray uniform, Captain Jones knew by the man's southern accent and strong bearing he was a former officer during the Civil War. But he reminded himself the war was truly over and his men were all guests. Even Lt. Gray, who was still bandaged up, displayed a high regard for these people, including the Blacks.

"Only a very short time, Mr. Blake and admittedly, I can say this desert is very misleading. I have two scouts with me, from Tucson, who know the region quite well and were in the process of leading us to the border, which was the limits of our patrol. Now we can take Lt. Gray and the surviving soldiers off your hands, and with the assistance of one of your wagons, will take the wounded back to Fort Defiance for the doctors to observe."

Before JW could reply to the captain's absurd request for one of his wagons and four of his black Percherons, the army's two scouts rode up and began their report to Captain Jones. But suddenly, JW and then Lt. Dreeke drew their Colt .44s from their holsters, cocked their hammers and aimed them right at the two scout's stomachs.

Captain John's shouted, "What is the meaning of this, Gentlemen? If I give the order I can have 32 rifles aimed at you and awaiting my next order to blow you out of your saddle…unless you plan to murder me, too."

"Captain Jones, before the Arizona Rangers were dismantled in '62, I was its commander, this man with the Colt .44 in his hand was my MSgt and all these others were Rangers. Only 30 Rangers patrolled this entire territory of Arizona and at last count we weathered over 100 engagements against the warring tribes. Our very last engagement was against more than 60 Apache warriors on their way to attack Globe." JW lifted the barrel of his .44 to lift the brim of his hat. With all the sweating he was doing his flat-brimmed hat had slid down a bit to cast a shadow over his vision and he wanted clear vision over these two owl hoots.

"Yes, as you most likely suspected, we road for the south and joined with General Hood's Army of Texas and my scout unit were captured before the major battles were fought for the City of Nashville. We spent the winter in that hellhole the Union called El Mira Union Prison Camp in New York. A lot of good men died in that camp…But I am getting off the subject at hand."

He brought Lt. Sampson up and asked him to recall these two men, even though both had grown beards. But one had a serious scar down the left side of his neck and another had the top of his right ear lopped off. They had both been knife fighters, but rather poor ones. "Captain Jones, Lt. Sampson handled the Tucson Office for the Rangers and saw the wanted posters for these two animals. I want him to identify them and tell you what these two…chunks of human waste are wanted for. I am amazed your Headquarters never checked old wanted posters, both had $5,000 rewards on them…each, alive or dead."

Sampson road up beside them and with his Colt pulled, he carefully removed the knives and Navy Colts the two men carried. He also pulled out the Sharps 50 caliber Buffalo rifles from their slings and handed them to a nearby soldier he knew—PFC Sharp.

"Yup, Captain, this is them…They're those brothers…The Calvin and Alvin Zed…Zedekiah Brothers. Their mother should'a drowned them at birth. Sorry, took me a long moment ta recall their Biblical names. But not what they're wanted for. These slime are both wanted for more than one murder and both for hold-ups of stores and stagecoaches, where they usually killed everyone aboard for the sheer fun of it. They'd only leave the small boys alive to wait for a rescue party. But they're wanted for molesting women and the young girls before killing them…Whites and Indians. Then when the Rangers made it too hot, they fled the territory to join up with the banditos and went into cattle stealing along the border.

Last we heard in Tucson they were down in Mexico City. I jus' can't believe they were stupid enough ta come back here and go ta work for thu Union Army." Sampson uncocked the hammer on his Colt .44 and then whipped his arm around to nail Calvin Zedekiah to the left side of the head and knocked him off his horse.

"Sampson, that man is employed by the U.S. Army, he and his brother will have his rights to a trial by a jury," Captain Jones said.

"Captain, one of my Rangers, PFC Ringer, had his sister on one of those stagecoaches. He was in the rescue party and when they found her naked out in a small gully, these two animals had taken their knives to her. Had he been here right now, there would've been no trial. But he died as a Ranger and I hope to represent him and his sister at that trial to ensure these two coyotes are hung by the neck until dead." Sampson glared at the other brother and then rode off to cool down.

Later, once the two new prisoners were well tied up, Captain Jones, Lt. Sampson, Lt. Dreeke and Lt. Gray, who was carried over to the fire, where they were meeting, covered with a blanket, along with MSgt. Gary Wells, MSgt. Michaels. They met with a worried JW Blake

"What are your plans, Captain Blake…concerning this wagon train?" Captain Jones asked.

JW gritted his teeth and tightened his grip on his holstered Colt, before replying. "Seems the smartest thing to do is follow the new wagon trail up to this Fort Defiance and give your Fort Commander a total briefing on these two dogs and offer my expertise on what I know of this area. Since I've shown your scouts to be unreliable and at some point, even the possibility of leading you into a bandit or even a Comanchero attack." He saw the curious expression on the captain's face. "Comancheros are White men and Mexican who ride with the Apache, and their army is supposedly growing in number.

"I have never heard of them," Jones said in response, his eyes showing his honesty.

"I'll offer you the services of two of my men, Mr. Holloway and Mr. Jim Williams. Probably the two best scouts in Southwest Arizona. Then I will try to talk the wagon train occupants into following us to the fort, for they have no scouts. Thieves posing as scouts stole their money and abandoned them. We found them against a Texas River, about to be massacred by Comanche Indians. Thankfully, the Chief and I knew each other from a long ago meeting and he owed me a favor, so we were allowed-to pass. We built rafts and eventually picked up the old trail and proceeded west.

"Once we leave the fort, we'll take them to the Arizona and California border and send them on their way, with our best wishes. There are some courageous families in that group and a few of them have been slaves for over 80 years, still remembering how they came across from Africa on those stinky slave ships. I've talked with the seniors over several meals and listened to them and these were the lucky one who were bought by Christian people. Missionary schools, churches and medical treatment was provided, log homes and no one went hungry. There was never a whip used and his people produced the highest cotton crop in Louisiana all out of love. When they were set free at the end of the war the owner blessed them with $100,000 in gold coin to buy those wagons, horses and supplies. He advised them to travel to California where several minorities are making futures."

"They are the rare ones. We have a couple dozen Blacks who have made a fine show of themselves and I've heard the Ninth and Tenth Cavalry or combined Infantry will be formed up of all Blacks, with White officers. But most officers feel this is a dead-end for any future ambitions, yet I'm not sure.

"I worked for my Dad in Missouri, we made Holy Bibles and various other books. A real hit and miss business. But we employed a dozen Blacks and they were harder workers than my Whites. I had one who was a book keeper, where he had learned his trade in England and had also studied for the law. An extremely intelligent man. I believe he would've made a fine senior officer given the chance."

"Your statement forces me to re-evaluate my character study of you, Captain. There is more to you than I thought," JW said, with a smile to his words.

"My father was always after me to broaden my mind, but understanding the Indians of Arizona is a challenge. I've read some books by earlier explorers who had lived with the Apache, Navajo and Ute, and those who even lived with the Comanche and it makes me wonder how they could have accomplished it?"

"Captain, you're sittin' 'fore ah legend of sorts. Captain Blake, he has lived wit' three of thu Apache tribes, for ah think dere are seven of dem in all, an' main Comanche tribe on Nort' Texas. Thu good Captain has lived wit' thu Navajo an' Ute, an' spent ah few weeks wit' ah Pueblo tribe 'fore he left ta make its journey into deep Mexico." James Dreeke was pointing a burning stick from the fire at JW.

"Dere ain't ah man on dis desert dat knows more 'bout dese people, mostly 'cause he treats dem like people," James said, and then added, "He treats 'em all wit' respect. He learns deir languages 'til he is fluent an' learns deir customs. For dis, dey done honor him. Comanche refer to him as 'Man Who Follows', 'cause of his Ranger duties. Apaches, will dey call him 'Ghost in Desert Wind'. But ah can't recall what thu Navajo or dose Ute named him. But since he was an adult, when he came to dem, his name always follows wit' wha' he does an' out of respect."

"Can you tell me what this was like," Captain Jones asked in a sincere tone. Blake could see he really wanted to know.

"If you're an invited guest, you are forever safe in the encampment and treated as royalty. No, they do not send you a woman, but you are well taken care of and in the camp, they have five and sometimes six meals a day. As a guest, you are invited to ride along on hunting party, with the best hunt being the one for buffalo. Here you will witness the skills of one of the finest cavalries in the world. Nothing is wasted on a buffalo and one eats until one is ready to bust a gut. When it is time for you to leave, they will escort to where you are safe and give their goodbyes. I was with a photographer and an artist, acting as their interpreter and we visited the three Apache tribes. There was no war going on between anyone it seemed, a truly peaceful time, so the men and young men trained daily for the coming of war. We visited the Payson Apache in the center of Arizona, the Colorado Apache on the border with California — but the great Colorado River separated the two territories, and then I took them to see the San Carlos Apache." JW took a breather and swallowed some of his now getting warm coffee, and asked for a refill after he poured the contents out and he held his tin cup up for the cook, assigned to Jones' patrol to refill it.

"Fortunately, while we were visiting the San Carlos Apaches, the famous Cochise, renegade Apache Leader of the Chiricahua Apaches, arrived with 100 warriors. I will admit, it was a frightening moment until he learned the three of us had been allowed into the village and how I spoke Apache as if I was an Apache.

"Well, a few moments later, I stood before the Great Cochise and worked hard to keep my knees from rattling. He was not a big man. His hair was beginning to turn gray and his eyes revealed to me a man of great intelligence. He gave me a hard once over and tested me for knowing their language and then their customs. He smiled when he heard my Apache name, 'Ghost-in-Desert-Wind'. Then I explained to him, maintaining my honesty with him, how I was an Arizona Ranger Captain, who had been assigned to journey with this painter and photographer and act as their interpreter. To show there was no dishonesty on our party or secret plans."

JW took another drink of hot coffee, which burned his lower lip and he sucked on it briefly. His story so far had so impressed Captain Jones, he wished he had a written story of these events to show his father back home.

"We stayed there three days as guests of Cochise, but also the Chief of the St. Carlos Apache Tribe. The artist made numerous drawings, but the photographer was not allowed to take any photos. The St. Carlos medicine man had ill feelings about this camera device and told Cochise it threatened his power.

"Cochise and I spoke of the future of Arizona and the American Indian and I continued to remain truthful with him. This left him dismayed. But to have said even one lie, and he would see it in my eyes, all three of us would've been tortured and killed. When the three days were up, I was given an invitation to return to St. Carlos, but then the Indian Wars intensified and I could see no future for me ever meeting with my earlier friends in peace. Some of the Apache I have killed were ones I have shared ceremony water with, watched their children be dedicated by their medicine men and even stood by as they were married. I truly hated war.

"I had heard that Cochise's Co-War Chief, Mangas-Coloradas, had been killed, and this left Cochise as principal chief of the Apache warriors. The Union troops were busy in Arizona, New Mexico and Texas, rounding up the wild Indians to place them on government reservations. Some of the Great War Chiefs were being transported by train to Florida to keep them from organizing a breakout. But Cochise remains out there, with over 200 desert warriors and I felt it was doubtful he would ever surrender. So, Captain Jones that is who you must watch out for and when he strikes it will be like a rattlesnake hitting you from the shadows."

With the wounded men and knowing we had just come from the border, Captain Jones saw no reason to continue to the New Mexico Border. They would now turn around and head back to Fort Defiance with their prisoners and wounded troops. Holloway and Williams were sent out ahead, leaving a good two hours before the patrol departed. Behind them came the wagon train, followed by the three Ranger wagons and their extra mounts.

The Union soldiers had seen all the Winchesters and JW's Henry Repeater and had not asked any questions, other than to hold one and explain how it works. Captain Jones was also very impressed by the 12 mighty Percherons. He had seen such animals in Missouri, but never 12 matching Black ones. The two prisoners, bound up, road in the back of the Union supply wagon, along with a trooper who had his orders to shoot if the men tried to make their escape. Those orders were also written into the unit's log book.

CHANGING THE ROUTE

When JW asked Juke, Zeke and Abraham about changing the route, people began to get all excited. Jonathan, a 58-year old carpenter, said the direct route to California was the best way and they shouldn't trust the Union Cavalry. But JW appeared before the wagon committee and explained, "You can leave at any time, you're not responsible for us, nor are we responsible for you. Only out of friendship have was stayed together. But I must travel to Fort Defiance to ensure those two men stand trial for what they have done. Believe me, I want to go home, and this travel takes me farther away from my family and my land. But I have promised to take you to the California border.

"Now without scouts you'll have a hard time finding the route to the south and you're liable to run smack into the Grand Canyon and it will take you weeks to find the crossing over the Colorado River to enter California. Plus, you'll have my Ranger to escort you. But I needed an answer in 15 minutes because Captain Jones is getting ready to leave."

Now the three parties were headed west, at a slightly north angle. JW had never seen this Fort Defiance and now he's been told a new fort was about to be built only 65 miles away from Fort Defiance and it would be called Fort Apache. This second fort was to be finished and occupied by 1870, with another three forts to be constructed in the next five years to handle the Apache problem.

"People are moving west, JW and these settlers want to feel safe." Lt. Sampson said.

"But what about the Indians? They're feeling pressured and now see themselves losing all their hunting grounds to the encroachment of the White and now the Black settlers. Who will speak for them?"

"Maybe you can...We cun get yuh elected guvnor of Arizona, once we become a state." Leo D Wakefield said from the front wagon. "I'll make your posters!"

"You all forget, I'm a rancher, husband and father, hopefully a Ranger again, but no to politics. Thank you, gentlemen...Now let's ride."

White Stallion or not, JW's Appaloosa was demonstrating its love for the desert country. High stepping like a Tennessee Walker, he walked as an emperor of all he prevailed. When JW needed some speed, the mounts rear flanks kicked into gear and caused JW to hold on or fall off. While galloping, and needing to clear obstacles, all JW needed to do was give the horse clear rein to move quickly enough through the danger area. Yes, the white stallion had great forbearance, speed and never lacked for courage or strength, but the Appaloosa side provided exceptional desert intelligence, a deep care for its rider and understood what the partnership meant between horse and rider. There was no horse faster in the unit and only the Percherons showed to be stronger in weight pulling contests.

Although he had always wanted to find such a horse to call is own, he had never thought it was possible. But the strange set of events put into play by the actions of the Civil War had brought them together in a Pennsylvania horse farm. JW had tried so many names on their way home, but nothing seemed to have worked and even the horse disliked them. Finally, as they approached Fort Defiance a name came to his thoughts and he rolled it around before he said it out loud to his mount, "How about 'Cochise'? Would you like that that, to be named after a famous Apache War Chief. His hair is all white in color now, but I found him to be a man of honor. Okay, 'Cochise'?"

Utterly surprised, Cochise nodded his head up and down four times. Oddly enough when he thought about it, JW recalled how the number 4 was important to the Apache and most all Indians. They saw this as a lucky number. JW ran the number through his memories when he had lived with the Apache and other tribes and recalled how small hunting parties were of four riders and often four separate hunting parties going in the four directions of the wind. He tried to see the number four in other things, but then his mind was directed to his scouts riding in to make their report.

Captain Jones, JW, Dreeke, Sampson and three upper NCOs met with the scouts. Everyone was now dismounted, standing behind the trooper's supply wagon and listening, "We made it to within visual range of the fort, but everything looked wrong," Holloway sad. His mouth was dry and Jim Williams, who had taken a couple sips, handed his canteen over to his friend. He'd wait, let his partner make the report, he was a better speaker.

"Thanks, mouth was all dry." He took one more sip and began, "We rode up slow, pistols drawn. Yankees in the towers, but they weren't no one movin' ta challenge us. One side of the gate was open all the way and other side jus' part way. So, after we talked about what we should or shouldn't do, we went to the gate and looked in. Bodies everywhere, not a soul left alive in the fort. Looks like the Union boys put up one heck of a fight, but the Indians burrowed a hole in the back corner. This went right into the barracks, where no one would be. Once they got through, my guess it was all over. By all the horse prints, JW, I estimate more than 300 Apache, but they carried off a lot of dead. Found blood trail for nearly a third of the attacking force. My guess it was Cochise, he's their smartest one."

"But why the fort?" Captain Jones asked. "We're here to also protect the Indians."

JW thought for a moment and then nodded his head, he might have an idea. He looked to Captain Jones. "Sir, when you received your orders for this patrol, did these two men come up and volunteer to scout for you?"

"Why, yes, they did," Jones replied. "But they were on our list of scouts."

"Captain, out here you just about have hog tag a scout, drag him out of a bar or a jail cell to get him to go for you. No one just volunteers in Indian country, too many never come back."

"So, you think these two might have something to do with what happened at the fort?"

"I'm just guessing here, but to protect us, I'll need to go have a talk with Cochise and I'd like to have some knowledge with me. No let's ride ahead. We need to get those bodies moved and ready for burial in order to get all these wagons inside." JW then grabbed Holloway by his arm and asked, "Were they all scalped?"

"Nope, that's what's strange…No one was scalped and it don't look like any trophies were taken, but guns. They took the rifles, but left the cannon."

"Thanks, I know that must've been hard on you."

"Sir, I hope it never gets easy," Holloway said.

He and Jim Williams rode ahead to open the other gate wide and take up position in two of the towers. They needed to watch over the desert to ensure the Apache were not headed back yet.

JW road over to where Juke set on his wagon seat with his elderly wife, Sarah. JW could see how she had been a lovely woman in her younger years and still carried eyes that could dive into a man's soul to view his state of mind. He knew from their first meeting she was a woman he needed to watch himself, for she could probably read his very thoughts and desires.

"Juke, we've got a serious problem up ahead and I need you to keep all your members in hand. I know you've seen a lot worst in your long life, but maybe for not sometime. But we have a lot of dead bodies up ahead and I will need all your menfolk to help us bury them, their families and whoever else died in an Apache attack. They've killed everyone in the fort," JW stopped when Sarah sucked in a deep breath of air and then closed her eyes to begin praying.

"I don't have a count left, but out Captain Jones and his 31 troops are from that fort and he can help us deduce the numbers. We will have-to record names, remove valuables and box them up for family members. For all of this we will need your help. Once we have the bodies removed and placed outside for burial, we will bring our wagons inside. Until then we will form another one of those rectangle formations, with your horses inside. Now will you help?"

"It would be our Christian duty to assist in any way possible. As soon as we have the train in position and horses unhooked and secured for the night, I will put eight guards on duty with two at each corner."

"Thank you, Juke," JW said and then rode his horse into the fort, where Cochise demonstrated his feelings concerning the stench of so many dead before him on the sand. He stopped cold and then rose on his back two legs, then whinnied for all to hear. But JW brought Cochise back down and patted his neck for comfort and led him over to the wagon Liam had driven in. There was an inner fort corral, where all the horses had been stolen from and now Cochise was released into along with the 12 Percherons, horses from the Union patrol supply wagon and eventually most of the horses the Rangers and the Union Patrol had with them. The extra ones were tied up to the nearest pole or whatever worked to secure them. The hay barn was nearly full, which surprised Liam, and he went to feeding all the horses. He didn't want to handle any bodies, especially all those ones that had been outside in the sun for some time.

JW and Captain Jones walked over to the Headquarters Building, stepping over numerous dead soldiers. Arrows had been removed so they could be used again, but bodies showed evidence of being shot, knifed or speared. There were tomahawk wounds and a couple bodies that showed not a mark on them. Women folk were dead, but they were not abused. JW found that Holloway was right, not a person in Fort Defiance was scalped, no clothes were ripped off and not a sign of torture. Rifles were gone, but the Navy Colt pistols remained on the ground or in the men's holsters. Boy and girl children lay dead, but not a mark on them and JW believed they had had their air ways closed off and died of asphyxiation.

When they entered the Colonel's office they found him sitting behind his desk, an open record book in front of him and three arrows in his chest. These arrows they had left and JW was not sure why. Jones dragged the record book over and read the last entries out loud. He read the date and the Colonel's name, and then, "Fort Defiance, they have come three times and each time the same command. But they do not believe me. I suspect Cochise is behind this as I see a whitehaired Indian directing their attacks. This man could be considered a general.

"I never should have hired those two men. My gut instinct said they were trouble. But we needed scouts and I had to send my first patrol out with Captain Jones to show the people we were here, to show the Indians. So, the two men went with the patrol and they were all these Indians would take. I offered to surrender, but they killed my representatives…Four men slaughtered under a white flag.

"I have lost over 200 men, women and some of the children. A fire broke out in the chow hall, over 20 people died there. I expect the next attack at any time. But I find it strange, if anyone reads this, no one is being scalped or their bodies mutilated. Each time they come they ask for these two men by name, which I believe now are fake. I've even told them to come in and search, but I will not release this horde upon a patrol of 32 men. I can only hope my different riders have made it through.

"Noise, screams they've breached the walls in the barracks. Tell my wife I died as a soldier, tell her I lov…" He never finished it.

"If we are to leave here safely, and you are now responsible for 22 wagons, also, then I need to take these two men to Cochise. I also believe I am the only man who can because we have talked and broken bread together. But we must continue to bury the dead, for it may be tomorrow or possibly next week before his next war party returns. But he will return. Will you give up these two or lose everyone here, including your new command. Your Colonel appeared to be ready to give them up, but he had sent them with you. I am thinking once you got clear of the fort, they probably took off, but the Indians forced them back to you. They were especially happy to see our added number, but they were not expecting Rangers."

"Which wagon do you want to take?" Jones asked. He left the Colonel sitting there and walked out in front of the desk to lean back against it. "Who are you taking with you?"

"I'll take your wagon. I don't want to lose our Percherons. Now if you see them take us away and not kill us on the spot, we have a chance. But I could be gone for three to four days. Don't do anything until the fourth day. If after the fourth day I have not sent you any word, I'm dead and the gruesome twosome are dead. Then it's up to you to decide what happens next. But keep getting those bodies buried, or you'll not be able to handle the stench."

JW Blake glanced about the orderly room and set down to write a letter to his wife. "I'll give this to Lt. Dreeke and he'll make sure my wife gets it." He then engaged his writing brain to enter a one-sided conversation with his wife. Once he was done and he had composed three pages to her, plus one page to each child, he placed then into an envelope and went to find Jamey.

When morning came, the two prisoners were in the back of the wagon, with nearly 20 feet of rope binding each of them. Both men had scarves worn tightly over their eyes and another scarf worn tightly over their mouths. That made JW happy, for if they were going to be killed at least he could go in silence. He then saw the White sheet pole attached to this new wagon, with a new white sheet which bore a different diagram.

This one showed the lines of a cloud formation in one corner, with four broad lines coming out of the clouds to simulate wind and underneath it a simple diagram of a white horse with black spots on its flank.

"It's to say 'Ghost-in-the-Wind', and hopefully Cochise will see it and know this is you. He might let you talk, then," Lt. Sampson said.

"Four days, and you are in command of Rangers and possibly the wagon train. I gave them my word to get them to Colorado River and California border. Holloway knows how to find it. If you can, deliver this to my wife or have Jamey do it. Liam will be a bit broke up if I don't come back, so take care of him. Have him take care of Cochise. He's to be taken to my son. Liam already has a great horse. Give my Henry to Jamey, but you can have my other Colt .44. You always looked like a two-gun man." JW then went down the line shaking hands with all his raiders, some of the Union men and the people of the wagon train.

"Mr. Blake, our prayers go with you and your valor and your kindness will forever travel with us. Thank you, Sir." Juke said as he shook JW's hand and, then he laid his other hand on top of both of their shoulders. "Mighty is the warrior who walks with God."

"Thank you, Juke and good luck on the trail ahead." He then climbed up onto the wagon seat and wondered where Liam was. He expected the boy to be out here, but with all the working he did yesterday he probably slept in. But JW guessed it was better this way. He looked down at Captain Jones, "I got enough food in back in case I'm out there for a few days?"

"Sure, you have enough to feed twenty men for ten-days, plus two water barrels," Jones replied.

"I'll go straight out from the gate for a thousand yards, then wait. If nothing happens, I'll camp out there and move another 500 yards tomorrow. You should be able to see me from the tower with binoculars."

"Watch your back, Captain," Lt. Sampson said.

The ride out was only slightly bumpy and JW thought about the cavalry who had ridden outside the fort to drive the Indians off. But they were overwhelmed by mounted men and foot soldiers. According to the report, 63 men were killed out here, a full company of Union cavalry. He looked over his shoulder and down at his two prisoners and his brain burned up in wondering what these two might've done to cause this war. With so many people killed, he figured these two could burn in the pits of Hell and it wouldn't bother him. Evil was a subject he had once dwelled on, how it struck some people at a certain age and avoided others. He had known of evil men and women who had been completely changed by an encounter with God, but he had known Bible carrying preachers who spoke works of gospel and then led a sinful life in the backgrounds. It confused him so. He had stepped into churches, heard the word spoke and felt his presence all around him, and he'd felt the creator's presence when he rode through a mountain pass and laid by a mountain spring. He truly didn't think of himself as a sinner, but he had killed more men than he thought he could sit down and count. Nor was he the type to put notches on his gun, knowing that was for fools.

"What!" a sharp bump brought him back to reality and his mind centered on this open desert he was riding over. He looked back over his shoulder and figured the fort was about 1,000 yards back. Now he simply had to worry about being at the receiving end of an arrow or whatever weapon one might be using. If he had to guess he suspected there was a dozen or so tarantula holes all around him. But he might as well and carry on as if everything was just all hunky-dory.

He went back to ensure the two men were still bound up well enough and then went about building a fire. After giving a drink of water to the criminals, he opened his food and supply box to find, by great surprise, Pvt. Liam Blake lying there in an uncomfortable position. He was also armed with two Colt. 44s, extra cartridge belts and two Bowie knives. "Get out and leave the weapons inside there. Don't you realize I'm under a White flag!?"

"They sent a couple different White flag teams out and all of them were gunned down. I just wanted to make sure you were covered."

"Liam, what am I supposed to do with you?" JW asked. "Chances are I'm going to die with these two animals, but you weren't. What if I get taken to the Indian camp, do you think they'll let you play games with the kids your age. No! They're liable to tie you up to a tree, have you hanging and let the teenagers practice their spear drills by sticking them into your stomach." JW popped the lid wide open and then open the front that exposed the kitchen drawers or shelves to be used.

"Now you roll out and hustle your butt back to the fort. Don't worry about the guns, I'll bury then under the wagon. Now move!"

Liam, a tear in his right eyes, turned toward the fort and began to run, when he stopped dead. "Captain, we're too late."

JW looked up from the cook box and saw a line of Apache warriors coming their way. He only had enough time to close the weapons and belts inside the cook box and close it up. He then pulled the back gate up and latched it into place. "You stand by me. If you utter one word I will back hand you. For you to speak is a sign of disrespect to me and I must be seen reprimanding you and it won't be gentle. However, it will keep you alive. So, silence unless I speak to you. Got it?"

In response, Liam nodded his head twice.

As they came, JW hoped the men at the fort were watching all this. A good sign was that the Apache were not charging, but simply walking up in single file. He hoped his flag had helped him.

At the fort, Captain Jones used the Colonel's binoculars, which were quite a bit stronger than the ones Jones was issued for patrol. From his left frontal tower, he could count 18 Apache, each carrying shields and long spears. "I think this is a good sign, the Apache appear to be in ceremonial attire. Each one is armed with a long spear and a decorative shield. Oh, no! Liam is out there...He's standing beside JW, who is resting his right hand upon Liam's right shoulder. I am betting JW would like to throttle that boy right now, but he may be keeping him alive with friendly gestures." Jones was speaking to a good-sized crowd. By now they had moved all the wagons inside, but bodies were still stacked up outside and it was decided mass graves for three to four bodies would be used. Families would be buried together also and the whole business had rattled everyone involved.

"There's now one Indian who is speaking and making aggressive movement to the back of the wagon. It appears Liam was directed to climb into the wagon and remove the scarves from around their eyes and mouths. Then another two Apache are summoned forward, but behind Captain Blake are half-a-dozen. I'm not sure but it looks as if an identification is being made by the twosome and the others are there to keep the Apache from killing the two animals. I gather something else is waiting for them." Right then even at that distance, some of the people could detect the feint scream of an extremely terrified man.

JW stepped up into the wagon, looked at the one Apache, said something and then gave both men a strong right cross before he secured their scarves. He then ordered Liam to join him on the wagon seat and they prepared to follow the Apache.

"As per my agreement with Captain Blake, the time begins now. We set four or five days as the maximum we will wait for him. With the ceremony provided I feel five days should be granted. If in that five days troops arrive to man Fort Defiance, my promise is to get this wagon train to the California border. He would not include you Rangers in that promise and leave it up to you on what you wish to do.

"If in five days there is no sign by the sundown of the fifth day, we will leave this fort and first head to Tucson by the most direct route to file my report and then escort these wagons to the California border. Again, you Rangers have your own decisions to make. I will at least need Mr. Holloway and Mr. Jim Williams to scout for us to Globe...After that we can follow the stagecoach line to Tuscon. But in the next four days, we must make this fort livable, if in the event troops are sent here and all the bodies are buried. Wagons should be repaired as needed. I know we have a fine blacksmith shop here if anyone in the wagon train is a smithy?"

"Yes, we have numerous trained people from carpenters, smiths, tins-men and tailors. We even have two armors who repairs the owners hunting weapons and a fine assistant veterinarian. There are numerous people trained in providing medical assistance, gardening and the cooking of very large meals. We have bakers, kitchen staff, two chefs trained by the French and a fine butcher. You'll find there is little the people of our wagon train cannot do in domestic and outside skills," Juke said with pride.

"What about a nice lunch, Zeke?" Juke asked his dear friend.

"Already in the works and lunch will be served at 12:30."

"Be careful, Zeke, you spoil us too much we may have to hold you here." Jones said in jest.

"Ah-h, your President Lincoln has already taken care of that, Sir." Juke said and then dropped his head to add, "And he paid for it with his life. We will never forget him."

RIDING THE TRAIL DOWN INTO THE PINE FORESTS

JW Blake knew where he was, he had ridden through this land on more than a dozen occasions. Sometimes in friendships and sometimes in pursuit of half-breed criminals in hopes their Apache side family may hide him, even possibly to go so far as the kill the Ranger in pursuit. This section of Arizona was through the upper hills and mountains of the Arizona Territory. Here, in the center of Arizona, was where several of the Apache tribes lived close together. Tribes such as the White Mountain Apaches, San Carlos Apache and the Chiricahua Apache. But just below the San Carlos Apache were the Yaqui Tribe and to the east were the Ute. The Payson Apache, Colorado Apache and to the north always stood the Navajo and Hopi.

JW knew where he was going now, he was on his way to the mountain fortress of Cochise and it was not a location he wished to go to. To learn of this location could mean a quick death for both he and Liam. He glanced over at the boy, "Whatever you do, do not lose your nerve. You may be tested, so be brave...I'm just not sure how far Cochise will take this. We know nothing, so there is nothing for us to tell him. This can be good, or bad. Just remember to remain silent and follow my lead."

Liam nodded his head. He only hoped JW couldn't see how jittery he was. But this was now the second day of travel, but up ahead he could see smoke from many cook fires, many-many cook fires and he stopped counting at 200.

Liam had attempted to feed the prisoners, but one of the warriors knocked him away and tossed the food into the fire. The Indian then said something to JW, which in turn he shared with Liam. "Prisoners may not eat, waste of food. Die soon."

"Nice to see they're letting us eat," Liam said to JW with a tone of sarcastic wit.

"Careful, Liam or you will kill us both," JW said and he shot Liam a fatherly look he used on Steven and Jessie to let them know they were walking the line way too close.

"Sorry," Liam muttered.

On the third morning, they pulled into the Chiricahua Mountain Fortress. JW gave it a good look and could see why the army had never found it. This place was impregnable from the front and both sides. Only from the rear could this place by defeated. He estimated there was at least 1,000 or more people here, but he didn't know how many were warriors? He was then helped down from the wagon seat, and he looked over to see Liam had received the same courteous treatment. More and more it appeared he and the boy were being looked upon as friends of the Apache.

He did recognize several of older men as warriors he had met in prior visits to other encampments. But he stood back as the two criminals were dragged out of the wagon by their bound ankles and with long staffs shoved through their ropes they were carried upside down by two strong men each, over to three large pine trees. Liam had seen large wooden spikes had been hammered into the trees, each at an upward angle. The first prisoner was lifted up and placed upside down between the spikes of an outside tree to a center spike. Then this movement was repeated for the second man. Once secured and hanging upside down, a warrior walked over and removed the scarf from the man's eyes, so he could now see where he was and who was now around him. Then the warrior, who was armed with only a small knife, walked over and repeated this move for the second prisoner. Both men now looked up at Liam first and then JW.

They tried to plead, but they could not speak through the scarfs. They tried chewing on them, hoping to wet them down and spit them from their mouths, but their mouths were much too dry from nearly three days without water. By now even their throats felt as if they were closing, causing panic, from a lack of fluid for fear it would soon mean their death from oxygen not reaching their lungs. Their minds were already being effected, providing illusions as delirium became a constant partner. They fought against their bonds until their strength had given out, but still they lived on and Liam wondered how they could do it.

"JW, three days without food or water, now hung upside down like a deer waiting to be gutted and skinned. How can they still be alive?"

"Hate mostly," JW replied. "An innocent man would most likely be dead by now, standing before the Lord God for Judgment. But these men know where they're headed an' don't want to go. Hell, ain't no spring day up here in the hillsides, flowers blooming and all the critters waking up from a winter's nap. No sireee, I read it's a place made for murderers, women molesters and nasty jerks who'd steal the gold out of a fellow's teeth before he shot him, just to hear him scream. Now it gonna be their turn ta scream."

They then watched as two Apache women approached the men and set up a tripod built from branchless tree limbs about five-feet long. They used a longer leather strap to tie the top together and then planted the ends in place to make sure both tripods were firmly in place. Then two other women came forward and hung a water bottle, made from a buffalo stomach, from both tripods. But rather than open the bottles, they used a fine wooden needle to pierce the downside of the bottle and allowed for mere drips of water to escape. Once a drip splashed on the man's face, or usually taking several drips over a period of two minutes, the man would suddenly catch on and fight frantically to get their mouths under the drops.

"I thought the Indians were trying to kill them, but now they give them water...sort of," Liam said in a voice of confusion. He glanced about, he had never been surrounded by so many Apache before but in one way he was developing some respect for the way they have lived for so long and how the family is such a working unit. In so many ways, they were similar-to a farmer's family. He also noticed how a lot of the young men were looking at him and there was not a lot of hate in their eyes, except for a few who looked as if they wanted his blood, scalp and to roast him over a fire.

Liam sat on the wagon's gate, as JW chatted with a few of the Indians he knew and gradually he learned why these two men were wanted so badly by Cochise and his tribe. But the attack on the fort was not explained and JW was told only Cochise would provide that information to him, if he saw fit. Until he appeared before the Chief of the Apache Tribes, he could consider him and the boy as guests of the camp. Their departure would also be decided by Cochise, but their stay here could last for weeks if Cochise so ordered it.

JW and Liam were assigned to an Apache Wickiup; a grass hut with a stick frame and made by the women and young boys and girls of the

tribe. The Wickiup is the primary housing for the Apache family, unless
the Buffalo hunting has been plentiful and then teepees are made with
excess leather, not needed for Buffalo robes. A well skinned and treated
buffalo robe could last for several years and into decades, but teepee
leather, which constantly faced the elements, including travel, rarely made
it ten years.

The Apache Wickiup was considered a permanent lodging because
it was never moved. Though strong once it was finished, the Wickiup
would fall apart once a family tried moving it.

They had only been inside their Wickiup for a short time when two
women brought them food and water, including fruit and meat. JW looked
over at Liam and said, "This is really something, Liam. We're being given
the best of guest treatment for bringing these two varmints to them, even
though we had little choice. But you can't get better than this unless they
send us a couple ladies to keep us warm for a cold night, but I'd have ta
refuse that and with your young age and my being a married Christian we
wouldn't offend anyone."

"But JW, there's some really cute girls out there an' I'm still a
virgin," Liam face flushed red.

"I'm glad you got embarrassed saying that to me, so I know it's true.
But, boy, you're going to stay that way until you meet that right girl or my
wife would tan my hide. Now hush and finish your food."

"I'm finished, but will you tell me what these two did that got the
Apache all stirred up?"

JW remained silent for a moment as he poured a handful of berries
into his mouth and chewed them down, then he nodded he would. Once
he took a drink, he began, "You already know why the authorities have
wanted posters out for these two…right? And you understand what those
charges entail."

"Yes, Sir," Liam replied. He then added, "What I didn't understand,
Lt. Dreeke explained to me."

"Okay, this is much of what Cochise wants them for. Now, do you
recall those two big Indians who really wanted their hands on those two,
but they were dragged away to keep our prisoners unharmed for now?"

"Yeah, they were white hot angry. I thought they were gonna tear
those two apart. But it wasn't jus' those four Indians, it was also the voice
of some Indian standing on a rock overhead."

"That's Geronimo, he's a sub-chief under Cochise; and, also very
important to the Apache Warrior Society. I've already fought against him
once…maybe twice, he's smart as a whip and when Cochise dies I see him
taking over as senior chief."

"So...what happened?"

"Oh...sorry, I forgot, I was flashing back to my last engagement with Geronimo." JW took another drink over water from a gourd and then continued. "Well, those two are brothers and there used to be a third brother. Their sister-in-law was out berry picking, with her two daughters and one son, all under eight-years old. Then these two came along. The final screams were heard by a teenager out guarding his family and he rode his horse over there. Seeing the White men, he began hollering and other young braves on guard duty came a running and those two were chased away, riding their horses until they vanished in some tall pines.

"They left behind a real gory scene with the woman, who appeared to have been raped, but the medicine man found it hard to tell because she was nearly split in two with a knife or tomahawk. Both little girls were badly cut up and molested, but the boy, his head was cut off and he was scalped. Makes me sick just retelling it and I've seen some bad scenes by Indian, Mexican and White man. Evil is evil, it don't care who it uses."

"Was one those men the father...and how did they identify these two as being the suspects?" Liam asked. His eyes were now showing the revulsion he felt for what was done to the woman and the three kids. He wanted to walk over and kill both of them right then.

"No, there was a third brother. But after losing his whole family he gave everything away to his brothers and friends and insisted to ride in the first attacks on the fort, if the men were not given up. As to identifying them, they were not finished with one of the girls, when she screamed out and the braves closed in from three directions. So, when they took off, one of them had left his britches. His name, Alvin Zedekiah, was marked in there for the yearly laundry job he got done on it. Wasn't hard to figure out who the second man was, but Cochise used his fort Indians, to get the information for him. Those fort Indians should be better known as Apache Intelligence Personnel. Soldiers think they're tame, but it's all an act." JW picked up the gourd and took another sip, but then opted on another handful of the sweet berries.

"So, the husband was killed in one of the attacks? Right?"

"Appears so, but Indians do not like to discuss the dead, so they clammed up on me for that part."

"But they wouldn't say anything about the attack on the fort of why they killed everyone?"

"Not yet," JW replied. "Now I'm gonna lie back and catch some sleep. When Cochise is ready to talk or the execution begins, they'll come get us."

"Aren't you afraid they'll sneak in here and slice our throats," Liam asked.

"We're surrounded by a thousand Apaches, Liam. If they wanted to we'd be hanging up beside those two. But we're are being treated as guests. No one is going to slice out throats, at least not until we leave this stronghold and all bets are off. Now catch some sleep."

It was restless night for Liam who imagined Apache's coming in from all sides, or his imagination creating a beautiful maiden who snuck in to lead him off to some forbidden waterfall, where all his dreams were fulfilled. It was during that fantasy that JW woke him up with a slap to his chest and he was suddenly back inside his smelly Wickiup, in the middle of the Apache nation.

"Time to go, lover boy," JW said in an amused tone of voice. "Hated to make you end that dream, but I should warn you that you talk in your sleep. That one was a dizzy."

Once again, Liam was speechless as he wiped the sleep from his eyes. With a light mutter, he whispered, "Where we going?"

"Cochise is apparently a morning person, he wants to see us," JW said. He then chuckled as he watched Liam's eyes bulge wide. "Let's go, kid. Don't wanna keep the big chief waiting."

When they came outside there were two Indians with long spears there to escort them over to a large teepee. Once inside, JW whispered to Liam, "Don't say anything unless asked. This is a big shindig."

The center fire, surrounded by medium sized rocks was shooting up flames only ten to 15 inches, but adjacent the ring's rocks, only embers were smoking. Heat being produced by the fire worked its way out of the teepee through an opening at the top, but the teepee was designed in such a way that the heat could be maintained to keep the occupants warm. Plus, with all of the men in the room, body heat made for quite a toasty meeting place. Except it was so warm, it caused JW and Liam to begin sweating.

A circle of Apache warriors surrounded the fire and JW identified Cochise of course and Geronimo, plus he recognized the two brothers who tried to attack his prisoners. But the rest of the men he had no idea who they were. But Cochise remedied that by gesturing JW to sit in the open space provided and allowed for Liam to sit behind him. JW had earlier explained how Liam was his adopted little brother and the Apache fully understand adopted family members as this is done often in the Apache world, as well as other Indian Tribes.

JW learned the other men were senior elders, one was the tribal medicine man and two were sub-chiefs of the warrior party. Cochise had already explained to his tribal council who JW was and how long he has helped, chased and been involved with the Apache and had been given the name, "Ghost-in-Desert-Wind". Also, that he was very fluent in their language and the language of other tribes. "Ghost is a very strange White man, but above all I find that I can trust his words, even if I do not like them."

Once the two were seated, the pipe was passed around, but Liam was not allowed to participate. He grumbled, but only JW heard him. Then Cochise looked to JW and asked, (speaking Apache), "Why these two of coyote dung your prisoner?"

"My Rangers and I return from White man's war in the east. We become scouts for wagon train of Black people who leave east to travel to California. Along the way, we run into Army patrol of 32 men. Then these Scouts appear, but Rangers know we have life or death papers out for them and we took them prisoner. From what I have learned what those two have done to your people, they have done many times to White people. We were told they had fled to Mexico and our law no good down there. We were surprised to find them working for Army, but we believe it was lie to escape Arizona for fear of the Apache. They have killed more than a dozen people we know of and a half of them children. I was taking them to the fort to have them hung."

Cochise as he heard JW statement and he believed it. "You know why we wanted them, so I send Apache to fort to ask for them. But Colonel say, No!" Cochise pounded the ground beside him. "We had said them by name and what they had done to my people and he still say no."

Cochise stood to his feet, a look of frustration on his face. "I no want to kill soldiers. I only want two men. I went back with twenty Apache and set on my horse outside the gate with White man's white flag. I ask once more for those two men, but they already gone. Colonel no tell me that, he still refuse. When I threaten to attack fort with 600 warriors he laugh at me and told me to leave before he shoot my men. So, we left. We knew a small patrol on horse was out there on way to New Mexico border, but we not know the two we want had run off to join them.

"When sun rises the next day we attack with 600 warriors. Very little battle, but many brave soldiers who fight for coward leader. We find him in office, too scared to even help his men fight. My warriors angry over what happen to our children and women, they think of their own children womenfolk. They kill everyone, but I give order not to scalp anyone, even coward colonel. We take guns and horses and our own dead. But we respect the fight the little put up against the big. Do you understand, Ghost-in-Desert-Wind?"

"Yes, I do. But what will you do with these two. The quick kill or the slow kill?" JW asked.

"I leave that up to the two brothers as they will be the ones who will deliver death. But I insist you watch so you may tell soldiers of why it had to be done this way. If anyone can explain it will be you."

"I, Ghost-in-Desert-Wind, will tell your story of what happen at Fort Defiance and with these two coyotes. But know this, with the war to the east over, more and more White and now Black people will be coming here or traveling through to reach California or even Oregon. This will mean more and more Army to protect them from Comanche, the Ute and Navajo, and you, the Apache. Too many people in the east do not know how fierce the Apache and Comanche truly are. They fight Indian foot soldiers until Indian no more, but here the Indian wars will be a mighty thing. To the north, it will be the Crow, Pawnee and the Sioux who will meet the Army." JW stopped for a moment and looked hard around the circle and then he continued.

"You know of me and I have fought you and lived with you. I have great respect for the Apache people. But I warn you Cochise, great and wise Chief of the Apache tribes, yes, you can put 1,000 warriors on the field of war, but this is nothing. In the Great White man's war to the east, we called the Civil War, I saw 100,000…that is 1,000 at 100 times fight on one side and still lose. Yes, we came to the battle field with 30,000 Cavalry, 60,000 Infantry and 10,000 soldiers who were with the cannons. But the Yankees had 300,000 men and we lost in one battle. In one three-day battle, over 500,000 soldiers fight and over half of them died. This is why my side lose. The Union Army, the men in blue, had too many troops. They can send many-many thousands of troops here if they need to. Or to Texas to fight the Comanche. This is not the time to make war, it is the time to make peace, with conditions that help the Apache people. If you need me I would speak with you or for you at any time. I hope to be a Ranger again, but I will never fight the Apache unless it is a bad Apache. I will protect all Indian people in Arizona, as well as White and Black People. That is my word."

The men in the circle did not speak. Numbers given by Ghost-in-Desert-Wind baffled them, but they read his intent in his eyes and would talk more with Cochise to have the big numbers explained.

Cochise nodded his head several times and with a half-grin of appreciation he came around and grasped arms with Ghost and added a nod in Liam's direction. "We have their deaths tonight, then tomorrow you may leave with my escort to ensure you make it safely to the fort."

"Thank you, Cochise." JW replied.

When they came out of their Wickiup after a dinner of venison meat, bread and mixed fruit, their two escorts were there to take them over to where their wagon set. From there, they glanced over to where the two prisoners had been flipped over to where their heads were on top, but their arms were spread out, tied to long wood poles. Their legs were also tied together to a heavy wooden pole behind them. This was all spiked into the large trees they'd earlier been held by. Scarves had been removed from their eyes and mouths, and they remained hungry and thirsty.

"Why did they give them those drops of water, Captain?" Liam asked

"Add to the torture. Just keep them alive long enough for this event and worst torture of all, it gave them a spark of hope. Now it's gone."

Alvin Zedekiah spotted JW and yelled, "Captain Blake, we were your prisoners, aren't yuh gonna do anything to save us for our trial?" His voice was crackly from no water and JW saw it hurt him to scream out like that. But an Indian stepped forward and hit him in the chin with his staff, which nearly knocked Alvin out. After seeing that, Alvin wasn't about to say anything.

Cochise then stepped forward and the area turned silent to hear their chief speak. Instead, he summoned JW over to him. This got the whispers going between the families in attendance.

Cochise put his hand on JW's right shoulder, which was a well-known sign of respect or friendship, even both. He then said to JW, "Because you speak truth in our Holy Circle, I give you permission to tell these men why they die and give them a brief-moment to make peace with the creator."

"Can you tell me if quick or slow death?"

"Brothers both decided death by a thousand cuts, but they no last that long. But it satisfy the tribe. I have let be known these two were to be killed by White Law for killing Indians and White people. That you, Ghost-in- Desert-Wind, was taking them to be hung. This made them happy with you and little more respect for white law. But you must watch this to show you are strong. Even young one must watch. No get sick, warn him."

"I understand. Thank you, my friend." JW left Cochise and approached the two brothers.

JW briefly thought of all the Indian he had learned over the years and wondered when he might slip up and use Navajo when talking to a Comanche, or Comanche to an Apache. His Ute was still a problem and he never did learn any of that Choctaw. Then his thoughts refocused and he glared at Calvin, who focused his look of pure hate right at JW.

"You can keep that hate going or you can use the next minute to make your peace with God. Cochise is letting you have that out of regards to me. As to your death...execution, you're going to die slow...death of a thousand cuts it's called. But no one ever make it that long and no one is actually ever counting. Maybe you can think of the Indian maiden you split in half and the three children you then murdered. I won't even mention all those others you murdered and robbed. But the family carrying out your sentence, those were the kid's uncle and the wife's brothers-in-law. So, make you peace, Calvin and you, too, Alvin. I'm not sure how God will handle you two, but Judgment is all His department. So long."

"You can't leave us like this, we deserve a trial. Our rights demand it..." Alvin shut up when he spotted two old Apache women coming their way with butchering-type knives. He then noticed each of them wore belts with knives of assorted sizes.

JW turned and said in a raised voice, "These were the children's aunts and you'll find them a might testy over what happened. Behind them are the two uncles, they get everything above the waist."

JW summoned Liam to his side, "You've got to watch this with me. It is Cochise's order. But if you upchuck or feint, we're dead. We have-to show our strength all the way through or until Cochise leaves. You understand me, Liam? This is really important and it could involve everyone at the fort."

"I'll certainly do my best, Captain."

"Look to the side if you need, but do not look away. This is an important trial for us."

The screams began and they were the most horrid sounds Liam had ever heard because of the length. These women seemed skilled in hitting the pain centers with the points of their knives, until they began skinning the meat off the legs. Both men had passed out and cold water was thrown over them to wake them back up.

"Liam, try to think about all the people these two had killed in just this fashion and even worse," JW whispered.

After spending a good amount of time on the two men's feet, removing each of the toes and a good amount of skin and meat, the two women looked to each other, selected their special knives and began working on the men's manhood in slow precise cuts. This was when Liam began looking higher up on the tree.

JW had seen such punishment handed out before and they were never pretty and when finished had depressive effect on the tribe, but he did not think that would happen with these two. These two White men were looked upon as being devils and they were now slaying the devil in heinous ways to keep the evil one from returning to their tribe. But within days an Apache warrior would go out to slay a prospector or some settlers, and once more the evil was back to haunt their tribe.

Though there had been missionary schools among various tribes, the Christians, from Baptist to Presbyterian, and the Catholic priests, had tried to reach the warrior clans of the Apache and Comanche, without success. JW hoped Christianity could find a breakthrough, knowing it would help with the peace process. But as JW looked to the future, giving him something to think about as the executions were carried out and now the two Apache men were busy on the upper body, he saw little of the desert set aside for the Apache and Comanche. He pictured reservations, in Texas, New Mexico and Arizona, where the great tribes will be confined and their economic needs provided by the U.S. Government. No more buffalo hunts, no more rifles and probably no more secret rituals the White man cannot understand so he fears it. White man schools for all the kids, but jobs will be scarce.

Soon the execution was over both men had died. Calvin had died first, which surprised JW. He thought the man's hate would keep him alive longer. With both dead, their heads were cut off, placed on stakes and placed at the entryway into the Fortress. The rest of them was thrown into the gorge in front of the fortress for the predators to consume.

Cochise came over to JW and Liam, "Young brother has shown to have guts. You be proud of him." He then looked in JW's face, "You leave in morning. Party of ten warriors, my protection. They escort you Fort. You tell Captain to leave fort. If other Apache see I allow fort in my land with only 32 men, they see me weak and Indian war be fought. Large force of 300 soldier return...I no attack and meet with leader to make peace. But only 300 right now, more-later...maybe. He go south with you, and Black wagon train, No one attack. You go to Globe see family. It is good to have family. I will miss you, Ghost-in-Desert-Wind. I hope we never fight."

"It is my hope we never fight, too. I give your words to Captain at fort, but he may be gone. He was to only wait five days and then leave if not heard from me."

"Not to worry, I send word to fort you stay with me a couple days and then you come back. Indian return that message was delivered."

"You a wise Chief, Cochise. Makes me happy we not fight when both you and me were young braves."

"Me too happy, me not want to kill friend." Cochise said with a smile.

JW laughed out loud and put his arms out to arm grasp Cochise in saying so long for now. Cochise nodded twice and grasped his arms, which they held tightly and looked in each other's eyes.

Both knew if a war came, they would both fight for their people and this meant trying to kill one another, but they would do it with honor and respect.

FORT DEFIANCE

They made it back to the fort without a single difficulty and waved so long to their escort, when they came within sight of the logged fortress. JW thought they should change its name now, since it had already fallen so shortly after being constructed.

The gates were open and they were met by a crowd of over a hundred people, full of congratulations and questions concerning what had happened. JW kept smiling, though his backside was turning raw and sore from all the back slaps. Then he got with Captain Jones and requested he get a Commanders Call called so they could make some plans. He asked that both Zeke and Juke be invited to this. Jones agreed and he sent a Corporal to make the notifications.

Soon a couple fiddles got going, a banjo and even a guitar were playing and the people were dancing about the big communal fire. Everyone felt safer knowing JW was back and that the Indians had escorted him in.

Of course, the number of girls to men was a bit one sided against the White troopers. There were a dozen or so single Black gals standing around waiting to be asked, but most of the men were married and they were caught up in the moment with their wives.

One of the Union PFCs kept his eyes on this very attractive Black girl, granddaughter to Abraham, who had once been in-charge of the cotton field. But, then his age got the better of him and he was retired to live out his life on the plantation in his same home he had lived in for over 70 years.

The young PFC from Illinois looked up at his best friend and asked, "Do you think Old Man Abraham would have a heart attack if 'in ah asked his granddaughter fer a dance?"

His friend was shocked and his faced radiated with it, "What, you wanna go dance with one of those Black women. Ain't you afraid of what the other guys will say?"

"Look, I may get an Indian arrow in my chest tomorrow, but at least I danced with a pur'ty girl tonight. Dang what color she be." He stood up and first approached Grandpa Abraham and asking politely wanted his permission to have a dance with his Granddaughter. "I'm from Illinois, Sir and my parents raised me to ask the parents first and I understand you are her next of kin."

Abraham rocked in his chair, that didn't move and gave the boy a real eye over. He knew time were a-changin', but he wasn't sure tonight was the night to start things off. But a lot of these good men had died and been wounded fighting for their freedom. "Young man, I am not sure how my Granddaughter will respond to your invitation, but I thank you for your politeness and you do have my permission. I wish you good luck."

When the first mixed race couple joined the dance floor everyone stopped, including the musicians. That is until Grandpa Abraham stood to his feet and said, "Is this a dance, or was I mistaken?" That's all it took. The musicians began until they were playing together and then the dancers were rotating around the fire. Within 15 minutes six mixed-race couples were on the floor and it appeared everyone was having a good time. Some of the soldiers left, unable to except the mixed racial affairs, but they were less than half. Some of the men were chatting with men they had met on the trail and were talking about California, their run-in with the Comanche and some of their skills. For the first time, some of these northerners learned how these cotton pickers of Louisiana were a whole brew of a different lot then they were first told. They were not stupid, ignorant, weak minded or devil worshippers from Africa. They were strong willed men; and, also, strong of body, quick witted and could be equally polite to the opposite race. That once dance and the days to follow became a real eye opening experience for both race.

At the Commanders Call, JW told everyone what transpired from the time they left to when they returned. Jones and Sampson were somewhat stunned by the meeting he had had with Cochise and what had transpired between the Colonel and Cochise. Though on one side it spoke the hostility the Apache felt over what had happened to the family killed by the two Zedekiah Brothers, it also spoke to them of the honor of the Apache in how the respect was shown to the men and their families by withholding mutilation and scalping. The three arrows in the Colonel were to show the three times Cochise had come and the Colonel treated him as an ignorant savage and rebuffed his attempts to avoid a fight. It made Jones angry but in time his anger shifted to the idiotic Colonel.

"His reason that you must leave is respect. He cannot allow you to hold this fort with an inferior force as he would lose respect with the other tribes that now honor him as making him Supreme Apache Chief…They describe it in other words but that's about what he is. He is over seven tribes and if they lose respect of him he could lose it all and the White man will be in severe trouble."

"But why a force of 300," Captain Jones asked.

"By bringing in a superior number force, twice of what you had here, you show him respect and this is good medicine for him. You've got to remember, these chiefs are also politicians, but instead of argue thy fight battles and sometimes wars. He wants peace. I've told him of the numbers he could face and he still cannot believe such numbers. I tried to describe to him some of the Civil War Battles, including Gettysburg and their eyes looked those of little kids lost in toy factory. Ten thousand to 100,000 toys compared to 100,000 soldiers and still more. But sadly, I could not tell him the future, for it would hurt him deeply and a warrior would want to go out fighting."

"What kind of future do you speak of, Captain?" Zeke asked.

"Indian reservations, where the tribes can no longer hunt their buffalo because we can no longer allow them to have guns. Only bow and arrow, but few horses. They can hunt deer and elk, but only if the animals cross their reservations. There'll be Federal Tribal Police to watch the reservations and maybe someday those will be Indians, I don't know. But warriors will have to become farmers to help supplement what the government brings them to eat. And if I know the government, there'll be corruption involved. Always seems to be."

"But you said they'll let the train and the troops move south, with no desire to attack us…why?" Juke asked. "They have killed everyone here, why not destroy us and gain everything we have?"

"Juke, Cochise has an encampment in a mountain stronghold that can only possibly be reached by one side, but that side gives them enough notice to clear out or set up defenses to stop any attackers. I actually saw a thousand warriors, so you think this fort would stand up to a thousand warring Apache. No, we'd actually have a better chance moving with the wagons and Cochise knows this. He only attacked the fort because the Colonel could not simply meet with the Indian chief and give him a tour of the fort to show the two animals had escaped. But the Colonel tried to show his superiority at the wrong time. Cochise didn't want a fight, but he had to show honor to his people. He could not turn his back on this. If the Colonel had backed down this fort would not have been taken. There would be no reason to take it. This is why he even allows a force of 300 to return to the fort. The man does not want a war. He has lost to damn many warriors and families. We also need to leave here, as soon as possible, we've got a couple creeks to pass. I am hoping they have water in them."

They took a quick vote and the encampment would be leaving at daybreak. The Rangers would lead the way, with the wagon train in the middle and the troops bringing up the end. Holloway and Williams take off on scout a half-hour before the train left.

When the meeting broke up, JW drank and walked over to find something to eat and some of that punch he'd sampled moving across New Mexico. When he walked up to the kitchen area and looked out over the dancers, he was floored. He came close to dropping his plate. Both Juke and Zeke were standing beside him and they too were speechless, for by now there were nine mixed race couples dancing and one was Liam, with a very pretty girl of equal age.

"My-my, I sure had not expected that...at least not yet." JW said and then he started laughing, but not out of racial disharmony or anything that had to do with the mixing of races. He was simply overjoyed to see Liam dancing and laughing with a pretty girl. Soon enough, Old Juke was laughing too, but not Zeke. No, he had too many memories of what real life was outside the plantation and the mixing of races was a surefire way to bring death to the Black wagon train.

Zeke wouldn't say anything tonight or the trip south, he knew he owed these folks his life and the lives of this train. But once they were back of their own, he'd straighten those kids up right away. Especially, those girls. He knew it always began with the girls, but he didn't want it to happen this time. Zeke had lost his first fiancé that way, killed dead by a boozing white man and Zeke was nearly hung for beating up the man who killed his woman. But a kindly sheriff broke it off and later opened the cell and told him to skedaddle, "You get back to your plantation, I won't be able to stop them when they come after to you tonight. Now get!"

His fiancé wanted to see something more than the Wilkerson Plantation and ran off. Took him five weeks to find her working in one of those houses in New Orleans, selling herself to white men. When he reported back to Mr. Wilkinson, he explained what happened to her, he was made to work extra hours in the fields, two hours a night, until his time was made up. But because he was working so hard, Mr. Wilkinson sent him to the missionary school to receive an education. This was where he met his Roberta and they'd been married nigh on 40 years. Zeke had five sons, who produced a crop of 31 Grandchildren and now he had his first Great-grandkids out in those wagons and there were times he just couldn't believe what the good Lord had blessed him with. When he prayed, he tried to remember to thank that kindly sheriff for saving his life and setting him free and now they were on their way to California. There was some mention of Los Angeles and another of San Diego, but Zeke had taken a love for this desert and he'd heard rumors of a new town growing in a place called San Bernardino. He might just check that out and see how many other wagons wanted to go with him.

That next morning with horses fed and watered, scouts out on the trail south, Captain JW Blake, reined his beautiful White Appaloosa stallion, Cochise into two circles, waving his right hand to get everyone's attention. Then he stopped and waved forward, they were now on the move south.

A mile from the fort, the Rangers picked up an escort of 20 Apache Warriors, with shields and spears. They would remain with the wagon train until Globe was within sight. They were told to eat their meals away from the others, but often JW and Liam would journey over to chew the fat and show them some hospitality. At one point a platter of pan-fried doughnuts was produced for the Apache, with appreciation for their escort and after that the Apache moved in closer to where they were within spittin' distance of the Rangers. Having the Union guards walking around bothered them not at all, for they knew out a couple miles or so was another force of 60-some warriors, just in case the White man had lied. This was an agreement Cochise was forced to meet with the senior elders. They all liked JW, but he was still a White man.

CHAPTER TWELVE

"They showed me their pretty tin badges and i just had ta show them my pur'ty Colt.44."

INFORMATION

Arizona was part of the Country of Mexico from 1822 until the Mexican-American War, when in 1848, the US took possession and made Arizona a part of the New Mexico Territory. But in 1863, the U.S. Congress organized the Arizona Territory. Although most of the people of Arizona felt they were already standing on their own and had little to do with New Mexico. A Census was done in 1860, which showed that only 6,482 people lived in the Arizona territory. This did not take into-account any of the Indian tribes, the Mexicans or Latin's living there, nor the slaves owned by the wealthier land owners. This census was only the Whites. Another Census would be done in 1870, which increased the number of Whites to 9,658. Even though the slaves had been freed, they were not being counted in the Arizona Census.

TWO MILES NORTH OF GLOBE TOWNSHIP, JANUARY 4TH, 1866. A TIME TO SAY GOODBYE

With his escort of Apache warriors having already departed once they could see the stove fires of Globe and everyone waving them on to show their thanks, the wagon train moved along until Scouts Holloway and Jim Williams came riding up and their faces looks as if they were the harbingers of doom.

"I thought I'd probably find you two in the bar..." JW stopped when he read disaster and grief in their eyes and eyed the other Rangers who circled up. "What's wrong?!" JW asked.

Jim Williams glanced to Holloway, who could only shake his head. This left it now in Jim Williams' hands and he didn't want to play with no hot potato. But he owed it to these men to be a straight shooter. "The Globe before yuh, ain't thu Globe you all remember. Most all our friends is long gone, pushed out ah guess by the Yankees. There's hundreds of government troops hangin' aroun' an' some sort marshals staff that work for a large group of those carpet baggers we done heard 'bout up north. They're seizin' up land left an' right accordin' ta Preacher Joe, who is one of the honest people stickin' it out. They're out collectin' all the property taxes owed for four years an' they want it all now, or they jus' seize the property with those sheriffs an' troops ta back 'em up.

"They tax you on how many cattle you have, how many acres you got, horses, sheep and goats...probably chickens an' ducks, too. They built two huge hotels, usin' big city money an' now they're buying up all the ranches and farms in rigged court auctions."

Now Holloway spoke, but quietly, "Seems most of this area is now owned by those who live in Boston, Philadelphia and New York City. They've bought it up cheap."

"I'd better light a fire under Cochise and get home," JW said.

But Holloway blocked him with his horse, which was about the same time Liam came walking up from climbing down from his lead wagon. "Why are you stoppin' me, Holloway...give it out...all of it. We'd been friends to long for yuh to think I need somethin' sugar coated. Now give it out or get out of my way." JW shot Holloway a hard glare, but he didn't put his hand on his .44 to threaten him with.

"Captain, Sherry Ann is dead...died shortly after your ranch was hit hard by bandits. With so many old Rangers gone, after losin' their own places, there was jus' no one to watch thu outlying areas. Your boy, he put up a brave defense from what Preacher Joe said, but he went down shootin'. Your daughter, she was a taken but Preacher Joe says it don't seem the feds are all that worrisome 'bout a rebel's daughter. Preacher Joe, he said he buried both proper on the hillside above thu house. He thought that's where you'd like it."

"Where is Preacher Joe?" JW asked.

"Where else, at his little church...still tryin' ta hold on," Jim William said.

"Okay, this is my last order. Go home...check on your families and your places. Liam will come with me with one wagon, you guys decide on the other two. If you guys end up with similar problems as mine, try to recover what stock you can and find some of the old Rangers still around here. We will meet at, or in, hidden valley in the Superstition Mountains. You all know the place. You single fellas, help-out some of these married boys. I've got ta go speak to the Army boys and then the Wagon Train people before we leave, but you can take off. Just don't get into any fights, I've got some plans for our future but they won't help any if your dead."

Liam was leaning against the wagon, blubbering over Sherry Ann and Steven's death, also the kidnaping of his little girl. But he had some talking to do so he let the boy cry it out for now. For himself, he had too much anger simmering inside to weep any grief out.

He rode up beside Captain Jones and shook hands with him, "This is where we part company, Captain. Seems like the Revenue people have taken over this section of Arizona. Bandits hit my home, kilt my wife and son, kidnapped my daughter…she should be about 11 or nearing 12 by now. Probably sold to the Mexicans, so I'll be going after her. From what I've been told, hundreds of troops are hanging around Globe, but there wasn't a fort there before we left. Lots of carpet baggers, supported by federal marshals laying claim to the land with east coast money. I'm sure my place was taken for back taxes but maybe not my stock. I'm going by the house to see my family graves. I just wanted ta say, play it smart with Cochise. He'll be honest with you, if you'll be honest with him. But lie to him once, you've lost his support, forever. You might share that with your Colonel or whoever gets orders for Defiance. With what I see coming now, with the federal government turning on its own rather than forgive and grow together, you'll see the big Indian wars hitting in the '70s all along the Midwest. We won't see the Comanche, but we will see all of the Apache tribes and the Ute. As to the Navajo, be watchful, they were old cousins of the Apache until around the 1400's and then suffered a family break-up and the two have been quarrelsome ever since."

"What are you going to do with the wagon train?" Jones asked.

"I'm going to suggest they take the wagons around to the west of globe and set up for the night. I know they'll need supplies, but with all those northern boys in there fresh from the war fields, it might get really rough." He put out his hand and Jones shook it.

"You're the nicest rebel I ever knew," Jones said.

"Back at you, Yankee. I only pray we're never on opposing side again." He then waved and turned Cochise around to ride toward the wagon train. There, he tied his reins to the lead wagon and asked the leaders to join him for a talk. He then glanced over his left shoulder and watched the Union patrol ride toward Globe with their one patrol wagon and a couple of wounded still aboard. One was still Sgt. Rimes, who hung out over the back gate and waved to JW. When he spotted him, he waved on back and did his best to smile in return. But the longer he put this off, the harder it was getting to stick around. Yet he knew his responsibilities and he also knew his Sherry Ann would expect this of him.

"All right, gentleman, our scouts found that Globe has transformed into a Union stomping ground for US Marshals, who are serving carpetbaggers from the east coast rich people. They're all over the south, including right here in Arizona, buying up all the land owned by Rebels, under assumption we owe taxes for the last four years on newly created war taxes. This is to help pay for the war. I sincerely hope your Plantation owners escaped in time to miss all this, otherwise he wouldn't have had the money for a taxi across the street. But as to us…us farmers and ranchers have been wiped out. Now I want to again warn you, because of your skin color, not only does the south dislike you but a good share of the north dislikes you for all the brothers, sons, nephews and grandsons lost in the Great War to Free the Slaves. They will not be your friend. Oh, you will find the occasional Christian here and there, but you must be careful. You will also find a bushel basket of land schemers out in California ready to take your money for this or that perfect plot of land. Most of the time this will be utterly worthless. A good percentage of the people in the city don't want you living near them, so you may have to create your own town. Just don't be too quick to spend your money and be extremely careful where you buy supplies. Do not take any more money into a town than you absolutely need."

"Why so much concern for us, Captain?" Zeke asked.

"Zeke, I never knew people of your color, but I see an integrity, a grit in you I seldom see in the White race. Over-the-times we have spent together, I don't want to hear or read about your wagon train being wiped out because you trusted the wrong people again. Now if you need supplies, you wander into town with a group of ten healthy men, but Juke and Zeke, you leading the way. You have one wagon with you and inside that wagon you carry those Winchesters and ammo I've given to you. I don't want them back. I want them to keep you safe. But do not display them. Now let Zeke and Juke do all the talking. Their age may keep you from getting into a big brawl or worse, a shootout. Keep your women folk back at the wagon train and have all rifles loaded in the event the Union boys decided to pay a little visit for some horsing around. Or those Federal Sheriffs come around with eyes on seizing all-of-your property...wagons and horses...everything. They might even try to sell you to the Mexicans. Yes, I am trying to scare you, but the bandits that hit my place have never come up this high before. They hit my farm and ranch, my wife died, my son was shot down and killed and my daughter kidnapped. Now I'm going after them."

"We're so sorry, Captain and here you are taking care of us. Truly I am sorry, Captain," Zeke said. Zeke's eyes were watering up, "For so long I have hated the white man, except for my owners. But you have again shown me skin color is not the man." Zeke reached forwarded and offered is hand, which JW shook carefully because of the man's advanced years.

"When you get into town, go to the small church and you will meet Preacher Joe. Tell him you are the wagon train I helped bring across the Southwest and he would appreciate if this man could help you pick up the needed supplies. Also, be warned, this man often rides with the Rangers and he is one tough old geezer, like you two. Now last of all, leaving Globe is two roads; the one stagecoach road going almost directly south, but be ready for robbers. But it is a good chance they'll leave 22 wagons alone, unless they're US Marshalls posing as a gang of bandit and for them you'll need to shoot to kill.

There is also a second stagecoach road that follows the southern course for the Pony Express. Word is, the stage route to California will be using it pretty soon. But it should work for you. But you'll have to decide. If you head due south try to turn off before you get to Tucson so you can escape the same mess Globe is in, but bigger.

"Now If Liam and I ever make it to California, we will stop by. Get Preacher Joe's mailing address and let him know how you're doing. I'll keep him advised of what we're doing. Now I gotta go. No time for long good byes. I've got 12 miles to go and I'll be coverin' that ground fast. God bless!" He climbed aboard Cochise, reined his horse up on to its back two legs and then rode off at a fast clip. Liam waved to everyone, especially the young philly he had danced with most that night. He didn't think he would ever forget her. Now he had to catch-up with two wagons and his four Percherons, which were misbehaving to show they were not very happy with these speeds expected of them.

Liam kept yelling until he finally got JW's attention and slowed down. He then waited for JW to ride back and asked, "What's the matter?"

"We keep going like this and I'm going to kill this four Percherons. They're built for strength, not the speed of your Stallion."

"Okay, I'll slow it down…you want me to take two of those mounts over?"

"Nope, the speed is the only problem and the way you're were flyin', I was waitin' for Cochise to break out wings."

"Sorry, kid…wasn't thinkin'. Besides, speed don't really matter much now anyway."

"We will find her, Captain, no matter how long it takes and even if we have to go down to Mexico City."

"So, you're thinkin' she was taken to be a slave for a rich person's house?"

"With her hair color an' beauty, she would get those scum, $5,000, easily and that means they won't touch her. Probably got $500 at the border and the slave traders going south will ask $5,000."

"How'd you get to know so much about the slave trade," JW asked.

"Hanging around Preacher Joe and then Lt. Dreeke. He's a fountain of information."

"Let's ride and try not to lose all that gold you're carryin'. It's gonna have-to support us for a while. No more rangers for this corrupted government, at least not until those Federal Marshals and civilian money baggers leave the state, and I'll do everything I can to help them along."

It was later in the afternoon when JW and Liam came slowly riding into the ranch yard, only to find the door to the barn hanging wide open. On the front of the right side barn door was a yellow US Government Foreclosure Statement provided by the Department of War Taxes Reclaiming Board. As Liam pulled the wagon up he spotted three horses inside the barn corral, but he was pretty sure he recognized one of them. "There's three horses inside the barn's corral, but I think one belongs to Lt. Dreeke. Looks like his new roan, five gray spots on the right hip and...yup, six gray spots on the left. The other horses I've never seen before."

"Hey, Cap, c'mon in and meet your guests. Appears they or others like them have been waitin' for yuh to show up. I been watchin' them, so I didn't walk up to pay my respects, but I'll wait until you is all done. But you Liam, you get ta wait behind me." He gestured for Liam to take the mounts inside the barn and after he walked around a bit to get the muscles yanked back into place from that ride across the desert, he told him, "Water and feed them after takin' the saddles off and take care of your Percherons. I gotta watch these dangerous partners we have inside."

"I'll trade you," Liam offered.

"Now I'd feel damn silly if one of those big bad Federal Marshals talked you out of your gun and somewhere along the line I got shot in the back."

"How'd you ever take two of these big bad dudes down?"

"When I rode up, they pointed their pistols at me and got all unfriendly from the start, wanted ta know what my name was. Ah told them I was Chet McFarland from down the river and was a wonderin' why my water was shut off. Told 'em these dang rebels were always turning my water off as a prank and I was getting tired of it.

"They told me the Federal Government had closed off all the water in the valley until they figured out who deserved what. They then asked if I knew where that dastardly dude JW Blake was they might make it worth my while and I told 'em he was supposed to be dead. To which the smaller guy said, 'I hope so, I heard he was one tough customer'. But the big dude, spinnin' his silver plated .45 Colt on his fingers like a real trick gunman, he bragged a bit, 'Well I had hoped to catch up with that Ranger Captain and show him a thing or two. We're not going to put up with all their shenanigans. Hearing that he finished his spinning, which weren't dat bad and re-holstered his gun. I was then told to clear out by the little man, who also holstered his much smaller and newer western style Smith & Wesson

.38 revolver, and then they showed me their real pretty gold-colored tin Federal Marshal badges an' ah could see how proud these men were. But they showed me their pretty tin badges and I just had ta show 'em my pur'ty Colt. 44.

"They were then suddenly looking up at the barrel of my Colt.44 and neither man had a smile on his face for my surprisin' dem so good. Oh, I warned dem not ta go for their guns, cause ah woulda' kilt dem stone dead. Had 'em each, one at a time disarm themselves. Then thu little guy tied up the big guy inside the house, might as well be comfortable until you two got here. Then I tied the little guy up. Dey made sum threats, but I clopped the big dude on the head and things got real quiet. Little guy, he's nice ta talk to. He's from Boston, got sent down here by his Investment firm ta work security. He was expectin' Injuns, not this stuff. But he's got a wife and five kids to support."

"Did they bury her proper, Jamey?"

James gave the boy a hard eye for calling him by his family name for him. Only JW and his family had the okay to call him, Jamey. Yet, the lad was now considered JW's little brother and he's been through the same Hell the whole unit has plus the visits to the Apache fortress.

"Only when you an' ah is alone or in thu Captain's presence cun you call me that, got it?"

"Sure, but what about Sherry and Steven, are their graves done right?"

James nodded his head as they walked together into the house to make a check of the Federal Marshals. But both men had nodded off. "Ah es'pected it, dese guys don't get paid enough to play hog in a real gunfight wit' Rangers. Not when deres three of us now."

"About the graves, Lieutenant?"

Oh, sorree, lad, thu graves…Preacher Joe, he done a real smart job. When my time comes, Ah hope he's 'roun' ta bury me. Ah was told he spoke real pretty words for both of 'em, an' thu whole town turned out…even those Yankees over dere. Preacher Joe offered up a beer party an' barbecue. He told me he hoped ta get some information from dose Yankees when dey get drunk. He don't think it was real bandits. They come too far north and too many Yankees around and when told 'bout what happened, an' how little girl was kidnapped, dey jus' set on deir arse countin' tax money comin' in. Nearly every piece of land owned by a Confederate has been lost. Those who resist, never make it ta court. Dey're either in prison for years, or shot down dead."

"I don't understand, Jamey, how can these men be Federal Marshals and be allowing this. Troops are all over Globe, why aren't they out on patrol protecting the ranchers an farmers?"

Walking through the yard after leaving the house and heading over to the wagon to unhook the mighty Percherons, who were now cooled down some, James spotted a stone in his path and kicked it toward the barn. "Preacher Joe says thu troops are here ta work with thu Federal Marshals and now ah'm bein' told a Federal Marshal doin' this kind of work out here is not the same as a US Marshal. While the US Marshal does what we used ta do as Rangers, a Federal Marshal is a security guard and he'll escort pay and gold shipments for thu government and sometimes escort federal prisoners. So, it appears these two here was actin' outside deir…realm of responsibility. Bein' big-shots, almost got them dead."

It was while they were finishing feeding the last of the horses, when a blurry-eyed and rosy-cheeked JW walked down the hill, his hat between his hands. He felt he was about all cried out, when he came to the barn door and stood there and for a long moment in silence. It only registered then that Jamey had two Federal Marshals tied up somewhere around here and then he recalled Jamey having them inside the house. He looked about the barn, ignoring the Foreclosure Posted sign on his barn door and another on a porch post. But later, he'd see how the Federal Marshals had wired them on the fences, nailed them to the coral rails and on to trees.

"Liam, you can go on up now…there's some wild flowers blooming on the hillside, if you want to put some on their graves. You take your time. I know how much they both meant to you. Jamey an' I need to talk some about our future…but don't fret none. If you want to be with me, you're comin' along."

"Thanks, Captain…I'll be along in a…" Liam didn't finish but ran up behind the house to where he found the grave markers. He picked the light blue wild flowers and some yellow ones and placed them into two small ceramic pots provided for that purpose. He took notice of all the flowers already there and knew it was a lot more than what Jamey and the Captain could've put there. There were also white and red ribbons laced about the two wooden crosses. He dropped to one knee and looked behind him, now recalling the time he had wandered over this same hillside, semi-incoherent and blood all over him. How this beautiful unknown woman had made life whole again with love and tenderness, and how Steven had become his little brother and when he wasn't learning cowboy ways the two of them would be off fishing or critter hunting. He could see Steven standing there with a rifle in hand protecting the ranch, his mom and his sister. He was such a threat the bandits had gunned him down, rather than rope him up to be sold as a slave south of the border.

Liam patted the top of Steven's grave and whispered in an emotional voice, "I'll really miss you, Steven, but I know you did your Dad proud. There was just too many of them. He and I will never ever forget you, of course your bond with him is closer than ours, still you meant a lot to me. I looked forward to the day we'd be a Rangering together. But on those lonely nights, you might hear my voice, if it makes it to Heaven, because I'll be talkin' to you and Mrs. Sherry. And don't worry, I'll be doing my best protecting your dad. He's the only kin I have now, my adoptive Big Brother is how we figured it out. I was hopin' to come home and tell you how you were my nephew now." Liam broke down crying and fell forward onto Steven's grave, with his right hand clamping a large white desert rock on Sherry Ann's grave only inches from her son.

Each grave was dug nearly seven feet deep and Preacher Joe had lowered coffins into them. He then had a one foot deep layer of dirt put on top the coffins, followed by about two feet deep of smaller desert rock dug from the springs nearby. Then the rest was dirt, with the graves finished by a two-foot high mound of fist sized and large white rocks. Preacher Joe figured it would be nearly impossible for any coyote or wolf to now reach the Captain's family. The grave was finished by two handmade wooden crosses, with name plaques in the center showing full names and date of birth and date of death. Preacher Joe had used the family Bible from inside the ranch house to locate the date of birth for both-of-them. The bottom of the plaque for Sherry Ann read, "Beloved Wife, Mother, an Arizona Ranger in Heart and Soul. She is missed." Steven's plaque read, "A Brave Son Who Stood His Ground to Protect Family, Land and Rights."

When Liam came down the hillside he was amazed to find several more horses either tied up to one of several outside corral rails or running loose inside the larger corral without saddle and blankets. Water troth was full and James was shoveling hay into the feed bins for both the corral rails and inside the big corral.

Liam counted the new horses and came up with seven men and once he was back down in the ranch yard, without the house blocking his view, he recognized Holloway, Jim Williams, Brady Williams, John Gibson, Andy Salcedo, Gary Wells and Wallace Michaels. But within the evening hours, Chad leaders and Lawrence Coon had showed up. Leaders had dropped a buck deer on the way here and gutted it, but he waited to skin it here and then have fresh meat for a barbecue. But everyone was too hungry to wait for barbecue, so the meat, combined with beans and wild onions was made into a stew, and cooked over the fire by hanging in an eight gallon cast iron pot from a short steel three-legged spit.

Gary Wells had volunteered to make the coffee inside the house, while Jim Williams made Navajo flat bread. With all the smells being produced, it had all the Rangers salivating.

Then from out of the darkness came a rusty old black buggy being pulled by a large dark brown mule. Preacher Joe had now arrived. "You best save me a dish of that, I've been smelling it for the last 15 minutes or so."

"Not quite ready yet, you, old fart," Wallace Michaels said and then he stood up to give Preacher Joe a hard look.

Joe stretched out his neck to see who was standing there in the shadows and calling him an "old fart". He had one hand on his whip and the other holding his reins, but JW stepped forward. "Michael, you've earned our respect over and over again, but we do not bad mouth Preacher Joe, whose helped us here...a lot, especially while we was gone. Okay?"

"Captain, Sir, I got nothin' but respect for you and these boys, but that man in that buggy over there is a disloyal SOB and I've been tracking him for the last 17 years. Now I found him and he's just shown up as you please right at our fire." Michaels stepped forward so Joe could see him better, but he never reached for his side arm. "You recognize me now, Joseph?"

"Michael...is that really you?"

"Yup, the family sent me after you 17 years ago when the Old Man kicked off. You were supposed to take over, run the family business, but you ran off...Why?"

"How'd you find me?" Preacher Joe climbed out of his buggy and walked straight up before Michaels.

"Providence, Big Brother...providence, fate and a whole lot of luck. I had joined the Confederacy, thinkin' you might have gone with their side just to get back at the whole family...but to become a Preacher...that's even worse. Our cousins are just gonna all die from heart-attacks." He looked to the Captain. "See, Sir...the family is all Jewish...devout Jewish. Except I've had a hard time keeping up my faith while running across the west and fightin' in that war.

"Anyhow, when I joined up I told them my name was Wallace Michaels, instead of Michael Wallace. Where I'm from Wallace accounts for a lot of Jewish from Scotland and Ireland, who came over here to get away from the oppression. Then the family made their fortune in making footwear, men's leatherworks and eventually western wear and even saddles. One of you may have a Wallace saddle or cartridge belt, maybe your boots. But I digress, when I heard through the grape vine you men were Rangers from Arizona, I thought I'd get assigned to you and it could save me a trip here. But then I found brothers, friends, but low and behold my big brother suddenly appears…it's got to be fate. But what do we do, Joseph?"

"I preach the Word of God and I help people, Michael. That's what I do and that's what I'll continue to do. I live rough and enjoy it. I'm not going back there to where I'm forced into an office, have 200 employees under me and stress that can kill an ordinary man within a month.

"You can go back and tell the family you found my grave marker and people said I died happy. Okay?"

"Joseph, I'm not going back either. Like I said these men have become my brotherhood and Mr. Gary Wells over there is my best friend. After riding a horse across this land day in and day out, facing the Apache and helping that all-Black wagon train. Going back to my office would become a cage. Nope, were both here in Arizona, but I just had to vent some of my anger over some of those not too agreeable years I suffered looking for you. So, we'll both vanish out here…okay?"

Preacher Joe grabbed his little brother by the shoulders and hugged him fiercely. He then turned around to face the Rangers and said, "This here is my Little Brother Michael."

Everyone began to laugh and they slapped both men on the shoulder. They could understand the deception on both men's part, but beyond it all both men had stood up beside the Rangers and faced Indians, Yankees and now an unknown future.

As everyone took a serving of stew, flatbed and a second cup of boiling hot coffee, Gary Wells sat down by Michaels, who still preferred going by that name and asked him, "Just how rich are you and your Brother?"

"Most of the money is tied up in the Wallace Corporation and the Wallace Investment Company. There's also the Wallace Bank and Loan, plus miscellaneous smaller businesses we own a big share. But it's more than just Joseph and I, the whole family network is made up of six Wallace families. But he was the oldest Wallace and by our rules and bylaws he was and is supposed to be the General Manager and Chairman of Wallace Incorporated. We had the Pinkerton Investigations looking for him for five years, too. But living poorly as a Christian preacher was something no one expected, especially in a backwater Arizona town."

"But, let's say if we worked it out with you and Joseph, I have a hard time calling him that…heard too many stories about him from the others. But say we sent word we kidnapped you, how much cash could the Family put together quickly, to get you two released?"

Michaels thought about it for a minute and then replied, "If they so desired to do it, which they wouldn't because we have such a rule against bowing to the wishes of thieves, kidnappers and killers. Still, if they were to give in, I think the Family could put together $12 Million dollars within 48-hours."

Gary sputtered the figure, "$12 Million…dollars, I've never even seen more than $50,000 and it was on display in a Nevada bank." Gary thought more about the figure and while Michaels was drinking his coffee, sips at a time because of the boiling temperatures. Gary looked over and asked, "So, next time we get into a town you can stand me for say…a Dollar. I got this sweet tooth an' some of these towns have a candy counter."

Michaels started laughing, accidently gulped his hot coffee and burned his mouth and was now spitting in all direction, while Gary set back laughing.

Preacher Joe was with JW inside the house, feeding the prisoners, who were released temporarily to eat. Once they finished, they were tied back up and each one received a blanket for their shoulders. The desert could get real chilly at night and drop below the freezing mark. Even in the barn, Sherry Ann, Steven or JW would normally put winter blankets over the horses to keep them warm. But for JW he wore long-handles sewn by Sherry Ann, with extra padding in the backside to help with all the saddle work and at night he'd snuggle in with her under two wool blankets and her handmade multicolored padded quilt. Now that time was over, but the quilt was still on the bed, but he would sleep in the bunkhouse with Liam.

"The carpet-baggers came in by the three's and four's, acting all friendly, but full of questions. Sometimes they said they were cattle buyers or land agents and paid good Yankee money to have someone take them around ta show them the farms and ranches. Next came the new Union court; couple judges, court officers and five office people to work with the people. A week later the Tax people showed up…about a dozen of them, but they showed up on special stages escorted by three dozen of these new Federal Marshals. They had a brand-new building put up for the territory's new federal court, a new office for taxation and enforcement, and a larger office and ten cells for the Federal Marshals. I'm just not sure how many people they thought lived up here in Globe."

"When did the Union Troops come in," JW asked. He was scooping down his stew like a starved man and was already desiring a second plate load.

Preacher Joe thought about it for a moment, glancing out the window at the Rangers and then said, "I took a total count of a cavalry regiment, along with a dozen wagons. They often assign a Yankee patrol to support the Federal Marshalls when they do a confiscation and make an arrest of a man or even a family for Failure to Pay Owed War Taxes."

Before he got up for a second trip to the stew pot, he looked over at Preacher Joe and asked his old friend, "As long as we've know each other and you never said a word…that's okay, we all have something in our past. But why's you really runaway, leave your religion and take up livin' in our little hamlet?"

"I hate my job with the family from when I was old enough to have my own desk and then my own private office. Fifteen hours a day I was trapped in there, carrying out the Old Man's orders and I did my best to satisfy his whims. He was a real hard man on the employees and how they spent their days, but ignored the family members and how much time they wasted on their own personal projects. Sometimes I was ordered to hire Pinkerton Agents to follow senior employees and observe if they were sharing secrets with our competitors. But even when I knew a family member was having lunch with another company's employee, and advised him of it, I was told to forget it. I watched him age, become meaner by the week and I believe that's what killed him. He became heartless. The employees probably held a party to celebrate his passing. That's when I was told I was expected to step into his shoes the following Monday.

"Well, I slept on it and then ran for the harbor to work my way to Brazil. I've had all kinds of jobs, JW…I've been a cowboy and rode the Boseman Trail, fighting Sioux and Blackfeet. I've prospected and logged in Oregon. Rode as a stagecoach guard in Texas and worked a gambling boat on the Mississippi River handling stock and whatever. Spent a hitch working U.S. Mail, fought a war in Brazil and sailed home on a Spanish Clipper, teaching the skipper how to handle cattle on board and how to play a decent game of Canasta with his officers. But it was in New Orleans I was hit by the Lord…He hit me or I hit him. Either way, I turned my Jewish scarf pin in and learned the secret Christian handshake. I was sold."

"Christians have a secret handshake?" JW asked.

"Naw, I was simply telling you how the Lord transformed my life and eventually I became a Preacher and I was directed to this little hamlet of yours. But it has been exciting. Lately I've been compiling all the evidence to eventually bring these federal officers to a real federal court for violating the rights of American citizens. I also believe they were involved in the attack on your ranch…not directly, but they allowed it to happen. You need to capture one of those bandits, which I believe are operating in the old bandit area of Arizona's southeast. The Army seems to be ignoring this entire area and it could be the banditos have some kind of agreement with the Apache."

Once dinner was consumed, JW led the men into the barn, but he left Liam on guard outside with a loaded Winchester 30-30 Rifle in his hands. He would get Liam up to date after the meeting, with all that was said by the others. Bales of hay became chairs or couches, and the smell was building from horses that all needed a good grooming and wash.

"You all know about what happened here and how Jessie, who should be about 11 years old, was kidnapped. Sherry Ann and Steven were buried up on the hillside behind the house, a favorite spot of Sherry Ann. Bandits hit, but I am not so sure they were bandits. Right now, I'm considering these might've been Comanchero, working in conjunction with corrupt Federal Officials. Bandits have never worked this high before. But I am going after my daughter. Lt. Sampson, the Wakefield Brothers are escorting the wagon train down to Tucson or directly to the California border. They will then hit Tucson and investigate the happenings there. At some point, they will join us and give us a full report.

"I know you all returned to your homes and found the same foreclosure notices for unpaid war taxes. I've been told I owe $60,000 on the ranch alone for four years, plus $25.00 a head of cattle, for each horse and $10 for each ram, ewe and 50 cents per chicken or duck. Now it's impossible for me to count-up what I had, so I have-to accept their total after they moved all my animals to a new communal ranch land for an upcoming auction. So, according-to my notice, they want another $43,678.50 for me to have the return of my animals and then pay a yearly tax, plus penalty for whenever I am late. Total owed is $103,678.50. How about the rest of you?"

Holloway replied first and his voice radiated with the anger he felt for the Yankee government, "They took everything and somehow my home burned down, plus the barn. I owe a total of $84,565 and my payment date is now a week away."

Brady Williams then spoke up, "They want $48,965 from what I've built up."

"Yeah, when I got home the family was all gone and the neighbor had a note for me, they'd gone back home and I could come or stay here to play Ranger. She was really upset when I followed you, Captain, off ta war, but I learned most women were. But my note said my amount due to the Federal Government was $39,245.50. Now where do they think we're goin' ta get that kind of money?"

"Captain, do you suppose they know about us?" Michaels asked.

"Naw, they have no idea who you are or Preacher Joe and even if you'd come up ta pay that money, they'd find another way to take our stock and land. That's the whole thing, they want this land for the big investment companies in those rich states, and they want the herds we've built up. They're simply using bought and paid for Federal Court officers, tax lawyers, these Federal Marshals who are supported by Yankee troops. No, this is a no-win situation right now, but I keep thinking about all the Arizona ranchers; small hard rock farmers having to cut through volcanic rock to find suitable soil. They're spread miles apart and open targets to the Apache and Ute, Mexican Bandits and slavers, also these Comancheros, who need to be hunted down and drowned, or shown the errors of their ways in some selective way."

"What are we going to do for money?" Brady Williams asked.

"How much gold have you got left?" JW asked

"Oh, sorry, Captain I forgot all about that Gold."

JW glanced over the men then down at his feet and held his voice for a moment as the barn set through a moment of silence. Finally, he shuffled his feet and spoke, "Gentlemen, we now ride the finest horses we have ever seen and we now carry the best rifles in the west. I estimated we still have about $45,000 in gold coin in our wagon and that's the most any of us have ever had. It will keep us in ammo, food, feed for our animals and whatever else we need for the next ten years. But what I am suggesting could get us all killed or hung, but we will ride again illegally as non-authorized Arizona Rangers and be here to help the settlers of Arizona until new legal Rangers are installed once again. When this occurs, what gold is left will be divided up among you. If you do not wish to follow me, we will divide the spoils right now and you can ride back to Texas or hit California with that wagon train. I've sent word to Lt. Sampson and hope fully that he will be with us once he finishes his job in Tucson. I don't know how many men he'll bring back with him. But they will not have a share of this Gold when we divvy it up."

"Captain, will we keep our Ranger or military ranks and be assigned to one of two separate squads?" John Gibson asked.

"I think we will keep it Ranger style, in this people will recognize us. We will behave as Rangers and treat our prisoners as if we were authorized law enforcement officers. I am thinking we will drop the offenders off in the town's center plazas, and then ride out. In this way, the courts will have-to ask and just maybe, Washington will hear about what is occurring our here."

"Tonight, we gonna sleep, for tomorrow we is gonna ride south an' it's gonna be a hard ride," Lt. Dreeke said in his typical drawl. "Now check dose weapons an' let MSgt. Wells or Michaels know what you all may need. If a knife needs sharpening, then do it! If a saddle needs sewin' or a blanket needs replacin', fix it. Check your field pack, make sure canteens are full an' you got three days' worth of hard tack in case we get stuck. One-hundred rounds rifle ammo, 60 rounds revolver ammo will be daily issue, replace as needed. See Liam if' in yuh need more. Finally, check dose horses an' clean deir hooves, comb deir manes an' tails. Dose horses wort' a parcel of money…Now you're dismissed!"

John Gibson looked over at Chad Leaders and said, "So glad we is out of that Army stuff, oh Lieutenant might 'a added us to wash behind ours ears an' wear a clean shirt in thu morning."

Suddenly another booming order, "Make sure you all get a bath down in thu spring. Might be a bit 'fore the next one and thu Apache can pick up this stench from a day ride away."

"Hush-up, John, 'fore he has us shin' our boots…we is back in the Rangers, officially or not. Welcome home."

During the evening the men each took their turn visiting the grave site for Sherry Ann and Steven. Over the years, she had become like an adopted sister for most of them or a dear friend and confident for the rest. Every Ranger always knew he was welcome to stop by for a meal or just coffee, have a chat and almost all of them had talked with her about the Civil War issues long before they discovered they were being disbanded and contemplating joining. There were some of the newer Rangers who pulled out when the South fired on the North. Sherry Ann knew these men had hurt her husband's feelings by leaving, but they hadn't been with him long enough to develop any loyalty. Now, JW wondered how many of the youngsters might have survived the four years of bloodshed and mayhem. He knew he had averaged more engagements with the Northern boys every month than he ever did as a Ranger facing the Indians and bandits back here. He had hoped to have seen some of the kids he sent off after taking their resignations, but he never did. Now he couldn't even recall their names.

With his termination as the Ranger Commander, he had sent all Ranger records to Tucson, to be filed away in hopes they would someday become a part of Arizona's Historical records. They were loaded into the boot of a stagecoach and sent south. Now he wished he had held on to his personal note books and his diaries. But at the time he thought they might be of more importance to the state. Except now, seeing what was going on, he imagined all the stuff he sent south was piled into a funeral pyre and a match was put to it.

NEXT MORNING—THEY RIDE SOUTH

At daybreak, JW was already up making breakfast of frying up the leavings of last night stew and the remainder of the venison. Plus, he had the coffee on, which began to wake the Rangers up with its hot aroma of real coffee beans beat to death with a three pound hammer the night before. One of Liam's chores was to get a ten-pound bag of coffee grounds ready for the trail and it took him better than an hour, plus a sore wrist and shoulder.

Their prisoners were awake, so James cut them free and took 'em out back for nature's call. "Look, boys, you is getting' released today, don't be stupid an' try ta make a play. There's 12 of us and you'll be dead. Most of us can drop a man at a-1,000 yards, we've had ta learn how. You play nice an' ah won't have ta tie you to a house or porch support. Okay?"

"Yes, Sir. You've all played square with us, so you'll get no gripe from either of us," the shorter Federal Marshal said. The bigger man simply nodded his head in agreement. He was too busy scooping down the beans.

The wagons, one being an old lighter eight-footer now pulled by the Federal Marshal's horses, was loaded down with food stuffs, dry goods, sleeping rolls and the men's field packs. Normally the field packs were saddle bags on the back of the man's horse, but when the Rangers had a wagon coming along they piled their goods into cloth bags and kept only their emergency supplies; very basic first-aid bandages, one pint of wood grain alcohol for wound treatment, a small but highly sharp cutting knife for surgery, extra ammo, that would not be touched unless he was down to his last cartridge and was surrounded by a band of roaring Apaches, and a black powder kit if he had a Sharps long rifle with him and a small Holy Bible. Thanks to Sherry Ann's teachings almost every-one of them could read.

Liam's wagon carried the gold, dispersed evenly in the bed of the big wagon. He carried the rest of the general supplies, extra saddles, boxes of 30-30 Winchester Rifle and Colt .44 ammo for revolvers and JW's Henry, also two casks of black powder and a case of mini balls, plus loading and cleaning supplies for the six Sharps Rifle, carried in the second wagon. Three were in .30 caliber, two were .50 caliber and one was a sniper's .54 caliber. They had extra knives, revolvers, a set of matched dueling pistols that belonged to JW and were hidden in the barn in the event the Yankees visited. He warned Sherry Ann, "Union boys coming this way from California, so hide our finest silver and whatever, in that place I stuck my family's dueling pistols. No sense some Yankee First lieutenant or some damn corporal from Los Angeles finding our best stuff."

Knowing how most people were a might fussy with animal leavings, JW had dug a hole underneath the poop dump and kept the articles in a sealed container. Then even more poop was placed over the top and this was the family's fertilizer makings for their next year's gardens. A lot of farmers were in to composting with steer and horse fertilizer, even chicken and duck leavings. But it was messy.

The box was lifted out and put into the big wagon. Liam had the four big Percherons hooked up and they were ready to go to work. Liam had learned these big draft beasts did not like sitting around too long. He had made sure they had their morning water and feed, and then noticed they had left behind a new supply dump for the Blake compost bins. He made sure his own rifle was strapped into place, using an old rifle boot he had found in the barn. He had his canteen and a day's supply of hard tack, hard baked with ground turkey bacon and some ingredient he didn't want to identify because it had an awful smell about it. The hard tack needed to be sliced with a sharp knife, put in the mouth on sucked on for a time. Chewing on it right away was a surefire way to break a tooth, just like the jerky they lived on before.

JW was spending his last moments up on the hillside, saying his good byes, he hoped someday he and Liam could return and work their Ranch. But he told Sherry Ann he was out to rescue their daughter and help all the people of Southeast Arizona, who he knew were being ignored by the Territorial Government and Union Troops. He then blew both of them a kiss and wandered down the hillside to find his men standing by their horses and wagons.

JW wasn't all that surprised to find that Preacher Joe had now planned to go with them. He wanted to be with his Little Brother, plus he knew these Rangers would be needing his connections with the Good Lord. But he was also a pretty good doctor when it came to bullet and arrow wounds, plus some sewing work. So, he abandoned his buggy, grabbed the two bags he always carried with him; one medical and one for church uses and took over the reins of the other wagon. He tied up his old mule to the tailgate, knowing the beast could shed a few pounds from a 300 mile journey south.

James came out of the house, holding the two Federal Marshals at gunpoint. Both men had been released of their rope bonds. They waited on the porch for JW to make his appearance. Upon seeing the two Marshals he gave them a hard glare, which frightened them, but his look softened a bit and he stepped up before them. "I never planned to harm you, but I needed time. I figured you were waiting out here for me, so no one was missing you yet. But, I gotta take your horses, I can't have you riding in to report what you've seen until I've had time to vanish into the desert. But you tell your bosses, I'm headin' for California and how I know more crossings of the Colorado River than he's got troops, so not to bother coming after me. But I'll be back someday to hang every-last one of them. I hold them in the same contempt I hold the men who murdered my wife, my son and kidnapped my daughter. But I also got'ta take your guns. But don't fret, I won't have you crossin' the desert to get back to town without firearms. They'll be on the side of the road, along with the costs of your horses down the road about one mile. Look for a dried spring with a steer skull on the right side of the road. You'll find what you're looking for underneath it. I won't leave it out in the open for some Apaches ta find. But do not leave here until we've gone and I want your word on that…or I'll leave a man back here to babysit you."

"No, Sir…you have my word and once I get back to Globe, I'm quitting and heading back east. This Old West stuff isn't for me. I can bluster, but I got no starch up against the likes of you men. And I don't want my wife hearing how I died in some Indian fight. But I'd like one thing from you, I'd like to shake your hand, Sir. Sitting back in there I've listened to you men and I'm proud to have known the likes of men like you. I can't wait to tell my kids about the Arizona Rangers." The short Marshal offered his hand and both JW and Jamey shook it.

"I'll tell you something, those big cities terrify me," JW said and then walked away.

James looked at the two men, smiled again and said, as he dropped his smile and glared at the big guy, "Jus' t'ink, he was killin' Yankees a year ago. Men can sure change."

Big man never opened his mouth, but he shot the small guy a hateful glance and then watched as the men formed up and rode out of the ranch yard. JW and James were in front, with Liam's wagon right behind them, then Preacher Joe, followed by MSgts. Wells and Michaels. Then came four spread out strings of extra mounts, roped together to keep them from running off in a surprise Indian attack. This meant four rangers were stuck on horse duty and the first shift fell upon Coon, Leaders, Gibson and Brady Williams. Holloway and Jim Williams were riding scout up ahead and this left Andy Salcedo to bring up the rear, but he stayed in tight. Numerous times either Michaels or Gary Wells would drop back to ride with Salcedo and keep him company. For this was only a 12-man Ranger force and it was unknown if and how much larger it would become when they met up with Lt. Sampson in the Town of Benson, which wasn't much larger then Globe the last time JW had ridden through it.

The firearms were wrapped in an old blanket taken from the barn and buried under the skull marker. He placed a $40 gold coin in the bottom of each holster, which was a lot more than what their two horses were worth.

The marker was also used by the locals to show where an old cattle trail ended here on their road into town. JW looked south and could see his two scouts wandering easily, using the old trail to make their tracks harder to read. Mostly it was only the locals who knew about the historic trail, which had brought cattle up from Mexico, moved down through Globe and upward to Nevada and other parts unknown.

JW wasn't expecting any Indian problems this side of Tucson, but one thing he learned about fighting them for so long is they had a habit of showing up when one least expected it to happen.

They made camp in an ancient buffalo wallow, big enough to hold both wagons and all the horses. Rock walls were put up on the edges for firing positions, just in case. But they never needed them and we're out at daybreak, hoping to make another 25 miles.

Each day was another day of hot dusty travel and the water barrels were becoming ever lighter. The men were down to rationing their water, but not the horses—at least not yet. Then finally on the tenth day they came into the sleepy Hispanic and Indian Catholic missionary community if San Manuel. The only thing left standing of the mission was the original church building. JW had been through this way nearly ten years before and knew of the community's famous wells, two said to have been blessed by a Saint and had never run dry. JW didn't know about the Saint business, but here was evidence of it. Still, he figured the wells dug into an underground river. Ancient legends spoke of several large underground rivers that traveled underneath Arizona and were known about during the time of the Great Aztec and Inca worlds. JW often wondered if they fed into the upper Colorado in the deep areas of the Grand Canyon, but he was no geologist or ancient history fan. He just wondered about things.

They found the old priest he had met last time he was here still carrying out his duties and they were made welcome. When it was learned all these men were in fact Rangers and not Union soldiers or more prospectors, the town of 354 people all came out to welcome them with food and gala events. This was an unofficial holiday for San Manuel.

"The town was named after a Hispanic Saint...one of those from Old Spain, but like all Spanish communities, this town was started on a legend. I heard the story last time I was here, but some of you were with me even back then...makes me feel old."

"What's the story?" Liam asked.

JW grinned. "Seems there was a notorious bandit in these parts who robbed from everyone, but never harmed anyone. But the people had so little, even a peso was too much to lose to a freeloading bandit. Then one day, this bandit was found unconscious on the steps of the church being built...that one over there, same one. He was in rough shape, having been chased by the Mexican Army for days on end. He had made the mistake of stopping a rich coach and stealing the necklace of the Governor's daughter.

A highly valued piece of jewelry because it not only carried a rich gem, but it had belonged to the girl's dead mother.

"The troops could not allow him to escape and we're closing in on him when his stolen roan horse simply collapsed from sheer exhaustion. The man, his leg pinned under the dying mount, his pistol tossed aside in the fall, he laid back to await his fate. But then he saw a flash of bright light and a man in bright illumination appeared and offered his hand. He thought it was the Lord Jesus coming for him to take him to his Final Judgment and he knew where he would be headed then, into the fiery pits of Hell for his life of crime. But though the Lord had seen everything this bandit had done, Christ had also seen the love and care he had for his people. Many times, he had helped them with back breaking labor when the man was laid up, never revealing who he was. He had shared in his loot stolen from the oppressive government with the people and helped them pay their taxes. He had carried medicines great distances and even deliver Christmas to the poorest of peons.

But when his hand touched the lighted man, he passed out and awakened on the freshly built steps of the adobe church. Then a voice spoke to him, telling him to serve His people as their Priest and Father God would do the rest. All evidence of ever carrying a firearm was gone, his horse could not be found and the story says the girl's necklace showed up in her jewelry box that same day. Two days later, a traveling Priest came by who was not expected for another six months. But he had received a dream message to come here right away and begin teaching a new man what it was to be a Priest. One that did not need official seminary because he was following God's orders. So, he finished building the church, the Mission school and was then directed in a dream to dig two separate wells, each 40 feet deep. He was told where and you can see them, still there; plus, according-to the legend, water exploded out of the wells like an oil gusher, at the same moment and were instantly full."

"So, this robber become Father Manuel or Saint Manuel?" Liam asked.

"That's the story, but it was well over a 100 years-ago. But I will add, the community has never again experienced bad guys. Oh, they hit the cattle herds outside of town passing by, but the town here actually appears blessed...accept by time. The Catholic Church has all but forgotten it, moving their priests out to larger communities and a traveling priest comes by. But they've never suffered a bandit raid or an Indian attack since the day Manuel first appeared here in his new profession. I also was told the much older priest who taught him, elected to be buried here and years later, Father Manuel elected to be buried beside him."

311

"Wow," Brady Williams said. The men were sharing in beans and corn with the locals, while music was played and several couples were dancing.

"So, Captain, you think Catholic have the only real religion?" PFC Coon asked.

"My wife would teach our Sunday lessons and she would say, 'Religion belongs to churches, but the love of God, His Son, Jesus Christ and Holy Spirit belongs to everyone. As-long-as we separate ourselves by our beliefs in the same things, the very same Father, Son and Holy Ghost, then the Promised Chapters in the Book of Revelation will fall upon us.' She had me read them, and though most of 'em I cannot understand, what I can understand sound really scary. Like ten million warring Indians coming at you and you've got no place to go and hide."

"But…" Liam wanted to ask another question, but JW stopped him. "We are back on the trail tomorrow, enjoy yourself while you can." He turned and walked away, over to be with Cochise and share a sliver of dried apple with him. Apples and carrots, Cochise loved his fruits and vegetables.

Three days after they had left the community, a large Union patrol entered San Manuel, but was unable to learn anything from the locals. But the community leaders smiled when they observed the patrol head east. For they knew their friends were en route south to Benson.

A week later, Holloway and Jim Williams rode in to report sighting Benson through the low hills up ahead. "Towns grown some, Captain…spread out a bit," Jim Williams reported.

"How many miles up ahead," JW asked.

"I'd say from here 'bout 15 to 20 miles," Holloway replied.

He thought about it briefly, chewing the figures over in his head, as they rode along. But he didn't want to stop the procession. Once everyone joined up, got the news and asked their questions, they would lose an hour of travel.

"Okay, find us a campsite ten miles south of here and we'll make our encampment. You two will go in tomorrow, take Liam and Preacher Joe to load up on our food needs. We'll take the big wagon in the next day or so, once we empty it, to buy our feed and top off the water barrels. The four of you, especially with the sprout and the geezer, shouldn't shake up any alarm. But we play it smart. If Sampson is there he'll be in one of the eateries, a bar or even in a hotel. He won't make it hard to find him and he's traveling under his own name. Most connect his name with the current government, not knowing he became a Ranger first."

312

"You got it, Boss," Holloway said. They then rode back to jaw the fat with the others for a moment before riding on to find that encampment.

The next day in Benson was a big surprise. Benson had become a boom town for gold and now the report of a silver lode. Liam estimated over 10,000 people in town and Union troops were camped only on the outskirts, but in a two-company force of cavalry. But it was Jim Williams who noticed these troops had taken up a permanent posting here. He didn't see a single patrol leave Benson while he was off riding alone. All the horses were kept in wired off horse corrals with large wooden water troths and walk-in barns were built for the hay. He figured the only thing missing here was an actual fort being built. But he knew no sane Indian tribe was going to attack a town this size. In fact, there were dozens of Apache Indians leaving a couple trading posts carrying black powder rifles, shot and powder horns. He couldn't believe his eyes. They were actually selling rifles to Apache warriors, instead of shooting them. Then he learned about the gold nuggets they were bringing in and it all made sense. White man was selling death and destruction and it would be the Arizona settler or passing wagon train who'd pay the price. This made him sick.

Unarmed, the Old Geezer and the Sprout, took a walk about town after leaving their wagon at the delivery stable. Cost them $20 to leave their wagon and have the horses fed and watered. Back in Globe it would have cost maybe a whole dollar. "That sure took care of a $20 gold piece...And did you see the look that stable man gave us. I bet our whole wagon's being searched for where we might have more gold stored."

"JW knows these people and keeping the gold on us was the best thing but let's be careful how we show it and spend it. I don't want anyone fallowing us out of town to see where we're holed up."

Holloway checked the hotels, the eateries and a couple fancy cafe's and just finished his last hotel, but no Bret Sampson. When they met together to get the wagon loaded, Jim Williams noticed how the stable hand was having a friendly chat with three other saddle bums. When he spoke with Geezer and Sprout, he and Holloway learned about how the stable hand was paid with a gold coin, it was all they had. "No one's got any Yankee cash and our confederate paperback are just good enough to be wall paper on some cabin wall," Liam told him.

"Tomorrow, whoever we send in should go to the bank and change some gold over for paper, so we don't have this problem. Now you two ride on ahead, but get your guns back on." Holloway dug into his saddlebags and handled each of them their weapons and belts. "Once you move up ahead a-ways, those three or four will began following. Then me and Jim, here will get behind them to have a little chat."

"You two get all the fun," Sprout replied.

"We do, huh? Maybe next week I'll have you and Preacher Joe take the scout, while me and Jim here drive the wagons and rest up all peacefully."

"I'd do it, but you know the Captain won't do it," Liam said and then Preacher Joe added, "Bring me my mule and the two of us will show you two how to do a proper scout. Why, I was scoutin' down the Boseman before you two was out of your swaddling clothes."

"If we get some more Rangers, I'll ask the Captain to let us take you two on a scout with us. Preacher Joe, you can teach us how and Liam, about time you learn how and what makes this country worth fightin' for. Now get a movin' but not too fast. I want you leading them, not them chasing you." Holloway pulled off and traipsed up to where Jim stood behind a building as to not be seen by their quarry.

"You ever notice the longer we spend talkin' with the sprout, the more Northern we take off sounding like?" Holloway asked.

To which Jim replied, "Taint so." They both chuckled and then checked the loads on their revolvers. They knew this was going to be fun and in their job, they had to get their chuckles when and where they could. An Apache arrow could come on all sudden like and that was it for a Ranger, or anyone in the wilds of Southwest.

After Liam and Preacher Joe left Benson, moving slowly with a heavy wagon and heading north on a new miner's trail they had discovered coming into town. They would use the hard-packed earth for as far as the roadway went north and drive off it once the road veered to the west toward the hills. Then they would simply follow their tracks back to where the Rangers were waiting for them. Meanwhile Holloway and Jim Williams were quietly closing up the distance between them and the three men following the wagon. Both Rangers had their Winchesters out and sitting across their laps.

When they reached a small dry lakebed, Liam moved into it and stopped halfway across, tied the reins off and turned around with his Winchester resting a top a big 100 pound bag of beans. He had it pointed at the center rider, while Preacher Joe had his long double-barrel 12-gauge shotgun pointed at all three horsemen. When they turned to ride away, they discovered both Holloway and Jim Williams were now within 100 yards behind them and their rifles leveled in their direction. This was not the situation they had expected, for the stable hand had never warned them of an additional two riders.

Holloway rode up to within 25 feet and yelled at them to cautiously and very slowly pull their side arms out of their holsters and throw them a good distance from their horses. This was followed by their black powder rifles, which were carefully dropped to the ground. A cocked black powder rifle could easily go off and send a bullet in all sorts of directions and a mini-bullet might hit one of their horses.

Jim Williams was now up to the wagon, staying ten feet behind and to the left of the wagon. "If one of you even think about jumping one of those riders, I'll shoot you out of the air with buckshot and leave you out here for the buzzards," Preacher Joe said.

"Now slowly, climb down from your horses, but you can hold the reins," Liam said in a loud voice. He then dismounted the wagon and after leaving his Winchester in the seat, walked around collecting up the older black powder rifles. He had each of the three men back away, with their mounts, moving about 50 feet to the west of the wagon's tracks. Once he had loaded the rifles into the wagon, he went back to collect the men's revolvers. "You men need to take better care of your weapons, one of these might blow your head off if you fired it. They're filthy." Liam said and shot the men a dirty look. He had developed a real respect for firearms since being with the Rangers and in the war.

Holloway then rode up to the three standing men, who were acting as if they were about to be executed or their horses taken and left to die in the desert. But Preacher Joe relieved their worries. "Gentlemen, we're not going to shoot you or take your horses, but we are taking your rifles. You see, we work for the Federal Government, out of the Denver Mint, and they have us down here checking on the quality of gold coming out of this Benson gold and silver strike. So, we ended up paying the stable hand you chatted with a $20 gold piece. That's how we often get paid, but your prices down here are a lot higher than we expected.

"Now our encampment is generally located so we can reach most, if not all, of the mines in less than three days, but we prefer that no one else knows where we are for now. If need be we can always have a troop of cavalry with us, but those horse soldiers make a lot of noise, when ones trying to sleep. And to help your curiosity from not over ruling your judgment, we do not carry the actual gold with us, only our reports. Otherwise we'd have those troops to protect us. But almost every member of our group, except for those report writers, is a long experienced Indian fighter and can drop a man at 800 to 1,000 yards. Any questions, Gentlemen?"

A tall lanky man with two weeks of growth of a dark brown beard and a heavier moustache, held up his right hand. He wore a filthy brown and red plaid long sleeved shirt with rolled up sleeves, a dark blue dust scarf covered in sweat stains, black slacks that showed a lot of wear and emphasized his thin legs, inside scuffed up brown leather boots. His cartridge belt, at one time tan in color, was now stained dark brown and covered in dust. Their horses looked all done in and they had come only ten-miles or so at an easy walk. "I got a question...sir, he asked.

"Go ahead," Preacher Joe said and he added a couple nods.

"What 'bout our guns...an' us?"

"Well, you keep the horses to ride back to town, but not the rifles and I'm not sure why'd you want to. Whoever sold 'em to you, sure saw you coming. As to your Navy Colts, one of these fine young men is going to ride them back a mile and drop them off on the trail. You can pick them up. In each holster, will be a $20 gold piece to cover your time and the expense of your rifle. Now I expect to see you walk back for those pistols, because if my good man here sees you at a run, he'll drop the three of you in mere seconds." He gestured to Holloway and asked him to hold up his Winchester.

"Men, this weapon being held up that three of them are carrying, is the brand new Winchester 30-30 caliber repeater. It fires six cartridges before reloading. Highly accurate and at present time only being issued to important government units. In a couple years, it will be generally issued to the U.S. Army and I expect a year later, for sale to the general population at a very high price. We have already demonstrated it against the Apache and Comanche, driving superior numbers off with overwhelming fire power. So, our little encounter here has probably saved your lives, but now we must move along. Now you may see us in town time to time, but please ignore us and you'll also never know who and how many of us are in Benson. Please take care."

Liam and Preacher Joe began to move ahead at a slow rate, waiting to see the return of Holloway. Meanwhile, Jim Williams, who was mounted and staying 50 feet away from the three dismounted men, stayed, while waiting for the return of Holloway. They attempted to engage Williams in conversations, mostly how he got this job, how much it paid and where to inquire, but William remained silent until he spotted Holloway returning.

"All right, you three can ride back to Benson, but slow-like. Count your lucky stars, had it been me, you'd be feeding the buzzards. My job is to keep him alive, that's all. But he's a gentleman. Don't let me see you again, in Benson or otherwise. Might be a good time to visit Mexico or California. We'll be out of here in a month. Now ride!"

The men kept nodding as they rode and Holloway gave them a wide birth. The rest of the trip back to the encampment was trouble-free and it was pancakes all around, with maple syrup.

CHAPTER THIRTEEN

"We don't need no stinkin' badges!"

TOWN OF BENSON, ARIZONA TERRITORY, RANGER'S ENCAMPMENT NORTH OF BENSON

Several of the senior men were sitting about a low campfire, surrounded by large rocks, with a three-foot tall three-legged spit holding up a four gallon blackened coffee pot. By now most of the coffee had boiled away and the men were talking quietly about past events and wondering how much longer they should wait for Bret Sampson in Benson, or should they send a couple of the men to Tucson to see if he was there and possibly in jail.

"If Bret don't show up in Benson in two days, we'll send a couple men to Tucson. If he's not there, we'll leave for the southeast when they return. We can give them two days, so that's six days in all we'll have to wait," JW said.

"Do anyone else need ta go ta Benson for a bath, a nice dinner or what ails yuh?" Chad Leaders asked.

"Well, Liam sure ain't had a chance wit' one of dose dark ladies of thu night," Holloway added, which brought a smile to everyone's face, except for Preacher Joe and Captain JW Blake.

"Liam will find true love when he's old enough to know what it means and not some pasty-faced $5 an hour spoiled feather," Preacher Joe said.

"Joseph, in Benson it's now $20 an hour since the gold strike. I can see you've been living a pastor's life…makes me proud of you, somehow." Michael said to his brother.

"Let's change the subject, before the kid comes in from guard duty. I hate it when he blushes and tries to hide his face inside his underarm. Most innocent kid I've ever known," Brady Williams said with a laugh.

"Yeah, ol' innocent who kilt over a dozen Injuns an' never once ran away from a fight. I'd rather have him beside me than most men," Lawrence Coon said for everyone to hear. He was on cook duty and was now cleaning up.

"Yuh got dat right," James added.

When Liam came in relieved by Chad Leaders, he went directly to where JW was laid-out but still awake looking up at the stars. He opened his eyes wide when he heard the shuffling feet moving around the fire and trying not to step on anyone. Then Liam dropped down on JW's left side and put a hand on his arm, gentle-like. "It's me…Liam…you awake?"

"I am now, so what's up?" JW asked. He didn't sit up yet because he didn't want to disturb the others until he knew what the boy wanted to tell him. It had to be serious to wake the boss-man up, though.

"There's something or someone out there, JW. Coyote went all quiet, some time ago and I haven't heard a wolf all night. Now the horses are growing nervous, especially the Percherons. Those horses are high stepping here and there, acting mighty uncomfortable…all the horses are acting scared-like. I don't think its Indians, but I can't put a nail on it."

"Did you tell your relief?"

"Chad knows."

JW mumbled something under his breath, "Wake up Preacher Joe and Gary Wells, get all the black powder rifles of 50 and 54 calibers loaded quickly, with extra loads ready. Have Michaels and the Wakefield Brothers get those extra torches lit and placed on the wagons to light up the area now."

"Do you know what it is?"

"I'm thinkin' we may got us a big Grizzly and when he decides to come, they're almost unstoppable. Like a wild buffalo. Our Winchester won't stop him, but those old black powder Sharps have the best chance if we don't panic. Now get everyone up and tell them to move Injun style."

Coon thru extra wood onto the fire and eight torches were lit on the four corners of the two wagons. A second large fire was built up across the encampment and dried brush was thrown to get a raging fire going with flames hitting four and five feet in height. The Percherons were manhandled by two men at a time to bring them inside the interior area of the encampment. The personal mounts, which included Cochise were already tied off on a ground line between the wagons, but they were sure jumpy.

Then everyone heard a loud shout and part scream coming from Chad Leaders, who was now just south of the encampment, "Grizzly! We got us a…" then they heard the horse let out a terrifying scream that few men ever hear. The sound of a horse being sliced apart by the deadly claws of a massive silver-back Grizzly boar.

The men couldn't worry about Leaders for the moment, they had to protect the encampment and the horses inside. The experienced men knew that bear would attempt to kill as many animals as possible before it would bother to carry off any meat.

Then came four shots of a Colt .44 and they knew Leaders was still alive and putting up a fight, but the roar of the mighty bear was terrifying. Five men now held the .50 and .54 caliber black powder Sharps Buffalo Rifles and they now stood side by side. It was Gary Wells, Preacher Joe, Liam Blake, Leo D Wakefield and Michaels, who stood beside his brother. On each side of the men were lit torches to illuminate the encampment. JW was armed with his .44 caliber Henry and he was ready to pump all 16 rounds into that behemoth, but they would only have mere-seconds before the bruin would tear into them.

Another horse went down, one of the beautiful roans from Pennsylvania and it never made a sound before a massive paw whipped around and busted its neck. They just didn't have time to get all the horses moved and Liam began to blame himself for not acting sooner.

Right then the bore raced by one of the torches and it gave JW and two others a quick view of its size. "We got us a big one, so avoid head shots and go straight for the heart and lungs. His skull is two inches thick and he's gonna die hard," JW hollered. He then added, "Don't shoot unless you got a target!"

A third horse went down but it wasn't pretty or silent as most of its right hip was clawed right off, and both legs were shattered and broken. But then for some reason, the boar raised up on its two rear feet and began to approach Cochise. But unable to run off, Cochise turned its back legs around to kick out at the bear and the third attempt struck the bear in the bottom of its jaw and knocked it on to its backside. But as the angry bear whipped around to charge the horse, six men fired as one into the belly and chest of the bruin. While the men did a fast reload of their black powder rifles, JW continued to drive .44 caliber bullets into the bears throat, chest and bowels. The others were ready and they fired their second load of heavy mini-balls into the bear. This time it worked and the bear now lay on its side, its heart beating slower and slower. But Preacher Joe wasn taking any chances, he leaned his rifle against the wagon and rushed up with his double-barrel 12-gauge shotgun. He stuck it into the bear's enormous ears and let loose with both barrels. Blowing the top of the skull off the bear. The silver-back Grizzly, estimated at over a ton in weight and eight-foot, nine-inches. tall, was definitely…dead.

They found four horses, dead. More than they had figured on and Chad Leaders was still alive. Though his horse had died, it fell over the top of Chad, keeping him from being torn up by the bear. His right leg was broken by his horse and he sustained a couple broken ribs and a dozen bad cuts and scratches, but he was alive. A place for him was set-up in the big wagon to use until he could once more ride again. But everyone was relieved he had made it.

Andy Salcedo and Brady Williams were given the assignment to skin the bear and clean the bear skin for a rug. JW wasn't sure, but he wasn't going to leave such a valuable bear skin out here in the desert to rot. Bear meat needed to season for a couple days, but a lot of Rangers didn't cotton to bear. But they all knew the Indians held great respect for the silver-backed Grizzly in making trades.

The next morning, Liam had the chow line to run and JW noticed how down in the mouth his little brother was acting. So, after breakfast he took him for a walk and asked what the problem was and it was what he had expected. "Captain, I nearly got Chad killed and we lost four horses. You nearly lost Cochise and my Percherons almost became dinner for that monster. I should'a acted sooner."

"Have you ever seen a Grizzly in the wild before?" JW asked him.

"No, Sir…saw a Black Bear up on a hill top one time, but it just sat there and watched us go by."

"Could you see the bear out there in the dark?"

"No, Sir," he replied in a solemn voice.

"Did your orders as a guard allow you to leave the encampment to wander off to check out every strange sound?"

"No, Sir."

"You did precisely what you were supposed to do. Now a more experienced bear hunter might've known right away what was out there. After you described the sounds and actions of the horses I hazarded a guess and I was right. But had you gone out there, you'd be dead and we wouldn't have been warned. Grizzly is famous for coming out of the dark, quick and silent to make a kill. A lot of people call them Satan's beast or just Satan for being the devil from Hell.

"You heard Chad and he's got a lot of desert experience. Everyone did their job last night and stood their ground. No one panicked, not even you. If you hadn't given us a warning, there is no telling how many of us and our mounts would've been killed or wounded badly. Yuh did good kid."

"Thanks, JW that really means a whole lot to me to hear you say that."

That evening after chow a Rangers ceremony was conducted and two necklaces of bear claws were handed out. The first set from the two frontal paws to Liam for giving the initial warning and the second rear set to Chad Leaders for screaming out the Grizzly had arrived. It made for laughter all around, but both men were proud to be wearing the leather stringed necklaces. The remains of the skull and jaw bone were stored in the small wagon. When they got to where they were headed, the bone fragments would be placed in the dirt for the bugs to clean. After a year, the bone would be dug back up and made into pieces for knife hilts, for the Ranger's Bowies. But only for the men who were present that night.

MOVE ON TO BISBEE, ARIZONA, NORTH OF THE MEXICAN BORDER

Because of the Civil War, the Rangers had not been down near the border town of Bisbee for nearly five years. Since Bret Sampson had not shown up, he was not sure what had happened to him and the messengers he had sent. But if the messengers got through, then Bret knew that if he could not find JW in Benson, he was to move south to Bisbee.

Bisbee was well known as a bandit haven where stolen cattle was brought to be moved across the border either into Mexico or stolen Mexican steers moved into the US of A. There was also Naco, a smaller, sort of an armpit of an outlaw's last stop before leaving the United States, while on the run. A lot of wanted cowboys died in these two communities from knife and gunfights. Even with all the criminal activity on both sides of the border, the Mexican Border Police and Mexican Army never seemed to be around. But the United States Army also failed to make a showing, preferring to stay in Benson and Tucson. This left the American ranchers and farms helpless to raids by the larger groups of bandits, banditos and Comancheros

On the way to Bisbee the Rangers encountered two banditos gangs, who were greatly surprised to see any form of law enforcement in southeast Arizona Territory. Some of them recognized Captain Blake and others. The two groups had independently struck two ranches. Both had previously been hit a year earlier and workers murdered and cattle stolen. During the recent attack, they had attempted to steal over 100 head of cattle, some horses, raped a few women and murdered half-a-dozen workers and family members at each location for those who had put up a fight and wounded three of the banditos. One at the first ranch and two at the second one. The first gang, caught in an ambush as they attempt to leave the farm numbered 14 Banditos. The second gang was caught at the ranch, in the process of carrying out their crimes with apparent little concern for any interruption by US law enforcement butting in. Six Banditos were killed right away in a quick gunfight, with Brady Williams, the only Ranger receiving an arm wound.

At both locations JW conducted thorough interrogations of the Mexican Banditos. He noticed how some of them were wearing highly decorative sombreros with gilded gold thread and thick rope-like silver colored thread, which were made by gifted craftsmen in Mexico City. So, with some added pressure, he had learned these men with the fancy hats had been in Mexico City, after a run around mid-Arizona to fulfill specific orders for a slave trader. The men involved were now only semi-conscious when James pulled him out of the room. "You'll kill 'em, Capt., an' you'll not fin' anythin' out. You've beaten 'em wit'in an inch of deir life. We still need ah bit more an' den we cun hang dem for what dey done here an' to our homes in Globe. Now, you let me finish, while you cool off. Okay?

JW couldn't reply, he was bloody, though none of it was his and sweaty, but he placed his hand on James' left shoulder, patted it and then walked outside. He walked over to a troth to where he found some of the prisoners and for the first time he noticed how young some of them were. He also noticed their hats were flat brimmed cowhide hats and their cartridge belts were made of simple leather design.

"Where's their pistols," JW asked Lawrence Coon.

"Over there in a pile, unloaded. Pieces of junk, nothing like we took off those you got in there."

After one more look at the prisoners he went over to where the pile of weapons lay and checked them over. He saw that Coon was right, half of these wouldn't even fire. Two of the cylinders wouldn't rotate and one had a broken firing pin.

"How many of them had rifles?" JW asked.

"None of these. Only ones with decent weapons were the ones we killed in the gun battle and those in with James right now. These are just cannon fodder, used to help the older ones make an escape. But we literally caught them with their pants down."

Yeah, some women paid for that, Lawrence, don't jest about it."

"I'm sorry, boss, just unwinding."

"Yeah, I know, we get pretty tight at times. But I want to have a chat with them."

"They're all yours." Coon backed up as JW approached them, but he kept his Winchester ready.

JW gave the young men a hard eye, trying to figure out why kids this age would end up riding with Banditos — stealing cattle, murdering and raping. But it appears, maybe so far none of these kids had made the move into the serious side of the job. They were being used as throwaways, to show larger numbers as they rode up to instill fear.

He switched back over to his Mexican and asked who had made the trip to Globe last year to bring back White Americans for slaves to rich Spanish people in Mexico City. They all shook their heads, finally one said how this was the first year they had gone out with the leader and have seen their mothers and their Priest would not allow them to have confession if they were to learn of this. But they were lost, they didn't know what to do.

JW asked them and watched their eyes, concerning the murders and the rapes, to which they each replied they killed no one and they were kept from the women folk. But rape in the eyes of God, they would rather die than have their mother learn of such a thing. He could see how frightened they were, but not of him, but of God. He had to force himself to keep from smiling, knowing these boys were just sprouts caught up in a poor situation. But he would remedy that.

Speaking Spanish, he asked another question. "How many of you are from Naco?" Two men nodded their response. "Have you ever been there when your gang leader has brought white women, young white girls through Naco and stopped for a night to rest?"

One man replied. "I have seen this happen for three years as they stop at my mother's farm to give his prisoners water and food. Four or five…sometimes seven…women and girls, but no men. Last year, there were nine young girls, all of them crying and if they did not stop a small fire was built. A piece of smoldering wood was brought very close to the bottom of their feet until they screamed and stopped crying. A couple of the men speak good American."

"Did you ever hear the name Jessie used?"

"No, Sir. No names,"

"Did they cross the border at Naco?"

"No, I do not think so, I often hear the men speaking of going to Nogales. Something always special there. We was going to Nogales after these raids, but now we go to jail or be hung."

"Someone's going to be hung. But talk around with your friends and see if anyone can remember a destination in Mexico for these slaves. It's important to Arizona."

"Are you Federal soldiers, or Federal Marshals?" the boy asked.

JW grinned, "No, we are Arizona Territorial Rangers and we're here to stay."

"They tell us Rangers all gone, no more law in Arizona."

"Well, you know better now don't you," JW said and he walked away. He could hear his young prisoner tell the others these are Arizona Rangers and a state of awe came over the young ones. They had grown up on tales of the Rangers and now to meet them, but they also knew they must pay for what they had done and repent their sins before the Lord. If they were to survive this they would have to ride home and face their mothers and the town Priest, and some of them wondered if hanging might be easier.

James came outside, his knuckles bloody and face splattered with blood from the men he had questioned. He took a seat under a tree beside JW and accepted a canteen. "I think we are getting too old for all this," JW said.

"Speak for yuh self, ah'm good fur 20 or 30 more days at least." He tried to grin, but failed.

"What did you learn?"

James shook his head, "These some hard men, but dey blame everyt'ing on thu kids. No guts for 'ceptin' blame ta save dese kids from thu rope, but hard. But I did learn dey take thu prisoners over to Nogales an' hold 'em dere 'til dey met by slave traders from Mexico City. But one man, he tells me thu best of thu Anglo- children, dey are transferred on board big ships. He t'inks back ta Spain, or even thu Spanish Islands down below Florida."

"Shoot the one who gave you that information and we'll hang the rest. Have the kids' watch, so they can see what awaits them, then send them home. Give them each a $20 gold piece to give to their mothers and warn them, we'll be passing through their community and that money had better have been given to their moms or I will hang the lot of them."

James went into the large ranch room where the prisoners were collapsed and quickly shot the one prisoner as he was ordered. He knew it was a less harsh execution over being hung. He then had five of the locals, with Ranger help drag the semi-conscious banditos out to a large dead tree. The banditos, with hands tied behind them, were set backwards in their saddles and ropes secured to their necks by James and Andy Salcedo. There was no priest handy, so Preacher Joe said a short prayer over them, as a whole. The Rangers watched as the locals all crossed themselves as Catholics would. But before the horses were whipped with short ropes to speed them away, JW had Rangers dump a gallon of cold well water into each of the banditos faces to wake them up. JW had the men mounted backwards, so they could see the locals they had robbed, hurt and violated and the rope whips coming down to drive the horses forward. And they screamed.

He had men or strong heavy-set women behind each of the boys to make sure they were unable to turn their faces away as then men dropped from their horses, necks snapped and the effects of hanging to the human facial features became visible; eyes bulging out, tongues forced out and face turned a flaming red as blood swelled up into the cheeks and ears from the arteries being choked off. For those who did not die right off from a broken neck, the suffering was tortuous to view, but JW made the boys see it all. He had a point to prove, that bandit work was not a healthy lifestyle and he wanted them to view the final ending for these desert coyotes.

When it was all over, the boys bury them, before JW sent them on their way. Each boy had his horse and a $20 gold piece, but no firearms. Before they left, the boys went up to Preacher Joe and asked for a prayer for safe traveling and he blessed them all and a change in their lives. And to the surprised of the locals, the boys held their hats in front of them, against their upper chests, and asked forgiveness, which was granted. They had all been told the boys had no dealing with the sins committed by the old Banditos, except guard the horses and cattle.

The last thing they did was offer their hands of gratefulness to JW, who shook each of their hands and in Spanish, he told them his 12-year old daughter was kidnapped and he would be coming to Mexico to find her. If they heard of anything, her name was Jesse Blake.

"Then you be the legendary General Blake?" One of them asked.

"Only a captain, young man, but I've been around for a long time. Now be good to your mothers and get going!" He gestured over their heads toward the south and they rode off.

"Then you be the legendary General Blake?" Liam started laughing.

JW shot his adoptive brother a hard glare, "I guess it is time you pulled some scout, maybe all by yourself!"

"Aw, c'mon, Captain, it was funny. You've got your own hero worshippers now...You're bigger than Wyatt Earp up in Dodge City."

"Earp is a marshal and a fast draw. Sooner or later he's gonna be gunned down by some 16-year old kids with lightning reflexes out to earn a name. Two years later, that kid will go down in a hail of bullets by another 16-year old. Nope, I'd rather be slow and known for Rangering duties, even if it isn't authorized."

John Gibson walked up and asked, "Since we is unauthorized, how about us getting some of those fancy badges like those Federal Marshals cart around."

Before JW could respond, Jim Williams popped off, "We don't need no stinkin' badges!"

A lot of the Rangers were nodding their agreement and then JW answered, "Badges give the other guy something to aim at. Maybe someday, but not now. Besides you guys didn't think too highly of those tin badges they were showing off. If we do ever get a badge it'll be a homemade job, simple and easy to make."

"Chad Leaders was walking pretty well now, still used his mount for any travel over ten yards like most cowboys, reported that each of the young bandits had a full canteen and enough food to get them home by tomorrow night. "It's a shame though, maybe we could've used them with this outfit."

JW thought about his response for a moment and the men waited, seeing he was in deep thought and then he replied, "I'm not saying this to sound all anti-racial, that isn't the point here, but I want the Arizona Rangers to be citizens or those seeking to be citizens of the United States. Now if those youngsters come across, seeking us out and demonstrate a desire to become members of the US of A, and a note from their mother, I'll take them on for menial duties and we'll train them. I would like to find a location and build a secret encampment, where the Union boys and these Federal Marshals cannot find us. But I doubt they'll be working the Southeast Arizona Territory for some time. No, we'll continue with our jobs and accept our pay from what we were blessed with. I simply wish we could get another squad of cavalry at least. But without any reports on Lt. Sampson, we'll have to carry on without him.

"Where to now, Captain?" Chad Leaders asked.

JW looked about the ranch and decided it was time to go before they ate up all their stores. They would leave behind a 100 pounds of beans and a 100 pounds of flour. They also had the weapons and fancy clothes they can sell in town. Soon word would spread that Captain Blake had returned with his Arizona Rangers and they had just hung nine Banditos.

"Let's head east, over to a wagon road the Mexicans use for coming into the USA. When we reach it, we'll either come across a stick in the road they had planned to name McNeal or we'll be closer to the border town of Douglas. McNeal used to be nothing more than a bar-trading post and a few desert cabins." He looked over at James and asked him, "You remember that place, right?"

"Dat thu poison palace dat blinded me for two days?"

"Yup, that's the one. We were new Rangers back then, made some stupid mistakes. My gut hurt for a week. We learned they made their whiskey with rattlesnake venom. Both of us wanted to go back and kill the owner, but the sergeant said it was a learning experience. A couple months later, he was killed by the Yaqui Apache and I was made a Captain due to my prior Union Army rank. Mr. Dreeke here refused his previous rank of Lieutenant and continued to babysit me. Turns out our grandma here was worried about getting promoted to Captain and sent elsewhere in the territory. Back then we had more Ranger Companies; A, B and C, all led by a Captain and the Colonel worked out of Austin.

"Now Douglas, that's another outlaw border town, with half-a-dozen bars, gaming joints and two or three of those palaces of sinful pleasures. Now I wouldn't trust the booze, the women and be wary of the men who hate strangers. But one night in either place, depending on where we come out of the desert and then we head north for a building community of Pearce. Could be dead too, depending on the Apache Nation. But if it's there, it might be more civilized than the border towns. But I want to camp north of town, up in the rocks. Plus, we avoid trouble in all the towns right now. But we will become involved if we come across settlers, wagon trains, farms and mines under attack by anyone, using military tactics.

"I'm thinking about us obtaining some Yankee uniforms, which might help us work easier and enter these towns. A Special Unit assigned to whatever Army is handling the Southern Territories of the US of A. We're out here to make contact with the various Indian tribes and deal with the bandit problem."

"Sir," Brady Williams asked, "are we moving north to that new wagon road running between Wilcox and Tucson?"

"Eventually we will be using it. Why?" JW asked.

"There's some high hills north of the wagon trail you might find suitable for our new Ranger Station. I went through there on a special assignment for you, just prior to us being made civilians and we left for the war."

"What was that assignment?" JW asked.

"Me and John," he was pointing to Gibson, were keeping an eye on a special stage coach making the long route on the old roads. Wagon trains are coming in on them if they're entering Arizona to the south and hittin' the north part of the road, going to Globe, if they entered Arizona to the north. You know they all eventually head south because of the Colorado River and Grand Canyon."

"If'in we ev'a find a way ta bypass dat Apache fortress, we cun build some big cities up dere to thu north, way up dere above dat place dey want ta build Camp Verde," James added into the conversation.

"Okay, enough hopes an' dreams, when we gets everyone back, let's move." JW ordered.

"Captain, you know what I'd like ta buy before we engage the Apache again?"

"No, Liam, what would you like to buy before we engage the Apache?"

Liam's face opened with a big smile and he replied, "I'd like to get one of those new Gatling Guns we went up against at the end of the war. Can you imagine what that kind of fire power would have against the Indians, or facing large numbers of banditos…or those Comancheros?"

JW was thinking about his daughter and what exactly he could do to find her, not knowing where she could possibly be. He figured with her being such a cute little thing she was probably kept for the Spanish, but was she in Mexico City, Spain or Cuba.

"Did you hear me, Captain?"

JW didn't respond at first, so Liam began to back away, when JW's mind returned to the now and he replied, "A Gatlin Gun? Where are we going to get one of those?"

"I figured that if you'd agree, we give that little assignment to MSgt. Gary Wells and Preacher Joe. Those two have an art for scrounging and might jus' find one of those Gatlin's down south of the border. The South captured a few of them toward the end of the war from what we heard in prison camp and I am betting they sold them off across the border, rather than hand them over to the Yankees. A lot of our people needed traveling money to escape the south and all this northerner persecution."

JW stared at Liam for a brief-moment and then replied with a remark that caught Liam off balance. "Liam, I always hoped my son would grow up to have your education…For a Southerner you sound as if you just walked off one of those fancy northern colleges."

Liam dropped his head and whispered, "I'm sorry to have reminded you of your son, Captain. It was not my intention."

But when Liam looked back up, he saw a grateful grin on JW's face. "Liam, I think of my Sherry Ann, Steven and Jessie every single day. I continue to pray for my Jessie and that someday we will find her, but until then we have a duty to defend the people of Southeast Arizona from the renegade Indians, Bandits and Comancheros. And if locating one of those Gatlin Guns will help, then we'll turn MSgt. Wells and Preacher Joe loose on the border towns. But I'm sending Holloway behind them…just as a backup. This will give Lt. Sampson a few extra days to meet up with us."

"Where are we goin' to hold up, Capt?" Brady Williams asked.

"I plan to move our unit, what's left of us, up north…Take up a position in the Texas Canyon, within eyeshot of the New Mexico to Tucson wagon trail. Stage coaches are using it now and I imagine someday it will become a real road. But I want word to go out among the former Arizona Rangers that we're down here and in need of volunteers and supplies. Our purpose is to protect the Arizona settlers, their ranches and farms."

"Sure, sounds good to us, Sir, especially the supplies part. Food will be running short real soon and I don't know about the others, but all these desert critters begin to taste the same," Liam added.

"Don't fret, I'm sure we can get one of these ranchers to donate us a steer before you all start starving to death. They know were out here and why, and they appreciate any help we can give them. Since we've been gone, they've been losing over 1,000 head a year over the border, which has put the smaller rancher's right out of business and that, was before the carpet-baggers even hit.

IN THE WEEK TO FOLLOW

Set up on the ridgeline on the northeast rim of Texas Canyon, out of rifle shot range of the wagon trail, but still within visual range, the Ranger kept an eye out for the Rangers returning from Mexico and Lt. Sampson returning from Tucson with volunteers. Two-hands from the Big A ranch brought over a 1,000 pound long horn for them to have for rations and water was no problem.

Late in the week, Holloway led a flatbed wagon, driven by Preacher Joe, with a long sturdy box and two extra wagon wheels strapped down on top. On each side of the box were two medium size boxes wired shut. Then MSgt. Wells came riding up behind, pulling Preacher Joe's horse.

They were met by Jim Williams, who led them to the trail, but the wagon was too wide to make it to the top. So, Chad Leaders and Liam came down to help, bringing a lengthy sturdy rope tided to the back of a tall black Percheron, that scraped the sides of the rocks as it made its way down the rocky trail.

It took all five men to unload the Gatlin Gun, which was only semi-used during one of the last battles of the Civil War—according the arms dealer in Nogales, who had cousins in Mexico. The weapon was brought across the border after the gold was exchanged, along with extra coin for 1,000 rounds of ammo—500 rounds per box. The wagon wheels that supported the weapon were added for free, in hopes of future arms trade. MSgt. Wells told the Mexicans they were dealing with a new band of Comancheros. He knew the three of them would have been gunned down had there been any suspicion that the three of them were law enforcement officers.

The trip back had been wearisome and they were all hungry, but the weapon still needed to be lifted up to the rim and for this task a block and tackle needed to be built on top the wagon and another up on the rim. With this, the two draft horses used to bring the weapon up from Mexico, in which wagon and horses had cost dearly, along with the much stronger

Percheron in the lead, pulled the boxes up. First the gun and then the ammo and wheels, but after five hours of drudgery the weapon now set on the wheels in the middle of their small plateau for all to admire. Preacher Joe had taken a somewhat brief familiarization course on putting the weapon together and firing it. He had put 100 rounds through it and was extremely impressed.

Each man was shown the basic needs for loading and unloading, firing 20 rounds and assisting Preacher Joe as an Assistant Gunner if called upon. The Gatlin would be taken off its wheels and hidden in the supply wagon and the wheels attached to the sides to appear as extra wagon wheels for the supply wagon or water wagon.

"Now just so everyone understands me...I never plan to use this weapon or any of our weapons against U.S. forces. The war is over and though we may be looked upon as renegades, I do not wish to have the people of Arizona see us as treasonous raiders. We are here to protect the Southerners, as we swore to do when we went to war. Our enemy is the banditos, the Comancheros and those renegade Indians on the warpath. As we all know, there are a lot of peaceful Indians out there and the citizens of this country must learn to live with them, to bring them on board to become citizens." JW stopped to glance about, looked in the eyes of the men listening to him.

"Now I know all of you, but people change. We're working without pay to help our territory grow. We'll survive on what food the locals will bring us or the money we make from the horses and guns we sell from the battles we have with Arizona's enemies. Is there anyone who needs to leave, you may leave now with all our respect and thanks."

No one left. These men had nothing to go home to and still looked forward to the day they could see this corrupt federal territory government be brought down for its corruption in illegally collecting war taxes to break the backs of Southern settlers so Northerners from the east could buy them at exceedingly cheap prices, or buy steers at 20 cents a pound and sell them at $10 on the market in Kansas City. Thousands of Southern families that had made their home in Arizona long before the Civil War had lost their livelihood and their children's future turned dark and bleak.

Then on the sixth day of occupying the plateau, JW was awakened by Liam with a report of a good-sized force of horsemen riding east along the roadway. Two men were out front on scout, two men were acting as flankers, and two riders were riding as tail behind the main body.

Liam brought JW his binoculars, as he finished climbing up upon a large rock. This gave him the best view of Texas Canyon south and across the well-traveled dirt road. The horsemen were now moving to the right, off the road, to give room for a small wagon train of 18 wagons on its way to Tucson. And those wagons made it hard for JW to focus on the front riders to see if it was Lt. Bret Sampson. He could see the riders were all in civilian clothes, so he knew this wasn't an Army Unit, unless the Army was going out into the field in civilian clothes on a job to trick the Indians. But riding military fashion had already given them away. Still, Rangers always rode this way and they used this fashion to intimidate the enemy.

JW pulled out his four-inch by four inch signal mirror and began flashing it at the position of the lead party. Fortunately, a young boy in the back of a wagon was watching the bluff for Indians and saw the flashes and he pointed it out to the riders, "Look, Indians!"

Sampson read the message and said to the boy, "No, boy, that's part of our outfit. We wondered where they had moved off too. Thanks for spotting them for us." Sampson gave the young boy a casual salute and led his unit forward until they reached a dry spring bed and turned to the north. "We're camping tonight, Boys!"

Once again it was Liam who went to the bottom of the ridge trail to find the new fighting force and he was so happy to meet up with Bret. Boy, young man, and a weary-eyed soldier hugged one another, slapped each on the back and Liam led the way up. As each rider came upon the plateau, the original unit was stunned by the number of new recruits Lt. Sampson had brought with him. As it turned out, these new recruits were former members of the Tucson Rangers, or their younger brothers and even a few of them were the oldest sons of Rangers lost in the Civil War, but were now 18 years old.

"We heard what happened up at Globe, and it was nearly ready to become a real city. Well, same thing happened in Tucson and the valley all around it. Federal Revenuers came in with this new war tax and wiped out farms and ranches. Only a few real large settlements could keep going but they had partners in the north. All the law enforcement officers were fired and these federal men put in their place. The U.S. Cavalry supports them, but a lot of the officers don't like what they're doing and some have refused. But rather than risk the publicity of a court martial they're reassigned to Montana to work against the Sioux. I've heard the Sioux are pretty unhappy up there, right now," Bret Sampson said, as he sat around a small fire with JW, Dreeke, Liam and MSgt. Wells.

"With the men you've brought us, we've got two full companies of Rangers…A and B Companies…Sixteen men per company. I can't believe our good fortune. You really did well, Bret."

"Thank you, Sir. But I can't take the credit. Word is simply spreading about what your intentions are. But the U.S. Cavalry has also picked up on it. There are reward posters out for information concerning you. Right now, it's only $100, but it will grow with time. You need to watch out for who comes along...We could end up with a Yankee spy."

THE FIRST MEETING FOR THE "NEW RANGERS" COMPANIES "A" AND "B"

Making breakfast for 32 men was an ordeal and it involved five volunteers, but each man was required to handle his own horse. JW planned to send Company A out today, which was made up of mostly of the old group, but they had the most rest. Still, Company B would be required to provide a four-man guard posting and two men posted with the Gatlin Gun. Last night the men of B Company and those of A Company unfamiliar with the Gatlin were given the course. In the process, they frightened off a scout of three Apache who had been checking out the fires a top the ridge line. With such firepower, they were not sure of how to report it to their war chief, but they knew there was no way any brave would survive going up against such a lethal weapon.

Two men were also to keep a look out over the roadway below, to report any problems observed to Lt. Sampson and let him decided if Company B should respond to give aide.

"I'll make this meeting short," Captain JW Blake said in loud harsh words. "I am the commander here. Lt. Sampson is my Second-in-Command and Commander of B-Company. My Second in Command of A Company is Lt. James Dreeke, who is also third in line for command of this unit. MSgt. Wells and MSgt. Michaels are A and B Company First Sergeants and you will see them before moving up your chain-of-command.

"So you see, we continue to run this unit as a military command, it help make things work easier. Now if you are having troubles, even with another man or officer, you may talk with me directly, but use the chain of command. If the NCO or officer fails to move you along, he will no longer hold this position and they know this. Now there will be times when you may talk to me directly and you will be notified of these times in advance. I hope to have these once a week. We will also hold BS sessions around the fires, but this is for general complaints and not private ones. A general complaint is one that concerns our direction, our problems, chow, safety and work load, while individual complaint is against a person, or your problem with the unit.

"Now each A and B Company will be made up of 16 riders, which is much like the number of riders before the war, except we had a C Company, and though I commanded all the Rangers in the Arizona Territory as the only Captain, C Company was my baby up at Globe township. We were not fully developed yet, but Globe was rapidly growing into a good-sized city.

"Now we have no administration support behind us, but we do have the people. We will patrol the wagon trail road all the way to New Mexico border and making a stop in at Fort Bowie for supplies and water. We'll be going right through the land of the Chiricahua Apache, one of the best guerilla fighters in the world. But be wary of all the Apache, they are a fearsome fighter and born to the horse. If you are forced to fight them, never assume your opponent is dead. They will often play dead and then kill you. Make sure he is dead before you approach him.

"You are to travel north for as far as there are settlements to ensure they remain safe. Lt. Sampson has maps and compass and he understands that you are not to go north of the west of Tucson. Those areas are patrolled by the U.S. Army. When we begin seeing the U.S. Army patrolling the roadway below, we will move further east. For now, the Gatlin Gun will remain up here with a security force of four men to support our retreat if needed. We have also built a back way, but right now it's covered in rocks until we need to use it. Now any questions?"

A new man held up his hand and he was acknowledged by JW with a hand gesture, "Sir, what do we tell people if we are asked who we are?"

"Tell 'em the truth, you're New Arizona Rangers. But if they ask us if we have anything to deal with the federal government ruling the state, you tell 'em we're here to uproot this new evil that has attacked our country from within and toss the corrupt politicians and these foul carpetbaggers out on their ears and to spread the word we're back."

The men all applauded to this, which stirred the blood in JW's system…He was ready to ride now.

CHAPTER FOURTEEN

"Castles In The Sky"

SULPHUR SPRING VALLEY, ARIZONA TERRITORY, SWISS HELEM MOUNTAINS, 7,185 FEET

Eight days later, B Company helped two broken down wagon-loads of Italian immigrant settlers put one wagon together for their long journey to West Arizona. They planned to grow date palms. The people would walk, while the baby palms would ride crowded together in the one wagon. They had left the Texas sea docks in Galveston aboard eight wagons, with guides, but Comanche had reduced their numbers to two packed wagons, 14 people afoot and four men mounted. They had tried to hook up with a long wagon train en route to California, but they were unable to keep up and eventually the weight in the two wagons became just too great. When Lt. Sampson found the party, they were just off the wagon road and had been encamped for the last nine days.

Though there were farmers and cooks aboard and a few hunters, there were no carpenters. The elder of the group would not allow one or two of the horsemen to ride off for help, for fear he would be killed by the Indians. They decided to wait for a wagon train, but were greatly dismayed when Lt. Sampson advised them the next train could be more than two weeks away.

"Most of the wagon trains are taking the northern road into Arizona to avoid the Apache. Your guides displayed little experience for Indian fighting and paid dearly for it. Your Comanche roadway leads right into the Chiricahua Apache and they're considered just about the worst of the Apache tribes," Lt. Sampson said.

MSgt. Michaels walked up right then, "Zebulan and Foster say they can fix it, but it will leave 'em with only one wagon. They have to use the parts off one to get the other rolling. But we should get them moving by tomorrow."

"Really!?" The elder asked in wonder.

"Seems so, those two were carpenters back in Tucson before the war. They know what they're doing," Lt. Sampson replied and then slowly rode off to get his guards posted. He sent a three-man scout out and they found enough Indian signs to keep him worried and to have his guards posted in doubles and their horses brought in to keep them close by.

Once the immigrants were mingled in amongst a lengthy wagon train, they were on their way to Tucson. From there they would locate a settler's train en-route to Northwest Arizona. They had bought their land grants in Galveston at prices nearly three times the value of what they were worth before the war. They were also going to be billed taxes on this property. Lt. Sampson was happy to see they were not bringing a herd of beasts with them, for he knew the new war tax for each steer and cow may have broken them.

It was two weeks later when B Company was riding deep into the Sulphur Spring Valley, attempting to locate an old cattle ranch known to run over 800 head of cattle. Before the war there were 22 hands and a family of five on the River Wire Ranch. But no one had heard anything from the ranch since the third year of the war.

The first sign something was wrong was when Daniel Boon, distant relative to the historic character, came upon two skeletons lying in the trail. An hour later, Boon and his added scout of Tariq Striker, entered the valley that opened into the ranch area. It was hard for both men, for they knew a massacre had occurred here within the last couple of years. There were a dozen skeletons left laid out on the ranch yard, their firearms all gone. All the animals were stolen and they knew this also meant the herds out on the back country.

Tariq agreed to ride back for the Lieutenant, while Daniel entered the ranch house. From what he could see, the Indians or raiders had hit hard and fast during the night. Husband and wife were killed in bed, along with the older two children. But he searched and searched and could not find the third child, a daughter, who was said to be less than nine years old. The Ranger now suspected either she was taken by the Apache for slavery or to eventually become a wife, or taken by the Comancheros for white slavery. But by the shape the skeletons were in, they had been and gone too long ago.

When Lt. Sampson and the others arrived, a secondary search was made for the girl's skeleton and none was found. They knew it was possible she was small enough to have been carried off by a bear, but it was the not knowing that created knots in their stomachs. Three men were found in their bunks and each one had had their throats severed. But they were not mutilated. Had this been Indians, the bodies of the men and woman would've been terribly mutilated — even to the bone. Sampson also noticed another thing. Of the reported 22 ranch hands, only 20 skeletons were found. Two skeletons were missing.

MSgt. Michaels walked up to Sampson and verified the count, "Twenty ranch hands and four family members, Sir. I've also found that all 22 beds in the bunk house have been used. Our Secondary search for the little girl's body did not turn up another two ranch hand bodies. Those two men are missing.

"I've double checked the bodies and I've found bullet nicks and holes on all the bodies, accept for the three in the bunk house, which is leading me to believe two of these ranch hands might have been involved in this attack. Unfortunately, the Rancher hired a couple Comancheros, who silently killed these three men and then possibly rode out to relieve the rode guards. At the right moment, the both stuck knives in their backs and signaled their comrades to come on in. The ranch hands never had a chance. It was probably the two pretenders who ran into the house to warn the family and then shot four of them. After that, they had all the time in the world to loot the Ranch and steal all their cattle."

"Get a mass grave dug for the ranch hands and a separate large grave dug for the family. We need to bury them all before we leave and stop by Fort Bowie to report all this. We need to get a report out on this little girl and I'll search around to see if I can find a photo of her, possibly some address to family members. This ranch should be passed on to someone, even without the cattle."

A high-powered rifle shot struck the ground right between Sampson and Michaels, and neither man knew exactly where it was fired from. But both dived for cover just before a second shot struck the water trough inches from Sampson's head. Had there been water in it, he would be receiving a shower right now.

"Whoever's doing the shooting is dang good!" Jordan Akers yelled to be heard by all, and the shooter must've heard him because they put a bullet two inches from the toe of his left boot.

"Keep your mouth shut, Akers, before they put one between your teeth," Michaels shouted.

Lt. Sampson realized that with such fancy shooting, that whoever was doing it could've killed a third of his force by now. But they chose not to. So, taking in a deep breath and slowly exhaling it, he stood to his feet and raised both of his hands. "I don't know who you are, but we are the Arizona Rangers. We came out here to investigate why no one has heard from this family for over two years. No one new about these killings and we are about to bury the Ranch hands and the family. You can come down and watch, or help us and maybe tell us what happened. But we suspect Comancheros were involved and possibly two of the workers were part of the plan. So, please stop shooting because you are terrifying my men."

There were no more shots and he had his Rangers continued with their work. Suddenly, Ranger Mark White, who was working security, shouted toward the ranch, "We have one coming in and she is still armed. Young female, very frightened."

Lt. Sampson was called out of the house and he slowly walked toward the 12 to 13-year old girl, who was armed with a Sharps 30. Caliber Rifle and carried a leather pouch over her right shoulder for her ammo and powder, and a water bladder over her left shoulder. A homemade leather belt sheath held a knife and an old trade tomahawk, with ancient feathers tied to it.

"Miss, I am Lieutenant Sampson and I command B Company of the Arizona Rangers. We have just reorganized following the end of the Civil War. From what I have seen here, you may not be aware that the Northern forces have defeated the South and we are attempting to rebuild the Union. Now would you answer a question for me, please? Are you the young daughter of this ranch...a Miss Kathleen Legends?"

She didn't answer right away, but her eyes began to water up and then she saw four blankets being carefully carried out of the house and she knew this was her father, mother, older brother and much older sister. Now she broke, dropped to her knees and began wailing. It was then that she let go of the rifle. Michaels caught it before it could strike the ground. It was a good thing because the rifle was loaded and charged and would've gone off upon striking the ground.

Lt. Sampson knelt to the ground to comfort her, but she instantly whipped out knife in her right hand and took up an aggressive position from her knees. Her blue eyes glared into Sampson's face, with a look of utter hatred and not an ounce of fear.

"Kathleen, I am not going to hurt you. I was only offering you my arm as a way to help you handle your grief. I did not mean to scare you, or wish to hurt you in any way. No one will ever hurt you ever again. You are now under the protection of the Rangers. Do you understand this? You will not be alone out here. You will not be hurt. You will be coming with us so we can help find other family members. We also hope you'll be able to help us find the men who did this, so we can punish them. So, please try to understand me. You are safe here."

Her glare softened and a moment later, she sheathed her knife. She then tried to speak, but it had been two years since she had spoken a word or sung one of her songs. "This will take you time, Kathleen, you need not hurry. But are you able to go back into your house to help me locate important papers?"

It took her a moment, but she followed Sampson in to her father's business office. She had spent a lot of time in there, helping her father file papers alphabetically in the big cabinets. She also remembered where his hidden safe was, which was missed by the thieves. It wasn't in his office. He only kept his locked files there. But his important papers, cash and deeds and water rights, were kept in a large floor safe under his wife's dresser, hidden beneath a pile of Japanese decorative boxes he had brought back to Arizona from San Francisco 12 years prior to the attack. Because he was beginning to lose his memory from growing old, he kept the combination for the floor safe in a file folder, mixed with other random numbers that only the family would be able to separate from a normal bank transaction report. Thankfully, even Kathleen knew the combination and all the valuables were removed and placed into a locked metal box. Both keys to the heavy metal lock were given to Kathleen. A single wagon was found on the ranch and two of the Ranger's horses were assigned pulling duty. One man would drive the wagon and the other would ride on back with a rifle pulling guard duty.

Over time, while they reviewed the documents and counted the funds from inside the hidden safe, Sampson learned of how Kathleen had escaped the Comancheros. She did verify these were in fact the raiders and estimated their numbers in the excess of 40 riders. She was awake when the attack came and was up on the roof of the ranch house, where she often went to view the "Castles in the Sky". She explained how these were the rugged mountain tops of the Swiss Helm Mountains. Her father had once told her the tallest peaks reached 7,185 feet and to her these were where the ancient gods of the Norsemen — Vikings — had lived. He would read to her tales of Odin, of Thor and the mischievous Loki. He had told her how the Norsemen had once come to this western world of ours and sailed up the great Mississippi River.

It took her long moments to relearn her words but the more she talked the easier it came and soon she was speaking like a nine to ten-year old and before they were finished her tone was clear.

"I was up on the roof top, dreaming of my castles and how someday Thor would come for me. But then she heard a commotion and looked to the road to see a large group of riders come charging. Gunfire all around, everyone shooting. I watched as two of our workers ran inside the house and I heard more shooting in the bedrooms. Now I was scared…scared! I had no gun, but my father, he teach me how to shoot real good."

"Calm down, Kathleen, your use of words is becoming bungled up again. Take a drink of water and then we'll continue. There is no hurry," Sampson said. He knew reliving the incident, even two years ago, was causing her problems.

"I hide behind a smoke stack. They cannot see me. Soon they kill all my people, but we kill some of theirs, too. They take what they want, but I know they can't find my dad's safe. I come down next day to make sure they left before I do. No more horses, no more cattle. Even take sheep, chickens and…my mom's prized turkeys. But they shot all the dogs, even my dogs. But they couldn't find the hidden door to the attic, in case Indians come. Up here I find three rifles, this knife old tomahawk my grandfather or his father carry in French-Indian Wars. I used rifle to shoot game, plus I know how to build fishing pole and catch a lot of catfish. I live in my Castle in the Sky and watch over land. I wait for those who hurt us to come back, but you not look the same, so I warn you to go."

"Your voice is tired. Tomorrow, I'll send some men up with you to remove whatever you have so you can take it with you. Today, you choose whatever is in the house you wish to take with you. There are still a lot of valuables here…some very nice paintings, sculptures and family photos you may want, for when you become an adult. You may or may not be returning here, unless to come back here as an adult with your family to show your children the Castles in the Sky."

She smiled at him and went about inspecting her home. The next day he was amazed to find out how many items she had removed from her Ranch house and dragged up over 6,000 feet to her fantasy home. There were fancy lamps, a tabletop Grandfather clock, expensive gold and silver frames missed by the thieves because they were in the hidden attic. Lt. Sampson couldn't wait to tell this tale to JW, but it ended up being more of a show & tell afternoon.

When B Company reached Fort Bowie they found it occupied by only a small force of men; a sergeant and seven enlisted men. A brand-new Lt. Colonel from Washington D.C., who had never seen a day of combat during the Civil War, had taken over command of Fort Bowie. The man had absolutely no respect for the Apache and hoped to win his Colonel's eagle by forcing the unruly Chiricahua Apache to return to their reservation. Once again, Cochise and 200 warriors had left the reservation because of treaty violations on the American side.

The Lt. Colonel had taken all but a single squad to chase down these "unruly children" and ignored all the comment made by his staff and threatened to jail most of the officers. Had Fort Bowie been a location where dependents were allowed, the Lt. Colonel would've ended up locked up, but the men followed him out, since their families were safe back at Tucson.

As for the sergeant and his squad, they had six five-pound howitzers loaded and ready to repel the enemy. One cannon was placed on each corner tower and two were sitting on the ground to be fired at anyone coming through the front gate. Beyond that, the men had all developed a keen prayer life.

Lt. Sampson knew he couldn't leave the Legend girl here and he couldn't leave his 15 Rangers here with a chance of taking on 200 Apache. There were still a lot of settlers out there and with Cochise jumping the reservation, both companies needed to be out in the field instead of one at a time. He also knew that Gatlin Gun could come in real handy against 200 Apache. He'd also wanted to get his hands around the neck of this idiotic Lt. Colonel. "Typical Northern Army, to get him some battle experience by sending him to the west to lead men against the most fearsome foe on this continent and possibly the world."

B Company got turned around and was now making 40 miles a day, to make it back to Texas Canyon before Cochise wiped out a third of Southeast Arizona. Not to mention the possible slaughter of the 200 troops of Fort Bowie.

But the soldiers of Fort Bowie never found Chief Cochise and five days later found their way back to Fort Bowie, where a frightened but thankful rifle squad was on hand to meet them. The Sergeant however, who was at the point of ready to shoot the Lt. Colonel, was hustled away by two captains and a lieutenant. It was that very evening a rider came charging in from the wagon trail, where he had left a wagon train under siege. Cochise and his 200 warriors, along with another band of some 50 warriors, had attacked a California bound wagon train with 102 wagons stretched out along the roadway. Over 30 wagons were afire when the scout rider took off for Fort Bowie, having to kill two Indians to get clear. One cattle herd and a small horse herd had been stolen and the messenger had no idea how many settlers were killed or wounded, plus children stolen.

When the Lt. Colonel was awakened, he was greatly troubled by the news and made the command decision that it would be better and safer for the troops if they left Fort Bowie in daylight hours. When it was pointed out that continual action going on meant more deaths and how word of their coming might cause the Indians to flee, he ordered his officers to prepare his troops for a morning departure. At this point, the Major had the doctor proclaim the Lt. Colonel unfit for military command and he took over as Commander of Fort Bowie. The major looked to his officers and head NCOs, "We will depart in 15 minutes for a forced drive to reach that wagon train as quickly as possible. I know the men are tired, but lives are at stake...and First Sergeant, select another rifle squad to hold the fort. Make sure the armory and powder room is set to blow, if trouble reaches here."

"Yes, Major," the First Sergeant replied.

TEXAS CANYON PLATEAU

From wagon train to pull-carts, riders to the walking immigrants with massive packs on their backs, word of the attack on the wagon train traveled west like a windswept wildfire. For over 17 hours the Apache battle waged, while the first two-thirds of the wagon train proceeded west. A lot of the men stayed behind to fight alongside their new friends as wave after wave of Apache cavalry swept in with fire arrows to burn the remaining wagons to the ground, but the settlers refused to give up their goods needed for a new future. Amongst the burning wagons were 100 pound bags of seeds and grains, most of them now smoldering and potted grape branches, apple trees and those of orange and pear that would never see California.

Telegraph lines were not available to Fort Bowie, so Fort Bowie's new Commanding Officer had no idea that three companies of U.S. Cavalry were just now being dispatched from Tucson, once a weary and saddle-sore scout and his sweat-lathered mount rode in to report the Indian attack of the wagon train. He had been doing his Paul Revere imitation all along the way and word quickly reached the plateau via Arizonians helping the Rangers. But Captain Blake knew by the time the Tucson troops arrived at the scene of the battle, the Apache would be long gone and over 30 wagons would be blackened ruin and the families all killed and scalped.

But Tucson's U.S. Cavalry Command and the troops of Fort Bowie didn't have any knowledge of the Arizona Ranger's A and B Companies, who were already now en route from the Texas Canyon Plateau. Captain Blake, leading both A and B Companies to the northeast of the wagon train road, left behind a squad escort for the Gatlin Gun, under Jim Williams' command, while the Rangers rushed ahead to reach the wagons. This powerful automatic weapon and its ammo, plus the wheels strapped down with the mount for the weapon, were being carried by the very same wagon left down at the foot of the rocky mountain trail for the rapid response to the East. The wagon would be pulled by those same two black Percheron horses, which had made the rapid decent down the rocky trail, scratching up the wheels and causing several abrasions to the hides of the horses. But these were tough giants and nothing seemed to stop them or even slow them down.

Once the Gatlin Gun was secured to the wagon, the procedure accomplished in record time, the heavy weapons detail was less than an hour behind A and B Companies.

As it stood, the men of Camp Bowie were coming in from the east of the ambush site, while the Tucson troops were rapidly responding from the west. But with the distances involved, it would take the Fort Bowie

Command to arrive first in approximately five hours from the time they hit the Tucson Wagon Train Road and the Tucson forces Yankee troops close to 22 hours from the time they departed Tucson City. Captain Blake estimated his travel time at just over five-hours and he planned to have Jim Williams and his new squad of Gatlin Gun experts take up position right on the Tucson Wagon Train Road to smash the Apache force if they attempted to further pursue the remaining wagons, as A and B Companies engaged the Indians.

While en-route to the battle scene, Captain Blake and Lt. Sampson both wondered if they had done right by the Legends girl. With this sudden situation sprung upon them, they didn't have much time to talk things over with her. All Captain Blake could do was find a local family Lt. Sampson had known from his Rangering days, who had a small homestead nearby and asked them to take custody of the girl until they got back. In doing this they picked up three more cowboy volunteer fighters to ride with them. They would also picked up an additional 11 riders willing to volunteer to fight against the Apache. Everyone knew how if the Apache were attacking a wagon train they would soon be turning on the ranches and small communities.

BATTLE FOR WAGON TRAIL ROAD

The wide valley floor where Cochise led his Chiricahua Apache against the back third of the settler's lengthy wagon train to California was now filled with dark gray and blackened plumes of acrid smoke. Less than three dozen immigrants were still capable of putting up a fight, with another 107 lying about wounded, and cared for by the womenfolk and the older children gathering up weapons and ammo for the survivors. Not a single wagon was left on its wheels, with most of them reduced to blackened ashes and small flames still present among the rubble. All the horses and cattle were either dead or stolen. There was even a couple dozen dead dogs lying about with arrows in them or they had been killed by gunfire. High up above the smoldering debris flew assorted layers of black desert vultures in widening out circular formations. All in all, this was a scene of death and survival to the last fighter.

Cochise, mounted upon his favorite brown and white pinto, looked down from a slopping ridge to the Northeast. Behind him were better than 100 Apache warriors, while beside him were his various war chiefs. It was no secret Cochise had desired a quick victory, for his people were hungry and they needed food for the winter. But now, except for the cattle and horses, all the grains and warm clothes they had hoped to seize were now burned up and he had lost nearly 100 of his warriors.

He was told the people of these wagon trains were weak, not trained in fighting and would most likely panic, leaving their wagons and animals behind to flee the Apache. But this didn't happen. They had made a stand and a brave one at that. He watched as women stood and shot down his warriors, or young teenage boys unhorse a warrior with a burning piece of wood and use a large axe to finish him off. Everyone in the family was fighting and he had never fought such people before. They were frightened, but most of these people did not panic.

Yet there were a few men, who ran, even leaving their families behind to ride off and he was happy to see his warriors shoot these dogs down. No, there were several Whites he would have escorted out alive if it had been possible for such displays of courage.

But before he could signal his last attack and then head south, away from the wagon train, a scout rushed up with a panting pony to report a large mounted force of blue coats coming this way from the east at the gallop. The scout estimated the force to be 150 to 200 troopers in size.

Cochise quickly looked about and knowing the east was now cut off, he would take his force west until he passed the next ridgeline and then quickly move south toward Mexico via a large riverbed. The rest of the wagon train was making a run for Tucson, so the road would be clear and it was doubtful anyone was coming this way from Tucson. If the Army had left the big city, it would be hours yet before they could block the Wagon Train Road off and by then they'd be close to Mexico. Going to the north was a possibility, but they would have two separate union forces right behind them and another northern unit blocking them in the Globe area. There was also the addition of those new Federal Marshals, who were killing off a lot of his tribes-people. No, Mexico was his best decision.

So, bypassing over 30 burning, smoldering wagons, nothing much more than a debris pile, Cochise signaled with the spear in his right hand and took off at a run for a gradual decent to the Wagon Train Road. He wanted his men to stay out of range of the American's rifles, for he could not afford to lose another warrior.

He was now entering a wide canyon and as he led his warriors around curve, where his visual range was reduced by a sheer granite cliff, he came out on the Wagon Train Road to find himself facing a civilian force a couple hundred yards straight ahead. Piles of rocks were slid out onto the roadway to make a four-foot wall and now a small number of men were behind them. He also noticed this strange looking cannon in the middle of the road, pointed right at his force. He couldn't help but laugh, thinking these Whites, actually thought they could stop him with such a small force and this single cannon.

Stopping long enough to check the area for a trap and finding no evidence of one, he waved his warriors on with his spear and kicked the sides of his war pinto to feel it spring forward. With this came the war cries, battle shouts and shots of rifles being fired at the small Ranger force blocking the road.

Ranger Jim Williams ordered the men to hold their fire until he opened up with the Gatlin Gun. Their horses and the wagon were hidden behind another ridgeline, but these men wouldn't have enough time to reach them if this Gatlin Gun malfunctioned. Williams had with him, Rangers Matthew Bender, Phillip Champion and Jimmy Sitter, Timothy Whitefall, Luke Rogers and Judah Spurrier. Jim Williams was operating the Gatlin and Spurrier was assistant gunner and loader.

The new men were getting bad cases of itchy trigger-fingers as they watched the mob of Indians charging at them, but they obeyed orders and waited. In a short time, they had gained a real respect for the older Rangers and they all kept their fingers completely off their triggers so they wouldn't make a mistake for fear Williams might shoot them out of hand.

Finally, when Williams estimated the distance between the Gatlin Gun and the charging Apache to be roughly 75 yards, he opened fire with the first magazine of ammo by turning the rotating firing and loading arm. For the military, the Gatlin Gun was the first heavy machine gun on the field of combat and it caught the Apache completely off guard. In support, the other Rangers were using the Winchester lever action 30-30 rifles.

The onslaught dropped the first three lines of Apache, even killing Cochise's war pony and sending him rolling across the desert. He made it behind a large boulder, where first one attempt failed to retrieve him and then a second attempt failed, killing both Indians. But while changing ammo in the Gatlin Gun, a third Apache Warrior dashed in and scooped up Cochise and another war horse was quickly found for him. By then the Apache had fallen back and the war chief knew he had no choice but to proceed north and try to get lost in the desert before Union Troops were upon them. But as the Apache made a mounted move up a dry wash, Cochise suddenly found his way of retreat blocked off by a force of mounted civilians. He estimated the line of horsemen to be 22 to 24 in number, but they were not moving.

Suddenly, he recognized the leader of the riders as Captain Blake, a Texas Ranger Chief. This was a man he had shown great respect for over the years they had fought and during those years of peace. Still, Cochise had nearly 60 warriors against Blake's 24 men. But right then, before he could come to a decision concerning the best way to handle Captain Blake, the Rangers slid off their horses and formed two lines. Front row was kneeling and back row was standing, while the horses had stepped behind the men.

Once more, Cochise had signaled the charge in the same fashion, using his spear. Thirty Apache warriors rushed forward on horseback. Amidst a graying and brownish cloud of foul smelling gunpowder and the horrendous death throes of nearly 18 mounts, plus 28 warriors killed or wounded, the first 30 warriors went down or fell off their mounts and ran back. Cochise realized these new rifles the Rangers were using could not be beat. Not wanting to risk losing the rest of his warrior army, he ordered his mounted force to use side trails to escape. For those men on foot, he ordered them to escape by any means but to withhold entering a shooting match with these new rifles. They were to eventually meet at their northern fortress, but to travel in small parties to escape notice. They were to also hunt game as they drew near the fortress as food supplies were low.

It would be sometime before Captain Blake would see Cochise again, but for the moment he needed to get his troops out of here before the U.S. Cavalry showed up. The Gatlin Gun was all secured and en route back to the Texas Canyon Plateau. Then by the time the Fort Bowie troops arrived, the Major could figure out what had happened here. He had dead and wounded Indians spread across two separate battle scenes and no report of any dead or wounded military or civilian forces. The only evidence at the scene on the roadway, where the Gatlin Gun was used, was Jim Williams and his squad's failure to pick up all the leftover cartridge shells thrown from the Gatlin Gun as the bullets were fired at the Indians. A couple hundred or more shells were found in the middle of the road and several dozen were taken into evidence.

Two of the officers from Fort Bowie instantly recognized the ammo and advised their Commander, who ordered them, "For the time, we will keep this between us."

The major then ordered his command to return to Fort Bowie, with the ranking captain in temporary command, while he and a single squad journeyed to Tucson to report on the condition of the relieved commander, of what took place to have caused such a drastic action and to request an ambulance to return with them to take custody of the senior officer. He took with him a Staff Sergeant, one Sergeant, two Corporals and five PFC troops. The remainder of Fort Bowie's Command returned to where the wagons were attacked and the soldiers assisted in the burials, with all the graves being placed on the south-side of the Wagon Train Road and well marked by wooden crosses and a few Stars of David.

Open wagons came back from the wagon train and all the survivors were carried back to the rest of the wagon train. People put together what they could for the survivors to help them survive their ordeal and if they so wanted, to continue with the wagons or take transportation back east. Each family had deposited their traveling funds with the wagon master and he now returned it to them. Once they reached Tucson, numerous old wagons could be purchased, along with horses, especially if two families were now sharing together.

Out of the survivors, only four people opted to head back east with other travelers who had given up on their California dream. But within a week, the wagon train was leaving Tucson; heading west for the border crossing into a new growing community of Blyth, California. The bridge work crossing the Colorado River was log built and in constant need of repair work to handle the constant flow of wagons. A couple hundred miles to the south was another crossing near Yuma, Arizona. This was where the new Federal Prison was being completed and Captain Blake had escorted many a prisoner to that bare island in the open desert, where escape only meant death out on the sweltering desert. Captain Blake had told Liam that Yuma Prison was one ghastly storage tank for caged humans and if it ever was to occur, they being caught by the feds and tried in a corrupt court, and sentenced to Yuma Prison, he'd find a way to kill himself first.

"But, I'll take some of these phony federal marshals right along with me," JW added on.

BIG SURPRISE AT THE PLATEAU

When the Rangers returned to their hideout sight atop the Texas Canyon Plateau they found two men with rifles guarding the mouth of the trail leading up the ridgeline. Both men had been in hiding but came out slowly when they both believed this was the Rangers and not some militia force working for the Federal Marshals. They wore dark brown cowhide vests, blue cloth shirts, and newish denim jeans and scuffed up black leather boots. Each man had on his head a well used flat wide-brimmed cowboy hat, and strapped around their waist a cartridge belt for their side arms. Neither man had shaved for a while, nor their longish dark colored hair washed in the last week or so. They were both filthy, but the desert was hot and water was scarce to come by.

They held their rifles easy and kept their hands off the side arms, not wanting to cause a shooting with these suspicious Rangers coming back from a major battle with the Apache.

"Captain Blake, I'm Jake Wilson and this is my brother, Sam. We were asked to pull guard duty down here until you arrive and keep anyone else from nosing around. The young lady who recruited us, said to tell you that the Federal Marshals and the Yankee boys are out in force trying to locate you. Why, you've already got a $10,000 reward on you and the rest of the Rangers go at $2,500 each once positive identification is made."

Blake remained mounted and made hand gestures to Dreeke and Sampson to have the block and tackle set up to lift the Gatlin Gun up to the plateau. JW didn't want to cause anymore skin or foot injuries to the Percheron Horses by them carrying the loads back up the trail. JW knew going downhill was a sight easier than making the overburdened hill climb to the plateau.

"First off, who is this young lady you're speaking of," And as soon as he spoke those words he knew who they were talking about. *Kathleen Legend!*

"Why, she says she is your niece...Kathleen Legends. Told us her folks were killed and she was saved from the bandits by you and your Rangers. She had been riding about looking for former Texas and New Mexico Rangers, or former law enforcement officers who refused to work with the new Federal Marshals, Union Army or any sheriff's department who would work with those crooks. Like yourselves, we came home from the war to find our lands forfeited due to this tax now one ever mentioned at the time of surrender. Our families were gone...wives run off with other men or joined with those dang Federal Marshals. Some of our families were killed by the Comanche or Apache, even raiding Comancheros. Farms and ranches burned to the ground and no one back here to protect them, while we rode off to fight with General Hood...just like all of you from what your niece says."

JW shook hands with both men, reading the same pain he felt in their eyes and offered his welcome, "Well, how many troops did my niece bring here?"

"There are eight of us, all veterans from the Army of Texas. We have one former major with us, but he knows this is your operation and will offer you all his support. He worked in General Hood's Headquarters...some kind of plans and tactics man. Long before the war he worked with various sheriffs or state marshal's department. He showed a lot of guts during the Battle of Nashville, when he took over a company of cavalry after the top three officers were killed on the fourth day north of Nashville. That was my company and it shocked most of us to see how much a staff officer knew about cavalry tactics. He saved our hides several times over the next couple of days."

"We were riding scout for General Hood at Nashville and walked right into a Yankee trap. Next thing we know we're on our way to El Mira Prison Camp in New York...a hell hole if you ever saw one. We finally staged an escape about seven or eight months later and were on our way south when General Lee surrendered."

Sam Wilson stepped up, his two hands resting atop of the barrel end of his rifle, with the butt down between his feet. "Yeah, they finally caught the two of us, along with the whole company, when we were a foot. Marched us to the Nashville Train Yard and filed us onto these foul smelling cattle cars. There was cattle crap all over the hay floor, not that they allowed us to sit down. We were shoved in there so tight a man would have to lie down on five people heads to get a nap. But those cars shook so bad the only real sleep we got was standing up. Tempers flared, but there was no room to fight.

"But then we were in the middle of Pennsylvania when the train stopped, they unloaded us all and told us the war was over. There was utter silence and then shouts of 'Liar', or worse. But then the Yankee guards filed on the train and we were told we were on our own. We were later told this saved a lot of processing in New York, just by letting us go."

Jake jumped in to say, "But someone forgot to warn the farms and ranches, the communities and towns as over 10,000 starving and ragged rebels were set loose for the long walk home," Jake Wilson said. "Now I'm not sure if and what kind of violence was committed, but the men needed to eat and they stripped the field of melons, corn, apples and anything edible. Men's clothes, boots and shoes were stripped of clothes lines and out of sheds and barns. A lot of horses, wagons and buggies were taken and it demonstrated the US Government had not made the best decision involving the prisoners of war. Similar situations occurred at the prisoner of war camps, where Yankees and Rebels passed each other on the roads, but mostly everyone was brain-tired of the fighting."

JW glanced about and saw that they had the block and tackle almost set-up, so he ordered the Rangers up the path. He also advised the Wilson brothers to go on up, "We do not normally keep guards down this low, but Kathleen was not aware of this." He was now wondering just what he was going to do with this Ms. Legends, who was going around posing as his niece. Of course, eight new Ranger was a big help, but he would've liked to have checked the men out before bringing them to their new hideout.

By the time JW reached the top he found Kathleen waiting for him at the main corral, wearing a 'cat that swallowed the goldfish' smile on her face. She knew she was in trouble, but hoped the adding of eight new Rangers would help her cause to remain with the Rangers. She did not want to go anywhere else and she knew Captain Blake would have a hard time getting rid of her now — or so she had hoped.

"I see your Rangers have returned victorious, once again," Kathleen said. She walked over to climb up on the corral and sit down on the top pole and be closer to JW. But JW was horse weary and he dismounted and handed his Ghost over to MSgt. Gary Wells. "Give her some extra salt and a whole apple, if we've got it to spare. She deserved it today."

"Are you going to ignore me, Captain?" Kathleen asked in a raised voice. This produced smiles on a dozen or so cowboys, who heard this exchange going on.

"I'll respond to you in accordance with my camp priorities, which means we shall have a talk tomorrow at noon. So, good day, Ms. Legends."

Then, right before Kathleen could explode into a juvenile tantrum, Liam suddenly appeared in front of her, with a big grin on his face and said, "Ms. Legends, before you put on a childish display of juvenile hysterics, that you will later hate yourself for demonstrating in front of all these cowboys, why don't you and I take a walk. I can show you our overview, where we can keep an eye on the wagon train road and, also a couple hundred miles surrounding this plateau."

"I remember you, you're Liam, adopted brother to Captain Blake. We met last time…" She stopped talking and provided a gentle smile. She then put her two arms out and Liam helped her to the ground.

There was nearly a five-year difference between Liam and Kathleen, with him at 19, and she a whole 14-years old. But Liam was the one-Ranger, closest to her in age. The next oldest Ranger was 24 years old and he was already a widower.

The two kids spent the next hour or so walking about the ridgeline, while she explained how she escaped the people Captain Blake left her with and then went on a crusade to enlist new Arizona Rangers. She understood the need for secrecy, but she also understood the need for additional Rangers. She was also working on gathering a herd of riding horses and cattle, goats and sheep, pigs and chickens to bring to the plateau to provide food for the Rangers.

But now as she looked around the plateau, she knew this secret base could no longer be used as the main Ranger base. It was rapidly closing too small, especially when she considered the animals to be brought up and additional troops.

Once she had heard about today's battle against Cochise, she knew for the Rangers to effectively do their job, their numbers needed to be over 200 fighters. Liam said this would mean four heavily re-enforced Ranger companies. He also hoped they could lay their hands on another Gatlin Gun, but they had spent all the gold coin they had brought with them from their journey south from New York. Of the original Rangers, the men were down to less than a $100 each in gold coin, but they all liked how they had spent the money and offered no complaints.

The plateau could remain as an advance base, or position of retreat when fleeing from the federal government's troops. But locating a new main base would take time, a location unknown to the Indians and the Arizona Government. Liam told Kathleen he would bring these things up when he talked with JW later tonight.

"Do you think he'll send me away, again?"

"Why do you want to stay with us? We bathe seldom, our cooking can poison the average person and there's always someone out there wanting to kill us." Liam walked over to the firewood supply bins and carried away an armload for the dinner fire. They only had fires at night and they knew the flames could not be seen; as-long-as they made them low to the ground Indian-style. The smoke couldn't be seen at night, nor could the glare of the fires, shining off the clouds. Riders had been sent out surrounding the steep ridgeline to verify the fires could not be seen, except if a fire was built during the day and then the smoke would be seen.

"Why don't you chow down with us tonight," Liam asked her and she agreed. But he made sure to add, "No questions for JW. He needs to relax."

"I'll agree, I can understand him needing some light social time to relax. Was that way with my Dad, but he'd yell at us to all leave the house so he and my mother could sneak a drink or two after dinner. But we all knew they drank, so it was sort of like a game."

Liam could see her face droop, her eyes water up as she recalled her folks and that last night of sheer horror. She still hoped that someday she could find the two men who had killed and mutilated her family, and it was by her hand they would die. She didn't share this with Liam, but his eyes told her he already knew this. For she had learned of his story and how they tracked the murdering Indians down and killed most all of those involved in murdering his family in their small wagon train.

"Right now, I need to ensure all the animals have been fed and watered, all the troughs are refilled and there are horse blankets on the backs of the mounts. We all have small tasks to perform and that's one of mine. MSgt. Gary Wells handles the guard duty roster, MSgt. Michaels works the armory, while Chad Leaders works in the smithy, making horseshoes and shoeing the horses, cleaning their hooves and even brushing their teeth. Two other men work the butcher shop, and we have a rotating KP roster and a five-man firewood detail when the bins get low. We now use the wagon that's on the canyon floor below to help gather the wood and hoist the bundles up with the block and tackle set up. But there are also lots of other jobs popping up. Lt. Dreeke is in charge of those. This keeps everyone busy and no time to get bored."

"Any idea of what we're having for dinner tonight? Kathleen asked. She was headed back to her new tent and Liam was escorting her, though he knew not a man on this plateau would lay a hand on her. They all knew JW would hang them over the canyon floor for the vultures to feed upon.

JW, Dreeke and Sampson met with the Wilson Brothers, the two new men they had already met at the mouth of the plateau path, but now they were meeting Justin Regant, a 47-year old Rebel Cavalry Staff Sergeant, who had previously spent five years as a Sheriff's Deputy in Austin, Texas. His wife had run off with their savings.

Robert Jefferson, 36-years old, formally a member of Army of Texas Rebel Artillery, a widower, who left his four children with his Uncle and Aunt in San Antonio. He had worked as a Sheriff's Deputy for four years then took up a job as Stage Coach Guard for the increase in pay, but resigned when Fort Sumter was fired on.

Todd Hood, a distant relative to General Hood, had grown up in Virginia, but came to Texas with the Union Army. He was stationed in San Antonio when war broke out and separated to join the South. As a First Lieutenant in the Union Army Infantry, he instantly became a First Lieutenant in the Southern Infantry. But he was wounded in the first year and retired, classified as not being able to fight with his serious wounding to the left shoulder and stomach by rifle fire. But he forced himself to improve and soon became a railroad detective operating between Florida and Georgia. On his own he learned how to ride and became a member of the Georgia Militia. When the war ended, he was soured on the South and decided to move to New Mexico. But he soon lost his various jobs to immigrants coming west from the North.

Frank Ware, 39-years old and his younger brother, Jerry Ware, 37-years old, grew up in rural Texas. The rode with General Hood and had never surrendered. Both had been shot during the war. They came home to find their shared ranch burned to the ground by unknown parties. Too many storms had come and gone, so it was impossible for them to identify if Indians ponies were used or bandits. They had lost everything, from their families to stock, but at least someone had come by to bury their dead, though they never found out who had shown the kindness. They first got jobs guarding mine payrolls, and then being company guards on the railroads, which was then followed by sheriff's deputies in New Mexico and were once more looking for work in law enforcement, when they heard a young lady and some men who were looking for volunteers for a dangerous job. Unable to find any work, they decided to check it out in hopes the job would at least provide meals and feed for their horses.

Abe Wilcox, who was really Abraham Wilconski of Germany, and a Jew, had been a Texas Ranger in the earlier days, but resigned to keep his wife happy, had been a Union officer in the Mexican-American War and promoted to the rank of captain. He had found a home working on a commander's staff dealing in tactics, but after the way he had separated, again to keep his wife happy. But when the Civil War broke out his convictions told him to join with the Army of Texas and he became a member of General Hood's staff in the Office of Tactics. He rose to the rank of Major and lost his job, when one afternoon he found himself too close to one of the battlefields north of Nashville, when command of a cavalry company landed in his hands. He turned out being a natural horseman. With his knowledge of tactics, he led his men to repeated victories, up until General Hood resigned his commission for the loss of Nashville. When Abe returned home, he found that his wife had taken their son and daughter and returned to Germany to remain with family. It was during a drunk, when Abe ran into the Wilson brothers, who he had recalled and bought them several drinks to regale the war. They had found him and sobered him up, dragging him with them to check out on this word of mouth operation.

MOVING TIME...AGAIN

Dinner that evening had been a quiet one and JW was surprised Ms. Legends had showed some self-control and not pestered him with questions. But watching her make moon-eyes at Liam most the night he could understand why, and it surprised him even more for all the grins and smiles he was responding with. It appeared his Little Brother was smitten and that just gave him an idea. So, he soon excused himself and returned to his tent to spend some time with the new maps Lt. Sampson had brought him from Tucson for the Territory of Arizona, Southern California and New Mexico. There was even a map of Texas. The maps pointed out the known roads and where the townships, communities and recently created Indian Reservations were. The maps also pointed out particular God-made landmarks and new towns being built, along with points in the territory where known mines were being worked by large companies.

JW was surprised to notice that Globe was listed under the growing community ledger, where he would've thought it was an established city. But they still weren't incorporated as the territorial laws saw it, and having not voted in a mayor and city council, no legally established school and no territorial appointed sheriff's department. Globe began as a trading post and then added a smithy. Then came a café, a stage stop and a hotel. A town had begun...

But they couldn't return to Globe, plus it was too far away from where they needed to be. For two hours, he looked at those maps until he wore a scowl on his face and totally ignored the natural landmark that stared right back at him. Running against his normal procedure to operate alone he summoned Abe Wilcox, the former Major to his tent. He wanted this former officer, reportedly a fine officer, also assigned to tactics on the General's Staff, to review these maps and give him his opinion.

Using an empty water cask, Wilcox set down opposite JW at a table small enough to be used for a large doll's tea party, and reviewed the maps. He was familiar with the Texas maps and some of Eastern New Mexico Territory, but this was the first Arizona Territory map he'd seen and he found it interesting. He asked JW to mark down the known Indian strongholds and their tribal names, which JW accomplished in under ten minutes.

"These are the ones I know of, but there are over a dozen smaller tribes out there I've never seen, but I've found evidence of when they moved their villages." JW said, as he put his pencil down.

"Wow! That a lot of Indians. Good thing they never joined together, they could wipe us out."

"Indians just don't think like us, Major. They'll fight a battle together…mixed tribes and all, but they consider that single battle the war. Once they defeat that enemy in the one battle, they separate and return to their own hunting grounds and camps. No campaigning like we'd do."

Wilcox gawked in response and then nodded his head, "I guess that's what happened against the Spanish. When the Spanish fired their guns, and displayed their horses, the Indians simply went home in mass. If they had simply rushed the Spanish, possibly losing their front line to gunfire, they would've seen the last of the Spanish soldiers and history would've been altered for all of us."

"Well, I don't know about you, but there are no Spaniards in my heritage, but I do love my horse. So, I thank them for that. I would've hated walking across this desert. But now back to work, have you discovered a place that would work as our new encampment?" JW asked.

"Captain, first of all, my days of being a major are lost forever. You command this outfit and rightfully so. If you want to make me an officer, then I suggest a Second Lieutenant under First Lieutenant Sampson. I also understand why the Rangers continue using the military ranking system. It works. Now as to the maps I believe you've already selected the right place and for some unknown reason you have doubted yourself with your decision. But I agree your best choice is the Superstition Mountains. I know little of the location, but what I do know I doubt the US Army or the Federal forces will search us out in there."

"Well, you got me there, Lieutenant, that place has given me the willies more than a few times. Apache Indians say its haunted and those ghost stories kind of stick with you when you're in there, late at night and one of those desert storms is kicking up outside on the valley floor. It used to be an Apache fortress, but the men couldn't handle the ghosts and they boogied out one night."

"Who are the ghosts that haunt the mountains?" Wilcox asked.

"Supposedly, the major story concerns this Dutch miner, who had hit the motherload in those mountains in a deep mine he had dug out by himself. He'd loaded down half-a-dozen mules with the gold and was on his way to the trading post where that Community of Phoenix is growing. But the Indian wouldn't let him leave, they had gotten used to the Dutchman, but they didn't want their sacred mountains filled with gold miners. So, they killed him and slaughtered his mules. Gold meant nothing to them, so they tossed it aside. But before he died, that tough old Dutchman yelled out curses in how his mine would never be found and his spirit would haunt the Apaches who visited this mountain."

"What about other stories?"

"Another major story came about in the 1850's, when supposedly a large Mexican family and their paid guards had taken 750 horses to the Army in Nevada and accepted only gold coin for payment. They were said to be en-route back to Mexico when a large party of Apache attacked, chasing them into the Superstition Mountains. They eventually found a cave, where they carried in their sacks of gold coin and tried to move their horses inside. But the horses would not enter the cave and they ran off, while the Apache were preparing their next attack. Now, according to the son of one of those Indians involved in that attack, it took them over a week to kill that party, but some were found dead due to lack of water. What was strange was how they discovered the cave to be a working mine, with old equipment, support beams in place and dried up lanterns hanging at various places. When the Apache realized that they had entered the accursed miner's cave, they took off running to escape the curse. But the young war chief, who would one day be known as Geronimo stayed long enough with four of his closest advisers and friends to climb above the cave entrance and cause landslides to seal off the opening. The father said they had not seen any gold coins, but the family most like carried the treasure back into the cave to give them as much room for fighting.

"However, in 1860, before everything blew up in our faces, the Territorial Governor asked me to scout for three companies of soldiers. They were supposedly out looking for a large gang of cattle thieves, who were taking their stolen beeves into California to sell. The governor didn't think the Rangers were big enough to handle such a large group of crooks.

But I learned later, after the war began, there were no thieves. These soldiers were here to escort a group of officers…men assigned to a growing corrupt government. President Lincoln was busy fighting his war and had no idea what was going on. But these men were here to review the number of farms and ranches, especially those owned by Southerners or Southern sympathizers, and the size of their cattle herds. Growing communities were being checked out to see if they were Northern or Southern hotbeds, plus to review the Indian situation and to make suggestions of the best way to handle their red brothers.

"However, when I told them the tales of the mine as we rode past Superstition, they insisted on riding in to see if they could find the old mine site. So, I took them all in, deeper and deep into thru the Mountain pass. But then came a certain point where a strange wind began to blow, causing the horses to go crazy — even mine. Mine stood up on its back two legs, began to let out screams and wiggled around sharply. I couldn't hold on any longer. Then she was gone and I couldn't recall when my mare had behaved in such a weird manner. I looked around for a bed of rattle snakes, but didn't find anything. Then I noticed how nearly every other troop was on foot or on his butt, and a few other still fighting with their mounts. But before long our cavalry unit had become the infantry.

"Now I don't know if this had anything to do with that curse, but we had to walk over 20 miles before we came out of that pass and found all of horses chowing down on the desert salads."

Wilcox shook his head and laughed quietly, but then apologized. "I'm sorry, Captain and please understand I am not laughing at you or your story, but in my life I have come up against such things many times and now once again it seems I am being tossed into the fray of good versus evil. But I am ready and I believe you are too. This will be an interesting ride, Captain…But, let's move our main force to the Superstition Mountains. It appears the Indians will ignore us and I doubt the US troops will bother with us. Plus, we're close enough to our post here to back them up if needed within 24 hours' notice or less.

"Have you decided who you'll leave here to man the plateau?"

"Not yet, but do not worry. You're too new and I'll want you up with me for a while. You can report to Lt. Sampson to advise him that you'll be his second-in-command. And while you're out there, will you locate Liam and Kathleen and ask them to report here, pronto?"

"Yes, Sir," Lt. Wilcox replied as he stood to his feet and offered a proper salute to his new commander.

The salute was returned and then JW was back looking at his maps.

SPIES TO TUCSON

The large wagon was a loan from a family that had long supported the Arizona Rangers, especially after the wife was brought back alive when Banditos had kidnapped her and wanted $10,000 for her return. Unfortunately, the Banditos had remained on the American side of the border and they came under American law, instead of crossing the to be under Mexico's Laws. There, they might have seen ten to 30 years in prison, or if they had bribed the judge maybe only a year. But for kidnapping a woman in Arizona, all five men were hung within a week of the trial. Women out west were looked upon special and the punishments were often more severe.

Four all-white draft horses came with the wagon, they were all gelded males and made strong pullers.

But when Kathleen was asked to pose as Liam's wife so they could spy on Tucson and check on the local happening, possibly pick up another volunteer or two, she burst out laughing. This seemed to upset her pretend husband and he asked JW, "Do I have husband's rights to paddle her when she needs it. She might realize that posing as her husband is not all that exciting for me. And Captain, does this job come with a husband's bedroom rights?"

Kathleen glared at Liam and wagged her right index finger at him, "You touch me outside of holding hands to show were married and I'll take one of your guns to blow your head off while you're asleep. This is a pretend marriage, no church and no minister. You just remember that...Got it?"

"Little fiery thing, isn't she?" Liam said and then asked what the rest of the plan was.

"You broke away from an Oregon train to check out Arizona. Both of you are young missionaries, who were on your way to Portland, but felt the call to drive south. You'll be loaded with empty casks to be filled, which the plateau, here, will need. I'll have a list for you to get filled and the money you'll need. But the main thing is to keep your eyes open and your ears. I want to know where the carpetbaggers are moving in the Southeast, and any troop movements.

"Kathleen, you might be able to get a part-time job at the trading post, a café or one of the other stores. Look for where the soldiers visit or their wives. You're both smart enough to figure this out, but do not do anything that might make the federals curious about you. If someone gets nosy, move out. That's why I want the supplies filled first, just in the event you have to leave in the middle of the night."

"What about volunteers?" Kathleen asked.

"Be particular. We want ex-soldiers and ex-lawmen. I don't really care which side they rode for, or what race they are. I'd like a couple more men who speak Indian. No drunks, gamblers or womanizers, you can't trust 'em. Watch out for feds working undercover, they out there looking for us and that might be a good way to catch us. I know that's a lot to ask for, but you might turn over a rock and find someone special."

"Sir, where are we going after the plateau? I understand most of us are moving on to a new post, but no one is sure on the place and we'll be gone."

"Sorry, Kathleen, but you two will be told the location and directions to find it once you reach here. In the event, you're taken and tortured by the feds, its better you don't know the location. Too many good men could be lost if a couple hundred Feds descended upon us. Okay?"

"Yup, I didn't think about it that way."

"Last item...I hope, I'll be sending six riders with you. You'll go right across the desert so you can enter the roadway north of the city to make it look right. If anyone asks you can just say you got lost and some Mexican pointed you in the right directions. Your escort will leave at night, so they won't be seen, but they're only along in the event you encounter any Indians."

"Makes me feel safer already, Romeo will actually behave with a crowd around," Kathleen stabbed with.

"What do you think, Cap, should the two of us practice our kisses before we get seen in public?"

"Captain, he may or may not come back to you, but if he keeps this up he'll be singing soprano...Is that the one with the canary voice?"

Liam burst out laughing as he held the tent flap open for her and shook his head at JW before he walked out to prepare for leaving. He wasn't sure who his six riders were, but he'd find out soon enough.

JW then summoned a guard and asked him to locate Lt. Sampson, "Ask him to report to me, please."

He would have Lt. Sampson choose the seven men he would share duty with on the plateau, until he was sent for to join with them at the Superstition Mountains. But he himself would choose the six men to escort the couple to Tucson. Brady Williams, John Gibson, Chad Leaders, Joseph Coon, Luke Rogers and Matthew Bender would be picked, with Chad leaders as the leader for the detail. He needed to promote Leaders, for the man had the time in service, experience and took care of his men. Still, he would talk it over with his officers and senior NCOs. Rank didn't mean anything pay-wise right now, but it did have a status in the new Rangers, even if only their fellow Rangers knew of rank.

The men were summoned and briefed, but sure enough it was Brady who complained about being so close to Tucson and not being able to ride in and grab a beer.

"Brady, you're a well-known bar character and you've made your share of enemies, so try to imagine what $2,500 might mean to them if they spotted you," JW said.

"Thanks, Cap, I sure don't feel all that thirsty now." This produced a round of laughter.

Later that evening, JW dismissed his outside guard, "Come back in two hours."

"Yes, Sir," the guard replied and went over to have his evening chow.

JW then waited for his senior staff to show up for Commander's Call. This was Lt's. Dreeke, Sampson and Wilcox, MSgt. Michaels and Gary Wells, JW covered the escort detail for Liam and Kathleen into Tucson and why he felt the kids would accomplish the job better than anyone else in camp, and they agreed. He then explained his reasoning behind moving a larger force to the Superstition Mountains and ended up telling the stories behind some of the legendary curses.

"I do not plan on using that same pass. Superstition is massive. The mountains are tall, wide and there is plenty of room for us to move around. But the Apache still avoid the whole thing. Occasionally a miner or two still go up there, but few come back. You can make a wrong turn and take a 900-foot fall or get lost, and some of those smaller valleys have more than their share of rattle snakes. So, keep your eyes open all the time."

"Now Lt. Sampson and his force are to map the southeast, showing the farms and ranches we need to know about, river beds and such and anything else we should know about for responding to help these people. Visit with these people and see who they are and what they may be in-need of. Knowledge about the bandits would be helpful, but be careful, they may be working with the bandits. Find out if they have any kids missing, recent raids on them or someone they know. Also, if the feds have been around demanding and taking anything."

"Tough order, Captain, but we'll get it done. I'll need MSgt. Wallace Michaels, Jordan Akers, Eli Foster and Daniel Boone, Tariq Striker, Eric Bear and Joe Link. Okay, Sir?"

"That's okay, Lieutenant, that will leave me with 25 Rangers to move to Superstition, along with the Gatlin gun, our herds and supplies.

I'm going to try to move across the desert and stay off the roads, until we reach our new mountain stronghold. Lt. Wilcox, you will take over B Company and do you have any idea who'll you'll like for a First Sergeant?"

"Captain, I believe I'd like to have Sam Wilson. He is a sound man of great courage, intelligent and he cares for those who serve with him. He is assuredly First Sergeant material."

"Then you got him and tell him he had just been promoted to Master Sergeant, without a raise in pay and no stripes to sew on his sleeves."

"Thanks, Captain, I know he'll appreciate the promotion. I'll have to admit, I have a feeling being a Ranger lieutenant will mean more to me than wearing my major's gold leaves."

"Even if it means being hung by these federal marshals the government sent to Arizona, not having a single idea what was going on down here and how many people were being hurt by their lack of foresight."

"Captain, our country is rebuilding and you know as well as I do this project will take years. In this process a lot of people will lose everything they own, be hurt and God forbid, killed by the corruption that is allowed to prosper. It happed before, right after the Revolution and our second War of 1812. There were always those who prospered off the wars. You saw this down here in the Mexican-American War as a lot of Mexican were forced to give up their vast ranches and farms to the carpet baggers of that time, even when some of those Mexicans fought with us. Not to forget the Whites only who tried to push all the Mexicans out of Arizona, New Mexico and Texas following the war against General Santa Ana and the fall of the Alamo. People died and corruption reigned. But now there is a fighting force down here, one that will grow to prevent the large-scale events from happening and protect the smaller people who've been offered no protection by the government. The new Rangers will be their safeguards and I for one am proud to become a member of this group, and I would be happy to ride with you even as a private...But lieutenant always sounds better."

"You must be thirsty after that mouthful, but I only have whiskey to offer you."

"No, Sir...I've got a new company to inspect, once this meeting is over and my men would think poorly of their new commander if he shows up with whiskey on his breath and none to share with them."

"We'll all have a drink before breaking up and heading our different ways." Captain Blake then moved on to supply needs, water needs, ammo and horse needs for the two main units. It was decided the black Percheron monsters would go with the men heading for Superstition, packed down with supplies or pulling the Gatlin Gun wagon. Four regular draft horses would pull the kids' wagon into Tucson and they would return on the well-used wagon train roads to Superstition. Both Liam and Kathleen would be armed with two of the lever-action Winchesters, but those would be kept hidden unless needed. Otherwise, they'd have a single shot 12-gauge and an old Sharps .50 caliber buffalo gun up in the wagon seat with them. Both Winchesters would be wrapped in blankets right behind the wagon seat, but reachable if suddenly needed in the event of bandits or Indians.

"The unit proceeding north will lead out with Holloway and Jim Williams on scout, two men on right and left flank, and Andy Salcedo and this Jake Wilson on tail. I heard Wilson was a pretty good scout, so I'll have Salcedo check him out first to see how observant he is. This will leave us with 15 riders and one man driving the gun wagon. Any questions?"

MSgt. Michaels had his hand half-way up and waited for Blake to gesture to him, "Sir, are we going to wear uniforms…shirts, or carry a banner to identify ourselves to the locals when we respond in force. It might save us from being shot."

"Arizona Rangers have never worn uniforms, we wanted to be looked upon as different than the regular army and I believe that should be especially true with all those federal marshals riding around causing all their problems. Someday, we might have badges, for those times in the future when a Ranger responds alone to tame a large situation…Like those Texas Rangers always like to say, 'One town, one Ranger'. But that's in the future. But I can agree with a banner, like our companies carried in the war to identify who they were." He looked out over his senior staff and said, "You all come up with some ideas and bring them to me, then we'll have one of our local womenfolk sew a couple up for A and B Companies. Better have one drawn up for a C Company, too. I have a feeling we're about to be seeing some enlargement soon enough."

There were no more questions so JW released his staff to complete their duties. The whole unit, minus guards, was to meet after chow for a final briefing. Then the kids, plus their escort were to leave under the cover of darkness to reach the farmer's homestead to pick-up their wagon, empty barrels and draft horses. It was believed it would take them three days to reach Tucson and they planned to stay in town for up to two weeks to gather information and pick up supplies for Superstition Mountains and possibly another day to locate the Rangers' stronghold.

CHAPTER FIFTEEN

"Marrying a fourteen-year old girl should be illegal and a hangable offense"

MAIN STREET, TUCSON, ARIZON

Liam and Kathleen had been in town only two days and his temper was getting mighty riled over the way all the single men were glaring at Kathleen, especially those who hung around outside the bars and taverns. It began right off, when they drove the wagon into town and looked for a place to camp their wagon. Some nasty words were spoken from the drunks and it took Kathleen's strong two arms to hold Liam in his seat. He was ready to teach a few of those men some proper manners.

"These are not Arizona men, Kathleen. Men out here respect women and men with their mouths would usually end up scraping the boards with their teeth by now. City is changing, outsiders becoming the majority and Main Street isn't a proper place for womenfolk."

Through a series of inquiries, they found a spot to camp their wagon, but the price shocked them. It took them a $5 gold piece for two weeks of dirt space, with no water or outhouse facility. When they walked through the three supply stores they could find nearby, the prices for their needed supplies left them both speechless. But they realized Captain Blake had expected the rise in cost by all the remaining gold coins he had provided and some silver they had taken off some dead Mexican bandits. They picked out what they needed among the three stores and had it delivered to their wagon on the same day. Liam made sure they would be there to take delivery and have the men help them empty the 100 pound bag of grain, beans and salted bacon and pork into their barrels. In this way, they could return with the big bags to be used once again.

One of the delivery men, a young boy not a year older than Liam, asked about Kathleen, "How old is your sister...Mr. Rogers?"

"Mah sister? Why, Mister, this here is mah wife, Kathleen an' she's jus' turn 14."

"Fourteen!? Why that's illegal in mos' states...Ain't it?" The man asked.

"Not in Tennessee," Liam replied. "Why I got two cousins 12-years old who jus' got hitched. They jus' real happy, but still livin' wit' her parents." Liam turned to Kathleen and tossed her a wink.

The young man gave Kathleen a hard gaze and asked her, "But why so young?"

She didn't answer right away, but then replied, "Cause of all the feudin' in the hills, then the war. Too many menfolk lost, new babies needed ta grow up an' do thu farmin' and keep thu family honor upheld. Some thu family feuds on hold, waitin' for new blood. Me and Liam, we didn't want our sons dyin' for a piece of rocky hillside, covered in tree roots and dead bodies. Feudin' goin' on so long, cemeteries too full, they just start plantin' 'em everywhere. So, we took off for thu west. Raise our kids out here and give 'em a chance."

"I'd heard about your mountain feuds, but out here we have Apache Indians, Bandits and Comancheros to deal with. We also got these accursed Federal Marshals and the tax collectors, so you both get your wagon out of here before some tax man comes after your wagon and demand some sort of war tax. Looks like you were too young to fight in the war, but that won't matter. I've never seen such a ruthless bunch of men in all my life."

"How long you live in this Arizona," Liam asked.

"Not long. My family came down from Maine a couple years ago, but the Sioux hit our wagon train and burned most of us out. Survivors kept together and went south, hoping to reach Southern California or Virginia City, Nevada to hunt for silver. But my brothers and I only got as far as Tucson. We needed supplies and thought we'd get some work here for a month and then head west for Los Angeles. But plans can always change…Can't they?"

"How many brothers?" Kathleen asked.

"There were six of us when we hit the plains. Dad took a Sioux arrow in the heart and mom, she just seemed to up and die that night from heart break. We buried them side by side. So, the six of us rode south with the new and much smaller train, which was now being escorted by a company of U.S. Cavalry. I lost one brother when we crossed a nasty river, never did find his body. A month later, we were in this small town of…of Globe…up north of here and my oldest brother, Tom, was gunned down by three federal marshals. They had no reason to shoot him, but a whole platoon of army soldiers was backing them up, so we put his body on a horse and rode on. We buried him south of there, a lonely spot of ground off the road and now that left four of us."

"You know our names, but what is yours?" Liam asked.

"What happened to your Tennessee accent, Liam…your sounding like a fellow northerner…East coast northerner?"

"Comes and goes as I need it. I work with some men who could use you and your brothers, if you're interested. If you meet with us tonight, here, I'll explain more. But be careful not to be followed. The US Marshals are a crafty bunch and if I find you're working for them, our fellow Arizona patriots will make you pay."

"My name is Randy Wagner and my brothers are Wes, Billy and Timmy. I'll talk to them and see, but I'll be here. You have got my interest."

"Great," Kathleen said.

The next day inside the Apache Junction Tavern, located on Main Street in Tucson, Liam and Kathleen were having a tin plate of the tavern's buffalo stew, which Liam knew was only steer meat. But it tasted pretty good. Randy Wagner had told his boss he was quitting, but would stick around for another week, while the owner found someone to replace him. But it was during lunch they found out that one of the other workers, a man from Colorado, had overheard part of Liam and Randy Wagner's conversation.

The man wandered over to table of five men playing poker, on their second bottle of locally made whiskey and in a loud voice, he said, "Married life with a 14-year old should be illegal, if you ask me. Some places even consider it a hanging offense I've heard."

"What did you say?" The gambler who usually ran the table asked the loudmouth. By now both Liam and Kathleen had dropped their spoons and were glaring at the mouthy one. Randy Wagner had vanished, but he had gone back into the supply closet to lay his hands on his pistol belt and wrapped it around his waist. He placed a sixth round into the open chamber, rotated the cylinder of his .44 Colt and then returned to observe the happenings.

"I'm not even sure why you're pestering us with this, but if that young couple got themselves legally married in Tennessee and came west to find a new life, then, Mister...Butt out and let us play cards. This is America, fresh starts is what this country is all about."

Kathleen left her table and dashed over to the gambler to kiss him on the cheek, "Thank you, Mr. Gambler."

The man touched his cheek, smiled and said, "Best pot I've won all week, fellows. Now whose deal is it?"

Big mouth shook his head and walked back into the back room to hide his shame, but unfortunately, he still had to face Randy Wagner, who desired his pound of flesh for embarrassing and possibly frightening his new friends. Later that evening, when the young trouble-maker came to, he walked back out into the tavern café area with a face of bruises and the loss of two front teeth.

As for the gambler, he was still at his same seat and when he saw the facial damage, he grinned and then returned to his cards. He was holding three queens and two tens and there was $200 in the pot. It had been a good day for him and now he was thinking of moving on to Wichita. His name…Some called him Doc, but they were his friends. Others simply stayed out of his way and his lightening draw with a .38 caliber revolver with ivory grips, which he preferred to wear in a left-sided shoulder holster for a right-handed draw.

TWO WEEKS LATER

The ride across the desert to Superstition Mountains had been one of blistering heat, water rationing a brief running battle with a band of White Mountain Apache, who had jumped their reservation for a raid on passing settlers making their way north towards Phoenix. MSgt. Gary Wells picked up an arrow wound to his left arm and Phillip Champion took a bullet between the ribs, but both would be fine with some decent doctoring.

News was learned from some friendly Apache of how a Navajo war had started up in New Mexico and over 10,000 Navajo Indians were involved in the battle. No one seemed to know what the war was about, but it had stirred up some of the other tribes as well in the region.

Even up in Wyoming and Montana, a battle over the Bozeman Trail intruding into Indian lands had brought the Sioux, Arapaho and Cheyenne to the warpath against the U.S. Cavalry and local settlers. Chief Red Cloud was leading the Indians, who for the moment out-numbered the U.S. Army, but additional troops were being brought in, along with cannon and the fearsome Gatlin Guns.

Chief Victorio, Cochise, and Geronimo continued stirring up the Arizona Apache Nation, giving rise to various break-outs from the established reservations and continual raids coming down from the Apache fortress of Northern Arizona. So far, the U.S. Army had yet to penetrate its stony mountain face and surprise the Apache in their homes.

But the Main Ranger force had established its new headquarters deep inside the southeastern section of the Superstation Range. Observation posts were set up on all four corners of the mountain range and a mirror communication service was used to warn of any approach, but this took a total of eight men per week, with two men per post. Communication check in was every four hours, unless an emergency popped up. If nothing was heard within eight hours, JW was notified and a patrol was sent out. They all knew it was possible for the Apache to pick up their mirror service and though they usually didn't attack at night, they would often move into position to attack at sunrise. But JW continued to hope their fear of Superstition would keep them away. His main reason for the observation posts was to keep an eye on the desert roads and trails, settlement fires and cavalry troops riding about.

It had taken them two attempts to reach the two observation posts on the far side of the range. One man in each group had taken bad falls and broken a leg, which got some of the others a bit jumpy concerning the ghosts. Weird noises became the norm and an Irishman, who had recently joined the group, had said it was the sound of the dreaded banshee. "T'is the black spirit who appears b'fore…You'd call it the death hearse, to carry the dead away."

"Knock that stuff off," MSgt. Michaels ordered. "Besides, I'd rather face one of your banshee's than a raving bunch of Apaches, any day."

Once a week the big water wagon they had acquired from a friendly farmer, who was greatly appreciative when the Rangers saved his family from a murder raid, left the post and made the 46 mile trip to the nearest clean river. Besides the driver and a helper, it was escorted by ten riders. Water was to important out in the desert and JW didn't want to lose the trailer or his men. They were all armed with the new Winchesters as an added plus.

Cover over by a tarp to protect it from the sun and the rare rain fall, their Gatlin Gun was set up behind a rock wall. This was one of a dozen walls and trenches they had set up and dug at their post. Their corral, deep in one valley, with only the entry to pass the horses, now held over 200 assorted breeds. Each man had his two mounts, the draft horses and extra breeds they used for trading with locals. They now had a herd of nearly 400 head of cattle, which was held in the next valley over and kept under a four-man watch around the clock. Chickens roamed free, except for the layers and goats and sheep were kept in a small corral beside the horse enclosure.

It didn't take any time at all for the Ranger Station to get built, with JW having his office and a briefing room for his command staff. With both Yankee and Southerners on the force, it was decided for now no U.S. Flag would be flown until politics were no longer a topic of interest. But the old Arizona Ranger flag, removed from the pole in Tucson, now waved on the post flag pole, positioned in the center of the yard. An empty pole stood beside it, waiting the day for when the U.S. Flag would be flown.

The Ranger Company banners for A, B and C Companies were sewn, simply signifying the company name in blue material on a background of light gray. The banner was nearly two feet long and ten inches wide where it was attached to an eight-foot long pole. This pole was carried by a man who volunteered and he rode beside the company's MSgt. and right behind the Company Commander or Second-in-Command.

With the return of Liam and Kathleen Legend, a celebration of sorts carried on with a whole steer being slaughtered and one of their precious kegs of beer being rolled out. But Liam surprised them with the addition of two more kegs of beer in the front of his wagon bed. The Southern roadside observation post settled in 600 feet or better up a hard top lifeless mountain, spotted them coming with the help of their binoculars and sent word down with flashes of sun light. The wagon was loaded, which required another set of horses and the addition of a two wheel wagon cart attached to the back. The post also reported ten additional horsemen and this surprised JW and his senior staff. They had expected maybe three to four riders, but not ten.

JW directed Lt. Dreeke to use five men to disarm the ten men and escort them to headquarters for a talk. "Now be nice, Jamey, these could be good recruits, or one or two could be spies. I also want to talk with both Liam and Kathleen in my office right away."

"Yes, Sir," Lt. Dreeke replied and began to leave.

"Jamey, you know when we're alone you can call me John or JW. We've known each other a very long time."

"No, Sir," Lt. Dreeke replied. "Ah might slip an' call you dat durin' a formal meetin' an' it wouldn' be correct. You're puttin' togedder a fightin' unit here ta help thu Territory of Arizona become a state someday. Ah figure when we is both retired, sittin' in our rockin' chairs on some porch, like two toothless an' senile cowboys, then I'd call yuh JW."

"Get out of here, Lieutenant…before you sour mah beer."

Liam had the ten men lined up at the end of the room, opposite JW's ancient looking gray desk. A former rancher's desk, it had been taken out of a burned up home after all the bodies were removed following an Indian raid. The desk was cleaned up and made a surprise gift for JW on his birthday. He was deeply moved by the gesture.

"Captain, four of these men I can account for. These are the Wagner Brothers." Liam asked them to step out so JW could see which one these were. "Oldest one is Randy Wagner, then Wes, Timmy and Billy is 18 years old. Wes has already helped me out some, when help was needed and they've lost their parents and two oldest brothers in coming to Tucson from the Northeast. They feel like us, to serve in the Rangers is a chance to transfer a territory into a state, and in the process, stop a lot of people dying from corrupt officials and Indians. Their oldest brother was gunned down by Federal Marshals because they wanted his wagon."

"How'd you meet the other six men, Liam and do not be shy on the details.

"Word of mouth, asking around people Lt. Sampson gave me names for people he knew well in Tucson. I kept an eye on them, watched them working on this ranch or another, while I looked into buying small herds of cattle for my new dirt ranch up north. Mentioned how I was looking for some pretty fair cowboys who'd been working the range for at least two years. These six men came up with the best credentials and while three fought for the South, three of them fought for the North. I thought it was a good balance."

"What did Kathleen think of them?" JW asked.

The men stood quietly, holding their hats in their hands in front of them. JW could see they felt a bit fidgety standing around armed men and not having their own shooting irons wrapped around their hips. In his case, he would've felt plum naked.

"Well, Sir, we had an 11th man, but he got to where he began misbehaving a bit with my wife and the Wagner Brothers interfered and took him out for a long ride and came back without him. I was on the other side of town and I guess the man felt this was his opportunity to see if she was that kind of woman...and she wasn't. Now they promised me they didn't kill him, but I gather he might be pulling cactus quills out of his behind for a week or so."

Everyone started laughing, even JW, who was very fond of the young Kathleen. He looked up her as a girl who would've been a close friend for his daughter. He also knew that if Liam had been there, he would've blown the man's brains out. He knew how fond his little brother was of Ms. Legend. But he wasn't so sure in how she felt for the young Ranger.

"Gentlemen, over the next week, you'll be introduced to your fellow Rangers and come to understand how we operate. Certain jobs you will not work until you've been accepted into our...Band-of-Brothers. It's a line from a famous poem. But this is what we are. We fight trusting one another to watch our backs. When you've been accepted, you'll get your shooting irons back. Unless we come under attack and then everyone is of course armed.

"The thing to remember is how we share in everything because we do not work for pay. Sometimes we find things that are impossible to return to a relative or partner. Other times, people give us things to say thank you. But we are out here to effect a change in how things are being done down here in the Territory of Arizona. Most of us came home to utter destruction, our ranches and farms seized by the federal government and

our herds all forfeited to the US tax collectors for a war tax we knew
nothing about. Our families were butchered by the renegade Indians and
killed by disease, and while we were gone no one seemed to care about
Southeast Arizona. Oh, Fort Bowie was here but 200 troops to manage
such an area was just impossible. We saw a recent example of that when
Cochise attacked a 100 wagon wagon train and burned over 30 wagons to
the ground and killed…a lot of people. Fort Bowie attacked once they
received word and troops from Tucson also launched their attack, but we
were the closest, but none of us arrived in time. But we hit them. We may
have been late, but we saved some and decimated Cochise's strength with
our force and a little surprise we had for him. We have recently gained the
strength of a Gatlin Gun and this weapon terrifies the Indian.

"Now, please don't misunderstand me. I have been a wagon scout
through this territory, an Army Scout and I've led hunting and trapping
parties all over this land. I served with the earlier Rangers and formally
commanded the Arizona Rangers before they were disbanded by this
corrupt government. I also spent two years riding scout, with many of the
men here, for General Hood and his Army of Texas until we were captured
at Nashville and sent to the prison camp at El Mira, New York. We
escaped from El Mira and was returning to the war when we received
word General Lee had surrendered, so we decided to return home. Now
during my 30 plus years in Arizona I have come to know some mighty fine
Americans, both northern and southern. For me, the war is over and I
desire both sides to bury the war to become Rangers.

"But to better understand me, I have lived and hunted with the
American Indian. Here in Arizona I have found them to be an intelligent
and caring people. No, they do not think the way we do, but why should
they. They are a different people, much as if we had gone to China. They
have a code of honor that far surpasses ours and there is no word for 'lie'
in their language. All the women and children, plus old people eat in a
village before the men do, but at the same time they look upon horse theft
as an honorable thing…A test of manhood of sorts and a way to provide
for the families. Now, I've lived with the Pima, Navajo, Ute and Papago,
spent two months with a Pueblo tribe up north and they helped me over a
sickness I might not of survived. As to the Apache, I've spent time with
nearly every tribe, but I know Cochise and I've shared numerous meals
with Victorio and found him to have a keen sense of humor. My only
problem with the Apache is when they break a promise and go renegade,
but this is most often the young ones. Cochise was with this last bunch, but
he probably left with them to keep as many of them alive as possible.

"The problem lay in that we have pushed the Indians as far as they
can go. Indian wars are popping up all over, from Montana and Wyoming

with the Cheyenne and Sioux, to New Mexico with the normally passive Navajo. But you cannot go out and kill Navajo medicine men and expect the Navajo not to react, they're a very religious people. We may not understand their beliefs, but I can sure tell you they have no handle on ours either. Now it's a mite better in California, where the Catholics and other religious missionaries have made a big change in the Indian people's lives. But not here in the Arizona Territory or the plains. Now I've heard a big Indian War is coming, one that could involve the whole mid-west and that'll bring out 100,000 troops. Some of the Indian prophets see it, coming with the end of the buffalo and that could be right around the corner. Yet, still the settlers keep coming. They've got silver and gold mines springing up all over and these people expect protection. I doubt the US Cavalry and us can provide that much help.

"Now my other concerns are the Mexican bandits or banditos, even worse are the Comancheros...Those Whites and Mexicans who work with the renegade Indians. My own 11-year old daughter was kidnapped by them and I have yet to learn of her location, though I've offered a $1,000 reward for proof of that location. But I am afraid it could be Cuba, Spain or a far-off island.

"But these bandits and Comancheros also steal herds to sell in Mexico or steal in Mexico to sell here. We will stop it going both ways and try to catch the Americans involved with it on this side. When possible we will find ways to turn people over to US Army or US Deputy Marshals, and I do not mean those fake Federal Marshals the US Government sent down here. I'm talking about real deputies, with real jails and real hangmen's ropes. Sometimes we may have to be judge and jury, but we will take all possible means to provide a legal and just trial for a suspected criminal. As to Comancheros, I hope to question each one myself, if the situation allows in hope of finding some bit of information concerning my daughter. I can't give up, not yet...It's only been three years or so.

"I also have contact with certain Mexican Police Officers we can trust who will take the prisoners over and try them in Mexico. Most are hung, but it is legal. The herds are then returned to their rightful owners.

"Last of all, I know you are growing weary of my lecture, but remember, in joining us you have already picked up a $2,500 reward on your head and that is dead or alive. I have $10,000 for my head. By coming this far, you have learned of this location and cannot return...I am sorry for this. If you are rejected for suspicion of being a spy, you will be shot. If you attempt to flee into the desert, you will be chased down by our best desert wolves and shot. We will give you every opportunity to measure up, but if you fail, you'll become part of the general staff. No, we won't shoot you for that, but you'll learn to cook, mind the goats, the chicken and the sheep. To do whatever is needed of you. Some people cannot be hunters or killers, and this is what is required of a Ranger.

"Oh, one thing more, there are women about, but these are all wives or daughters and off limits. You'll have times to visit Mexico to shake the dust off your boots and you might even locate a settler widow or an older daughter. But keep your hands off all the women here and as for Ms. Ledgends, she is like our camp mascot and my adoptive daughter. Besides, she is probably a better shot than most of you, believe my men. I learned that the hard way. Now, go get something to eat and meet the people."

After they had filed out, Liam walked up to JW's desk and set on the empty corner top. "So, how'd we do?"

"Not sure yet, Kid. I do like the cut of the Wagner's, you did well with them. But I'm not so sure yet about a couple of those men. I watch the eyes, see if they have trouble looking at me…Which usually means they're hiding something. Those Bush Brothers look like a couple of stage robbers operating up in the Oklahoma before war broke out, but I can't remember their name. All my wanted posters got burned up a long time ago. But we'll keep an eye on them."

"You going out to eat?" Liam asked.

"I will, but I want to get a few things written up from what you brought in. How'd you score on that box of Gatlin ammo?"

"Wagner boys heard they had a couple of the guns in supply on their way to Fort Yuma, so they made a late-night withdrawal and scored on one box of that ammo and two boxes of .44 ammo."

"Sure glad they didn't get caught…But now, how is you and Kathleen getting along…Any courting bells startin' up?"

"What are courting bells?" An embarrassed Liam asked.

"No such thing, just wanted to see the look on your face when I said it. So, you do really like her, don't you?"

"Captain, I'm too old for her…I got five years on her."

"So, when your 23, she'll be 18 years old and that will be perfect. You two can court until she's 18, if you can last that long." JW now had a big smile on his face.

"JW, if in it weren't for what I owe you, that $10,000 reward might be tempting right now," but, then Liam burst out laughing. "But you're right, I'm not sure I could make it five years. What am I gonna do, and worst yet, what if she says no?"

"Well, you can keep being sweet to her, taking her for walks, maybe hold her hands and sit with her at meal times…Even going for a ride or two, maybe by the time you're 22 years old and she's 17. You two can be wedded and I can become a grandfather someday."

"Why, You, old coot, you've been planning this all along just to have a grandchild and I'm the one to suffer through married life."

"Well, I could marry her off to MSgt. Wells or maybe that handsome Bret Sampson, you could even pick the prospective suitors for me."

"You're a mean old man...Let's go eat before I get a firing squad for attempting to strangle my Commanding Officer."

TEXAS CANYON PLATEAU

It was late in the afternoon when Ranger Jordan Akers, was on duty as guard, half-way up the mountain pathway leading to the Ranger's Plateau Post. With the sun, still an inch above the horizon, Akers had enough reflection to send a mirror shot up the hillside to the second post atop the plateau. There, Daniel Boone saw the reflection and alerted Lt. Bret Sampson of the relief column's approach. The other men were then alerted so they could prepare their belongings and then get their horses saddled.

Lt. Wilcox and his seven-man squad arrived at the foot of the path without incident. For this first trip, they were escorted by Holloway who saw this ride south as a comfortable ride in the country. They had met up with over a dozen settlers' wagons and separate small groups of horsemen headed for Phoenix and further destinations north. A couple groups had silver on their minds, and were headed for Nevada.

Riding with Lt. Wilcox was newly promoted MSgt. Sam Wilson, his brother, also newly appointed SSgt. Jake Wilson, Justin Regant, Robert Jefferson and Todd Hood, plus Frank and Jerry Ware. They pulled behind them five pack horses with their supplies and recently filled water bladders. They'd fill the water wagon up on top the plateau and sometime this week half of the team would go to the river for more water to load down the pack horses. Even the men's horses would be carrying water bladders to top off the water trailer. With the trailer brought up empty by the block-and-tackle rig, it was kept in under an overhang to keep the water cooled off.

Lt. Wilcox and MSgt. Wilson met with Lt. Sampson and MSgt. Michaels in the Command Tent, while the others shared information about the last two weeks of activity. Lt. Wilcox's men were all new, so this gave them time to tell the others who they were and something about why they decided to join the outfit. Then the oldsters replied with their own stories. What the men found amazing was how some of the men had survived battles where they had faced each other from opposite armies and were now fighting together as Rangers. Hands were shaken and coffee was passed all around. The war was truly over with this group, now they had new enemies to deal with to save Arizona.

INSIDE THE COMMAND TENT

Lt. Sampson was running the briefing for the moment and using a large hand drawn map to show what they had accomplished in the last two weeks. Sampson had obtained the blank news print paper from the Tucson newspaper office for $1, telling the salesman he needed to work out a mapping of some new mine section In Northern Arizona.

"This newsprint rolls up fairly nice and this thick cardboard tube will keep it safe, but I'd advise you to use this smaller art book to take down your facts, any settlements and roadways. Lots of washes, dried riverbeds to draw down, which probably fill up with flash floods. Then there's the hills, ridges and mountains. But some of these peaks that shoot right up to touch the stars, you almost feel like you'd like to climb every one of them.

"But over here you've got the Chiricahua Apache Reservation and from what I've picked up those young bucks are always kicking up their heels and leaving the place for a horse thieving raid or another murder raid. Up above them you have the Pima, but right now they're quiet and growing their crops. Ute are on the war path, but they always seem to be mad at everyone. It's a good thing their tribe is such a small one, otherwise they'd knock off both the Apache and the Comanche.

"We've had two small settlements raided, but not by Indians. A herd of maybe 400 to 500 cattle was moved south, but the men were in the 30's and way too many cattlemen for such a herd. I think these were Comancheros, but that's only a guess.

"However, we did chase down a small raiding party that was attacking three settler wagons heading west down below us. Our arrival ended the attack and identified the Indians as Chiricahua. We killed six of them and the settlers took care of 13 during the chase. I'd say about 15 took off south, but we didn't give chase. We helped the people with their wounded and buried their dead. Four men were lost including their patriarch, an old man of some 86 years. Two women were also killed when they took over for their husbands, but not a single child was hurt.

"Where are they headed, Lieutenant?" MSgt. Wilson asked.

After finishing off his cup of lukewarm coffee, Lt. Sampson replied, "They were Mormons headed for San Diego. They left Florida four months ago, and broke away from their 123-wagon train for a stop at Salt Lake

City. They left there, three weeks ago, with seven wagons and this was their fourth skirmish with the Indians."

"That's a sad story, Sir," MSgt. Michaels said.

"Sure is, Wallace, but I told them this should be the last of the Indians, but to watch themselves for the banditos and Comancheros. I also warned them about the White trouble-makers in Tucson and some of the larger towns. I warned them to find their church people in Tucson before making any deals for camping overnight and gave them directions to the Mormon Church and for the same thing in San Diego. Those bigger cities of San Diego and Los Angeles are going to be the Devil's playground, where new settlers will find all their money taken over land scams, men will be shanghaied for the long sails to China and Japan. Wives and kids will be walking the docks looking for their fathers, never to find them.

"I've heard San Francisco is a haven for boat captains to pick up free crewmen that way, just a knock over the head or something dropped into their drinks. Later, they wake-up in the ship's hold and the boat is 20 miles at sea," Lt. Wilcox mentioned and Lt. Sampson nodded his head in agreement.

"Me, I'll just stay here in the Arizona desert," MSgt. Michaels added.

"When do you plan on leaving, Lieutenant," Wilcox asked Sampson.

"I think tomorrow morning at sun-up. I'll advise Holloway he can pull out a half hour earlier to scout ahead. One thing I've learned here; you cannot trust the Apache to do what you'll think he'll do at any given time."

ALARM

During the evening meal, Lt. Wilcox advised Lt. Sampson of the new recruits Liam and Kathleen had brought back from Tucson and he provided the names to him from a notebook he kept in his left shirt pocket.

"I know the Wagner Brothers and they're a good bunch," Lt. Sampson said..." They all showed up about the time I came home. But that Zack and Wally Bush, if they're the same two I'm thinking of, both are wanted men for bank robbery and murder up north. I don't know the others, but I've been gone awhile and a lot of good and bad people have moved into Tucson."

"Minus the Bush Brothers, this will give us 48 Rangers and that is a sizeable unit," Lt. Wilcox said with enthusiasm. "We'll have two complete A and B Companies. Captain is even having Company Banners made up for one of the men to carry, like our company banners we had in the war."

"With such a force, we'd be able to take on any problem, even an Apache outbreak, as long as we have our Winchesters," Lt. Sampson said.

Suddenly, one of Lt. Sampson's men, Jordan Akers, burst into the tent, came to attention and reported, "There's an alarm out, Sir. We've got a fire burning in the distance and it appears to be a ranch house to the Southwest...Sir."

"Boots and Saddles, Akers...we'll be going out strong with both units." He looked to Lt. Wilcox and asked, "Okay with you, Lieutenant?"

"That's what we're here for," Lt. Wilcox replied. He then turned to MSgt. Wilson and ordered, "Get 'em mounted and make sure they're well-armed and canteens full."

"Who do we leave here," MSgt. Wilson asked. He then added, "To pull security of the post while we are gone?"

"We have our local crew who live here now, which one of our men supervises. Plus, we will leave four former Mexican Policemen who we rescued from being hung by their own sergeant because they refused to partake in his corruption. They can shoot, but still need a time of healing. But once healed they planned to ride to Mexico City to report on the corruption in the Border States. I only wish I could send half a dozen Rangers with them for escort," Lt. Sampson said.

"They won't steal the place dry?" MSgt. Wilson asked as they walked out the tent.

"No, this is the only place of safety they have ever felt and we pay them well, plus we house and feed them. No, they will protect this place with their lives. This is why they are armed with our old rifles. But they have no knowledge of the Gatlin Gun or how to remove it from the plateau. Now let's ride!" Lt. Sampson ordered.

Sixteen Rangers rode down the mountain path, which left abrasions and cuts on a few riders' knees and horse's flanks. Once the men and horses were spread out on the desert flatlands, Lt. Sampson ordered them into two ranks. Lt. Wilcox would ride beside Lt. Sampson, and behind them would be MSgt. Michaels and MSgt. Wilson, and while in the back, the tail role would fall on SSgt. Wilson, who would take the rider beside him to fall back 100 yards. Meanwhile, Holloway would already be out a good mile in front of the detail scouting for possible enemy troops.

At this moment, the wagon train trail was deserted, but the Ranger with the binoculars up on the Plateau had seen the flames be ignited at the great distance, only he couldn't see why or who was involved.

"It's going to take us four hours or a bit more to reach that ranch. It was on the other side of Texas Canyon, so I didn't include it in the mapping. However, I know they run a lot of cattle there," Lt. Sampson said.

"I thought the Indians didn't fight at night," Lt. Wilcox said in a raised voice to be heard between the galloping horses.

"They don't...Think this is bandits after the cattle, only 40 miles to the border."

"Think we'll reach them in time to do anything?" Lt. Wilcox asked.

"Depends on what kind of defense they put up, now let's ride!" Lt. Sampson shoved his heels into his mount, sinking his spurs and his horse jumped ahead.

Most of the troops new from riding in the dark like this they could easily run into a tarantula hole, varmint hole, crush a rattle snake and have it lock its venomous fangs on the horse's ankles, or ride into a cactus or cacti and be thrown from his mount. The only thing helping was the nearly full moon that provided some limited degree of night vision. But the rider had to stay within earshot of the horse's backend in front of him, or possibly be lost forever in the dark desert.

Most often a patrol would be carrying torches or walking their horses, but it seemed Lt. Sampson knew this trail quite well. But the men had forgotten they had actually mapped the Texas Canyon, or at least some 60 miles of it and knew that until they reached a wall of rock diverting his ride to the right, he could lead the company. But then Holloway, who should be waiting for them there, would have to take over and they would have to slow their pace down.

Lt. Sampson had slowed the pace as he felt the rocky ridgeline to the left of him and he knew he was rapidly approaching where he would come upon Holloway. Twenty minutes later, approximately, he did walk right into the side of Holloway's horse and feel the barrel end of a Winchester Rifle pressured against his chest. "What's the password, Greenhorn?"

"How about 30 days in the guardhouse for threatening an officer, Mr. Holloway?" Lt. Sampson replied.

"You may pass...But you sure need ta work on your sense of humor...Sir," Holloway said, as he removed his rifle from blocking Lt. Sampson's advance.

"What have we got up ahead?" Lt. Sampson asked his point man.

"If we stay in the wash for another three...maybe four miles, we should be right close to the ranch house. But we'll never get our horses over the ridges. We'll have to climb hand and foot and then probably make an infantry charge once we see the enemy. Do you want me to go ahead, Lieutenant?"

"Yes, but I want another man to go with you." Lt. Sampson sent the name down through the ranks and SSgt. Wilson showed up. It had taken him a few minutes to come in from riding tail-end Charlie.

"Sir, I could've been following Cochise out there and wouldn't have known it," SSgt. Wilson said in jest.

"You just keep that sense of humor going, because you're going to need it. I want you going on scout with Mr. Holloway. He'll explain everything to you and he's in charge, understand?"

"Yes, Sir…I understand the order," SSgt. Wilson answered and the four people nearest him could hear the dry gulp in his throat.

Nearly two hours later, the 16 men were lying in the warm desert sand only 100 to 150 yards from the ranch. They now knew a battle was still going on between the attackers and several riflemen in the large bunkhouse. The Ranger horses were tied off to Chola bushes growing on the sides of the wash, and now they were afoot, or more exactly on their stomachs.

The Main Ranch House had nearly been burnt to the ground and through the glow of the dying flames the Rangers could see several bodies and one or possibly two were female. Lt. Sampson took a count of the attackers and came up with 11 riders and by the same glow of the burning ambers they didn't appear to be Indians, but wore the large sombreros of the Mexican bandits.

"Lieutenant, you take your men to the north of the bunk house and watch for when I light a match. That's the time to charge the riders. Keep calling out Rangers so the men in the bunkhouse don't shoot at you or us, and we'll do the same. But watch for the match light…I'll give you five minutes, so please hurry," Lt. Sampson whispered to Lt. Wilcox. Sampson then grabbed Holloway by the shoulder.

"Mr. Holloway, take SSgt. Wilson with you and make your way over to that other dark building. Must be a hay storage room or for leather tack. Make sure it's empty and get on the other side. I want you two to shoot down anyone trying to escape. I know they'll be hard to see, but listen for their horses or the rider's yells. Mexican Bandits love to yell. You have five minutes, and the clock starts now…Both of you have watches, right?" Lt. Sampson asked, wanting to kick himself for not asking that sooner.

"I've got my watch," Lt. Wilcox answered.

"I've got a pocket watch," Holloway answered.

"Then get moving!"

The shooting war going on was a noisy one, with the Bandits whipping around the large bunkhouse like Indians around a wagon train. But in the dark, it was nearly impossible for the men inside to hit one of the riders and for some reason the riders had not set the bunk house on fire, which had Lt. Sampson confused. He wondered if there was cash inside or a particular person they needed to rescue. But they would know soon.

"You men get ready to go and slowly move to the top of the ridge so you're ready to reinforce the other unit. Remember, no shooting to your left as Mr. Holloway and SSgt. Wilson are down that way. We will attack in a flanking movement, take ten steps and assume firing positions with two roles. First row on one knee and second row standing. You've practiced this enough and you know how to do it and how the concentrated fire is fearsome. Also, don't forget to continual use of the yell, 'Ranger'. I don't want to lose anyone to some guy in the bunk house killing one of you by accident."

Lt. Sampson covered over his watch and let the moonlight provide the time. He still had two more minutes. He only hoped his men would survive this first action, because they still had to locate the cattle and bring them back.

Seconds went by slowly and finally the moment came. As the minute hand reached the top of the watch, Lt. Sampson ignited a single match and waved it over his head. This apparently caught the attention of a Mexican Bandit because a shot zinged right over the top of Lt. Sampson's head.

"Rangers! Rangers!" was screamed out from both positions as both units approached. They then assumed their shooting positions and began firing with their Winchester repeaters. Horses were heard dropping and men were screaming and the intense rifle fire did its job. Two riders tried to escape to the south and were shot out of their saddle by Wilson and Holloway.

Finally, a "Cease fire!" was yelled out by Lt. Sampson and the men stopped, but continued to hold their rifles at the ready. Then first one and then a second torch was lit on the porch of the bunkhouse, followed by several others that were soon handed out to the Rangers. Bodies were located and injured horses were put down. With the two down by the tool shed, both men dead, the Rangers had accounted for 11 bandits. The cattlemen had earlier killed six Bandits, but the herds had not been touched yet. By morning the Rangers were out searching for other bandits, but none were found and there was no evidence the Bandits had any intention of taking any cattle, at least on this trip.

The old man who owned the Ranch, buying a Spanish Grant from the original owner 38 years ago, when the man wanted to go back to Spain, had lost his wife in the first moments of the attack. The Bandits had ridden in and demanded the original deeds, water rights and any gold, cash or gems the owner had on hand. When the owner came out with a shotgun and blew the leader out of the saddle, another Bandit killed the wife. Another woman, who was the wife's cook and dear friend of over 20 years, was also gunned down when she tried to escape the main house.

The owner tried to reason with the remaining Bandits, telling them all his important papers, large amounts of cash and jewels were in the bank in Tucson. That was when they set fire to the house and the owner, plus two of his men were able to escape to the bunk house. Like typical ranches in Arizona, the ranch house and bunk house were set up to repel Apaches. Window shutters had firing ports, entry doors were heavy and braced so it was nearly impossible to break through them. Fire was their major enemy, but the Bandits wanted to capture the owner alive. They never did learn why, whether it was for revenge for killing their leader or some other devious act.

Other cowboys were now able to come off the land to see if their boss had survived. They had stayed with the cattle, which was their main responsibility last night and the owner wasn't mad at anyone of them. He started everything off and he knew he should've gotten his wife inside the house before opening up with his 12-guage cannon. But he figured they were all dead anyway and wanted to take out the leader first. Now he had two sons to tell their mother was dead. Both of them were back east in college. He had hoped they would take over the ranch some day and know how to run the operation within all these new-fangled laws and keep a good accounting of the books. The Halverson Ranch went for 300,000 acres and the 26,000 head of cattle wore the Triple slash-arrow head brand. There were two lakes on the land and two major rivers, which kept the cattle in drinking water.

Old Man Halverson couldn't understand what a bunch of Mexican Bandits hoped to do with his land deeds and water rights, unless he agreed to sign them over. But to be upheld legally, both sons would have to sign off on all the deeds also. He had made them full partners when they turned 18 years old.

Upon hearing this, Lt. Sampson suspicious mind began to go to work. All though investigations were not part of their current job, he was mighty curious to find out if the brothers were still at college or possibly living high on the hog in Mexico, possibly Nogales, Senora. This could be the classic case of the two sons weary of their father's hard ways, attempting to sell off part or the entire ranch to continue living in the matter they now enjoy. But he could fire off a letter to the U.S. Attorney General and request an investigation by the lawful U.S. Marshals. He'd have to clear it with Captain Blake first, but he was pretty sure JW would agree.

Just before sundown, the Rangers had arrived at the plateau. Lt. Sampson and his men had to ride back up to gather their belongings and were soon going back down for the long ride to Superstition Mountain Range. Holloway had ridden on ahead and the squad was riding in a loose formation because everyone was tired.

With a full moon, the road was easy to see and the men voted to continue riding until midnight, then grab a few hours of sleep and make the final ride in one ten hour piece. There was no fire and at 4:25 a.m., they began the remaining long ride in hopes to sleep in their new encampment tonight.

But at 0803 hours, Chief Victorio had other plans when he attacked a small column of Union Cavalry. One Platoon of new troops en route to the newly constructed Fort Verde, with over 500 miles of travel ahead of them, believed they were taking a shortcut to Phoenix Township, after the lengthy ride from Texas. Instead, they had ridden straight into an ambush, with some 40 warriors attacking a relief patrol of 20 untried raw cavalry.

With Lt. Sampson shaking his head in wonder, he ordered his men into a flank of eight horsemen, including himself and a doubtful Mr. Holloway. The patrol was at the bottom of a gully, surrounded by their dead horses, returning fire. Of the 20 troopers, 14 were still able to shoot and give an account of themselves.

"You all ready for Act II of this play," Lt. Sampson asked his weary-eyed men.

"Rangers...do or die!" Daniel Boone exclaimed.

"Let's do it, Lieutenant," said MSgt Wilson.

"Rangers, CHARGE!" Lt. Sampson yelled and the horsemen rode over the desert knoll to sweep down on the backs of the Apache Indians. Caught by surprise, Chief Victorio and his two top advisors stayed around long enough to see five of their warriors be cut down by these cowboys. He ordered a full retreat, but as the Indians fled another three Indians were taken down and then it was done. The shooting ceased.

Lt. Sampson ordered Holloway and SSgt. Wilson to the hill where Chief Victorio was sitting upon his war pony, to ensure the Indians were still running. He then went down to check on the conditions of the new troopers.

"Sir, you have just saved our lives. Thank you...I just don't know what else to say, but you have saved 14 of us and maybe one or two more if we can get them to a doctor." A very young second lieutenant said. This was his first command since finishing West Point. "We headed west with a much bigger unit, but we continued to drop them off along the way. True, we had a brush with the Comanche in New Mexico, but there were still a-100 of us. But then we had to drop off most of them at Fort Bowie. I was told about this shortcut we could take and miss Tucson for our way north for Camp Verde, it's a brand new post."

"Lieutenant, do you know me?" Lt. Sampson asked.

"No, I don't think so."

"Then please explain why you are telling me US Army information I have no reason in knowing about."

"Sir, I thought you to be a scouting unit for the army, I apologize for my mistake, but I am still very much in appreciation for what you and your men have done for us."

"Lieutenant, I am a former First Lieutenant with the military, but currently I am a First Lieutenant with the Arizona Rangers and we were on patrol when we spotted you in trouble. But our unit is small and we welcome the additional U.S. Army troops into Arizona. But before I leave I'd like to offer you a word of advice: As a new officer, you will be challenged at every corner to become a member of the corruption in the U.S. Military now assigned here in Arizona. This is mostly senior officers. Keep your eyes open and you will find corruption in the court system, law enforcement and federal office of taxation and their U.S. Marshals Services assigned to the Tax offices. This is why I resigned. But it's only advice. When the war was lost, southern land owners came home to find their farms and ranches seized for overdue war taxes they had never been told about. Small and large herds were seized by the taxation people, as well as wagons, belongings and anything of value. These US Marshals, which is different from the US Deputy Marshals, who mostly work alone and never enforce this tax law, carry out all the weight, but the Taxation people then work with the carpetbaggers coming down from the Northeast. Big money coming here to buy up these ranches and farms, and all these herds, who will eventually sell the beef to the Army at triple the price and it will be taken out of your pay.

"I know men who came home to find their families killed off by these federal marshals, or watched as three marshals gunned down a man with no gun to seize his wagon. This is what is going on in Arizona and why the Indians are out in force. The carpetbaggers want all the Indians killed off, not just put on reservations and small patrol like yours will be the ones to suffer.

"Now before we leave I'll let you in one thing, so you'll understand I am telling you the truth. Those Federal Officers applied pressure to have the Arizona Rangers disbanded, leaving the settlers wide open to be killed or run off by the Apache, Mexican Banditos and Comancheros. When the war ended, we came back to restart the Arizona Rangers. We work without pay and we have two Cavalry companies to help the people of all South Central and South East Arizona. So now the Federal Government has rewards posted on us. I am worth $2,500 and our leader, the former Company Commander and now again our superior officer, is worth $10,000. But the people love us for what we do. We are here to help the Territory of Arizona.

"Now get your men together and we'll escort you up to where I'll have horses waiting for you. By then, you'll be out of Victorio's range. Well, that's not exactly the truth the whole territory, is his range, but he mainly centers on the Southeast. Okay?"

"You'll have to excuse me, Lieutenant, I seemed to miss hearing that part about some people being wanted and as to the other advice, I will keep my eyes open. My degrees are in Law, and political science, but I desired the Cavalry and finished in the top five percent of the class and received the orders I wished for. Of course, I might have seen all those college hours wasted had it not been for your timely arrival, so please remember, you have a friend."

"Thanks. Now how can we help with your wounded?"

When the detail was ready to move, some of the men walking, wounded lying in homemade stretchers lashed between two horses and others riding as flankers and point. Holloway was sent forward at all capable speed to bypass the Apache and reach Superstition. A message was written out for Captain Blake, explaining Lt. Sampson's needs for saddled horses and two wagons for wounded men. An eight-man volunteer outfit was also recommended to escort the detail further down the road, at least to the big open desert where it would be hard for the Indians to sneak up on the unit. Lt. Sampson advised where he would wait for the requested supplies, adding the request for extra ammo as he was personally down to four 30-30 rounds for his rifle.

Five hours and 24 minutes later the slow-moving patrol rounded a corner to find the Rangers waiting for them with everything Lt. Sampson had requested. One of the men who was the closest they had to a doctor, Greg Sacker, was on-hand to take the bullets out, arrowheads and bandage the men up. It wasn't easy on the victims, but the travel would soon go easier for them. Wounded were moved into the wagons, two men to each wagon, along with two water barrels strapped to the sides of each wagon.

The draft horses were being used, but they would be exchanged for the riding horses when the Rangers ended their escort.

Lt. J.B. Newhall was amazed to hear that he had another escort to take him to what they call the big desert. He was told to ration his water for the men, but not the wounded or the horses, for they had a ways to go to reach Phoenix and then Camp Verde.

"Now remember, Mr. Newhall, no matter what you hear about me, I never did murder a bunch of nuns, set fire to an orphanage or cheat at poker…No, never did. But I have killed a lot of people as a soldier and as a Ranger. But my boss, who sent you those horses, wagons and supplies, he came home to find his wife killed, his son murdered and his young daughter kidnapped to be sold into slavery. He lost his entire ranch, his herd and he had yet to kill a carpetbagger, one of those fake Federal Marshals or a tax man. He even had his hands on two of them when they set an ambush for him at his own property when he went to put flowers on his wife's grave. But he didn't kill them, only popped one in the nose who tried to back shoot him. He is a bigger man than I'll ever be, but if he does ever cut loose he'd burn those revenuers to the ground. Almost every Ranger in our group suffered like that, but they've put Arizona in front of that hatred. This is why this territory will grow to become a state and a proud one at that. Good luck to you, Sir." He shook hands with the young officer and rode off with his command.

CHAPTER SIXTEEN

"Buffalo? ain't no stinkin' Buffalo in the Arizona desert! You been sucking that prickly pear juice again?"

SUPERSTITION MOUNTAINS, ARIZON

Three weeks after Lt. Sampson had returned to the Ranger's Superstition Fortress, a package had arrived for him at the Halverson Ranch. By the time word got to him and it was his rotation at the Plateau, a month had gone by and he was about to return for Superstition Mountain. Mirror posts had been set up at various locations along the southern wagon train roadway going and coming from Tucson. These mirror stations were hidden, but known to members of the area who might need to contact the Rangers. The Observation Post on the Plateau routinely kept an eye out for these various posts. It might be a sighting of banditos or Comancheros, stolen herds being moved, murders riding through on a rampage or Indian raids, or in this case notification of a mail delivery.

Lt. Sampson asked MSgt. Wilson to go ahead and take the unit back and explain to Captain Blake he needed to ride to the Halverson's Ranch for some information and should be in the next day.

When he reached the mirror station he found one the Halverson's cowboys waiting for him, with a good size document mailer. "Mr. Halverson was not aware if you needed to come to the ranch, where of course you are always welcome, or if it was better you just get it here."

"Let me look it over real quick and then I can decide." He dismounted from his horse and walked over to sit on a rock with a shady overhang. He went through the papers, shaking his head with a hard look of disapproval on his face. He then found a single piece of paper that caused him to glare at it for a moment, before he folded it up and placed it inside his vest inner pocket.

Lt. Sampson stood up and walked over to the cowboy who was dismounted and curry combing his beautiful roan gelding. "We need to see your boss. He'll want to see this."

"Then let's ride."

They rode hard and by the time they arrived both horsemen were carrying lit torches to guide their paths. Lt. Sampson was surprised, in only a month the burned debris had been pulled away and the first floor of the Ranch House was already built out of cedar logs. Lt. Sampson knew when finished this house they would have a beautiful scent from the cedar.

He just hoped the news he carried wouldn't kill the old man and the ranch never be finished.

"Welcome, my dear friend, I am pleased to see you decided to ride back here. But I do not wish this packet of mail is what brought you back and that it might be bad news for you or your family...Or the men you ride with. If so, I do have legal counsel in San Antonio and Mexico City who might be of hope," Mr. Halverson said in sincerity as he came out of the bunk house and offered his hand.

"Normally, I would treat my guests to some wine in my dining room and a platter of Mexican sweet fried bread my cook could prepare so well, but I am now without a cook and my wine cellar has been destroyed. But I have sent my ranch manager to Mexico City to find me both a well-trained cook and can prepare the French and Mexican dishes I have come to appreciate, as well as barbecue a thick steak or pork chops. Then there is the wine, brandy and sherry list he is to fill and the guards to hire. I will then bring them on as new ranch hands if they appear suitable.

"Now, my good friend, what may I do for you, for we owe our very lives to you and we will move mountains to assist you in any way, "Mr. Halverson said with that big grin of his on his face and his arms outstretched.

"Sir, I hope you feel the same way in a few moments, for I bring you bad news," Lt. Sampson said. "Could we take a seat on the bunk house porch, just the two of us?"

"Of course, besides the men have plenty of work to do and he waved them all away. They knew he was safe with the Ranger lieutenant; they were just interested in what the packet contained.

"Mr. Halverson, when we were here during the attack, things you said and how the attack was conducted put my investigator's mind into thinking how things were not adding up. The Banditos were not acting in a normal faction and they set fire to the ranch house if knowing your important papers and major cash was not stored inside there. By all the evidence shown in their attack it looked like you were the focus, they wanted to kidnap you and possibly your wife but one of the banditos got mad when he saw their leader get blown away by your shotgun, he took it out on your wife. Your cattle were not even touched and they never set fire to the bunk house. No, they wanted those land deeds and water rights, but they seemed to know they needed you alive."

"Yes, I too have been wondering about this."

"I am sorry, Sir, without asking your permission as to not cause you greater pain, especially if it turned out to be unwarranted, I contacted a Federal Officer I knew very well outside of Arizona, not desiring to conduct any business with our current Arizona government who would like to see the Ranger before a firing squad or hanging from a tree for refusing to remain disbanded and letting the these tax people and Federal Marshals destroy our Territory."

"Lieutenant, we can discuss politics later, you said you had something for me?"

"I apologize, Mr. Halverson, the current situation has led to the death of a lot of dear friends and their families. But, in your case I asked for the true whereabouts of your two sons and any information about them they could offer." Lt. Sampson stopped when he saw Mr. Halverson's expression turn to one of anger and he launched into, "By what right do you have to…" He stopped. "I apologize, Lieutenant. You have every right for you and your men coming to our aid and attempting now to once again help me. May you now tell me what you have found and I can tell from the size of the mail packet it is significant."

"Sir, I'll leave this packet with you, there are no copies. But your sons dropped out of school over a year ago and now live in Mexico City. They have become greatly involved in the evil forces attempting to steal the Arizona Territory away from the settlers and long term ranchers and farmers. They have also accrued some heavy debts with the people who operate the Northeast banking chain, which provides all the money to the carpetbaggers to buy up the land from these illegal tax sales, which are supported by these corrupt Federal Marshals, who are also on the payroll of these same bankers.

"I believe, to get out of these debts and give them millions of dollars to live on, they planned to kidnap you and their mother and use her to force you to sign over his third of the land ownership and water rights. With her dead, all they could do was possibly threaten you or use your grief to simply hand it over. But in this packet, you will find a copy of the court paperwork filed in Mexico City and in Santa Fe, making the initial declaration of the attempt by the Banking Chain in the American North East to purchase your land, cattle, buildings, plus water and mineral rights. Someone must think you have silver or gold on your property. But as to why the declaration was filed in Mexico City, I'm not sure because your land is all in the Arizona Territory…isn't it?"

"No, Lieutenant Sampson," a weakened older man said. He rested his jaw in the palm of his right hand and began to slow rock back and forth in a handmade pine rocker. His eyes had watered up and Sampson remained silent.

In a moment, Mr. Halverson spoke in a quiet voice, "Across the border in the State of Senora, my property continues for another 200,000 acres, including a hot-springs. I have a second ranch over there and here is where I keep most of my horses, especially my Appaloosas. I've been breeding them there for the last 20 years and move them up to Texas or New Orleans."

"One of the finest horses...Captain Blake rides one of the most beautiful ones I've ever seen and he got his in Pennsylvania...I believe. A stallion that behaves like a brother to Captain Blake."

"My wife spoiled the boys. I wanted to make them ranch hands, bring them from the ground up to learn the animals and the men, but she won the argument and sent them off to Europe for boarding school when they both turned eight years old to obtain a proper education. They sure got a proper education all right...They knew their math and reading the classics, but knew nothing about the world and especially how men needed to be led. They both got their butts kicked by ordinary hands and never challenged for a rematch. Oh, I expected them to lose, but I needed them to keep coming back until the cowboys respected them for their effort. But they ran and Mom sent them off to the Northeast, some fancy college."

"I'm sorry, sir to have to be the one to tell you this," Lt. Sampson.

"Don't you see, Lieutenant, it had to be you. Anyone else and I would've shot them for just making the accusation. But I was in debt to you and needed to hear you out. I guess you can say this was providence...fate. Now I owe you even more, you've saved my home."

"Mr. Halverson, there is no debt. I am a Ranger, here to serve the people of Arizona for as long as I am alive. But may I ask what you may plan to do, now?"

"Well, off the top of my head and I usually follow up with these quick leaps of faith, I'll contact my lawyers once again and if they're not aware of this Declaration to Purchase filed in Santa Fe and Mexico City, they had better get off their butts and request a file the same day they hear from me or find a different client. But I'll ask the Mexico City lawyer to find my boys and make this deal to them, that I will give them the land and horses in Mexico to sell or keep. I figure this will pay of their debts and give them a fortune to live on. They won't choose to keep the ranch, but they'll live in Mexico City. Then I will move forward to disown them as my legal Aires to keep them from ever claiming this land, which I will probably donate to the Territory of Arizona and divide up my stock to my hands who have been so loyal to me."

He then glanced around, with a small smile coming to his mouth, "I think this place would make a nice park for the people to visit. We've got several old ruins here from the ancient Pueblos or those once known as the Anasazi, the tribe who mysteriously just up and disappeared; another one of those desert legends." But one of the things he didn't tell Lt. Sampson concerned his shoot to kill order if his sons came across the border and entered this land. He never wanted to see them again, but if it was to occur he would bury them beside their mother. He knew she would want it that way.

SUPERSTITION MOUNTAINS

When Lt. Sampson rode up into the new Ranger headquarters he was surprised to see four trailer loads of cedar longs coming in and then he saw the foundations being built for the kitchen and a large bunkhouse. He knew it was only a matter of time before log homes would be built for the married couples, headquarters and supply. The Cedar forest was not that far away and a detail of ten men plus three drivers went out every three days to log the desert forest.

Captain Blake estimated by the time they had all their buildings constructed the forest would be mostly stumps and it would take another 20 years before they could call it a forest again.

Oddly enough with all the noises they produced in the logging they had no problems with the Indians. The detail reported not laying an eye on an Indian scout, which made JW wonder where Victorio, Cochise and the new buck Geronimo were.

Lt. Sampson reported in to Captain Blake and explained why he was late and allowed the detail to come back without an officer in charge. JW was not happy, but he eventually agreed with Lt. Sampson's decision to return to Mr. Halverson's Ranch. He then learned that Mr. Halverson was going to have his lawyers in Santa Fe, look into the possibility of having Captain Blake's Rangers being made an extension of the Santa Fe Reserve Militia on active duty.

Formally, Arizona Territory was only called that by word of mouth, but officially in Washington D.C. Arizona was only part of the New Mexico Territory. But New Mexico openly preferred Arizona to become its own territory because of its Indian problems and settler troubles needing expensive assistance from the territorial government. But if the Ranger could be made a part of the New Mexico branch of legal law enforcement, all the arrest warrants would be dropped and the Rangers could continue to act without worry from the Federal Marshals going after them. Unless they, as an individual Ranger or a small group broke a federal law, then they could be charged and arrested by the federal authorities.

Still, JW was not very hopeful. He knew New Mexico had done its level best to stay out of Arizona politics. But they would wait and see how the Santa Fe lawyers handled it with the Santa Fe legislature.

"I've got something else for you to see," Lt. Sampson said and after he took his riding gloves off, pulled out the folded paper he had removed from the mail packet he had been sent to the Halverson Ranch. His address was the only location he knew where it was safe to receive confidential mail, and no one had attempted to open the packet because the seal was unbroken.

"This came with the mail I requested on the two sons...I had the two Bush Brothers checked out and asked for their wanted posters showing their pictures or accurate drawings. We got photos."

JW remained in his chair, behind the old, school teacher's desk and he opened the folded paper. Almost instantly a soured expression appeared and the two hands holding the paper were squeezed tight enough into fists his knuckles were turning white. Only through self-control he kept from ripping the paper in half, but Lt. Sampson was really glad this man's anger was not focused on him. He knew the boss had high hopes his inner voice might be wrong on these two men because every troop mattered in the growth of their Ranger Companies.

With a strained voice, JW called for the outside guard, who also acted as an orderly at different times. "Get me MSgt Wells and make it on the double!" He ordered.

"Want a drink? One of our patrols picked up a case of 35-year old Bourbon from a wagon crash. People just gave up on searching it and this one case survived. Rest of the Bourbon was broken glass and liquid pouring into the sand from the report. We'll probably get some nice smelling flowers there in a couple months. Nice reward for the men. I kept one bottle for the Command Tent, so only one ounce, Lieutenant." JW was now under full control of his senses and he carefully, but casually poured the Bourbon into small brandy sniffers. In this way, the wine would last longer and the men were advised to do the same. One third of what was left went to the married people, one third to the single troops and one third to the civilians who worked here. With such a small capacity, Liam made sure Kathleen got her one ounce in a tin coffee cup. It was measured out in another Brandy glass about the size of a large thimble.

Once they had finished their Bourbon and the bottle was put away as to not tempt them for a second glass, MSgt. Wells came into JW's office and then moved into the Command Staff area when he saw both JW and Lt. Sampson there. "Sir, MSgt. Wells reporting to the Commanding Officer as ordered." Wells presented a crisp salute, while he remained at attention.

"Gary, I have informed you in the past...several times, if I recall, you need not salute me and report officially when you come into my headquarters. We only request it outside to keep military protocol in the ranks."

"Yes, Sir, but I see Lt. Sampson is here and I was not sure how he would've felt about the lack of protocol between us."

"MSgt. Gary Wells, I feel a more relaxed headquarters between the Command Staff members producing a higher functioning unit. All right, Gary?"

"Thank you, Sir, but to keep me from slipping outside, I will still address you by your rank, Sir."

"Okay, Gary, now I've called you in here for a very important job. But before I send you out, tell me the shape of our new jail." JW inquired.

"Sir, as you know we located a nice one-way cave that goes in approximately 30 feet. Some miner had dug away and it looks like he did some blasting, but he gave it up. His wood piling work is very sound, with reinforced six-inch beams every four feet to keep the roof from falling in. Once it was decided to make this our jail, we began building a stone wall at the 20-foot line. A couple of our civilians know how to work with stone and adobe, so we now have a four-foot thick adobe wall, mixed with heavy stone from floor to ceiling. Though we have no beds yet, but that's not a serious problem, yet. We have miner's lights filled with candles to provide illumination and not be dangerous to a guard. The door is made of cedar and there is a view window with an outside door for only the guard to use and two heavy outside door bolts unreachable by the prisoners."

JW walked back over to the desk and picked up the flyer and then handed it to Wells, "Take a look at that. We had a hunch and Lt. Sampson checked into it. Remember, it's that kind of follow-through that makes a good Ranger. The future of Rangering is far above town taming and Indian fighting. We all have to become investigators, but by that time, Gary, you and I will be planted in a piece of land and this here Lieutenant will be a Colonel of a Rangers Regiment, and Arizona will be a state."

"How do you want me to handle this?" Wells asked.

JW took the flyer back. "Two Bank Robberies, suspect in a Train Robbery where a US Deputy Marshal was killed. A Second Town Sheriff killed in Ohio, and a Family of five Butchered in Southern Ohio. Suspect in Three Separate Women Being Raped and Murdered in New Mexico, and a Trading Post Robbery Where the Unarmed Owner Was Murdered.

"These are a couple of hardened criminals and I am really surprised they're hiding with us. Might be they think strength in numbers will protect them, or they hope to claim the reward for us. They might believe the authorities are too ignorant, or stupid to have wanted posters. But now we do.

"So, Gary take four men with you, disarm them and conduct a thorough search for knives and a second gun or derringer...Check their hats and inside their boots. Then bring them here. Pick four men you trust to get the job done," JW ordered.

"Good luck, Gary…You might have two of your men come from another side as to not warn these outlaws," Lt. Sampson said.

"Sir, no offense, but I've been doing this sort of work when you were still throwing rocks at little girls to demonstrate your undying love."

Nearly ten minutes later, both JW and Sampson heard a single shot, causing them to dash outside to see if one of their men was hurt in making the arrest, but it was Zach Bush who was being escorted with a bandaged wrist. JW sighed with relief and Lt. Sampson nodded his head with satisfaction.

With the escort standing behind them, the Bush's firearms, knives and a hideout derringer, were now locked up, Lt. Sampson displayed the wanted poster to both fugitives. But the men had no reply, but to only glare at Lt. Sampson and Captain Blake.

"You two fugitives, wanted for various robberies and murders, are to be held in our new jail until we determine what we will do with you. Any attempt to escape and you will be shot immediately. I do hope you both understand this." Captain Blake said.

"Captain, what can you really do with us. We are wanted felons and once you turn us over to the proper authorities you risk us informing on your location. You can't just shoot us, not and still uphold your Ranger oath. So, why not jus' let us head for Mexico and we're out of your hair and you know we'll avoid the authorities."

JW smiled at the two men, which made both of them uncomfortable. "You both violated your oath when you failed to advise us of your criminal past, at which point I may have simply sent you on your way, which gives me grounds to shoot you down like the snakes you are. Or I could leave you out in the middle of the desert without guns and water, to let God decide your fate. But, I haven't decided what I will do.

"Until then you'll be the first occupants of our newly completed jail. You can move your mattresses and blankets in with you, but nothing else. Food and water will be provided until which time we've made our decision.

"But please, let us know how you feel about your new lodgings, so we can improve on them for future prisoners," JW said. He then gestured to MSgt. Wells to take them away. "Make sure you get his wrist cleaned and bandaged before locking him up and he'll probably need some extra water for the first two days."

"Yes, Sir," MSgt. Wells replied. He then called the detail to attention and escorted the desert slime out of the building. All told, there were ten rifles aimed at them for the moment, but both men wondered if an attempt to escape might make it a quick ending. But they were cowards without their firearms and so they walked along with their escort.

"Any ideas, Captain?" Lt. Sampson asked.

I have a copy of Arizona Laws and will search them through and see what my options are and then I'll know how to answer that question," JW answered. "Now, you'd better check on you're A Company and I'll have Lt. Dreeke notify you of a Command Staff Meeting tonight at 8 p.m.

"Yes, Sir," Lt. Sampson said and he presented a casual salute, to which JW responded with his own.

Now left alone, he walked over to a rusted blue painted four drawer file cabinet salvaged from a burned-out church building, where the Apache had struck a small town. The men had scrubbed off all the blackened smoke and some of the rust. The cabinet was aged, but it did the job for JW's needs. JW also picked up a case of file folders from when his men took a trip into Senora to investigate the Comancheros operating in that particular-area. Now he opened his 18th file folder and placed the Bush wanted poster into it and would soon add a written report.

He would let Lt. Sampson write up his own report on the Halverson Ranch investigation, but they would add it as an amendment to Report # 12. One of the things he realized he needed to procure a large order of writing paper and find out how many of his Ranger could not read and write, so they could begin school. He had it in mind to have Liam and Kathleen teach the First Ranger School of academics. If he knew his men, Liam would need to carry a club and they would have to attend without firearms. Kathleen's good looks would soften the edge on the men, but Liam might need a whip and a chair to harness in these mountain cats. But JW wanted everyone of his Rangers to be able to write a report, so they could interview witnesses and not have to wait for the officer or senior NCO to handle the chore.

This was one of the items he wanted to discuss tonight at the staff meeting, along with other matters.

COMMAND STAFF MEETING

JW was running the meeting, which was conducted around an old wagon plank board table top. Lt. Dreeke and Lt. Sampson were present, along with MSgt. Wells and MSgt. Michaels. Both Lt. Wilcox and MSgt. Wilson were out at the Plateau and would soon receive this briefing when JW inspected the position in two days. For tonight though, JW had also asked Liam and Kathleen to be in attendance during part of the meeting. There was enough Bourbon, mixed with water, for each member present to have a single ounce, if heavy on the water. The bottle was then to be used as a candle holder. Two of the wives who had learned the trade in candle making were actively pursuing their craft with all the wax found in the various burned out wrecks along the roads. JW hadn't thought of how easy melted wax could be turned around to form new candles and the talents of these women amazed him. They soon realized the candle lanterns lasted far longer than the oil ones and much easier to come by. Soon all the empty Bourbon bottles had become decorative candle holders, which added to the atmosphere of the married quarters and the men's chow hall.

First thing to be handed out at the staff meeting was the new Post Duty Roster. JW commanded the Rangers, with Lt. Dreeke being carried as his Executive Officer and C Company Commander. Orderly as assigned was Liam Blake, who was also official messenger for the Rangers.

"A Company would hence forth be commanded by Lt. Wilcox and his top sergeant will be MSgt. Wells. Sixteen Rangers are assigned, plus the Lieutenant. You'll notice both A and B Companies have two scouts each, but currently C Company has none. But I will get to that in a moment.

"B Company is commanded by Lt. Sampson and his top sergeant is MSgt. Michaels. B Company also has 16 members, plus the Lieutenant. Now you will see A Company is somewhat rank heavy and that's because these men have been fighting together since long before the war, in the old Rangers. If I was to separate them now, I might have a mutiny on my hands.

"Now as to C Company, for the moment this company under Lt. Dreeke is responsible for our fortress here, pulling security and manning our observation posts. When one of the other two companies is in on its rest periods, half of them will proceed to relieve the Plateau force, while the other half will assist in fortress security and helping to man the observation posts here, work the cattle and just assist as needed.

"As to the primary patrol on duty, we are to patrol south to the main Tucson wagon train road and then head east for the Arizona border with New Mexico and then return, making side trips as necessary, but to be back here within two weeks. If you have not returned, an eight-man unit with two wagons will be en-route to find you. Leave markers we can identify whenever leaving the main roadway and any other markings that might help to locate you.

"If you have questions about Ranger assignments, bring them up now. No, good! Let's move on to the next detail, then.

"We have two prisoners in our jail, men who joined us to become Rangers, but we have found them to be fugitives. I will not bring up what they are wanted for as some of you might become members of the jury. I have recently read that in the absence of an accredited law enforcement authority, a militia force made up of the majority may conduct a lawful trial and either release the prisoners or conduct sentencing and carry out same. This was recorded in Arizona and has not been repealed, so this leaves it still in effect for us to use.

"So, we are going to hold a trial here in one week. A jury of six to 12 men will be selected from the civilians and Rangers here to make the trial legal. I will perform the office of the Judge. Two of my officers will be the prosecutor and the defense lawyer and I will demand that both men will do their level best to carry out the duties assigned to them. If I find the Defense Attorney slacking, he will lose his position as an officer and be demoted to a Staff Sergeant."

JW slapped a deck of cards on the table top, for he had been holding them in his back pocket and waiting for this moment to shake the meeting up. You two officers will draw one card. High card is the prosecutor and low card is the defense attorney. When Lt. Wilcox returns from the field he will then draw his card. So, who feels lucky?"

Dreeke reached out and pulled five cards off the deck and lifted the fifth card up for all to see, it was a Jack of Hearts. Lt. Sampson then picked halfway through the deck, which he spread out across the table and selected his card, which ended up being the 8-of-Spades.

"Well, this still leaves it wide open, but Dreeke, you're favored for prosecutor position at this point. Now, some additional information, you may only interview your men in the jail, with the door open and everyone ten-feet from the opening. Four armed men will be present, but they will not be allowed on the jury and they will be sworn not to speak with anyone else in camp about what they overhead. If their word is broken and they will be forewarned, they will face 25 lashes with a cowboy's whip and the trial redone.

"Only the jury will be present for the trial and any witnesses who might be called. During the sentencing and the carrying out of the sentence, all will be required to attend, except for the women and children."

JW pulled a second note piece out and added, "For the length of this investigation and hearing, I am appointing Kathleen Legend to assist the Office of Prosecutor, while I am appointing Liam Blake to assist the Public Defender. Before you both badger me with complaints, I will add that both of you know how to read and write, and have some understanding of the Law. You will carry out these duties as ordered by the court."

"We don't get to draw cards to see which side we enter into battle for?" Liam asked.

"No, I do not wish to have Kathleen around these...subjects. Are we understood?"

"Yes, Sir and thank you," Liam added on.

"Next item: once this trial is over with, I want to start up a school for our civilians and especially for our Rangers. All of these people need to be able to read and write. Ignorant Rangers make for poor Rangers and I see no reason why this school cannot take on these civilians. We have a couple dozen kids and some adults in need of book learning. I already know we have several women who have home taught their children since leaving their homes to head west. So, I want a school built with a heavy stone foundation and cedar walls, it can operate as a second function by being a reinforced bunker if the Indians ever do decide to raid us. Now as to those people in charge, I am asking for Liam and Kathleen to head the school and decide how many pupils they can handle from the Ranger ranks?"

"What?" Liam blurted out as he jumped out of his chair, but a hard look from his superiors put him right back down.

"Sir, I'm no teacher..."

"Need I remind you that I am also no judge, but we do what we must do for the Territory of Arizona? Imagine educating 30 Rangers, who may eventually pass these skills on to 30 more. We can be a state of ignorant people, led by corrupt officials, or we can all learn to read the law books and see what our U.S. Constitution gave us and our eventual State Constitution will give us as rights to live by."

Liam was quiet for a moment and then he nodded his head in understanding. "Yes, Sir, I'll do my part to teach these bow-legged lunkheads how to add and read their Psalms."

"Thanks, Liam. Now you and Kathy can leave, the rest of this meeting is sort of boring."

After they left JW had Lt. Sampson brief the staff on the Halvorson case, afterward he explained, "This is a major turn for the Rangers and law enforcement in general. We're not Pinkerton Agents or even Wells Fargo Agents, and I haven't seen a one of you wearing a Treasury badge. This kind of investigative service is brand new for a cowboy cop. But this is where old west meets the new west is all about. We have to learn how to go with our hunches, conduct background investigation and conduct interviews with people, of how to handle evidence to obtain a guilty plea in a trial. Why, I even read how they're comparing types of ammo to see not only what type of caliber of bullet was used in a shooting, but the various markings on a bullet and then comparing it with a bullet fired from weapon seized at a murder scene.

"They also have something new coming into play called fingerprinting, but it might be a ways off...But the article spoke of how every human in the world had their own finger prints and it's not repeated on another human. So, human finger prints left on the surface of a murder weapon could logically identify the killer or make sure they have the right guy in custody. It rattles my mind to think where law enforcement ideas are going. We now have air balloons that flew above us in the battlefields, but now that Army lieutenant we helped said they have those things in all sizes crossing above Europe and new wars are breaking out all over there."

"Maybe we can ship them our Apaches," Lt. Dreeke asked.

"You try to gather them up and I'll ask," JW replied.

"Oh, Mr. Halverson told me something else that might give you a laugh, he read in a month-old copy of the New York Times of how the U.S. Army is planning an experiment in the very near future involving the use of Arabian camels here in the Southwest by the Sixth Cavalry."

"What's a camel?" Lt. Dreeke asked.

"Well, it's a desert animal used by the Arabians in North Africa...To go across the major deserts of Egypt and such. They're bigger than horses, really ugly, with extra-large hooves so they don't sink in the sand and they can go for long periods without water to survive between watering holes. They can store the water in this natural store tank called a hump, it's on their back. Really hard to ride, so I doubt any cavalryman is going to handle one."

"You're joshing me, right? This thing really exists?"

"Jamey, you've heard of elephants and they come from Africa, along with lions. Well these camels also come from there and they're not nearly as strange as some elephant. Remember how we used to say, we've gone off to see the elephant when we went to battle."

"Sure do, but I sure hope the Rangers never get any of these camels, next thing you know they'd be asking us to eat one."

JW let the laughter die down and then asked, "Wonder if the cavalry will get the one-hump or two-hump version of camel?" The question sucked Jamey right back in again and he had to ask, "You're telling me they come in single or double humps...well, which one is easiest to ride?"

"I don't know, Jamey, but knowing the Army, they'll order the single 'humpers' to save money. Government is always tryin' ta save money and the first place is with the Department of the Army. Personally, I'd like to see the bill for bringing a herd of these critters all the way over to our desert here, plus someone to train the troops how to stay on top of one." JW replied.

"Personally, I'd like to be nearby when one of those animals, with some greenhorn lieutenant was aboard, came face to face with one of our silver-back grizzlies. I sincerely doubt they have bears like ours over there…or any buffalo," Lt. Sampson said, shaking his head and slapping his legs when he burst out into laughter.

"Buffalo? Ain't no stinkin' buffalo in this Arizona Desert…not any more, at least. Cheyenne and Arapaho doin' their level best to keep 'em up north, leavin' the desert antelope and White man's cattle for the Comanche, Apache, Navajo and Ute. Too bad really, I could really use a new Buffalo robe coat and knee-high moccasins for the next winter. My old winter coat is going into its 12th winter and I sure can't afford no East Coast coat for $20.00," MSgt. Gary Wells said. He had to wipe his eyes after laughing so hard about the camels. He sure hoped JW never thought about having the Rangers try a couple of those, 'cause he'd just have ta refuse. Sitting up nearly seven to eight feet in the air, a man could break a leg falling off from one of those, maybe even a few ribs or his whole back. *No sireee!*

TRIAL OF ZACH AND WALLY BUSH

Unlike city trials, there was no formal arraignment, as JW considered the arrest and review of the charges the two men were wanted for as detailed on the Wanted Poster and confirming the warrant was still active, was arraignment enough. Lt. Wilcox drew a King of spades and assumed the duties of local prosecutor, while Lt. Sampson, with his low card, of an 8-of-Spades became the Defense Attorney for the two men. It was first established that neither men wished to plead guilty before the court, which contained the lawyers, their assistants, the judge and his court officer, who was Lt. Dreeke, and the jury of ten-men chosen from a pool made from a bean collection. One hundred white beans and a dozen black beans were placed in a large pitcher. MSgt. Gary Wells, who carried the pitcher and escorted by Lt. Dreeke, to verify the pool was done in all fairness, went around the compound to allow the eligible men to draw a bean.

Selectees must be 18 or over, men only, race had no effect on being selected, but they must understand fluent English and be able to bring forward a capital punishment if same is warranted and the subjects were proven guilty. It took less than an hour to select the ten men, which was made up of nine Whites, two Mexicans and one Black man. But the Black man was removed on the basis the prisoners felt he might be prejudicial toward the brothers for the way they had treated them in the past because of views toward ex-slaves. JW didn't want to release him, but he had to under the jury laws he reviewed in his law books. His head was bursting from all the long hours he had put into reading all the laws and taking notes. He now hoped this was the last trial he ever had to conduct for the Territory of Arizona.

JW now sent MSgt. Wells back out with Lt. Dreeke to select four additional black bean jurors. No other jurors were chosen, but JW read about the need for alternate jurors in the event of a juror falling ill or any sort of problem developing where a juror needs replacing.

Once back in court, all the jurors were advised of their responsibilities and the punishments they could receive for violating said responsibilities. He then ordered the prisoners to stand and confirmed both men still wanted to be tried together, rather than separately. Their only argument was they held this trial was illegal and they wanted to be taken to Tucson to be tried by a state court.

Judge JW again advised the prisoners that due to their own decisions to make false statements to this organization and to become members of said organization, they had received access to secret information which could endanger the entire Ranger organization. "You knew this going in, so now you get to finish out the battle. Either you're guilty or not guilty, it's up for this jury to decide and the laws of this territory uphold such courts. Now keep quiet while the Court Officer reads your charges out loud for the jury to hear.

"But before he does I want the Prosecutor to state before the jury how the arrest warrant for the accused was obtained..." JW stopped when Lt. Sampson stood up and declared, "Objection your honor, this evidence should be presented during court and not prior to it." Both of the brothers were nodding their heads in agreement.

"Will the lawyers please approach the bench," JW stated. The bench was JW's school teacher desk and the lawyers were sharing the Command Staff table. Jury members set against the large tent wall in two rolls of recently made benches. As court officer, Jamey set to the right side of the desk. The lawyers were seated with Kathleen on the far left of the table, then Lt. Wilcox, then Liam and next to him the two Bush brothers, who had their waists secured to the chairs by rope to make it harder for them from high-tailing off, then came Lt. Sampson. Behind them, by good six-feet, stood five Rangers with rifles from the current security post detail. No firearms were allowed in the court, other than those carried by the guards, JW and Lt. Dreeke. If the brothers made any attempt to run they would both be shot and found guilty as charged.

After a short chat with JW the lawyers returned to the table and JW announced the warrant poster would be identified by the prosecutor during his presentation. So, it began and for the next three hours it was a battle between the lawyers, with a flow of constant objections from both sides and by noon, JW had a grinding headache. He had no idea this hearing or trial would last so long, but Lt. Sampson had sincerely done his best as a Defense Attorney to show the wanted posted should not be enough to execute these two men. Although, secretly, Lt. Sampson felt both men should be hung that late afternoon. He had spent several hours talking to them and learned what kind of people they were and the act they had put on to enter the Rangers and for that alone they should've been dragged by a horse across the desert or maybe left in an Apache camp as a gift.

During the trial, the Prosecutor produced a bank bag from one of the very banks they were accused of holding up, where a security guard was killed. They had also found a deerskin wrapping in one of their saddlebags that contained three Indian scalps, which in some locations were going for $25 apiece and paid for by the federal government. But the Rangers didn't scalp and one of the reasons why is due to the barbarous and horrendous taking the scalp of Mexican women and children, saying they were Apache and for most people they couldn't tell the difference. This was causing a lot of border trouble, as well as Indian trouble inside Arizona.

When the jury was given the facts and arguments, and released to a temporary tent put up for the trial and under guard, JW set back and finished off half a canteen of water. The prisoners were taken back to their cell and fed an early dinner. But the jury used less time than JW expected after such a well presented case by both lawyers. They had been in the side tent for less than an hour, which was just enough time for the two brothers to finish off their dinner of roasted chicken.

Twenty minutes or so later, the two brothers, now untied, stood before JW and listened as the jury brought forward the guilty plea and the recommendation of capital punishment. Zach Bush, who had killed the most people between the two brothers, fell to his knees and began weeping, but it was Wally Bush who began yelling and threatening each member of the jury and the court. But when he threatened to rape Kathleen and leave her for the coyotes, Liam dashed over and laid the man out with hard blow to the right eye. This left the dangerous man unconscious, leaving Liam shaking his head for he had hoped the man would get back up so Liam could finish the licking the man needed.

When JW offered the brothers, who were now tied up, the option of a firing squad or hanging, they chose the firing squad and JW authorized it. Lt. Dreeke picked out eight-men for the duty. Once the chore was carried out, the two men were carried over to two new graves freshly dug in the recently built Ranger cemetery. JW read from the Word of God and the Lord's Prayer was read over them by all those present. A wooden cross was put on each grave, but no names. JW had ordered that and he told MSgt. Wells, "They hadn't died as Rangers and don't deserve to die as one. We only had to bury them up here to keep our location secret…for a little while more at least."

"You're looking tired, JW," said by his friend Wells.

EPILOGUE:

Captain John Blake had not realized it, but in time he would be asked to hold additional court hearings, because people respected his honesty and they no longer trusted the Territorial Government. A new location had to be found and it ended up being a newly constructed school house built south of the Tucson Wagon Train Trail, when slowly a community was built that came with a brand-new school house. This township would eventually become Benson, Arizona. JW continued looking for his daughter, having to make several trips to Mexico City and one long sailing to Havana Cuba, where he would end up rescuing several kidnapped American young ladies. The people of Arizona grew thankful of JW Blake and sought to make him their first U.S. State Senator, but he felt he was too old at the time, now in his early 90's and refused. Besides, he felt his war against the federal government had not ceased and he did not want anything to do with politics that would tie him into Washington D.C.

The unauthorized Arizona Rangers continued riding, growing to well over 150 Rangers and their main post remaining in the Superstition Mountains. But eventually it would be moved into Phoenix, with posts in Flagstaff and Tucson. The reward offered for JW continued to grow, the funds being offered by the carpetbaggers, who operated for the bankers in the Northeast.

And meanwhile, Chiefs Victoria, Cochise and Geronimo would continue their wars against the U.S. Army and the White settlers, until Geronimo only remained. Then he and only 30 Apache, including women and children, led the U.S. Army on a lengthy chase, with over 5,000 U.S. Troops and 3,000 Mexican troops in pursuit. At the time, these 5,000 U.S. troops made up one fourth of the entire U.S. Army. But it was only after a few years were the Apache scouts able to talk Geronimo into surrendering. When he did, the Commanding General in charge of operation, placed him and his top warriors under arrest and shipped them to Florida, but also arrested were the Apache Scouts, who were once again lied to by the U.S. Government. However, the Arizona Rangers refused to partake in this operation and continued to deal with the outlaw problem, which the U.S. Cavalry didn't have time to deal with.

Arizona would grow as the Southwest became a continual destination for European immigrants and survivors of the Civil War poured in. As for Liam and Kathleen, well, their courtship would blossom and Blake's War would continue on.

Historical Notes

Arizona Rangers came and went in the Arizona Government due to a lack of funds. They were reestablished in 1882, but money eventually did run out and disbanded once again until March 21, 1901, when a new company of rangers were formed and paid for by the Arizona Territory Legislature. Fourteen men staffed this new ranger company.

Badges were first "issued" in 1903 as a solid five-point star. Officer badges displayed his name, while enlisted badges bore the man's ranger number. In 1903 the number of rangers increased to 26, with Theodore Roosevelt and many of his rough-riders served in the ranks.

But in 1909, the act that established the Arizona rangers was repealed, once again disbanding the unit. In seven and a half years, 107 men had served in the Arizona Rangers.

In 1957, the Arizona Rangers were reestablished by a few surviving members of those 107. But the present-day Arizona Rangers are unpaid, all-volunteer non-profit law enforcement support and assistance civilian auxiliary and under control of established law enforcement officials. Youth support and community service is one of their aims to preserve the traditions and honor the history of the Arizona Rangers. Eighteen satellite companies of rangers are known by the local law enforcement agencies and today's rangers receive extensive training.

A little-known fact: In 1902, a U.S. Supreme Court decision in Washington D.C., determined that congress had the inherent right to unilaterally break any treaty the government signed with any American Indian Tribe. Over 320 treaties were made with the American Indian and every single one was broken by the US Government.

In 1924, law was passed finally making American Indians citizens of the United States. In 1950, privileges of Social Security were extended to American Indians — 26 years after becoming citizens.

Two-hundred ninety-three Tribal Reservations in the United States are handled by the Bureau of Indian Affairs (BIA), reportedly they continue spending one-billion dollars to ensure poverty continues among the Indian people as only ten percent of these funds designated for the Indians reaches them.

The End

Thank you for reading Blake's War. The author and publisher would greatly appreciate it if you would consider posting a review.

ABOUT THE AUTHOR

William Casselman was raised in Southern California and he enlisted in the U.S. Air Force in 1971 to become a Law Enforcement Specialist/Military Working Dog Handler. He served the next ten years in the military and met his lovely wife, Mona Sue, at Eielson AFB, Alaska.

A Vietnam veteran, he left the service to become a police officer in Dillingham, Alaska and spent the next twenty years in Alaskan police work. From patrolman to investigator, he has worked with four police departments and became Public Safety Director for the City of Whittier during the tragic Exxon Oil Spill of Prince William Sound in 1989.

William, a 36-year Christian, retired as Senior Investigator for the State of Alaska gaming program. With 40 years in Alaska, six children and 22 grandchildren, and two great-grandchildren, William and Mona Sue now live in rural Alaska.

Other Titles from

ALASKA DREAMS PUBLISHING

By William Casselman

Apache Snow

Search of Honor

A Coming Storm

Titles by other authors from ADP

My Life In The Wilderness

All Over The Road

Ghost Cave Mountain

Inside the Circle

The Silver Horn of Robin Hood

Alaskan Troll Eggs

Through My Eyes

The Professional Ghost Investigator

The Adventures of Jason and Bo

Please visit www.alaskadp.com and sign up for the ADP mailing list to be notified of future titles by Alaska Dreams Publishing.